THE DEVIL OF BLACKHILL HALL COLLECTION

ELIZA CARLTON

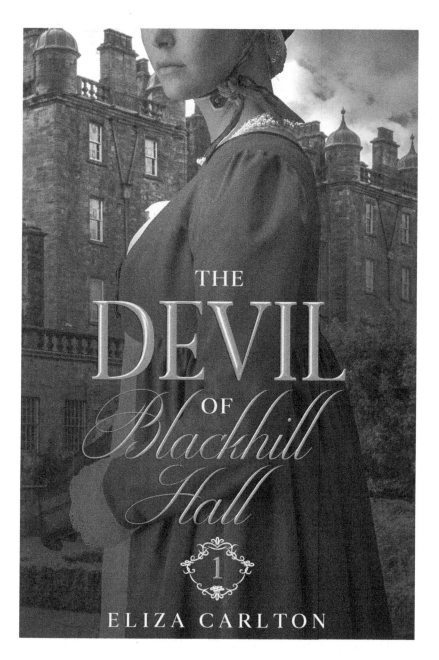

THE
DEVIL
OF
Blackhill Hall

1

ELIZA CARLTON

PROLOGUE

~October, 1815~
Richmond, Virgina

The band struck up a waltz, and the familiar strains wound around Caroline, threatening to pull her back to her memories.

The ballroom was crowded: expensive dresses swishing, elaborate arrangements spilling over polished surfaces, jewels glittering in the light of the chandeliers, where masked and costumed revelers painted a surreal, swirling vision, monstrous and beautiful at once. Some masks covered their wearer's nose and chin concealing all but mysterious voices, whilst others revealed much more, delicate as a spider's web, disguising only the eyes coquettishly. Caroline's was golden: an intricate fan of sculpted lace that veiled her features, tracing her eyes, which shone blue and green like jewels against the gold. Her dress was simple, its soft empire waist draping closely down her body, with layer upon layer of gossamer white fabric trailing romantically behind her. Upon her back, feathered wings rose large and dramatic.

Standing by the edge of the dancefloor, she saw Julius Caesar approach and smiled at him.

"Lady Caroline, may I have the pleasure of this dance?" he asked holding his hand out to her. She was just about to extend her own when a familiar voice cut in; and, in that blinding instant, shattered her heart like teeth through spun sugar.

"I'm sorry to be the bearer of bad news... but this dance has been promised to me." His voice was light, but there was steel just underneath, and her new dance partner did not seem the type to argue, accepting his rejection with a smile, he bowed, and departed swiftly.

Turning slowly, she crossed her arms protectively over her chest and found herself face to face with the Devil. All in black, his breeches and fitted coat were dark midnight, his boots gleaming. His coat fitted him high to the neck, then tight across his broad shoulders, tapering down to a narrow waist. His mask was also black, without detail, and covered the top portion of his face, more black against his burnished golden hair and bronze stubble. There were gleaming back horns, large and curling, which looked as though they were carved from bone. Though, knowing him, she wouldn't have been surprised if they were. His mouth was the same full, pink smile, which knew too much about her. He had always been able to look at her, and make her feel naked under his gaze, as though they were the only two people in the room... in the world.

He extended his hand to her, and she knew she shouldn't accept. She wanted to hate him, to slap him, to ignore and hurt him, but she moved to him against her will, as if

in a trance. Their fingers touched and she felt his energy course through her skin. Leading her slowly onto the dance floor, he gently pulled her close and they began to dance, their eyes never leaving each others.

"I thought all your dances were mine," he murmured softly.

She kept silent, not trusting her treacherous heart to speak. All her dances had been his for as long as she could remember, and he had walked away from her.

"You planned this?" Caroline asked, an accusation.

"You've always been the saint to my sinner. It seemed appropriate," he answered, pulling her a little closer.

4

When the song came to an end, they remained close. He held her tightly, and she tried to build up the will to leave. The draw of him, his lingering blue gaze, his hands on her, the smell of him: it was all too much. Suddenly, his attention moved to her hand held in his, as his fingers caressed hers through smooth silk gloves.

"Your ring," he remarked, looking back at her with renewed intensity, and she felt heat rise in her cheeks.

"I am a widow," she said softly. "Or, did you not know?" She felt his hands tighten on hers, but he said nothing, his eyes reflecting a fathomless emptiness that threatened to undo her hard-won resolve.

"Caroline?" she heard a voice at her side and pulled her hand from his grasp.

"Please excuse me," she said, already turning to hurry through the crush of people. She quickly ascended the stairs, feeling the slow fading of his presence like a wound that refused to close, a throb, each step more painful.

Turning on the top step, she couldn't help but look back down at the ballroom: the dance floor, a riot of colour and sound, of joy and laughter she felt so far from.

And, as though she had imagined him, he was gone.

CHAPTER 1

~ April, 1809, London~

"They are not hot enough!" Katherine exclaimed as she winced at her face in the looking glass. "Put them back in the fire. I do not want frizzy curls within the hour. I shall look like a sheepdog!"

Caroline sighed.

"If you want to have any hair left at all, you will quiet your harping." Caroline gave a slight tug on the irons. "Oops," she smirked in the looking glass.

"Ooff!" Katherine gasped dramatically and scowled at Caroline's reflection before they shared a grin.

"There. Happy?" Caroline said as she slid the perfect curl from the iron, and arranged them prettily around Katherine's face. While her friend admired her handiwork, Caroline stole the opportunity to retreat, and flopped backward on the bed, tired by her efforts, and gazed at the ceiling.

"Finally! Though, I know not why you like to make it seem so hard," Katherine said, arching an eyebrow at her friend lying exhausted on the bed. Caroline snorted. "A sound like a little piglet," Katherine teased "You're lucky that Lady Ann was not here to witness it. They already think us crass as it is."

"Well, in that case, she probably shouldn't witness your ability to empty the sugar plum tray when it passes," Caroline said, rolling over to look at her friend struggling with her short stays.

"Help me with this, will you?" Katherine asked, squeezing the stays mercilessly.

"I shall never understand why you insist on tying these things so tightly," Caroline said, pulling.

"Mother insists." Katherine made an unflattering impersonation of her mother's voice. "'What is the sense in breathing when you could be swooning into the arms of an eligible bachelor?' Besides, how else am I to make a bosom, if I don't squeeze everything else in first?" Katherine laughed, her chest pulling tight at the ribbons.

"Well, luckily for me, your mother does not much bother about what I wear," Caroline said happily.

"She does care, she just cannot see past marrying off Eva and me. Once that is settled, she will turn her full focus on you, and then you shall be sorry," Katherine grinned.

"Yes, but I should very much like to get married *before* I reach my fiftieth year," teased Caroline. Before Katherine could let loose her retort, they both turned at the sound of the door. It opened quickly admitting Eva, who hurried in looking a little scared, closed the door in a rush, and leaned against it with her eyes closed.

"Mother is in such a temper today, I do not know how I might have upset her. She has been so strict with me all morning, watching my lessons," Eva shuddered, and Katherine shrugged and turned back to the mirror.

"Do not let it bother you, sister- mother must have someone to bark at. It makes her feel complete," Katherine said lightly and Caroline was struck as always, by the difference in the sisters.

They both shared the same beautiful features, large, bright-blue eyes, glowing skin, and long, strawberry blond curls. However, you need only know them a day to see that the resemblance ended there.

Katherine, the younger of the two, was loud and outgoing, confident to a fault, and a constant headache to her parents. She loved to make mischief. She rarely studied during her lessons, running off at any given opportunity. Caroline loved her dearly with all her heart, but Katherine could be a test to anyone's patience.

Eva was the opposite, and only tested Caroline's heart, in so much as it felt for her. After a childhood of frightening health scares, the dear girl was prone to nerves and had very delicate sensitivities. Eva felt the plight of every unfortunate creature they walked past on their outings-she would give the very shoes off her own feet to the match girl who stood on the corner and walk home barefoot in the snow if someone did not prevent her. Eva took every word from her bossy mother's lips to heart and tried time and time again to please her. Margaret Fairfax, their mother, was a vain woman, who longed for nothing more than to see her daughters married into aristocracy, simply so she could be the envy of all her friends in Virginia.

Caroline immediately felt bad for such faultfinding, when the Fairfaxes had been so kind as to take her in. Her own mother and Margaret had been childhood friends, and Caroline knew it had been Margaret who had insisted to her husband John Fairfax that Caroline become part of their family; though, she must have had little resistance, as Mr Fairfax was a kindly, soft-hearted gentleman. They had even promised her the sum of her parent's estate, which had passed to them when they took up her guardianship, to be given as a dowry when she married. Though, from the state of things lately, Caroline had seriously begun to doubt that the day might ever come. As the Season moved from winter to spring, it was clear to Caroline that she was not to the tastes of the London Ton; her looks were unusual, and her dowry small- an unforgivable combination it seemed.

They had been in England since winter; Mr Fairfax fortune-hunting, searching for investors, and making business connections between cotton plantations back home, and mills in the north of England. Finesse was needed, time and patience were required, and social connections were intrinsically necessary. This suited Mrs Fairfax down to the ground- as her business in England was in husband-hunting.

Shaking such thoughts away, Caroline went to Eva's side and grasped her hand, surprised to feel it trembling slightly. She led her to the bed and helped her lie back on the pillows. She went to the washstand and poured some cool water from the pitcher into a large porcelain bowl, and added a few drops of lavender oil, which Eva often found soothing. The aroma curled from the bowl, thick, sharp and fresh- a tincture for the troubled mind. She wrung out a cloth and put it to her friend's hot forehead. Eva sighed and squeezed Caroline's hand in gratitude.

"Well, how do I look?" Katherine asked, twirling around in front of them, showing off her new dress, which Caroline knew had cost the earth. It was of a creamy color, with broad blue stripes that made the most of her eyes, and a bodice tight and low enough to reveal more of her chest than was entirely appropriate so early in the day.

"Disreputable," Caroline replied wryly as Katherine dabbed a little too much tint on her lips, and smiled at her reflection.

"Precisely what I was going for." Smiling wickedly, she swept out the room and downstairs to meet whatever poor chap Margaret had planned her to take tea with. Caroline watched the closed door a while, rewetting the compress now and again, and finally felt Eva drift off to sleep.

Getting up quietly she went to the dressing table and began to put away Katherine's powders and rouges, all the little pots and brushes that were usually left out, then carelessly lost. She wondered if Margaret would really help her to find a husband once her daughters were married, or if it was a futile hope. She would never stop being grateful for the life they'd given her. The chance to come to England and the opportunity to have real sisters, to be part of a family. But, in that tiny, dark part of her heart where she kept the memories of her parents, she longed to know what it felt like to have a mother fussing over your studies, choosing dresses with you, trying to find a husband for you, and a protective father who kept a close eye on which gentlemen came to call.

Rising, she cast a last glance at Eva, then quietly opened the door, deciding to go to the library and continue her study of French in preparation for her lesson tomorrow. In truth, it was Eva and Katherine's lesson, but she was permitted to join in as well, albeit with less forceful demands made on her progress from Mrs Fairfax. She started down the gracefully curved stairs to the lower level. While they did not have status in London, they had money from America, and they used it to elevate themselves with the finest rooms that they could afford.

They rented an elegant townhouse right in the fashionable heart of London. It was exquisitely and fashionably decorated and contained not only one, but two drawing rooms, to Margaret's delight, the walls covered in expensive Parisian damask, and the ceilings with a lace of beautifully carved plasterwork. The parlour was to the back and used exclusively for the family, and it separated Mr Fairfax's study from the dining room, which connected to one of the drawing rooms. It was toward the study that Caroline now went. She knocked softly, and hearing no answer, carefully opened the door and entered. It was quite empty and she went to the section of wall lined with bookshelves.

Sliding out the volume of poems by Voltaire, she heard voices coming toward the door. They seemed to stop just outside. Starting forward, she stopped again in shock as she heard what was being discussed.

"It is for the best, John. She is old enough to marry, and she is far too shy and nervous to ever encourage a gentleman sufficiently to attract their singular attention. And if she were to marry into that family, it will throw Katherine into the path of other highly eligible gentlemen-titled gentlemen, if there is any God up there!"

"But, why not Katherine? She is not so shy and timid as Eva, surely she would make a better wife for the man."

"Katherine will never agree, and nor would he. You know that. She is far too foolhardy and stubborn. I'm not quite sure where she gets it from."

"Indeed," Mr Fairfax said dryly. Caroline, frozen in the middle of the room, heard a hand upon the doorknob. She had already heard too much, they would not be pleased to find her within earshot. She ran to the window, lifting back the curtain, and pressed herself against the wall behind it. She let the heavy velvet drapes fall over her, wrinkling her nose against the urge to sneeze as the material tickled her face.

The door opened, and their voices got louder as they moved into the room.

"My dear, I do not wish to upset your careful planning, but I cannot warn you enough against this match. The things I have heard about his man are not for a lady's ears. Eva is as delicate as a kitten. Please believe me, this man is no gentleman. He could crush our little girl under his boot."

"He is an Ashford," she trilled. "That is all that matters! She will survive it, no doubt, and have the name she needs to be truly accepted in society. To be invited to all the right balls and onto all the right committees, she never needs to feel the pain of being cut in public or of waiting for invitations that never arrive," Margaret's voice trailed off, and even Caroline behind the curtain could hear the pain in it.

"I'm sorry, my dove," John said quietly, moving to her. "I am sorry you have suffered because of me."

"Do not be ridiculous. I could never have been without you. But that does not mean we cannot do our best for our daughters. All the Ton gossip is exaggerated, I'm sure. I have met his sister, and she is a fine and respectable woman. If he really is as bad as you say, then our daughter will not be burdened by his presence often, but she will enjoy the privilege of status that only a name can bestow. Please, Mr Fairfax... I know I am right about this." She spoke with such conviction, even Caroline felt inclined to agree.

"I shall meet with his father tomorrow then, as you ask. After that, I shall tell you my decision." He came to an abrupt stop as a loud crash sounded from another room.

"What in God's name?" Mr Fairfax said as he started out the door, Margaret hurrying after them. Caroline took the opportunity to slip out the door and avoid the commotion in the drawing-room, where servants were now hurrying with buckets of water. Katherine ran out of the room, her new dress spoiled by a black scorch mark down the front. The young man she was entertaining was making for the door hastily, whilst Katherine's chaperon directed the men with the water, and Eva looked on flustered and embarrassed. Margaret scolded Katherine, while John went into the room to check the damage.

"I just wanted to see why men love smoking pipes so much... I must say, it tastes utterly revolting," Katherine exclaimed between coughs, as Margaret's face looked likely to burst into flames at any moment.

❀

The next morning, Caroline waited for Mrs Fairfax to retire to her correspondence, and as soon as the room was empty, she and Katherine clutched at the carefully ironed society pages in tandem.

Her eyes skimming over the smudged words, Caroline's eyebrows rose higher and higher, until she finished, dropping the paper to her knee. Katherine who had been scoffing at each sentence shrieked in exaggerated desperation.

"This cannot be true! Mama and Papa would never allow it. He sounds like a devil himself!"

"Yes, he does, doesn't he," Caroline agreed, wide-eyed.

"What will we do? I have to warn Eva!"

"No. Do not tell her just yet- you will only worry her. You said your father was not yet decided. Let us see what comes of meeting him, and what your father thinks. Besides, perhaps she will like him."

"What?" she shrieked incensed. "You would have us do nothing, and let Beelzebub take poor sweet Eva for a wife?"

"No. I am just saying, let us not frighten her for nothing. Gossip is not always trustworthy. I trust Mr Fairfax to be level-headed. Let us all see for ourselves who he is tomorrow before we plan an attack against the poor man."

Katherine let out a lung full of air when she failed to find the appropriate response. "Well... I will hold my tongue this once if you insist upon it, Caroline, but let it be on your head if Eva dies of shock on the night of her wedding!"

Caroline chuckled quietly. "Oh, it's unlikely that we will ever get to that. Come now, let us go find Eva and ring for some tea and cakes. That should soothe all our worries."

CHAPTER 2

*W*hen Lord Lucian Ashford came to, he felt the previous day's excesses weigh down on him instantly. His mouth tasted of cigars and whiskey. His eyes felt like sawdust, and his body hurt all over. Opening his eyes in the dim light, he became aware of the female smell in the room. Like all ladies' boudoirs, it shared a childish, girlish fragrance of flowers, so nauseatingly sweet that his stomach turned, of talcs and powders, and all the other things the ladies of the Ton seemed to think men found attractive. Then, he thought wryly as he turned and looked at Olivia, a beautiful redhead sleeping naked beside him, why wouldn't they? Men hardly gave any indication of their true desires with their wives, never mind their lovers.

Wives. At the thought, his hangover increased in force. He recalled the talk with his father that had led him here.

"You will court her, propose to her by all means, but it has already been decided between her father and me. You are to marry Miss Eva Fairfax of Virginia, make no mistake. Our families combined will be a powerful union. Their money and American connections, our name and status. I do not have the time nor the inclination to argue the matter."

Lucian had sat, his head in his hands, trying to comprehend what his father was telling him. He was getting married. To someone he had never met.

"Father, I do not want to marry. I have never even set eyes on this girl," He ground out in as reasonable a tone as he could manage.

"Lucian, have you ever done anything for our family? Ever benefited us in some way? Paid us back for taking you into the family? Housing and clothing you? I think not. You have been nothing but a drain, and an expensive and embarrassing one at that-"

"But-"

"You dare to interrupt me, boy!" Silus's roar snapped Lucian's head up and he saw the sudden violence on his father's face. "You bring disgrace to our family with every breath. Do you want your sister to be a spinster? For no man will approach her with the reputation you have given the Ashford name." Lucian dropped his head back into his hands, guilt filling his heart, quickly followed by anger.

"Why do you hate me so?" he said quietly, though he already knew the answer, and waited as Silus composed himself and sat behind his desk, turning his attention to his correspondence before him.

"I do not hate you, boy. I feel nothing for you," he said cruelly, as Lucian's hands tightened into fists.

"Why me? Why not Wesley or Charles? They would make better husbands than I," he tried one last time to appeal to the impassable man.

"Do you really think I'd let my own flesh and blood marry some new money husband hunter, whom they have no genuine feeling for? What kind of father would that make me?" he smiled sadistically at the boy in front of him, enjoying every second of his misery. "Now, get out. I've work to do. Tomorrow, you shall call on Miss Fairfax," and he dismissed him with a glance.

Dragging himself out of bed, throwing off the clinging satin sheets with disdain, he searched the floor for his clothes. He dragged on his breeches, his undershirt and waistcoat, he then considered tying his cravat but decided instead that he didn't care who saw him in his state of undress. People already expected the worst of him, why spoil their expectations. He sat to pull on his long boots, one by one, and suddenly felt female hands, with long nails like talons reaching into his hair. He jerked away from her and stood, collecting his personal items from the nightstand.

"Lucian, why do you leave me so soon? My husband will not be home for hours," she simpered, pouting all the while. Her milky white skin was creased with hours of lying, and red in places, pinched and scratched, blue in others- bruises of their night of lust. Lucian fought down another wave of hangover, and the revulsion he now felt looking at Olivia, the horror that he would soon be shackled to his own hateful woman. She started to slip hands down her body, looking up at him, coyly, though he knew what an act that was. She was anything but coy.

"Please– do not embarrass yourself. Let us forget this indiscretion," he said curtly reaching down for his overcoat. As he swung it over his shoulder, Olivia made another play, this time by standing up, naked in front of him, and pressing her soft body against his, looking up with desire-laden eyes.

A flash of anger shot through him, as he grabbed her arm whilst she attempted to pull his head down to hers. Jerking her close to him, he leaned in and spoke in a voice that was completely devoid of feeling.

"Touch me again and it'll be the last thing you do," he warned, enjoying the fear in her eyes for a moment, squeezing her arm, hard enough to leave another mark, another trophy for her collection, for her wall of conquests, the brute, Lucian Ashford, then he threw her roughly back on the bed. It was certainly less aggressive than he had been the night before, but this time there was no lust behind it, only contempt.

"How dare-" she gasped out, tears threatening. Her face reddening angry, her sweet expression already slipping into one of haughty disbelief. Whirling around, he left the room, hearing a bottle smash behind him as she threw it at his departing back.

"Missed!" he called joylessly as he swept out of the wide front door, passed startled-looking servants, and onto the morning streets of London.

He walked with his head bent, avoiding curious looks. This would hardly damage his reputation, in fact, if experience taught him anything, it would probably only make him more popular. He wondered what it was about women of privilege, who liked men who would hurt them, then brushed away the dark thought.

The bright sunlight on the fresh May morning pierced his skull, making his head throb. He thought of all the awful things he'd been called over the years, the tears he'd caused, the heartbreak and hurt. He deserved it all. In some ways, he really was Silus's son.

The walk did little to restore him, instead, the clean air seared his smoky lungs, and each step on the hard ground sent a jolt through his pounding head. He rounded the park, seeing his townhouse close at hand, nestled on the edge, he hastened on, his step faltering as he spied a carriage drawn up in front.

Two tall figures waited by it in the blinding light, the door open and he recognised his father's crest on the door. He considered turning around, disappearing before his two brothers spotted him, and clenched his fists in frustration as the elder nodded a greeting in his direction. He had been spied after all.

Approaching them, he saw the judgment in Charles's eyes and the amusement in Wesley's.

"Do not dally, Lucian, we are already late." His older brother's voice was a reprimand, a tone too familiar to him of late, and he made to go past them.

"What is it? I'm tired and you cannot need another lesson in the art of lovemaking quite so soon," he slurred, eyes narrowed in mockery.

"Lucian, even you cannot have forgotten. You are to call on Miss Fairfax today. In fact, we are already late," Charles stated with a tightness that belied his calm tone and herded his younger brother toward the carriage before he could refuse.

Lucian stopped, suddenly remembering his father telling him to visit his intended today. He must have expected him to be late or dismiss it altogether, so he had sent his more trustworthy sons to help keep him to heel.

Well, he decided grimly, he would visit. And, he would make sure that Miss Fairfax knew exactly whom she was marrying.

aroline had passed the point of nervousness, as she glanced up at every carriage that sped past. The clock hand indicated the lateness of their guests and she felt each second as though it were a personal insult. The nerve of this man was unbearable. Making the sweetest, purest girl in the country wait, unaccountably, for him. A girl who still had no idea what the future might have in store for her.

Finally, a passing carriage stopped, and Caroline leapt to the window to see it. It was tall and impressive. Black horses, with black plumes, snorted and stamped as the doors opened and three men descended.

The first gentleman was tall and upright in his standing. He looked at the house, and Caroline thought immediately what a noble brow he had. He checked his pocket watch and suppressed a look of annoyance. The second man jumped down more carelessly, longer, foppish hair, carefully coiffed, he seemed to be buzzing with contained energy and when he looked around, he grinned. The third stepped down from the carriage slowly and seemed to prowl forward, his body tense, with an aura of controlled power.

As they turned toward the door, the third man suddenly glanced at the window, catching her eyes. Caroline gasped and turned abruptly, rushing back to her chair and her book, which she now buried her blushing face in. Margaret fussed around Eva's hair, then threw herself into a seat assuming a casual pose, all ladies creating a tableau of graceful repose, before a servant knocked on the door and announced their guests.

Katherine, Eva, Margaret and Caroline all rose to their feet, putting aside their books and needlework. Each man to enter was as handsome as the last, there was no denying that, Caroline thought. Tall and broad, they radiated energy, and it seemed strange to see such pure examples of masculinity in the exquisitely delicate feminine room, with its floral, hand-painted wallpaper, and dainty furniture.

"The Lord Charles Ashford," the servant announced again as one of the brothers stepped forward. He made a short formal bow and the women bobbed in return.

"The Lord Wesley Ashford." Caroline fought the urge to sigh as they all bobbed again.

"And the Lord Lucian Ashford." The man bowed lazily, surveying the women before him with hooded eyes. Caroline felt cold settle in her stomach, this was to be Eva's betrothed: a fierce-looking man, cruelly beautiful, without a hint of a smile for any one of them, who looked as though he had not changed his clothes from the previous night- a rough night, by the looks of it. Lord Charles stepped forward, speaking to Margaret.

"Mrs Fairfax, it is truly a pleasure to see you again. What a beautiful home you have."

"And what beautiful daughters!" Wesley commented amiably, making Eva blush and Katherine snort. Charles cocked his head at her slightly, looking bemused while Wesley simply laughed good-naturedly. Margaret made the usual introductions, introducing her daughters first, then Caroline.

Silence ensued as they waited for Lucian to make some kind of sociable comment so that they could all sit down. Caroline shifted around from foot to foot, tired of the tension, and watched as he looked around, with an insolent glaze, before spying the whiskey decanter. Walking over to it, he lifted the stopper and smelled the dark amber liquid, and looked back to his waiting audience.

"May I?" he asked, already pouring himself a generous measure.

"Of course," Margaret said smoothly, indicating for the girls to sit down, who were then followed by Wesley and Charles, the latter watching his brother through narrowed eyes.

Caroline sat again, settling her hands on her knee and watching the various interactions going on around the room. Margaret was clearly not about to be put off by a few bad manners and was engaging in light social conversation, somewhat forcefully. Eva was politely listening to her mother, and trying to ignore Lucian as he wandered around the room, drinking and looking at the room's accouterments. Katherine was sitting back, watching the drama unfold with an interested look on her face, raising her eyebrow at Charles when he glanced at her.

Caroline became aware that Lucian had stopped walking around and was now looking at Eva. He walked toward her and sat next to her on the settee. Eva, unsettled by his proximity, immediately shuffled over to the other end, her face blushing brightly. He smirked and sat back, gulping down more of his drink, and shaking his head slightly.

☙❧

*R*aising his eyes, Lucian skimmed languidly over Charles and Margaret making small talk about the Season, past Katherine who had engaged Wesley in conversation. Then, he suddenly became aware of being watched. Sliding his eyes her way, he met the stare of the other girl in the room.

Miss Caroline Lesage, Mrs Fairfax had called her. She met his gaze directly and stared right back. What an unusual creature. Amused, he let his eyes stay on hers a while longer, watching to see how long it might take before she grew uncomfortable and looked away. She was quite lovely, he realised, as his eyes took in the pile of her thick, raven black hair, and the slanted hazel eyes which seemed to glow against her olive complexion and striking cheekbones. He had traveled widely and seen more than his share of exotic women, but he had never seen anyone in his life quite like her before.

She was looking at him with a touch of hostility, tinged with curiosity, perhaps. Utterly unafraid of him, or in awe of him, or even attracted to him, he could not tell. In fact, she was looking at him as if she might like to hit him, a look he rarely encountered from women, before he'd bedded them anyway, and her boldness delighted him.

He attempted to unnerve her, an easy trick in his repertoire; he let his eyes drop lower, to stray on her lips, appetisingly full, distinctively wide, dark pink in color, and perfectly shaped, he thought, with a small jolt of lust. Whatever must those generous lips feel like to suck between his teeth? Rather than blush and look away, as most ladies her age would have done, her eyes narrowed challengingly. He smirked a parry, and let his eyes stray lower to her shoulders to look at the tantalising glimpse of gently tanned skin there- terribly unfashionable of course, but oh how she made the other ladies look like paintings that had been left in the rain to fade and drip their colour away, leaving only the ghostly pale indiscernible from every other lady of the Ton.

His eyes moved lower again, would that smooth milk and honey skin stretch across her entire body, or just where the sun had touched it? Her slender body was free and uninhibited under her gown. She was like nothing he had ever seen- a rare and beautiful bird brought back from distant lands, and next to her, his intended was but a sparrow.

Suddenly he became aware that Charles was addressing him.

"Pardon, brother?" he asked, finally moving his eyes from her and round to the rest of the gathered company.

"Mrs Fairfax just enquired if you plan to attend the Season much this year," Charles repeated

"Yes, as we heard you were hardly in evidence at all last year," Margaret stated, clearly implying that as her daughter's fiancé, she would like to see him there.

"My brother does not care for such things much, but the rest of the Ashfords will be more than happy to escort your three charming daughters wherever they should wish to go," Wesley said extravagantly.

"Oh! I only have two daughters, Lord Wesley, Miss Lesage is our ward," she explained. Lucian watched as a tinge of pink stained Caroline's cheeks at the conversation, though she still did not drop her head. He had wondered about the lack of family resemblance.

"Oh, but she is our sister, in everything but blood," Katherine added quickly.

"And, you are also from America?" Charles asked politely to the unusual girl who had not yet spoken. She smiled at him.

"Yes, my Lord. From Virginia," she said, her voice was deep and steady, her accent soft, in a dragged lilt, rich and sugared.

"And do you miss it much? Do you not find England terribly cold and dull?" Wesley continued. "I would not blame you!" he chuckled.

"No, not at all," the girl answered smoothly. "In fact, I quite enjoy the cool weather. Home can become almost insufferably hot and..."

"Sweaty?" Lucian interrupted rudely, raising an eyebrow insinuatingly at her. Caroline levelled a look right back at him.

"Quite," she said sharply, then, she turned deftly to the other brothers and continued. "Though, I must admit we are all looking forward to the balls this Season."

"Absolutely, all those eligible bachelors to dance with," Katherine exclaimed to her mother's horror.

"My word, Katherine! What will our genteel company think of you, I do not know."

"Oh come now, mother. Let us not pretend. We all know that is what the Season is all about. Why, it's practically a cattle auction, with the most thoroughbred specimens being sold to the highest bidder," she broke off with a triumphant smile.

"Katherine," Eva whispered.

"Well, I could not have put it better myself," announced Lucian, sitting forward in his chair, smiling at Katherine. At that moment, a knock sounded and maids arrived with the distraction of tea, sparing anyone from having to remark.

*a*s the tea was laid out, Margaret stood, forcing all the men to stand with her, and there was a small reshuffling of seats. Wesley and Charles drew Katherine and Caroline aside, to give Lucian and Eva a chance to speak, though it seemed a clumsy formality to Caroline, who was finding the social subtleties of London already to be burdensome.

"And what say you of this proposed engagement?" Katherine asked abruptly, causing Charles to look at her in surprise, and Caroline's eyes to widen.

"Proposed? My brother is under the impression that it is quite final," Charles remarked. A smile played around Katherine's lips.

"Rather like a death sentence?" she said and laughed as Charles choked on his tea in surprise, giving Caroline enough time to shoot her a censuring glare.

"I'm beginning to get the feeling you rather enjoy doing that," Charles said, displeased, but with a hint of interest, Caroline suspected.

"Oh, I only do things which I rather enjoy. Luckily, that is a great many things..." she said with a wicked smile causing Caroline to make free with her elbow before things were allowed to get any worse.

"Ouch, stop that."

"Well then, behave yourself. He is to be your brother-in-law," she whispered fiercely, glaring at her until Katherine sighed. Caroline turned then, and caught Eva's eye. She was staring disapprovingly at her, with a look Caroline recognised well. Excusing herself, and ignoring Charles's air of disapproval she went to her friend's side.

"Caroline!" Eva exclaimed just a little too loudly, making it obvious how uncomfortable she was.

"We were just talking about Virginia, will you please keep Lord Lucian entertained, I'm afraid I should help mother," she said, her eyes begging Caroline as she moved away. Caroline found herself alone with Lord Lucian and quickly made her inspection up close. His clothes were wrinkled and slept in, his face unshaven and his eyes bloodshot. He was on his fourth glass of whiskey now, and she could smell it on his breath. Haughty, disgraceful and inexcusably rude; the rumors were true, it seemed.

"So, the lovely Miss Eva was telling me about the differences between Virginia and England. It was absolutely fascinating," he sighed as he stood belatedly to excuse his fleeing future wife, indicating that he had thought her quite the opposite. Caroline could not believe his nerve. He swayed slightly on his feet, and she realised he was probably still drunk.

"Well, in that case, let me go on, Lord Lucian," Caroline said primly. "In Virginia, gentlemen are not usually late to call on their intended. They also make time to bathe and dress in clean clothes before arrival. They usually add to the conversation, instead of stalling it, and do their best to say something intelligent, if they are capable of it. I see that London is quite the reverse, with the exception of your charming brothers, or should I instead believe *you* to be the exception?" Lucian's face took on a subtle shift into something more feral as he heard her words. Gripping his glass tighter, he swayed toward her a little.

"Oh. I do like this game. If I should follow your example, I should believe that all American girls are impertinent, rude, and outspoken, with no regard for their station or respect for their betters," he said condescendingly, hitting his mark. Caroline fought to keep her face indifferent.

"Show me one, sire, and I shall act accordingly," she said,

He narrowed his eyes, incredulous, no doubt, that such a girl was refusing to be intimidated by him, nor show any deference for position or rank. In response, she smiled pleasantly and turned to accept a cup of tea and sit beside Eva on the settee, leaving Lucian to sit alone, awkwardly without company, in an armchair.

"The first spring ball will be in only two weeks, I can scarcely believe it," Margaret was saying.

"I love the first spring ball. It is always great fun," Wesley agreed, his eyes twinkling.

"Yes, anything is better than sitting around at home constantly, waiting for people to call," Katherine huffed, and then laughed at her mother's expression. Charles's face though was a picture as he watched her. He looked as though he'd like to scold her, and Caroline could tell that propriety was very important to him, probably especially important in a new sister. Well, Caroline decided that it did not matter, since Eva could not possibly marry his insufferable cad of a brother anyway.

Suddenly a loud snore rent the air, and they all turned toward Lord

Lucian, who had made himself comfortable in the chair, and now appeared to be sleeping quite soundly.

🍀

*K*atherine paced. She could not settle. Caroline had told her to be patient, to make her own assessment of the man, rather than let her head be swayed by gossip. Well, now that she had done as advised, she had made her own appraisal, and it was not as bad as she had feared- it was far, far worse! He was a beast, entirely without consideration or gentility. He would drive a saint to rampage. And, where Eva's health was concerned, Katherine did not care to tempt fate again.

She had been six, to Eva's eight, when Eva had almost died in her arms. They had run into the fields of a hot spring day, the Virginian sun bright and blistering, heating the sweetness of the blossoms, and carrying their perfume on the air to tempt the bees.

Katherine had chased Eva, though she could not now remember the reason, and Eva could not catch her breath. She had suddenly dropped like a doll in the grass, her white cotton dress splaying around her, clutching at her throat, rasping and panicked, unable to get enough air. Her face had gone pale, and her lips blue before their mother had been able to make it across the field to reach Katherine's screams.

As she grew older, her attacks had grown less and less frequent, but sometimes because of the flowers, sometimes because of the heat, a friend's beloved pet, or sometimes when emotion overtook her, they lost her again. And, every time it brought Katherine back to that field when she was six and had nearly killed her sister.

Eva had always recovered quickly enough, but the doctor had warned she suffered from a weakness of the heart as well as the lungs, and that one day it may fail her. He recommended smoke to strengthen the lungs, but while Mrs Fairfax forced her to smoke once a week with Indian hemp, or pure tobacco, Eva could not abide it. Chloroform was also recommended, but Eva seemed to manage her condition best by avoiding things that had triggered an attack in the past, and controlling her emotions as best she could.

She had spent many years in relative safety, but while Miss Fairfax

24

was adamant that the ailment had finally left her for good, Katherine could not find it in herself to believe in such good fortune. She worried. She always would.

🌸

The weeks leading up to the opening spring ball were a flurry of activity for the girls. Dancing lessons were doubled, visits to the dressmaker demanded, as Margaret caught wind of the new style of dress that would be worn by the elite this season. Mrs Fairfax had already hinted to Caroline that she was to act in a chaperoning capacity for both her girls and not to leave them alone, especially Katherine to keep her from trouble, though Caroline thought that may be asking the impossible.

In her free time, Caroline scanned the papers for any news of the Ashford family. It seemed they were rather infamous. Three sons in total, and one daughter, all of which were out in society and unmarried. They had been predominant figures of the Ton for years and were frequent members of Almack's; though, none were as infamous nor as gossiped over than Lord Lucian, the second son. The wildest rumour had that he was a bastard of the Prince Regent, George IV, others that he was the son of a pirate, and Caroline had even read that some attributed his existence to the devil himself. He certainly behaved like him, Caroline thought, as she heard wild tales of his excess and escapades, his countless conquests, his drinking and gambling, his unbeaten record in dueling, and multiple illegitimate children. Caroline tried to imagine a worse suitor for Eva, and found it far beyond the capabilities of her imagination, though Mrs Fairfax was as convinced as ever that this match was perfect, and took every opportunity to reinforce such opinions loudly, provoking Katherine to contradict her even more loudly at each turn.

Eva had taken the news well, the only sign of her devastation, a paling of the cheek and a slight trembling of the fingers as she busied herself with her needlework. But, she withdrew, and became gradually more fragile, it seemed, and both Caroline and Katherine began truly to worry.

They had cause for such concerns. Eva's health had always been delicate, less so as she had grown older, but she remained the family member most carefully coddled, and most fussed over, which she endured with her usual quiet grace.

Both her sisters tried, in turn, to convince Eva to ask her parents to spare her the fate of marrying such a man, but she would not. She was rigidly dutiful. She knew well the importance of the union to her parents, to her father's business interests, and though she did not say it, Caroline guessed that Eva felt duty-bound to the marriage prospects of her little sister as well. The fates had dealt their cards, and she would sacrifice her own happiness for the lot of them.

The man who was the cause of such worry did not return even once in that time, and Caroline was glad of it. Eva was in mourning for her life, and seeing him would only make it worse with his hateful personality, and lidded, jaded eyes.

The only bright spot was the arrival of their dear friends from Virginia, the Taylors. A family that had grown up as their neighbours, and had decided to join them in London for the Season, as Mr Taylor's business interests were closely linked with Mr Fairfax's. He had brought along his two grown sons, who were excited to be exploring the world for the first time.

Isaac and Eli Taylor had known Caroline, Katherine, and Eva since they were all young and silly. Caroline couldn't have been happier that they would be attending the same functions in the coming season. They would be a sanctuary in a swirling ballroom full of unseen dangers. Unfortunately, this also meant that they knew Eva far too well for her to successfully disguise her evident pain with her usual stoic silence, and even Isaac and Eli, merry as they always were, could not fail to be upset by it.

It had been some time since she'd last seen her old friends, and she was surprised how much older they looked. They had become men in the time since she had seen them, and now she struggled to remember the carefree little boys or lanky teenagers that they had been. Isaac, ambitious and sharp as a whip, was still the entertainer, keeping everyone laughing long into the night with his wild stories and jokes. Eli, if anything, had grown more introspective, sensitive and earnest. He was learning his father's business and took his work seriously. Always the sensitive one, he took Eva's pain the hardest, and Caroline could see a true vulnerability in his eyes when he looked at her. Now, there was the perfect suitor for Eva, Caroline thought, watching them together. Though between the two of them, they'd probably give all their worldly possessions to the needy and live happily penniless and selfless.

The only brush with the Ashford family came unexpectedly. Caroline had decided to go to the haberdashery with Katherine and Eva, and they had run into Isaac and Eli on the way, and being the gentlemen they were, they had immediately offered themselves as escorts. Walking together, the five made a merry party and decided to stroll the park on their way back.

It was a warm afternoon for England. They laughed about the weather, comparing it to Virginia, and Caroline felt as if a little bit of home had followed them to London. They stopped to buy some cool drinks from a seller when she spotted a familiar pair coming toward them on the same path. Feeling her heart sink, she wondered if she could change their course so they might not be seen, or else be able to politely pretend. At that moment, Lord Wesley Ashford's head swung toward hers, and she saw a smile of recognition spread over his features. Changing course, he intercepted them and smiled amiably and stopped in front of them, removing his hat as he bowed.

"Miss Lesage, the Miss Fairfaxes, how wonderful to see you all! I was just mentioning to my brother that we have been absent inexcusably long from your fair company," he said warmly, waiting to be introduced to her friends. Caroline took a breath, watching as Lord Lucian sauntered unhurriedly over, looking her up and down before a slow smile melted across his chiseled face. He did not bother to remove his hat. Caroline ground her teeth at his poor manners. As Eva introduced the Taylors, Lord Lucian looked them over with an assessing glance that had a slightly possessive feel to it, if Caroline was not mistaken.

Both parties spoke of their mornings, and Wesley demanded to see what the ladies had bought at the haberdashery. Eva obliged with a shy smile, and Lord Wesley kindly acted as if he were being shown artifacts of great interest rather than lengths of ribbon.

Lord Wesley continued to hold up their side of the conversation single-handedly and in good spirits, engaging the Taylors about their journey, and then inquiring after their family, and talking about their respective family business with Isaac. While Eli took the opportunity to sidle closer to the sisters to share a conversation about the various sites on offer in London, Caroline found Lucian's eyes uncomfortably heavy on her, and she met them challengingly.

"Lord Lucian, is there something the matter?" she asked in a marked tone, widening her eyes, as he looked at her closely. His lips quirked slightly, though he did not speak. "Perhaps you are suffering somehow—your face suggests that you may be in some digestive discomfort," she continued dryly, hating the way her words made his smile spread. "Or, perhaps you are just wondering about the health and happiness of your much thought-of fiancée?" That struck a nerve, she thought triumphantly, as his face darkened. "Ah, I see that is it. How sweet of you. Well, worry not, she is quite well, I assure you, though the last few weeks have been difficult for her. She has had some devastating news to adjust to of late," Caroline continued, watching as he sighed, tucked his hat under an elbow and ran his hands through his hair making it stand most rakishly. It glinted like tarnished gold in the sunlight, and reminded her of the rumors over his parentage, seeing it now in stark contrast with his dark brother.

He returned his eyes to hers, burning into her, and she ignored the little thrill which antagonising him gave her. Her heartbeat picked up a little, and maddeningly enough, he smiled slowly, as though he knew the effect he was having on her.

"You are quite impertinent today, Miss Lesage. Unbecoming of a lady, some would say."

"I think you shall find that whether or not I am becoming to you, or anyone else, is of no interest to me, Lord Lucian."

"Is that so, Miss Lesage? I find it difficult to believe. Do you not worry that you are on Mrs Fairfax's list of ladies to marry off? That you may be next? Then you will have to learn to curb that tongue, or end up with a husband who enjoys teaching you," he taunted, his eyes darkened wickedly for a moment. Forcing herself to sound carefree and ignore the strange sensation in her belly, she replied.

"That is not something which concerns me."

"No? I think you are mistaken, Miss Lesage." Caroline sighed at the unpleasant task of having to discuss her marital availability with this man, but anything to prove him wrong.

"It is difficult to find time to be a chaperon and companion if one is married. I do not think Mrs Fairfax is in any hurry to take me away from her daughters until they themselves are wed, and I am in no hurry to leave them. You see, I am far luckier than most of my sex, as I have been promised a choice in the matter." Caroline's eyes strayed to Eva pointedly, before turning back to Lord Lucian to ensure that the insult had been received.

"You will choose spinsterhood then? I must agree, you have the disposition for it, but do you not want a family of your own?" he asked coolly.

It was that step too far. He knew it, they both did. She stepped closer in and spoke quietly in the hope that the others would not notice her tone.

"Lord Lucian. I may be new to your city and customs, but I would still prefer to be treated with some decorum and respect *if* you are at all capable," she said, a harsh note in her voice which she hoped would provide the slap on the face she so longed to give.

"I shall be happy, Miss Lesage," he said, finally doffing his hat with a slight bow, "to introduce you to this city and our customs, as well as *any* other thing which you may not yet have experienced in your short, sheltered life."

The condescension in his tone was thick and unmistakable, and Caroline bristled at it, almost as much as she bristled at the crooked smile and intense gaze that was making her flush. She lowered her voice again and moved closer.

"My Lord Lucian, if you think that I am a shrinking violet who will blanch at your rudeness and cower at your lewd suggestions, then you will find yourself quite mistaken. I will not be bullied or shocked. Do not ever think that you can speak so to me again, nor to either of my sisters. Why, if you had any honour at all, you would have the grace to bow out of this betrothal that our parents seem so set upon, when it is so very clear that my sister neither likes you nor wants anything you have to offer. I will not have her hurt by you. I will see to it myself if I have to." Her breath was coming a little fast as Caroline finished, realising that she had said too much. Something had changed in Lord Lucian's demeanour. His smile was now as wide and unfettered as she had ever seen it, and his eyes crinkled at their corners with what looked like genuine mirth.

"Protective little thing, aren't you? A force to be reckoned with," he whispered, raising his eyebrows. "I quite understand, Miss Lesage, as I myself have always been fiercely protective over my own siblings. You do yourself credit. But surely I do not deserve such damning condemnation when I have been the very image of gentility."

A fierce little thing! He spoke as if she were a terrier for ratting. Rather than warn him away, as she had hoped, she had given him more cause to bait her. For a second, she could not help but try to slap the smile from his face.

"You do not deserve anything so much as a swift kick in the teeth from a horse, Lord Lucian."

He laughed, and that inappropriate stare returned to flush her hot skin.

"Would you not prefer to do it yourself, Miss Lesage?"

She opened her mouth to retort when Eva's soft voice broke in.

"Dear Caroline, you look quite overheated! I think perhaps we should be getting you home to cool down, do you not agree?"

She dragged her furious gaze from Lucian and managed a smile to meet Eva's worried face. "Yes, I would, thank you. I am very much in need of a change of view, I find."

"So, will we have the pleasure of escorting you, and the Miss Fairfaxes to the ball tomorrow night?" Wesley asked.

"Fortunately, that pleasure already belongs to us, I'm afraid, Lord Ashford," Isaac said, and his arm lifted for Caroline to take it.

The smile on Lord Lucian's face melted in an instant, and a frightful look of icy disdain replaced it as he turned slowly to Isaac. "Well... I am not sure how I feel about my fiancée being accompanied to a public event on the arm of another gentleman," he said darkly, causing everyone to look at him. Wesley, in particular, looked surprised.

"Well, I am quite sure Miss Fairfax's dance card shall have a space or two which you may yet steal," Eli said, with an edge to his voice that quite surprised Caroline. Lucian said nothing for a moment, locking the other man in his narrowed stare.

"Of course. No matter." Lucian finally said, tossing his hand as if it was nothing at all to him, and his face took on the look of a man bravely enduring a most tedious encounter.

However, after they had said their goodbyes, and parted ways, Caroline walked alongside the elder Mr Taylor, who offered his arm over a patch of mud. He made a remark about the superiority of Virginian mud, and she threw her head back as she laughed. As she did so, she caught sight of Lucian's eyes trained on them both, with a look like storm clouds.

❀

"*Y*ou seem anxious tonight brother," Isaac Taylor remarked as he watched his younger brother make yet another mistake with his cravat. "Here, let me," he said, coming forward and untying it. He glanced up at Eli's face and wondered what was going through his brother's mind, or *whom*, he corrected

"Is it because you are escorting Eva tonight?" he asked mildly.

"We are escorting the family. I am hardly escorting Eva," Eli said, scoffing uncomfortably.

"I feel sure she would be most charmed if you did," Isaac said, watching the tiny flare of hope appear in Eli's eyes. "Most charmed to have your hand warm about her waist, pulling her close for a waltz...giving that English barbarian a run for his money."

"Don't speak like that," he said, his soft expression wiped away. "Eva is a lady. She doesn't think of me so. Anyway, she is engaged to be married, and from what I have gathered, it is quite settled," Eli said stiffly, turning back to the mirror, brushing Isaac's hands away.

"Oh? Have you been making inquiries then?" Isaac asked, one taunting eyebrow cocked.

"No, of course not. She is a dear childhood friend. I worry for her happiness, that is all."

"And would you like to be the one to make her happy?" Eli ignored him. "Over and over again..." Isaac added.

Eli's face flashed with anger before hands shot out quickly and grabbed his brother by the neck, bending him over, and pulling his jacket over his head in a practiced move from many years of rough-housing.

Isaac laughed and twisted away from his tight grasp before tugging Eli's neatly tied cravat loose. "Unhand me, you villain! You will destroy my beautiful hair," he said, smoothing it back into a fashionable angle, "and then all the ladies of London will be furious with you."

"A risk I'm willing to take," Eli warned, readying for another attack. "No lady worth her salt would even look twice at you."

"There must be many an unsalted lady in London then," Isaac said, running around the table just out of Eli's reach, "because my dance card is already full, and you shall have to stand by and hold my coat and fetch me punch to keep me from collapse." He dodged another lunge and yelped.

"You are a ridiculous buffoon!" Eli finally laughed, gathering his things. "Come on then, let's not keep our ladies waiting."

🍥

The assembly rooms chosen for the ball were grand indeed, Caroline thought, as she stepped down from the carriage. The Season had various different events throughout the year, and Margaret had been carefully preparing her girls for this, the most exclusive event, with the most beautiful gowns that any of them had ever seen, prompting Caroline to wonder how long she had been planning Eva's engagement, as there were several other balls that night, but, following the announcement of Eva's engagement to Lord Ashford, they had been invited into all the most fashionable despite their newness to London, and their lack of family.

The road was clogged with carriages, and servants helping women cross the cobbled street. Lit lanterns glowed above wide and gracious stone steps, beckoning excited ball goers like moths through the pillars at the top and into the glittering opulence within.

Whilst the Fairfax ladies had been to neighbourhood balls in Virginia, and even occasionally to Richmond, the balls of London could not be matched for grandeur. The exquisite rooms sparkled with thousands of candles, fresh flowers adorned the surfaces and balustrades in fragrant abundance, and there was enough fine food and punch for all of London. Majestic columns decorated each grand room, bringing one's eyes to the chandeliers which dripped crystal and gold from the high ceilings.

Underneath, glittered the Ton; its beautiful young ladies and gentlemen polished and in their very finest silks, while the older crowd were draped in the most beautiful and expensive jewels that Caroline had ever seen.

The massive assembly rooms had several floors, each designated for different purposes. The entirety of the ground floor was set aside for dancing, another floor for eating, drinking, and resting, and it was already filling up with elderly chaperons awake past their bedtimes and drowsy with punch. Another floor was set aside for the gentlemen, with smoking tables and games of poker already springing up.

Katherine's eyes danced as she squeezed Caroline's hand. They stepped in and worked their way along the introduction line. Mr Fairfax and Mr Taylor had already excused themselves for the upper level, while Mrs Fairfax had spotted some ladies she wished to be introduced to. Caroline tagged along after everyone, looking around at the splendour, unable to take it all in. For the next hour, she dipped and bobbed in response to countless introductions, trying to remember all the names being thrown at her. A while later, she found herself at the refreshment table with Isaac and Katherine. Thirsty from the endless introductions and platitudes, she quickly drank her first glass of champagne, then reached for another.

"Caroline! I shall start to think I have been a bad influence!" Katherine exclaimed, raising her glass in a toast. Eli smiled.

"Ladies, let's not do anything foolish just yet, you have not even danced, nor eaten," he reminded them, urging them to try some of the lavish food that was spread out over the banquet table. Caroline, who had never felt less hungry, continued to sip her champagne, turning this way and that, still taking in all the new sights. A couple of young socialites stopped near her, engrossed in their conversation, and Caroline could not help but overhear.

"Rosemary swore it was true. They are here! All of them. And she said he was mere steps away from her," the girl gushed, her cheeks pink with excitement.

"I heard tell that he has not shown his face at a ball in years. It must be because he is engaged now." The other girl sighed, sounding positively jealous.

"Well, surely you've heard about the man he killed just last winter. Shot in cold blood!" The girl leaned closer to her companion, and Caroline strained to listen. "They say the poor man walked in on his wife with him doing the most *unspeakable* things." The girl gasped behind her fan and then giggled into her punch.

"It's not fair! Why can't it be me? He has finally decided to take a wife, and he chooses an American, of all things," the girl whispered the salacious news.

There was a pause, then Caroline started as one of the girls let out a small squeak, which was instantly shushed by her friend.

"It's him. It is definitely him. I think he may be the most handsome beau I've ever laid eyes upon. My word, I think he's looking at us!" The other girl also squealed in excitement, and Caroline could contain her curiosity no longer. It was obvious who they were talking about, but she couldn't quite stop herself from following their tilted heads up to the inner balcony which ran around the gentlemen's floor. Two floors above her, the balcony looked down on the refreshment and resting area, and she saw the figure that had caused so much excitement.

He was impeccably dressed unlike the last time she had seen him; his tailcoat a rich, deep blue, buttoned tightly over his firm, narrow waist. His waistcoat was a creamy white, as was his elaborate cravat, and his black hose were tightly fitted to his muscular legs.

He leaned on the balustrade casually, and Caroline was too far away, and in too dim a light to make out his expression, but found that she too could not help but be struck by his beauty. When she had first met him, she had found him soulless, and unrefined, and not nearly as handsome as his brothers. Now though, seeing him there, in all his state, his unruly thatch of golden hair messily coiffed, wicked blue eyes, and almost wolfish virility, she could not ignore his obvious appeal. She raised her glass and took a quick gulp of champagne to dispel the feeling. She risked a last glance upwards and was surprised to see him raise his glass to her, as he continued to stare down. Looking quickly away, she returned to relative safety behind a group of fanning ladies.

Finally, they were moving together into the ballroom. The place sparkled and danced in a sea of moving bodies. A band played at one end, and upon their arrival, Eli immediately asked Eva for her first dance. Waiting for a reluctant nod from her mother, she accepted, very gladly, Caroline noticed, and they disappeared into the mass. Caroline smiled around and thought how lucky she was to be there. Even if she should spend the entire evening watching the others dance, and not stand up herself, she would still leave with a dazzled smile on her face.

"May I be so bold as to claim this dance?" a deep voice drew her attention, and she looked over to find Lord Charles standing by Katherine, who was grinning unreservedly up at him.

"Absolutely," she purred, long and suggestive, causing him to raise his eyebrow, before leading her out into the crowd.

"Lady Caroline. You look splendid. I trust you are enjoying yourself?" Lord Wesley asked pleasantly. "Please, allow me to introduce my sister, Lady Rebecca Ashford," he said and Caroline turned her attention to the startlingly lovely brunette standing by his side. Greeting her, Caroline reciprocated and introduced the rest of her company.

At that moment, Mrs Fairfax appeared, and Wesley gallantly asked her to dance. Flattered and flushing, she accepted, and soon their group was once more reduced. Caroline turned to Lady Rebecca and smiled.

"You are so very lucky, Lady Ashford, to live in London, to be able to attend these types of functions frequently."

"Actually, I just arrived from the country this morning, and am already wishing to go back. I don't care much for cities," she said haughtily, making Caroline want to roll her eyes.

"Still, it must be wonderful always having a range of friends and escorts to call on at a moment's notice," Caroline continued, determined to make polite small talk.

"If you insist." She actually rolled her eyes in disdain, and Caroline thought maybe she was starting to see the family resemblance, with at least one of the Ashford clan anyway.

A waiter passed with champagne and Caroline turned to fetch them a couple of glasses, as she turned back, she saw too late that Isaac had asked their surly new acquaintance to dance, leaving her alone. Trying not to seem embarrassed at being left alone, and holding two glasses of champagne no less, she looked around for somewhere to set one down.

"Let me get that for you," a familiar-sounding accent said behind her, transporting her back home in an instant. Spinning around, she was met with a new face- a handsome, dark man, with smiling eyes and white teeth. She looked around quickly for help and could see no one she knew.

"I know. We have not yet been introduced, therefore, I should not speak to you. That's the way it works here, right? You must forgive me. I can not keep up with all these rules," he laughed, and Caroline relaxed a little. Curiosity getting the better of her.

"Where are you from, Mr...?" she asked.

"Tennessee. Mr Lee. Joshua Lee," he said, and took one of the glasses from her hand and toasted her glass, with tilted head in silent question.

"Virginia. I'm Miss Caroline Lesage," she added conspiratorially, "just in case anyone asks if we've been introduced. Now we have," she said, and enjoyed his playful laugh.

"It's a pleasure to meet you Miss Lesage," he said, his dark eyes dancing. They each sipped their champagne and watched the floor. Most of Caroline's friends had stayed and were beginning the next dance.

"When we finish this drink, I'm going to be even more improper, and ask you to dance," he said seriously. Caroline laughed, then assumed a serious expression.

"Well, in that case, I'm going to behave unforgivably and say yes..." she said, feeling her cheeks grow warm as their eyes locked for an instant. Clearing her throat slightly, she dropped her gaze and suddenly became aware of being watched. It was a slight crawling sensation on her skin, a light prickling at the nape of her neck.

"Miss Lesage." She turned slowly to meet his predatory gaze. Up close, he was even more powerful looking and exuded an energy that she found overwhelming. Bobbing politely, she plastered a smile on her face.

"Lord Ashford, how... delightful it is to see you," she said, reciting one of her standard phrases from Margaret's patented polite English introductory lines, while gently implying the contrary. His eyes lingered on her face, before making a leisurely survey of her whole body, she felt the blood start to beat in her cheeks.

"As it is you. You look exquisite," he said, his voice lingering scandalously on the last word. He then looked to Mr Lee and Caroline realised that it may be her responsibility to introduce them.

"Mr Lee, this is-"

"Lord Lucian Ashford," Joshua finished, reaching his hand forward to shake Lucian's. Lucian smiled lazily.

"You know of me, I gather."

"Only by reputation."

"Well, one cannot believe everything one hears."

"I sincerely hope not," Joshua said shortly before he turned to Caroline and extended his arm. "You will please excuse us, we were just about to dance," he announced to Lucian, his eyes fixing on Caroline and smiling. "Miss Lesage..."

She smiled shyly back. They moved out into the crowd and she could have sworn she felt his eyes on her back, then on her often during the dance. Ignoring the odd feeling, she concentrated on her partner and was soon laughing and dancing, until she was out of breath.

Mr Lee's company was as easy as a breath of fresh air after all of the strict rules and restrictions that had been put on her recently. Dancing with him, she could imagine she was back home, where people had known her family, and where she was not made to feel completely insignificant.

When the song came to an end, without leaving the floor, she was asked to dance by Lord Wesley, as Mr Lee offered to dance with Mrs Fairfax, rather bravely, Caroline thought.

Caroline found herself warming more and more to the youngest Ashford, and found him comfortable company. He joked about his family and their childhood and politely inquired after hers.

At one point, Eli and Eva danced past, and Wesley turned his head to watch them.

"I am sad to say that till tonight, I did not know that Miss Fairfax had such a lovely smile," he noted, and Caroline glimpsed her friend, who truly did look happy that night, in her childhood friend's arms. "Do they know each other well?" he asked and Caroline wondered how to answer.

"Longer than she has known her fiance, that is certain," Caroline said with a light laugh, trying to ease any tension which might arise at the situation.

"Well, that is not difficult, is it?" Wesley rejoined, turning his eyes back to her.

"I suppose not. And your brother? Does he smile often? Whenever I see him, he always seems to be in a terrifying mood, or else smiling at the torture of lesser mortals," Caroline teased with a smile, hoping she was not causing offense.

"Lucian? Lucian is a very complex man," he answered seriously. "He had a harder time than the rest of us growing up, and those days still torment him now. But I believe the right woman will be good for him. It may just save him," he said almost to himself, leading Caroline through the choreographed steps easily, for which she was thankful.

"Does he need to be saved?" She asked, surprised by the choice of words.

"Very much," Wesley returned, his eyes meeting hers, his smile slipping a little.

"May I ask from whom?" Caroline hoped to get one last answer out of him, as she sensed his growing reluctance to share. Her mind swam with many of the dark rumours she had overheard that night and wondered what nasty trouble he might be in.

"Himself, for the most part," Wesley finished, giving her a wry grin. "Or perhaps that's just champagne talking."

The music changed, and she continued to change partners, dancing with Isaac, Charles and Joshua again. As she whirled around, having more fun than was proper, she glimpsed Eva dancing with Lucian, and suddenly grew nervous.

Eli was leading Mrs Fairfax around the floor, oblivious to her chattering, as he turned his head, taking every opportunity to watch Eva with Lucian. To be fair to him, the infamous playboy seemed to be behaving quite well that night, Caroline decided, thinking maybe she had judged him a little too harshly.

By the end of the next dance, Caroline felt exhausted. It was amazing how others managed to keep up with all the demands of socialising, gossiping, flirting, propriety, and all while dancing a quadrille. It was very warm in the ballroom, and the fresh air of the balcony beckoned to her.

Mercifully, the band was taking an interval, and Caroline excused herself and went upstairs with Eva and Katherine to the lady's room. Katherine talked brightly, and a little loudly, causing Caroline to wonder how much champagne she had had, as she shot off in search of more. Eva was subdued, even for her, and Caroline did not doubt the reason for it. Sitting beside her on a soft divan, she clasped her hand.

"Are you well?"

"Yes, I should not complain, really. It is such an exciting night," Eva said, but her voice lacked the luster of her words.

"However..." Caroline prompted, and watched in dismay as tears filled her friend's eyes.

"He terrifies me. Even just dancing with him. In a room, full of people. How could I ever be alone with him?" she said brokenly. Caroline wrapped her arms around her friend, grateful that this particular room was relatively quiet and they could speak without interruption.

"This is all very new. It's normal to feel this way," Caroline lied, trying to soothe her fragile sister. Eva shook her head vigorously.

"No, it is not. He's different. Savage. I can just tell. The way he touches me pulls me too close. The things he says..."

"That's the difference between men and women. Men are rougher, they enjoy hunting and other physical activities. Women are gentler and more refined. It is to be expected," Caroline tried again, thinking she would not mention the extreme physical activities she'd heard Lucian preferred.

"But, not all men are like that. Some of them make me feel safe, like father, and..."

"And Eli?" Caroline finished for her, watching Eva's shoulders shake with sobs.

"Hush now, sweetheart. We can fix this."

"No. We can't," she said, her voice breaking. "It's too late. It's all too late."

Lost for words, Caroline hugged her hard and waited for her to regain her composure. Her blood began to boil. What had he done? What had he said? Why was he so incapable of acting with any care for others' feelings? With her it was different- he didn't scare her, she could handle herself. But Eva, Eva could not, and he knew it.

"I discover you at last! What is taking so long? That insufferable Lord Charles will not let me out of his sight. He's a stricter chaperon than mama! I've only managed to have one glass of champagne in as many hours. I am in desperate need of diverting conversation," Katherine said, as she burst into the room. She reached out her hand to her older sister, and finally, calming somewhat, Eva took it, dried her eyes and stood up. Together, she and Eva reached the door, but Caroline hung back.

Someone would need to speak to Lord Lucian about Eva. This would not do, and she would be damned if she could watch a most beloved sister scared to tears, and say nothing. He must be spoken to. He must be gentler with her. She thought of asking Lord Wesley to speak to him, but he would probably think it was not her place, and he would be right. But Eva's happiness was far more important than propriety, or Caroline's discomfort. She had watched Eva grow more fearful every day, and she could not go on seeing her so unhappy, not when she might be able to help. The champagne sparkled in her belly like fuel on a fire. And, Eva wasn't wrong. Lord Lucian *was* different. He seemed to enjoy terrifying people, and Caroline had a thing or two to say about it.

"I'm going to find some food. I'll join you shortly," Caroline said, avoiding their eyes as she told the lie.

She glanced in the mirror as she left the room. The dancing had heightened the roses in her cheeks and her lips were flushed pink, her hair, too heavy for its pins, had begun to surrender in a tousled mess. Maybe it was the champagne running through her veins, but she felt the braver for it.

CHAPTER 3

There was no sign she could see of the notorious bachelor in the resting area, nor the ballroom, as she ducked around, trying not to catch the eye of her group. That only left the garden and the men's floor. Approaching the terrace doors, she sincerely hoped he could be found in the garden, as she had not the slightest idea how to look for him in the men's quarters, and the garden was reckless enough for one evening.

As she stepped out onto the stone terrace, she felt the cooling breath of the breeze soothe her. It lifted the damp tendrils of hair off the nape of her neck and caressed the gap between her sleeves and gloves. Quickly, raising the edge of her gown, she carefully descended the steps into the garden. She could see the odd group of people, sitting by the fountain, or walking in the arbour. Some scandalous couples, too drunk for their own good, giggling as they disappeared into the maze. She trod the gravel quietly, hoping not to draw attention to herself and the fact that she was alone.

After a quick pass of the perimeter of the garden which was lit by torches, she walked to the maze. She had made it this far, and could not turn back now. Taking a deep breath, she marched into the carefully pruned bushes and started turning left and right, quite at random. She began to wonder if she had drunk too much for her own good.

It was dark inside the maze, with an occasional flaming torch, and plenty of alcoves for couples to hide in. Every time she passed by a woman giggling, she pushed on a bit faster, mortified, her illusions of the uptight English social elite crashing down with each step. After what felt to be an hour, but was probably mere minutes, she had to admit she was lost. The walls all looked the same, and as music had restarted inside the assembly rooms, the maze had gotten quieter, with couples rushing back to dance.

She continued her pace faster than ever. She felt as though the shadows and belated worry were chasing her. This had been foolish. Stupid. Dangerous. Suddenly ahead, she heard steps on gravel. She moved forward a little, scared to interrupt someone, but also afraid to be lost and alone in the labyrinth. Turning the corner quietly, her eyes took in the sight before her, long before her mind was able to comprehend it. She fervently wished she had turned back, or better still had never come here in the first place.

It was that wolfish manner of his that gave his silhouette away even in the dark. His movements languid, but filled with controlled menace.

He was kissing, most inappropriately, a woman whom she had never seen. Then, he broke away and shoved her savagely against the hedge. She let out a low cry, and he closed the distance after her, pressing her hard against the branches, and Caroline watched in shock as he roughly clamped his palm over her mouth. Her bodice was open, and her pale breasts shone in the moonlight, and she saw Lucian's hands scrape across her waist, leaving marks behind that could be seen even from where she stood. Caroline watched, paralysed, unable to tear her eyes away as one of his hands went to her breast, touching them so roughly, that the woman writhed in pain, Lucian's mouth at her neck. Cupping the other breast in one hand, he lowered his mouth to her nipple and bit down. The woman screamed through his closed fingers, still clamped tight across her mouth, as he pinned her arm back with his free hand, and ground his body against her, pressing more savagely than before, the branches of the hedge scraping her exposed skin.

Going cold, Caroline suddenly realised that she was not witnessing a mutual act of love, but a violation. Her heart started to pound in her ears. Pulling herself up to her fullest height, she scanned the ground, her eyes finally adjusted to the moonlight, and picked up the biggest rock she could find.

Creeping up quietly behind them, she tried to reassure the girl with her eyes that she was there to help as she raised the rock high in the air and brought it down with a crack on Lucian's head.

He staggered to the side, went down on one knee, holding his head, swearing. Caroline wasted no time pulling the girl from her prison, and trying to help her stand, hurrying to cover her bare breasts.

"Quick, we must make haste. He will recover in a moment," she said, not understanding why the girl refused to move faster. In exasperation, she pulled at the girl's arm.

"May I ask what exactly you think you are doing?" The girl's voice was tight with contempt.

Caroline looked at the girl in confusion.

"I am helping you to escape. He will not get away with this. I will see to it," she said slowly, thinking it obvious. The girl studied her in silence for a moment, then threw her head back and laughed, a throaty, mirthless scrape in the quiet night air. Slowly tying her dress closed again, all the while, smiling at Caroline in a patronising manner.

"Let me guess. This is your first Season? Perhaps even your very first ball? Little fool..."

A low voice interrupted her from behind.

"Lydia, leave her be. She thought she was helping you," he said dryly, and Caroline turned to look at Lucian, who was closing his breeches, causing her to whirl back around.

"I did not think such simple-minded naivete was possible. Darling, I must go, my mother will be searching for me," she smirked and walked off into the maze. Caroline stood in silence, her face blazing until she heard her footsteps fade completely. Wanting to leave, but not wanting to follow the girl too closely, lest she be the focus of more ridicule.

She heard a soft chuckle and turned furious eyes to Lord Lucian.

"Don't be upset. You arrived just in the nick of time to preserve her virtue," he mocked, and she felt the blow of it, though his voice was not unkind.

Her head spun with adrenaline and alcohol. Sitting on the cold stone bench, she pressed her hands to her cheeks and tried to cool the fire in them. She was mortified, but after a moment's thought, she accepted that she had merely disturbed two lovers, and while she hated that one of them had been the man promised to her dearest friend, she also knew it to be common behaviour for men of his class. Perhaps it would be better for Eva if he were to take his interests elsewhere. Too many thoughts. She wasn't sure which ones were correct. She felt her stomach roil in protest, and swallowed hard, praying that she would not embarrass herself further.

After a time, Lucian sat down slowly on the bench beside her.

"I'm sorry-" he began but she interrupted.

"You should be." She frowned after a moment, thinking of his head. "I am too. Truly. It's just. Well, it looked like you were hurting her," Caroline's words tumbled out clumsily. He sat quietly beside her for a moment.

"I was," he replied evenly. Caroline's chest filled with another deep breath.

"Did she want you to?"

"Yes, she did. She begged me to."

"Lord Lucian, please take this in the way it is intended..." she steadied herself, trying to match her courage to her reserve, "but you cannot touch Miss Fairfax like that."

"I would never dream of it," he said, putting his hand to his heart.

"I'm afraid I'm going to have to hold you to that. If I should hear from her that-" she started gravely, and he chuckled.

"Please, do not worry, Miss Lesage. You have my word."

Leaning back a little, she released a breath that she had been holding, and trying to calm herself, she looked up at the starry sky, her eyes widening with wonder. As always when she looked up at the night sky, she felt peaceful, forgetting herself as the stars swam quietly in their velvet, the world spinning slowly around her as if she were the center of it. Everything else seemed so small, so far away: the shocking spectacle which she had just witnessed, her desire to be away from this man, the ever-pressing urgency to return to her group, and indeed, the life-altering consequences should she be discovered in the maze alone with the most infamous rake in all of London. Champagne swam in her veins, and she felt like the stars themselves twinkled under her skin.

The night had grown still around them, and she realised that Lord Lucian seemed a lot closer to her arm than he'd been before. Suddenly, she felt his fingertips slowly trail the gap in fabric above her glove, bringing out goosebumps. Her response sluggish, she looked down at his fingers, then up at his face.

"Why do *you* not fear me?" he asked, almost a whisper.

"You are assuming I do not," she replied, her stomach starting to coil with nerves.

"I think you would not have come here alone if you did, unless... unless you are not so unlike Lydia? Perhaps you came to the maze alone to seek out my company," he whispered, moving closer still.

Before she realised what was happening, she felt the cold, hard stone of the bench against her back. She opened her mouth to stop him and felt his lips come down on hers. Her head spun, her body weakened, her fingers plucked weakly at his clothes. His mouth was hot, hard and insistent on hers, and as she tried to clamp her lips shut, his lips moved away, to her neck, and she felt her senses returning.

"Lord Lucian! Stop!" she gasped, suddenly terrified he was too lost to stop. He continued to kiss her neck and she stopped trying to push his solid chest and slid down dropping her hands to either side of the bench until she could reach the ground, searching frantically over grass, twigs and leaves. Something rumbled in this chest appreciatively, as he mistook her sudden change in posture. Finally, her hand closed around something solid, just as he raised his face to hers.

"Miss Lesage, I have dreamed of this," he said passionately, his eyes boring urgently into hers, as she brought her hand up to the same side she had hit before, slamming the rock hard against his skull, for the second time that night. He rolled off her, falling to the ground, and she felt the cool night air enter her lungs with a rush. Sitting up, she immediately took off through the maze, running past his prone form on the ground.

"Miss Lesage... wait!" he called, but she sped faster, hoping that the knock to the head would slow him down, turning left, then right, and then left again. Completely disorientated, she stopped for a second, breathing hard, trying to get her bearings, trying to listen carefully past the drumming in her ears for footsteps, for music, for voices. The maze was dark and silent, when she heard the gravel crunching, she took off again. Suddenly she rounded a corner and saw the lights of the party in the distance, she had found the exit.

"Miss Lesage," Lucian's voice came from directly behind her, and she cried, spurring herself on toward the gap in the bushes. Just as she was close enough for her fingertips to brush the free air, she felt his arm go around her middle and a hand around her mouth. She tried to scream, but no sound escaped, and wriggling made no impact as he bore her back into the darkness.

❀

Stilling, but continuing to hold her tightly against him, Lucian lowered his mouth to her ear. She shook her head violently, causing him to hold her mouth even tighter until she gave up. Standing still, she listened to his urgent whisper,

"Listen to me, sweetheart. Do you hear them? They are looking for you out there. If they find you coming from the maze, your reputation will be tarnished beyond repair before the night is over. If they find us together, you will be ruined," he muffled her exclamation with his hand.

"I have no idea where she can have gotten to," a shrill voice rang out, Margaret's voice. It sounded irritated, probably at missing the ball due to her ward's carelessness.

"Indeed. I am sure she just felt unwell and took the carriage home early. Champagne can do that to a young girl who is unaccustomed to it," Charles's voice floated back.

"Still, she should have informed us, this is so unlike her," Margaret said crossly and Caroline could hear them moving back toward the assembly rooms.

She made to move forward, but he pulled her back, motioning to be quiet again. There were other voices further away that she could not place. Lucian had been right about the audience who would see her emerge, disheveled, from the maze. She waited in silence, her heart pounding, her breath burning in her chest, his arm, still a steel band around her middle. He lowered his mouth to her ear again and whispered.

"I'm going to release you in a moment, but before I do, I have to tell you most fervently, that I am sorry. I know you will not listen to me after, so I say it now. I thought... it matters not. I was wrong. I am sorry. You are safe, you have my word. Now, please take a moment to think carefully of your next move, Miss Lesage, for it may determine your future." Slowly he loosened his grip on her mouth, and she immediately began to squirm in his arms.

"Put me down," she hissed at him, wishing she had another rock. Finally released, she turned around and slapped him, with a resounding crack that threw his head to the side. He closed his eyes, slowly bringing his face back to hers, and smirked.

"I suppose I deserve that."

"What is wrong with you? How could you? What gave you the right? And you are engaged to my sister!" she said incredulously.

"Not by choice," he reminded her, his voice dropping as he rubbed his cheek.

"So, that is an adequate excuse to try and take advantage of an unwilling-"

"I did not realise that you were unwilling."

"You thought I would enjoy that? Being forcibly disgraced outside on a bench?"

"You would be surprised," he said in a low voice.

"And what possible indication could I have given you? Because I tried to be civil to you? Appeal to your better nature?" His clenched jaw loosened with a lopsided smirk and she scowled. "I see now that you don't have one, do you?"

"I suppose Miss Fairfax will be telling you soon enough," he answered smartly. Anger flashed across her face, more enraged than he had seen it before. When she came upon he and Lydia, she had been reasonable, when he had made unwanted advances on her, she had protected herself, but this throw-away comment about her sister had been the thing to send her over the edge. She was a mystery.

She turned around wordlessly and marched out of the mouth of the maze. When his hand touched her arm, she whirled furious, and his eyes softened, as he raised his hands up in quiet supplication.

"I just wanted to point out that you do not have a method of returning to the ball without your absence and appearance being noted, nor going home without going in to request the Fairfax carriage. The streets of London are hardly a place for someone such as yourself to be wandering at night. I can escort you safely." She raised her eyebrows at this, and the irony of the statement.

"Are you trying to convince me that I might be safer with *you*? Stay away from me, Lord Lucian or I shall tell your brothers and anyone else who will listen of your behaviour here tonight." She turned and started off toward the carriage entrance, her shoulders squared and proud. He followed behind her, making a final plea.

"Look, allow me to escort you. I have my carriage. I arrived separately from my family. We can slip out undetected, my carrriagemen are trained for discretion. Your reputation shall not be questioned. It is the least I can do," he offered, and, to his surprise, she paused to consider it. Biting her lip, she looked back toward the glowing lights of the party before turning back to him with narrowed eyes.

"Yes, it is the least you can do," she confirmed frankly, and turned from him, calling back over her shoulder. "However, you are more animal than man, Lord Lucian, and I trust the streets of London more than I would ever trust a blaggard like you."

❀

*G*lancing back after a while, she saw that he had gone, and she hugged her arms tighter around her and considered what to do. The Fairfaxes townhouse was not that far away, and the streets still seemed busy with carriages and groups of people walking. She was glad that her face was a new one in London; while she would make a strange sight walking home alone, her anonymity should, she hoped, keep her safe from gossip. This length of absence had been inexcusable, and she would never manage to fix the state of her hair or dress without a long stretch in front of a mirror. She didn't want to embarrass the Fairfaxes after everything they'd done for her, and she knew that the repercussions could be far, far more grave. She could paint the Fairfaxes in scandal, ruining their new business connections here in England, and worse still, not only ruining her chances but also tarnishing the girls with her ruined reputation all because of a sudden foolishness decision. This small mistake might ruin Katherine's chance for a good match, or make Eva an outcast, trapped with a beastly Earl she feared, and with no chance of being part of society.

No. Better perhaps to disappear unnoticed from the crowd and claim a sore head. The Fairfaxes would no doubt have angry questions for her in the morning, but others would be far less likely to notice her disappearance. Steeling herself, and arranging her shawl around her shoulders, she slipped past the entrance with its carriages and started home.

The streets were lit with lamps, and people talked merrily, laughing and joking as they walked around her. Spying a group ahead with three young ladies, and a couple of older companions, Caroline walked as close to them as she dared, hoping it would look as if they were together. She managed to draw near the townhouse in this way, and she was almost congratulating herself when the group suddenly turned toward a brightly lit house, ascending the steps without a backward glance, leaving her to continue alone. She pushed on, close now. Her feet hurt terribly, and she could feel blisters forming as her feet slid around in the thin fabric of her new slippers. The pleasantly cool breeze from earlier had turned into something bitter, and she hugged her shawl closer wishing that she had been able to retrieve her coat before leaving.

Turning down her street, she realised how quiet it was all of a sudden, and cursed the length of fashionable London streets, as she picked up the pace a little. A shadow moved beside her and she jumped, turning abruptly, her breath caught in her throat. A tall tree waved its leaves in front of a lamp, casting shadows over the pavement. Laughing nervously, she turned back and continued, a little faster than before. In the distance, she thought she could just make out the shape of her terrace.

Suddenly, the quiet of the street was broken by a rhythmic thud, harsh and loud.

Footsteps. Someone was hurrying toward her.

Picking up her pace even more, she clasped her skirts in one hand, her shawl in the other, she was almost running, her whole body prickling with nerves. She glanced back, but the street was shrouded in shadow apart from the spaces directly under the street lamps. The footsteps were getting louder, closer, running too now. The last of her nerve broke and she began to run as fast as she could. Her feet hit the hard pavement through the thin soles of her slippers, each step sending heavy jolts through her whole body, making her legs feel like lead, and her teeth clatter.

Suddenly, her foot descended into a cold puddle, she gasped as she felt a sharp flash of pain shoot through her ankle and up her leg. Throwing herself to the railing, she held on, and took the weight off of her ankle, breathing hard, taking a moment to try to get the pain under control while she scanned the street frantically. The footsteps continued to get closer, and in desperation, she pushed off, hobbling toward her house, which she could see now. Each step sent a crushing pain through her ankle, but she gritted her teeth and continued. Ahead, she saw only one more side road she needed to pass before reaching her home, and relief started to pour through her.

The feeling of relief was quickly replaced by apprehension, when she saw two men stagger out of the dark street to her left, clearly drunk, slapping each other, laughing loudly, and swearing. She considered trying to cross the street, but then one of them looked up and noticed her.

As she skirted to the side, almost hopping on her good leg now, she stiffened with alarm as one of them immediately acknowledged her, and crossed the street to her.

"Why! Fitz, what do we have here?" his voice was educated, apart from the drunken slur. She saw he was indeed wearing gentlemen's clothes, albeit wrinkled and askew.

"It seems we have a little debutante butterfly... who has fluttered away from her escort," his partner confirmed with a tisk, swaying toward her.

"Hmm. Oh, very careless indeed," he tisked again.

Caroline ducked her head and kept moving. She would be near enough to home soon if she could just manage to get past them.

"My lady, you are hurt? Allow us to escort you," the first said, hiccupping a little.

"There is no need sir, I have all but arrived," Caroline said, stopping as he stepped in front of her.

"But you must, it would be a mark against our honour!" his friend exclaimed, suddenly grabbing her arm. She gasped, pulling her arm out of his grasp, and accidentally putting weight on her ankle. Crying out, she reached for the railing again and was intercepted by the first man, who seemed to have recovered himself somewhat. Holding her steady, she realised how close he was holding her, far too close to be proper. Flushing, she tried to push herself away from him.

"Thank you, you are too kind." Her back suddenly came up against the second man's chest, who had moved right behind her, her palms sweating and adrenaline coursing through her veins.

"Please-" she started, stilling when the first man put his fingers to her lips, shushing her gently.

"It's alright, little one, we'll take good care of you." He reached out then and stroked the side of her face, while she felt the man behind her place his hands on her waist, and Caroline knew then with a sickening thud of her heart, with the slow-moving clarity of an unthinkable certainty, that they would make sport of her, and that she, wounded as she was, would be able to do nothing about it.

The man behind her clasped a hand across her mouth, and before she knew it, they had pulled her into the central garden in the middle of the square, and her muffled screams and her thrashing silhouette hidden behind the hedges, would not even draw glances from the windows.

CHAPTER 4

"$\mathcal{I}$ do hate to interrupt, but perhaps you chaps could be so good as to tell me where a gentleman can get a stiff drink around here," Lucian's light tone cut through the tension, and Caroline swung to face him, terror written across her face.

He sauntered toward them, his mess of hair golden under the lamplight, and the two men tensed, holding Caroline a little tighter.

"At the end of the street, a smashing place. They have women too," the first man said.

"Right then. In that case, gentlemen, might I suggest that take your hands off that lady immediately and get yourselves to the end of the street to enjoy a pint, and hire the services of a willing woman before I personally see to it that you can do neither ever again," he said very calmly, as he removed his gloves unhurriedly.

"We could. But then again, we've got a woman right here, without the extra block's journey. Don't let's be greedy, my good man. You're welcome to join us," he offered, nodding his head toward Caroline.

"That lady is not for your lips, nor mine." He whipped his jacket off in a fluid motion and tossed it to the ground, his hands loosening his cravat. "I give you one final chance," he said. She squirmed again in the man's arms, trying to break herself out of the hold, but drunk as he was, he was still stronger than she was.

"Bugger off then," said the second man, turning away from him. To Caroline's mounting horror, the man stuck his face in Caroline's hair and breathed deeply. "Mmmm" he murmured, starting to run his hands up from her waist, then looked down in surprise as his hand was caught in an iron-like grip.

Lucian looked at him intently, clearly enjoying the man's drunken confusion, as he twisted his hand into a lock behind his back, and the idiot's mouth fell open in pain as he let go of Caroline and started to swing at him with his other hand.

Lucian's smile became feral. He pushed the locked wrist, slowly and deliberately, until a crack sounded, so loud it shook the first man from his stupor. The second man started to scream in agony, and Lucian delivered a quiet, but terrifyingly efficient strike with the edge of his hand to the man's windpipe. Gasping and coughing, the man sank slowly to his knees. The first man, realising what was going on, grabbed Caroline roughly, spinning around to face an advancing Lucian.

"Don't come any closer," the man shouted at Lucian, and when he failed to stop, put his hand around Caroline's neck, squeezing until she coughed, and Lucian finally halted. He looked at the man, calculatingly, his head to the side. Then his eyes dipped to Caroline's face.

Caroline steeled herself, prepared to do something, anything to help herself. Without warning, she threw both her hands back, at her attacker's face, and scratched at his eyes. Taken by surprise, he swore, his grip on her loosening and Lucian moved.

Wrenching Caroline forward, he ducked quickly under the man's punches, before rising in front of him, and firing a sharp uppercut. He fell back on the fence, his head hitting the railing hard. Breathing heavily, Lucian crouched over him and continued hitting him, until Caroline saw blood start to stain the ground.

"Stop! Stop! Enough! Lucian!" she called desperately, seeing her words have no effect. Lucian stood over the man, and delivered an almighty kick to his head as Caroline screamed, the sound of it hanging in the air.

Struggling to stand, her ankle gave out and she screamed. Lucian's head whipped around, and his face cleared as he saw her, clasping onto the railing, disheveled and pained, trying to stand. He moved quickly to her side, putting his hands under her arms, pulling her upright. She caught sight of his face then, and it chilled her. His blue eyes were wide, dazed and his face was covered in a fine spray of blood. He looked barbaric.

As she stood, safe in the circle of his arms, locked in their shared gaze, she felt safe again. Heart pounding, she felt like she was being drawn into his eyes as they filled her vision.

A sound from the street caught her attention, and she stepped on her ankle once again, swearing loudly. Without asking he suddenly whisked her up into his arms and began toward her home.

"That is a new expletive for me, I confess, and I had thought myself quite the expert," he said, smiling slightly. She trembled in his arms, the shock of the entire evening, the cold, the intensity of his close proximity. As they came to her steps, she squirmed until he put her down gently. They stood before each other in silence. She saw humanity returning to his face, but couldn't forget what she had seen before.

"Miss Lesage... I-" before he could speak, she turned from him, without a word, and carefully ascended the steps, opened the door, only to step back in surprise as Lord Wesley and Isaac Taylor stepped out.

"Well, what the devil happened to you two?" Wesley exclaimed loudly.

⚘

*C*aroline spent the next day in bed, resting her ankle, and trying to come to grips with everything which had happened to her. She was thankful and relieved, at least, that the fallout was not as dramatic as it might have been. The night before, Lucian had left with his brother, annoyed that the two gentlemen had left the ball in search of them, but Isaac had waited at the Fairfaxes' townhouse. Mercifully, the Fairfaxes had not yet returned, and a man was sent quickly to the ball with a message of Caroline's whereabouts and safety.

Leaving out Lucian's attack, she told Isaac that she had taken too much champagne and gotten lost in the maze, turning her ankle in the dark. Lucian had found her there, and brought her home, with the intention of returning to the ball afterward to inform the others.

Isaac took in her disheveled appearance, and red-stained cheeks without comment. If he had noticed the blood across Lucian's face, he did not say. When the rest of the family returned home, they found him reading in the drawing-room, Caroline safe in her bed, explaining that he himself had escorted her home when she had hurt her ankle. Margaret, satisfied, but irritated all the same, barely glanced in to check on her, for which Caroline was glad.

After lunch, as Caroline lay under her cozy blankets, reading and trying to soothe her frayed nerves, the maid entered the room and announced the arrival of a doctor.

"But, I've only turned my ankle," Caroline exclaimed, upset at the needless expense the Fairfaxes had gone to.

"Well, I heard Mrs Fairfax wasn't going to be calling any doctor, but come on his own he has!" the maid said excitedly as she helped Caroline sit up, and cover her thin nightdress with a shawl. She returned to the door to admit the doctor, and Caroline heard voices downstairs.

"Betsy, who is that downstairs? Do Eva and Katherine have callers?"

"Yes, Miss. Miss Eva's gentleman and his brother, they brung the doctor with them, you know," she said and disappeared into the hall. The door stood ajar a second longer, then a soft knock admitted the doctor and Caroline lay back, her mind absorbed by the group in the drawing-room.

✿

*T*he next evening they were invited to another ball, which Caroline was not able to attend due to her ankle. The doctor had informed Mr Fairfax that the ankle was not broken, but merely sprained and swollen, and complete rest was necessary, for as much as two weeks. Caroline had borne the news well, she did not feel ready yet to face the world, and was not particularly eager to spend another evening in the company of the Ashfords again quite so soon. Another night of dancing, and pretending her dear sister was not marrying a brute, was too much to bear.

She was shaken. She had always been the calmest of the three girls, especially cool in a crisis, but she had never been directly attacked before. She had never before feared being taken by force, and in one night it had happened with three different men. There was a defining moment in which she truly feared for her life, but that terror had abated when Lord Lucian had arrived. She knew then that she would be safe, at least. People were always talking of how wild America was- a savage and dangerous place, yet she had been in London for less than four months, and this was the first time she had ever truly feared another human being. Three so-called "gentlemen", no less! Were there any truly decent men at all? Or, had she finally seen the truth that lurked within every man?

She soaked her sore body in a warm bath, took tea on a tray in her bed, sipped hot cocoa, read several novels, and reveled in the quiet. She did still worry over Eva, but from this distance, she could allow herself the hope that attending balls together, night after night, might draw Eva and Lucian closer. She hoped that he would see the beauty of her, and learn to treat her with respect and compassion.

Her mind wandered occasionally in the low light of the fire, with the household still, and the clocks softly counting down the hours. She wondered over her future. With thoughts of Eva's imminent wedding and Katherine's determined husband-hunting, it was hard not to imagine her own and wonder if it would ever come to pass. The Fairfaxes had always been clear that they would not force her into marriage. That she, unlike their own daughters, they neglected to add, would be free to choose her match. She knew that it was a privilege and a luxury that few women had, but it also left her unaided in what would surely be the most important decision that she might ever have to make. And, she was no longer feeling inclined to be trusting where the honor of men was in question. Now, as time sped ever faster, she felt it might perhaps be safer not to marry at all. She felt genuine relief that she could choose to remain unmarried if she wished.

After all, how might she ever be sure of a man, if society afforded young couples so little time in each other's company? It was a horrible risk to ask of two young people who knew yet little of the world, she thought, and she had seen first-hand so many couples shackled by unhappy marriages. Of course, she wished for a family of her own- as her own family had been taken from her- but not without security, not without control.

Her mind drifted, with a rueful smile, to a memory of her youth, not quite a child, not quite an adult, when the three girls had saved their coins and snuck away to visit a visiting fortune teller against Mrs Fairfax's explicit disapproval. The old crone had looked bored, and painted generic images of happy futures to Katherine and Eva, with handsome husbands and plump babies, but her eyes had darkened when it was Caroline's turn, and she had spoken of happiness, but also of hardship and misfortune, claiming that Caroline would be married twice in her lifetime. This had upset Caroline for many years afterward until she had convinced herself that the entire adventure was nothing more than a bit of fun, and the crone nothing more than a charlatan, though the girls still teased her goodnaturedly about her two husbands from time to time.

Thoughts of their happy childhood brought her home, and she thought of Virginia. She missed it. Things seemed simpler there.

Sometimes she thought of Lord Lucian. She felt sometimes grateful to him, and at other times consumed with rage at what he had done. And yet, other times her mind lingered on him, curious, attempting to unpick the riddle of him; but, she pushed him from her mind again and again, telling herself that it was for Eva's sake that she thought of him at all, and that she would be better off without his presence, even in her thoughts.

🐚

*F*inally, the two weeks of recommended rest were over, and the Ashfords had invited them to a dinner party, to be held at their own townhouse. A party such as this was very exclusive and would confirm to the world the union that was being planned. Caroline was not alone in her lack of enthusiasm, as Eva was lower than ever, and even Katherine seemed less than enthused.

That morning, however, a package arrived at the door, and the girls were all in a flurry to discover who it was for. Still walking carefully, Caroline followed Katherine into the drawing-room as she hurried to rip open the box and pull the wrapping aside.

It was a dress, a beautiful dress, eggshell blue, with gold thread woven through to make it shimmer. It was low cut at the breast and then flowed out artfully in gauzy embroidered layers.

Katherine returned to the box, searching for a card, triumphantly found it, and read it aloud.

"Dear Miss Lesage, simply gilding the lily. -An admirer," she turned it over and frowned.

"That's it!" she screeched. "Where is the name? It must be a secret! Caroline, you have never told us about an admirer," she accused, her eyes going to Caroline and watching as heat warmed her cheeks. Eva touched the dress softly.

"It is beautiful, Caroline. You must wear it tonight," Eva said, picking it up carefully and holding it to Caroline's face.

"Oh, no. I couldn't possibly. I do not know who it is from!" She said, though she had a discomfort in her chest which suggested she did.

"You must! It makes your skin radiant, and brings out the blue flecks in your eyes," Katherine gasped. "It's perfect for you. Whomever he is, he must have made a very careful study of your colouring," she added in a suggestive tone. Caroline scoffed, and they all laughed.

"Katherine's gold slippers will look so well with it," Eva continued looking over to her sister. Caroline looked up and caught Katherine's look of disappointment for a moment, then it was gone.

"Of course, and she must wear them," Katherine said.

"Girls, Girls!" Caroline laughed. "I cannot and I will not. I will be wearing the green muslin, just as I planned."

❀

The day passed in preparation, and finally, the evening came, and with it Caroline's apprehension about the dinner. She had not told anyone the full story of that evening with Lucian, and certainly no one of what had happened in the maze. She had run over every scenario in her head but could come to no better result. The Fairfaxes knew of Lucian Ashford's reputation as a rake, she had even heard them discuss it on more than one occasion. While Mrs Fairfax seemed to think that "a bit of philandering" was to be expected in an unmarried gentleman of his age, Mr Fairfax seemed mostly to wish to please Mrs Fairfax, and Eva, as always, said nothing against her parents' wishes.

He had also come to her aid, she reminded herself, so he could not be all villain. Telling Eva, indeed, telling any of them, would not change their plans, but only serve to further frighten Eva, whose nerves seemed to be growing more fragile by the day.

The dress fit beautifully, as though it had been made for her, she admitted, looking in the mirror as she got ready. It was not a color she often wore, as it made her skin look a little more tan, she thought disappointed, but it also made her almond eyes glow in light browns, blues, and greens, glittering like the golden thread. She took it off after another admiring look and replaced it with the light green muslin. Sitting to rest her ankle, she pinned her hair up herself, coaxing loose tendrils to curl around her face.

She was apprehensive about seeing Lucian and Wesley. She didn't know what Lucian had told his brother had happened that night, but considering his state, he could hardly pretend it was nothing. He had probably told him about the attack of the men, but probably not of the maze, she guessed, just the thought of it sending heat to her cheeks.

He made her nervous, he had from the start, but now it was another thing entirely. She could still feel his hands on her, his lips on hers, the whispered words of passion. She could remember the smell of his skin. She was somewhat naïve about the affairs between married people, but now the thought of it seemed to resurface again and again.

Did all men enjoy the same things as Lucian? Or was he peculiar in his tastes? She didn't know, and had exhausted herself over the last few weeks trying to forget that night; however, she couldn't quite escape the feeling of fear that the memory gave her and the knowledge that inside him was another person, someone other than the somewhat restrained, and vaguely polite man he usually was around his family and Eva- someone darker, more animalistic- someone more difficult to control. One thing was for certain, she planned to make sure she was never alone with him again.

They all rode in a carriage to the party and were simultaneously silenced as the carriage came to a stop in front of the Ashford's townhouse. It was far grander than any place they'd been to since arriving to London four months before, and Mrs Fairfax let out a sigh of ecstasy. As they descended from the carriage, Caroline tried to force the slight flutter of worry away. She set her shoulders and raised her chin, determined not to let herself be so affected by anyone, least of all Lord Lucian Ashford.

CHAPTER 5

*L*ucian heard the carriage pull up and waited for the servants to open the door and announce their arrival.

The last few weeks, he felt as though he had been slowly going mad. Since the night with Caroline, his brothers had had him at a disadvantage and had used it to force him to behave. He had spent ample time with Eva Fairfax now, and he felt frustrated that she still wasn't warming to him. What more did he have to do, he wondered. His new fiancée was a dull, cowering mouse, with a harpy mother, who would no doubt follow them everywhere, and an outrageous foghorn of a sister. It was maddening! How could he be tied to such a woman? And, of course, he hadn't had the fascinating distraction of Miss Lesage to help him forget his painful fate even for a moment. There had been barely a bottle of whiskey untouched in the whole of London, a high-class brothel unvisited or poker table unplayed.

Miss Caroline Lesage. He hated to admit he had thought of her all too often over the past weeks. It had been only a fleeting moment, but he could remember the feel of her supple body under his hands- the silk and chemise between her skin and his, hinting temptingly at the shape of her. He could remember the moment when she was soft and pliant, welcoming him, it seemed, and then the furry that flashed in her eyes a heartbeat later, filling her with rage, and life, and fire. He remembered her intoxicating smell. Those full lips had been everything he had imagined, and he ached to feel them on his body.

He knew the taste of her.

He had imagined it again and again, letting his mind wander into fantasy. He wanted to taste the skin of her neck. He wanted to feel her nipples harden under his tongue. He wanted his mouth on her sex, where he would take his time savouring the taste of her while she grew slick and wet with the wanting of him.

He was accustomed to getting what he wanted; however, instinct told him that this girl may be the exception. She had surprised him. She was brave, outspoken, but something else too, independent, a quality he could not quite remember seeing in an unmarried lady of her years before. She was strong-willed, outspoken, and handy with a rock.

"The Fairfaxes and Miss Lesage," a servant announced from the door and he stood slowly, feeling anticipation rise in him. Then they were there, and she was smiling mildly, bobbing in front of his brothers, and being introduced to his father. She was exquisite, and he wondered why he had not before noticed quite how bright her eyes were. He hung back and, after encountering a dark look from his father, made sure to greet Eva first and foremost. As conversation swirled, genuine laughter exchanged, he felt himself start to relax, tonight would be a not-unpleasant evening, and he would find some time to speak to Caroline alone, one way or another.

❀

*D*rinks and canapes were served and Caroline, engaged in conversation with Lord Charles, realised she had missed some of the Ashfords after all.

"Our company has been greatly reduced without you, so I am most glad to see you so recovered," he said and she smiled.

"Lord Charles, you flatter me. I am sure the Miss Fairfaxes have kept you quite occupied." She watched as his mouth quirked a little.

"Well, one more than the other perhaps. Miss Eva is a wonderful model of good conduct in society," he said with obvious appreciation and Caroline agreed, watching Eva standing dutifully at her mother's side, her eyes downcast and modest. "While her sister is..." Just then a loud laugh interrupted the conversation, and Caroline turned to see Katherine bent over, in a most unladylike way, laughing with Lord Wesley. Turning back to Lord Charles, she noticed his expression and felt intrigued by its intensity.

"Allow me to introduce you to our father, his Lordship, Silus Ashford," Charles announced, escorting her over to the tall, forbidding-looking man who was speaking to Mr and Mrs Fairfax. She bobbed at the introduction and smiled pleasantly.

"Ah yes, the ward," he said, without rancour; however, Caroline fought down an instant feeling of dislike. He looked her over in a perfunctory way, his eyes seeming to communicate mild surprise, or perhaps distaste, at her unusual features, before turning back to Mr Fairfax to talk about business. His face was handsome and showed little of his age, still smooth and unworried by lines she saw on Mr Fairfax, as though, perhaps he was not accustomed to smiling often. He seemed a cold, hard man and she remembered Wesley talking of his brother's difficulties in childhood.

As Caroline listened to the small talk being exchanged, she noticed Lady Rebecca standing quietly to the side, studying her glass of champagne. Excusing herself, Caroline approached and smiled.

"May I join you?"

"I cannot stop you," the brunette said quietly, her face dark tonight, and Caroline wondered what could possibly make someone so beautiful and privileged, so unhappy.

"Perhaps not, but your attitude is doing a fine job of it at present," Caroline scolded, shocked at her own boldness, and watched as surprise dawned on Rebecca's features.

"I'm sorry, I suppose I am not much used to company," she said, indicating for Caroline to sit beside her on the divan.

"I cannot believe it, Lady Ashford. I'm sure your brothers are beating callers away with a stick," Caroline said kindly and saw a small smile appear on Rebecca's face.

"Well, I wouldn't be so sure. I rarely receive callers," she said after a pause and looked up at Caroline with a slightly challenging look on her face. Caroline decided to be honest with her.

"Neither do I. In fact, I do believe I have never received someone calling for just myself, though I am often present when callers come for

Katherine and Eva." At her words, she saw the defensive look on Rebecca's face soften slightly and she even gave Caroline a little smile. It was a sunrise, lighting up soft and gentle features, hidden behind her usually churlish façade.

"Well, we may have more in common than I'd thought, Miss Lesage."

"Please, call me Caroline."

"Caroline then, and I am just Rebecca," she said, her smile warming still more. "My brother told me that we could be friends. I am sorry that I did not believe him." Caroline felt her heart beat a little faster at that confession.

"Oh? Did he? Which brother said that?" Caroline asked lightly.

"Wesley," Rebecca replied. Caroline's heart calmed, and self-rebuke followed. Why should her heart beat faster when she thought of him? She felt wretched and confused. He scared her, yet when he looked at her, her whole being was aware of his eyes, as though his glance bore physical weight. It was impossible to explain. She knew he was in the room, however, she had yet to look directly at him, and planned to avoid doing so for as long as possible. She could hear his low voice, laughing and talking in that distinctive rumble.

Just then, a servant appeared with a bell, announcing dinner. Rebecca stood quickly, waiting for Caroline, her sweet smile still in place.

"Come, we shall sit together at dinner and ignore everyone else," she said impishly, leading the way through to the dining room, as the only female Ashford.

As they approached the table, Caroline could see Rebecca giving quick instructions to the servers, and realised she was urging an impromptu rearranging of the seating. Caroline fought a smile, Rebecca was obviously used to getting her own way in this house.

As the ladies stepped forward, the servants pulled their seats out for them, Caroline was seated beside Wesley on one side, and across from Katherine. She felt someone approach her chair from behind her, and her neck prickled in that way it seemed prone to whenever he was near.

"Miss Lesage," his words poured ice down her spine, and her hands clenched in her lap. Next, he was there, sitting beside her, his arm brushing hers, as he waited for her to acknowledge him. Lifting her glass to her lips, she sipped some water and took a steadying breath.

Preparing to meet his gaze, she turned just in time to see Rebecca bearing down on her brother.

"Lucian, I shall sit beside Miss Lesage. You must sit near Miss Fairfax, of course," she said pleasantly, in a tone that brooked no disagreement. Lucian did not hurry but looked to Caroline, who had finally met his eyes. "Lucian..." Rebecca urged.

Tearing his eyes away, he looked to his sister and smiled, agreeing to her demands, which Caroline suspected to be the usual way of things.

"Of course, dear sister." Standing, he waited for Rebecca to take his seat and pushed her chair in himself, walking to the top of the table to sit near Eva, her parents and his father. His face, she thought, had taken on a grim expression, but before he sat, he had turned to look at her once again, and Caroline felt, with that look, entirely certain that he would be seeking her out again at his first opportunity.

⁂

*A*s the main course was cleared away, Katherine glanced over at Caroline, Rebecca, and Wesley and thought how much fun they seemed to be having. Rebecca was like a different person tonight, Katherine mused. She glanced to the top of the table and noticed the tense stillness that surrounded Lucian and her sister. Eva was listening politely to Lord Silus Ashford talking about something or other, whilst his son was aimlessly toying with his food and frequently glancing down the table toward them.

"And has coal been more lucrative, do you find, or has your copper had a better result?" Mr Fairfax was asking.

"Ahhh, well that all depends where your mines are, and the state of the market," Lord Ashford went on, while Margaret prodded her future son-in-law for information.

"And you, Lord Lucian, do you enjoy speculation?" she asked politely. Lucian went to answer but was interrupted by his father.

"Oh, my dear Mrs Fairfax, you'll soon discover that my son has a limited capability for mentally demanding pursuits, however, I hope that this marriage may change that. At the very least I shall expect some grandchildren out of him. That he should manage just fine." He laughed toward the end, but it could not distract from the shocking words nor the dark tone beneath them. Margaret, determined to smooth any unpleasantness, interjected.

"I myself cannot wait for grandchildren. The more the better. A full home is a happy home, I have always said." Eva blushed hotly and did not look up from her plate.

"Miss Fairfax. I must congratulate you on tonight," a deep voice cut in and pulled Katherine away from her eavesdropping. Slightly flustered, she turned to Lord Charles, who was sitting beside her.

"And why would that be, Lord Charles? I have done little of note this evening."

"That, Miss Fairfax, is precisely why I am congratulating you. You have acted well within the bounds of societal propriety," he remarked, bestowing a rare smile on her.

"Ah, yes. Propriety. That is of the utmost importance to you, is it not, Lord Charles?" Katherine said, watching the well-mannered handling of his cutlery and drinking glass.

"Of course. It is a mark of good breeding, proper education and, I believe, even a measure of a person's very moral fabric. If seen as such, I fail to see how anyone could not hold it in the utmost importance," he finished earnestly, and Katherine held back a roll of her eyes at his seriousness.

"Well, I am afraid I must tempt your disfavour by disagreeing with you, my Lord. I believe there are several things more important in the measure of a person."

"I see. May I enquire as to what they could be?"

"You may inquire, however, I must decline to answer or risk losing your newly-won congratulations." Her eyes widened suggestively, and she saw the shock of her words in his. His smooth neck, barely visible under his starched collar and cravat, tinged a slight pink, as he picked up his wine glass a little roughly, taking a large draught. Putting it down he looked back to her, with a dry look.

"Miss Fairfax, you seem to enjoy provoking me."

"And you, my Lord, seem to enjoy censuring me," she said lightly, with a warm smile at him, and watched his dark eyes finally crease in a returning smile.

"Well, it seems we are quite the pair," he murmured in a voice that sent shivers up Katherine's spine. Instead of answering she took a drink and fought the blush that threatened to betray her.

❦

*D*inner finally finished, with the ladies withdrawing to the drawing-room and leaving the men to their cigars and cognac.

Caroline had barely made it onto the divan before Rebecca was at her side urging her up.

"Come. Mrs Fairfax gave me permission to show you around the house."

"Oh," was all Caroline could think as Rebecca propelled her from the room. They ascended a very long, white marble staircase, gracefully curved, its royal blue carpet secured with glistening brass. Walking along the hall, Caroline noticed a series of family portraits on the wall, and she was able to identify every Ashford sibling in them, except one.

"Is this your mother?" she asked, stopping in front of the painting. Rebecca stilled beside her, quiet for a moment.

"Yes. Though I scarcely remember her face, so I can only look at this to remember," she sounded a little defensive again, and Caroline took a deep breath.

"My parents are also lost to me. In an accident, when I was a child," she finished simply. Hearing it out loud, pained her still.

"I am sorry, Caroline. I did not know," Rebecca said and surprised Caroline by slipping her hand inside her own and squeezing it.

"Why is there not a portrait of Lord Lucian here? Can he be found elsewhere?" Caroline asked, seeing something fall over his sister's features for a moment before she hid it and replied breezily.

"Oh, he does not care to sit for such things. And father does not care to make him," she said, in a tone that discouraged further questions.

She opened a door and pulled Caroline inside. It was a beautiful room, full of feminine things, papered in delicate peach and ivory, with hand-painted birds and butterflies. A large canopy bed sat in the center, and off it, she could see a dressing room, which looked fit to bursting with beautiful clothes. There was a divan in the window and an ornate dressing table, with gilt-edge glass and countless perfumes, brushes, and pots.

Rebecca threw herself onto the divan and stared out at the city, her face relaxed.

"Your room is quite lovely," Caroline remarked as she walked around it, before sitting on the divan with Rebecca.

"Yes, a lovely cage for a flightless bird," she said, and Caroline was alarmed by her expression.

"But surely you cannot mean that. You have a beautiful home, and a loving family," Caroline said as she searched the tight expression on Rebecca's face, and watched how the shadows of the window panes cast dark shadows against her fair skin.

"I have an expensive prison and a broken family, held in place by a tyrant."

"Do you mean your father?" Caroline asked.

"He is a hard man. Yes, he loves me in his way... but, he sees his family as possessions, to do what he wishes with."

"I must confess to overhearing some conversation at dinner. Your father and Lord Lucian seem to have a difficult relationship."

"Difficult would be a generous term," Rebecca said. "I'm sorry. What a tedious host, I am," she sighed dramatically. Then, seeming to shake herself out of melancholy, she turned and smiled. "I can do better. Wait here, I want to show you something." She hopped up, not waiting for an answer. "I'll be just a moment. Do make yourself comfortable," she called over her shoulder.

Alone in the huge room, Caroline went over to the window and looked out over the city, much as Rebecca had done, kneeling upon the divan to get a better look at the lights spread out below. It was breathtaking, even in the dark. Hearing the door open softly behind her and click shut, she remarked over her shoulder,

"I do not think I should mind living in a cage if I was able to see the world such as this, laid before my feet." Suddenly warm hands touched her shoulders gently. Warm, large hands. Unmistakably masculine. She froze.

"Who would dare to cage you?" his voice was a caress. Too intimate.

"Lord Lucian!"

Caroline stood, whirling to face him, her eyes wide.

67

"Please call me Lucian."

"You took me by surprise," she accused, moving away from him. "What are you doing here? We cannot be here together. And alone, with the door closed behind you!" She scowled at him and moved quickly for the door.

He stepped to block her, holding up his hands in a gesture of peace, and backing down, sat at the dressing table.

"For that I am sorry, that was not my intention. When I saw you lost in contemplation, I simply wished to know what was in your mind," he explained.

"And may I ask what your intentions *are*? Why would you put me in such a position? If someone were to find us-"

"I merely wanted to check on your health, and to apologise further for my rash behaviour the other night," his eyes softened, and she believed him, for the most part at least, but it did not make the situation any less compromising for her.

"You thought to make amends for rash behaviour, by conducting yet more?" she said incredulously, still backing away, feeling a little safer when the bed was between them. "I should leave this instant."

"We shan't be caught here. Do not worry, Miss Lesage. I would not endanger your reputation twice in the same month." He attempted a smile, a mischievous one, though it failed to move her.

Silence fell between them, as Caroline was unsure what to do. Lady Rebecca was sure to return at any moment, and she worried that her disappearance would disappoint her when she might just wait a moment longer. And, though she knew better, she could not pull herself from the curiosity of what he might say.

"So, it seems my sister is quite taken with you. I am not surprised. Rebecca is an excellent judge of character."

"I would have to disagree, she seems to care for you, inexplicably," Caroline said shortly. He threw back his head and laughed, a deep, throaty sound.

"Ah yes, well, perhaps I am her weak spot." He smiled.

"I shudder to think how many women may make that claim," she threw back and looked indignant as he laughed again.

"Miss Lesage. You do not give leeway easily. I am quite the villain by your estimation. There I thought that perhaps my sister's recommendations might work to endear me to you, ever so slightly."

"I prefer to make my own judgment, based on first-hand experience."

"Ah, therefore I am fated to forever remain a villain in your eyes, am I?"

"Yes. Until you prove otherwise, if you are capable of such a thing."

"But, to prove otherwise, you would need to give me a chance to change your opinion, would you not?"

"I suppose. However, I must confess, I fail to understand why you should care. Surely there are many more than I who do not hold you in high regard."

"Alas, yes. A great many." He smiled. "However, and I confess I am at a loss as to why, but I find the absence of your regard particularly hard to bear." He looked up at her, his eyes full of unspoken intent, his face full of artful hollows and reflections in the candlelight. She felt her heart speed up. That look was so personal, so intimate, it made her whole body feel overheated, as though she was standing too close to a fire.

"I should hasten back, Lord Lucian."

"Please don't. I saw Rebecca just moments ago, and she told me to ask you to be patient."

"I am sure she did not know what she asked."

"I promise my best behaviour, Miss Lesage. You are quite safe with me. Have I not proven it?" She hated this mention of the night in question. She hated the disadvantage it put her in, and most of all, she hated that she had felt safe in the end, in his arms. Turning away, she sought to change the subject.

"Your portrait does not hang with the others. Was it too discerning a painter to capture your likeness?" she needled and watched as he bit back a smile.

"He did capture it, however, the painting was damaged, and father got rid of it." At the mention of his father, his face lost a little of its ease.

"I met your father tonight, he seems... a very capable man," she finished lamely, suddenly unsure of what to say.

"Is that really how you would describe him? I guess he is indeed very capable. And well he knows how to wield it," Lucian said bitterly.

"Lady Rebecca told me that you do not enjoy a good relationship, I'm sorry to hear it," she said, unable to think of an adequate way to express her sympathy. He looked at her, his face almost curious.

"Even with your low opinion of me, you are still capable of feeling sympathy for me? You are quite the lady, Miss Lesage."

"I am not a lady, Lord Lucian," she said modestly, surprised by his low tone.

"You are indeed a lady, and no doubt you shall one day be in title also, and leave the rest of the men in England to pine."

Silence fell between them and Caroline felt her conflicting emotions bubble to the surface. Where was Rebecca? Would she not hurry?

"You should not say such things," she whispered, looking away from him.

"I know. I am sorry, I cannot seem to restrain myself around you. You intrigue me. Like Icarus flying too close to the sun."

This declaration tightened her stomach, with worry or excitement, she did not know. Of course, he had attempted the other night to make love to her, but then, she had assumed that that was nothing more than opportunism. Tonight, he seemed to be singling her out. Seeking her out.

"Then you must restrain yourself, Lord Ashford, for you are promised to a most beloved sister. And Eva is good and sweet... sweeter and dearer than I could ever be."

"Too good," he said, slowly rising, and making his way toward her. "You are not sweet. There is no simple word to sum up your attributes. You are maddening and brave, outspoken, challenging... intoxicating."

She was shocked, but her loss for words did not last long. She had been warned that men pulled tricks such as these to tempt women to lose their reason. She knew him to be disreputable. She knew him to be practiced. Unscrupulous.

"You are quite the poet, Lord Lucian-"

"Lucian,"

"Lord Ashford, and if I wasn't quite so, what was it- challenging?- then maybe I would fall into your arms. However, I am not as easily taken in as your usual dalliances, it would seem. So, I must decline your advances, and advise you not to make any more in future, as they will all be rejected with increasing severity. How is that for outspoken?" He raised his eyebrows but said nothing. "The very most which you can hope for from our relationship is friendship, and even then, I cannot simply forget what I have learned of your character. Even if attacking me was a misunderstanding, there is no denying your inclinations. Maybe one day, when you learn to control yourself, you will make a good husband to Eva and a good friend to me."

"Until then?" he asked, challenging.

"I am simply a sister of your betrothed. That is all." She stood then, and slowly walked past him.

"And if that day never comes?" he asked roughly, standing as she passed him. She fought down the urge to hurry away and stood her ground.

"I believe it will."

His eyes grew soft at her words, sentimental perhaps, or pitying, or wishful, she could not tell. But he looked as if he wished to come closer.

"I must go, Lord Lucian. Please give your sister my apologies. And kindly refrain from sending any more gifts."

CHAPTER 6

Stepping out into the bright hall, Caroline gasped as she walked straight into Rebecca just outside the door.

"Oh gosh! You startled me. I was afraid you would never return," Caroline said nervously, trying to seem relaxed, though she wondered if Rebecca had just overheard everything.

"Sorry! I was detained in the kitchens. He was eating," Rebecca smiled, and Caroline felt her clenched stomach relax.

"Who was eating?"

"Louis!" Rebecca exclaimed, pulling her hands from behind her back, revealing a large birdcage, with a dainty bird inside.

"Oh! He is beautiful," Caroline said, then taking Rebecca's arm started to direct her downstairs,

"Come, let's show Eva, she loves animals."

Later that night, so late the darkness was beginning to lighten, Lucian lay watching the day start through dirty, smeared window panes. His body was tired, but he couldn't sleep. He sighed, shifting on the hard bed, stirring the woman sleeping beside him.

"Hhmmm, awake already, Milord? You are quite insatiable," she stroked her hands down his chest, and he caught them and turned to her. Her pale skin was not soft, and it was marked by her hard life. Her dark hair was brittle and probably full of living creatures.

He fought down his anger and gently placed her hand on the cover.

"Don't," he said, and then flinched as she whispered to him.

"What's wrong... do you want to call me by her name again. Shall I beg you, like last night, tell you how I want you," as she spoke she started kissing his ear. His disgust at himself and her overwhelmed him, and he pushed her away, hard. She fell from the bed onto the hard wooden floor, the breath knocked out of her.

Standing, he threw on his clothes, ignoring the woman as she sniveled in the corner, going to the door, he looked back and saw Caroline for an instant, her head lowered, arms wrapped around her knees. It was like a fist crushing his windpipe, as he went back, and grabbed three times over the amount of money he'd already paid from his billfold and put it on the window ledge. He started to speak, then getting a grip on himself, turned on his heel, and walked out into the dawning light.

❦

A couple of days after the dinner party, Caroline was busy with lessons and helping Katherine and Eva with their studies, when Margaret came to the door of the parlour.

"Caroline, there is a gentleman here for you," she said, not bothering to disguise her surprise. Caroline looked at her blankly, her mind unable to come up with whom it might be. There was only one man she could imagine but hoped that she was wrong. "Did you hear me, Caroline? You have a caller!" She clapped her hands. "Eva, Katherine, and I shall keep him occupied whilst you... fix yourself up," she said, waving her hand in the general direction of Caroline's hair. Jumping up, Katherine rushed through, with Eva a close second, and Caroline stole upstairs to make herself more presentable.

She took only a few minutes, slipping into her nicest day dress, modest but new, and pulling her hair up simply before she went back to the drawing-room.

Her heart pounded for a moment at the view of muscular legs by the fireplace, then raising her eyes, she found herself in the warm, embracing smile of Mr Joshua Lee.

"Miss Lesage! I am relieved to see you so recovered," he said smoothly, moving toward her, bowing low to kiss her hand.

"Mr Lee, such European manners," Margaret purred, thinking of his prospects, no doubt.

"Well, I have been travelling extensively, though I am more glad than ever that I managed to return to London before the Season is ended" his eyes captured Caroline's as he spoke. Katherine whistled appreciatively, and her mother elbowed her sharply.

"Have you been enjoying this Season in particular then, Mr Lee?" Katherine asked leadingly, causing Caroline's cheeks to flush a little with her insinuation. Joshua simply smiled confidently.

"Well, it started well. Sadly though, I have been deprived of my dance partner for a few weeks now," he said. "In fact, I was rather hoping Miss Lesage would accompany me to the opera tomorrow night," he stated calmly, despite looks that passed around the girls' faces at the request. "With your permission, of course, Mrs Fairfax."

"Ah. I am sure Caroline would love to accept, however, we have already agreed to go with the Ashfords, and Caroline could not possibly accompany you unchaperoned."

"I had planned for us to sit with my parents in our box. I believe it is right across from the Ashfords. The Taylors will also be joining us." Seeing the indecision on Margaret's face, he carried on. "Perhaps we could pick her up in our family carriage, and I assure you, my parents would not let her out of their sight," he smiled winningly. "You will practically be able to see into our box." Margaret finally gave in.

"In that case, Mr. Lee, I think I might be willing to make an exception," she said.

"What? You would never allow me to go out unchaperoned," Katherine pouted.

"Dear, this is a completely different case, as Mr Lee has just illustrated," Margaret said pointedly.

"Excellent! Most excellent," Joshua said, making to leave, sending the girls all rushing to their feet. "Mrs Fairfax, Miss Fairfax, Miss Katherine, it's wonderful to see you again, and I no doubt shall repeat the pleasure tomorrow at the Opera. Miss Lesage, I wait in anticipation of the morrow. And, at the risk of sounding too bold, I hope to see you in blue... blue with gold might suit you perfectly," he smiled, his white teeth shining against his tanned skin.

He left with a jaunty bow, whistling as he strolled out onto the busy London street, leaving the girls giggling behind him.

"Caroline! Mr Lee is your admirer! How wonderful," Eva said happily, squeezing her hands.

"Yes, he is rather handsome is he not? I do love dark good looks on a man," Katherine commented, as she peaked out at the street and Joshua's departing back.

"How fortunate that you did not wear the dress the other night! Now it will be the first time, with the man who gave it to you. How romantic," sighed Eva.

"I spy the Taylors!" Katherine said from the window. "I wonder that they did not tell us of Mr Lee's intentions sooner, for surely they must have known. Did you know they were coming to visit today?" She glanced to Eva and the telltale flush on her cheeks.

"Of course not," she said weakly, sitting down and arranging her dress. Caroline caught Katherine's eye and shrugged helplessly, sitting beside her. Feeling her emotions swirl inside her in anticipation of an exciting night, where her company had actually been requested.

"Caroline. I do believe he is going to sweep you off your feet," Katherine sighed, falling back dramatically against the armchair.

"I agree. First the gift, now the opera. He has set his hat at you!" Eva exclaimed, much cheerier now they could hear the Taylors ringing the bell.

"But, we have not asked Caroline what she thinks of the man. If you do not find him charming, then I doubt much foot sweeping will occur," Katherine pressed, leaning in, watching Caroline for her reaction.

"I find him... very pleasant indeed," Caroline said with a smile.

ovent Garden was a writhing mass of Season goers the night of the opera. Carriages filled the streets, lamps flickered over silk cloaks, and fine jewels, and music was already filling the square as they arrived.

Caroline did not think that she had seen anything so splendid in all her life. Crimson velvet draped in waves, softened the cavernous expanse of the room, every detail framed in gold; and, so high above her that it felt like the vault of the heavens, was a glass dome, decorated in elegant gold detail. The room glowed.

The Lees guided them toward their private box, introducing her to people as she went. They were warm and kind with her, and she liked them instantly. She settled and stretched to see if she could spot her sisters. Laughing with surprise, she saw they were indeed extremely close, and Katherine waved at her, and then laughed at something Lord Charles said.

She could see Rebecca sitting with Lord Wesley, and received a lady-like smile from the brunette, and a wide grin from the latter. Waving back, she turned her attention down at the stage and the pit, soaking it all in. Joshua was conversing with his father, and when Mrs Lee started to reminisce about home, Caroline joined her.

Isaac and Eli entered, and Caroline soon found herself between Joshua and Eli. She spoke with them both, and the only hamper on her happiness was the tightening of Eli's hands in his lap when they saw Eva enter the opposite box on Lucian's arm. Eva was pale, a soft smile affixed to her lips, but her eyes were lost.

Lucian, on his best behaviour, escorted her in and ushered her to sit next to Katherine, leaving himself alone at the end. Settling back in the chair, his eyes roamed over the hall, and Caroline felt an immediate jolt when his eyes found hers. She quickly looked away and spoke to Eli who had fallen silent.

"Do you know much of this opera? *Acis and Galatea*," she asked, and watched sadly as he tore his eyes from Eva and turned to her.

"I'm afraid not. I know it is about love, and that is all. I am quite the fool in matters of the heart, so I'm afraid I cannot give you any guidance," he said with a wry grin that did not reach his eyes, and Caroline's heart went out to him. He was clearly in anguish, to the point that she wondered why he had come, and put himself through it. Flipping open her programme she skimmed through the description.

"Well, apparently, Galatea is a fantastical creature, who is in love with the shepherd Acis. They are very much in love, and live in a rural setting, happily together. Polyphemus is an evil demon, who is also in love with Galatea. He will try to destroy their happiness," she said, turning back to Eli. "There! Does that not sound entertaining and dramatic?"

"I prefer stories that do not so closely echo the tragedy of real life, I think," Eli said grimly. Reaching out she put her hand on Eli's until he looked up at her through pained eyes.

"Dear friend. I believe you do know of matters of the heart, and now you are receiving the cruelest education. But, you must forebear. For yourself and for her too. She will need you as a friend, her trials have not yet begun." Eli's hand clenched in a fist beneath hers.

"If he hurts her-"

"Hush. Do not let us talk of hurt when we have no cause. She is braver than she looks, maybe even braver than she yet knows," Caroline soothed, as she heard the bell ring for the beginning, and saw people start to settle in their seats.

Once all was quiet, the sweet strains of the orchestra warming up filled the air and she relaxed and started to enjoy the wonderful experience. She determined not to look at the Ashford's box, and to concentrate on the opera.

As the first act went on, she found herself utterly captivated by the characters, the songs, and dances, even the costumes. Laughing at the physical jokes, and blinking back tears at the love songs, she felt a hundred emotions in that short time and when the interval came, she was ready for a rest. She elected to stay with Mrs Lee, who was not inclined to go out into the mob. The Taylor boys and Joshua joined the throngs of people collecting outside, as they offered to brave the crowd in search of refreshments. Caroline fell once again into easy conversation with Mrs Lee until a knock on the private door of the box surprised them. As it opened, she was happy to see it reveal Rebecca and Wesley on the other side.

"Rebecca! How lovely to see you. I did not know you were coming tonight until I spied your radiant face across the room," she said with a genuine smile, thinking of how girlish the formidable and statuesque woman in front of her had looked when she had held her birdcage up with both hands and a childish glee.

"I decided to come and keep you company before you made other plans," Rebecca admitted.

Remembering her manners, Caroline immediately introduced Mrs Lee to the Ashford siblings.

"Where has Mr Lee got to? I must have a word with him about stealing my friend, and leaving me all alone with my brothers," Rebecca said lightly and Caroline laughed.

"Lady Rebecca, we have a spare seat. Why don't you sit with us for the second act? I am sure Miss Lesage is awfully bored, surrounded by men there," she said politely. Rebecca hesitated, looking to Wesley.

"Why, I think that sounds like a capital idea," Wesley said, helping his sister into the chair previously occupied by Eli. He sat down on the other side of Caroline and she felt her heart lighten in their company.

"Well, you are quite the topic of conversation this evening, my magnificent Miss Lesage," Wesley said, with a quick waggle of his brows.

"Whatever do you mean, Lord Wesley? And, call me Caroline, please. Are we not nearly family?" Wesley smiled at the invitation.

"Oh, our box has been alive with the hum of your name since you arrived looking like an angel visiting us grubby mortals for an evening."

"Lord Wesley, please. You perjure yourself unforgivably!" she laughed. "Would you be a dear, and do it a little more loudly next time?"

He chuckled back. "I am but your humble servant, my lady."

"Well, I must confess, you've piqued my interest, which I've no doubt was your purpose, you scoundrel. Has there been anything said of me that you might be willing to repeat?"

"Oh no, Miss Caroline, I could never. I am excellent at keeping secrets, you know, but I find that it is only fun if others know that you are in possession of them."

Below a bell started to ring, signaling the end of the interval and Wesley stood up.

"Ladies, thank you for the refreshing company. I shall collect you after the performance, dear sister," he said, leaving the box, meeting Isaac and Joshua as they returned with drinks.

Isaac sat next to Rebecca and Joshua beside Caroline, the lights already dimming as she twisted back around to the door.

"Where is Eli?" she whispered to Isaac, watching as his lips tilted downward.

"He decided opera is not his to his tastes, I'm afraid. He went home," Isaac said, shrugging. She sighed and turned her attention to the stage, where melancholic notes and minor keys were preparing the audience for the destruction of Acis and Galatea's innocent love.

⊛

*T*he blue dress fell perfectly over her slender form and made the blue of her eyes glow even at this distance. Lucian stared openly. Half of London was in this room, preened and bejeweled, and wearing their fortunes, and yet she stood out against them all. No one had a face like that.

Her smile, so carefree and wide, pulled at him, and he longed for it to be directed at him. Like a child, begging for attention, he moved distractingly in his chair, causing Eva to look at him askance. Stilling as the lights fell, he realised he would see not one moment of the opera, nor hear one note of song.

She had barely glanced at him all evening. Only that first moment when their eyes met, and she had looked away immediately, and spoken intently with the youngest Taylor. Now, she smiled and whispered with Joshua Lee who, Lucian felt, was sitting rather too close. He glanced angrily at Mr and Mrs Lee, cursing their lax chaperoning skills.

Next to her, the company of the Fairfax women grew ever more insipid.

"A dress like that does not come cheap, no indeed. I dare say it is the most expensive item Caroline has in her wardrobe," Margaret's grating voice filtered her crass statements through his black mood, though he paid more attention at the sound of Caroline's name.

"And the colours suit her so well. He must have spent a good deal of time to consider which hues would match her so beautifully," Eva said, brightening ever so slightly.

What were those idiot women talking about, he wondered, as he suddenly saw Caroline's dress in a new light. A new dress that someone had chosen for her, apparently. A man, dammit all. Joshua Lee had presented her with a gift and now she was wearing it. He felt a wild sense of possession, that he couldn't remember ever feeling for a

79

woman before. After all, one must care something for a woman in order to be jealous, and it had been all the effort he could muster to try to remember their names. He felt like Lee had personally insulted him, though he knew it was absurd. Taking a deep breath, he scrubbed his hand over his face trying to dispel the uncomfortable feelings but found his mood darkening nonetheless. Childish, he chided himself, gritting his teeth as they droned on beside him, right over the music of the opera.

"I wonder how much he paid for it," Margaret said. Would she never shut up? "I haven't seen finer lace or silks since I was a girl." He shot them a cold, stern look, but it seemed to go unnoticed.

"Did you see the sheen on the silk?" Katherine chimed in now, leaning back to participate. "I could practically see my face in it! It's beautiful with her dark hair."

When he was married to the girl, would he be tortured by Margaret's voice, and the sound of their incessant, inane chatter in his parlour, at his table, and ringing through his halls? He grimaced, and it was a full-bodied thing, making his toes curl.

"The gold embroidery, I think, is the most exquisite part. So fine, the leaves and flowers. And as she moves, it shines under-"

"Shhh!" It was a harsh thing, a reflex, and Eva turned to him, her eyes round as a mouse. He moved his face closer to hers to be heard and spoke quietly enough to avoid the others' notice. She would be his wife soon, he was well within his rights to censure her, but he did not want to make a lengthy spectacle out of it. "Honestly, woman. Will you not be quiet? It is a fine dress, we have all seen the wretched thing for ourselves, damnit. Could we not now listen to *some* of the opera?" Her mouth fell open slightly, and she looked as if she may cry. She had better not, he thought, infuriated by the sight of it. "Please, madam. Control yourself," he said with distaste, turning away.

Her breath started coming fast, and he considered storming out for the pub before a dramatic scene could be made which he, no doubt, would have to answer for.

Katherine, oblivious, leaned over to catch her sister's attention. "I think we shall be hearing of an offer of marriage from the dashing Mr Lee within the fortnight!" Her voice was high with the giddy thought. "What say you? Should we place a coin on it?" Lucian saw red.

"I would give you a coin, Miss Fairfax," he leaned over Eva in order to hiss, "just to shut up! I would give you my whole purse, goddamnit, if you and your goose of a mother, would collect the quivering mess of your perpetually-frightened sister, and remove yourselves to another box so that the rest of us might all have some goddamned peace."

Katherine gasped, and a look of fury settled over her face- nostrils flared, eyes like fire. "How *dare* you?" she said lowly, picking up speed and volume as she went. "And you call yourself a gentleman? You are nothing but a brute and a boar, and if my sister is frightened-"

"Hey? What is going on here?" came the voice of Mr Fairfax, but they all fell silent, as the sound of Eva's breathing became increasingly difficult to ignore. It had started as the heavy breaths of someone shocked and upset but had become an urgent, wheezing thing that could be heard even over the raised voices. Her eyes were huge and terrified like Lucian had never seen them, and she clutched at her throat in panic.

Mrs Fairfax threw herself at Eva's feet, kneeling there in her own panic. "She's having an attack. John! Do something. Calm down, sweet girl," she was trying to soothe between her own upset shrieks.

With Katherine next to her, and her father behind her chair, his hands on her shoulders, speaking steady instructions in her ear, Lucian stood and drew the curtains closed, giving them privacy. The other Ashfords were also on their feet, asking what they might do, and Wesley left at a run in search of water, though Lucian doubted that the girl would be able to drink it.

To Lucian's surprise, Mr Fairfax struck a match and lit a cigar, which he held hurriedly to Eva's lips, imploring her to inhale, though she was not able.

Pale, and clammy, her head began to bob as she lost consciousness.

"She's dying, John! She's dying!"

"No No, Margaret. She's just grown dizzy. She's done this before. She's calming even now- listen."

And she was. She had fainted, but her breathing was slowing now, and did not sound so laboured. Mrs Fairfax had picked up her limp head and was now cradling her in her arms as she wept.

Caroline arrived then, throwing the door open, no doubt having seen the commotion from across the theatre before the curtains had been drawn, and with her, rushed his own sister, one of the Taylor boys, and blasted Lee. Everyone was talking at once. Wesley arrived with the water. He heard his name cursed on Katherine's lips, and saw Caroline's face snap up, her eyes locking with his for a moment.

He bowed stiffly, turned on his heel, and left.

❧

*L*ucian sat at a gaming table and stared at the cards in front of him. He felt heavy with the whiskey he had been drowning his sorrows in all night, and his father's words whirled through his mind, adding to his shaken nerves an engulfing sense of dread and horror he had been desperately trying to avoid.

"*W*e need to talk about this blasted wedding," Silus said shortly, barely glancing up.

"What about it?" he asked, his hands tightening on his knees with the thought of impending doom.

"I am tired of waiting, I need their American connections, and we need that girl's dowry now to make good on a new deal in the East Indies. I want you to push forward with the date. You shall marry next month," he announced curtly, finally looking up to enjoy the scowl on Lucian's face.

"Next month? But, that is not enough time. Mrs Fairfax has been planning a big wedding. They will never agree."

"They already have. It is settled. To hell with her blasted wedding plans. I hold that family by the strings, and well they know it. Now, all that is left is for you to climb on top of that sweet bride of yours," Silus said, with a laugh.

"She is not strong, father," he argued, knowing that his desperation to escape the marriage made his point sound pathetic. "We should not force her. Or hurry her. With time she will grow accustomed to the idea, and you will have every penny you wish."

"Why should I have a care over her health, you fool? So much the better, in fact. If she perishes from the shock of you, then you shall be free all the sooner. Perhaps to marry into another rich family. We could make quite the business of you, boy," he laughed, nastily, raising his glass of sherry in toast, and finishing it.

. . .

*T*he queen of hearts came out the deck and Lucian stared at it blankly. The queen of hearts. It was like Caroline. To suddenly appear from the deck and make all the other cards he held worthless. Good God, but he was drunk. Pushing his chair back, he swayed away from the table and staggered in the direction of the exit.

God knows how much he had lost on the tables of late, he didn't bother counting. No amount of money in the world could buy him what he wanted, and no sum could save him from the dull-witted, dead-eyed Eva.

In the street, a carriage brushed past him, and he swore as he pulled himself back from the road.

As he turned toward home, the streets swinging before him, he didn't notice the shadows detach themselves from a dark lane and begin to follow him. In fact, he had no idea that he wasn't alone until he came to a particularly dark street, where even the wind didn't howl. His alcohol consumption softened the first blow, and the second, and was undoubtedly the reason why he didn't even raise a fist in response or defense. He recognised the men, the ones he had saved Caroline from, but they were not alone this time.

He fell to the ground and felt their vicious kicks vibrate through his body. As he let his attackers do their worst, he realised he welcomed their blows. It felt almost good, satisfying even, to mirror his inner torment with outer pain, let his body reflect his ugly soul, his corrupt, hideous self.

He would be the death of that poor, weak little girl, he thought grimly, just as his father had been the death of his mother.

As he lay there, long after the beating had ceased, whilst his blood wept into the pavement, he realised he didn't want to be found. He didn't want to move, didn't want to be helped. He looked up at the stars, so brilliant against their velvet background, and felt peace. He remembered the night in the maze, with Caroline and how she had smiled at him under the same sky. He didn't want to wake to see the next dawn. The realisation was startling, and yet somehow a relief. A deep sense of exhaustion overwhelmed him, and he let his eyes close, and felt his consciousness float away.

CHAPTER 7

*L*ady Rebecca Ashford rose promptly each morning at eight
o'clock. She washed, dressed, and took her breakfast with her
father. Sometimes her brothers joined them, though more
often she would read the society papers whilst he read the news, and it
was usually a very somber affair, with only the clinking of glasses and
cutlery as company for the silence.

A couple of days had passed since the attack on her brother, and she
hated that she could do no more for him than sit by his bedside and
read to him, or talk to him if he woke. She knew he was not without
enemies, most of them jealous husbands and lovers, but she had never
seen him truly hurt by them before. It had been Charles who pointed
out the oddness of his injuries, in that no defensive marks seem to have
been made. Rebecca had guessed what that meant.

Her dearest brother, the most lost and damaged of them all, hadn't
bothered to protect himself. The news had hit her hard, and she still
found herself worrying over it constantly.

This particular morning, as she prepared to sit in the drawing-
room, catching up on her correspondence and watching the window
for callers, a knock at the door startled her. Rising, she watched a
servant come in to announce them.

"You have a caller Milady, Mr Isaac Taylor." Rebecca frowned, unable to imagine what he could possibly be calling on her for. The servant settled into the corner, as a chaperon, and the man in question arrived at the door, smiling his big smile, his hat in his hands.

"Lady Ashford, how good of you to see me."

"Mr Taylor, what a pleasant surprise," she said smoothly, sitting, and watching him pace a little around the room. The silence drew out between them, as she waited for him to say something- instead, he just looked increasingly agitated.

"May I enquire after the health of Lord Lucian?" he asked.

"He recovers, slowly, but the doctor does not think him in any further danger," she replied and waited for him to speak further. Silence stretched out. "Was there... something I can help you with?" she asked politely, sure that this wasn't exactly a social call, considering they had barely spoken since their introduction.

Isaac came to halt before the fire and looked at her in the mirror above it before his eyes darted to the footman. She waited expectantly.

"Do you care for your brothers?" he asked suddenly, and Rebecca's face reflected her bewilderment.

"Why, of course, I do," she said, leaning back a little as he spun around and faced her. His face animated; alight with something tanta-lising that she was now ever more eager to know.

"Exactly. And, you want them to be happy, of course, and would do anything for them," he continued, looking searchingly into her eyes. She fought down her confusion and retained her gentile facade.

"Their happiness is of the utmost importance to me." Her words set Isaac's head nodding as he resumed his pacing in front of her.

"I believe that. I have seen you with them. They dote on you and you on them." That is why I came to you.

Abruptly he sat down. Looking into the fire, he finally spoke.

"I love my brother. He is the youngest, so I suppose I would have always felt protective of him. But it is his character too. He is moral and honest and far better a man than I, I confess."

"How... lovely," Rebecca said evenly, unsure of what was being required of her.

"But, you see. He is completely capable of ruining his life... of missing his chance at happiness, just by sticking to his damned moral code, if you'll forgive me, which I promise you, would make a nun weep." Rebecca laughed and then stilled as she felt Isaac's piercing eyes on hers. He pinned her down with just a look, and she was caught in his stare."Lady Ashford, I need your help..." he started and what had begun as a somewhat strange and brief social call, became something else entirely.

☙

Charles looked out over the countryside as it moved slowly past, the driver making every effort not to jostle the purpose-made bed inside which carried his brother. Gently drawing the cover higher over him, Charles leaned back and let his mind wander back over the problem he had found himself contemplating at every given opportunity lately.

His brother was a deeply unhappy person; he had been since a young age. Fiercely protective of his siblings, he had always shunned the company of others, even resisting falling in love, reserving women as an indulgence of the physical nature, never involving himself too much, and never lingering too long. Now, his father was forcing him into this match, with a completely unsuitable girl. Eva Fairfax was as soft and delicate as a hothouse orchid, and his brother would crush her before he even realised it, and then he would only hate himself the more.

Her sister, Katherine, would stand a better chance against him, though the very thought made Charles scowl. No, Katherine was too badly behaved, she needed a good example in a husband, someone to carry the mantle of respectability for both of them, instead of dragging them both into indulgence and destruction. As Lucian's wife, they would end up being thrown out of all good society, a disgrace to their families, and surely hating each other.

Whilst Lucian was not sensitive enough for someone like Eva, nor respectable enough for someone like Katherine, he desperately needed someone to love, who would love him in return, unreservedly.

Lucian shifted in his slumber, murmuring something. Charles leaned forward to catch it.

"I didn't- don't-" he muttered, his head shaking from side to side and Charles frowned, leaning forward he placed a hand on his brother's arm, feeling his hot skin under his palm. He pushed open one of the windows in the carriage.

He wondered if he had done the right thing, allowing Rebecca to talk him into having the Fairfaxes join them in the country, along with the Taylors no less. It was their tradition to host house guests at their country home every summer; however, with his brother's condition, he wondered if it was still appropriate. He worried over Lucian's reaction and had decided not to tell him until he was recovered a little. He wouldn't be aware of their presence until he was well enough to leave his rooms at the very least.

Rebecca had become very close to the Fairfaxes' ward, Miss Lesage, and he hated to see his sister alone so often, so granting her request had been a foregone conclusion really. Taking a deep breath, he tried to imagine spending time with Katherine Fairfax in close quarters, day after day, without losing his calm.

❀

"Are you nervous?" Caroline asked Eva, as their carriage rolled through a small village near to the Ashford's estate. Eva looked at her, her face still lost in the thoughts Caroline had pulled her from.

"A little, of course. Though I expect we shan't see Lord Lucian until he is recovered somewhat." As she said it, the relief on her face was palpable.

Caroline looked away, her thoughts betraying her for a moment, in a pang of sadness for an injured man, whose own fiancee was relieved at not having to see him sooner than necessary. He deserved better than that, Caroline thought of the way he had protected her that dark night weeks ago. They both deserved better than they would be able to give each other. Turning back to the window she lost herself in the overwhelming charm of Wiltshire's rolling green hills as the carriage turned into the long driveway toward the manor.

Blackhill Hall was grander than she might ever have imagined. Sitting amongst emerald hills, with beautifully manicured gardens and a lake like a jewel in the middle of them, the house rose, grey and imposing, with more windows and chimneys than she had ever seen on one building, matching spires and turrets, like a castle from a fairytale.

The manor was just as breathtaking inside as it was out, Caroline thought as she walked into the entry, which seemed big enough to fit their entire London townhouse inside. It had high gracious ceilings, with elegant stairs, splitting, and curving in tandem up toward the higher levels, the floors were a pale marble that gleamed in the sunlight, streaming in from the long, plentiful windows.

After being shown to her rooms, Caroline went directly to the large window where a setting sun was casting warm, golden light, tinged with pink, spilling over the fabrics of her elegant testered bed. The lake lay before her, glimmering in the light, and as she watched a heron, graceful and serene in its flight, glided over the water, before landing gently at its edge. She closed her eyes, and drew a deep breath, feeling the perfect tranquility of the moment fill her, her smile irrepressible as she felt the tensions of the city melt away.

When she turned, she found herself looking into another window, from her room's west wing position, and gasped as her eyes met inquisitive blue ones. The room was dark, with only flickering firelight glowing from deep within and Lucian's face was shrouded in shadow, but his eyes, catching the last rays of daylight, blazed at her. Looking closer, she realised it was not simply shadow darkening his features, but bruises. Vivid purple, fading into yellow and black, cuts lined with dried blood.

She fought down the expression of horror she instinctively felt, and offered a tentative smile, raising her hand in a small wave. His face, regarding her speculatively, relaxed at her smile, and formed a small one of his own. He glanced down as she watched him, and she saw he held on his knee a sheath of paper, on which he was working with charcoal. Glancing back at her, his hand continued to move quickly across the page, and she wondered what he was doing. A knock sounded at the door, and she turned toward it, waving goodbye to him, leaving him unmoving at the window.

"Miss Lesage?" a maid said as she pushed open the door and came in."I've come to unpack your clothes."

"Of course, thank you," Caroline said, preparing to help.

"Shall I draw the curtains, Milady? It'll be dark soon." Coming to join her at the window, she leaned over a little and saw the chair in the window was now empty.

❀

*E*va started a little as someone walked past the outside door and continued down the corridor. She was sitting in a drawing-room and had been speaking politely to Rebecca, thanking her for inviting them to stay and expressing her concern over Lucian's health. They had been joined by the Taylor brothers, Eva's heart beating faster as she had returned Eli's smile with a shy one of her own. Everything had been going along quite nicely until Rebecca suddenly remembered a word she had to have with the staff, and Isaac went off to retrieve something important in his room. Mystified at their sudden departure, Eva realised that she was alone with Eli, for perhaps the very first time.

He cleared his throat nervously, as though the same thing were occurring to him. Looking around, her breath caught as he suddenly stood up and moved beside her on the divan.

"Mr Taylor!" Eva said in a loud whisper, scooting away from him a little, her eyes widening as he took her hands. His ungloved touch was so warm and soft, she stared at their joined hands, quite disbelievingly.

"Eva. I can bear it no more. I must tell you how I feel. I could not endure it if you were married without my first confessing how much I admire you. And love you. Eva, I love you." His voice was ardent and earnest, choked at the truth of it, and she simply stared at him incredulously. She opened her mouth to speak, but no words would come out. Her heart soared at his words and twisted at the hopelessness of her situation.

"Eli-'" she breathed

"I know you are engaged, but I truly believe your father would release you from it if we were to explain to him how we feel about each other...would he not?" he continued, squeezing her hands as he spoke.

"But- " she started again and saw red start to creep up his neck at her hesitation.

"Unless... you do not return my feelings. If that is the case, I promise you that I shall never speak of them again," he said, the red reaching his cheeks.

"Oh, Eli," she whispered, and gently raised her hand to his cheek, her eyes growing misty. "I-" she did not get a chance to confirm her feelings for him, as the door suddenly began to open. As quickly as he had arrived by her side, he was gone, sitting back in his armchair, an open book on his lap. Rebecca and Isaac returned, smiling pleasantly. Rebecca sat down, arranging her skirts carefully, as Eva tried to calm her furiously blushing face, and blink away any tears before they had a chance to fall.

"So, what have we missed?" Rebecca asked sweetly, her eyes missing nothing of Eli's frustration or Eva's fluster. As Eva and Eli stole glances at each other, Rebecca's gaze met Isaac's, her mouth curving in the slightest smile, his intense stare warming her though with their shared secret. She felt a blush of her own threaten, and dismissed it, she was only doing this for her brother. Spending time with Isaac Taylor was merely a byproduct. She rang the bell for tea and wondered how a mere byproduct might be so distracting.

*D*inner was served promptly at eight, and Caroline prepared for dinner with anticipation. The country air and the long travel had left her hungry and eager for conversation. As the group gathered, she saw they were all present, excepting Lord Lucian, who would take dinner in his room.

The Fairfaxes were ecstatic over the house, and Margaret had dropped several fishing questions as to how Lucian's own estate might compare. They were to depart the next day, for Mr Fairfax had business affairs in the north, and Margaret had grudgingly agreed to accompany him. If Katherine happened to be compromised by any of the Ashford boys, she had said to Mr Fairfax's dismay, she would only be achieving her objective all the faster.

Dinner was a lavish affair, consisting of seven courses, and by the time it was over Caroline felt she would not be able to eat for a week. She had greatly enjoyed the company, taking the opportunity to speak to Wesley and Charles, who were pleasant and entertaining, as always. They had discussed Lucian earlier, and she had seen the shared look of concern pass between the brothers as they thought of him. One part of the conversation was particularly disturbing.

"Has he spoken much of the incident? Does he recall his attackers?" she had asked.

"He told us he did know them. He said he probably deserved the beating," Wesley said, with a humorless laugh.

"I do not see how he could mean that," Caroline responded.

"My brother often expects the worst from people. He is usually more surprised by kindness than brutality, unfortunately, and often finds the latter easier to deal with," Charles said matter of factly. Caroline sipped her wine and glanced up at him, a frown creasing her face.

"I am truly sorry to hear that," she said sincerely.

"He would be happy to hear it, Miss Lesage, though, I am sure he would not admit to it,"

"Sympathy, I am speculating, is not something he is familiar or easy with. I imagine he finds it synonymous with pity," Caroline said softly.

"How is it that you are blessed with such insight after knowing him for so short a time, Miss Lesage?" Wesley said, his eyes earnest. "I could not have put it better myself. It is not the physical recovery I worry over. My brother is strong, his body will heal and be as good as new in no time at all..." Wesley said, and Caroline nodded encouragingly, sensing his willingness to talk.

"Then what worries you? That his attackers will return?"

"No, I doubt they would be so foolish. Lucian let them go this time. Another time would surely be their end. No, the worries I have are more of his mood. He is terribly low. I don't believe I have ever seen him so unhappy. I do wish we could find a way to cheer him up. He seems disinterested in getting better, which will not heal him any the faster." Caroline sipped her wine but did not answer. "You are wondering why I am telling you this?" Wesley said, smiling at her as he guessed her thoughts.

"I confess, I am not sure what I can do. Perhaps Eva could..." she trailed off as Wesley shook his head, and looked at her frankly.

"Come, Miss Lesage, we both know that they do not comfort each other. I am not sure he can even look at her, after the evening at the opera. No, he needs someone to laugh with him, to make him smile, to help him forget his guilt, and lighten his heart. I believe you could do that, Miss Lesage. It is a special ability you have, to make the people around you happy."

Her cheeks flushed, "You flatter me too generously, sir."

"I speak the truth, dear friend. Your powers affect the old and young alike, of both sexes, and I shall not be dissuaded," he warned, smiling brightly at her until she laughed.

"Very well, I concede to your compliment, however unfounded it may be, and thank you for it."

"Good, I like a woman who can graciously accept a compliment which she has earned. Now, will you be my accomplice or no?" She took a moment to answer. "Unless..." he went on, brows drawn, "unless you have not forgiven him for the upset of Miss Eva?"

"Well. It is a difficult thing to accept the way the two of them seem to be so ill-suited. And, of course, I am disappointed that he has not taken more care with her. But, as for forgiveness, I have thought over the matter, and I believe that I have. He was not aware of my sister's condition, or her particular need for calm."

"Of course, Miss Caroline. Or course your heart is too generous to condemn a man forever, even one who has acted like a brute. Perhaps you might even see a little of the goodness that we see, though, I must admit, he does his utmost to hide it!"

"I cannot argue with you there, Lord Wesley," she laughed.

She thought of Lucian, alone in his room, his mood black, his face battered and bloody. She thought of Eva's relief at being free of his presence for a while longer, and the lonely, guarded look on his face as she watched him through the window. She was at a loss for what she might possibly do, and discomfited by the need for close proximity, but it had only been a few weeks since he had saved her when she had thought that all was lost, and she felt bound to at least try to do the same for him.

"Miss Caroline Lesage," he shook his head, "you are a true friend, though I have barely known you a summer," his eyes softened.

"I would grant you any favour after such a compliment, Lord Wesley," she smiled. "Yes, I will help Lord Lucian if I can. Just tell me what it is I am to do. Though I insist that you not hold me responsible if I have no effect on his mood. You may overestimate the esteem your brother places on me."

"That, my dear Caroline, would be impossible," he said with a triumphant smile, clinking her glass with his and drinking deeply.

※

*L*ucian found recovery a slow business, and it gave a man far too much time to dwell on the sorry state of his life. Away from his usual mindless pursuits, the futility of his situation was painfully clear, and he spent long days staring into the darkness of a future without hope or anticipation.

The night of the attack was still a blur, but he did sometimes find himself wishing that his assailants had done a better job of it. His only regret would have been not seeing Caroline Lesage again, a thought that sent scorn rushing through him. Yes, she was interesting, and certainly lovely to behold, however, if life with his father had taught him anything, it was that women could not possibly be a source of happiness in your life, only one of suffering, humiliation and pain. And he was not an easy person to love, his father had taught him that well enough as well. Besides, what could he possibly have to offer her?

He shifted on his bed and sighed, the pain in his back lancing through him. Eva was to be his wife, and nothing he could do would change that. As she was, his life would probably not change dramatically anyway, as she seemed to hold no desire whatsoever to spend any time with him. If he must marry a woman that he did not like, at least she was not the forceful type who might set herself at reforming his bad habits.

Outside he heard the sound of feminine laughter and resisted the urge to get up and see who it was. He hadn't seen anyone except his immediate family in days, though he now knew the Fairfaxes, Taylors and Miss Lesage were all there.

He had not seen Caroline in person since the night of the opera, her beautiful face twisted in worry and confusion. He could imagine the telling of the story, of his beastly behaviour over and over. He could vividly imagine Caroline's face when she heard it, her hatred growing with each retelling. How she must loathe him.

Though, the memory of her face when he saw her at her window gave him some small hope of forgiveness which he could not quiet. She had smiled at him, a smile he had sketched quickly, a desperate effort to keep it a little longer, to have some token he could look at when she was gone.

It had come out too rushed, forced, and he longed to redo it, wishing he could ask her to sit for him. Though he reminded himself if he was asking anyone to sit for him, it should probably be his fiancee. He groaned at the thought, remembering his father's disappointment that the wedding would have to be postponed for his recovery. If his father had his way, he would be limping down the aisle tomorrow. He clenched his fists at his side, wishing more than ever that he was allowed a decanter in his room, which had been strictly forbidden by the doctor.

Wesley had been quite the constant companion, as he did not have responsibilities around the estate as Charles had, and had gotten into the habit of bringing him new objects to draw every day, yesterday a flower arrangement Rebecca had made, fruit the day before. It was hardly a challenge, but it was better than sitting alone in his room.

Rebecca usually read to him, which he enjoyed very much, though her concern for him was so evident that he exhausted himself trying to keep up the facade of positivity around her. Especially the way she looked at him lately, as though she saw right through it. He was accustomed to disguising his unhappiness around his siblings, as he had always done since they were children, but for some reason now it was starting to show through. Perhaps, since the attack, stripped of all his usual distractions, with his impending marriage, his act was starting to lose its brilliance, or perhaps he had just grown tired of pretending.

A knock at the door sounded, and he tried to find the energy to sit up and look enthusiastic for whatever tat Wesley had brought him to draw today.

"Brother. How are you feeling today?"

"Better, thank you. I will wish to leave this room soon, you know," Lucian warned in a slightly menacing tone.

"We shall see. When the doctor deems you ready. Though I do know how it bores you, so I have brought you a special treat today."

"More flowers?" Lucian teased lightly, trying to inject a note of happiness into his tone.

"Of a sort," Wesley said, stepping aside and turning toward the door. Lucian's breath caught. There would be no reason to feign interest.

"Well, come in, he will not bite, you know. Probably," Wesley said laughing, and Lucian felt a jolt of excitement run through him as Caroline appeared in the doorway. She had her gaze lowered, dressed in a simple white day dress with light sleeves, which nipped in close to her body beneath her breasts, her long dark hair was not pinned up, as he had always seen it, but down, and caught back simply with a ribbon. She looked indescribably beautiful. He pulled himself up further, arranging the covers hastily, and pushing down the escalating beating of his heart. He waited for her to look at him.

"Miss Lesage," he said gently, suddenly feeling self-conscious of his beaten face. She bobbed respectfully, finally raising her eyes to his.

"Lord Lucian. I do hope I am not intruding. Lord Wesley said you would not mind the company," she said, her eyes searching his.

"Quite the contrary. Though, I am afraid I am not on top form these days. I hate to keep you from the beautiful day outside, I am not quite so pleasant to look at, now more than ever," he said ruefully.

"I don't know, I would say you are much improved," she said seriously, and he gaped at her until she let out a laugh. He relaxed at the sounds of it, feeling warmth spread in his chest.

"Miss Lesage, I see that my present state still does not earn any sympathy from you. One cannot help but wonder what a man must do to gain a second chance at your good opinion. Nay," he said gravely, "a fourth chance if I count them correctly."

"You must win one with your drawing, brother," Wesley said as he settled on a chair by the window.

"But first," Lucian said, sitting up straighter. "Miss Lesage, I am afraid I owe you and your family a most sincere apology. Words are… not enough."

"Let us not dwell on it, Lord Lucian. While I would ask you to be more tender with Eva in future, now that you are aware of her delicacy," she said, meeting his eye seriously for a moment which made him feel truly small at the memory. Yet, her stern eyes gave way to softness, and her brows drew together for a moment before a smile broke through, and lit her face from within. "But, I have long since forgiven you, my lord, and so has my dear sister. And you can repay us with your swift recovery."

"I dare not hope that you, nor she, could be so compassionate. I do not deserve such kindness."

"Ah, well there we can agree, finally," she teased, and he chuckled back at her, overcome with gratitude at her light attitude. It felt like a temporary reprieve from the mood he had jailed himself inside of.

"How is Miss Eva? Is she well?" Lucian asked, his eyes intent on her face, unable to break from her smile.

"She is good as new. Worried about you. As we all have been."

"I am sure that my company has been much pined for by the Fairfax women this week," Lucian said, raising an eyebrow cynically.

"Well. In truth, the Miss Fairfaxes do not have the strong constitution I have for hideous, battered beasts," she said, and he laughed, leaning back, enjoying her unflinching acknowledgment of his condition.

"Well, I guess I am lucky then, that you are able to stomach me."

"Quite," she said primly, folding hands on her lap, but her eyes sparkled at him.

Silence descended over the group, and Lucian watched as Caroline walked to the window, enjoying the view, following her with his eyes, doing the same. Abruptly she turned and broke the quiet.

"Well! I was promised a picture," she said, and Wesley hopped up to collect Lucian's materials. Putting them within his brother's reach he stepped back, and sat in a chair near the head of the bed, so he could watch his brother work.

"Where would you like me?" Caroline asked sweetly. At that, Lucian's beastly nature took over his thoughts, and he realised belatedly, it must have been painted across his face.

"Lucian, please do *try* to act like a gentleman! You are setting an example for your younger brother," Wesley reprimanded him with a smooth smile.

Lucian cleared his throat, and ran a hand over his face, waking him from the vision.

"I apologise. I am but a weak man," he said with a lopsided grin. "In the seat near the window please, and can you arrange yourself so the light falls on your face." He selected a pencil and straightened the paper before him. She sat down, a little self-consciously, facing toward the window, then looked back to him.

"Like so?" she asked, but he had already started drawing, lost in the clean, bold lines of her face, the gentle sweep of her hair and curve of her cheek, the golden arch of her cheekbone.

Wesley watched as his brother recreated Caroline on the page, effortlessly, with the perfect precision of someone who has studied the detail of their subject in great depth. Suddenly, Lucian discarded the picture on the floor and started again, and Wesley noticed with interest that he was completely absorbed with his task.

His blue eyes kept returning to her, and she met his gaze unflinchingly, their eyes like magnets drawn together time and again. Wesley felt the change in the atmosphere of the room, it felt charged with energy, the air hummed with it, and he realised that he felt like an intruder. He wasn't sure exactly what was going on, but one thing was for sure, he didn't dare leave them alone.

❀

It was a drizzly day, and the three Fairfax girls had stayed inside for the quiet afternoon while Lady Rebecca visited her brother, and Lord Wesley had taken the Taylor boys to town to see his milliner.

A fire had been lit for the girls in a parlour set aside for the particular use of the ladies of the house. The walls in soft pink damask reflected the light from the large bay window, lending the room a sunny warmth, even in the poor weather. The furniture was Parisian and decadent: the delicately turned woodwork, gilded in gold, framed the floral silks of the settees, armchairs and chaise. They sat in quiet companionship, each at their own task, and enveloped in their own thoughts.

Eva cleared her throat nervously, looking down at her needlework, and without looking up, asked in a quiet rush, "How long until Lord Lucian shall be fully recovered, do we think? Will he join us? Shall it be... shall it be soon, do you reckon? Has anyone heard anything from his sister, or brothers... or Dr Winslow?"

"Oh, Eva, is there no end to your goodness? How you must worry,"

97

Caroline soothed. Katherine looked up from her fashion sheet to see Caroline moving to sit next to Eva, and caught the wretched look of guilt on Eva's face. "He is young and strong, and I am sure he will be back in fighting form before we know it."

Katherine scoffed. "Fighting form, indeed," she said, disgust undisguised. "I do not know why we any of us should worry over him. It might have been in all our interests if he had not been discovered at all, or if his attackers had been a little more... thorough."

At the silence, Katherine looked up and saw a look of fury on Caroline's face, Eva's hand clasped tight between her own.

"And you would choose that fate for him, dear sister?" she asked thickly. "You would be so unforgiving? Because a man lost his temper and said some careless words at an opera, you would condemn him to this?"

"I am only saying what I am sure everyone is thinking," Katherine defended herself smartly, surprised at the vehemence of Caroline's anger.

"We have a man who was beaten to within an inch of his life upstairs, fighting day and night not to be swallowed up by the darkness of it, and you sit here in his parlour, reading his novels, eating his cakes, and wishing for worse injury?" Her voice rose with her anger. "I had not thought even *you* could be so foolish, Katherine. So unfeeling. It is monstrous." It was scathing. Katherine had never heard Caroline speak like that in all their years together, to anyone.

Caroline stood abruptly, kissed Eva on the forehead, clasped her worried face between her soft hands, and looked into her eyes with barely contained emotion. "Excuse me, my heart. I cannot stay in this room a moment longer. Forgive me," she said, and then turned to wither Katherine with a glare. "Never utter that foul poison again in this house, do you hear me?" Katherine gaped, unable to say anything before Caroline stormed from the room.

Alone with Eva, Katherine puffed. "Well. What has gotten into her? It was just a joke... mostly."

"Hmm. I cannot help but notice that Caroline and Lord Lucian have formed some sort of... friendship. Perhaps she has seen something in him which we have not. The heart is an unknowable mystery," Eva said pointedly, and Katherine's brows drew together. "And it is just like

Caroline to come to his defense. She is always prepared to think the best of people. Besides, you know how she dotes on a wounded thing."

"What sort of friendship?"

"Have you not seen for yourself the way they speak quietly together when others are busy with conversation. And surely you know that Lord Wesley asked Caroline to sit for Lord Lucian to draw her likeness yesterday?"

"What? Why Caroline?"

"I confess, I was asked first, but felt... unwell," Eva flushed.

"As well you might! I should not wish to spend one minute more with him than I had to. But soon you will be married, and there will be no escaping him then," Katherine said, desperation rising in her voice. "Eva, what are we going to do? There must be something, if only you will try. It is not too late!"

Eva looked down at her needlepoint. This had been a conversation that they had had over and over, with the same result.

"Why will you not listen to me?" Katherine pleaded, her voice growing more desperate. "Your wedding is less than a month away, and your beast of a fiance is upstairs bruised and beaten in a violent fight, which he no doubt instigated, on the very same night that he almost killed you!"

"It is not so bleak as that, Katherine. Let us not get carried away. It was just a little episode. I am quite fine, as you see. He will be more gentle now, I think, and with time I shall learn to endure him, I am sure."

"And if you do not? We have worried over your health all these years, and now you are just to be thrown to that man like a sacrifice? This is ridiculous! Why will no one listen to any sense?"

"Please, do not worry so for me, Kitty. All will be well, I am sure."

Katherine could hear no more. Weeks of mounting worry, and heartache had exhausted her. She had tried talking to her parents, to Eva, and even to Caroline, but each had their own reasons that they would not listen.

"Has everyone gone mad? You cannot do this! It will not all be 'well'. Do not pretend to me. He will crush you, Eva!" Tears broke and rolled down her cheeks, and she brushed them away with an angry hand.

"Hush, my love. Hush now. I will not let that happen. Lord Lucian is not yet recovered enough for a wedding, and who knows when it shall be, maybe not so soon as all that." Eva held on to her sister and spoke the words that she hoped would be true. "And... anything might happen until then," she said. "Perhaps..." she whispered, "perhaps it shall never come to pass at all."

᪥

*T*hey eased into a pleasant silence, the fading afternoon sun stretching its long legs through the window.

Caroline was roused from her daydreams by a quiet, contemplative voice.

"It's the shape of your eyes. I cannot manage to capture it truthfully. It drives me to ruin," he said softly, and Caroline looked over to find Rebecca asleep in her chair. She let a gentle smile warm her lips, and he continued to sketch, looking up from time to time, the focus on his task knitting his brows together. "The colour and depth, I do not dare attempt. That is why I use pencil instead of paints."

"Oh, they are mostly just a muddy blue, I think. No great feat."

"Utter nonsense. They have blue, yes, and perhaps if one looked carelessly from very far away, and if one were very stupid indeed, that is all that they might see." Her short, dry laugh urged him onward. "For the rest of us, however, they are a painting all unto themselves." She said nothing, and he did not rush but carried on at his quiet, easy pace while focusing on the page. "The blues are threaded through with brown, and amber, radiating outward from its middle into flecks of gold. There is a lot of green as well, a lush, leafy green at the core, which gives way to a creamy, light green as it mixes with the blue like a sun-lashed Caribbean sea viewed from above. Indeed that is how they look sometimes. As if light were shining from within rather than from without." He pulled the paper from his notebook and started again.

"The Caribbean sea?" she laughed, matching the quiet of his tone, equally unwilling to wake their chaperone. They had spent several afternoons together, when she had sat for him, and mild discomfort or awkwardness had given way to an enjoyable friendship. "Now who is speaking nonsense, Lord Lucian?"

"A man could make a study of your eyes, Miss Lesage. I know I have only just begun mine." Her smile stretched wide and warmed her voice.

"I will not fall for your blather, my Lord. Look now, and you will find me quite unmoved."

"Ah," he said looking up, and narrowing his eyes in careful scrutiny, raking her from head to toe. "It is as you say. You are far too smart for me, Miss Lesage. How very disappointing. I think... I shall draw... a mustache."

Caroline barked a sound of laughter that Lucian had never before heard from her, and he grinned as if he had won a prize. Rebecca stirred in her chair, but to her relief did not wake.

"Could you forgive me, Miss Lesage, if I asked to know more about you? You see, you have these cheekbones... that nose, and such a mouth, if you'll forgive me saying so, a strong, stubborn jaw, and those most incredible, luminous eyes." He carried on, his voice just as low and even as before, as if he were saying nothing shocking: nothing untoward, or intimate in any way. "The Americas are a strange and wondrous place, which I have not yet set foot upon, but I have met many an American abroad, and never have I seen anyone in my life with such a remarkable collection of features. Where does it come from?" he asked, but before she might answer, he went on. "Your skin... it is not so much tanned- it is light in colour, and not quite olive, but nor is it pale and ghostly like the ladies here. It is... a little bit golden, I would say. Another colour which I would struggle to match on my pallet."

She said nothing for a moment, but her mouth tightened, and her eyes looked from him to the window. He did not push her but drew and waited.

"My parents," she said. And it was all she said for a time. Her voice was new. Heavy. Thick. Far away. "My mother's family was English, and not in the colonies long- Thorntons, from Oxfordshire. My father's family had been French, and had come over nearly a hundred years or so past."

"I see," he said. "Though... the French and English have spent centuries fighting, and hating each other, which of course, resulted in swathes of French and English babies..." he said, not finishing the thought.

"It was my father's mother. She was of the native people there in the mountains," she said and stopped. She waited. It was like it always was when she thought of her childhood or spoke of her parents. She wanted to stop, to not put herself through the discomfort, but she pushed on. "I did not know her at all, but there were always stories of her."

"Would you tell one to me?" he asked gently, tentatively. "My mother used to tell me stories, but… but I have not had one in a very long time."

Caroline exhaled- less a sigh, and more because there was a pain in her chest that she wished to ease. It was a love story, the way she had heard it. One which had been passed down from her grandmother, to Caroline's father, who had whispered it to her mother on cold winter nights while they lay under the blankets. Her mother knew it so well that she, in-kind, told it to Caroline, sometimes as a bedtime story, or when a storm had frightened her awake. The way Caroline's mother had always told the story, it was long and slow, winding this way and that, focusing in on tiny details that gave colour and life to an old, dead tale.

And Caroline decided that she would tell it, as best she could, exactly the way that she had heard it many times, many years ago.

⚘

*T*he afternoon had grown to evening, and as Caroline had told her story, they had moved from the window to sit by the fire. It had been excruciating for her at first, the unwrapping of a seeping wound. The thought of her mom curled under the blankets of Caroline's bed until she would fall asleep, seared through her, and stung her eyes. The sound of her voice still echoed through the story as Caroline told it. She never spoke of her parents to anyone; but, she had heard things from Lucian about his father. Painful, twisted things that so affected him that they seemed to draw him back into darkness at times. She felt somehow that he could listen, and know that she hurt, and understand.

As she eased into the tale, so too did her heart ease, and the pain soften. When she had finally finished, she felt drained, and tired, but somehow lighter. She had shared something from home. A piece of her that was dear, and heavily guarded. And while thoughts of her family brought them fresh to her mind in a way she had not allowed for years, she found that the burden of her pain, having been shared with another, was lessened.

"I feel as if I know them," he said softly. "You have given me a gift, Miss Lesage. It will not go unpaid." The look which passed between them was all that she felt needed to be said. They sat silently by the crackling fire and waited for Rebecca to wake.

***

*C*aroline spent a lot of time in Lucian's company, Rebecca noticed. And while it was remarked upon, in hushed tones, by both sets of siblings, she carried on, aiding to plan and chaperone the visits, despite the growing impropriety. Mr and Mrs Fairfax, who might have discouraged the meetings, were not there, and her father seemed to care nothing for any of them and was seldom seen at all, even when he was at Blackhill. The Fairfax sisters did not complain for fear that they would be made to take Caroline's place at Lucian's bedside, while none of the Ashfords, not even Charles, could see fit to quell the friendship, for the remarkable effect it seemed to have on their brother, who had been all but unrecognisable of late. Each new visit gave Rebecca a silent thrill that her scheming might yet be successful.

***

*L*ucian flung himself out of bed and went in search of drink. To hell with the doctor's cursed advice! He could go hang, for all Lucian cared. He could not sleep. Night after night, he could not sleep for want of her. The story of hers had opened the gates. They both had begun to speak more freely, and share their pasts with each other. It had opened some part of him that he had not known that he had. He spoke of his mother and her love, of his father and his cruelty. He spoke of past adventures and past mistakes. He told her about the hidden place under the trees where he hid for comfort when he was a boy. He shared the darkness with the light, and she did not flinch from it. It seemed that there was no end to her capacity for compassion, her ability to forgive. And, all the while, she had become more human to him as well. Not only brightness and strength which everyone saw, but darkness and vulnerability too. Human complexity personified, and all the more glorious for its imperfections.

And yes, dear Christ, he wanted her. He had stared all day at her form, studying it, trying to sketch the curves and angles, imagining what might lay underneath her gauzy summer gowns, all under the steady gaze of those remarkable eyes. To be watched while he wanted her was intoxicating. He was sick with longing, to have her skin under his hands, her lips between his teeth, the taste of her on his tongue, but it was much, much more than that. He wanted to consume her- body and soul. He had never connected with a woman emotionally the way he had with her, perhaps he had never connected with anyone that way before. And the more he got, the more he craved, the more he needed. And, by God, if he had to drink an entire bottle of whisky to finally get some damned sleep; then, bloody hell, that was just what he was going to do!

&

*C*aroline pinned her hair up more carefully than usual perhaps, though she denied the thought even as it formed. Being drawn would make anyone more conscious of their looks, she thought adamantly.

She had kept Lucian company several times, thrice with Wesley and four or five times with Rebecca over the last few weeks. He had also received other visitors- Eva had eventually come, though those visits were more stilted and formal, and seemed to exhaust everyone involved. Katherine flatly refused. He was healing well, and would soon be out of his rooms, as it was, it was difficult to contain him to bed any longer.

Caroline had yet to see one of his sketches, though he had shown Wesley. When she had visited with Rebecca they had read out loud one of his favourite plays, with Rebecca proving a natural actress, her voice changing with each character, Caroline smiled at the memory. It had been a very sweet day. Lucian had listened attentively, sketching at the same time, placing Caroline on the page as a character in the play, he said, and now Caroline practically burned with curiosity to see the results.

She determined that day that she would insist. She had also allowed his request that she wear blue, as today, he was going to teach Rebecca to mix watercolours, and she had agreed to sit for them. The only blue gown she owned was the one from Joshua, and she smoothed her hands over it nervously, aware of how formal it looked.

Leaving her room, she met Rebecca in the hall.

"Caroline, that looks gorgeous! I do hope my brother is able to help me. I confess to be quite terrible at mixing colour," Rebecca said breezily as she knocked on Lucian's door, and entered without waiting for a response. Caroline followed slower, giving Rebecca a chance to start conversation and check her brother was decent, the thought bringing a flush to Caroline's cheeks.

"Miss Lesage," he said warmly as she entered and she noted with surprise how well he looked. She hadn't visited him in a few days, and now, she could see the handsome, virile man whom she had first met, returning to his face. The bruises had faded, his eyes back to their icy blue, his hair, once again a tousled mane of gold atop his head. She bobbed politely, smiling back at him, and watched as he surveyed her dress, a shadow crossing his features.

"So, brother dear, shall we start?" Rebecca said, crossing to an easel, with a small table set up before it, holding brushes and bottles of paint, to stand beside him.

"Indeed," he said shortly, turning his attention away from Caroline to look critically at the window, moving a chair before it, this way and that, until he was satisfied. Gesturing to Caroline, he stood behind her as she sat, a little nervously in front of him, turning her head to look up at him. She practically jumped when he placed his warm hands on her shoulders and turned her gently around, and then on the soft, sensitive skin at the line of her jaw, to reposition her head.

Caroline's eyes flew to Rebecca, to see if she had noticed his inappropriate touch, but she was absorbed with filling bottles with water from a pitcher in the corner. His hands still rested on her shoulders, and she felt a tremor run through her.

Why did her body respond with such intensity, she wondered. Perhaps because he had almost hurt her once, she thought, but then, the feelings were difficult to define, they seemed to blur the line between fear, and excitement, to the point that Caroline preferred to keep distance between them.

"Relax," his low voice purred in her ear, and she felt goosebumps spring out from the point of her skin where his lips had once grazed. She nodded dumbly and waited for him to move away. Finally, his hands released her shoulders, and the cool air on them burned her skin. He walked back to the easel, turning at the last moment and smiling at her, so very... intimately, she looked away. She had never met a man who managed to make her feel quite so naked under his gaze before. And he was a different man again today. Someone whom she did not recognise from the easy visits they had enjoyed before.

The afternoon light was very warm on her, as the sun moved across the sky. At one point, she rested her head back against the chair, the soft warmth of the sun, the quietness of the room, the soft chatter of Rebecca and Lucian, all conspired to drag her eyelids down and before she realised it, she had fallen asleep.

When she later opened her eyes, the first thing she noted was the relative darkness of the room, compared with the dazzling rays of sun which she had fallen asleep to. Coming fully awake, she sat up and looked around.

"Good evening," a warm voice teased, and she turned her head toward it, finding its owner sitting in a chair by the fire, a few feet from her. He sat with his leg thrown over the chair arm, his shirt unbuttoned at the neck, and his sketch pad once again in his lap, his fingers blackened with charcoal, and some streaks marking his face. She suddenly realised they were quite alone.

"Where is Lady Rebecca?" she asked, forcing the disquiet from her voice as she smoothed her mussed hair and dress.

"She is only gone momentarily. She asked that you wait for her. She was reading to me, and went in search of the next title," he supplied, swinging his leg back to the ground and stretching. As he stretched, his body realigning agility, she couldn't help her eyes from sliding over the full muscles of his arms and chest, his shirt clinging to them.

"I should not stay without her..." she said, looking away as his eyes met hers with a contemplative gaze.

"Come, Miss Lesage, do not worry so. Have I not been a complete gentleman of late?" he drawled lazily, standing and carrying his sheath of paper to his desk.

"I suppose," she admitted, standing to stretch also, her body coming back to life after her nap. Turning she found him watching her, his eyes narrowed in disapproval.

"What is the matter?" she asked, as his eyes slid down her dress, while she brushed at the creases.

"That gown. I do not care for it," he said, draining the bottom of one glass of whisky, and turning to the decanter, for another. Caroline raised her eyebrows in surprise at his cutting words.

"Well, that is not really my concern, Lord Lucian, though I only wore it because it is the colour you requested," she said acidly, as he turned to her, a strange expression on his face.

"Are you in earnest, Miss Lesage? Are you sure there was no other reason you chose to wear that dress?" he spat.

"What other reason could there be?" Caroline asked, defensive.

"Perhaps to stimulate jealousy?"

"Jealousy? From whom?" she asked, surprised, and stepped back as he advanced toward her around his desk.

"Certainly not from Rebecca," he ground out as he stood before her.

"Lord Ashford, just tell me your meaning in plain words. I am tired of trying to understand your games and foul moods today," she shot out angrily and had to force herself to stand her ground as he leaned closer to her, his eyes raking uncomfortably.

"Ah, back to 'Lord Ashford', I see. My meaning is this: I know who gave you that dress," he said darkly.

"I did not know you were in the habit of gossiping about women's clothes."

"And I did not know you were in the habit of accepting gifts from men you hardly know," he said bitingly, and she pushed down a retort.

Swallowing, she smiled coldly at him. "I wouldn't say that I hardly know Mr Lee. In fact, I have been spending time with him, and I find that I like him a great deal," she said, her chin raising with defiance. "Though I cannot see why our friendship should have anything at all to do with you."

"Is that so?" he said, moving closer still. He raised his hand and stroked a finger along the line of her jaw where his hands had touched briefly earlier. She felt that thrill of emotion that she had felt before-fear laced with excited anticipation. She pulled back.

"Do not do something we shall both regret, Lord Ashford. You are still engaged to my sister, and I have not forgotten your previous behaviour," her tone held a stern warning as she turned away from him, and made toward the door. He moved to grab her wrist but stopped his hand.

"Damnit. Caroline, Miss Lesage, wait." His face crumpled from its usual haughty confidence. "I'm sorry." She stopped, and he let out a breath he had been holding. "I have felt as though a friendship has been developing between us of late, and now I... well, I would hate to jeopardise it." He scraped a hand over his mess of hair. "I am a petty, jealous man by nature, even over my friends it seems."

She did not move, so he went on, trying to get his words out before he lost his chance or his nerve. "You don't deserve my foul mood. Your company has been the only light since I arrived here. Truly. I'm so grateful for every minute you are here with me instead of enjoying an afternoon with your sisters or playing tennis outside with the others. And yet, I cannot seem to stop humiliating myself around you. I have been a brute. Please forgive me." His tone was so conciliatory, she turned, crossing her arms over her chest as she regarded his expression. The silence dragged on a long painful moment. She did not need words to chastise him. Her shoulders eased.

"Well... I suppose I shall forgive you," she said. "Despite my better judgment. But, I want something in return."

"Anything," he promised.

"I want to see the product of all this sitting I've been doing." He took a deep breath, and she could see the indecision on his face as he looked at her. She made to leave again, and his face conceded.

"Very well, though they are a very poor imitation, and you shall probably never sit for me again," he said as he picked out some papers, and shuffled them uncomfortably. Caroline sat down again on the divan, the offense overshadowed by excitement. She had waited for this. She had never sat for a portrait before and hoped that Lucian may let her keep one if it was a good likeness.

Coming over to her, he sat on the divan beside her, and with a sigh, handed over the notebook. Caroline turned to let the firelight hit the papers and looked closely at them.

She was speechless, he had caught her wonderfully, if too complimentarily. She slowly leafed through the pages, her eyes lost in the beauty of his work. The fine lines, shading and shadow- he was a gifted artist, she realised. This was how she looked to him. Strange, she thought, to see one's own face reflected through the eyes of another.

"Lord Lucian, these are... beautiful," she said softly, looking up at him, and finding him studying her face.

"The subject is breathtaking, I merely tried to capture a glimpse of that."

"You flatter me."

"I flatter no one, this is a poor rendering of how I see you. Your beauty is uncapturable... it is blinding," he said, and Caroline felt heat travel over her skin from his direct gaze and soft words.

"Lord Lucian," she said frankly. "We cannot enjoy a friendship of any sort if you do not desist in these intimacies."

"I cannot," he murmured.

"You must. Soon you will be married," she said, fighting to keep her heart from clambering out her mouth at his proximity.

"That does not have to change anything." He reached out to touch a fallen tendril of her hair, slipping the smooth silk through his fingers. "It will not change the way I feel about you."

"What can you mean?" she demanded.

"I mean that I cannot pretend to feel nothing for you. I am consumed by thoughts of you, Miss Lesage, you must know that. And you spend so much time here with me that I... well, I begin to wonder if you do not feel for me also." She stared straight into him. Eyes wide. Speaking neither to confirm or deny his suspicions. "Miss Fairfax and I will only have the minimal marital relations we must, for appearance's sake and to beget children. I would take care of you... your own home, carriage, servants...we might still be together. And you could enjoy certain freedoms and independence that most women cannot dream of," he trailed off, watching as his words sank in and her eyes met his.

"Are you... Lord Lucian, am I correct in understanding that you are proposing that I become your mistress?" she asked slowly, her eyes narrowing at his words.

"You are all I need Caroline. If I had you, I could survive anything else."

He had barely finished when her palm connected with his face. Frustration coloured his cheeks as he turned back to her.

"What they say about you is true. You really are the most despicable creature I've ever-" she said, then gasped as he suddenly grasped her arms and pushed her back into the divan.

"Yes, I probably am. So why do you toy with me? Why do you tempt me, and treat me like a man, if you will never see me as one? What do you want from me!" he growled, his face inches from hers.

"I certainly do not want to be your mistress! How could you ever propose such a thing? Do you think I am the kind of woman who wants to be misused and hurt by a man while I am ostracised by all society as a wanton reprobate? And for what? Again, sir, you mistake kindness for interest," she spat, pushing her hands against his hard chest.

"I wouldn't hurt you, don't you see... I would worship you. I would love you." His voice dropped low as his eyes fell to her lips. She pushed harder.

"You are not capable of love! You only look to others for what you can take from them. What would the price of your love be? To be the mistress to my own sister's husband? You house a devil in your soul, Lord Lucian, one who only takes... no matter the cost to anyone else. You have no idea what love is," she said desperately, twisting her face away from his, looking to escape his iron clutch and searching eyes.

"You could teach me... if I had you-" he murmured.

"You will never have me," she cried. His face took on a look completely foreign to her, and suddenly fear ignited in her chest.

"I could *make* you have me... *make* you love me." His face came toward hers, and she flinched. She took a ragged breath and forced herself to calm her escalating panic.

"Lucian, if you do not desist this instant, then there is no chance for us, no friendship, no acquaintance even. I will truly despise you," she said firmly, her eyes locked to his, challenging him. Never run from a wolf, she remembered her father saying.

She saw her words finally register there. Halting, he slowly drew back and she pulled her arms from his grasp, rubbing where his fingers had dug into her soft flesh.

He turned away from her, toward the fire, cradling his head in his hands. She did not run, but stood by straight-backed and waited. She saw the crazed look fall from his face, and regret and reason return.

"You have bewitched me, I am not myself. I don't recognise myself anymore," he muttered. Standing, he went directly to the decanter, sloshing a generous measure of liquor into his glass.

"Lucian, I could not find-" Rebecca pushed open the door, and stopped as she took in the scene in the room. Caroline brushed past her out of the room, but not before a sudden rage took Lucian. He roared as he threw his glass into the fire, where it exploded, the flames leaping high, the splintering of the crystal screeching into the night.

❀

*C*aroline ran for her room, her face flushed, her heart pounding. She was reckless with the effort to put a locked door between her and Lord Lucian, and reach her room before her tears began to spill. She turned a corner and smacked straight into a tall, solid body. Looking up, she was horrified to find Silus Ashford staring at her with a considering expression.

"Miss Lesage, is it not?" he asked, taking in her mussed hair, and general state of disarray. She swallowed her harsh breath and forced all emotion from her face.

"Yes, my Lord Ashford. Forgive me, I-" she started, wildly trying to think of a reason she might be running through his house in such a state.

"Have you seen my daughter? I wish to speak to her," he interrupted abruptly, and Caroline stopped.

"I'm afraid not," she said shortly and stepped back as he pushed past her, and disappeared around the corner without another word. Taking a deep breath, she continued on to her room, entering and locking the door behind her. She laid down on the bed and calmed herself, slowly regaining control.

She closed her eyes and tried to avoid thinking of Lord Lucian's lips inches from her own, his hard body pressing her down. She could not quiet the same combination of fear and excitement that sent lighting up her spine. She had not been afraid that he would hurt her physically, not after what they had shared together over the past weeks, not now that she knew him. But, she was afraid of what he might do and afraid of how she would respond.

He was frustrating, and complicated, and altogether too tortured to even try and understand. He was also exciting, passionate and brilliant, and looked at her like no man ever had. Now she found, perhaps for the first time ever, that she no longer understood herself either.

She pressed her palm over her pounding heart and squeezed her eyes shut. Control was important to her. Stability was vital. Those things had been taken from her once, and she had fought and clawed her way back to them.

She had to stay away from him. He was too dangerous, he was all passion and fire, and he would burn through her until nothing was left but ash.

CHAPTER 8

*T*he dappled horse snorted as Katherine ran her hand over its neck, appreciating the elegant beauty that masked its pure power. She hummed low in her throat as she continued to run her hands over it, brushing its mane back from its large, soft eyes. Since Silus had arrived, the house was not the peaceful retreat it had been for everyone before. Now she preferred to get out as early as possible, and spent many a day riding alone, exploring the estate, unlike Eva, who had always been happiest indoors.

This morning she had ridden until she had reached a river, and dismounted to rest the horse, and stretch her legs. Smiling, she thought of the groom's reaction to her riding clothes, men's breeches, allowing her to ride astride the animal. It was fairly common at home, at least in the country where practicality was vital, and where there was a certain amount of lawlessness that she felt made her blossom. Sidesaddle was uncomfortable and dangerous, she reasoned.

She unbuttoned her jacket and tossed it on the ground, looking longingly at the clear water of the river. She sat on the river bank and pulled off her socks and riding boots, rolling her breeches up to her knees, her toes rejoicing in the fresh air. It could be suffocating in that house, with the growing tension, so many unspoken words, and the crushing weight she felt of the upcoming nuptials.

Walking forward, she gasped at the shock of coldness, then advanced further into the lush, rejuvenating water. Blessed freedom! Her hair, which had become unbound during her ride, now pulled on her scalp sagging from its pins. She pulled them carelessly out, collecting them and pushing them into her pocket. She combed her fingers through her waist-length curls and left it strewn around her shoulders. Closing her eyes, she hummed slightly, moving her legs through the water, letting the sun dance on her face.

A sudden noise made her eyes shoot open and she looked around. There was no one. She looked closer, and spied a horse, moving through the trees. The rider had not noticed her, and she froze, recognising Charles's upright figure. She cursed herself, thinking of the good impression she'd been making lately. She wasn't quite sure when it had happened, but his good opinion of her had become strangely important.

He was about parallel to her now, and she started to move stealthily forward, aiming for the shore and a well-placed tree. His horse abruptly jerked its head her way, and she froze again, though he just pulled it back and continued. Starting off again, her foot suddenly slipped on a slimy rock, and she felt her balance go. Her arms windmilled, but she couldn't catch it and hit the water face first with a loud smack. The shock of the cold water opened her mouth and she immediately swallowed a lung full.

She felt strong arms go around her middle, coughing and spluttering, as her body was hauled out of the water and held tight against a strong chest. Charles laid her on the grass, and she proceeded to cough up the river, no need to worry about losing her ladylike demeanour now, she thought sourly.

"Miss Katherine! Are you well? I shall help you back to the house."

Katherine pushed herself up on her elbows and swallowed hard.

"There is no need, Lord Charles, I am fine," she said, pushing herself roughly to her feet. Charles stood back, perplexed, regarding her, and she stood before him, soaking wet. His eyes widened as he took her in slowly- men's trousers rolled to expose a great deal of skin, wet fabric hugging her legs tightly. His eyes stopped at her white shirt, which clung to her like a second skin.

"I am hardly a delicate flower, and I have been in worse scrapes I can assure you," she was saying, pulling her long hair over one shoulder, wringing water out of it.

Without warning, Charles reached out for her, his hands grabbing her by the upper shoulders, and pulled her to him in one fluid motion. The breath left her body. She found herself pressed once more against his hard chest. With one hand, he tilted her chin up, and all at once his mouth was on hers.

Hot and insistent, his mouth moved against her lips, and she surrendered to it. He ran his hand along to the back of her head, where his fingers grasped her heavy, wet hair, using it to press her closer, bending her to fit him.

Her body was a mass of conflicting sensations, her wet clothes rubbing against her burning skin. Their kiss built and built, until his mouth broke away, and moved to her neck, turning her head to allow him access. She gasped as his teeth scraped her skin, nipping it.

Her horse snorted and Charles pulled back suddenly, the unexpected loss of contact making Katherine gasp. He looked at her, his eyes clouded with desire and need, roaming over her, his breath coming fast, his brow creasing. Pushing himself back, he put his hands to his head and ran his fingers through his hair. He finally met her gaze.

"Forgive me," he muttered, and suddenly he was gone, pushing through the trees back to his horse. Mounting, he turned the beast, and then all Katherine could make out was the thundering of galloping hooves.

She sank down, her heart beating as though it would break her chest. What had just happened? She buried her face and laughed. She could never have seen this coming. It was insanely frustrating that he would turn and run from her. She had to fight down the urge she felt in her bones to follow him, to confront him.

Steadying herself finally, she took a deep breath and returned her gaze to the glimmering water. She would confront him, but she would choose her time, she thought, already smiling in anticipation of the torment she might cause. After all, why give away such a gift before you were able to enjoy it?

*I*t was three whole days after her encounter with Lucian when Caroline came face to face with him again.

She had avoided him as much as possible. The doctor had granted permission for him to leave his rooms, but she had not seen him much and when she had, she barely met his eye. With his father at Blackhill, Lucian was being more attentive to Eva than ever under his father's ever-watchful eye. Eva, in response, had been even more preoccupied and nervous than usual, and Caroline despaired that she still had not accepted her impending wedding day. Silus had taken control of the arrangements, and their wedding would be in two weeks.

On the third night during dinner, as they moved to the dining room, footmen showing them to their seats, Caroline cringed when she saw that she was to sit between Lucian and Isaac, across from Rebecca. When dining so often together it was customary to change table seatings regularly, so that conversation topics were not rehashed too often. As the footman pushed her chair in, she felt the men sit at either side, and she turned to Isaac almost immediately.

"Mr Taylor, why, I have not had the pleasure of your company in quite some time," she said politely, hoping her eyes did not look too desperate.

"Yes, Miss Lesage, how unfortunate. It seems you have been quite busy. As have I. Let us do what we can to rectify the situation," he said warmly.

"Pray, do describe what has been keeping you so occupied."

"Well, apart from basking in the collected beauty of you and your sisters, Miss Lesage, I am very happy to report that the hunting here is most excellent."

"It sounds fascinating. I confess I have always been curious about it, and why exactly it is that men enjoy it so."

"The thrill of the hunt- it is a pleasure as old as time itself," Lucian's dry voice came from her other side, and she now had no choice but to sit back and allow him into the conversation. "Miss Lesage," he said warmly, waiting patiently for her to turn to him.

"Lord Lucian," she said stiffly, giving him a courteous, brief smile before turning back to Isaac, who she now saw had fallen into conversation with Rebecca. There was an air about them of not wanting to be disturbed. The first course arrived and she smiled graciously at her server.

"Well, this shall be a long evening if you refuse to speak to me," he said quietly. "Hunting is a thrilling sport. I could take you sometime, if you wish."

"Ladies do not hunt."

"Oh, quite the contrary, Miss Lesage. It is quite the thing in the country, women even have special riding habits. Rebecca loves to hunt. I'm sure she has a habit that you might borrow," he said, watching as Caroline turned a little to him.

"I confess I am not skilled enough on a horse to participate," she said shortly.

"I thought all Americans could ride?" he asked wryly, raising an eyebrow at her.

"I rode as a child when I lived in the country, but when I moved in with the Fairfaxes, I had fewer opportunities to ride, and chose not to pursue it," she explained, taking a long drink of wine, feeling dry-mouthed at his proximity and the way he kept looking at her with eyes like molten fire. "And I confess that I am weary to give over so much control to an animal... particularly one so strong and unpredictable," she leveled him with a pointed look.

"That is a shame, but something that could be easily remedied. We have an excellent stable here. And, I flatter myself, an adequate teacher."

"I think not. Thank you, Lord Lucian," she said shortly, remembering his scorching eyes and inappropriate words the last time they had been alone together.

"I see I have once again destroyed any goodwill that may have grown between us. For that, I am truly sorry. I confess to my head having been quite muddled that last night. I have not felt myself since the attack," he said with a tightness about his mouth.

Against her inner voice of caution, Caroline felt moved by the look of anguish that clouded his face.

"My Lord Lucian," she turned and addressed him squarely, speaking in a voice she did not think would be overheard. "I will not pretend that I have not felt a friend to you these last weeks. In those short hours together, we have shared much of ourselves. We have somehow defied all logic, and become confidants. I value our friendship, Lord Lucian, I will not lie to you." She pinned him down with a serious glare. "However, I must press in the most determined manner, that if you wish to continue our friendship, you must cease all talk of a romantic nature. It is an insult to both me and my sister and is below you, my Lord. Soon, I shall be your sister through marriage, and I do not wish for anything to inhibit me from visiting Eva when I can."

"I am quite chastened, Miss Lesage," he said with an easy smile, bowing his head in concession. "I will do my best to reform my unforgivably beastly nature."

🐚

*F*urther down the table, Katherine had become bored of listening to Lord Wesley and Eli talk to Lord Silus, and she slid her eyes down the table, where they rested for a moment on Charles. She was surprised to see his eyes already on her, and she automatically dropped them, feigning upset. Glancing back after a moment, she saw that he had become absorbed in his own thoughts, frowning. She hadn't spoken to him since their kiss, and she felt his frustration mount at each passing day. He wanted her to behave like a lady, well, she planned to do just that, especially when he was the one who had acted shamefully for once. She planned to make sure he tortured himself over their small, innocent kiss as much as possible. What she would do with him after, she hadn't quite decided.

She saw Rebecca deep in conversation with Isaac, and Lucian was saying something to Caroline that caused her to throw her head back in laughter. Noticing a small pause in Lord Silus's monologue, she saw his eyes sweeping over the scene, running over Caroline and her obvious effect on his son, one that no one could fail to notice.

"In fact, I have good news for you all. We will have an additional guest arriving tomorrow. Mr Lee, Joshua Lee. I have become involved with his father, our business affairs are quite connected, and when he mentioned that his son has grown tired of the city, I immediately thought of this cheerful little group Lady Rebecca has put together here." His tone was light, almost jovial, but he stared unblinkingly down the table at his second son, not unlike the way a boy with a magnifying glass looks eagerly down on an ant, Katherine thought, unwilling to miss a second. "And very soon after that, we shall be joined by Mr and Mrs Fairfax. Such fun to have so many… delightful people under one roof."

Something passed between Rebecca and Isaac in that moment. Katherine didn't understand it, but she could hardly fail to notice the look of worry in Rebecca's eyes.

☙

*L*ucian heard his father's words and felt a rage settle over him like the cold after a sunset, though he pushed it aside with his next breath. He must learn to control his emotions around Caroline, and he refused to give his father the satisfaction of this fresh torment. Joshua Lee, here. He fought to get his features under control and turned to study Caroline's reaction. Her face was pink-tinged, and he watched as she sipped her wine. Finding little else, he prodded her.

"So, it appears your admirer shall soon arrive," he remarked lightly, pleased at the calm in his voice.

"He is merely a friend," she said, just as smoothly.

"Well, I doubt he is coming all this distance for the hunting," Lucian said shortly, gesturing for more wine.

"Why not, I hear the chase is quite exhilarating," she said and smiled at him for a moment with such a mischievous quality to her blue eyes, that he found it difficult to stop his mouth from curling into a challenging smile. Gently setting his glass down, he smiled at her.

"Miss Lesage, I am glad we are friends again."

☙

*S*itting bolt upright in bed, Caroline clamped her hand over her mouth to stop the cry from escaping. She slowly came back to herself, finding the room quiet and dark, shadows from the fading fire dancing on the walls. She was at Blackhill Hall. Her brain slowly caught up with her consciousness and she pressed a hand over her pounding heart. Sweat ran from her temples, and her hair felt slick with it. She had dreamt of the fire.

She pushed the heavy covers off, the heat in the room suffocating, and went to the window. She struggled to pull up the heavy pane, and then instantly felt the cool night air cut through the thin, summer sleeping gown she wore. Resting her forehead against the glass, she felt the icy cold soothe her nerves and clear the smell of death from her mind.

Goosebumps traveled up her arms and she knew he was watching her. She breathed deeply, resigned to turn away and go back to bed, but she found that she couldn't resist the desire to see him. He stood in the pale moonlight, his arms braced on the window, and as her eyes met his, she felt that all too familiar jolt in her stomach.

From the other side of the glass, she looked like a vision from Lucian's dreams, ethereal in her thin gown, long raven hair falling in a thick wave around her shoulders, he had never seen it down before. It felt achingly intimate. His eyes searched hers and knew the look in them pleaded with her. The last few days had been a waking nightmare, his future was diminishing fast. The problem was not only Eva and his lack of feeling for her. It was also Caroline. Over these past days of being close to her, but not being able to see her alone, or speak to her- she had gotten into his veins, and he could barely think of anything else. He wanted her, he needed her. He had never felt anything as strongly as he did that. He also knew just as strongly, that she deserved better than him, so much better.

He saw her pale face, a fine sheen of sweat covering her skin, hands clenched as she had rested her forehead against the glass, and he longed to know what had upset her, to soothe her, to take away her pain. He took a deep steadying breath and, stealing himself, he tilted his head in the direction of the door. An offer. Of companionship... of the friend-ship she had offered him.

Caroline watched him steadily, considering his proposal. It was utter foolishness, she knew that beyond a doubt. But, the thought of returning to her fire-filled dreams, alone and afraid was too terrible to contemplate.

Feeling her heart in her mouth, she slowly nodded and tried to ignore the look of relief on his face. She went to the wardrobe and pulled out the thickest, most concealing wrapper she had. Before she could change her mind she stepped out into the dark hall and started toward the stair.

She found him standing there, waiting for her, his relief again palpable as she came toward him. Without a word, he turned and gestured for her to go first, and they silently moved through the house in the direction of the kitchen. The cavernous room was quiet, a drip of water, the growl of the stove all that broke the silence. It smelt of lemons, beeswax and tea, and she found it comforting.

She heard the flare of a match being struck and a soft glow filled the room as Lord Lucian lit some nearby candles. Feeling the chill of the stone floor, she perched on the wooden table, bringing her feet up to rest on the chair, pulling her gown tighter than ever around her. She felt her nerves grow as the silence stretched between them, as he busied himself, resting a pan on the stovetop and pouring some milk into it. Finally turning, he leant back against the stove and looked at her, smiling warmly.

"The perfect cure for sleeplessness... well, one of them at least..." he said with a smile, which widened with her expression.

"Sir, you are relentless."

"As are you in your resistance," he said with a smile.

"I had no idea you were so accomplished in the kitchen," she teased, watching as he occasionally turned to stir the warming milk.

"Well, I had an unorthodox upbringing. When you grow up with as many siblings as I had, without a mother, and with a father such as mine... you may have all the help you can buy, but sometimes nothing is more comforting than family."

"You took care of them?"

"Sometimes. When I could."

"They love you very much," she said, accepting a glass of warm milk from him.

"They do, though I have never been quite sure if I am deserving of it." He sat leaning beside her against the table.

"You will not take anything for your insomnia?" she asked

"I wish that my insomnia could be cured so simply. No, sadly, I have never been one for sleep or..."

"Peacefulness?" she supplied quietly, tilting her head to watch him as she sipped the warm milk. He slanted a look back at her, his eyes narrowed slightly.

"Miss Lesage, why is it that you seem always to cut to the heart of the matter so ruthlessly?"

"I prefer a direct approach I suppose," she said with a smile.

"That is very admirable. However, directness is not for the faint-hearted."

"I know you are right, and it is not proper in polite company... but amongst friends, I do not care to pretend," she said and flushed a little as she realised her words.

"Friends," he repeated, and Caroline could have sworn that he moved imperceptibly closer to her side. She kept quiet, looking into her glass.

"I am not sure if I merit your friendship, not yet anyway, perhaps I never shall. I have not lived a life I am proud of, Miss Lesage... though, until recently, it did not worry me much," he mused softly, and she saw his eyes were lost outside the window. "If you prefer directness, then I may apply it to you also, I presume. What troubles you tonight?" he turned his face back to her, and Caroline was sure he was closer.

"I had... unpleasant dreams," she said uncomfortably, and Lucian must have sensed her unwillingness to talk further of it.

"I see. Well, I will not press you if you do not wish to speak of it. Instead, may I ask you if you are looking forward to returning to the city?"

"I confess I am not. This place is a respite, I have truly enjoyed my time here. I shall be sad to depart for town."

"As shall I, though perhaps not for the same reasons."

"You still do not look forward to your marriage?"

"Miss Fairfax is a lovely girl. She would make most men extremely happy. Sadly, I am not one of them. We are destined to misunderstand each other at every turn, to hurt one another, to be trapped together in our misery. I feel sorry for her," he said.

"And what of yourself?"

"I am not convinced that a loveless marriage and a lifetime of soli-tude is not exactly what I deserve. I have done little to be proud of, my reputation is well earned. And, I am the man that earned it still, always. I have not the capacity for selflessness, compassion or love, truth be told." His voice was hard.

"I am sure that is not true," she said softly.

"Do not be sure- let us look at the way I have treated you. Abominably. Without question, yet, I would do it all again, for a chance to be here with you now," he glanced at her as he spoke and she felt a small thrill of alarm.

"Lord Ashford," she warned.

"Rest easy, Miss Lesage. I no longer want a stolen minute of intimacy from you. In fact, it might well destroy me. If I were not betrothed to Eva, I would make no secret of my intentions towards you, my father be damned." Caroline felt her face flush and tried to ignore the way her heart had begun to hammer in her chest.

"Well, I am convinced that we would make the most disagreeable match, so it is for the best," she said with a nervous laugh.

"We would? Yes, I suppose we would... you are far too good for me."

"True," she said with a smile, then continued "Moreover, it is not what I want from my life. Simply put, my choices are very important to me. I would like to return home one day, I would like to marry someone simple and honest. I wish to be my own woman."

"And you think I would restrict your freedom?"

"No, not particularly, but some people, when they are together, the intensity diminishes some parts of them, the sheer strength of it changes them..." she trailed off. Lucian was silent beside her, eyes searching her face.

"If I did not know a little about your low regard of me, I'd think you were implying that my love for you- our love- would be greater than you could manage."

She could feel him watching the side of her face. She hadn't been careful. She'd lost her head in the conversation, and she knew that things were poised to spiral out of her control. Putting down her glass, she briefly raised her eyes to his, forcing a quick smile.

"I apologise, being awake at his hour," she waved her hand, "has quite confounded my brain." She smiled through tight lips. "Thank you for the milk, and the company, Lord Lucian. I must return to bed," she said, in a tone that did not invite discussion, and walked away.

a soft knock alerted Rebecca to his presence at her door. Pulling her robe tighter, she crossed the room quickly and opened it as quietly as possible. A dark shadow moved in the hall, and just as quickly she was closing the door again behind Isaac Taylor. She crossed back to her bed and lit a candle that was waiting there with trembling fingers.

"Lady- "

"Shhh-" she said suddenly, hearing someone moving in the hall. Pulling him down to her side, behind her bed, she placed a slender hand over his lips, her eyes willing him to be quiet. She blew out the candle and waited in silence, straining to hear the person moving outside, terrified they might have seen Isaac coming into her room.

As silence met silence, and she started to feel safe again, she suddenly realised the closeness of Isaac to her shoulder and the sensitive skin of her neck, his face was practically resting in it, and his warm breath was lightly caressing her cheek. By simply turning her face, their lips would touch. Her heart started to pound, more forcefully than when she had feared being discovered.

Looking to the floor, she also realised she had grasped his hand in an effort to pull him out of sight. Now, she found his fingers were still entwined in hers. Slowly raising her eyes to his, she saw he was also looking at their locked fingers, with an expression that was impossible to read. He returned his eyes to her face, and at that moment she dropped his hand and pushed herself to her feet, putting some distance between them. She turned her back, busying herself with lighting the dropped candle. When she had regained her composure she turned to give him a speculative look.

"Well, Mr Taylor. It seems our schedule may have to change," she said as he came closer nodding. "When the Fairfaxes return, they shall be put next to Eva in the adjoining rooms, and I do not believe that anything would get past that woman's shrewd and determined eye."

"Indeed. Are you are still willing to do whatever it takes for your brother, as I am for mine."

"When the time comes, I shall not hesitate," she confirmed, her eyes evading his, she stood at the window and looked out on the moonlit lake.

"How shall we accomplish it though, before your father returns."

"He departs tomorrow on business, and will not return until the day before the wedding," she said, turning back. Isaac watched her closely as she raised her chin, hiding the moment of vulnerability he had seen when she talked of her father.

"He shall be very angry with you, you know." Isaac had not known Lord Silus long, but he seemed nonetheless to already be able to anticipate his ugly reaction.

"He will not hurt me, I am his only daughter. At the most, he would just send me away, marry me off to one of his elderly business acquaintances." He sucked in a breath.

"That does not frighten you?"

"Not as it once did. I feel I have to live my life and make decisions, even if they're dangerous, even if they're the wrong ones. A life unlived, a life constricted- that scares me more."

"A cage... like you said," Isaac said, trailing off as he noticed the gathering of tears in Rebecca's eyes. She nodded and turned back to the window.

"I may end up married to some old, wealthy man who has daughters of my own age, but at least I'll be free of him. He loves me, but even his love is controlling and manipulative."

"Would he never consider letting you marry for love?"

"I am embarrassed to admit it is not a question that he has ever been faced with. I suspect after he finds out my part in this, there will be no chance of it. My father is nothing if not vindictive."

"And yet, you still help? For all it shall cost you?"

"He is my brother. He has always protected me, now it is my turn. I must do this, I would never forgive myself if I do not. I want him to have a chance at happiness."

"It is worth more to you than your own," he finished softly for her, and she nodded imperceptibly, before turning back to the ghostly washed night.

"Now, let us plot and scheme, for the morning is not far, and tomorrow shall be the last day we spend as a contented household," she said.

CHAPTER 9

*I*t was to be their first day painting outside and the weather was sublime. Caroline sat in the shade of a tree to read a most scintillating gothic novel, while brother and sister set up their easels side by side and painted the idyllic scene. Caroline was growing tired of sitting, but reasoned that had she the afternoon to herself, reading under a shady tree in the fine spring breeze would probably be exactly what she would have chosen anyway.

Miss Branson, the housekeeper, had brought them some lemonade and cake, and they stretched for a break while they enjoyed it.

"I had not been to this part of the gardens before. I did not even know it was here, and I think it is quite the loveliest part," Caroline said.

"Oh, you must stick with me, Miss Lesage, I have lots of secrets to teach you," answered Lord Lucian with a sun-soaked, lazy tone that made her wonder if his words might not have an altogether different meaning.

"Don't be absurd, Luke. She must stick with me. I am by far the better of the two of us, and as no one would bother to gossip with you, I've far juicier secrets to tell," Rebecca countered, with a triumphant bite of cake.

"Oh, I disagree, dear sister, for who would choose a pale copy of an earlier masterpiece, which they might have the original?" he teased, and she threw a bit of cake that hit him squarely in the nose. He roared, and they all laughed to see icing smeared across his face. "Well, why don't we let Miss Lesage decide for us? What say you?" He smiled at Caroline, swiping his face with a large hand. "I will offer to share one of my secrets, and you shall offer one of yours, and we shall see who is the most compelling."

"Challenge accepted, for I know just what to show her!" Rebecca replied squinting into the sun as she chewed. "You have lost before you've begun, Luke. Now, Caroline. I happen to know of a fountain not far from here. And underneath the lilies hides a family of the largest golden fish you have ever seen, as big as your arm, some of them! And if we bring a bit of cake, we could feed it to their huge gaping mouths!" She opened her eyes wide, and clapped her mouth open and shut with a snap, in an imitation that made Caroline bark with laughter. Long gone was the rude and intimidating Lady Ashford that Caroline had first met. Once a person was admitted into her inner circle, Rebecca shone on them like the sun.

"Hmmm, perhaps you should not be so confident, sister mine." He took a long sip from his lemonade and chewed another bite of cake. "Fish? Really?"

"You see. He has nothing but complaints to offer, Caroline, just as I suspected."

"And no wonder- it would be difficult to top a family of fish with mouths as big as that!" Caroline teased.

"Let us not be hasty, ladies. Miss Lesage, if you would be so good as to recall, I once told you of a secret place, a hidden sanctum under the trees where a fairy queen reins and bestows her blessings and good fortune on all who visit her." Rebecca gasped.

"Not fair! You said you would never take me. To this day, I have never found it!" Lucian laughed and reached out to pinch his sister's cheek.

"That is because there is nothing so torturously vexing as a little sister." She huffed. "But, even still, if you behave yourself with decorum as a young lady aught, I will bring you there myself tomorrow, and we shall have a picnic. How does that sound?" She looked at him sideways.

"Agreed," she said grudgingly.

"Well, there you have it, Miss Lesage," Lucian drawled confidently, stretching his back against the bench, legs straight and crossed at the ankle. "Two rather tempting offers. A fairy queen, or... fish. Which shall you choose?"

Rebecca shoved her shoulder hard into his.

"Hmmm..." Caroline made a show of deliberation. She liked both options and did not wish to decide between the two, but Lord Lucian had told her of this place in his stories, and she knew that it was a precious place which he had never shared, and she could not turn her nose up at the gesture. "Hmmm. In all truth, it is nearly impossible to choose!" she laughed. "But, I am in sore need of good fortune these days, and I think that I cannot in good conscience turn the offer down, *even* if it means enduring your brother's company. Will you ever forgive me, Lady Rebecca?" Caroline laughed as Rebecca sighed dramatically.

"Oh, I suppose I shall." She brightened. "I could take you to see the fish after breakfast one day, and we can bring them a muffin."

"Oh, can we? Yes, please! I should love that."

"We shall," Rebecca said with a warm smile.

"Then I promise I will come back after visiting the fairy queen's court, and I shall sit for you again, for as long as you ask, more still than I have ever been in all my life."

❀

They had walked quite a way away from the Hall with Caroline's hand in the crook of Lucian's elbow. He had taken her down new paths, all in the fresh flush of spring, their flowers resplendent in a gaudy display of color. She didn't think she'd ever seen gardens as fine as these in Richmond, nor in London, and she wished that she too might learn to paint so that she could remember forever the magnificent beauty of it.

After some time that she did not feel Lucian was in a hurry to end: most of it in companionable silence, between small comments about the plants, or a folly, or a memory from childhood, they stopped in front of a lush, green tree, its limbs and leaves drooping down to create a thick green curtain around itself. She met his smile expectantly.

"It's a Camperdown Elm," he said. "One of my favorites." He reached out, and pulled some of the greenery aside, making a small gap in the curtain that one might slide through. "After you," he said, with a small bow. She smirked up at him. It would not be a ladylike undertaking, but she didn't care. She scrambled under the branches, trying not to rip her gown, or unpin her hair, and they both chuckled softly and the silliness of it.

But, she quieted as she was finally in. It was a magical, emerald room, a jewel. Under the sun the leaves became ethereal, velvet and stained glass, the roots and limbs providing buttresses, elegantly turned. Moss carpeted the ground in cool, plush jade, and at the center of it all, the fairy queen. A statue, long since forgotten, her face was all grace and soft curves, her hair so long and flowing, that Caroline found it hard to believe that it did not blow in the breeze. Soft green had grown on the stone over time, shading her, making her one within her viridian kingdom.

Lord Lucian had joined Caroline, though she had hardly noticed, and he lay now back on the moss, arms behind his head, looking up at the branches.

"It is enchanted," she said in reverent awe. "I am a little girl again."

"I am very glad to hear you say so." He had the smug, happy look of a contented child about his face, and Caroline could imagine him there, a young boy, hiding his most secret treasures here or coming for comfort when hurt and heartsore, and those times that the blackness of his father's actions had threatened to consume him. He had told her some of the stories of cruelty, of being willfully neglected, of a little boy who had lost his mother, and who was ostracized by his own father from the only family he had left. One who had sought comfort from a statue. No child should have to endure the emotional torment that he had.

She lowered herself down, and laid back, in the soft embrace of the moss, enjoying the new perspective from below. They sat there and needed to say nothing, for everything was perfect just as it was.

"Well," Lord Lucian said, stretching his long limbs after a time, though how long she did not know, "shall we bid adieu to the fairy queen, Miss Lesage? Rebecca will be fit to bursting with jealousy, and we should try to make it back to catch the last of the sun." He turned his body toward her, and looked across as one might do with a partner in bed, she thought. "Well, what did you think of my secret castle?"

"Oh," she sighed comfortably. "It is nothing short of magic here."

"Better than fish?"

"Better than fish," she laughed. "But please never repeat it to Lady Rebecca."

"I am glad that you were the first person to share it with me," he reached out in the space between them, and laid his hand on the moss, and without much thought, Caroline turned her body to face him, and did the same, laying her lace-gloved hand gently on top of his.

"I feel honored. Truly I do."

"Well, it is all the more magical for your being here," he said. giving her hand a soft squeeze. He stood in a fluid movement, and keeping hold of her hand, helped her up and back through the way they had come.

🍥

*W*arm, happily exhausted, and saddle sore, Katherine slid from her mount and decided to walk Circe the rest of the way back to the Hall. The late afternoon light was cool, much cooler than it would be in Virginia at this time, and she breathed deeply the wonderful sharp smell of the trees, earthy horse and late summer. Today, she had had a delicious ride and was already dreaming of the long bath she would indulge in before the dinner gong. It did her good to release some of her frustrations after the week of worry she'd had.

She turned at a movement in the far corner of her periphery, and stood in paralysed shock, as she saw Lord Lucian emerge from under some bushes, holding the hand of a lady who was definitely not her sister. Her heart stopped. Holding Caroline's hand. They giggled at one another and helped each other to brush the leaves and twigs from their tousled hair and rumpled clothes, making themselves presentable again before they set off towards the Hall.

🍥

*T*he next morning Caroline dressed slowly, looking forward to seeing Joshua Lee again. With all the upheaval of feelings here, all the emotions that whirled through her by the second, she

130

would be glad to have a distraction where she might safely focus her attention, and not be in perpetual danger of thoughts of Lord Lucian. Her attention had been straying dangerously and with increasing demand.

She attended breakfast with Rebecca, who seemed unusually subdued and nervous, and then went to help Eva with her fitting for her wedding dress. Standing on a stool, before the window, the fabric seemed to imprison Eva's petite figure. She had chosen an especially high neck and bulky fabric in an unflattering yellow, and Caroline couldn't help but worry for the girl, who hoped that adding extra layers would stop her husband from consummating their marriage. Especially considering who her husband was to be.

Katherine was out riding again, refusing to help with a wedding which she was still trying desperately to stop, and Rebecca was busily preparing for their new guest. As the dressmaker left the room, Eva sat on the bed, her eyes lost in the rolling green English hills basking in late summer sunshine.

"Do you miss it Caroline... home?" Eva asked suddenly.

"Sometimes," Caroline answered, sorting through the dressmaker's collection of gloves and pins.

"I miss it so. The warmth, the haze on the hills, the land. It shall always call to me. It is in my blood, I believe," Eva said and looked to Caroline from the window.

"Well, I am sure England shall become home to you too, after a time."

"No, I don't think it ever shall. It's not the same. I am not a fashionable or worldly person. I cannot change something so essential about me, and not lose myself in the process. I think the Eva who stays in England, she will be very different from the one she was at home."

"Do not be silly, my dear," Caroline said kindly. "You shall grow here, change and develop... everyone changes."

"Yes, I suppose they do." She was quiet again, turning back to the fields and valleys.

"You are my sister Caroline, truly. And I love you. I want you to know that. I cherish you dearly," she suddenly said, her tone so earnest Caroline ceased her search and came toward her, sitting beside her on the bed, and taking her hand.

"Eva, I know that, why do you speak of this now?" she asked, worried at Eva's detachment.

"I just... I do not know what is to become of my life. Each day brings new confusion and uncertainty. The only thing of which I am absolutely sure is that within a matter of days my life shall be irrevocably changed."

"Everything shall be well, you will see. Your Lord Lucian is not the monster that you fear he is. And, try though you might, it shall be impossible to get rid of me," she smiled, and as she hugged Eva, she hoped in her heart she was speaking the truth.

֍

*M*r Lee's carriage arrived at lunchtime, and Rebecca had organised for everyone to be present, as Lord Silus was leaving soon after.

Placed near Mr Lee at lunch, Caroline immediately relaxed in his easy company and found herself unwinding. Sitting near Lucian made her feel always on edge- the air was charged, lightning crackling between them, one look could stop her heart. Mr Lee, on the other hand, was like taking a stroll on a warm balmy evening in Virginia when the crickets sang, and the smell of honeysuckle perfumed the air.

He looked at her with his lively brown eyes for most of the meal, engaged her in conversation exclusively, outrageous behaviour for a luncheon, and then escorted her through to the drawing-room. Lucian and Eva were sitting near Lord Silus, who was taking his last opportunity to go over the wedding plans, probably less because he cared about the wedding arrangements, Caroline thought grimly, but more for the pleasure of tormenting the young couple who both looked as if they were marching to their own execution.

After lunch as the ladies were engaged in various pursuits, and the Taylor boys off fishing with Wesley, Mr Lee asked Caroline to accompany him for a walk, inviting Lord Lucian and Eva at the same time. Lucian immediately declined with a barely-concealed snarl, citing business he must attend to in his study. Eva asked Katherine to come, and soon the four were walking in the beautiful gardens to the side of the lake.

"So, Mr Lee, you simply must tell us of all the scintillating gossip that we have missed," Katherine urged.

"I beg your forgiveness, but I have none of note. I think that this gathering is partly to blame, for it has taken some of the season's most disreputable bachelors from the scene, as well as the much-lauded Americans," he said with a laugh.

"Do not tell me that without Lord Lucian in London, there is no juicy gossip to be had! I am quite disappointed in you Mr Lee. Do you not know that it is a guest's duty to bring intrigue to the captives of a house party," she said with a laugh.

"I did not know you felt that way, Miss Katherine. I thought you were enjoying our little gathering." Charles's voice rang out as he suddenly appeared, walking toward them over the grass.

"Well, I was... but I had an awful encounter the other day, and then the pleasure of it quite simply vanished for me," she said, turning to face ahead.

"An encounter, Kitty? Whatever happened?" Eva asked, concerned.

"I might suggest you ask Lord Charles," Katherine said, fighting her smile, and forcing a pained expression onto her naturally vivacious features. She felt him falter at her side. Clearing his throat nervously, he spoke slowly.

"I am not quite sure which incident you can be referring to Miss Katherine, though I am truly sorry if any upset has befallen you whilst you were my guest."

"My lord, you cannot possibly be in any confusion as to the incident I am referring to..." she turned and glanced at him as she spoke, again hiding her smile at his pained look, and savouring every moment of it. She looked to Caroline, all innocence, walking with Joshua, and wondered in a quick moment of anger if she might give her a similar fear of discovery. But no, she would have a quiet word with her as soon as she could, and see what she might say for herself. She wasn't sure yet what she wanted to do with the information, and she tried to remember not to act rashly.

"The one at the river of course!" Katherine said. She turned back around and continued walking.

"Well, do not keep us in suspense. What happened at the river?" Caroline asked with a laugh, pulling her arm out of Joshua's to turn and look at those behind her. Coming to a stop, they all looked to Katherine and Charles, whose face had actually turned a little pink.

"I insist that Lord Charles tell the story, for I do not think I can bring myself to say it," Katherine said, her face the picture of innocence. She looked to him then, as did the rest of them.

"Well, Lord Charles, put the ladies out of their misery, I implore you!" Joshua said, with a smile. Charles turned his tortured gaze to Katherine, pleading with her wordlessly before his face stilled with resolve. Clearing his throat, he regarded his hands as he started to speak.

"One morning I was returning from a meeting with the estate manager when I saw one of our horses tied up at the river bank. I naturally went over to investigate. I found it was Miss Katherine who had ridden it there..." he stopped, glancing up at Katherine again, who was now regarding him with amusement, her head to the side, enjoying his discomfort.

"And?" Eva prompted, eager to hear the rest.

"And she-" he started, and was suddenly interrupted by Katherine.

"Had fallen face-first into the river, and swallowed half of it! I thought I might have drowned if Lord Charles had not happened by at that very moment. It gave me quite the scare!" she said.

"Katherine! I told you that it was dangerous to go off alone every day!" Eva gasped.

"I am quite well sister, do not worry, though you may thank Lord Charles for my well-being if you have a mind to. I was very scared and shocked, and he behaved like a complete gentleman, put me at ease, and made me feel quite safe," she finished, flashing Charles a sarcastic look as she did.

"Well thank goodness for that. It seems you are quite the hero, Lord Charles." Caroline teased, "we should hold a parade for your gallantry," she smiled warmly at Charles. Turning she once again took Joshua's arm and started back toward the lake. Eva followed on and Katherine turned to go after them, jumping as Charles's hand suddenly clamped down on her arm.

"Are you quite finished toying with me, Miss Katherine? I shall not have the exposure of my bad behaviour dangled in front of me at every turn. I apologise for it, it was unforgivable. However, given your games, I have a hard time believing you to be upset by it."

"Is that so? You think I wouldn't be upset by almost drowning, only to be saved by a man who kisses me then leaves me by the shore, shaken and wet?" she said, raising an eyebrow and slipping her arm through his as she turned him toward the others.

"I apologised, and I shall do so again. I do not know what came over me. I have never acted so impulsively before, and I regret it deeply."

"Well, in that case, you really do have something to apologise for," Katherine bit out, glancing at the hard expression on his handsome face.

"May I ask what you mean?"

"You may, but I will not elaborate. Do you ever let someone in, Lord Charles? Or have you determined to live above everyone, looking down on them from your tower forever?" she asked, a little angrily.

"I do not think myself above you, Miss Katherine, in fact, I try very hard not to think of you at all."

"May I ask what you mean?" she echoed his words.

"No, you may not," he said, glancing down at her with the slightest smile, yet it sent heat flooding through her. Tucking his hand around hers, they continued after the others.

⚘

"May I ask when I shall have the pleasure of escorting you out in London again, Miss Lesage?" Joshua asked as Eva and Caroline finished filling him in on the wedding plans.

"I believe I shall return with Katherine directly after the wedding," Caroline said, not missing the red stain that appeared on Eva's cheeks.

"I shall look forward to it. In fact, I was hoping that we might spend a great deal more time together," he said, stopping and picking up her other hand, Caroline realised Eva had disappeared back to Katherine's side, and was some distance off.

"I would like that too."

"Would you? That means a lot to me, Miss Lesage. As I am sure you have noticed, I find myself quite taken with you." Caroline felt a warm, squirmy feeling in her stomach. It must be excitement, she surmised, though it did not feel like it usually did.

"I confess, I had not considered finding a suitable wife in London when I came to the Season," he said candidly, and though Caroline felt taken aback, she decided that she liked his candor. "I have specific requirements, and unfortunately English girls do not quite meet them."

"That sounds quite alarming, may I ask what they are?" she laughed, trying to keep her tone light.

"Well, I travel frequently for my family business, in fact, about nine months of the year, I am abroad. I want a wife who will happily stay with the children, run my estate at home in Virginia in my absence. Someone capable and strong, someone I will dream of every night while I am gone," he finished, looking closely at Caroline for her reaction. She tried to organise her thoughts, and process the information he had given her.

"I see, nine months is a very long time. Is it not?"

"I agree that it is, however, I see marriage as a partnership, a sharing of two lives, my wife will have her own duties and responsibilities, and I shall have mine. We may not spend as much time as I would wish for together, however, the time we do share shall be all the more special," he said confidently, and Caroline realised how much thought he had put into it. "Have I shocked you?" he asked, as the silence grew.

"No, not at all, I just wonder why you are telling it to me," she said, buying time, her thoughts still a blur. Joshua was offering her the life she had imagined. Getting to go home, running her own house, her independence, with a partner that she was completely at ease with.

"I should think that obvious, my dear Caroline," he said gently, his voice like honey.

❀

*C*aroline dressed for dinner, choosing the dress Joshua had given her. She felt nervous, though she was not sure why. Lord Silus had already left, though they would have only a brief respite, as the Fairfax's were to arrive in the morning with other guests for the wedding.

She pulled on long gloves, and stroked the dress softly, thinking of

Joshua buying it for her. She had been slightly taken aback by his reasonable and detailed layout of their future this afternoon, perhaps because she had no experience of that type of relationship, though she already knew it was what she needed. The reality would be more romantic than the proposition, she was sure, and what was romance anyway, other than the fine veil of deception people drew over themselves to hide the real state of affairs.

A soft rap came at the door, and she opened it to Katherine, looking beautiful in scarlet silk.

"Well, what a lovely surprise! Have you come to walk me down, Kitty?"

"Well, actually I was hoping for a private word," she said, and Caroline noticed a tightness in her mouth.

"What is the matter? Is everything alright? Is it Eva?"

The gong rang.

"Oh, I had better be quick. Well, no. I haven't seen her all day, actually. But no, for once it's not-"

"Look at you two lazy daisies whispering in the doorway," Wesley's voice came to them as he found them in the hall. "Mustn't keep the hungry lads waiting," he laughed and looped his arms through theirs before they shot a glance at each other and walked with him down to dinner.

When Caroline entered the drawing-room she was surprised to see that she was among the first to appear. Joshua was there, talking with Charles, and she saw Lucian's broad back stiffen in response to her arrival, from his position by the fire. Turning slowly, her eyes met his: his were cool, assessing as they swept her gown.

"Miss Lesage, you look stunning as always," Joshua said as he moved to her side, picking up her hand and kissing it. His eyes sparkled, and his smile glistened with the smug intimacy that she should wear the gown which he had selected for her. Caroline felt a blush sweep her cheeks, as she bobbed over the compliment, noticing out the corner of her eye Lucian turned back to the fire.

"Katherine, are you well?" Charles asked. "You seem..."

"I'm fine," she said with a brittle laugh, glancing around herself as she did. She watched Lucian, who had turned from the fire, and was now leaning against the mantle, inspecting them with a heavy stare.

"That man," she whispered. "How can someone send terror down your spine with just a look?" Katherine said quietly to Caroline.

"He is not as frightening as he would have you believe," Caroline said, wondering why Lucian seemed particularly churlish this evening.

"That, I shall never believe. You could be friendly with Lucifer himself, Caroline," Katherine said sharply in what sounded to Caroline's ears more criticism than compliment, and she assumed Katherine's sharp edges that evening must stem from her worry over Eva.

The dinner gong sounded again to draw them into the dining room, and Caroline looked around in surprise. Half the party had not yet appeared. Charles excused himself frowning, and Joshua and Caroline exchanged amused glances. Wesley returned to Katherine's side on the divan. Time played on, and the atmosphere in the room started to take on a strained air. Frequent glances were thrown to the door, and silences drew out. Lucian paced a little in front of the fire, before taking his leave and striding out the door. The remaining four looked between each other, in question.

"Perhaps they have taken ill?" Caroline suggested.

"I do hope not. My sister is the worst patient. She might yet make Lucian look like a saint," Wesley said with a small smile.

"I do believe that might be an impossible feat," Katherine said tightly.

*L*ucian strode down the hall, looking for his brother, or a sign of any of the missing guests. Reaching the study, he pushed open the door to find Charles sitting at his desk, a letter in front of him. His face was a white mask of shock. Feeling tension settle in his gut, Lucian advanced.

"Brother, what is it? What has happened?" he asked impatiently. "Where is our sister? Miss Fairfax? The Taylors?" Charles continued to stare at him, speechless, until Lucian slammed his hand on the table.

"Charles!" he roared.

"Gone. They are gone."

CHAPTER 10

*R*eaching Rebecca's room, Lucian wrenched open the door, a cursory look confirming that she was not there. Disbelief swallowed him, and his anger fought with worry and the need to do something, anything to fix it. What had she done? Glancing around, he saw a letter propped on the nightstand, in his sister's delicate hand.

*L*uke,
As you are reading these words, I must assume that I have now departed successfully, with Miss Fairfax and Eli and Isaac Taylor.

I do not know how you shall react at this news, though I can surely guess. You hate to feel betrayed, but know this dear brother, everything I have done tonight has been for you- for my love for you.

You cannot marry Miss Fairfax, and I can no longer stand idly by as the day approaches when our father will force you to do so. You have suffered enough, dear one.

Do not come after us, we will not stop until we reach our goal. I shall not write it here, though I am sure you can guess it.

I am setting you free. Free to follow your heart, wherever it takes you, but do not dally, as father's wrath is sure to burn.

Follow your heart Lucian, as I follow mine.

Your most devoted sister,

R

*H*e could barely comprehend the letter, so overwhelming were its contents. His sister was helping Eva and Eli Taylor to elope. They must be headed for Gretna Green at this very moment. It was madness. Silus would surely punish her in the worst way he could imagine. These thoughts all collided into one, along with the delayed realisation– that he would not have to marry Eva Fairfax. His wedding was off. He was free once more. But at what cost, he thought bitterly, thinking of Rebecca. He was supposed to be the one who looked after her.

And once Silus found out, it may all be for nothing, he could force Lucian to challenge Eli Taylor. He would have no hesitation using any weapons available to get what he wanted. He might end up married to Eva anyway, with blood on his hands.

He had to think. There had to be a way out of this mess... he looked up as Wesley suddenly appeared at the door, a soft, pitying expression on his young face as he came into the room, shutting the door behind him.

"What was she thinking? How could she do this?" Lucian thundered.

"She did it for you brother, can you not see that?" Wesley said calmly.

"She will be trampled under this scandal- ruined! And whatever is left for her, father will use to torture her with. And for what?" he yelled. "Will the Fairfax's even accept the union?" Lucian asked, watching Wesley settle down at his sister's desk.

"I believe they will once the shock has passed. Mr Fairfax has a particular fondness for Miss Eva, and we believe that he wants to see her happy at all costs. Though, this may cost them a great deal indeed."

Lucian sat also, shaking his head, the feeling of shock finally wearing off. He began to think more strategically. "Father shall never accept it. He wants the Fairfaxes' money. He will not stop until he gets it, or they are destitute for crossing him." Lucian said, watching his brother nod in agreement.

"He will try to force you to challenge Eli for her honour, I am sure. It would be the quickest way to reverse this. You have been engaged for months, it would be acceptable. Or... " Wesley trailed off.

"Or-" Lucian prompted.

"Or– there is always Miss Katherine," he said, his words ricocheting through his brother. Lucian dropped his head into his hands and squeezed hard, as Wesley carried on "Mrs Fairfax is as eager for a title as ever. It matters not which daughter you marry, and society would accept it as a suitable arrangement, considering her sister's behaviour," Wesley said.

His face twisted, and he growled out an angry response. "Rebecca has just condemned herself on my behalf! Would you have me betray her so quickly? She did not do it," he ground each word slowly, "for me to shackle myself to another Fairfax." The only sound in the silence was his footsteps and the gently ticking of the clock on the mantle. Wesley thought for a moment, then, making a decision, spoke on quietly.

"There is something else. It's Charles. He would not say so himself, but it has not escaped my notice that he is quite hopelessly in love with Katherine." Lucian looked at him in surprise.

"So our dear sister would sacrifice herself only to bring about the misery of *two* brothers instead of one," he said, turning again to the night, his mind racing. "Could he not admit to it, and marry her for himself?" Lucian asked, frustrated. Wesley blanched, as the silence stretched out.

"Father... he would not accept it." At the look on Lucian's face, he carried on. "I have heard him say that he would never waste his own sons on such a low-born match."

Lucian, his head in his hands, spoke quietly, "Then the noose tightens on all our necks." He braced both hands on the table next to him and stared out, lost, before bellowing a low, brutal moan- the sound of a beast with an arrow in its chest, and with a movement quick and destructive, he threw the table at the wall across the room, smashing everything in its path.

*C*harles pulled Caroline and Katherine aside and told them that their sister had run away with Eli Taylor.

Caroline had felt light-headed with shock, and sat herself down abruptly, quiet and contemplative, while Katherine had cried, the flood-gates finally having broken after months of worry clashed with relief and fear, and racked her slight frame with the force of it. Charles had knelt by her chair, her hand in his, and soothed her as much as he felt he could.

Up in her own room afterward, Katherine paced, her sobs having abated, the tears slipped silently and unnoticed now while she spoke to Caroline, trying desperately to find a way out of the reckoning that was headed their way.

Eva had left a note for both of them on Katherine's bedside, and Katherine handed it unopened to Caroline with a shaky hand, for her to read aloud.

My beloved sisters,

Oh, will you ever forgive me this betrayal? I am so heartsore with the thought that my actions may hurt you, or leave you feeling deceived and forsaken. You two are my own heart, and had I but known of the plans sooner, I would certainly have trusted you both with them. I was swept up by the determination of Lady Rebecca and Isaac at the last moment, and sworn to secrecy. Eli spoke to me of marriage weeks ago, but I could never have dreamt that it might be true. It pained me every day to think of his affection for me when we neither of us could ever have our heart's desire, so I spoke of it to no one, and nursed my broken heart in secret.

Unbeknownst to me, Eli had sent word across England to try to find Mother and Father to plead with them to break the engagement, but they must have been on the move, and no response ever returned.

Last night, Eli came to me and professed an undying love that burned so fiercely, that it had us both in tears. Then he got on his knee and proposed, and I confess that I was so overcome that when he offered me an option to elope, I took it without thinking.

With the wedding date moved forward, and Silus Ashford growing impatient, this was the only option left between us and a life of misery.

I am so very sorry. I know that Mother wanted this wedding very badly, and I know that she and father both will be upset and that I am leaving you both to deal with them. I hope more than I can say that my poor behaviour will not compromise your prospects, but Lady Rebecca has promised that she will

personally undertake any assistance in making introductions, and has quite
reassured me. I hope that I have not done the wrong thing, in my selfishness,
but I felt like my very life was being saved, and I could not look in Eli's eyes
again and deny him.
I will return as soon as it is done and safe from undoing, to face whatever
punishment that I must. Sisters, I believe I could face anything with Eli at my
side.
I love you with all of my heart.
Forever yours,
Eva

aroline sighed.

"Well, I must confess that I am somewhat relieved. I certainly would not be quick to condemn her to the life which she was headed toward- not when she might have a real chance at happiness," Caroline said. To this, Katherine's tears began again, and Caroline moved in to hold her, stroking her blond curls.

After a time, when they both had composed themselves, they sat on the bed and spoke of what would happen next.

"What is to become of us, Caroline?" Katherine asked after they had exhausted talk of Eva and Eli.

"I do not know. Perhaps everything will be fine. Perhaps your parents will adjust quickly, perhaps Lord Lucian's relief will smooth the other complications," Caroline said, and carried on after a pause, with a less optimistic worry. "I am afraid to admit that I do find it a bit naive for Eva to think that it might be *she* who would be punished for this slight on the Ashfords." Katherine's brow drew together.

"Yes. Silus Ashford is a beast, from the things that I have heard. Father has everything but our dowries tied up in this business venture. Do you think Lord Ashford knows that?" Katherine asked.

"Oh yes, I think he does. It is probably why he is so eager to do business with your father. I suspect he likes to be in a situation where he might be the making of a person's fortune or the breaking of it."

"The breaking of it? Do you think it would be so bad?"

"Yes. I think it could be if Lord Ashford wished it. From what I have understood from Lord Lucian, his influence is widespread here, and he wields it mercilessly."

❀

*T*he crackle of the fire was the only accompaniment to Lucian's tortured thoughts as he sat in his study, the shadows shrouding the dark wooden panels of the walls, halfway through his decanter of whisky. He felt trapped. He was as dark as the stormy sky that night, and just as likely to strike.

He raised half-lidded eyes to the door, as Katherine Fairfax slipped in, and softly closed it behind her. He cocked an eyebrow, but she stood nervously in front of him and said nothing.

"Well, if it isn't the other Miss Fairfax. You appear to be in your nightclothes, Miss Fairfax."

She took a breath and lifted her chin. "I am."

"Well then," he said after another heavily-laden moment where he looked her over. He swirled the drink in his glass. "I suppose I should ask you if you'd care for a drink." She started to shake her head, and then stopped herself.

"Yes." she decided. "A large one."

"Ahh. I think I begin to know what you're about, Miss Fairfax," he toyed with her, as he poured, a mouse under his paw. "Though, I suppose it would have been difficult to miss the subtle seduction of your abrupt entrance into my study in your nightgown." She coloured, and reached out for the glass, but he held it back an inch. She snatched at it with a scowl and drank half its contents before she broke off coughing. Lucian refilled it with a dangerous grin stretched across his lips.

"Well?" She demanded when she had finished her brandy.

"Well what, Miss Fairfax?" Her face darkened with unsuppressed anger and humiliation.

"Do not make me say it," she snapped.

"Ahh... a temper," he appraised her in a way he knew made her uncomfortable. "So unlike your dear, meak sister, are you not? Though now that I think on it, perhaps it was all just an act to hide her duplicitous nature and disloyal heart. No, I think I would like rather to hear you say it. In fact, I think," he said each word slowly, watching his voice crawl over her chilled skin, "that I would like it very much."

Her eyes were like knives, and he enjoyed watching her struggle to restrain herself.

"Would you..." she ground the words like glass in her mouth, "have me instead?"

"Hmm," he sipped his drink and let the silence stretch. "And why would I do that?"

"Because. I come with the same dowry. We could keep the wedding date, and it could be yours as soon as it is done. Because you know as well as I do that it would save us from your father." He said nothing, and she went on. "Because maybe Caroline is right, and there is a soul in there somewhere, and you would not want to see us all drown for this." He had started at the sound of her name, and she had seen it. Had he not been so drunk, he would have been more careful. Negotiation was a delicate game, and one needed a steady hand.

"Is that the end of your overture, Miss Fairfax, or is there more?" He snarled in distaste and lit himself a cigar as if there was little else of any interest in the room. He heard the sound of a deep inhale; the exhale ragged and tight. When he looked up, she met his gaze, and pushed her thick shawl off, letting it fall to the ground. Her thick blond curls, hung over each arm nearly to her waist, she pushed them back, and then, she began to untie the laces at her neck, with shaking hands. He took a long drag of his cigar, and let it burn down his throat, as he leaned back against the leather, in deafening silence.

The laces loose, she pulled her shoulders free, and let the top of the gown fall to her waist. She stood back-straight in the firelight, bold eyes direct, mouth set firm. Her skin was smooth and white, and it shined in the glow of the fire. Her breasts were modest on her petite frame but no less perfect for their smallness. She waited for him, terrified, he was sure, but too angry, and far too proud to let it show.

Lucian drained the last from his cup, and he stood, the leather of the chair creaking underneath him. He prowled over to her, until within arm's length, and heard her breath hitch. Her eyes fluttered closed, resigned, it seemed, for whatever he would choose to do next.

He bent down, gathered her shawl from the floor, and tossed it at her. "Cover yourself, Miss Fairfax," he said, harsh and unkind. As she did so, he saw the tears glisten in her eyes, though she did not let them spill. He let the deep rumble of his laugh do its damage.

"So," she said, and his pulse quickened at the broken, helpless sound of it. "We are to drown then," she said, wrapping her shawl tight around her. He looked at her searchingly, trying to calculate his next step. Her desperation was exactly what he needed.

"Perhaps not, Miss Fairfax. You see. There is something that I want very badly, and I think that you may be in a position to help me get it."

❁

*W*hen the carriage rattled into Shrewsbury, Rebecca started to feel as though she had been born in the damn contraption, so dim was the memory of solid ground under her feet.

They had stopped only to change horses and the constant travel for nearly a full night and a full day without rest was wearing her to the bone. She guessed Eva must feel the same, but was so too saintly to complain. Rebecca, on the other hand, had no such qualms.

"Mr Taylor. I insist that we rest the night here. This is preposterous. My brother is not going to come after us," she said with a sigh, as she stepped to the door of the finally motionless carriage. As she made it to the first step, her underused legs suddenly buckled and she went flying forward, stopped short by a sudden impact with Isaac's chest as he caught her under the arms. Her breath flew out of her. Slowly lowered to the ground, she looked up and found him grinning.

"Do not suppose for one moment that saving me from falling flat on my face forgives you for forcing us to travel night and day in that horrible box," she said, flicking his hands off her disdainfully. Isaac bit back his smile and bowed in mock seriousness before her.

"Of course Lady Rebecca, rest assured that next time I shall not bother," he said and laughed as she smacked him hard on the chest. As Eli helped Eva down from the carriage, Rebecca turned purposefully toward the inn they were outside. It was small and quaint, with charming brickwork and painted wood. The courtyard was quite busy with other carriages rolling in for the night, stable hands caring for the horses and such. Rebecca strode across the slick cobbles. Isaac appeared at her side.

146

"Allow me to speak to the innkeeper," he said and received only a scornful glance as she strode on.

"Lady Rebecca, do you not think it wiser for me to make arrangements for us? It might look odd for a woman to be holding the purse strings in a party containing men," he said, barely able to keep the smile from his face in anticipation of Rebecca's reaction.

Stopping, she whirled to face him, about to tell him exactly what she thought of his suggestion when she saw several stable hands in the yard stop their work to look at them. It would not be helpful to draw too much attention to themselves. Forcing a smile, she turned her voice as sugary sweet as possible.

"Why yes, dearest *brother*, you always know best. Whatever would we helpless ladies do without you? Here you are, you forgot your favourite purse in the carriage. Wouldn't that be a shame? I do know how you love to swing it about and watch the beads glitter." She was pleased to see at least one patron turn to have a look at Isaac with an assessing glace as she stormed off and tried to hide her blush at his deep, rumbling chuckle.

"Lady Rebecca does punish Isaac something awful, doesn't she?" Eva said as she took Eli's arm over the slippery ground.

"Nothing more than he deserves, I am sure," Eli said happily, watching Eva carefully, ready to catch her if she fell. He had come this far, and defied this many people- her safety was in his hands. The enormity of what they had done, and where they were going was almost overwhelming, but as she looked up at him, when her foot slipped and his arm steadied her, he knew he would do it all again one hundred times over.

His only concern was the wreckage they had left at home.

🐚

*C*aroline heard a soft knock on the door. Shifting, she felt the book she had been reading when she had drifted, fall to the floor.

"Yes? Who is it?"

The door opened, and Katherine stood in her nightdress, with two steaming mugs in her hands, and heartbreak written all over her face.

"I cannot sleep. I thought... could I crawl into bed with you, my darling? I brought us some drinking chocolate." She held it up.

"Of course, Kitty. It would do my heart good."

Katherine slid onto the bed, with a kiss on Caroline's forehead, and curled her feet under her. Together they sipped and let the chocolate's creamy warmth soothe their shattered nerves.

"I love you, Caroline," Katherine said simply.

"I love you too, dearest."

"Please tell me that everything will be alright."

"Of course it will. Everything will be alright."

They curled into each other's arms under the covers, warming themselves through- the comfort sorely needed. Caroline felt her head swim, dizzy, and so very sleepy.

"Caroline?" Katherine's voice came to her from a long way off.

"Yes?" she was dimly surprised to hear that her voice too sounded a long way off.

"Caroline. Do you care for Lord Lucian?"

Caroline let out a soft mumble of a sound, and let the velvet black consume her. Katherine shook her by the shoulders, rousing her. "Caroline, please! Not yet, love. Do you care for Lord Lucian, Caroline? Tell me." she shook her again.

"Hmm? Please. I cannot," she answered. "I cannot."

"Do you care for him? Tell the truth to me now, if you have ever, Caroline. Please." She sounded so desperate that Caroline cracked her eyes- they were so very heavy- and she saw that Katherine was crying. She pressed a soft kiss upon her wet cheek.

"Yes. Yes. I do," she closed her eyes. "So much it frightens me."

*T*he sun filtered through the velvet drapes and cast the room in a green glow. It looked late in the morning. How could she have slept so late, Caroline chided herself, with so much going on, and no doubt much to do. Katherine still slept next to her, and Caroline stretched out and wrapped her arms around the soft, sleeping bundle of her.

Caroline gasped and tried to scramble from the bed, but a large hand grabbed hold of her wrist.

"Shhh, sweetheart. Calm yourself."

"Lucian! What are you doing?" she yelled before she brought her voice down, afraid they would be found. "Let go of me," she said as loudly as she dared, pulling at her wrist, but his grip was tight as a shackle, and it did not take much effort for him to hold her.

"I am not going to hurt you, Caroline. Be calm."

"How did you get in here? Why are you here?" She put her hand to her neck and found her nightclothes had not been tampered with. "What is this, Lucian? What in God's name are you doing?" she forced any sign of trembling from her voice, standing her ground. He smiled a little sadly at her.

"Surely you must know that already."

"Do you mean to ruin me!"

"I do, my love."

"What? What are you saying? Is this some sort of sick revenge for Eva?"

"Of course not, Caroline. How could you even think it? Eva's elopement will not be challenged if I am married myself, and of course, my father will be angry, but this will protect the Fairfaxes somewhat- he will find some way to punish them, no doubt, but he would not destroy them completely if they are tied to us through marriage, or he'd risk bringing us all down. It can work. We will have each other, Caroline. We can be together."

"Was this your plot all along? I would not have you, so you take my choice away?"

"No. Not all along," drawing the veil back over his face at her reluctance. "It was a streak of good luck. Though, I must admit that I had some help at the eleventh hour."

"Katherine," she whispered. "How could she?" She shook her head, and the room swelled, heavy and distorted. She reached her hand up to steady her head. "What is this? What has she done to me?"

"It is only a bit of laudanum that the doctor left me. Perfectly safe. It'll fade soon, I should think."

She could not bring herself to believe it. The searing pain of betrayal burned in her chest, unbearable, and tears sprang to her eyes. He reached out for her with his free hand.

"Don't you dare touch me," she spat and recoiled from his hand.

"I am sorry, Caroline. I have been rough with you," he said. Letting go of her wrist, and holding his hand up in supplication. "Please listen. I'm sorry that I asked you to be my mistress. How could I ever have even thought such a thing? I want you to be my wife, Caroline. Please. I cannot... I cannot live without you." Caroline stood and tried to move, but the room spun around her, and she nearly collapsed. He stood before her now, in her path to the door, and he caught her elbows to keep her upright, to keep her close. "Caroline. Say you will be my wife."

"And this is how you ask it? To a captured woman whom you had to drug to be near? Do you see? I could never be your wife! I *will* never."

"I know. Not of your own volition, at least," he murmured, and to her horror, he reached up to his neck and started to untie his cravat. Her eyes widened as it fell to the floor. Backing up, her eyes never leaving his, she held her hands out in front of her, trying to force a reasonable, light tone.

"Lucian, don't. What will become of me? Your father shall never accept me. I am an orphan, I am nothing," she said.

"You are everything," he breathed, still advancing toward her.

"Please do not do something we shall both regret."

"I shan't regret it," he said, his jacket joined his cravat on the floor, her eyes widened again.

A feeling of terror shot through her. She could not flee- she wasn't strong enough; she could not scream- that would only bring the scandal quicker to her door. What was he prepared to do? She looked frantically for an escape but found none. "What about me? What about what I want?" she cried.

"You want me, you are just afraid of it, you said so yourself. I will make you happy, and you will love me back, in time," he said as he unbuttoned his waistcoat.

"I cannot love you!" she cried, lunging to the right, hoping to get around him. She screamed as his arm shot out, pulling her roughly to him, her body pressed against his. Up close, holding her face near his, she saw his tormented eyes, bloodshot and pained. He smelled of whisky.

"You can. I have to believe that you can, my love. If you cannot... I am lost," he whispered and lowered his mouth to hers. Her protest was swallowed by a kiss, a kiss that sent stars spinning behind her eyes, her head swimming. Her knees gave way, and she found herself folding down like a puppet let off its strings. His strong arms were there to catch her, and she felt him lift her, and then the soft bed was under her back, but he did not break his kiss- hot, urgent, and desperate. His lips teased and pulled at hers, demanding acknowledgment.

"Caroline- you are meant to be mine, as I am meant to be yours," he whispered, his hands cupping her face, and his eyes intent on hers.

Coming back to her senses, she gathered her strength and slapped him as best she could. His head turned and she tried to roll off the bed. Someone would have heard the scream, she thought frantically. She had to get out. As her feet touched the floor, she made to flee, suddenly realising that Lucian had a tight fistful of the long fabric of her nightdress, and was holding her in place, effectively imprisoning her in the garment. He would always be stronger. Her arms dropped, her legs stilled, her breath came out in a shudder of surrender. She turned to face him, feeling tears threaten.

"How can you do this to me? Someone will find us. I was to have a choice... don't take it from me... it's all I have," she whispered.

"You will have so much more. I want to give you the world, family, love... everything you dream of."

"I do not dream of that kind of love. It is not what I want!"

"Why? Why does it scare you?"

"Why do you ask when you do not care?" she shouted back, frustrated.

"How can you say so?" his voice cracked. "I would do anything for you, Caroline. Even this. I will make myself a monster if it is the only way. My life has been long, and dark, and you have been the only light."

As much as she wanted to run from him now, she heard the sincerity and pain in his voice, but what she said was also true, she had to make him understand that. Perhaps no one would come to find them. No one had yet. Perhaps there was still time to reason with him. Never run from a wolf. His arms went around her, and she spoke softly.

"It is not so, Lucian. You will see. You are not so lost that you cannot be found," she said gently, feeling his arms go around her. "Lucian. I cannot deny that I feel for you. I am not a liar, and it's clear to both of us that there is something between us. Yet, we are not meant to be man and wife. We would destroy each other."

"You are wrong, man and wife is exactly what we are supposed to be. If only you'd stop denying it to yourself. I know it, Caroline, even if you do not. You will understand it in time, and by the time my father hears of all of this, it shall be too late. No, it must be now," he said, and she had barely a moment to look to his face before he drove her back to the bed once more.

She cried out as his strong hands came down on her shoulders, pinning her under him. All thoughts flew from her mind as she saw him kneeling over her, his face more set than she'd ever seen it.

"Lucian!" she pleaded.

"I'm not going to hurt you, I'm not even going to touch you. I just need to wait for them to find us," he murmured back and she saw the single-minded determination in his eyes and felt it in his hands.

This was the man who hurt women sexually, a man who bedded whomever he wished regardless of what marriage he would destroy, or what man he would have to kill afterward. This was the man she had first met, the selfish monster who took what he wanted, everyone else be damned. All trace of the man whom she had grown to care for was gone from him now, and she had been a fool to think he was different toward her, that he could be anything but a beast. Holding both her hands with one large hand, he ran his fingers down the side of her cheek, and her heartbeat shuddered in response.

She ignored the melting of her traitorous body and waited until his hand was level with her mouth, turning her face to his palm, surprising him with a gentle kiss pressed on to one of his fingers. He let out a soft sound of relief, of desire. Without warning, as his guard was dropped, she latched onto his finger with her teeth and bit down as hard as she could, tasting the metal of his blood. He let out an almighty roar, and let go of her hands.

Seizing her opportunity, she kicked at him with all her might, finally freeing her legs. She stood and whirled back just as he jumped off the bed, bringing her knee up as hard as she could, she connected with his groin. His hand clutched her gown as he sank to his knees, his eyes pleading with her. But his hand held fast and shackled her tightly in place. She swayed, her vision blurring. She was trapped. She looked into his eyes, so blue, and could not tell if the sight made her want to scratch them out or to weep for him.

"Caroline– do not do this. We have a chance. It is now. Do not throw it away."

CHAPTER 11

The common room was loud and crowded, and Rebecca pressed herself against a rough wooden beam to avoid a couple kissing on a bench. Inching around them, she found a table that looked relatively clean, and was thankfully empty, and sat at it, looking around her for a server of some sort.

"I thought I asked you to wait for me to escort you," Isaac's voice veiled his anger at her venturing into a public common room alone, as he slipped into the chair opposite her.

"Well, I was hungry, and I grew tired of waiting for you. It really is shameful when a man's toilette takes longer than a lady's," she said sweetly. "Was it worth it, do you think?" she asked, nodding at his artfully coiffed hair, and noticing, with a fluttering flush of satisfaction, a telltale tightening of his lips. A serving girl rushed over and plonked two overspilling plates in front of them. Her smile soon vanished as she inspected the food.

"What is this?" she asked, wrinkling her nose. "Slops?"

"That is what the majority of your countrymen eat every day, better, in fact, this actually has some meat in it. Now, be a lady, and don't embarrass the hostess," Isaac said, tearing a thick chunk of roughly hewn bread and dipping it into the stew. Rebecca watched as his eyes closed in bliss as he put the steaming hot morsel in his mouth. Copying his actions, she pulled a piece of bread off, and soaked it in the hot, oily stew, before putting it in her mouth.

She chewed slowly, swallowing to find Isaac's eyes watching her speculatively.

"Well?"

"It is not too awful," she said, reaching out for a larger piece of bread. "Eli and Eva seem to be unable to eat at all, so full of love, they are. Those two are truly a perfect match," she said sometime later as she wiped the last of the stew from the bowl, a little disappointed that it was finished so soon. "While other people are just *impossible* to get along with," she smirked at him.

"Don't I know it!" he laughed. "Here, this should make me easier to bear," Isaac said as he grabbed a couple of glasses of ale from a passing girl. "Try it."

"What is it?"

"It is certainly not champagne, but it shall help you relax and sleep well tonight."

"I should think just being allowed to lie in an actual bed might have the same effect," she said, raising the glass to her lips. As she sipped at the drink, she tilted her head back and looked at him searchingly. It had been a long road since they left Blackhill, and she felt like everything had changed because of it. A bit of ale would do her some good, she decided. "Well, any regrets?" she asked. Isaac shifted down in his seat becoming more comfortable.

"None. Though I cannot help but be apprehensive of your brother's reaction."

"Naa. We shall be fine. You'll see," she pushed down her own worries.

"What will Lord Lucian do? How can you be sure that he will not challenge Eli?" Isaac said, gripping his glass. "Eli would have no chance against Lord Lucian, if it came to that."

"We've been through this many times. He shan't. He never wanted to marry Eva. He will be glad of the freedom. I believe he has other interests to protect."

"And your father? He is not a man to trifle with."

"He is not, it is true. But, if my brother and yours both refuse to fight, there is nothing he can do to them," she stated adamantly, with more confidence than she had. Isaac shook his head at her a little.

"You really do not understand men, do you, my lady?" Rebecca, whose own worries roiled under her skin, felt chided, and found her strength for optimism wearing thin.

"I understand my brother," she said shortly.

"You implied he has other interests?"

"Yes. Caroline Lesage," she said, unable to contain a smirk at his surprise. A secret shared was always twice as sweet. Perhaps, someday soon, her close friend would become her sister as well.

"Caroline? You know this for certain?" Isaac said, leaning back as Rebecca nodded. "And the lady? Are you sure she returns his affections?"

"How could she not?" she said, as much to convince herself as him. "Given time, she will love him, Lucian has a way with women- I have witnessed it often enough. She already feels for him and once he wins her over... they are sure to be a happy match."

"What of Joshua Lee? Or have you forgotten about him?"

"I have not. I confess, his arrival Blackhill was disappointing, but he has met Caroline so few times, there is no chance of a proposal before my brother has time to woo her, her heart is already open to him. I have seen it myself."

They had been over it several times before, but she could not blame him for the need to repeat it again. She admitted to herself that she did not know if anyone would come to stop them. If they would have time. A single brother on horseback could travel faster than a carriage of four, but they had had a head start of nearly fifteen hours, she hoped, and that time would be difficult to make up, especially when they could not ride through the night without rest as the carriage had, swapping drivers.

What would happen if Charles arrived, or Wesley, or worse, Lucian... she didn't like to think about it. Worse still, the thought of her father brought ice to her blood. She wasn't quite sure about his where-abouts. Had he been north when word reached him, he could surely cover the distance in time. But what would he do to them? She dreaded to think.

"I hope, for all our sakes, you are right," Isaac said, sipping from his mug. "I, for one, should not like to have an angry Lord Lucian Ashford hot on our heels."

❀

*C*aroline tried to blink away the tide of the laudanum as it attempted to pull her down, along with Lucian's grip on her nightdress. Clothes were strewn all over the room, and her dressing gown was torn along the side, the laces coming undone. She knew how it would look- the tableau of the two of them, Lucian at her feet holding on to her ripped gown- garments ripped off in passion.

"I don't understand where my daughter is! I demand that someone tell me!" an angry voice rang out outside her door, getting closer.

"Please, Mrs Fairfax, if you would just allow me to show you to your rooms..." Caroline heard Charles's voice as it came to her door.

Fear shot through her, she tried again to escape, to run, and he shot up, and locked his arms about her waist, pulling her down on the floor with him. He pinned her body down under his, large hands clamping her arms to her side, legs stilling her, hips pressing hers into the Persian run beneath her. His breath came hot and fast as he stared down at her, unmoving, eyes pleading.

"What have you done?" she cried, struggling underneath him.

"What I had to," he whispered back, his face pained.

"I shall never forgive you for this," she promised as she raised her eyes to the door. With a click, it opened.

It seemed to her as though the next few minutes unfolded as though she was watching a play. All the characters said their lines, performed their actions... but none of it was real, and she was merely a spectator.

Margaret Fairfax pushed past Charles into the room and screamed so loudly that the windows should have broken. It was deafening, and John followed right behind her, his angry voice cutting through the scream.

"Katherine, go to your room. You shouldn't see this!" he roared, his eyes fixing on Katherine as she watched open-mouthed while Caroline lay writhing on the floor underneath their daughter's betrothed.

"Where is your sister?" he shouted again, to Katherine who had made no move to leave, wrapping his arms around his wife, who was moaning loudly, as if wounded.

"She is gone," Katherine whispered, very quietly, however it was enough to still Margaret's sobs as she lifted her head and pinned her daughter with a furious look.

"Gone where?" she barked.

"To Gretna Green... with Eli Taylor." Katherine dropped their eyes, her cheeks glowing bright red, her hands twisting. Margaret's eyes bulged for a moment, and without another sound, she fainted dead away into her husband's arms.

Cursing, Charles rushed to help John hold her up, turning to call to Wesley who was now standing in the door next to Katherine.

"Fetch cold water and smelling salts. We shall take her to her rooms, where it is quiet," Charles said as he cast his eyes in the direction of the rug and the scene that had just exploded all of their lives. Wesley left quickly, and Charles and John picked up Margaret, as footmen came in to help.

Try though she might, Caroline could not free herself, and Lucian had stayed firmly in place while the others collided, making sure that the staff saw, staking his claim. Making toward the door, John turned on the threshold, his eyes raking over Lucian and Caroline's tear-stained face.

"You are the devil made flesh," he said, encountering a closed and aggressive look from Lucian, as he sat up slowly. John turned and left with his wife and Charles. Silence surged back in, though Caroline was sure that the horrific scene would stay with her always.

A strangled sob erupted from her shuddering chest as she ripped herself from under Lucian's broad form, now that the fight had gone from it, and he no longer held her down. Katherine rushed forward, picking Caroline's dressing gown off the floor and put it around her shoulders.

"Caroline. I am so sorry. Please-"

Caroline took a moment to breathe, pushing her tears aside, whirled around to face Katherine, her face carefully blank of emotion.

"Please what?"

"Please forgive me," Katherine said pitifully through her tears.

Caroline looked at the girl who had been a sister to her. The girl who had always been a little too impulsive, a little too reckless, and whom they had all allowed to believe that her actions had no consequences. The girl that Caroline had loved with all of her soul. Katherine's hands were still on her shoulders, and Caroline picked them off.

"Do not touch me. We are not friends. Not sisters... not anymore," Caroline said, watching the moment that her words broke Katherine's heart.

"But I did it for you, for Eva... I love you both. You said you loved him! What good would it do anyone with Eli dead, and Lucian forced to marry Eva anyway? What of Eva's heart? And what would his father have done to daddy?"

Caroline turned away from her and went to the window, looking for the comfort she usually found in the cacophony of green that always greeted her there. But nothing greeted her that morning but rain. The clouds were grey and the wind lashed the rain against the glass. The lake was a murky, dull colour that reflected the state of her soul.

"Leave," she said shortly, ignoring Katherine's sobs. Turning her head slightly, she caught Lucian's eye as he leaned back against the bedpost, naked to the waist, silently observing the exchange between the girls.

"You can leave too, now that the two of you have done your worst," she said coldly. Before he could respond, a knock at the door sounded, and Charles stepped back into the room. Quickly surveying the mess and Caroline's tears, bruised skin, and ripped gown, an expression of compassion came over his features, his face crumpled under the pain and pity.

Crossing the room, Charles poured a glass of water for her, and set it in her hand, then urged her to sit, draping a blanket over her lap.

Turning he strode to the bed in a couple of steps, and grabbed his brother, hauling him up, he growled, "What have you done, Lucian!" he held him at arm's length shaking him, and his brother, surprisingly, did not try to escape.

"It is none of your concern, brother," he said, with almost a smirk, and that small expression was too much. Charles raised his fist and connected it with Lucian's face in a flash without mercy. Lucian stumbled back, steadying himself before he stood again and smiled.

"Is that it, brother?" Lucian jeered.

Charles hit him again, his anger greater than Caroline could have imagined. He paused as Lucian went down on one knee. Katherine, who had pressed herself into a corner, with her hands covering her mouth, tears still running down her face, screamed as Charles landed a final punch, which connected with Lucian's nose with a solid crunch.

Fighting for composure, Charles stepped back, holding his knuckles, and watched his brother struggle to raise his head. Blood flowed freely from his nose. He stood slowly, swaying, his hands and face covered in blood, it dripped down his bare chest.

"Well, well. Where is my ever-appropriate and restrained brother today? Perhaps we are not so different after all, you and I."

"Do not insult me. I already long to finish this."

"So finish it," Lucian said, his voice thick with blood. Charles saw Caroline still sitting in the window, her eyes were glazed, as she looked over the scene completely without interest, reaction, or emotion. Charles swallowed his anger and went to Caroline, replacing the blanket that had slid to the floor.

"You are not worth the trouble, Lucian," he said calmly and then walked to Katherine's side who was shaking, crying almost uncontrollably.

"And she is? Why don't you ask little Miss Katherine Fairfax about her part in this?" Lucian taunted, watching as his moral brother stiffened with surprise and turned to Katherine.

"What does he speak of?" he asked, his tone insistent.

"I..." Katherine trailed off shaking her head, tears rolling down her cheeks, caught in Charles's gaze.

"Did you have something to do with this?" Charles said slowly, looking between Lucian's gloating look and Katherine's incredibly guilty one.

"I- I had to do what was best," Katherine whispered. Charles smashed his fist into the wall beside her, and Katherine jumped, her eyes flung wide in terror, but did not scream.

"You think this is what was best for her? She is your friend... your sister, God damn you!" he roared as he turned away from her, disgust pulling his face into a snarl. "I have misjudged you, clearly. You are nothing that I thought you were." Clearing his throat, he went back to Caroline's side, putting a comforting hand on her shoulder.

"Miss Lesage. Is there anything I can do? Anything at all?"

"Just, take her away, I cannot look at her," she said quietly, and Charles nodded. Moving to the door, he grabbed Katherine by the elbow and jerked her with him.

"And him? Shall I throw him away with the refuse where he belongs?"

"Miss Lesage is my concern now, so just leave us, unless you'd like to finish beating me bloody," Lucian said menacingly.

"Prepare yourself, brother," Charle's voice was still and dangerous. "I do not know exactly what has happened here, but if it is as I fear, then you had better run because I will kill you myself."

Caroline stared out of the window and ignored everything but the rain. She wished herself away from there so fervently that the voices behind her seemed as if they called to her from far away. She did not turn around when Charles addressed her directly again. She did not care.

"Miss Lesage, I will remove Katherine from your sight, as promised. I will return shortly to check on you myself. Should you need any assistance in the interim, call for me," he said gravely.

Caroline was aware of Lucian's voice as he grew nearer to her, but not close enough to make her worry that he might touch her. She continued to stare out of the window at the rain, and thought of the mid-summer thunderstorms of Virginia, with their dark skies and crackling lightning, and the booming of thunder, like a battle raging overhead. She thought of the way the rain had pelted the slates of the roof of her childhood home, not unlike the sound that the rain made now against the window panes, but back then she had never been afraid- her parents had always been home to keep her safe. She dimly made out words from Lucian who pleaded with her desperately. Forgiveness. Love. Marriage. Salvation. Atonement. They washed over her like the waves above a sinking ship, as it floated to the sand below.

Lucian had stayed for some time. He had begged, and shouted, and beseeched her, but she did not listen and was barely aware of the lack of him after Charles had returned and dragged Lucian from the room.

As the sick feeling started to pass and she slowly came back to herself, an anger unlike any she'd ever known welled up with threatening swell. She had never felt so betrayed, nor so lost in all her life. She was terrified of John and Margaret's reaction. What if they thought she had wanted him? If they thought she had betrayed Eva? She couldn't stand the thought of them all here, those she had hurt, and those who had hurt her.

But Lucian– there was no mere hurt in relation to him, there was anger, so pure and hot, the warmth of it fuelled her as she dressed, severely, in the darkest outfit she owned. She pulled her hair back sharply and sat and looked at herself in the mirror.

He thought he had bested her, that she would meekly agree to be his wife now that he had ruined her. Her hands clenched in her lap at the thought of his face that morning- so sure that his repugnant plan had worked. He would soon find that she was not so meek as he expected.

❀

Katherine sat by the fire, sniffling into a handkerchief as her mother's eyes finally opened and she looked around the room. Her father stood before her mother, his hands behind his back, his face stern.

"She's awake. Are you well, dear?"

"Well! I could only be well if you were to tell me this was all a cruel dream," she said, struggling to sit up, wiping her face with a hanky. "How could your sister run away with that Taylor boy? How could she? Everything was perfect..." she cried, blowing her nose.

"No it wasn't, mama. Eva was miserable and frightened... the marriage would surely have killed her."

"Nonsense," Margaret huffed. "No worse than me on my wedding night. She has been fine. She would have adjusted," she said stiffly.

"She would have diminished to a shadow of herself if her weak heart had not given out first!" Katherine insisted, quieting when John raised his hand, signaling silence.

"And what of that ungrateful slattern?" Margaret shrieked. "She has ruined more than she knows. Selfish little fool. To think we took care of her for all these years!"

"Enough! I will not listen to anymore," John warned his wife and then looked to his daughter, whose eyes had filled with tears again.

"Katherine, tell your mother what told me," he said sternly.

162

Margaret's brow creased with confusion as she listened to Katherine rush her story out through her tears, stumbling over her words.

"So, you are telling me that Lord Lucian is in love with Caroline, our Caroline. And he sought to ruin her, so she would have no choice but to marry him?"

"With my help..." Katherine looked down shamefully, her eyes spilling silent tears even after she thought herself beyond crying.

"Why would you do such a foolish thing!"

"What a mess, what a damn mess," her father cut in. "This is what comes of trying to force people's affections. We should have been gentler with Eva. Perhaps if we'd listened to your concerns sooner..." he looked at Katherine. "But, we cannot change what has happened. May God help us when that man discovers the insult and scandal we have caused his family. He will make it his mission to destroy us, and with our fortunes tied up as they are, it will not be hard." John sat in a chair, dropping his face into his hands. "And what of poor Caroline? Silus Ashford expects that dowry. He will never allow his son to marry a ward with no family, no title, and little to her name," he muttered, leaning back in the chair, "She is ruined. Truely. With the way that gossip spreads downstairs, servants from four households, I would not be surprised if word has reached London already," he said grimly, deep lines of worry crossing his face. "You have stolen her future from her, Katherine. You and that blaggard."

Margaret sniffled into her hanky, and tidied the curls around her cap, as Katherine's calm dissolved again into sobs.

"Well, she is not exactly penniless," Margaret's voice came softly.

"Of course, we can put up as much of a dowry as possible, but I fear it will not be enough to satisfy that man. I suppose we could get in touch with the executor of her parent's will, the one you spoke with, to see what, if anything, remains of her parents' estate. Perhaps the land might be sold, though I had wished to keep it for her if she should ever wish to return to it, and I am not sure what price it might fetch without the house. I am sure it cannot be a match for Eva's dowry," he said, shaking his head doubtfully. Margaret cleared her throat.

"As I said... she is not completely penniless..."

"*W*here is she, Charles? Do not toy with me today, I am in a black mood," Lucian snarled as he threw open the doors to Charles's study. Charles was sitting at his desk, writing, and looked up with a disdainful expression.

"I have no idea, if I may assume you mean Miss Lesage."

"I cannot find her in this house, and I have looked everywhere."

"Please explain to me, dear brother, how it is my responsibility to keep track of the women you destroy- there are so many, it would be a full-time pursuit."

"Do not push me, brother," Lucian growled. He had been looking for Caroline for over an hour. When he had cleaned himself up and returned to her rooms, hoping she had calmed down, or maybe that she would be willing to talk, he had found her rooms empty. Going to the Fairfaxes' rooms, he had been met with a slammed door by Margaret. He strode around, finally ending up at Charles's decanter. Pouring himself a glass, he resumed his pacing.

"If it would hasten your absence from my presence, I can tell you that a carriage departed for London, a few hours ago." Charles dipped his pen in ink and blew on the nib. Lucian stilled, gripping his glass tightly.

"Who was on it?"

"I cannot say for certain. But I do know whose carriage it was..." he said, raising an eyebrow at his irate brother.

"Tell me, Charles," Lucian warned.

"Joshua Lee's," Charles said, with a satisfied smile as he saw the information hit its mark.

"I will not push you. If you want to tell me what happened, that's fine, but otherwise, just rest." Joshua's voice was soft and she felt it warm through her weary bones, trying to smile at him in gratitude, but not succeeding. The carriage swayed a little, and Caroline felt the sick feeling, which she had been struggling to keep at bay, rise up.

"Can we?" she asked quietly, gesturing to the window. Joshua leaned forward and pushed the window up for her. A cool breeze filtered in and she sighed. It was such a relief.

She felt Joshua's eyes on her, and glanced up, touched by his smile. He had come to her that morning, he wanted to check on her, worried for her. He did not know everything that had happened, but he knew Eva was gone, and that the engagement was broken. Maybe he had picked up on the energy of the house or had heard of what happened from the servants, but he had offered Caroline a ride back to London, and she had accepted.

Settling her head back on the rest, she tried to force the painful memories from her mind. In the carriage with them was Joshua's valet who had joined as chaperone. Caroline was grateful that even when all was lost, Joshua still did not compromise her. He was an altogether different man than Lucian. She might have dreamed of a life with Lucian before, in her most private thoughts, but he had ruined that now. How could she ever accept a man whose love was so ruthless that he would betray her to keep her? It wasn't only what Lucian had done, or hadn't done- as may be the case; it was that he would manipulate her so terribly and brutally to get his way. It was calculating and selfish, and so fiercely possessive. That was what scared her the most. He wanted to consume her, to own her, to have her at all costs, and he was willing to go against his father, a man she knew he hated and feared in equal measure.

She worried over Eva and Rebecca. What would befall them after such recklessness? They would not go unpunished, either of them. The question was, would any of the Ashford men reach them in time to stop the wedding, or perhaps in time to challenge Eli afterward? If they did, someone would die. Probably the new groom. What would Lord Silus do to them all? What would he do to the Fairfaxes? It was enough to break her heart.

"Why don't you get some rest," Joshua suggested, his warm brown eyes making her feel safe. She nodded gratefully and felt a fresh onslaught of tears threaten at his kindness.

She would run from Lucian. She wished never to see him again. He was too dangerous to be near. Though, even if she could get out of marrying him, what respectable man in England would look her way now? There would be nothing for her in England after the scandal spread. Her chances for a happy life there with the Fairfaxes were gone. She had lost a family once, and now she was losing another. It had taken no more than an instant.

She would return to America alone and start over. What other choice did she have? The story would travel, no doubt, but it would take its time, and the tarnish of it would be nowhere near so dark by the time it found her. She was not a woman of means, but America was a wilder place, and she would be allowed to make her own way there or to try at least.

She knew of some distant cousins, sisters, who ran an inn further west, and she would go there first and ask if they might give her work for room and board. It would be a safe place to start if they would have her. Perhaps she might even find a man who would not care much about this scandalous episode in her life, distance and time would, if not wash her clean, at least help her to fade into anonymity again. She could be small there and live a quiet life, out from under the oppressive microscope of the London Ton. It would be a relief.

She closed her eyes and dreamt of a modest home, with children running in the fields, and chickens, and she might stand on her porch drying her hands in her apron after preparing a meal for her family. It was not the life her parents would have wanted for her, she thought with a new wave of pain, her chest curling in on itself- it would be quite a fall in her fortunes. But, somewhere deep down she knew that she could still build a happy life if she tried.

Caroline listened to the wheels over the road and thought of one path ending, and another beginning- the future she was racing towards, vast and unknowable, each revolution of the carriage wheel bringing her closer.

But, when she closed her eyes, all she saw was Lucian's blue eyes, pleading with her. With so much love. So much pain. Fighting in desperation like a cornered animal. It made her heart twist painfully in her chest. She knew what it would mean to him to lose her- the blackness that would consume him. She also knew that his father would attack him mercilessly for having lost Eva's dowry. More than that still, the feeling that she wished most to fiercely scour away was that Lucian had already begun to carve out a space in her heart, it seemed, and he would not easily be removed, even after the horrors of what he had done. She knew in some unforgivable part of her, that thinking back on what had happened made her cheeks burn, not only with hot anger but also with desire. Caroline scolded herself harshly for her stupidity and roughly forced the thoughts away once again.

She cracked her eyes open again, and they came to rest on Joshua, quietly reading his broadsheet in perfect serenity after all that had happened, while her heart was in a turmoil so violent that she might be torn in two. There he was: steadfast, turning the pages gingerly, so as not to disturb her. He was safety. He was security. He was already looking after her. She wondered if she might still dare to dream of him- by her side, building a beautiful life, with his hand in hers.

*L*ucian paced like a caged panther.

It would take a day, at least, to ride to London, if indeed that's where Caroline and the bastard Lee, were going. He wondered if the two of them would instead head straight for Gretna in a sweet, patched-together wedding, and the image of it, so clear in his mind, boiled bitter fury inside of him, thick, hot and poisonous. He grabbed the decanter and smashed it by the neck against the wall. The piercing sound of its destruction was satisfying, and shards flew to shower the stone floor, one of them slicing a cut on his forehead. He stood, with both hands braced against the wall, fumes of whisky hanging sharp and heavy in the air, and he breathed it in, trying to clear his mind, trying to think, while a small trickle of blood dripped through his lashes and into his eye.

Where would they go? Would they elope? Would Lee even have her now that she had been ruined? He wasn't sure. But even if he would, Lucian didn't think that Caroline would be in any fit state to want to marry after what she had been through, despite her reputation. He had seen the state of her. He had caused it.

Lee. Lee, Goddamnit! He wanted to beat him into bloody oblivion. And then he wanted to grab Caroline by the arm, and drag her to Gretna himself. Maybe he would.

He needed to calm his pulse enough to think. He needed to be smart, he needed to be fast. He couldn't lose her- a day or two and she might be halfway to the continent, for all he knew! Whatever he did, he would need to act fast before his father returned, before he knew anything about it.

Yes, he needed to think, but he couldn't allow himself to feel.

Emotion was swelling threateningly, a familiar beast waiting to consume him. Without Caroline, he felt like his lifeblood was oozing out of him, like without her he could never hope to be whole, to be human. He had had, in the dark misery of his life, some small moment, a life with her, however short, a flash of light, of safety, and he would cling to it like a man drowning. He would not, even for a moment, entertain the idea of a life without her. If he lost her, he would go to his grave torturing himself for what he had done. There was no life without her. She was his now. He had tried to make sure of it. Giving her space and time to recover had been the error of a soft-headed fool.

He breathed out slow and steady. He would take the gamble and go to London. She would want to be home, he thought, she would stay there and wait quietly for her fate, or if she was going to run, she would need to pack, to plan, to prepare. No one would be at the London townhouse, he realised. The Fairfaxes were at Blackhill.

He had better be right. If he was fast enough he could catch her there.

And when he did, she would not get away from him a second time.

End of Book 1

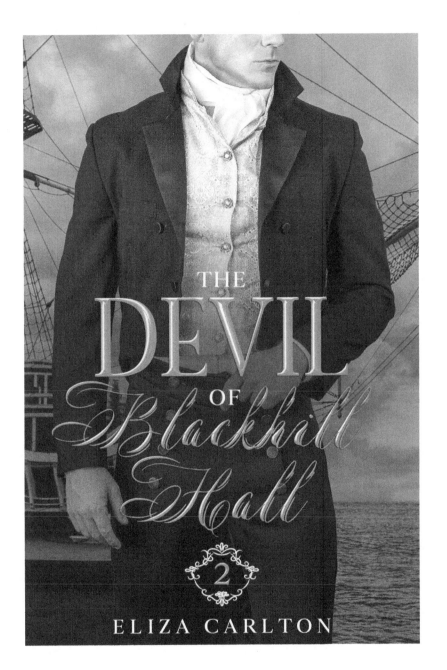

THE
DEVIL
OF
Blackhill Hall

2

ELIZA CARLTON

CHAPTER 1

~September, 1809~
Wiltshire

*I*n Lucian Ashford's life to date, there had been few things he'd known for certain. That he was a bastard in more ways than one, was a certainty. That he was destined to be hated, and resented was another, for who but family, would suffer him. Jaded, violent and broken, he wasn't a man who'd expected love, nor had any need of it. Or so he had thought. Until her.

The thought of Caroline, *his Caroline*, escaping him at this very moment, in the company of another man was enough to send bloodlust pounding through his body. After everything he had done to trap her, everything he had done to capture her, she thought he would just let her go? His sweet girl was still so naive and innocent. She still thought there was a way out that he would allow. She hadn't realised yet that the monster whose attention she'd attracted played by no rules. Yet, he would remind her as soon as he got his hands on her. She was destined to be his, and he would let no man stand in his way.

✿

"*M*r Lee, I cannot express to what extent you saved me today."

"Please, Miss Lesage, it was my pleasure, as it always is," he said smoothly, and she turned to leave. "Miss Lesage, wait, if I may have one more moment of your time," he asked suddenly, his brow crinkling. Startled by his tone, she turned back.

"Of course."

He stood, his large brown eyes studying her a little in the lamplight, and tilted his head. Joshua nodded, his face twisting a little, he seemed nervous. Suddenly collecting himself, he smiled and reached out for Caroline's hand.

"I do not fully know what happened last night, between you and Lord Lucian, between you and your family, but there is one thing I am sure of... I still feel the same. Nothing has changed for me." He swallowed, his large eyes dark and vulnerable. "And... I would still like you to consider the things we talked of by the lake."

Caroline felt her mouth fall open slightly and had to close it and take a moment to cover her bewilderment. He would still have her despite what it might do to his name? He did not care even to ask if she had been taken, had been forced, or even gone willingly to Lord Lucian's bed?

"But, Mr Lee-"

"Joshua."

Caroline blinked at the informality but carried on.

"Joshua... last night-" she started as he squeezed her hand and shook his head in a signal to stop.

"I do not need to know. I am not some stuffy English aristocrat, Caroline. If you want to tell me someday, that is fine, if not, I will never ask. I just want... you," he said, with a slow, warm smile. She felt overwhelmed, and so very confused. "I shall call on you tomorrow and you can tell me your decision, following that I shall speak to Mr Fairfax directly if I have need to... and I sincerely hope I will," he said, slowly raising her hand to his lips and pressing a kiss into the back. He descended the stairs in a couple of steps, and practically bounded back up into the carriage, turning to wave as he pulled the door shut.

Caroline stood a moment collecting herself, watching his carriage roll away into the night with a man she could hardly dare to believe existed. When she went inside the house, she gave Betsy strict instructions that no one except immediate family was to be admitted and went straight to her room. Pulling off her clothes, she thought about Joshua's stunning proposition. It was astounding. Completely unexpected. She had hoped, of course, with time, much time, when gossip eventually died down and they had returned to America, that he might come around; but, this immediate disregard of what was sure to be a scandal fit to cross the breadth of Britain within the month, was incomprehensible.

It was her way out, her chance at the life she dreamed of. As she slid into bed and blew out the candle, she stared up at the ceiling, trying to untangle the mess of her emotions. Joshua was offering her everything-why didn't she feel happier about it? Perhaps the events of the previous night had ruined everything, and now the hideous tinge of it had infected even the happiest news. Sleep pulled at her, and feeling finally safe, she abandoned herself to it.

※

*L*ucian had been on the verge of leaving, his horse saddled and ready, when a carriage pulled up. Cursing, he saw his father's crest on the door and realised he had missed his chance at leaving that night. He had to see her, and while he wanted to chase after her as soon as he had heard of her departure, he had decided that having her things packed, and bringing her trunks to London for her, might just open a door to him that would surely otherwise be slammed in his face. It had cost him too much time, he realized grimly.

The door banged open and Silus stormed out, and up the steps, a quiet rage suffusing his face. Stopping in front of his son, he curled his lip at him with such hatred that Lucian thought for a moment that he might attack him here in front of the staff, but instead, he turned on his heel, he strode toward his study.

"Bring me John Fairfax," he shouted over his shoulder, slamming the door.

*T*he clock ticked in the lounge as Lucian paced, counting the minutes of his agony. He was still wearing his riding clothes and planned to leave that night. He just had to wait for his father to see him first. If he inflamed his father's ire now, defied him openly, it would surely have severe consequences, for himself, but also potentially for Caroline who would, he was sure, attract his father's vengeful savagery just as surely as the Fairfaxes would. If Lucian survived the encounter, he would depart for London directly afterward.

Finally, the grandfather clock chimed eleven, the door to the study opened, and John Fairfax came out. Looking beaten, Lucian watched as Fairfax trod up the stairs, pausing occasionally to grip the barrier. Stealing himself, Lucian went to the study, knocked and waited to be admitted.

"Come," Silus's low voice called from within and Lucian opened the door, feeling as though he was going to the gallows.

Silus was standing at his brandy, pouring two glasses and he raised an eyebrow at his son and his clothes as Lucian moved closer.

"Going somewhere? At this late hour?" he said, chuckling joylessly, and then returned to his desk, placing one glass in front of Lucian. "Sit," he said, with a flick of his fingers. Lucian obliged, watching his father intently, looking for any sign of what might happen.

"Well, boy, I entrust you with one small task... and you cannot deliver even that."

"The rest of my life is hardly one small task, father," Lucian said, unable to stop himself. He scolded himself, picking up the glass and slowly taking a sip.

"Yes, it must matter to you, I suppose. Though, I confess that I did not much consider your feelings in the matter, as you have never been one to be affected by women. I truly thought it would not change you, or hinder you in any way. So I am quite surprised to hear what you have done, and to find you here, in all this state, desperate to run off after the object of your affection. It seems the *lady* is less inclined to the union. Perhaps last night was too much for her to stomach," Silus laughed and Lucian felt the brandy burning in his throat.

"You cannot expect much from them at the beginning, son.

Wives...they are not like pleasure women. You need to break them before you release yourself upon them- before you teach them how to please you. They will enjoy it, in the end, once they stop crying... your mother did. Oh, how she moaned and bucked like a tuppenny whore." Lucian felt his stomach roll and gripped the arm of the chair as Silus threw his head back and laughed. "Does it bother your delicate sensibilities when I speak of your mother that way? Come now boy, you will soon be a married man too," he said and Lucian tensed.

"Married to whom?" he asked, trying not to let any of his nervousness show. To this man, weakness was an intolerable fault, ripe for exploitation.

"To Miss Caroline Lesage, naturally."

Shock and relief took over Lucian's sense in waves, soon followed by the prickling of suspicion. Why would his father ever agree so easily to anything he desired?

"I have already come to an arrangement with John Fairfax. You see, it turns out that Fairfax really does think of Caroline as a daughter, so both our business interests are quite protected. And, also, most importantly..." Silus paused, swirling the brandy in his glass, "she is filthy rich," Silus finished with a flourish, raising his glass to his son's, sloshing a bit of Lucian's drink.

"Rich?"

"Why yes, it turns out that Miss Lesage's inheritance puts the little Fairfax girls' dowries to shame. Mrs Fairfax was hiding the fact, worried that it might affect her daughter's chances of landing a titled gentleman."

"Caroline... is rich," Lucian repeated to himself, trying to absorb the information.

"Rich indeed. Rich, and thanks to you, quite ruined," Silus said, settling back in his chair, a contented smirk coiling across his face. "Fairfax has given his consent, if not quite his blessing, and only has two conditions. Firstly, that the wedding should happen quickly, to minimise scandal, and his beloved daughter Eva is allowed to live with her *love*, unchallenged. Everybody wins really, except Margaret Fairfax, whose daughter will end up married to that American, and Miss Lesage of course, as she will be burdened with you till the end of her days."

"What is Mr Fairfax's other condition?"

"Caroline's consent... and he wants to hear it from her own mouth, boy, so you better hope that you didn't scare her too much last night."

"But... what choice has she? She will be ruined if I do not marry her," Lucian pointed out, fighting down a surge of anger as Silus looked at him condescendingly. Best not to mention Lee if his father did not already know.

"No woman with a fortune so immense has ever been ruined beyond repair. There will always be some poor, destitute sod who cares not whom she spreads her legs for." Lucian's hands clenched, and he stood.

"If I were you, I would get to London, and do what you must. And," Silus said, his face darkening, devoid of taunting or amusement for the first time. "I would warn against disappointing me again."

Lucian stood, bowing stiffly, picking up his leather riding gloves and hat, and went directly to his horse, still saddled and waiting, and set off into the night.

🍂

"*Y*ou have a caller, Miss Lesage- a Mr Lee."

"Thank you, Barnes. Can you please stay?"

"Of course, Miss," said the elderly butler smoothly, standing quietly in the background to chaperone. Caroline stood, smoothed her dress, and took deep, steadying breaths. Smiling somewhat nervously, she waited and then felt her smile become genuine as Joshua stepped into the room. She had almost doubted her memory this morning as she recalled their conversation.

"Miss Lesage, I am happy to see you rested and looking much more at ease."

"Thank you, Mr Lee. It is because of you that I do," Caroline answered politely, feeling her cheeks pinken.

"Well, I suppose it wasn't entirely selfless, spiriting you away from the Ashford's," he said with a smile, taking her hand and kissing it.

"Would you care for tea?"

"Certainly," he said as they sat. She rang the bell and then they fell into easy conversation while they waited for it to come. When the maid set down the tray, Caroline felt Joshua's eyes on her she carried out the small preparations that are a lady's duty in such social situations.

"You are very accomplished, Miss Lesage," he said admiringly.

"If you heard me play the piano, you would not be so quick to bestow that particular compliment, I assure you," she said with a smile.

"You have a grace of manner which only comes when natural elegance is paired with careful study," he maintained and she lowered her eyes modestly, deciding to accept the flattery rather than fight it.

"You are too kind, sir."

"It is the sort of elegance and manners I hope to bring to my home in Virginia... to teach to my children," he said softly, and Caroline stiffened with nerves. The moment had arrived it seemed. Setting her cup down she looked at him frankly.

"Mr Lee, we cannot ignore the unorthodox nature of this proposal. We are barely acquainted."

"When I feel strongly about something, I seldom wait-"

She held up a hand to stop him and continued, "There is also the matter of the incident at Blackhill. I could not be comfortable with any proposal if all the facts were not known," she said, holding his gaze unwaveringly. She saw him about to disagree before stopping himself.

"Dear Miss Lesage, if you think that it is necessary for me, you are mistaken. However, if it is something you require, I am ready to listen."

"Thank you. I know it is not something pleasant to talk of," and she proceeded to give him a very dry, factual version of events, from Katherine's part in the awful drama to waking up next to Lucian, making his intentions clear. Afterward, she was quiet as she waited, trying to read his face and imagine his thoughts.

"Miss Lesage, this changes nothing but my sympathy. As I have said, it makes no difference to me. I have not stopped thinking about you since first I met you. I cannot imagine returning home without you by my side."

Caroline fought back tears as she stared at him, his brown eyes earnest and soulful.

"So, tell me. Will you consider me? Will you do me the very great honour of being my wife?" he said, slipping onto one knee in front of her.

Caroline stared at him, speechless, unable to accept that this was truly happening. She waited for the feeling of elation she should feel at the prospect of marrying such a handsome and kind man, so generous that he would ignore even this. At evading Lucian. At going home. At running her own estate. A large and beautiful estate, if reports of Joshua's wealth were to be believed. It was more than an orphan dared to dream of.

"Miss Lesage?" Joshua prompted and she was drawn back to the present, to the man in front of her, offering to take away all her problems.

"Yes. Yes, I will," she whispered, her heart beginning to beat like a piston as Joshua broke into a wide smile, and leaned slowly forward, bringing his lips to hers.

The kiss was sweet and soft, and when he pulled away, her heart had resumed its normal rhythm.

"You have made me very happy, Caroline. May I call you Caroline, dear? Very happy indeed! I shall leave you now, and go to my father, he shall be overjoyed at our news!" Joshua stood with the energy of a boy, and Caroline stood with him.

"Of course," she murmured.

"I shall return when I may speak with Mr Fairfax," his smile was broad and Caroline followed him to the hall. Her emotions swelled but were no less confusing for their abundance. Turning on the doorstep he put his hand on her shoulder, squeezing it.

"You have made me the happiest man in London," he said and pressed a kiss to her cheek before turning and descending to stairs jauntily.

Caroline watched as the door slowly closed, and Barnes smiled at her.

"Congratulations are in order, Miss," he said happily. "Is anything the matter, Miss?" he asked then, catching her expression.

Taking a deep breath she pushed a smile to her face.

"Of course not. I'm terribly happy. It's an excellent match. Thank you very much, Barnes, for your congratulations," she said, and turned away, deciding that perhaps a lie down would help.

In her room, she let her hair down, as the tight pins seemed to be digging into her very skull. She loosened it around her shoulders, pulling her fingers through the heavy waves, massaging the back of her neck and temples. As she touched her skin, she felt a flash of memory surface:

Caroline – you are meant to be mine, as I am meant to be yours.

Catching her own eyes in the mirror, she stared at herself, unmoving, lost in her thoughts. Eventually, she brushed a hand over her hair and caught sight of a purplish mark on her wrist. Frowning, she looked at it, an ugly bruise beginning where he had caught her arm in the morning. It glowed darkly on her smooth skin. This was his legacy- his love made real. He couldn't love, he could only hurt. She thought of the wild and dark feelings that flowed through her when he kissed her- the desire, the urge to lose herself was so overwhelming. Joshua's kiss had taken nothing from her, it had not demanded anything... and it had been perfect. He kissed her and she remained herself, in control, intact. It was what she wanted.

She loosened her formal morning-gown and decided to slip it off. For the first time in months, there was a fresh breeze in London and a hint of the changing weather. The Season was almost over, soon the hunting season would begin in earnest and prominent families would depart for the country, to stay until the new year. She thought of Blackhill Hall, its beautiful land, welcoming library, and serene lakes. She felt a pang when she realised she would never go there again.

Marrying Joshua might keep her safe from the worst of the scandal, but it would not help to save the poor Fairfaxes from Lord Silus. She wondered if her duty was first to them, but she did not believe for a moment that a rushed marriage to a poor ward would stop a furious Lord Silus from taking his revenge on the Fairfaxes, or on her and Lucian if they were to marry. She feared for the Fairfaxes. Perhaps they too could return to America, and start over.

Sighing, she crossed to her bed and lay down, forcing her eyes shut, and took deep breaths to calm herself. She had a horrible sense of foreboding. She knew Lucian would not be happy about her marriage plans to Joshua, but surely he would see sense, once his passion had passed. Surely he would let her go to be happy elsewhere, especially once his father opposed the match. Would he feel betrayed by her? Would he hate her? Would he see it as proof that he was unlovable and should be alone forever?

She knew she should hate him, that she could never forgive him. But, at some point, he had gotten under her skin, and she could not fail to worry about the prospect of him being alone, hating himself, going from one heartless affair to another. But, she reminded herself firmly, a man must take responsibility for his actions. He might have been set on this path when he was young, but only he had chosen to walk it.

🦋

*A*nother night and another inn. Eva had lost count, but every step brought her closer to being Eli's wife and was therefore worth enduring. They had been staying as a family group, she and Rebecca sharing a room and Isaac and Eli lodging separately. She was still getting used to the shock and excitement of seeing Eli every day, and sitting in close proximity to him in the carriage was the sweetest torture.

She had been against his proposal, to begin with. There was no way she could betray her parents so. However, he had come to her at the last moment, having planned and plotted with Rebecca and Isaac, they had everything in order, ready and waiting for her only to say the word. And he had told her how much he loved her, and he had swept her off of her feet, and they had stood, clutched in each other's arms so that anything else but to accept him had seemed inconceivable to her.

Rebecca had told her that Lucian longed to be free of the engagement and assured her that her father would be reasoned with where her parents were concerned. She had promised to put it all to rights.

She thought of Caroline and Katherine at home with her parents. She dearly hoped that her mother would not make them suffer too much for her actions. She assumed they had returned to London once her absence had been discovered. It was a shame that Joshua Lee had only just arrived at Blackhill Haa, and Caroline and he had not had more time to secure a match. Would her outrageous actions affect her own sisters' chances of happy matches? Despite Rebecca's pacifications, she worried that she had brought shame to the entire family, and the burden of it weighed heavily.

In the carriage Eli was reading, his high brow furrowed in concentration. Rebecca had fallen asleep, and in the rocking of the carriage, had fallen a little sideways into Isaac. Eva watched as Isaac, clearly unaware of being watched, looked down upon her face, sweet in its quiet peace. He smiled softly to himself, and as heavy locks of chestnut hair fell free and slipped over her face, he gently reached up, catching each strand, and tucked them softly behind her ear.

✺

A knock at the door startled Caroline awake from her fire-filled dreams. Sitting up suddenly, she felt her heart in her throat and swallowed thickly before she could find her voice.

"Yes?" she called and heard Betsy's voice through the door.

"You have a caller, Miss," she said and Caroline frowned, swinging her feet over the side of the bed.

"What?" she said, still sleep dazed, passing her hands over her hair and casting about for her dress. "Who is it?"

"Umm... he brung your trunks, Miss."

"Betsy – who is it?" she called, shaking the fog from her head.

"Lord Lucian Ashford," Betsy said, her voice trembling a little. "I'm sorry, Miss. He told me not to tell you who it was. Only I could never do that to you, Miss Lesage, 'cause I like you ever so much, and there is something about that man downstairs that just ain't right."

Caroline felt her heart stop. He was here. Downstairs. Running to the door, she immediately turned the key, locking it. Panic blossomed in her chest. He couldn't be here, he couldn't, she thought, shaking her head. That bloody-minded man.

"Tell him I shall not receive him. He must leave," she said and heard the maid's hesitation through the door.

"You sure Miss? He seems awful determined like," Betsy said, her voice worried.

"I am certain."

She cursed herself for her carelessness. No one was meant to be at the London townhouse, and it was running on a skeleton crew, most of the staff having gone either to Blackhill Hall or with Mr and Mrs Fairfax on their trip. At this time of night, Barnes would have gone home to his wife hours ago, and Betsy was all that was left.

Running to the wardrobe she found her most somber gown, one she had had made for a funeral, and quickly stepped into it. At the mirror, she pulled her hair into a severe bun and steeled herself. If he managed to see her, she would not be at a disadvantage again. Spying her sewing scissors on the table she grabbed them up, opening them and holding them as one would a knife, she looked to the door and waited, her heart pounding.

What did he want with her? She had seen him when he was in a rage. It was a frightening prospect to imagine him heading toward her. Perhaps he intended to take her, to sling her over his shoulder like a caveman and drag her home. If so, she would not go without a fight.

"*P*lease Milord, Miss Lesage cannot receive you now. She is otherwise occupied."

"Otherwise occupied? What could keep a woman so occupied that she cannot receive her own fiance?" he asked irritably.

"She has taken ill," she said, her chin out, making the lie clearer to him than if she'd just told the truth.

"Has she indeed?" he said, his eyes narrowed at the cowering slip of a girl before him.

"Yes, my Lord. Real ill."

"I suppose, in that case, I should go up and check on her myself."

"Oh no! She wouldn't like that. It wouldn't be proper!" Betsy was aghast and Lucian hid a smile, thinking of how she would have handled finding them together the previous morning.

"Let me explain something to you. She is my fiance and I am not leaving until I see her. Therefore, in the interest of saving everyone's time, I am going to visit my beloved, right now, without delay, on her sickbed." His voice was dry as he spoke, stepping around the maid and starting up the stairs.

If Caroline thought she could hide behind servants, she was mistaken. They were a betrothed couple now. His rights had expanded exponentially. Of course, she did not yet know that he reminded himself and grimaced at the thought of her face when she found out.

----

*C*aroline stilled, the silence outside the door had not changed, it had simply become more charged. Looking down, she could see the shadow of someone standing just outside.

"Miss Lesage... sweetheart, please come down so that we may speak." His voice was calm, soft and she shivered at the tone. 'Miss Lesage', he called her - so he was being genteel now, was he? The man could go from gentle to madman in a second. She kept her mouth shut, and watched as the shadow moved, he seemed to be pacing back and forth in front of the door.

"Miss Lesage..." his voice purred her name. Her pulse raced and her palms felt clammy. "You will have to speak to me at some point, as I do not intend leaving until you hear what I have to say."

"I have no interest in anything you may have to say. None at all!" she shouted angrily, then cursed herself for breaking her silence. She could practically feel him grinning on the other side of the door.

"Come now. Let us put that nasty business behind us, and move on to more... pleasurable subjects. Such as the rest of our lives together."

"That prospect is certainly not pleasurable to me," she spat.

"I am sad to hear it, however, ever the optimist, I look forward to the day it is. I'm willing to wait for it... for you..." his voice dipped and trailed off in suggestion, and she looked away from the door, wondering how he could make her blush from another room.

"Well, you shall be waiting forever, Lord Lucian."

"Now now, did I not once warn you, about your sharp tongue, and the husband who would enjoy teaching you to curb it? I am delighted to be that lucky man," he said with a chuckle.

"Well, bridle your happiness, my Lord,– you shall not be that man. I have agreed to marry Mr Lee."

There was a tense silence, and Caroline could imagine the look on his face. She wondered if he would break the door down. His voice, when it came, was low and menacing.

"When was this? If I may ask."

"Mere hours ago, and before you mention it, he is fully aware of the compromising situation which you put me in. He does not care. He shall have me despite it," she said.

"Of course he will. Miss Lesage, you must come out to me, or allow

183

me entry. Come to the drawing-room. We should not talk about this through a door."

"It is the only way I feel safe," she answered, her voice a sneer that she hoped he could see.

"You will let me in. One way or another-"

"We shall see about that," she said. Inside the room she was tense, clasping her hands together, watching his shadow avidly.

"Do not push me, Caroline. You know what I am capable of," he whispered low, and she felt another wave of apprehension pass over her. Caroline didn't answer.

She kept listening, but a time went by where she heard nothing. He seemed to have left. Standing, she made her way over to the door and pressed her ear to it.

"Miss Lesage?" Betsy's timid voice came to her.

"Betsy? What is the matter? Where is Lord Lucian?"

"He... he left in a rage, Miss," Besty stammered, beginning to cry, and Caroline instantly felt guilty for exposing her to such a monster.

"Are you alright?" Turning the key, she opened the door, meaning to comfort the young girl. Betsy was standing, her eyes huge, round as saucers. As soon as she cracked the door open and saw her, Caroline realised her mistake. Betsy looked to the side, and quick as a whip, a strong arm flung the door open the rest of the way.

Lucian stood in the doorway. He looked furious: his eyes dark, his face lashed with mud, his breeches, riding boots and dark green tailcoat were also muddied and dishevelled. He held in his hand his riding crop, hat and gloves. He walked slowly into the room and Caroline backed away, her eyes never leaving his. Betsy whimpered in the doorway, indecision clouding her face, Lucian whirled on her, and she flinched.

"That will be all. Miss Lesage is not to be disturbed," he said tightly, and as she still hesitated, he put both hands on her shoulders and tightened, growling angrily, "Leave."

Berty cried out in fear, and at the sound, Caroline was shocked out of her paralysis and spurred into action. She rushed forward, and raising her hand, found the sewing scissors still there. She barely paused to consider what she was about to do, as she plunged them into the back of Lucian's large hand that held on to Betsy.

Betsy screamed bloody terror, and turned and ran away down the stairs. Slowly, very slowly, Lucian raised his hand to inspect it, blood dripped out of the wound, and Caroline saw she had nearly pushed the small blade halfway through. She felt fear course through her, as he calmly, without so much as a word, pulled the gold scissors from where they were sheathed in his hand.

Pulling her gaze away from the scene, Caroline started through the doorway but instantly felt his other hand on the back of her gown. He pulled her backward roughly, as he had done days ago, and she felt herself flying through the air for a moment before she landed on the bed. Sitting up, she watched as he closed the door, and locked it before removing the key, and placing it in his trouser pocket. Lucian moved toward her like a predator, suddenly grabbing one of her petticoats. She screamed, trying to propel herself backward, but he only sized the petticoat with both hands, before ripping a strip from the bottom. He held it out to her and pinned her with a stare.

"Bandage it," he commanded, his voice harsh. Blood ran down his wrist, dripping into his shirt cuffs and onto the bed underneath them. "Now," he growled, and she shuddered at the look in his eyes. Angry at his intimidation she pushed herself upright and grabbed the strip from him. She quickly wrapped it around the injured hand, and pulled it unnecessarily tight, though the only response was a slight narrowing of his eyes.

Throwing his hand away from her, she backed away from him on the bed, crossing her arms and raising her chin, determined not to show him any more fear.

He went to her dressing table, setting down his gloves and hat, his fingers lingering on the whip. Caroline flushed as she saw his eyes slowly travel down her body, his hand tightening on the crop.

"Go ahead, use it. What is stopping you? I couldn't hate you any more than I already do," she spat, forcing her eyes away from his dark gaze.

"Now, Miss Lesage, is that any way to address your fiance?" he said, softly tilting his head to the side.

"You are not my fiance. As I have already made clear to you, I have engaged myself to Mr Joshua Lee," she said, watching the flash of anger darken his features further.

"Do not speak his name to me," he warned, as he advanced on her.

She stood her ground, ignoring the writhing feeling in her stomach as he came closer.

"It is true. It is already agreed."

"Let me guess, he has not yet spoken to Mr Fairfax," he said.

"Not yet, but he shall as soon as the Fairfaxes return to London."

"Well, I see his enthusiasm has gotten the better of him. His time would have been better spent seeking out Mr Fairfax, than playing your knight in shining armor.

"What are you implying?" she demanded, suddenly frozen in place, as his eyes took on an amused glint.

"Only that, luckily for me, Mr Fairfax found time to meet with my father and-"

"Your father would never approve. You are lying," she said, backing away and shaking her head

"On the contrary, he cannot wait to welcome you to the family," Lucian said with a bitter laugh.

"You are lying!" she shouted and then bit her lip as he swooped forward and grabbed her by the upper arms.

"I wouldn't lie to you... Caroline, whether you believe me or not, I care about you a great deal."

"You don't know what it means to care about anyone," she said viciously, holding herself still, not wanting to give him the satisfaction of fruitless struggling.

"Perhaps – but, for the first time in my miserable life, I have found someone I want to learn for," he said, his tone starkly honest now.

Caroline's brow wrinkled in confusion. She looked up at him, possessive as he held her close. She felt the familiar pull she always seemed to feel near him. She tried to steady her pounding heart and became aware that his hands had softened their tight grip on her shoulders, that his whole body was no longer straining forward in anger. His breathing had deepened, and she felt as though she was being drawn minutely closer, with each passing heartbeat. Her breath was catching in her chest, and all she could feel was heat, trailing up her body.

She felt his finger under her chin, and with a gentle pressure her face was tilted up, so she had no choice but to meet his eyes. The look in them took her breath away. The need there, the desire... it was all-consuming and she felt dizzy with it, pulling her in every bit as much it urged her to run. He wanted inside of her, to absorb her, to be part of her. His face was lowering toward hers and she could feel his warm breath on her lips.

"Let me in, Caroline..." he whispered, and then his lips were on hers. The shock of the contact froze her for a moment. His mouth was hot and pressed against hers with urgent and needy. It caressed her lips, sucked them, teased them, lightly biting, until she opened her mouth in a gasp. Immediately, his tongue met hers, slow and sensuously, sliding against hers and causing the sensation to melt through her whole body. As her hands clutched his shoulder, he made a low noise of appreciation deep in his throat as he slid his hands up her neck, rubbing his thumbs over her jaw, tilting her head back, taking the kiss deeper, and she forgot the touch of her feet on the ground. Suddenly, the sweet torture was gone, and he was kissing her face, her closed eyes, feathering light kisses over her cheeks.

"You are mine, Caroline, and I'll kill anyone who tries to take you away from me, starting with Joshua Lee," he murmured softly as if he had spoken the sweetest words he knew. It took a few moments for his words to sink in.

"Kill?" she breathed, pushing him at arm's length.

"Your guardian has already agreed to our union, and Lee has proposed to you despite this, and without the permission of Mr Fairfax, alone, in a house not properly chaperoned. As your fiance... I am well within my rights to challenge him to a duel, especially if he does not desist with his farcical proposal at once," Lucian said. As she leaned away she felt her face flush, her eyes already snapping with anger.

"Duel? What are you talking about?" she said, pushing him away and turning to the window in a desperate effort to compose herself.

"The way I see it, that really depends on you, my dear," he said, turning away to walk a few steps. She could see that he was trying to control the longing that had hold of his body.

"What are you saying? I have no patience for your riddles," she snapped, resting her hands on the cool glass of the window, it cut through her hot, flustered skin, helping her to think more clearly.

"I am saying that if you do not inform Mr Lee of our engagement, and leave him in no doubt of our impending marriage, and tell Mr Fairfax that you simply cannot wait to marry me, I shall challenge

Joshua Lee to a duel, and I shall kill him, in cold blood, at dawn. Then, I shall marry you anyway. The choice is yours," he said calmly, pouring himself a glass of water and sipping it as she turned around to him. Her face drained of its warmth, and she felt a bit faint.

"You wouldn't kill a man," she whispered, wondering how she could have gotten so entangled with the villain before her.

"He would not be the first. Though, I might enjoy it more than any other," he said, smirking coldly, and Caroline felt that cold smile in her very soul.

"You are a monster. I was wrong... there is no better man within, there is nothing else, only more darkness," she bit out, feeling the utter hopelessness of her situation.

He refused to comment and continued to drink his water, before picking up his hat, gloves, and crop.

"What if I love him... do you not care?" she asked

"If you truly do, then I suggest you make the right choice. I am loath to herald my own skill, but I am known for my marksmanship. Joshua is a businessman with little time for sport. I have seen him shoot at Blackhill and he is no match. His life is in your hands," he said matter of factly, reaching the door, ignoring the sting of her words, he turned back. "The Fairfaxes will be home shortly, I suggest you make yourself presentable and speak to Mr Fairfax directly. I will be downstairs. I shall leave once it is done."

Caroline felt tears behind her eyes and fought to quell them, though when she spoke, her voice still held a slight waver.

"I hate you and I will hate you forever, Lucian Ashford," she vowed and saw him pause as her words hit him. He was still a moment and then grinned at her.

"Forever is a very long time, my dear," he said, ducking out of the room just as she sent a nearby vase crashing against the door.

CHAPTER 2

Katherine watched the townhouse come into view as the long and torturous journey finally ended. The carriage ride had been extremely quiet, she'd had altogether too long with her own thoughts, and she was feeling even worse now than she had before, though she had not thought it possible.

She thought of Caroline's face when she stood in the doorway and saw them both on the floor, and felt another surge of tears threaten. He had promised that he would be gentle, that he would not violate her, but whatever had happened, it had looked rough, and Caroline had wept bitterly. She had betrayed a sister, and she was only now truly realising what it meant.

She thought back to their departure from the Blackhill Hall. Lord Silus was very pleased with the outcome and had been quite jolly as they left, with plans to begin wedding preparations immediately from London. Wesley had been concerned, but kind- kinder than she deserved. Charles had come to see them depart, ever the gentleman, however, his eyes had been distant, and his mouth tightened in distaste as he had bid her goodbye.

He would be leaving immediately afterward to Gretna Green, in the hopes of mitigating any damage that would come to his sister's reputation.

"For young women these days do not seem to have a care for what ruinous damage their whims may inflict, nor whom is crushed in the process." He had thrown it at Katherine, and it had been a cut to an already bleeding wound.

The carriage halted and the party alighted, moving slowly into the house, each worn down by their various worries. Her mother still lamented the fact that Eva would not have a title, while her father said he felt as though he had made a deal with the devil. Katherine herself felt empty and broken, and as if she might never be happy again. If devils walked among them, surely there were none worse than her.

⚘

"Sir, there is a caller, waiting in the drawing-room." John looked in surprise at his wife and daughter, removed his hat and gloves, and went in the direction of the mysterious guest. Upon entering, he was perplexed to see Lucian Ashford, the very object of his strife and worry, standing casually by the fire.

"Mr Fairfax," Lucian said.

"Lord Lucian. To what do we owe this unexpected pleasure?" John asked cynically.

"I have come to ensure that the condition of your blessing is met to your satisfaction," he said.

"I see. Well, I have only just arrived home, Lord Ashford. I have not had the chance to remove my boots yet, let alone speak with Miss Lesage about the hopes of her innermost heart," John said, thinking belatedly that he should probably not bait the bear in front of him.

"Of course, I quite understand. I am willing to wait. No one need attend me," Lucian said as he sat down in a chair before the fire, and returned to his silent study of the flames. Feeling slightly as though he had just been dismissed from his own drawing-room, John left and made straight for his study, finding Margaret at his heels.

"Well? Why is he here?" she asked, flustered.

"He has come, because he is set on receiving my blessing today, immediately, to finalise our agreement without even another day's wait," John said sharply, settling behind the desk, feeling every one of the miles they had covered that day weigh down on him. They had

had so many hideous revelations to cope with. Riders had been sent toward Gretna Green, but he knew that they would not reach Eva and Eli in time, and even if they could, there could be nothing salvaged of her reputation if they did not marry. Failing any other conceivable options, the riders were ordered to simply see them all back safely.

"My dear, if she is not otherwise engaged, please send Caroline to me," he said and saw the stiffening in Margaret. She nodded and turned toward the door.

"Mrs Fairfax... be gentle with her. Try to imagine the fear and pain she must have felt at the hands of that ruffian... and our own daughter. A title is not an accolade for her. Be kind, you are the only mother she has left," he said as Margaret paused for a moment on the doorstep, then disappeared out the room.

🏵️

*T*he time had come to make her choice, though she could not help but feel that there really wasn't any choice to make.

She believed the worst from him. He wouldn't hesitate to challenge Joshua. Perhaps he was overconfident, and Joshua would prove to be the better marksman; though, that thought did not particularly comfort her either. She had scrubbed blood off hands and sheets already today, and would not choose to have yet more spilled on her behalf. Her thoughts were in turmoil, she couldn't imagine giving herself over to him, but there was no alternative. She was trapped. Again. He had taken her future from her, and she had no other option but to continue down that dark road.

A quiet knock at the door made her turn, and she breathed deeply.

"Caroline?" Margaret's voice was almost gentle as she came into the room and looked at her.

Margaret came up to her and pulled her close. She must be terribly disappointed about Eva losing her chance at a title, but even through all her crushed hope, and sore feelings, and the worry she must be feeling over her own daughter, she held Caroline tight and stroked her back.

"Are you well?" she asked, closely examining Caroline's face. Caroline gave a wooden nod. Margaret answered with her own tired, small smile, and stroked back wisps of escaped hair from Caroline's tightly coiled bun off of her forehead.

"You shall overcome this Caroline. You have your father's strength and your mother's wisdom. I know it seems that all hope is lost, but it is always there... your mother used to say there is always light in the darkness, as neither can exist without each other."

"Thank you, Mrs Fairfax," Caroline said, genuinely touched.

"And never forget, we are your family Caroline. We shall always support you." Caroline looked away at the words, thinking of Katherine, her heart contracting. "She loves you, Caroline, very very much. I still cannot believe her part in this, but I do know she is tortured by her actions," Margaret said watching as Caroline looked away and went to her wardrobe, pulling a shawl out and wrapping it around her shoulders.

"I suppose Mr Fairfax is waiting to see me?" Caroline asked.

"Yes, dear. He is in his study."

Slowly descending the stairs, she stopped at the foot, feeling her heart pound wildly. She leant against the wall for a moment, and breathed deeply, trying to stave off the faint feelings she had been fighting all day. She saw herself, reflected in the hall mirror. She looked tired, and haunted, her skin pale, her eyes dull. She hated her likeness at that moment. She noticed a movement to her right, and turning, she saw through the open door of the drawing-room, Lucian was sitting with his elbows on his knees, chin in his hands, and he was staring into the fire, lost in contemplation, so remote.

As Caroline's eyes lingered on him, he turned his face toward hers, and she saw for a moment the bare vulnerability of the man. The loneliness which she knew lurked within was laid before her, and she saw something else- fear. Fear that he could still yet lose her. For all his threats and bluster, he had no idea if she would capitulate to his demands, and it looked like this drawn-out moment, while he waited for his sentence, terrified him. She held that power over him, and for a minute, in his unguarded gaze, he pleaded with her.

She dropped her eyes, and turned toward the study, walking slowly, feeling a sense of finality in every step. Knocking gently, she waited, her heart in her mouth until Mr Fairfax's soft voice came to her.

"Come in, my dear."

✿

*M*r Fairfax studied Caroline carefully. She seemed hurt and tired, which was certainly warranted. She had accepted the news of her family's great fortune quietly, and Mr Fairfax decided that she must be too overwhelmed to feel much of anything else. But, she was also resolved.

"Are you certain, Caroline, you need only say the word I shall send this man and his bullying away forever."

"And have Eva and Eli bare the consequences of their broken promise... or Katherine? No, Mr Fairfax, I have thought this through from every angle, and I am afraid... there is no real choice to be made. Lord Ashford and his son are a determined pair, and I am really quite tired of eluding them."

"You remain dutiful to this family, though I fear we have done little to deserve it. The news of Katherine's involvement horrifies me the most. I am truly ashamed," he said, his heart squeezing at her faint, reassuring smile.

"Mr Fairfax, I owe you and Mrs Fairfax so much, for taking me in and offering me so many opportunities. I could never forget that."

"You are part of this family, my dear. That is all there is to it."

Caroline smiled at him and stood to leave. Hesitating, she turned back.

"When shall we be married?"

"As soon as a respectable wedding can be put together I believe. Eva and her new husband must attend, and soon all this ridiculous society will be quite without any scandal to keep them warm through the long, English winter."

"I see."

"Is there anything you'd particularly like? With regard to the wedding?"

"Well, I do not wish to seem ungrateful, but I would only ask that I be left alone, until the wedding, if that is possible. I need not receive calls from my betrothed, and I need not be involved in the wedding plans, Mrs Fairfax may decide for me... anything that needs to be decided upon," Caroline said, clasping her arms in front of her.

"Of course, my dear."

Caroline smiled a last time, and John was struck by the strength in the girl and her unflinching acceptance of her situation.

Once she was gone, he poured himself a large drink and sat a moment, gathering himself for his next visitor.

❀

*S*ometime later, John Fairfax found himself in a very similar position, sitting behind his desk, regarding the young person sat before him. In this case, however, the young person was rigid with repressed energy and nerves, his hands interlaced, a slight whitening of his knuckles. His face was carefully blank, and blue hooded eyes regarded him closely.

"Before I tell you of my conversation with Miss Lesage, I would like to hear your explanation of the events of the night that has damned us all," he said, reaching for his glass and watching a muscle tighten in Lucian's jaw.

"I cannot believe your daughter has not already done so," Lucian said woodenly.

"I wish to hear it from you. I wish to hear how someone who purports to care about another, could treat them so wickedly. Why did you do it?" John sat back and waited. The boy continued to regard him impassively, before speaking.

"Very well. I did it because I saw a window of opportunity, which was rapidly closing."

John watched him closely, waiting for something more personal to emerge.

"I did it because, almost from the very first moment of our acquaintance, I have held Miss Lesage in an esteem, unlike any other woman I have met, my sister, excluded. I did it because... if I have any chance at happiness, any chance of making a woman happy... it is her," Lucian said, looking away, clenching his fists, clearly uncomfortable by his own vulnerability.

John narrowed his eyes. Now the boy was calm, but he could see he was capable of great emotion and had a volatile nature. As he spoke of Caroline, however, there was no denying the emotion in his eyes. John was no fool, and he could see that the man before him cared greatly, perhaps more than he himself had even begun to realise.

"If what you say is true, I cannot understand why you could take everything away from her and paint her in disgrace, the way you have done. Where is your honor? Or human decency?" At the mention of his behaviour, the soft look disappeared from the young Lord's face, as though shutters had been drawn. "Have you no knowledge of the gentle nature of women? "

"I have a sister," Lucian retorted, angrily.

"And how would you treat her? If she went against you? If she disagreed with your orders?"

"I would do what was best for her..."

"Against her wishes?"

"If needs must," Lucian ground out.

"I see, and what of your mother, did she teach you nothing of the fairer sex?"

"My mother passed away when I was young, as well you know"

"Perhaps that is somewhat to blame then. For otherwise I cannot think why you would not show Caroline your feelings, draw her out, woo her. It is how one must treat women. They are our superiors by far. All we can do is treat them gently, cherish them, be tender with them - that is all we offer in return for all they give us. Really, they are the ones who are shortchanged by the set-up and we... we are the profiteers." John broke off, turning to the fire as he did, strange how the last few days had made him so sentimental, he mused.

He turned back to see Lucian listening respectfully, and John wondered how well Silus Ashford had attempted to prepare his son for married life.

"I thank you for the insight, and I can make a pledge to you... I shall never hurt Caroline again, I shall always protect her, I shall always value her... and I shall never stop repaying the debt I owe her for that night. It will not go unpaid... I promise you that. It shall never be forgotten."

"I am glad to hear it, though I am not sure I am the correct person to be saying it to."

"Then please, Mr Fairfax, end my suffering and tell me... will she have me?"

"She will. As I said, they are far too good for us, and you, especially, do not come close to deserving it. You do not deserve her. But, I think you realise that, and I pray you will spend every day trying to become a worthy man."

"I give you my word."

"And I shall hold you to it," John promised sternly as he stood, surprised by Lucian's suddenly strong grasp of his hand, and subsequent vigorous shaking.

"There is one caveat, however," he said as Lucian made to leave.

"She does not wish to be involved in the planning of the wedding. And she does not want to be called on beforehand. I think it a small concession to pay, considering."

*L*ucian stilled, feeling the elation and relief of moments earlier pull him back to reality, as a bird takes to the wing before it is shot and plummets back to the hard earth.

Caroline had agreed, but she still hated him. She loathed him and didn't want to see him for one moment more than was necessary. She despised the idea of marrying him, to the point where she was ambivalent about the wedding arrangements, which, if his sister was any indication, was every bride's joy.

He had wanted to give her everything, her heart's desire- the grandest wedding, in the biggest cathedral, attended by the best people, as only someone of his birth could. But, she didn't want any of it. She didn't want him. And forcing her into marrying him was not going to change that. She had wanted to marry someone else- Lee. She had even implied that she loved him. And now, by tearing them apart, he had probably made star-crossed lovers of them.

Nodding to John Fairfax, Lucian's mask once again in place, he took his leave and strode into the hall. When he walked past the drawing-room, he heard female voices inside. She might be in there. Hesitating outside, he abruptly turned and approached the front door instead. As a footman hastened to open it before him, he felt the rejection and the vile taste of envy at the back of his throat. Scowling, he waited as his horse was readied, and mounted swiftly. If she wanted him to stay away from her until the wedding, then he would not argue. There would be plenty enough open arms that would be happy for his company tonight.

The village of Gretna Green turned out to be quite pretty and with the long journey almost at an end, Rebecca allowed herself to relax a little. They had been traveling hard for almost eight days. She had lost count of the hours she had spent staring out of the window, watching the southern landscape melt into the rough north. The crowded towns were replaced by swelling hills carpeted in heather and craggy desolate mountains.

While she was afraid of her father, her brothers, and her fate when she returned, she had never before felt so free.

One night, as they traveled on a road that looked like a silver ribbon cutting through the dark moor, she had pulled the window down, and let her hand trail through the cool air, as everyone else was asleep in the carriage. She had leaned against the door, sticking her head out as far as she could. The wind hit her face, and her hair streamed backward, rising and falling in the air, pulled free of its bindings and constrictions. It had been so exhilarating. Closing her eyes, she laughed, a sound of pure joy. It was like flying, and at that moment, her cage had never felt further away.

Isaac and Eli were returning from the Blacksmith's shop, where the wedding would take place, while she and Eva were waiting with the horses outside an inn, one of the few in town. Crossing the street, the brothers came closer, and Rebecca watched as Eva and Eli's warm gazes met each other. That was love. That was what it felt like, she realised, and hid her own expression of envy for a moment.

"After relieving us of most of our money, we have managed to arrange a ceremony with the local blacksmith for this evening," Isaac started as he came over. "Apparently the town is preparing for a festival, and we'll be lucky to find room in the inn."

"Well, I'm sure a few shillings over the asking price can convince them."

"A few shillings? Perhaps you have not heard of our small financial predicament," he said, looking uncomfortable. "The ceremony is quite a bit more expensive than we'd imagined. Then there is the certificate and the rings..."

"Enough. I will pay whatever is needed. I do not care to know the details, only that what we came here for is accomplished," Rebecca said impatiently.

"There is one more expense... the wedding room in the inn," Isaac said, and Eva and Eli immediately looked to their feet.

"Brother, please do not speak of such things in front of ladies," Eli said rigidly.

"You will have to do a lot more than speak of it this evening, brother," Isaac said joyfully, clapping him on the back. "The smith was careful to tell us that the marriage is not final until consummated, under Scottish law. Something to keep in mind," he said with a wink, and Rebecca stifled a giggle at the look on Eli's face.

"Just a moment. If Eva is to sleep with Eli. Where shall I sleep?" Rebecca said suddenly, looking at the rueful smile Isaac gave her.

"Ah yes, well, of course, I asked for three rooms, the wedding suite, and two for single travelers." Rebecca smiled, relieved before Isaac continued.

"However, thanks to the festival, there is only one available room, which I took immediately, meaning to check the other inns in town. But-"

"They are all full?" Rebecca guessed, raising an eyebrow at the eldest Taylor, and huffed with exasperation as he shrugged innocently.

"One can only do so much," he murmured.

"Well, one must do much more, unless one wishes to sleep with the other pigs in the sty," she said with a sweet smile, before turning to Eva and looping her arm in her own.

"Come, we have lots to prepare, today you are a bride! Can you believe it?" she squeezed Eva's arm and they laughed together, starting toward the inn.

"Isaac, our bags," Rebecca threw over her shoulder, with a wicked glint to her eye. Isaac appeared to be fighting down his baser urges, this time probably to pick her up and dump her into the water trough.

❦

"*B*ut, Miss Lesage, Caroline... you cannot mean to do this! You are throwing your life away- on a libertine and a brute!" Worry etched his dark eyes. She held herself still and did her best to force a light smile.

"Mr Lee, please do not worry about me. What is done is done. I have made my peace with it. I realise now, that many of the soothing words I offered to Miss Fairfax, when in a similar situation, I can now apply to myself."

"What could possibly comfort you?"

"I shall have a distracted husband, who prefers his club and other social engagements over spending time at home."

"And this is what you want?"

"Well, I have not been offered husbandly accompaniment for more than three months, as it stands, so I was already prepared for an absentee husband," she said with a smile, trying to take the sting out of her joke, but she saw him wince nonetheless.

"You really compare what I offered you... to him?"

"No, I am sorry Joshua. You offered me everything I dreamt of, along with the independence I crave. He offers... something else, something I do not yet know. But, what I do know is that I have agreed, and arrangements are being made."

"I cannot accept it," he said, standing abruptly.

"You must," she said quietly. He paced the room distractedly. Whirling he knelt before her and grasped her hands.

"Caroline. Let us escape this cruel fate as Eva and Eli have done. I would risk everything, to see you happy and for us to be together. My father shall support us, I am sure of it. And Mr Fairfax will not object if you are happy."

"But the Ashfords shall... Lord Lucian would challenge you, and he would fight you without mercy, and his father would probably do worse if given half the chance," she said, letting go of his hands, and holding back tears, she stood and made for the door. "No. I shall not marry in secret and be ashamed of the consequences of my actions. They would jeopardise those I love. I cannot do that," she said, her look resolute, her hands finished in their trembling. "I beg you to forgive me and to excuse me. I must retire... I-" she caught his gaze for a moment, and she saw his disappointment, naked on his face. It touched her where his words had not.

"Caroline, please don't do this." His eyes were pools under a dark sky, and it hurt her to look at them. "I leave for the continent tomorrow. I mentioned my business there- I will be gone four weeks, no more, but I cannot delay my departure without risking my father's interests. I must press upon you that nothing short of ruin would keep me from changing my plans and staying here to convince you, but alas, fate conspires against me it would seem. If I stay, I would have little left to offer you," He looked at her as she stood. "Please. Say you'll wait for me."

"I am sorry, Joshua. I truly am," she said softly.

She reached for the door and closed it behind her quietly. Safely in her room, she fell face down on the bed and gave in to her tears. She cried for the life she might have had with Joshua, for the relationships she had lost with her sisters, and for her future she would have with a man that she couldn't seem to understand... and could never trust again.

⁂

*W*esley barged through the door of the brothel, ascending the stairs and pushing open the door of a room roughly. In the bed, there was a beautiful blonde, with silken hair, or she would be beautiful if not for the broken red veins on her face, her glassy eyes, and cheap underwear.

"Well, well, you should have waited your turn, sir... I'd take extra care of a pretty boy like you," she laughed, and Wesley felt the urge to wash, just from the salacious sweep of her eyes.

"Thank you, but you're not my type, sweetheart," he said grimly, and turning, spied his quarry in the corner, sunk low in a chair, cradling a bottle of some murky-looking alcohol.

Stepping over the female undergarments that were strewn around, he reached his brother's side. Shaking his arm, he realised that Lucian had managed to drink himself unconscious. Wesley hosted him up, and the bottle dropped from Lucian's hand, as the woman rushed over to save the last remaining drops in it.

"Oh, now I see, I thought it was just me he didn't fancy, now I see he prefers the likes of you," she snarled lazily. Wesley threw some money on the bed, and dragged his brother's heavy weight out the room, down the stairs, and out into the street. In the cool air, Lucian began to stir.

"What are you doing? Why are you here?" he mumbled.

"I am here, dear brother, because you have not been home in three days," Wesley said, staggering under Lucian. Suddenly, coming fully too, Lucian pushed off him and stood, leaning against a wall.

"Checking on me? You needn't have bothered. I am perfectly fine," he slurred.

"You do not look fine. You look like death."

"And I imagine there are quite a few people who wished I did not only look it," he sneered, before looking away into the darkness of the street.

"Caroline deserves better than this, Lucian... and you know it," Wesley reasoned slowly, his eyes raking contemptuously over his older brother.

"This is what I am. No one shall ever change me. You helped to organise our visits at Blackhill; served her up on a silver platter. Do you regret it now? Do you understand the depth of your folly?" Lucian sneered. Wesley felt as though his heart was wrenched in two as he watched the emotions run over his brother's face. "Do you think I want to be this man? Do you think I want to... to care? I don't. I have never cared about a woman, I *shall* never..." Lucian, slumped down as his voice left the air, his anger dying abruptly. "Do you think I want to... hurt... like this? To wander the streets, to watch her window... for just a glimpse... to see her face in a crowded market or street... and to find it is merely my mind that conjures her. To be unable to sleep, to drink or... even touch another woman... without feeling I am betraying her, without feeling unclean."

He now sat on a step and dropped his face into his hands. He was still, and Wesley approached slowly, not wanting to intrude on his brother's grief.

"I am not a good man," Lucian slurred. "I never have been, except, perhaps to you and Rebecca. I don't know how to be a better man... I don't even know where to start. Everything is so... spoiled... it is too late. She will never forgive me."

"Brother, if there is anything I can say about the female heart, it is that it is wise beyond our capabilities, and compassionate beyond our understanding. Do not assign yourself the title of blackhearted villain just yet. She will forgive you... *if* you show her you are worth forgiving."

"How?" Lucian asked, his eyes raw and bloodshot on Wesley's.

"That, I do not know... but I am certain this is not the way"

✿

The blacksmith's shop was small and smelled of smoke and sweat. Wrinkling her nose, Rebecca took in their modest surroundings. The walls were whitewashed, though coated in black soot and dust. Tools hung on the walls, various hammers, and moulds of several sizes and shapes. The floor was earth, bare and perfectly smooth with the weight of years of blacksmiths, and their sons after them.

As she entered the room, she saw that the Taylors were already there, and was thankful that they had taken the time to change from their dusty travelling clothes. They had attempted a morning dress, as was usual for weddings, however, modified slightly given the circumstances. They wore travelling trousers and boots, however, the top half was formal and expensively tailored and quite suitable for the task they had come to perform. Rebecca had managed to save aside a gown from the toils of the road and now she felt clean and fresh for the first time in a week.

Eli smiled and bowed slightly, his eyes looking past her nervously, while Isaac stepped forward to accompany her, his eyes moving over her in quite a surprising way. She schooled her features into ease and allowed him to lead her to the blacksmith's anvil.

"My lady, you never fail to enchant," he smiled appreciatively.

"Mr Taylor, I could compliment you similarly, however, it is not our wedding day, we should leave some compliments for the bride and groom to give each other," she said with a shy smile and a slight blush as he squeezed her hand tighter for a moment.

There was a quiet noise from the door, and Eva appeared. Rebecca felt her heart move as she saw Eli's face, the look he gave her, held in it more love than Rebecca had known in a lifetime.

She wore a simple, light pink day gown, but she had been working on it at night, embroidering small flowers around the collars and sleeves. It had a thin overlay, which softened the effect, and her natural curls were caught up loosely, where Rebecca had pinned small flowers, matching those on the dress. She looked, glowing in the light of the doorway, like an illustration from a fairytale.

The blacksmith was a small, broad man. Satisfied that everyone had arrived and that the marriage would go ahead as planned without either the bride or groom trying to run, he began removing his apron for the occasion. His hands were stained black, and his face was kind and welcoming.

"Now, it fair warms me heart to see love, in any shape or form. It's been bestowed on me, by the law of Scotland, power to officiate the marriage of this wuman and this here man." Eli took Eva's hands, and they stood side by side in front of the anvil.

"Will you promise, to take care o this wuman, to love er an care for er... till the end o yer days?"

Eli, clearly having an easier time understanding the man than Rebecca was, nodded confidently.

"I promise."

"An you girlie, do you promise to take care o im in return, to stan by im forever?"

"I promise."

"Good, good... now gae us the rings," he said, gesturing to Isaac who stepped forward and handed them to the blacksmith. He handed them out, and Eli slipped the heavy, beaten iron over Eva's delicate finger. She returned the gesture. They were then directed to a certificate, lying on the anvil, which they both signed. The Blacksmith smiled and continued.

"Who will bear witness tae this here union?"

"I, Mr Isaac Taylor, do," Isaac said, and raised his eyebrows at Rebecca for her to speak.

"And I, Lady Rebecca Ashford, do," she said, suddenly nervous at being included. Moving forward, she followed Isaac's example and signed the certificate lying on the anvil. The blacksmith inspected the names, then poured some sand on the glittering ink, shaking off the excess. He passed it to Isaac for safekeeping.

Turning back, he grinned broadly at the young couple in front of him.

"I now pronounce you... man and wife, by the law of Scotland and the testimony of these here witnesses. You can kiss er now, lad," he said gruffly as Eva and Eli looked at each other in joy. They moved slowly closer for the first kiss they had ever shared, and indeed, Eva's first kiss in her life. As their lips finally met, the blacksmith picked a massive hammer off the ground, and hit the anvil hard, hard enough to send sparks flying. All four jumped, Eva letting out a little squeal, which sent a worried Eli rushing to her side until he saw her laugh, and the blacksmith chuckled heartily. "It is done, you are joined in marriage, under God," he finished, hammering once again the anvil, the blow reverberating in the small room.

"And let no man put it asunder."

CHAPTER 3

The station was noisy and crowded, as Caroline pushed through the clamber to board the coach. The driver threw her bags on top, and she settled into a seat by the window, fighting down the nerves she felt. Whether or not this was the right thing to do, she couldn't imagine any other way. She wouldn't elope with Joshua in haste, and out of fear, and she could not meekly accept her fate with Lucian when alternatives still existed. And he would never let her go, even if she did marry Joshua, he had said so himself. Her only hope was to run away somewhere he couldn't find her.

When she had spoken to Mr Fairfax, she had fully intended to go through with marrying Lucian. Her options were all spent, and she was too hopeless to think of anything further.

The plan to leave, and the means to do it, had come the evening after she had agreed to marry Lucian. She had been lying in her bed, staring at the ceiling and the spidery shadows cast against it from the trees on the street. A soft whispering noise, of someone creeping about outside her door, had caught her attention. Raising her head, she had seen her door open silently. Outlined by a single candle, she saw Katherine's drawn face, her eyes dark hollows. They had looked at each other for an unknowable time, and finally, Katherine had come up to her, hesitant and trembling, and placed a packet in her hand. Before turning away, she clasped Caroline's hand hard, and Caroline saw raw love in that look. And just as suddenly as she had appeared, she was gone.

*D*earest Caroline,
    I cannot express here, with mere words, my regret over my behaviour. I do not deserve your forgiveness, and I think perhaps trying to earn it should be my punishment, which shall be exacted with my every waking breath, for the rest of my miserable life.

And so, it is not with words that I shall repent, but with actions. My father has now told you of your inheritance. It is more than you could ever dream of, and I wish you a happy life and that it shall serve you well. I have obtained the name of your family lawyer in Richmond, and all the funds are held in his name until you make arrangements for them. I have listed all the relevant details overleaf.

I have enclosed money, as much as I was able to raise, and it is more than adequate for a ticket on the New York ship. I urge you, brave Caroline, to seek out the life you deserve, and to reach for it fearlessly.

I accept the consequences of this action, Lord Silus Ashford may yet demand an heiress for his son to wed, and I shall not run. I robbed you of your choices, and I would sacrifice my own to return them to you.

Your bright and shining future, for mine. It is a fair trade and the only one I can live with. Though I know I do not deserve your consideration, I know you too well, so please, I beg of you, do not think much about me or the conse- quences... I shall bear them all with a smile.

Without fixing this, I will not know even a moment of happiness. You see- I am selfish to the end.

I shall keep your departure a secret for as long as possible, and I pray you will not delay.

I hope we shall meet again one day, my dearest sister, and beloved friend. Remember me well, and please let time soften my failures, for I shall only ever think of you with love and happiness.

    Your sister,
    Katherine

. . .

"*E*xpress to Portsmouth. Leaving now!" the driver shouted into the throng and Caroline braced herself as the coach lurched into motion.

"Wait!" a deep voice cried from alongside, and Caroline's stomach clenched in fear as she waited for Lucian's golden head to appear at the door, his eyes filling her with guilt. The coach stopped, and the door opened. She let her breath out in a whoosh as a dark-haired man stepped aboard and sat down, reaching for a newspaper and losing himself in it. When the coach started again, Caroline pulled down the window shade, complaining of the sun hitting her. The reality was, every person in the street that passed looked like Lucian. She closed her eyes to escape the wounded look of betrayal she imagined in his blue eyes and forced herself to think of the future.

Taking the ship alone to New York was dangerous, that she knew, but Katherine had given her more than enough for a private cabin. She would stay below decks as much as she could stand, and try not to attract attention. Katherine's promise, her sacrifice: it weighed heavily on Caroline, but, despite everything she had done to earn Caroline's scorn, Katherine was still her sister, and Caroline still cared for her. Yet, there was some small part of her that believed it might not come to that. Maybe it was in his tender words, uttered in moments of madness or anger, or his soft touch, or soul-searching kiss... she had come to understand that in his own twisted way, Lucian did care for her. He would not marry Katherine out of spite, she felt fairly certain of it, and perhaps Mr Fairfax would find a way out of this for all of them.

But she needed to get out as quickly as possible, as soon as possible. Lucian would find her, of that she was sure. The Ashfords would not be gentle this time. This final insult would not be borne, and Mr Fairfax would bear the brunt of trying to keep Caroline safe as they came at him with their teeth, bringing his family to their knees. She would use her inheritance to support the Fairfaxes if the worst happened - as soon as she could secure it, she would send it back to them, the price for freedom from the Ashfords.

She had sent a note for Joshua, and he would return from the continent to find her gone, but waiting for him in Virginia if he should wish to repeat his proposal. It would take time, but there was no rush. They could have a beautiful wedding in Virginia, in their own time. That is how their marriage would be: slow, unrushed, captured, hopefully treasured, moments between them, when life saw fit to bring them together again.

As she kept her eyes closed, and let her mind drift home, imagining the special, coloured light of a Virginian Fall, she did not notice the dark stranger, who sat opposite her with his intent gaze. Nor did she notice the small portrait, a simple sketch that he pulled from his pocket, comparing the likeness of it to the girl before him, before placing it in his pocket, a satisfied smile on his lips.

❦

"*I*s this really necessary?" Lucian said, irritated by Wesley's ministrations. Wesley stepped back, regarding his handiwork.

"You should know, you cannot reach my level of perfection without some effort," he said with a laugh, indicating to his valet a change of jacket. Lucian sighed and held his arm out. He had been allowing his brother to change his clothes, and toy with his appearance like a plaything for at least an hour.

"There, I think that should do it," Wesley finally pronounced, turning Lucian to the mirror. Lucian fought the urge to roll his eyes, and instead plastered a smile on his face. He was more dandified than ever, with every line perfect, starched and buttoned. His blue overcoat, cream waistcoat and starched cravat were immaculate, even his boots were gleaming.

"Now, what of his hair?"

"Wesley, you cannot make me into Mr Beau Brummel," Lucian said through clenched teeth.

"That man could primp all day, and not be as handsome as we Ashfords," Wesley scoffed. The valet approached with a hairbrush and withered under Lucian's glare. "Fine, let us not bother him further. His hair is probably a lost cause anyway," Wesley said with a grin. The chaotic mess of peaks and angles was rather in fashion lately, though Wesley would never admit it to him.

"Now, I have had some flowers delivered, which we shall take with us. And, a likeness of the horse painted."

"It is too much, she will find it desperate," Lucian said, trying to loosen his cravat.

"No, she will find it romantic! You told me she confessed to a lack of riding experience, despite a love of horses. What could she possibly want more than her own horse?" Lucian braced his hands on his dressing-table and took a deep breath.

"Can I have a drink now?"

"No. Absolutely not," Wesley announced cheerfully, slapping his brother on the back. "Now, let us go and woo your fiance."

"Against her wishes. She asked not to see me," Lucian reminded him moodily.

"Well, this is why we come bearing gifts," Wesley said, straining to keep up his positive cheer. Truthfully, the echoes of the awful morning, that he was sure he would never forget, kept haunting him. Lucian was right - he had served the poor girl up to him, knowing what his brother could sometimes be like, and knowing that there was a growing connection between them, he had nurtured it instead of putting a stop to it. He had been selfish for his brother's sake when he should have been more protective of Caroline. She had been a warm light in the darkness of Blackhill and had been punished for bringing them joy, rather than thanked for it. He could see no better way to make it up to Caroline now than to turn his brother into a man worthy of her, a process he was not certain was even possible.

*A*s they sat in the drawing-room, he began to feel his impatience build. Where was she, and why was it taking so long? Was she flat-out refusing to see him? He wouldn't be surprised, considering the last time he had called.

The clock ticked, and Wesley cleared his throat into the silence. They had been informed that Mr and Mrs Fairfax were not at home, though their daughters were, and so they waited with barely sustained patience.

Standing up, Lucian started to pace the room, nervously. A small creak from the door had him whirling around, and he spied the small face of the maid he had rather scared on his last visit. She saw him, squeaked with alarm, and disappeared out the door. Going after her, he caught up with her in the hall, catching her arm to stop her.

"Please, I am not here to harm you," he said as she quivered under his touch. "I am here to see Miss Lesage." The girl nervously dropped his eyes at her name.

"I don't know nothing about Miss Lesage. She is to be left alone. Miss Katherine told all the staff: leave her meals outside her room, she said. Do not disturb her," Betsy repeated faithfully.

"How long has that been going on?"

"Since... your last visit Milord," Betsy squeaked, the tray she held rattling. Lucian looked down at it, noticing it still held all its contents, untouched.

"Is that the tray from her room?" he asked. Betsy nodded.

"How long has she been refusing food?"

"A few days Milord."

"She hasn't eaten anything in days?"

"I– I'm not sure... I don't always collect the trays," Betsy said, tears springing to her eyes.

"Thank you," Lucian said abruptly, stepping back from the girl and starting toward the stairs. He took them two at a time and approached the familiar door. He waited outside, listening for the slightest movement from within, and when he heard none, knocked gently. There was no reply, and he stood for a good ten minutes more, knocking and waiting.

Nothing.

Taking a deep breath, he gently turned the handle, expecting to find it locked. It was not, it swung open easily and he walked into the room. The bright morning sunlight shone through the open curtains and spilled over the crisply-made bed. He walked further into the cold room and instantly felt an air of stillness, absence. She was not here, and it seemed she hadn't been here for quite some time.

He walked to her wardrobe and opened the door swiftly. The empty hangers that swung back and forth, mocked his foolishness. Turning to her bedside, he found a letter propped up against a vase of wilting flowers. Mr and Mrs Fairfax - It read.

He ripped it open and scanned its contents. She had gone, run off to

Portsmouth, alone... meaning to escape to America. The words turned him to stone.

She was literally risking her life to be rid of him. She had no idea of the dangers she was facing: not just in getting to Portsmouth alone, not just the dangers of the journey, but shutting herself on a ship full of men for two months without a protector. His stomach turned at the thought. He had done this, he realised then- this was his fault, and if anything happened to her, it would be on his hands.

He started down the stairs as fast as he could, straight out onto the street, he started for home. A horse would be faster than a coach, he just prayed that she would be delayed at the port, as the packet filled before the voyage, and that she would keep her head down, and out of sight in the meantime. She was no fool, but she was too extraordinary to go unnoticed for long.

*E*very sound outside the door made Rebecca jump. She tossed and turned in her bed. Isaac had not appeared, and she wondered if he would. She had been clear that she was not happy about the sleeping arrangements, and he had been very apologetic about the matter, whilst maintaining that there was nothing he could do.

Eva and Eli had vanished upstairs not long after they had all had dinner together. Rebecca had announced that she was also going to bed, and Isaac had urged her to go, without mentioning where he might be spending the night. One of the serving girls had then brought over an extra ale, setting it before the handsome, debonaire American with a giggle. He had looked up at her, his dark eyes warm, and Rebecca thought she saw something pass between them. Then caught herself staring, quickly hid her look of distaste, and had quite suddenly left, going upstairs without saying goodnight, pink-cheeked.

When she had stopped pacing, she threw herself into bed with castigations for her foolishness. Men like Isaac Taylor could always find a warm bed at short notice.

*C*aroline stood at the dock, fighting her frustration as yet another captain told her the same information, a four-day wait until the cargo hold was full enough to voyage.

She clamped her hand down on her hat, as the gusty port wind blew her skirts and hair about like a wild thing. It was bustling with sailors and crew, boats bobbed in the murky water and seagulls circled, crying out relentlessly in the damp, salt air. Cargo and luggage of all shapes and sizes lay on the dock, with nets holding them in place. Some ships were small, for fishing she guessed, others huge and exotic, bound for foreign seas and distant shores, and she couldn't help but wonder what sights they would discover.

Thanking the man, she turned and started back to her lodgings. She had found a respectable enough inn, where the female landlord had not pried too much about her being alone. She would stay in as much as she could, taking her meals in her room when she was able. She knew the dangers of staying alone near the docks, and just hoped the next four days would pass quickly without incident.

Carefully, she sidestepped a ginger cat with a scarred face tearing pieces off a long-dead fish. She wished that she had secured a veil to keep her face hidden. She felt each hour pass keenly as if Lucian was drawing ever nearer. Often, the image came to her of his mud-spattered face as he whipped his horse into a froth and spurred it on faster, focus and intention like ice in his blue eyes. She was a fox being hunted, of that she was sure, but what he would do if he caught her, she could not imagine.

❀

"*J*can't tell you nothing about specific guests," the maid said adamantly.

"How about now?" she heard the sound of coins clinking. "Can you tell me now?"

"Well... I can't say for sure if it is Miss Legrange, of whatever her name was... but she is dark, and she's alone. And she talks funny too... like a yank," the maid said.

"And which room's she in then?"

"Room five. But she isn't here now. Saw her go out meself this mornin. But she'll be back at night. She always stays in her room at night," the maid said eagerly, tucking the coin purse into her apron, looking around nervously.

"Good girl. Now, there is no need to mention this to anyone, right?" the man said and the maid laughed.

"If I value my worthless job I won't!" she said and resumed her sweeping.

❀

*I*t was the first time in Caroline's life that she was sleeping alone- without family or even familiar staff nearby, and in a totally unfamiliar place. She had to keep reminding herself to be bold, to put one foot in front of the other, and get on with it. She tried to think things through carefully, preempting any unknown dangers. Though the uncertainty was intimidating, the accents nearly impossible to understand, and the constant feeling of having to watch her back was unnerving; this was her life now, she was a woman on her own, and she would need to be tough, and she would need to be quick on her feet, or she would never make it.

The room was one of their best but, even still, it was modest. Small, and low ceilinged, the beams above seemed to cling to shadows and fire smoke. Worn wood paneling covered three walls, and a stone wall with a small window opened out to look over the docks and make the room feel a little less confined.

She had eaten a rather gristly dinner of unknown description and disconcerting flavour, but she was hungry, and it was cheap, and it would keep the hunger pangs at bay until morning. The blankets provided were not quite adequate, so she wrapped her shawl about her and laid in bed, listening to the bustle of the port, which it would seem, never slept, while she tried to imagine home until she could drift off.

She laid down and assessed the contents of her heart- all in all, she found that she was in good spirits. After all that had happened, and regardless of the obvious dangers of her ill-thought-out plan, she felt free and glad to be taking charge of her own life, while another part of her was enjoying the sense of adventure.

The sounds from outside the window became less noticeable, as a couple clambered in the room next door, bumping into furniture, knocking over candles, and laughing all the while. To her mortification, she soon discovered that the walls were so thin that she could hear even a heavy sigh. And oh, she began to hear many of them.

A pillow over her head seemed to achieve nothing at all but make it difficult to breathe. Hours later, the couple still unsated, and Caroline finally drifting off to sleep to the rhythmic thud, found that she could no longer chase away thoughts of what it might be like. What it might feel like. Though she was familiar with the mechanics of sexual congress, she wasn't sure that she knew exactly how it worked when it came down to the details, as she had only seen cows and sheep engaging in such activities, and she did not think that it would be exactly the same.

She did wonder if the act itself was pleasurable for the woman. When she had heard it whispered about or joked about, it seemed to be treated as if it were for the man's pleasure alone, and something that a woman must endure out of duty. But, she suspected that this wasn't entirely true- she knew that the girl in the maze with Lucian acted as if it was her own pleasure that she was after, and listening to the woman next door, the one who had been making a great deal of joyful sounds and grateful praises to God all evening, and who had just roused her partner into another session with promises, flattery, and sweet words, it seemed to Caroline that the woman seemed to be enjoying herself. Thoroughly.

Caroline knew too how she had felt her own yearning from time to time, one that was becoming more demanding than ever lately- one that cried out to be filled. She knew how the kiss from Lucian had ignited her entire body in the most uncomfortable and intoxicating way. It was all she could do not to lose herself entirely to it, despite the circumstances. She knew how it felt when her hand was in the crook of his elbow and they walked side by side, or how it had felt clutched inside of his hand underneath his tree- she was so painfully aware of every breath, every movement, her heart pounding. And through all the terror of being found, and of losing her reputation, she knew how she had felt on the floor beneath him, his body pressing down against the length of her, and while she was afraid of what it would mean, her body had not failed to register the smell of him, the feel of him, and call back in its own way- urgent, and insistent.

Here now, with the sounds of lovemaking ringing in her ears, and the dizzying, transcendent effects of the late hours of the night, she allowed herself to imagine. What would the male body look like naked, she wondered. She'd been to several museums and had a pretty good idea, but would it be different in person? She imagined Lucian's broad shoulders and then his hard chest. She thought of what they would look like, and then what they might feel like under her fingers. And then, what they might feel like pressed against her own naked chest.

What would it feel like to have a man inside of her? She had never been allowed near the type of novels that might have explained it to her, and there had certainly never been anyone whom she might have asked. But one day, perhaps one day soon, she would be a married woman, and she would find out. It seemed awkward, or maybe even painful, but then she listened to the sounds of the couple in the next room, and it gave her a little thrill in her stomach, and she found that that new but familiar tug of longing had returned to her own body, and was making itself known.

She closed her eyes tight in the darkness and tried to imagine it. Her body connected with a man's, his member- she had heard that it was meant to stiffen and stand, whatever that meant, being allowed into the most private part of her. She laid there, with her hands deep in her mess of hair across the pillow, and imagined them moving to the rhythm that drummed from next door, and the needy pressure of desire raced through her bloodstream.

She tried to think of Joshua's face, Joshua's body- if all went well, he would be the only man she would ever know. But while he was handsome and strong, with an easy smile, and big brown eyes, for some reason she found it forced and difficult to imagine. She tried instead to think of the body of a faceless man, but it was no use. She sighed heavily. Her mind kept returning to Lucian- though she tried to fight it. Probably, she guessed, because that was the only experience she had

had being close to a man. And because she knew the smell of his skin and the taste of his mouth. She would promise herself to never think on it again come morning, but for now, she would indulge herself a little bit longer.

※

*R*ebecca waited impatiently beside the horses, as their carriage was prepared. She had had enough of Scotland and travelling and she was quite ready to go home. She was sure her awful mood had everything to do with the lumpy bed and tasteless breakfast she had had to endure, and nothing whatever to do with a certain American, who had not appeared all night.

As though her thoughts conjured him, suddenly he was there, swaggering through the yard, smiling at her. He was wearing the same clothes as the day before, which was hardly surprising as his bags had been in her room all night.

"Good morning, Lady Rebecca," he said politely as she averted her gaze from him, and made a studied effort to look casual.

"Mr Taylor," she acknowledged curtly. They turned to look at the inn door, and Rebecca prayed that the newlyweds would appear as soon as possible, so they could be on their way.

"I trust you are rested?" he asked politely.

"More than you, I'd wager, given the state of you."

"Yes, well, sleeping in a stable is not something I would be quick to recommend."

"Hmmm, come now, Mr Taylor, I have four brothers, if you recall. You do not have to hide your promiscuity from me," she snapped.

"Promiscuity? Well, it seems your version of last night's events is a lot more exciting than mine," he laughed, surprised. "Pray, do not keep it all to yourself! Won't you tell me a little of what I got up to?" he leaned in solicitously, and Rebecca scoffed and shoved him away.

"What you do in your private time is no concern of mine."

"Would you like it to be?" he asked, his carefree grin fading, his eyes intent.

His words stole Rebecca's breath away, and she looked up at him, properly, for the first time that day. His eyes held hers, and her heart

216

pounded in her ears. What could she say? Her mind raced for words-any words.

"Rebecca," a deep voice growled, and she snapped her head up to see Charles, dismounting the back of his horse in a swift glide. He was hatless, dusty and weary from the road. He looked like he had not eaten or slept in days, and walked toward her like gathering storm clouds.

He grabbed her elbow and spun her back toward the inn.

"Charles! We were just-"

"I will change my horse, we will stay long enough for me to wash and eat lunch here at the inn. Then we will dine together in celebration of these nuptials, and make merry for enough people to see that I am here as your escort."

"But-"

"Do not breathe a word to me, Rebecca. You and I shall talk once we are home, and not before, when I have had sufficient time to gather myself and school my anger so that I do not tan your hide myself."

❀

"Who'da thought that one guest could double my income this month!" the small maid said with a laugh as she tucked his money out of sight. "I can only tell you what I told the other man," she said, leaning in, her eyes darting around, checking that no one saw her. "She's staying here alright. Room at the top of the stair. Don't say much about herself. Dark, American, pretty, if you fancy that type of thing," the maid chattered on as Lucian thought about what she'd said.

It had taken ten inns to finally find her- Caroline was here. He'd already been to the docks and found that there were still two days until the next ship left, so she was stuck until then. He had been riding for two days without pause, and his clothes and his mood stank. At the maid's words, his heart started pounding. Someone else was looking for her.

"This other man... what did he look like?"

"Well, I don't remember rightly... but I suspect he'll be back here tonight. I told him she was always at home at night."

"How helpful of you," Lucian growled. Turning from the woman, he ran up the wooden stairs to her room. Knocking briefly, he tried the knob and found it locked. He listened for any sound inside. She was not yet back. He debated what to do. If she saw him, she would likely run. Perhaps right into the other man who was pursuing her.

He walked to the hall window and looked down at the docks. They were filled to bursting and he couldn't make out any individuals clearly through the grimy windows. What did this man want with her? Unspeakable, horrible images began to flash through his head. And, Caroline was out there, somewhere, alone... the thought filled him with a desperate sort of fear and nervous powerlessness that left his hands shaking with unspent energy.

❀

*C*aroline kept to the shadows of the docks as twilight stretched into night. It was beautiful here, but also harsh, smelly, and gritty. Spires, grand and beautiful, pierced the skyline gracefully, and at sunset, they had been awash with startling golds and pinks, glowing red as they nestled in close to the water, the source of all wealth here. But, with the grandeur mingled the dirtier side, crushed in along the line of the water. Rats scurried about, gutted fish innards sat in the sun until the gulls or cats found them, and the workers: so many loaders, and sailors, captains, and errand boys; they were tired, overworked, unwashed and often drunk, noisy, and looking for trouble or women or both.

The ships were majestic, as tall as the buildings it seemed, and no less impressive. They moved in the water like living things, and in the docks, they bucked and jostled dangerously, like restless horses in a pin, churning the water into foam, rubbing and crashing against the dock with deafening moans. It was a city of contrast, at least the docks were, but she found them no less fascinating for all their grimy, glittering realities.

Restless, she had stayed out later than usual and now was finding it more awkward to return to her inn discreetly. The dock shifted as the boats were left for the night, cargo disappearing, and the pubs that ran along the side grew busy, spilling orange light and raised voices onto the swaying darkness beyond. The people had changed too, Caroline observed: louder, rowdier and a good deal more drunk.

Reaching her inn with a sigh of relief, she walked through the common area on the way to her room. The place was busy, given the late hour and the servers were rushing around the place, answering calls for more drink and food. She dodged, ducked and scurried her way through, grateful when her feet found the steps toward the upper levels and the guest quarters. She reached her door and inserted the rusty old key, rushing inside and leaning back gratefully against the hard wood.

Taking off her bonnet, and her cloak, she thought about dinner. She was hungry, but it was late, and she didn't want to risk going downstairs again. She peeled off her dress, which was almost stiff with salt from the clinging sea mist. She hung it and hoped it would not smell too awfully the next day, considering she wouldn't have a way to wash it for quite some time, but she reasoned that after a few days at sea, everything she wore would smell of salty sea air, and many other things besides.

In her thin chemise and petticoats, shivering a little, she pulled a thick wrapper around her shoulders and sat at her dressing table. Her hair had hardly fared better in the sea air. She pulled out all the pins and started to unsnarl the heavy tangle with her hairbrush. A slight noise in the room next to hers made her jump, and she laughed self-consciously. It was probably just last night's couple up to their old tricks. Still so nervous. She wouldn't stop being so until she stepped onto the boat, or rather, the boat left dry land.

She wondered about the state of affairs in London. Surely they would have discovered her absence by now, her mouth going dry at the thought of Lucian coming after her. It was the strangest thing... and she felt quite disarmed by the feeling herself... but there was something there, a sadness, at the prospect of never seeing him again after they had shared so much of themselves those long months. The truth remained that if he hadn't taken such drastic steps, she did not know how far he would have worked into her heart by now.

She caught sight of her expression in the mirror, melancholy and lifeless, and shook herself. She was setting out on her own adventure. She had plenty of far more important things to think about, she told herself firmly, turning away and lighting a candle by her bed. Blowing the others in the room out, she poured a small glass from a bottle of sherry that she had bought earlier that day to help drown out the noise of the docks, and anything else she might overhear. When it was done, she poured another. She picked up her book, already heavy in her hands, and tried to read: though, the long day outdoors, the hiding and constantly looking over her shoulder, were really very tiring. Before she had realised it, the book had fallen, and she had slipped into sleep.

*H*er dreams began as they always did, there was smoke and the sensation of not being able to breathe. Then the orange darkness, the acrid sting in her nose, and the crackling sound. As always in her dreams, she waited for her father to reach her, and felt the smoke pervade her young lungs. Coughing, she held her breath and waited. Suddenly, he was there, scooping her up, carrying her. His arms felt so strong under her, he felt so real.

She struggled to see through the smoke and make out her father's face once again. With a cry of shock she realised it was not her father who was carrying her, but Lucian.

He was untouched by the flames and smoke as he carried her, his face determined. She pushed against his arms in protest. This was not her memory, where was her father?

She came to suddenly, transitioning from her dreamlike state to one of full consciousness in a second, realising that the smoke and fire had remained in her dreams, whilst Lucian and his arms had not.

Opening her mouth, she managed to let out half a blood-curdling scream before he clamped his hand over her face, cutting her off.

She continued to struggle and had just managed to get her teeth around one of his fingers when abruptly she was dropped. She landed on a bed with a whoosh and instantly scrambled around, grabbing the candlestick off the bedside table to defend herself with.

"You!" she cried accusingly, pointing the weapon at him. He stood back from the bed, making no effort to come closer, and held his hands up in surrender.

"Shhh. Caroline, let me explain-" he began in a rushed whisper before she cut him off.

"You... you...unholy... rotten...madman!" she cried, feeling around for words to throw at him. He stood there, quite calmly, he didn't seem the least upset by her reaction, in fact, if she had to name his emotion, he seemed relieved.

"Caroline-" he started, stepping forward, causing her to shoot to her feet on the bed, her eyes widening even more, brandishing the candlestick like a sword.

"Do not approach me! No closer, I mean it!" she said and waited until he backed down, and then removed himself further and sat in a chair several feet away.

"Please, my dear, keep your voice down. Is this far enough? Should I move to the window?"

"Why don't you just jump out of it?" she lashed out, feeling her heart rate drop a little from its frantic pace.

"There are the lovely sentiments I have so missed in recent days," he said quietly with a lopsided smile.

"Why are you here? How did you know?" she asked

"I know because I read the letter that you left the Fairfaxes. And I think you know why I am here..." he said.

"I will not go back with you. I will marry Joshua Lee. I will not go with you, do you hear me? Not willingly, you'd have to tie me up and gag me- though I would expect as much from you," she said angrily, her mind spinning.

"As enjoyable as that sounds, beautiful, I actually have another reason for bringing you here tonight." Caroline finally looked around, realising they were not in her room anymore. "Welcome to room six," he said with a smile.

"You have been staying in the room next to mine?" Caroline asked slowly, horrified, her mind raced to what she had heard the night before.

"Only for the afternoon, you see, I had to hear when you returned home."

"What? Why?" she demanded.

"Because, my fearless girl, there is a man here asking about you, and he plans to visit you tonight."

"Who? You? You truly have gone mad!" she raised the candlestick again and jabbed it into the air.

Lucian suppressed a laugh when a soft knock sounded through the wall. They both looked at the door. The knock came again, and Caroline felt goosebumps travel up her arms. Someone was there at the other room, knocking at her door.

"Miss Lesage, dinner," a low man's voice said, muffled only slightly by the thin walls. She looked in alarm at Lucian, who put his finger to his lips, and walked up to the wall, placing his ear to it. He walked back to her and whispered softly.

"Did you request dinner to your room?" she shook her head silently, eyes wide. She felt the prickle of goose-flesh break out all over her body. Struggling to regulate her breathing, the next sound silenced her... the click of the latch, and the door dragging open over the uneven floorboards. Her eyes met Lucian's then, and she knew by his expression that stark terror was painted across her face.

Nextdoor, footsteps thudded into the room, over to the bed. Then silence fell. They waited, each moment stretching out until she was painfully tense. Then, just as she was about to move, the footsteps returned to the door, and it swung shut, the latch back in place, then the footsteps continued in the room, over to the other side. Probably to the armchair, she guessed, where they stopped.

Silence then fell and Caroline sank down slowly on the bed. Her head was swimming.

But for Lucian, she would probably have been asleep when the man had entered and consumed by sleep and sherry, or if she had stayed out later, she would just be returning now, finding him sitting waiting for her in the dark. She rubbed her hands over her bare arms, feeling cold to the bone. Lucian, moving quietly, grabbed a blanket from the bottom of the bed, and spread it around her shoulders. She accepted it, with a furtive glance up, wrapping it tightly around her. He then went and extinguished all the lights in the room, save one candle which burned lowly on the washstand.

"How-" she started, countless questions crowding her head, and stopped as he made a motion of silence. He stripped off his jacket and boots, allowing him to move more quietly, and came over to the bed, lowering slowly to sit on its edge, he leaned forward to speak in her ear.

She was so overwhelmed by the intruder that she barely noticed Lucian's proximity.

"We must be quiet. He cannot know that you are here." She nodded and leaned to his ear.

"Who is he? How did you know he was coming?" she asked.

"I do not know his identity. Somewhat humorously, I ended up bribing the same maid as he to find out if you were staying here," she leaned away and shot him a contemptuous look.

"Are you certain that *you* did not send him to have an excuse to drag me into your room?" she asked.

"Quite certain, though I'm flattered that you believe me to be so innovative," he said with a grin and she scowled as she pulled away from him. She needed to think, she needed some space.

She stood, holding the blanket around her, and paced soundlessly on the bare floor. The very man she had been running from, the crazed man possessed, had just appeared, and maddeningly, was speaking very calmly and logically and making her feel safe! He was acting as though it were normal for him to be here with her, hiding conspiratorially together, and not as though he had betrayed her and killed all her hopes and chances of the life she planned. She stood, indecisive, and watched as he rose and walked to her. He made no effort to touch her, just leaned in a little, allowing her to close the gap so he may be heard.

"We must stay here tonight. Tomorrow, I shall try to find out about him."

"I will not stay here with you! Just go there now, and demand to know who he is," she said.

"I suppose I might be pleased that you think me capable of defending you against our unknown adversary, without so much as a glimpse of the man, when I did not even bring a pistol with me. Need I inform you that this impromptu gallivant across the country began as a loving visit to my intended," he raised his eyebrows. "Or, might I surmise that it matters not to you who he is nor how he is armed, so long as he offers you an escape from me... in which case, I could save us all a lot of trouble and leave now..." he said slowly.

"No," she said quickly, annoyed that Lucian was making her admit that she felt safer with him than without. He raised one questioning eyebrow at her and she looked away. "Better the devil you know..." she muttered wryly.

"Right then. Well said. In that case, I'm going to try to get some sleep so that we are prepared for tomorrow. I'm well overdue for a wash, and then I will sleep on the floor between you and the door. Does that suit you, Miss Lesage?" he asked sweetly. She scoffed.

"Since when has that ever mattered to you?"

Caroline went to the bed, drawing back the covers, she settled in the middle, and threw a pillow and the blanket on the floor. She then drew the covers up until they reached her chin and watched Lucian as a mouse watches a cat. Crossing the room, his hands untying his cravat, he pulled it off, dropping it with the rest of his clothes, and started to take off his shirt. Averting her eyes, she heard the sounds of him filling the basin with water and splashing his face.

Curiosity overtaking her, she let her eyes drop a moment, resting on his broad shoulders, that tapered down into a slim waist. His muscles slid smoothly under his skin as he bent forward, stray drops of water coming to land on his arms. She wondered what the skin there felt like.

Abruptly, she realised the splashing had stopped and looked up. Her eyes collided with his in the looking glass. She felt her cheeks flame.

Turning over in bed, facing away from him, she hid her face in the pillows and heard him quietly blowing out the candle and lying on the floor. It squeaked under his weight, and she imagined it couldn't be very comfortable. Well, let it be the beginning of his penance then. Resolving not to care, she closed her eyes and tried to relax. It was impossible, she couldn't stop thinking about the man next door, and what might have happened if Lucian had not appeared. Who was he? How did he know where to find her? And what were Lucian's plans? She would have expected to be thrown in a canvas sack and spirited away by now.

"Why did you come after me? Why can you not just leave me be?" she accused.

"Because... I was worried about you." She scoffed.

"How saintly. I'm sure you had no intention at all of dragging me back against my will?"

"Do you have any idea how dangerous it is? To voyage alone? A lady such as yourself?"

"I can take care of myself, I'll have you know," she replied smartly.

"Oh, I do not doubt that. But, I..." he trailed off, suddenly uncertain.

"Yes?"

"I could not stand the thought of you being in danger... if I could still prevent it," he admitted.

"So, you only condone harming me, when it is you who benefits from it?" she asked bitingly.

"I never harmed you," he said flatly, and she pushed down her frustration.

"That is where we fail to understand each other. Maybe, one day, when you care more about someone other than yourself, maybe then you will understand how you harmed me," she whispered hotly, pressing her face into the pillow, fighting the urge to shout and rant at him. They remained quiet for a time, though it did nothing to help her sleep.

"What were you dreaming of before?" Lucian's whisper came to her through the darkness, and what felt like a great many miles away. She didn't answer. She was restless, and set her mind to planning. She considered the option of running once he fell asleep, but where would she run to? Lucian would find her quickly, she was sure, and if not him, then whomever the stranger was next door. Besides, if she wanted to leave for America, she would need to be on that ship. She stayed calm. She was physically safe at least, and she had no better plan. She would wait, and keep her wits about her for an opportunity. She tried to force herself to sleep, but it was no use. She would rather speak to the man she detested than be left with her own thoughts. Turning, she edged closer to the side of the bed nearer to where he slept on the floor, anxious not to make more noise than necessary.

"Nothing," she whispered back.

"It did not seem like nothing, you seemed quite... agitated," he said.

"It is private," she said and was met with silence. "It was only a memory. Of when I was a child."

"You were calling for your father."

"Yes... it was the night they died," she said, and Lucian did not pry any further.

"You never told me what happened the night that you were attacked," she said, curiosity prickling her. She felt bare and vulnerable after sharing the visions of her nightmares, and she welcomed a chance of settling the balance. As close as they had started to become to one another before everything fell apart, he had not spoken much about the life he had led in any real detail. "Who attacked you?" she prompted as he fell silent.

"I believe you might have recognised them from the other night, though not the friends they brought with them," he said, and she could hear his grim smile in the dark.

"The men you saved me from? What cowards!" she gasped angrily, thinking about those disgusting men who had begun to paw her on the street.

"Were there a lot of men?"

"There were... enough," he replied evenly. Caroline turned on her back, her thoughts reaching back to the dinner she'd had with Charles and Wesley and the things they'd told her about the fight.

"Your brother, he intimated to me that perhaps... you felt as though you were deserving of a vicious beating."

"Do you think me not?" he asked,

"Well, not then, perhaps," she said. "Now... I would rather not say."

"I'd call that fair," he said, shifting on the floor, creaking the boards beneath him.

"You did not try to defend yourself? Because you felt you deserved it."

"Well, I was rather drunk at the time."

"But, I cannot believe that even drunk, you would not try."

He fell silent for a moment.

"Once again, Miss Lesage, you cut to the quick of a situation... distill it down to its most vital parts," he murmured, shifting again on the floor.

"Is that an effort to avoid an answer?" she asked, more curious than ever.

He laughed quietly, but she could hear it held no humour. She waited, and just when she had given up hope of him speaking, his smooth, low voice broke the silence.

"I didn't fight back... because I didn't want to win. I didn't want to stop the beating, I didn't want to save myself even one blow."

"Why not?"

"Because I enjoyed it. I have not been a good man. Why shouldn't my outer self be as hideous and scarred as the inner?" he said, and she felt chilled by his words.

"You cannot mean that. What if they had killed you?" she whispered.

"I was prepared for that, even hoped for it, perhaps. I think my brothers knew, and probably Rebecca as well. It is what started this whole campaign to cheer me, which you got wrapped up in," he laughed bitterly.

Caroline kept quiet. Her emotions collided. She could not pretend that she didn't care for the man, even to herself. The events of recent days had horrified and disappointed her, but she had already known he was a man of duality, of hateful moments, and heroics, all in one turn. She could not forgive him for how he had treated her, manipulated her, but nor could she stop her heart from breaking just a little at his sadness and utter hopelessness.

"I am not sure that I could have recovered had it not been for you, Caroline."

Caroline lay in a stunned silence. She pressed her hands against her chest.

"I just wished for you to know that," he went on. "And after that, the thought of a life without you, nearly drove me mad, and I know it is no excuse for how I acted, but... I am not... experienced in matters of the heart," he said softly. Caroline stared up into the darkness of the room and felt her heart twist, wrung by a strong pair of hands. She knew he spoke the truth when she heard it. "'Sorry' is not enough, Caroline. I want to make this up to you. I want to spend my life protecting you and making you happy. I know that I can. I have been a monster, and I do not deserve the chance, I know, but I can be a better man if I am by your side. To make you happy... it's the only thing left in this life that I want."

She said nothing. She felt that there were no words adequate to respond when a man has in the breadth of one minute confessed that he wished for his own death and that he didn't want anything from his life anymore... anything, that is, but to make her happy. Perhaps, she thought, he said these dark and painful things to manipulate her because he wanted her to weaken, because he thought that that's what she wanted to hear. But, she knew it wasn't true. She had spoken to Lucian enough in those long, bare days of the summer at Blackhill, that she knew when he was airing his innermost thoughts. It pained her to accept the truth of it. She would rather it was a lie. At least his voice seemed to her to be a little less tight for having spoken its secrets into the night.

The crawling shadows cast by the boat masts swaying under a full moon leant an unearthly light to the ceiling as they both lay, quite separate in their thoughts, as the time ticked relentlessly on, bringing them closer to morning and the choices that would define them.

CHAPTER 4

$\mathcal{C}$aroline woke with a start, the memories of the previous night returning with force. She sat upright and scanned the sunny room. It was empty and quiet. It was quite bare of possessions, and she wondered what Lucian had brought with him, if anything.

She saw his hat and gloves resting on the dressing table, a stiff white corner of paper poking out from under them, and a day dress of her own lying on a chair, along with her sturdy, warm boots, hat and coat. She drew back the covers and gingerly put her feet to the floor, unwilling to slide from the warm bed and onto the chilly surface.

There was a substantial draft blowing across the rough floorboards from the crooked window. She glanced at the pillow and blanket that marked Lucian's bed and felt a fleeting moment of guilt at the icy draft that blew across her toes.

Reaching the dressing table, she carefully pulled on the white corner, and found it was her letter to the Fairfaxes. He had removed it. He didn't want anyone to know she had tried to run away. He must have thought he could bring her back, whether with force or free will, she couldn't guess, and he had planned to keep this little episode between them. He could have collected her forcibly like a willful child and brought her back to Fairfaxes. Was he trying to spare her pride or his own? He might yet force her to the church. But, she reminded herself, he had made no move to seize her, or force her in any way since he had arrived.

Hearing a noise in the hall, she hurried to the chair and began to dress as fast as she could, she jumped as a knock sounded at the door.

"Miss Lesage, Lord Ashford has requested breakfast in your room," a female voice came from the other side of the door. She deliberated. It was the same ruse as the man had attempted yesterday, however, given that her own clothes were here, it seemed that Lucian had already been into her room, and the man was gone. Also, the woman had referenced him by name. Her growling stomach was the last straw and she cautiously opened the door. The maid stood with a full tray, and she opened the door further to allow her entry.

"He asked that you eat as much as you are able, and then go and join him downstairs," the maid said, putting the tray on the desk. Nodding and thanking her, Caroline's eyes widened at the food. A steaming patter of kedgeree, a bowl of porridge with jam, bread with cheese, and some fresh fruit. Steaming hot tea also accompanied the offers. She locked the door after the departing maid and sat down, tucking into her first meal since that same time the previous day.

*A*s each mile brought them closer to London, and Rebecca to the consequences of her actions, the more she lost the fight to temper her fear, under her brother's steel gaze. Eva and Eli were quiet as well, though, with their hands clasped and fingers interlaced, Rebecca envied them their partnership against the uncertainty. No matter what the future brought for them, they would have each other.

She tried to still her pounding heart, looking out the window as country gently dissolved into city.

"So, my lady Rebecca, are you sad that our adventure is coming to an end?" Isaac asked quietly from her side once the brooding presence of Charles had succumbed to sleep.

"All adventures end, Mr Taylor," she said, forcing a light smile, though it felt strained.

"Well, I suppose one must end for another to begin."

"Perhaps for you, though... I fear that...my adventures are truly over," she said with a laugh, and a tightening of her hands on her lap. His eyebrows drew together, and Rebecca had to turn away from the look in his eyes.

"Come, now. You have proven yourself an adventuress of the first degree... I cannot believe the future does not contain more adventures for you," he said.

"Perhaps you should talk to my father of it," she said, her tone bitter, even to her own ears.

"Will he be very angry?"

"My father does not get very angry... he gets even," she said.

"You are brave, Lady Rebecca, braver than any woman I have ever known."

"Well, that is surely a compliment, given your vast troops of female admirers," she teased, but her voice was warm. "In truth, it is easy to be brave when you have nothing to lose," she confided.

"No. It isn't," Isaac disagreed softly and looked toward the city outside the window.

*C*aroline paced the floor, growing increasingly nervous as the dark gathered over the docks. She had spent practically the whole day inside her room and was tired of waiting. Lucian had positioned himself downstairs, and all day long they had waited for the man to return.

She had tried to set her idle mind to scheming her escape, but running from one man was better than running from two, and she decided she couldn't possibly leave until the man was caught. It would be foolish to attempt to run before she learned more about her mysterious adversary. Perhaps that night, after he had been questioned, or perhaps even while Lucian was distracted in the scuffle, if she kept her eyes open, she may just find an opportunity. If she was chased away from the ship, there would always be Plymouth, or Liverpool, or Belfast, if she must. He could not corner all the ports at once. She may just have to be patient.

She didn't like sitting in her room, like bait in a trap, yet she trusted that Lucian was watching and that he wouldn't let anything happen to her. It had killed a day of waiting for the ship, and Caroline's stomach tightened at the realisation that there was little time left. She had packed her cases, moving as though in a dream, her ticket waiting on the nightstand. She sat now and stared at it. Would she ever get to use it? It wasn't likely, but best be prepared, she decided.

She had hardly seen Lucian all day. After eating she had gone to the common room, and received a letter from him, explaining his plan that she wait for the man in her room. She wondered if he was embarrassed about the things he had said the night before. She had felt like him once, but she had learned to heal, and to move on as best she could, while Lucian had grown accustomed to the emptiness. The whole truth, she guessed, was that these feelings of his were not new, and had probably been building for a long time. She had heard it in his moonlight confessions, soft and sentimental, and the sadness of it had struck her with a force that she had not expected. She had been naive not to see before just how much the kindness of her outstretched hand had meant to a man who could not outrun his own demons. She could not help but look back over her memories of his wild actions in a more desperate light, a possessive fear of loss, and an absence of alternatives. She couldn't excuse it, but she began to understand it.

A knock at the door froze her to the spot, and she felt a chill raise the hair on her arms. Standing, she took a deep breath and listened. In the hallway, she heard sounds of a scuffle, and several grunts and smacks, the sound of fist meeting flesh. She pulled open the door, just as she saw Lucian haul up a man from the floor by the neck, and throw him toward her open door. Standing out of the way, speechless, she watched as he dropped the man in the centre of the room. He was doubled over into a ball, clutching his stomach with both arms, trying to get breath in, and his face was bloody, one eye already beginning to swell.

"What shall we do with him? Should we tie him up?" she whispered and coloured as Lucian raised an eyebrow at her, grinning slightly.

"We can if you'd like," he said slowly and she withdrew to sit on the bed, crossing her arms in front of her.

"It was merely a suggestion."

"Interesting," he said, clearly enjoying himself.

Turning back to the man, who was moaning, and moving on the

floor a little, Lucian lifted him by his shirt and made him sit up against a wall, then squatted in front of him, smiling pleasantly.

"Now, my good man, we have something to discuss. As I assume you can guess my line of questioning, why don't we get started without delay," Lucian said, resting his arms on his knees and waiting as the man recovered himself somewhat. "No? Alright then. Who are you, who sent you? And what exactly is your purpose here?" he asked, watching the man speculatively as he calmed his ragged breathing, and wiped some blood from his eyes. The man made to move away, but his movements were slowed and clumsy, and Lucian easily pushed him back against the wall, his head hitting the panelling with a loud thud. The man seemed to accept defeat for the moment at least. He looked away, his chin held firm in a deliberate silence.

"Come now, we both know how this shall proceed. You refuse to answer, I hurt you and ask again. Do we really need to go through it more than once? There is a lady present, I will remind you," Lucian said in a jovial enough tone, a light veil to the menace underneath.

When the man's silence held, Lucian picked up one of his hands, which lay beside his foot, and gently separated the fingers. He then held the pinky, for a moment, before pulling it in the wrong direction so quickly that Caroline almost missed it, but for the sound it made. The man screamed in surprise and then whimpered as Lucian dropped his hand hard to the ground, and put his foot on top of it. Shifting his body weight, ever so slightly, leaning forward, until Caroline heard a cracking. The man wailed piteously, and Lucian waited for him to stop before he tried again. Twisting his boot slowly, the man screamed, shaking now, and pleading as his bones were ground between boot and floorboard.

Caroline heard herself scream before she had even decided to.

"Stop!" It had been a pleading scream, raw and agonising. Lucian had heard it too- he looked up at her, concerned, guilty. She could not sit by, no matter the circumstances, and watch a man be tortured on her account. She felt as if she had broken his finger herself: felt the sick snap between her hands.

"Stop this, Lucian."

She brought a hand to her mouth and held back a sob. The look of agony on the man's face. It was all too much. What was happening?

This was her fault. Everything was happening so quickly: agreements made and broken, promises, deception, fortunes built and smashed, hearts healed and torn apart, lives forever changed. She felt swept away on a tide she could neither control nor escape. All their fates were intertwined, and she at the middle, with hardly enough time to guess at the consequences of her actions. She squeezed her eyes shut, and pulled a breath into her lungs that shook her whole body.

It had been all he had needed. The man on the floor had seen the moment when Caroline had captured all of Lucian's attention, and he had seized it. He had pulled his good arm free and grabbed a blade from his boot, or his belt, it was so fast that Caroline did not see, but the cold shine of its thick polished blade caught the light as he held it to Lucian's throat.

He angled the blade, and pushed up slightly, making Lucian stand with him, and then twisted his arm, turning him, and pinning Lucian tightly between him and the blade, at the mercy of one sharp movement. Lucian's eyes were wide, but his breath was calm. Caroline tried to scream but found that she could not breathe past the lump that had gathered in her throat.

"Don't make a sound," the man warned.

Lucian raised his free hand slowly, in supplication. "What do you want? I have money. I can give you whatever you want. Let the lady go." His head twitched toward the door. "Go, Caroline. Now." Caroline was frozen to her spot, unable to run, unwilling to leave him, unsure what to do.

"You're going to beg. You're going to bleed and she's going to stay right there and watch you."

"We will do business when the lady is safely away, you have my word."

"I don't want to hear no promises. I want to hear you scream, and I'm going to start with your fingers."

"Yes, fine, just let her go. I can double whatever you are being paid to capture her. Triple it." The man laughed, and it was a throaty, menacing sound.

"I haven't come for 'er, have I, Ashford? I came for you."

"For me?"

Caroline's mouth fell open. Who would have paid to have Lucian harmed? An angry husband? Were there unpaid gambling debts? Had he gone too far when some dark mood had taken him- threatened someone, insulted someone he shouldn't have, killed someone?

Caroline saw Lucien's eyes move around the room. Calculating. Searching for some way to turn the tables. He locked eyes with her again and flicked his eyes toward the door. "Run," he mouthed silently. Caroline made a quick, sudden shake of her head, just once, hoping that the man would not see it. She would not leave Lucian there with the blade.

"Yes, for you, my lord," he mocked. "But now I'm 'ere, and you offering a fortune, per'aps I'd better send an ear to your rich father and see what e'd be willing to pay to keep the rest of you intact." He laughed humorlessly. "And maybe a couple of fingers too," he said, holding up his injured hand, the little finger hanging loose and crooked. He tightened the knife into Lucian's neck, drawing a hiss from his teeth, and a spot of blood welled up against the shine of the blade.

"Let the lady go first, and I will not struggle, you have my word."

Caroline made to move, she was not sure where or what she should do, but she couldn't sit still on the bed and watch any longer.

"Sit down, you slut!" the man yelled, and Caroline stilled as she was told, her eyes on the blade as it jerked against Lucian's skin.

"That's right. Let's not be 'asty. Maybe I'd better do my job and finish 'im off first quick and easy. You'd be a lot less trouble on your own, I'd reckon. Pretty little thing, ain't ya?"

His arm tightened and drew a bit more blood. This man was going to cut his throat, Caroline thought. He was going to do it right in front of her.

Lucian reacted swiftly, grabbing at the handle blade with his left hand, he threw the man back against the stone wall, tossing his head back into the man's to ensure it connected with the wall. Caroline jumped up. There was a gush of blood from the man's nose, and Lucian's fingers were sliced by the knife, bleeding down his white shirt, while the man managed to pierce a little further into the side of his neck. Lucian trying to wrestle the blade away as it sawed into his fingers, let out an angry roar. They twisted together, stumbling away from the wall.

Caroline grabbed instantly at the ceramic pitcher on the bedside.

She rushed, swung wildly, and hit the man on the head, praying that the blow would not force the blade further into Lucian's neck and finish him off.

She felt time slow, and imagined all the ways that it might go wrong. It was a gamble she might lose, and it could all end here, in a gush of Lucian's blood. One stupid decision, too quickly made, and she could kill him just as easily as if she had grabbed the knife and done it herself.

The splintering crash of the pitcher was loud as a pistol shot, and the man crumpled to the ground. Lucian spun quickly around to her, white-faced, his hand going to his neck, the blood bubbling through his fingers.

She gasped, backing away from him a few steps, hoping it wasn't true, wanting to go back. Do it differently. He twisted his mouth in a grimace of pain but advanced toward her, her back against the cold stone wall now.

"It's alright. It's alright," Lucian said, but his voice was his own, not the whisper of a man seconds away from his own death, nor the gurgled rasp of a man whose vocal cords had been slashed and his mouth filling with his own blood.

She heard a little hiccup of fear escape her, and her hands went to his face, grabbing it firmly in a shaky grasp as her nerve broke, and she began to cry. She pulled his fingers gently away from his neck. There was a smear of blood, but it did not gush forth. The cut was not deep. More of the blood had come from his fingers. It was a slice, but a thin one. A red line. A scratch.

Her whole body shook with another sob, this time of relief, the proof in front of her eyes- she had not just killed the man that she loved with her own hands. She grabbed him, and he clung to her as if he too had thought they might both die there in that dark room.

He held her up. Their bodies drawing the last bit of strength from each other. Next to them, the body of the man lay on the floor inert, a trickle of blood slowly oozing from his head.

She held onto Lucian longer and tighter than she had ever held on to anyone- a lifeline as the world crashed down around her.

CHAPTER 5

"**You** were right," Lucian said with a smirk. "We should have tied him up."

He grabbed a rope used to tie back the curtain and tied it tight around the man's wrists and ankles. They needed more information from him. The head wound didn't look fatal, as far as Lucian could tell, but it bled a lot and made Caroline worry over him. In the hour or more since she had hit him, she had washed it and bandaged the wound as best she could with some old fabric while he was unconscious.

Lucian finally brought him round with some slaps to the face. The man moaned, and then his eyes opened. Seeing Lucian, he pulled back in fright, realising that he was bound, on the floor, bleeding, and entirely at Lucian's mercy,

Lucian gave him a moment to find his head. Then he took the man's own knife and lifted the man's chin with the flat of it. The man stilled, eyes wide and wild.

"Now. Let us try this again, shall we? Tell me," he said darkly. "Who sent you?"

"I'm not sure," the man stuttered. "It was 'is man came to me, paid me, told me what to do, I never met the actual gentleman."

"What did he want you to do?"

"Follow 'er, I have a likeness. They said I was to watch 'er house in London, and if she tried to run anywhere, they said probably the docks, I was to follow 'er, and wait outside 'er room, and follow wherever she went. Keep a close eye. Wait."

"For what?"

"For you. If you never came, no one would be any the wiser, but if you did, I was to get rid of you."

"To kill me?"

"Yes." It came out in a whimper, the confession of a man who feared what dangers telling the truth would cause, but was too afraid to lie. Lucian's eyes narrowed. " 'E said I was to be discrete, but I didn't 'ave time for that, did I?"

"Who is the man? What else do you know?"

"Nothing, I don't know any names... just... he was American, I suppose, at least 'is man was."

Lucian scrunched his brow, thinking. Who could this have been? Sure, he wouldn't be surprised to find that there was a number of people in England who wanted him dead, but what would that have to do with Caroline? American? Had John Fairfax been trying to aid in Caroline's escape? He was certainly not the type to have anyone hurt, even a man like Lucian. He looked to Caroline, but she looked just as confused as he was.

"What else?"

"Nothing else, sir."

"Nothing? I will not spare your life for nothing."

"There is only one other thing..." the man said, giving in at the expression on Lucian's face. "I followed the man back to an address in London, I'm quick see, and they were clumsy. Information is always worth something. You might know the place," he said, hurrying at the impatient look on Lucian's face. "St James Square, fifteen," he said. Lucian did not know it. But when he turned back to Caroline, he saw that the blood had drained from her face.

"Do you know it?" Lucian asked. She nodded at him, wordless, her confusion settling on her brow.

"That's... it's the Lees' address," she said in a whisper. He looked at her for a long moment before turning back to the man. "Oh God," Caroline said. "The letter to Joshua."

"I didn't think he had it in him," Lucian said.

"But he's on his way to the continent. He wouldn't have gotten it in time. His father must have opened it." Lucian turned back to the man with a sneer.

"You were to make sure that I stayed away? Make sure she gained the ship?" he demanded.

"He was trying to protect me," Caroline said, sounding unsure.

"She is supposed to be marrying the man's son. 'E was very insistent about that. 'E said you..." the man stopped, dropping Lucian's gaze, and shifted with a groan.

"What?" Lucian growled dangerously.

"Said you stole her once before, and the man wasn't going to lose a fortune to a dirty bastard like you. His words, not mine, sir! Forgive me saying so, sir."

"Anything else?" Lucian said, his voice as tight as a bow.

"I said to the man that it must be worth a lot to 'im, and 'e told me that wasn't the 'alf of it. Said that I ain't the only one. The man's got more hired men 'ere, and said there would be more men waiting when she got to America... protecting 'is interests, as it were."

Mr Lee senior was after Caroline's fortune and had pushed his son toward getting it. It explained the rushed proposal after a short acquaintance, and his easy acceptance of the scandal, and her loss of reputation. He looked at Caroline and could see by her expression that the very same things were occurring to her. She caught his eyes, and looked away, standing and crossing to the window.

"Did Joshua Lee try and convince you to elope with him?" he asked gently. She nodded slowly, her cheeks colouring.

"He did, and I flattered myself it was due to his... regard," she said, averting her face from Lucian's eyes. He left the man, stood and walked to her at the window, fighting every urge he had to take her in his arms, to soothe her somehow. No doubt she had looked on Lee as a savior from all that had happened to her, safe arms to run to, to take her home. Lucian choked on the guilt that rose up his throat. She had been so misused of late, mostly at his own hand, and he hated to know how much this probably hurt her already bruised heart.

"I am sure it was, in the end," he said softly. "I saw the man with you.

He was not someone acting impartially. I believe he truly cares for you," Lucian said, despite himself.

"Please, Lucian. Don't. It matters not. It is only my pride that is hurt. It is better that I know the truth so that I can live with it, no matter how painful." She stared out of the window, her voice even.

"Do you still care for him, then? Would you still go to him, if you could?"

"This information doesn't change anything. And, what difference does it make now, Lucian? You're hardly going to give me the chance to go, are you?" She sighed and looked behind her to the man on the floor. "Let him go. He has told us everything we need to know."

Lucian felt the sting of her words, like arrows through his flesh. This changed nothing. She wanted to marry Lee despite what they had learned of him. If he did not drag her from this place, she would sail tomorrow, her plan unchanged, despite everything, despite what they had shared not an hour ago, and she would marry Joshua Lee.

He walked numbly over to the man and took up his knife again, this time using it to cut the rope that he had bound him with. The man backed away, still on the floor, and then from a safer distance, put a hand to his head.

"Go. Do not come back here." Lucian rummaged around in his pockets, and the man flinched. Taking a coin out, he tossed it at the man's feet. "And have a doctor look at your head- there may be some sewing that needs doing," he said and waved his hand as if to shoo the man away. The man grabbed the coin, scrambled up, and was gone with a slam of the door.

🍂

*T*he night was closing in, and even the noise from the dock was growing ever so slightly fainter. He still had time, didn't he? Not much. Few precious hours to spend with the woman he loved.

She still wanted to go. She would still marry a man who was after her money if it meant escaping him. She had withdrawn. Her arms curling around her waist protectively. Hurt. Confused, he imagined. He hated to see it. All she had said that she wanted was a bit of stability, a bit of control, a choice, and yet nothing was ever in her control. She stood calmly and quietly, trying to hold things together.

Perhaps nothing had changed for her, but Lucian knew, with a nauseating swell of dread, that something had changed for him. He knew with a certainty that somewhere in those dark hours, clinging to Caroline who had not left him when she might have escaped, who stood by him, protected him, even when death was staring her in the face, who had saved his life, that he had made a decision then that would change the course of his life and damn him forever.

He would let her go.

He would not take her choice again. He would aid her journey in any way he could. Her happiness meant so much more than his. How could he have ever thought differently?

Crossing over to her, the only noise in the room came from the soft scuff of his boots on the creaky floorboards. He put his hand gently on her shoulder and saw her flinch.

"Caroline-" she pulled her shoulder away from him. "Please do not flinch from me, my love. Caroline, I ... I will not stop you tomorrow if you wish to board the ship and go to Lee." She said nothing, and his stomach sank like a lead weight. "We will sleep tonight, get some rest, and you can sail tomorrow as planned... if that's what you wish."

Caroline turned to him, silent, her slanted hazel eyes sharp, careful.

"Is that what you want?" he prompted. "Will you go?" She looked at him for a long time, or at least it felt like an eternity to Lucian as he held his breath and awaited his fate. She searched his eyes for something, taking her time to assess, though what she was looking for, he couldn't tell- disbelieving, suspicious of a trick perhaps.

"Yes," she said simply, and just like that, tore his hopes to shreds. He had thought, he had hoped against hope, that when she had risked her life for his, and when they had held each other as if one being, one soul parted too long and finally whole again, that perhaps she loved him, that perhaps she would stay. But he had been wrong. He took a shuddering breath.

"Caroline, if he was telling the truth, there may be men waiting for you, when you disembark."

"I am aware of that. But if that is true, then my safety shall be their primary objective."

241

His heart twisted at the finality in her tone. He tried to stop himself, he sounded like a petulant child, but he could not stop the words before they tumbled out.

"So, you will marry Lee then? Even after you were manipulated, lied to. You would choose to marry him, over me?" he asked, watching her reaction with pleading eyes. She left him, walked over to the looking glass where she sat down and began to unpin her hair. She said nothing, and it stung as if she'd slapped him.

"I do not wish to discuss it now, Lucian. Please. We have been through enough for one day. Our nerves are shot. Tomorrow," she said, softening. Her eyes turned to his finally in the glass and met them, gentle this time, clouded with emotion.

❀

Through the darkened silver stains of her foggy looking glass, she watched Lucian's face. He was working to control it, but she could still make out the way that the pain pulled at it, and she found that her own could not help but respond. How was she supposed to feel about the man? It was easier at the beginning when she could simply reprimand herself for thinking on him, or later when hate and anger boiled for him like acid in her belly, but now, so much had changed in only twenty four hours. But this - this declaration shattered everything they had always been to pieces.

He said that he would let her go. That he would *help* her to run into the arms of another man if she would allow it. Her heart had leapt when he had said the words - but not because she could go home, because the man whose selfish need to always take what he wanted was now saying that the choice was hers, that he would sacrifice his desires for hers. She let out a long, slow, steady stream of breath and emptied her lungs. It had been his selfish need to dominate her, to bend her to his will, that prevented them from the possibility of being together. But now, if he loved her enough to change...

Was he being truthful? Did it change anything? Everything?

Because she knew that she was in love with Lucian Ashford. Perhaps she had been for a long time. When she had almost lost him mere hours before, she had felt her world coming apart at the seams. Maybe now she could allow herself to dream of a different future, one where they could build a life together, one with trust and love and support.

It could be a trick. Perhaps this was all some scheme of his to soften her. She knew him to be unscrupulous when it came to her.

The ship would leave in the morning, with or without her. She didn't have the time she needed to make this decision - the decision of her entire life with this man... or an entire life without him.

She wanted to cry. She wanted to scream, and rail against him and curse him to hell. She wanted to run to him and be held tightly in the steel circle of his strong arms.

But, she didn't do any of those things. She needed the sanctuary of silence. Over time, she had found that she could be calm and level-headed in a crisis. She didn't tend naturally toward dramatics, and despite all the noise, the fear, the horror and trauma, and the great clamour of emotions of the last day, with a bit of inner quiet, she could right herself again.

She would have to decide what to do come morning, and she needed to be as prepared as she could be.

Her mind told her that despite the day's bitter revelations, Joshua still provided the safest option for her. Perhaps his feelings were genuine, and perhaps they were not, she could not tell, perhaps she never would, but it made no difference to the outcome either way. Between them, they would have enough money for comfort and stability, and provided that he continued to treat her with respect, and would give her the children that she wished for, feelings- love- was unimportant, she decided. Maybe it would even be preferable to have a straightforward relationship without the added confusion of strong emotion; regardless, he would be away for more than half of the year, and she could have her way with the running of the estate and the raising of the children. She had not yet spent much time with his father, and if what the man had said was true, he was a monster. But then, so was Silus Ashford, and it was not the father that she would be marrying.

Her heart longed for Lucian, now more than ever. She knew accepting him would be easy: for her, for the Fairfaxes, for Lord Silus- everyone could get what they wanted, she supposed. But, turmoil was part of Lucian's being, and for every bit that she was drawn to him, she knew that to be with him would mean a life untamed - at the mercy of his moods, his passion, his complicated family, at the mercy of her own love for him. How could one build a home over a faultline where the earth quaked?

Lucian was readying himself to leave her for the night, and her chest grew hollow at the thought of it - the silent room, the sleeplessness, the loss of him, she knew would settle on her like mid-winter, and that hollowness in her chest would gape open. The two of them were raw and bruised and bloodied, inside and out. She could not abide any unnecessary pain, not after the day that they had had.

⚘

Caroline had grown still, and pensive. How, he marveled, was she able to always be in such control of herself? Her inner peace was an incredible rarity that he could not begin to fathom. How was it that while he felt constantly in the merciless grip of his feelings, a pawn, no more able to control the storm within, than to hold back the rain; that she was the calm - the eye in the middle of the storm, graceful, and self-possessed, no matter what hell swarmed around her. Here she sat, this creature: delicate, composed, angelic, and stronger than he might ever hope to be.

She pulled the last pin free, letting her long twist of dark hair come to rest over her shoulders. He could smell the scent of it, even from where he stood- salt sea, wood smoke, a touch of jasmine, and Caroline. The unmistakable scent of her, that he craved like a starving man. Her midnight black hair shone in the candlelight. It was so beautiful. He longed to take the brush out of her hands and run it through her hair himself as she began to untangle the shining mass. He wanted the silk of it between his fingers, wanted to press his face into the bundle of it at her neck.

Clearing his throat, he moved to the door, dragging himself away from the last few moments that he might ever spend with her.

"Lucian?" she called as he put his hand on the handle.

"Yes?"

"Would you... stay with me?" she asked, and he froze, afraid to look back at her, afraid that he had misunderstood, afraid to break the spell.

"I thought to wait, in the hall, before your door. I shall watch over you, for as long as I am able," he said and saw her consider his proposal.

"I think I would prefer you here... if you do not mind," she stated. He felt his stomach leap at her words. She was putting her trust in him, and it was more than he deserved. At his silence, she went on. "Propriety seems... no longer important," she said simply.

"Of course," he said, gently. He took a breath. Then he turned back into the room, and saw her, going about her preparations, as if she had not just handed him a piece of the moon.

He moved slowly, aware of her eyes on him in the mirror. She stood, her hair now falling to her waist, and she moved smoothly to the bedside and lit a candle, before extinguishing all the others. His eyes adjusted to the new darkness as he saw her go to her trunk. She faced away from him.

"Lord Lucian. Would you kindly turn around please?"

Heat flashed through him, tightening this body, as he looked away, turning quickly to the wall. Feeling unsure what to do with himself, he removed his boots, unbuttoned his jacket, and cast it on the chair. His waistcoat and cravat followed, but he left his shirt sleeves and breeches. He felt at his neck. It was not much more than a scratch. He had been shockingly lucky - at any point during the struggle, the man might have tightened his grip, pulled his hand, and sliced his neck in an instant. He had been sure he would die in the scuffle. It would have been so easy. Perhaps his assassin was new to the trade. He flexed his hand, the bandages held, and the bleeding had stopped.

Her reaction had been so visceral, so raw. She had truly feared for him. He would have done it all again to have that time with Caroline afterward, everything else having fallen away, just the two of them at their most deconstructed- it was a rare moment to share with another person.

Even in the cool air, his skin prickled with heat, at the thought of her carefully removing her clothes in the same room, just a few strides away. The rustle of the bedclothes signalled to him that she may be ready, and he slowed, listening intently.

"My lord," she said, and he turned back, and caught at the sight of her, innocently smoothing the blankets, and tucking herself in, glowing golden under the light of the candle at her bedside.

He tossed his coat onto the floor and began to lie on it, grateful that at least the window in this room was keeping more of the draft out.

"Is it not cold?" she asked hesitantly, and he turned his head to see her, leaning on one arm, over the side of the bed. He smiled reassuringly.

"I've slept colder," he said, putting his hands behind his head as a pillow. She scrutinised him for a moment, before her face disappeared to the other side of the bed where he could not see her.

"Well, then you shall have the blanket." She tossed it, and in the darkness, it fell heavily on his face and swallowed him up. He sat up and laughed at the fright he had gotten.

"I most certainly will not," he said, affronted, and tossed it back up to her, hoping that it landed on her like a lead weight, as it had done to him.

"No," she huffed from under the blanket. "I have not just saved your life so that you might just freeze to death slowly on the floor next to me." Her face appeared again before him, and she threw the blanket down like a weapon. He laughed again, and it felt good after the day that they had had.

"Miss Lesage, after all of the innumerable and unspeakable wrongs that I have done you, I shall not *also* take your blanket. Not even should we be in Lapland in winter, and I without a stitch of clothing." She snorted.

"There is but one blanket, Lord Lucian. And two of us."

"Of that, I am well aware, Miss Lesage."

There was a silence then, that thickened in the cold room between them. She puffed out a breath.

"Right then," she said, her voice unfaltering. "Then there is only one logical solution. Let us not be delicate about it."

"No."

"Lucian, if you do not, one or both of us shall surely freeze here tonight. Do not now pretend to be a prig, for it may be the last thing you do. "

He smiled broadly in the darkness, and slowly stood up.

"That should be a terrible way to die- priggishly." She laughed again, a little more easily this time, and scooted across to the other side of the bed.

He gathered the blanket up from the floor and made a wave of it, spreading it across the small bed. He carefully slipped under the covers, keeping himself as far from her as he could. He lay there, his whole body alert and on guard, and felt that she must feel just as uncomfortable.

"Caroline, I am really quite well on the floor. You do not need to -"

"Hush. Anyway, it will not be the first time we have slept side by side. Though, perhaps I shall recall this time better," she said wryly, and he felt that familiar shame roll through him.

She raised herself up a fraction and blew out the candle.

Just the feel of her body shifting in the bed near his, not touching, not even brushing, just the mattress moving correspondingly, was something that would live in his memories, long after she had sailed to America.

It was silent for some time, but he could tell she was awake, thinking, fighting the urge to sleep, though her yawns indicated it was a losing battle.

"I could go with you. To New York," he said suddenly, breaking the silence. "I could see you home safely through the journey, and even all the way to Virginia if you'd like," he rushed on. "I could stop any interference from Lee. You need not marry him, you know, you are a woman of fortune now. You could be truly independent. I would help you either way." The seconds that passed stretched on, and he counted each one.

"And what about afterward? What would you do?"

"I would return home, I suppose," he said, already dreading two long sea voyages. He hated to travel by boat, more than anything.

"You would expect nothing in return?" she asked, critically.

"For you to be happy," he said simply, but the words felt heavy with unsaid things.

"That's nice," she whispered drowsily. She fell silent then and he felt her start to drift away, saying nothing more.

The quiet of the night crowded in, and he felt utterly spent. He was lying beside the woman he wanted more than anything in the world and he was about to lose her. Yet, he lay, calmly watching her sleep. He would go with her to New York, or on to Virginia, if it was what she wanted, and leave her there. Or, he would watch her go tomorrow morning and dwell on her decision until nothing was left of him. It would have to be enough for him to know that she had the things that she wanted. She would have a good life there, he felt sure.

The soft warmth of her body reached him from her side of the bed, and he thought of how lucky he was, when he might be in the hallway, when she might have left him on the floor, to be in this soft bed next to her, his skin warmed by her skin.

Perhaps, if he had handled the whole thing differently, perhaps then... but he would never know. The night stretched out before him, too short, too precious as he turned on his side, watching her face, heart-stoppingly beautiful as she slept, long, dark lashes feathered across her cheeks. There was not enough time to memorise every feature, to appreciate her closeness, her new trust in him. He did not know how long he watched her, as the moon slid over the water, and the sky started to lighten.

She gasped at one point during his moonlit vigil, her hand reaching out across the covers, finding his chest.

"I am here, Caroline. Sleep. I am here," his voice caressed softly, mourning the loss of her hand as it returned to her side, and her troubled brow relaxed back into sleep.

CHAPTER 6

*R*ebecca walked into her father's London townhouse, her stomach clenched like her fists at her side. She looked back before the door closed, catching a last glimpse of Isaac Taylor as the carriage drew away. She longed to run back out there, climb into it, and never stop again.

Instead, she turned around, and slowly started toward her room. A sound from the study drew her attention, and she glanced that way, stopping as she saw Charles. His face inscrutable as he approached her.

"Sister," he said, narrowing his eyes. She nodded, stealing herself to speak.

"Is father home?" she asked, haltingly, and felt relief course through her as he shook his head.

"You have some time," he said and then tilted his head to the side and leveled her with a stern look. "You will deal with me first."

"What is it, Charles? Just come out with your scolding, will you?"

"How could you act so rashly... so... inappropriately?"

"I did it for Luke."

"And you would allow yourself to be painted by the same brush as a couple eloping without their families' consent, but without the wedding to make you decent? You had no chaperone, Rebecca, for christ's sake!"

"What else was I to do? He couldn't marry Eva. He would have been miserable! He is in love with Caroline Lesage, and I believe she cares for him too," she said adamantly, pushing her chin up. "I am not afraid of the consequences."

"I forgot, you do not know."

"Know what?" she asked

"Come, sit down and hear about the impact of your plan on your dear brother... and your beloved friend."

🌸

*C*aroline woke early, the sounds of the docks pulling her from her dreams. Dreams where she ran through mist and fog trying to find the boat that would bear her home, but she could see nothing, the swirling fog hiding the shape and names of the ships.

She turned a little, seeing the cause of her confusion and heartache lying near her, asleep. She studied his profile, mesmerised by the vulnerability of the man in his sleep, stripped of his usual aura of power and confidence. His golden stubble, full pink lips, his tawny eyelashes, and smooth neck were all inches away; and she took her time over them, committing each feature to memory. The neck of his shirt was open, a smattering of dried blood dotted the collar, and she could see a small expanse of chest underneath: the shadows of the collarbone, the curve of muscle, a dusting of chest hair, she wished that she could press her face there and that he might bring his arms around her and hold her tightly again.

A soft noise came from his throat, and he stretched. She felt a knee touch her lower thigh and a length of calf rub sleepily and unaware against her own, and then still against her, its warmth sending a shock of electricity radiating through her body. Her breath caught in her throat, and she was afraid to move, or even to breathe, lest she wake him and he move his leg away.

She remained paralysed, while the sun crept brighter into the dark room, every move of his and every move of hers magnified, full of nerves and tension that made her feel alive and excited. The warm breaths that he exhaled in quiet puffs smelled good to Caroline, and for a moment she closed her eyes again and breathed in the air that he had exhaled, sending hers back to him, relishing in this secret intimacy that was hers alone- a memento to take with her, wherever she would go.

What they had done, sleeping here together, was an outrageous impropriety which most people would consider wrong, wanton, and immoral; and in the morning light, she was shocked by her own boldness the night before in asking Lucian to stay. But, she could not scold herself for it when it had brought them both comfort after the terror of the day before, and when it had made her feel the way that she felt that morning. She would give herself just a few minutes more to think of nothing but him, and then she would break the spell, and prepare for the day ahead of her.

Gently, she pushed herself up, pulling back the covers over him, and stood. Dressing quietly, while he still slept, she put the remaining items in her case and sat at the window, looking out at the ships docking, her mind running with all of the choices in front of her, trying to weigh them up logically and fairly one more time, trying her best to ignore the emotions that clouded her judgment, and following each path toward its suspected outcome.

A stirring came from the bed after a while, and she looked over to see Lucian rubbing his hands over his face, before looking to his left, at her empty side of the mattress. Suddenly sitting up, he looked around, instantly alert.

"Good morning," she said softly, and his head snapped to the window. Upon seeing her, his tense face relaxed and he leaned back on the pillows sighing.

"Good morning," he said, looking more closely at her, seeing her fully clothed. His eyes fell on the cases that sat packed by the door. His face was unreadable as he looked at them for a moment, and then he sat up and swung his legs over the bed, presenting her with his back.

"I'll be ready presently," he said, his voice cold. "Am I preparing for a voyage to New York?" he asked.

"No. Thank you, Lord Lucian. I have thought on it. It is a very kind offer... but I cannot accept."

He stood, and without turning to face her, gathered his things, went to the door, and closed it behind him.

Caroline turned back to the window, her serene posture hiding the panic she felt inside.

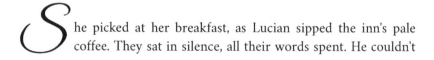

Lucian threw on his clothes, with little care for how the blood and general disarray made him look like a wild man. His anger and helplessness choked him. Her words rang in his hand, snapping the last shred of hope that he was holding on to. Not only would he be saying goodbye to her in a matter of hours, but she was gladly sailing off into danger, and a future where she would probably marry Lee. How would he go on without her? Not counting the wrath of Silus when he returned without his heiress, his father, he knew, would spend the remainder of his life finding ways to punish him for his failure, but worse, he knew that there would be nothing left to punish, as you cannot torment someone who has no happiness, and you cannot break someone who has no hope.

She was about to walk away from him, and he was about to let her.

He clenched his fists and again fought the overwhelming urge to go next door and drag her home with him. She was mere feet away, and soon there would be a vast turbulent ocean parting them. She cared about him, he could tell, even though the very fact of it bewildered him. He turned to the wall, and in his frustration, slammed his fist into the hard plaster. The pain sobered him, and he let his fists free against it, again and again, allowing the pain to ground him, to calm his urges to react rashly. He took deep, ragged breaths, seeing his blood smeared on the wall, and glanced down at his hands. The knuckles of both hands were bloody, the toughened skin broken. He turned and dropped his hands into the pitcher of cold water, feeling it burn through the cuts, as the water slowly turned pink. He did not want this version of himself to be her last image of him.

She picked at her breakfast, as Lucian sipped the inn's pale coffee. They sat in silence, all their words spent. He couldn't keep his eyes off her, aware that each passing second may be his last to look upon her. She was remote, her eyes full of unspoken things.

"Let me see your ticket," he said abruptly, leaning forward and holding his hand out for it. She looked at him warily.

"Why? What will you do to it?" she asked, slowly, retrieving it from its place in the dresser, and handing it over to him. Tensing as he opened it and read it through.

"You are in one of the best cabins, that is good. However, I will still need to board with you, and speak with the captain," he said squarely, handing her ticket back to her, and turning toward her luggage.

"Why?" She slipped the ticket into her reticule.

"He needs to know who his most important passenger is," Lucian said shortly, already planning how he would impress upon the captain the need to keep Caroline safe and unharmed. He looked up and caught her gaze, soft on him.

"Thank you," she murmured sweetly.

"Please– do not thank me now. We both know that I am not deserving of it." Suddenly, he stood up, grabbing his gloves, and looked down at her. "We should depart," he said, watching as she collected herself, and stood, breathing deeply, she seemed nervous.

Lucian called a man, directed her cases to be taken, and waited for her, each moment agonisingly slow. When she arrived with a soft smile, he was surprised as she slipped her arm through his, and they made their way outside. The cases were already on their way to the ship that would carry Caroline to New York and they slowly followed them, along the busy dock. She picked up one of his hands and looked up at him in askance.

"What happened?"

He shook off her question and kept walking. Whenever he thought to speak, it stuck in his throat. He was afraid of what would come out. Afraid he would beg and plead and her memory of him would be nothing more than a pitiable creature on the docks that had humiliated himself as she watched the place where she had experienced such pain fall away forever.

They fell silent, sharing a look for an uncountable length of time. The wind whipped around them, pulling at Caroline's hair, and birds cried overhead. A sound from the ship signalled passengers to board.

They embarked on the ship together, and once on it, Lucian made free with his title and military rank to gain a chance to speak to the captain.

❀

*C*aroline stood looking out at the sea. Home, Virginia, was so close only a day ago. Now... well, now she didn't know. Lucian had been very careful with her, not to touch her, not to get too close. He had been patient, and gentle. He showed no signs of trickery or deception, only of pain and loss and longing. How could she be sure? Was he right now arranging with the captain for some way to stay on the ship, or perhaps would he try to snatch her at the last moment, just as the ship was leaving, when his emotions became the master of him?

"Will I ever see this face again?" Lucian's unsteady voice surprised her from her reverie, and she turned to find him standing next to her at the bow, his gaze burning into hers. His hand reached up to cup her cheek gently.

"Whatever happens after you leave here, know that you can always call on me, should you need help... should you need anything at all." He took a moment and swallowed, and she saw that it was an effort for him to do so - too much of his heart had gathered there. "I love you, Caroline," he said softly. "Do not be confused by the things that I have done. By the things that Lee has done, or his father. You are, with no fortune at all, the most remarkable, most compassionate, most beautiful, wisest and bravest woman that I have ever met, and you are deserving of love and devotion. I am sorry," his voice thickened, "that I have not always treated you so. I have been a selfish animal."

The whistle of the ship sounded again, and Caroline jumped, nerves writhing in her stomach, heart splayed and naked in Lucian's hands. He breathed out leaned in closer and planted the gentlest kiss upon her forehead. Pulling back, he searched her face for one last time and caught her eyes.

"Good luck, my love. May the world give you every single good thing that you deserve." He stood for a moment, still, then he gathered himself, took off his hat, made a deep bow, and then turned on his heel, and made his way over the ramp and off the ship back to the docks as

Caroline watched his every step, feeling each foot fall in her chest as if it was the beat of her heart.

She wanted a moment to herself, to turn again to the sea, to look out over the water toward home one last time, and in that peace, make a choice. But she did not. Her voice ripped from her throat as if pulled out against her will.

"Lucian!" She screamed.

And she ran.

CHAPTER 7

*L*ucian walked as if in a daze off the ship and into the crowd. He thought to walk straight to his horse and ride until he dropped, or if not, walk straight into the sea, but he could not. He would still be able to see her from the docks, and he would not squander those last moments of her to pay homage to his emotions. He fought through the throngs to find a place where he could see her, and when finally he spotted her blue bonnet, he looked down to see a look on her face that he had never seen there before. She opened her mouth and screamed, and it was his name.

She began to run, and so did he, shoving his way through the crowd as best he could, gripped with fear, confusion. He yelled back to her, over the heads of so many that he was sure she could not hear, but it didn't stop him. The crowd seemed to work against him, a wall sometimes, a moving creature at others, keeping him from her. Then finally he got to the ramp to the ship and she was there.

"Caroline? What is it?" he asked, grabbing her gloved hand. They were both breathing hard, and she took a moment to collect herself.

Her eyes looked so green in the sun that struck the water before it shone back at them. They widened, and he thought he saw the black center of them stretch slightly as she stared directly into him, pinning him there with some unsaid, unreadable emotion that he could not understand.

In her other hand, she held her ticket. She looked down at it, and then for a searching second scanned his eyes, and then she ripped the thing right down the middle.

Lucian looked at her, his mouth agape. He watched her wordlessly as she ripped it another time, and another, and then let the pieces flutter away in the wind. They both watched them fly. When he looked back to her, her eyes were trained on him and filled with something that clutched at the very soul of him.

"Take me home," she whispered. Tears shone in her eyes and she reached out for his other hand, grasping it in her own. Confused and stunned, he stared at her mutely.

"Do you mean…"

"Yes," she smiled, and nodded.

Finally, he raised her hand to his lips, and kissed the back reverently, his eyes squeezed shut. Taking a deep breath, he lowered her hand, and moved it to his chest, over his heart, and spoke sincerely.

"Caroline… I will become the man you deserve, I promise you. If it takes the rest of my days," he whispered.

"I will hold you to that."

"Are you certain? Are you sure?" he asked, worry gathering his brow.

"I am decided." She nodded again for emphasis, and then a wide smile broke out across her perfect face. Lucian grabbed her in his arms, and spun her, as he laughed and held on as tight as he might without crushing her.

The whistle sounded again, and they broke their embrace.

"I'd better hurry to get your trunks. Wait for me there - I'll not be a moment."

Lucian felt as though he was flying. He ordered for the luggage to be unloaded and waited impatiently for it by the water, his gaze returning to Caroline constantly. He could see her, gazing out to sea, lost in thought. He could have run all the way there. His face hurt for the smile that pulled across it, so wide and unrelentingly happy that he felt like a fool, and decided that he did not care.

She had offered him a second chance. It was more than he had expected and far more than he deserved. Caroline would be his wife. The thought of it consumed him alive.

"Ashford," a deep voice cut through his thoughts and he turned toward it. Stiffening he saw his would-be assassin hidden in the shadows of another ship, holding his bandaged hand against his chest, hat pulled low across his bandaged head. Lucian glanced back at Caroline, wary of a plot, and then around the nearby crowd, and darkened corners.

"Don't worry yourself. I'm alone," the man said.

"What do you want? Your plan has failed, she is not going to New York, she is returning to London, with me. You can report that back to Mr Lee with my well-wishes, and the threat of my pistol should he ever wish to renew his interest in my wife." The man narrowed his eyes at him, leaning against the ropes, then chuckled darkly.

"Don't recognise me, do ya? I figure you owe me something, for the trouble you've caused me. Your father never mentioned being brutalised," he said, lifting his hand, and Lucian suddenly felt cold run through his bones. The flicker of recognition that he had first felt when he saw the man, and had dismissed, now flamed back into life.

"I do not know you," he said shortly.

"Oh, but I know you..." the man said. The cases were loaded onto the cart, and Caroline was waiting. Turning back to the man, Lucian sneered.

"I highly doubt it. And I care not. Get out of my sight before I finish last night's job."

"Oh, but I think you do care, Ashford. And you owe me something, also I can't 'ave you returning 'ome and not thanking your father."

"Thanking my father for what?" he asked, unwilling to accept the understanding which had already hit him.

"For pushing your reluctant bride into your arms, you fool."

"What are you talking about?" Lucian demanded. He already knew the answer, had already placed the man's hateful face in his father's study.

"It was all rubbish, weren't it. Everything I said. Clearly, the other fellow's the better man," the man said, laughing now at the expression on Lucian's face. "That's why you needed a trick to catch her."

Lucian glanced back at Caroline, seeing her start toward him. He felt panic explode in his chest.

"Unless you want me to 'ave a little 'eart to 'eart with your fiance, then you'd better pay up... the ship's not left yet, plenty of room for one more," the man said menacingly. Caroline called his name, close now, as he frantically pulled his billfold from his pocket and threw money at the man.

The man picked up the money and started to walk away. He gave one last crooked smile and disappeared into the throng, leaving Lucian speechless and frozen to the spot.

Lucian looked out over the murky water of the docks, his mind reeling. The ship to New York had finally finished loading, and the passengers were gathered along the railing to wave goodbye to those remaining on dry land. The ship let out short blasts of the horn, each one felt like an accusation.

Silus had manipulated them, and there was no doubt that the plot had influenced Caroline's decision to stay. He had time still to tell her... to give her back her choice, a genuine choice, a choice untainted by his father's lies. Now, he stood watching the ship getting ready to depart. There was still time.

His conscience writhed and wrestled with the information. He knew what was right, there was no doubt. But, his heart held onto her face, her words: *Take me home.*

His panic started to wear off, and cold certainty settled over him as he looked at the ship.

Turning, he saw her, almost reaching him now, smiling with an uncertain tilt to her lips.

"Is there a problem?" she asked, but he shook his head, silently forcing a smile to his lips.

"No, nothing. Let us depart," he said, scanning the crowd, the lies a bitter poison in his mouth.

"*R*ebecca, father wishes to see you," Wesley said softly, as he sat gently down on his sister's bed. She didn't stir, and he smoothed his fingers through her long chestnut hair, so rich and lustrous that it almost managed to hide her red and mottled skin. He brushed it back, and Rebecca's eyes fluttered open and looked at him, instantly filling with tears again.

"How could he? How *could* he ever do such a monstrous, grotesque, hideous, inhuman thing?"

"Becca..." he sighed. "You are not wrong. I confess, I do not know," and continued to stroke her hair. "I believe he thought she cared for him, if it makes any difference to you." She shook her head, violently.

"This is my fault. I never should have taken Eva away. Caroline will never speak to me again," Rebecca cried as she buried her face in the covers again.

"It is no more your fault that it is mine. We all of us feel guilty for what happened. If you are upset, blame Lucian. Lord knows I have had some strong words with him myself. Becca, I know you are upset just now, but father is waiting. You shouldn't keep him," Wesley urged, and Rebecca heard the unsaid words waiting just below the surface. He was right. Her father would only grow angrier if he was made to wait, and who knows how things might take a turn. Rebecca pushed herself upright. Taking a deep breath, she pulled her fingers through her hair, trying to restore order. She nodded numbly and stood, going to her nightstand, she splashed some water on her salt burned eyes and blinked them. Her face was a mess, but there was little she could do for it.

Afraid of waiting anymore, she shot Wesley a look of pained gratitude and left the room. She hurried downstairs to the door of her father's study and steadied herself. Her father hated to see her upset and was angry when she lost her composure.

Knocking gently, she steeled herself for what was to come.

"Come in." He was standing at a wall of shelves, hunting for a volume, and he looked up as she entered.

"Rebecca, dear. Sit down. Have you been crying?" he asked disapprovingly. She shook her head, tensing as she felt him walk behind her, coming around to his seat behind the desk. "Just up from a nap, father."

"Do not lie to me, child. Have you been crying?" he bit out each word and she nodded, nervousness beginning to override her grief and guilt. "Well, it is a pity when childish games end up with adult consequences," he remarked dryly, studying his daughter before him. "Well, what do you have to say to explain your actions?" he asked, his tone already implying he found her explanation lacking.

"There is nothing I can say, father."

"True enough, I shall speak in that case. I have realised that this childish action is not your fault. It is mine. You are too old to still be at home. You need your own home, your own children, your own responsibilities. It is a shame no suitor has come forward yet, though I would thank your brother Lucian for that. Who would want to be aligned to our family when he causes us nothing but embarrassment?" he seemed to be enjoying himself, she thought with distaste. "However, I do hope, at least his situation will be resolved by this whole mess if he can ever manage to do anything right for this family."

"What do you mean, father?"

"I mean, Lucian is going to be wed that little dark thing and her fortune will help to stem the losses of our foreign investments."

"But – Caroline..." Rebecca started and trailed off as she saw her father's warning look.

"It is unfortunate for your friend, but I am sure she shall forgive you eventually. In any event, we must get down to discussing your situation."

"My situation?" Rebecca echoed meekly.

"Yes. You are to get married, my dear daughter. Now, is there anyone that you would like to consider?" She bit her lip and shook her head. She knew her father would probably never let her have what she wanted now, and she refused to give him the information he could use to torture her with, or torture Isaac.

"In that case, I will be inviting some colleagues to dine for the next few weeks. Good men, some widowers, some bachelors. You shall take your pick, my sweet," Silus said cloyingly. "You see how I love you?" She shook her head. She knew that this would come, she had prepared for it. He did love her, in his own way, she knew, but even too much sun can wilt a flower.

❦

*T*he carriage swayed and Caroline swayed with it. She had given up trying to sleep, feeling far too nervous about returning to London. The brooding man sitting opposite her was not helping. Lucian had been quiet and introspective the whole journey, and she had tired of trying to make conversation with him. He seemed determined to sit in silence, stewing in his thoughts, and she was left to amuse herself. Rather than the relaxing, carefree company she had expected, the potentially romantic time alone with new circumstances, she was finding it quite the opposite.

Sitting across from her, his heavy brow lowered pensively, his cornflower eyes hooded, he seemed to emanate some forbidding power. She felt his eyes on her often, but when she met them, he simply looked away, still lost in his thoughts. It occurred to her then, that he had pursued her so purposefully and so single-mindedly, she wondered if the renowned bachelor had truly considered the implications. He would soon be a married man, held to a higher standard of respectability and accountability. She wondered if he was already mourning the loss of his freedom and wild ways. The game was over, the fox caught. Her stomach tightened at the prospect that perhaps he was not planning on ending those ways at all... but she couldn't quite believe it.

She did not know who this was that she sat across from now. She had been rash. A decision that would shape, from this day forward, every moment of her life, irrevocably- perhaps she had been a fool letting her heart decide what her head should have.

Though, when pushed to the wire, when the test had come, he had been self-sacrificing. She held onto that thought. That, more than anything, gave her hope that he was not wholly the monster he had shown her many times, that he was not so lost.

For, if he could be that man on the docks, the one she glimpsed in his moments of selflessness and love; if he could hold on to that man, then could they not still learn to be happy?

❀

*L*ucian felt her eyes on him and he dropped her gaze. He was afraid she would see his shame written plainly in his eyes, afraid that one proper look, with those eyes of hers, and he would confess everything. He would admit his selfishness had won in the end, his damn fear had taken away all the efforts he had made to be a better man for her, and he loathed himself for it.

She was easily convinced to travel through the night in an effort to minimise the worry to John and Margaret Fairfax. She seemed to want no one to know of her attempt to leave and he was happy enough with it. It would be simpler. Soon, they would be married. Then, perhaps, he could relax, tell her the truth... she deserved to know, of course, but he could not take any chances before their vows.

Closing his eyes, he feigned sleep, and let his mind pull him down into the writhing black depths of his guilt and insecurity.

❀

Caroline woke to the feel of soft arms around her, comforting and familiar.

"Eva!" she said waking suddenly at the revelation. "The sun is not yet risen. How did you get here so soon?"

"Katherine sent word to the Taylor's townhouse as soon as you arrived home, and the horses could not bring me fast enough." Caroline grabbed her by the middle and squeezed her until they both laughed, teary-eyed.

"You're a married woman now, Mrs Taylor," Caroline said, refusing to let her go. Eva blushed prettily. "Are you happy?"

"Oh, Caroline. So happy that I cannot speak it," Eva answered, her voice thick with emotion.

"Well then, I am happy and content in every possible way."

"But, Caroline, you must know that I hadn't any idea that any of... what happened, would happen. I cannot..." Eva broke off, tears began to roll down her cheek.

"Shhhh," Caroline hushed softly and hugged her again. "Do not fret. All is well."

"How can you say so? When I think what happened, what he... what they..." her voice choked her and she rose a hand to her mouth to hold in the sobs. "This is because I ran. I left you," she forced out through her tears.

"No no. Of course not. What happened was the act of two desperate people. It was a cruel and painful trick, a betrayal, but I will learn to forgive them both in time, I daresay."

"But, what has happened? Is it true that you are to marry him?" Caroline looked up and shook her head. At the sound of the words said aloud, her stomach roiled with nerves and worry, and her heart twisted with the tender memory of all she and Lucian had shared in the past few days. Everything else seemed so long ago.

"But why? You do not have to. He is a villain, Caroline. He cannot have you!"

"I know that I do not have to, but so much has happened. He loves me, Eva, I know he does. And my heart too has turned," Caroline said softly. "I tried to run away from him, and found that my heart would not let me."

"So you… truly care for him?"

"I do."

Eva sat silent for a while, wiping that last stray, silent tears with the back of her hand. She seemed to be trying to understand and accept what her brain told her could not be true. "Well," she said, and after a moment more, "I must have a word with Katherine, for I believe she is already planning your second escape. There is to be a highwayman this time, and a kidnapping." They shared a quiet laugh.

"No, there is no need. I have my hands full with just the one rogue, thank you."

"Oh!" Eva said, shocked by the unintended salaciousness, and they laughed again.

"Enough of this silliness!" Caroline said. "Tell me what happened in Gretna Green! I heard that Lord Charles gave chase. Did he not catch you?"

"He did. But his concern was for Lady Rebecca only. He never had any intention of challenging the wedding. He has been rather kind, actually, despite his disapproval of our methods."

"I am not surprised to hear it. He was kind to me also. And the ceremony?"

"I'll tell you more when you've had some sleep. But, it was small. Quiet. Perfect," Eva answered, with a new softness in her voice, as she fingered her new wedding band.

"And your health. I've been so worried that with all the commotion-"

"No, I've been just fine. It's true that there was much excitement, but Eli has known me since I was a little girl, and he's lived through several of my episodes, and somehow has learned how to calm me before things get too frightening. Also, if I'm honest, I think merely having him around soothes me, makes me feel protected, safe."

In her own way, Caroline understood that feeling. She'd felt it for Lucian when she was attacked that first night, and she felt it in Portsmouth.

"Well, Eli is perfect for you in every way," Caroline smiled, and Eva shook her head, ringlets shaking, her own smile warming her pale face for a moment before worry gathered at her brow.

"But, Caroline, what will happen between you and Katherine?" Eva asked,

"In truth, I cannot say," Caroline sighed, and buried her face into her sister's shoulder. "I have tried to forgive her. I know that she did what she did out of love for you, and she has come some way in trying to protect me too this past week. It is not fair perhaps to pardon one villain and condemn the other. I just..." Caroline shook her head, emotion choking her. "I just trusted her, loved her, with my whole heart. You two have been my sisters in every way, my saviors, everything that is precious to me, and I could never have dreamed that she could do such a thing. She has broken my heart, Eva. I just cannot seem to let go of the pain." Eva lifted her hand and stroked Caroline's hair until she closed her eyes.

"You take all the time you need, dear one."

"My goodness! Caroline, Mademoiselle du Blanc has arrived," Margaret Fairfax shrieked. "Tidy your hair, girl. Where are the ribbons I gave you? Lady Rebecca has come too." Caroline was still sitting by the fire with her book and Margaret pulled her from her chair, dropping her book and losing Caroline's page, and started fussing frantically over Caroline's dress and pinching her cheeks without so much as a warning.

"Well, come along! What girl could fail to be excited at having her wedding dress made by the most sought-after designer in all London, I do not know," Margaret chided, pulling the book from her hands and hovering over her. Caroline pushed a smile to her lips, but feared it would not fool Margaret for long, she knew her too well. "Please, Caroline. Do try to look excited, for Lady Rebecca's sake, if nothing else," Margaret said a little more softly this time. Caroline nodded and rearranged the pins losing their battle with her heavy hair.

In truth, she could not be less excited about being attended by the infamous designer. Barely two days had passed since she had returned from Portsmouth, and she was still weary from the road. To say that it had been exhausting would be an understatement of the highest order, and she was quite spent from the experience. But, as she did not wish to worry the Fairfaxes, she tried her best not to sleep solidly from sunrise to sunset, and to cheer her mood a bit, or at least learn to fake it.

It was true, also, that she did not want to disappoint Rebecca. Upon her return she had received a letter from Rebecca, informing her of her intention to call and to bring with her Mademoiselle De Blanc, a designer who never made a dress for any girl who approached unintroduced by a current or previous client. As Rebecca was a client favourite of hers, she had decided Caroline would have nothing but the best for her wedding. Rebecca had written eloquently, and sorrowfully, convincing Caroline that she had not been complicit in the scheme to force Lucian and her together. She claimed that while she would not lie about the fact that she wished to have Caroline as part of her family, and someone to stand by her brother's side, she had never anticipated Lucian taking such cruel and drastic steps. She was truly regretful and blamed herself if Caroline was now doomed into a marriage against her will.

Caroline had replied, trying to relieve her of her guilt. She urged her to forgive herself and put the blame firmly where it belonged... on Lucian's and Katherine's shoulders. At the thought of Lucian, her mind was drawn to the last time she had seen him.

"*L*et me do the explaining. I shall bear the brunt of their displeasure, and the consequences," Lucian said, escorting her to the door.

She looked up at him in surprise. It was the most he had said to her in their mad dash back to London, and she had half thought him struck mute by her decision. She nodded wordlessly and allowed him to lead her into the Fairfaxes' townhouse.

What a strange few days it had been: Lucian, as distant as a stranger passing on the street- feeling like the closeness that they had shared had been some fever dream. And for herself, the finality of her decision had continued to be felt, as though a large stone had been cast into a still lake, and her emotions were still caught in the ripples.

Her betrothed was not helping the situation, with his distance and silence. For once, he was acting like a complete gentleman and she almost missed his warm smiles, indecent jokes and longing eyes. Perhaps the chase of her was what had held him, a man used to getting what he wanted, a man not usually denied. Now, with his prize in his hands, perhaps his interest had waned. These thoughts flitted through her mind at night, as she tossed and turned.

Knocking on the door of the study, Caroline had stilled, her breath baited and she felt nerves roll through her.

"Come in," John's voice was muffled, and she glanced nervously at Lucian before she pushed open the door. John sat behind a desk groaning with papers and books, and his eyes showed his relief at seeing her there, closely followed by surprise, as Lucian had followed her into the room, closing the door softly behind him.

"Well, Caroline," he sighed. "I confess not to know the full extent of your actions, the past week, you can thank Katherine for that. I do not like to imagine how reckless and dangerous a plan you must have had to leave in such a way," he looked over the rim of his glasses at her, brow drawn together in stern worry, as he used to occasionally when she was a girl. "But," he exhaled more disappointment, "I am relieved to see you safe, unharmed and home at last. I suppose as you are nearly a married woman, you are too grown for me to scold."

"Thank you Mr Fairfax. I am sorry if I caused you to worry..." she trailed off, unable to think of what to say.

"What matters is this wedding next still weeks away. It is not too late to call the whole thing off. You need only say the word," he said earnestly, ignoring Lucian, whose face had adopted a glower, his whole body as tense as a spring.

Caroline took a deep breath, steadying herself, and cast a glance to him, seeing his hands, still scarred across the knuckles, curled in balls on his knees.

She could feel the hostility at John's question, and she glanced at his face, with a clenched jaw, and a muscle tightening slightly under the strain.

"Sadly, my reputation would not stand up to further insult, I imagine," she joked awkwardly.

"If that is all that concerns you, my dear, then do not proceed for society's sake. You owe them nothing Caroline, and you are probably a great deal too good, and too rich, to be thought of badly forever," John said. "Your options will be diminished, of course, significantly perhaps, but not lost completely."

Caroline looked toward Lucian. His panic and anger were clearly boiling close to the surface. For a moment, their eyes met, and she considered him. After that endless moment, she turned back to John.

"No, I have made a promise, and I shall go through with it." Lucian relaxed back in his seat.

"That is hardly a declaration that warms my heart, my dear. I should think most women dream of a match that is not merely... obligation, while few are truly lucky enough to have the choice."

Caroline felt her blood pound in her cheeks as she realised that John was waiting for more from her, some reassurance that she would not be unhappy in her forced circumstance. Taking a deep breath, she pushed the words out, refusing to notice the way she held Lucian's rapt attention.

"I know we find ourselves in an unorthodox situation; however, it does not mean that some understanding cannot be reached, that eventually... some mutual emotion cannot develop," she said, her face determined, and both of John's eyebrows rose a fraction.

"And you, Lord Lucian, what are your feelings?" John prompted.

"My feelings remain unchanged," he said at them both.

"Very well. If you are sure, the wedding will go ahead as planned. Lord Lucian, I believe, due to the unusual circumstances, and the damage which has already been caused by your... overzealous courting of Miss Lesage, that all appearances should be kept up for the remaining time. As I assume that you have just spent some time together, there will probably be no need of it before the wedding. Do we understand each other?" he asked firmly, and Lucian sighed at the chastisement.

"Yes, sir, we do. I believe I shall have many things to attend to in preparation for married life, and Miss Lesage will be extremely busy with wedding preparations... if she chooses to be involved," he said, leaving the suggestion to hang in the air. She made him wait as she took her time to answer.

"Yes, I shall be involved," she said quietly and saw a small smile finally break through Lucian's mood.

After leaving the study, they walked in silence to the hall, where he stopped and turned to her.

"Well, I do believe this shall be our last meeting, before..."

"Before I become your wife," she finished, meeting his eyes.

"Indeed, though it sounds much sweeter when you say it. I am very glad that you will be involved with the preparations. My sister says that it is something that all little girls dream of. I want you to have everything you desire, nothing is too much... please," he said, and she gave him a half-smile.

"I do not have extravagant tastes, and I fear I shan't be able to keep up with the expectations of London society," she admitted honestly.

"Caroline, you surpass expectations with your every breath, society will see that, and it matters not to me what they think. If it truly troubles you, my sister would love to aid you in every way possible."

"Society does not matter... rules do not matter... may I ask what does matter to you? I have yet to find something," she said ruefully, her smile freezing on her lips as he gently took her hands, peeling the soft glove back off one wrist and pressing a light kiss there.

"It has been a fairly recent discovery for myself also - a certain lady: outspoken, brave, direct...utterly captivating," he murmured and she flushed. "As for the wedding, I will settle for your attendance... it is more than I deserve, and I wish you to know that I am well aware of that fact. And I mean to change it," he said, releasing her hand, he pulled on his hat and gloves. Stopping at the opening door he turned back.

"Miss Lesage, I look forward to our next meeting, more than you can imagine," he said, bowing, leaving her standing there in the hall, her wrist held to her chest where her heart thudded.

*N*ow, following through on her promise to be involved, she was waiting to be prodded and pinched, stuck with pins for the next few hours. She had little interest in wearing a needlessly ornate, or terribly fashionable dress for the wedding, and given the extremely short notice, she wondered what kind of concoction this woman could pull off. She meant what she had said when she told Lucian she wasn't used to extravagance, and honestly, it was a little intimidating. She had no idea how to act, what to ask for and she hoped terribly that she would not seem like a country bumpkin to these Parisian seamstresses.

A footman arrived at the door, and Mademoiselle du Blanc entered behind Rebecca. After introductions were made, the seamstress bossily ordered Caroline upstairs, where her attendants would undress her and prepare her for the artist's arrival.

Nervously, Caroline started toward the door, and looking back, caught the look of disappointment from Rebecca. She had been nervous and fidgety, no doubt waiting for some time alone to speak or some sign that Caroline did not blame her.

"May Lady Rebecca accompany me?" she asked and saw Rebecca's face light up.

"If she wishes," Margaret supplied, looking back at the swatches the French woman had brought with her.

Rebecca approached her with trepidation, and Caroline pulled her forward, linking arms with her, and smiled as she pulled her up the stairs.

"Thank you.. for coming today," she said and was cut off by the sudden hug Rebecca enveloped her in. Caroline relaxed and felt the relief of her friend begin to warm that place in her belly where all her misgivings had taken up residence.

"Caroline, I am so sorry for setting into motion actions that have affected you so dearly. Can you ever forgive me?" Rebecca said, leaning away.

"Rebecca, I have already told you, I do not blame you. Your brother and Katherine are the only ones to blame."

"Caroline, if you do not wish to marry him, he will not force you... I believe he cares for you."

"You are kind, but it is too late, the decision has been made," she said and saw the torment in Rebecca's eyes. Turning away, she summoned her courage and spoke softly. "I am not unaffected by him, it would be wrong for you to think me so. I... do care for him," she admitted.

"I am so very glad to hear it. Well, now that I know you are not being sent to the gallows, we can start preparing for this wedding properly!" she said brightly, opening the door to let in the dressers. Caroline looked uncertainly at them as they started stripping her off her clothes.

A knock sounded at the door, and Eva stepped in, a smile already on her face. Her heart warmed at the smiles Rebecca and Eva exchanged, seeing that their trip had indeed brought them closer.

"Eva! Come and help us, I am quite clueless when it comes to clothes, as you know," Caroline said warmly.

"Nonsense, few people know what suits them better than you, Caroline," Eva said softly, looking around at all the extra people with wide eyes.

"I must admit this is a first for me, and I am quite overwhelmed by the whole thing," Caroline whispered to them as she stepped out of her dress.

"Worry not, dear sister. I shall take care of everything. You will be an Ashford soon," Rebecca declared with a large, contented smile.

Caroline smiled to Rebecca. She had begun to feel a bit like an Ashford, when Wesley had dropped in earlier that week unannounced. Caroline had called for tea and sandwiches, and they had talked, Wesley trying to make Caroline laugh, and studying her face carefully, it seemed to her.

"*Well, this is all rather English, Miss Lesage of Virginia and the southern wilds," he said to Caroline as she poured his tea into the fine bone china with its delicate, gold gilded floral pattern. "You've become quite the English rose in these short months."*

"What must you think of Virginia, Lord Wesley?" she smiled warmly. "I assure you that we are well supplied with tea."

"Do not attempt to deceive me! Why, I expect there are no tea and sandwiches to be found in all of the Americas, and that one can only drink strong moonshine in a saloon filled with dusty cowboys after a hot afternoon of gold prospecting, wrestling alligators, and driving steamboats. That is fairly accurate, is it not?" Caroline laughed and felt some of her worry lift.

"I am sorry to say this, but-"

"No! Please, I beg of you, Miss Lesage. Do not spoil my image, because that is the America of my childhood dreams. I have always longed to go there and ride with cowboys and drive herds of cattle in a massive hat."

Caroline could not help but snort at that. The image of the perfectly

polished and dapper Lord Wesley on a cattle ranch was even more delicious
than the sandwitches.

"Of course you are right, my Lord, as you always are, and I think you shall
look marvelous in a cowboy hat as broad as a wagon wheel and as tall as a
man."

"I am convinced of it!" he clapped and smiled, chuckling with her. But, then
his smile faltered, and after a quiet moment he leaned forward in his chair
pinning her with a concerned look. "I must confess that it is good to see you
laugh, Miss Lesage. I have been very worried about you these past weeks. Do
tell me... are you well? Are you happy?"

"I am. Thank you for asking. It warms my heart to know that you have
been thinking of me."

"Caroline? Is this what you want?" he asked more earnestly than he had
ever spoken to her. "Because, if it is not, I shall-"

"No, Wesley," she stopped him, her hand moving to his. "This is my deci-
sion. I care for Lucian. I hope that we can make each other happy." His eyes
softened, and he shook his head in disbelief.

"You are the best person I know, to have such a forgiving heart. He is... a
good man, for all his tempers and brash behaviour. He loves you, I know that
he does. And once Lucian has set his heart on someone, he will move heaven
and earth for them."

*W*henever Caroline would begin to fret over Lucian's cold
behaviour, she would remind herself of these words, and
be comforted. She was glad that Wesley had come, and that Rebecca
was holding her hand through all the difficult planning. She began to
feel the support and love of her family growing larger to encompass
new members, and her heart growing larger to make room for them.

*E*li Taylor felt as though fate had shone on him. Meeting with
his father and John Fairfax upon their return to London, he
had been fearful that Eva could yet be ripped from him somehow. He
was even more apprehensive of Lucian Ashford's actions, someone not
accustomed to being crossed. The man was dangerous and unpre-

dictable and the thought of him near Eva made Eli's blood boil. However, upon his return, he had been shocked with the ease in which the two families had accepted their hasty wedding, though Margaret Fairfax had made it clear more than once that she held his lack of title against him.

He and Eva had moved into the Taylor's townhouse as he made preparations to acquire his own property. He had learned that Lord Ashford would not be demanding satisfaction for his broken engagement, in fact, he himself would soon be married. The woman to whom he would be married was the only dark cloud on Eli's horizon. Growing up with Caroline, he thought of her more as a sister than a mere acquaintance, and he was sincerely worried for her happiness. How the whole torrid arrangement had come about, he had been horrified to learn from Katherine, who had the grace to hang her head in shame over her part.

"Good afternoon brother, I see *Mrs* Taylor has allowed you from her sight long enough to get dressed today," Isaac said with a smirk as he entered the parlour.

"Isaac, Eva is your sister now, and not to be made sport of, unless you fancy having your ears boxed, the way you used to," he lunged forward slightly, hands at the ready.

"Yes, I am so bored that I might welcome an ear boxing just to break the monotony."

"Well, perhaps you should get out of the house more- go and visit some of your lady admirers, I am sure they have all felt your absence keenly."

"I do not find myself inclined to call on them today," Isaac said moodily.

"Nor did you yesterday, nor the day before. And, I will wager," his voice sang up tauntingly, "nor tomorrow either, dearest brother. These are not the actions of London's newest flirt in residence. I begin to worry over your health. Whatever can have affected you so?" Eli asked as if asking a child where his nose went.

"Nothing. I am merely recovering from our trip. Or do you not remember, how you dragged us all across the country because you were too lilly-livered to duel with that Ashford fellow?" He shot out, clearly trying to get some of his own back, but Eli ignored this, to his irritation.

"Or... recovering from the particular company of a particular lady on said trip, perhaps?" Eli batted his eyelashes. Isaac looked over at him with a quelling look.

"Do not speak of what you do not know," he murmured and threw a cushion at his face. Eli's arm shot up just in time, a reflex perfected with a lifetime of practice.

"Well, I do know you, and I know there are few things that could keep you away from a beautiful woman, such as Lady Rebecca. I would never have believed that you bedded down in the stables over taking your chances with her unless I had seen it with my own eyes."

"And what would you have me do?" he burst out, frustration making his voice tight. "Disrespect her so? A woman like Rebecca is too good for the likes of me, and I would not offend her by hoisting my attentions upon her without invitation, and give her the tedious job of having to refuse them."

"And, you're sure that there has been no such invitation? I thought I saw invitations flying left and right when we were in the carriage. In fact, I was afraid of getting knocked over and pushed out of the carriage as you leapt into one another's arms."

"Enough. This is idiotic. I have things to do. Perhaps I shall call on some of my acquaintances after all. I am in desperate need of interesting company, and it seems that there is none at all to be found here," Isaac said, standing and shooting a last cushion at Eli, this time hitting him square in the face.

🍀

*K*atherine sat on her bed with a cheek resting against her fist, pulling her face into a misshapen, lopsided grimace, which was most unladylike.

"Katherine Margarita Fairfax!" Margaret trilled, snapping Katherine smartly on the head with the latest London scandal sheets. "Stop that this instant. You'll make wrinkles!"

"And what do I care about wrinkles?" she huffed and flung herself back against her pillows in a dramatic display of ennui. Margaret gasped.

"Well, what has gotten into you?"

"It's Caroline. We have barely spoken since she returned, I do not even know what happened when she was..." she caught herself, "away. What is her plan? And why the hell is she going ahead with her marriage to that monster?"

"I will not have that language in this house, young lady!"

"And now she is upstairs, giggling and laughing with Eva and Rebecca- who is not even her sister - getting fitted for her one and only wedding dress by Mademoiselle du Blanc! And I am sent away," Katherine finished, feeling very sorry for herself, and hating herself in equal measures.

"Katherine, our actions have consequences. It is about time you learned that. Caroline must forgive you as she sees fit, in her own time. It is selfish to push her."

"Ugh. I know," she droned out the last word with a whole lungful of breath. It did nothing to make her feel better.

"Why do we not instead turn our mind to something else?" Margaret said innocently, flipping through the pages. "Something diverting....like marriageable bachelors, for instance."

"What marriageable bachelors? I know of none. I have spent so much time at Blackhill Hall and plotting my own downfall, that I haven't had any time to encourage bachelors of any kind, marriageable or no. Now the season is drawing to an end, and I shall be an old maid for the rest of my life. Untouched! Pitied by all!" Dramatics suited her, she decided.

"Well dear, certainly you have met *some* marriageable bachelors in all these months? What of Lord Charles Ashford?" Katherine's mouth tightened.

"What of him? I haven't seen him since we left the estate, and in truth, I have little desire to do so. He is so... self-righteous. Truly, mother. He is really quite dull. Unforgivably dull," she announced, her voice ringing false even to her own ears.

"Hmmm, is he dear? That comes as a surprise. I did not think it possible to be dull with a face like that one and ten thousand a year."

"*I* am afraid Milady is not at home," a footman announced rather imperiously to Isaac as he stood outside the Ashford's townhouse. He nodded shortly and made to leave, wondering why he had bothered coming at all. Rebecca had probably returned to her frantic social life, their little trip long forgotten, and him along with it. As he reached the doorstep, he heard a low voice calling his name.

"Mr Taylor, to what do we owe this... pleasure?" Silus Ashford's voice boomed and Isaac drew a deep breath and fixed a congenial smile on his face as he turned to see the patriarch of the grand family walking toward him.

"I came to pay my respects to your family, my lord Ashford. I hope I find you well."

"And to see my daughter," Silus stated flatly, sizing Isaac up openly. He turned toward his study and called back over his shoulder, "Come. Join me for a drink."

Settling into a leather armchair in the dark room, Isaac watched as Silus poured two large glasses of brandy, setting one before him, and then took a seat behind his mammoth desk, though Isaac thought it an unnecessary tactic in intimidation when the man would have been just as intimidating in a seat by the fire with his stockinged feet up. He regarded Isaac with a twinkle in his eye, and Isaac felt a flash of unease.

"So. You are the man who whisked my daughter away, hundreds of miles in a carriage, countless inns and places of lowly repute, and helped his brother to wed my son's fiance."

"Well, if stated like that... I hardly dare to own up to it," Isaac laughed nervously.

"How else can it be stated?" Silus asked, with an edge to his voice. Isaac bit his tongue and kept quiet. "Relax, young Mr Taylor, luckily for you, things have turned out for the best. And luckily for your brother. My son may not be skilled at many things, but he is really quite brilliant at exacting revenge, and I believe you would be sat before me in black if Miss Lesage had not appeared," Silus laughed cruelly. Isaac cleared his throat and sipped the strong drink. It felt strange in his mouth at such an early hour, though he was glad now to have it.

"Well, we are a lucky pair then I believe," Isaac said, making his voice light and easy.

"Yes, indeed. Another advantage is the leverage you have handed me over my daughter. You see, it is beyond time that Rebecca was married. She has been stubborn and refused to put her time in at social functions. Yet, now that she is disgraced by connecting herself to this scandal, and the prolonged company of unwed men," he narrowed his eyes, "Rebecca has no choice but to marry," Silus said, watching closely for some reaction which Isaac tried carefully to keep hidden.

"I see. She has made no mention of a suitor to me," he said lightly.

"That is because she has not met him yet," Silus said carelessly, clearly enjoying Isaac's discomfort.

"May I ask who the lucky man shall be?" Isaac asked, his heart pounding uncomfortably. His glass felt like a weight in his hand, and he was not certain his face looked as nonchalant as he hoped.

"Perhaps you should ask again after I have chosen him. Or, you can simply find out for yourself on the wedding day. I shall take particular care over your invitation."

CHAPTER 8

$\mathcal{T}$he carriage wobbled over the country roads, making it impossible to focus on The Mysteries of Udalpho and Caroline began to feel as though she would not mind never to read another book in this fashion again. The past weeks had felt like a never-ending carriage ride over broken roads, her body and mind jostled and bruised, and she longed for some peace and tranquility.

In the distance, she saw the lake that lay before Blackhill Hall come into view. It was calm and serene and reflected the grand house sitting behind it, doubling its size. The sky was a deep blue, and the leaves were beginning to change, turning deep crimson, burnt gold and warm yellow. The air was crisp and brought with it the smells of woodlands and leaf fires burning in the distance. She glanced across the carriage and laughed at what she saw.

They had been joined by Margaret's younger sister, Eva and Katherine's aunt, as well as her husband, who had been travelling in Europe and now had come to visit them in England, the timing of which could not have been more fortunate.

Aunt Frances, as Caroline also called her, was large with child, and she and her husband Virgil would be staying with the Fairfaxes in London to have the baby. Virgil was a horse trader and had amassed quite a fortune. Travelling the world, he sourced the finest specimens and sold them, traded them, and bred them. Since he had married Frances, she had travelled with him, and Caroline enviously wondered at how many countries they pair must have visited together. They seemed to fit so comfortably together.

Frances was sitting, asleep despite the rocking of the carriage, and Virgil had taken this opportunity to lay his head near her stomach, where he was now whispering to his child, his face lighting up in excitement whenever he felt a movement. Caroline laughed at his dancing eyes.

"Laugh not, you may think me ridiculous now, but you shall be next Miss Caroline, and maybe you will not think your own husband such a fool," he said with a grin, though Caroline could not help the way her stomach dropped with disappointment. The scene was a happy one, and it should have raised her spirits, but instead, she fought back a sting of bitterness and disliked herself for it. The cheerfulness she was bombarded with from all sides, made her feel strangely flat in comparison.

As the carriage came to a stop, nerves clutched at her, and she realised that she had arrived here a girl, unmarried, a maiden... and she would leave a married woman.

The other carriages which had been in front of them were already opening, spilling out the Taylors, Fairfaxes, and Rebecca. The Ashford men would remain in London and arrive together the next day, leaving them one night before the wedding. Servants swarmed the courtyard as cases and hat boxes were passed down off the carriages, and footmen started showing everyone to their rooms. Caroline walked slowly after her escort, feeling uneasy as she realised they were taking her to the same rooms that she had been given before. She did not like the thought of facing the memories there.

Taking a deep breath she entered and waited as her cases were unpacked. Her wedding dress would be arriving the next day along with the rest of her marriage wardrobe. Peeling off her gloves and hat, she surveyed the room where Lucian had disgraced her. It was unchanged. And, as she waited for the suffocating memories of the ordeal to drain her of her remaining energy, she found that they did not descend as she thought they would. In fact, seeing how she had spent a good deal of time there, it felt quite homely.

Standing by the window, she couldn't help but glance at Lucian's window, remembering the first time she had seen him there, recovering from his attack, the memory of his longing look, and of soft secrets told, and the smell of warm milk. She turned her attention to the gardens, where she could see preparations being made for the wedding. A knock sounded at the door and she turned toward it eagerly, ready to be drawn out from her own thoughts.

❀

"*T*his game is too rich for my blood, I'm afraid," Charles said as he pushed his chair back from the poker table, grabbing his glass and standing. Lucian glanced up at his older brother, losing interest in the game immediately.

"I'll join you. Excuse me, gentlemen," he said, taking leave of the group. Walking away together, Charles looked at his brother askance.

"Now, Lucian, why walk away from the table with that hand?"

"I have no appetite for gambling tonight, I would rather spend time with my brother," he said tentatively, clapping him on the shoulder. Charles had been furious with him, giving way eventually to distant and disapproving, and Lucian missed his company. He knew he had disappointed Charles most gravely with his behaviour, and he hoped in time, once he saw how happy he would make Caroline, that he would forgive him.

They settled at the bar, watching Wesley trying his hand at roulette, and losing disgracefully.

"I have not forgiven you, you know," Charles said with a tired sigh.

"I know. I will make it up to her. I promise I will, Charles. You will see for yourself how happy she will be."

"I had better." They both sipped side by side for a time, quiet companions. "Have you decided where you shall live?" Charles eventually asked. Lucian swirled the amber liquid of his drink, his only drink so far that night, in its crystal glass.

"I have thought about it, but I want to decide with my wife- it is as much Caroline's decision as mine," he said.

"I am glad to hear it. Does she favour the city? Or country life?"

"I confess I do not know," Lucian said wryly, embarrassed about how little he really knew about the woman he was to wed by the week's end.

"She was happy in the country, at the Hall, I think."

"Will you take her to Westmere?"

"If she wishes. I do not know it is to her tastes."

"Who could fail to love that beautiful place? Does Caroline know of your... unique financial arrangement?"

"No. Not as of yet."

"So, she doesn't know about... father?"

"No, though I am sure she has heard rumours, it is hardly a secret."

"Well, with both your great fortunes combined, you will want for nothing, that is certain."

"Silus wants Caroline's fortune for his speculating," Lucian said, frowning. Charles considered him.

"And you do not?"

"Of course I wish to do what I can for the family, and a good season could mean more secure support for everyone, and for Blackhill. If I were able to put my own money down, you know I would. But I hesitate at the thought of giving away Caroline's parents' money to father, perhaps it is only pride, however," he said, studying his drink.

They sat together in silence, smiling as Wesley cried out for another roulette wheel to be brought, as this one had a personal dislike of him. Lucian saw his father bearing down on them from the corner of his eye and gripped his glass tightly.

"Charles, what kind of celebration is this? It's downright depressing! Where are the women? The drinks?" Silus demanded, swaying slightly on his feet, drink in his hand.

"No women tonight father," Lucian ground out, facing away from the drunken man.

"And may I ask why not? I know this night holds little significance in terms of preventing your voracious appetites, but the occasion should be marked somehow," he clapped him hard across the back of the neck, toying with the thin line always between them. Lucian ground his teeth and stood.

"I believe I have had enough celebrating. I will return home."

"I shall accompany you," Charles said.

"Well, well, whipped by a slip of a girl, and not even yet married, I should have expected as much. You are no Ashford, you have no idea how to treat a wife-" Silus was cut off as Lucian suddenly stormed back toward him and grabbed him by the shirt, hauling him around and bringing his face close to his.

"Like how you treated our mother? That is how a true gentleman acts?" he snarled and felt anger pulse through him as Silus laughed in his face, before matching him nose for nose, his expression menacing.

"That is how a real man acts. A real man understands that a wife is nothing more than a whore you cannot pay to be rid of by morning, and a servant who you must be polite to in public, and yours is no better than the filthy savages she came from," he spat and watched with satisfaction as Lucian's face clouded with rage.

"Lucian," Charles said quietly from Lucian's side.

"Lucian, let's go. It's boring here," Wesley urged, as the men in the gaming room had also stopped their activities and were watching them all intently. "If we sleep off the drink tonight, we will arrive fresher tomorrow," Wesley babbled on hurriedly. Suddenly Lucian let go of his father's shirt and spun around, walking away without a sound.

Charles and Wesley shared a glance.

"Charming, father. I hope you're proud of yourself," Charles scolded, as he and Westley started after Lucian.

"I don't know what you're complaining about," Silus called after them, "Look at all of this extravagance, all I have given him. What more can you ask of me? I treat your mother's bastard better than I do any of my own!"

🌼

The ride to the estate had been exactly what he had needed to brush away the soured memories of the previous night. The countryside was ablaze with autumn and the air was brisk. His father had been delayed and would arrive alone the next day, meaning the ride had been relaxing and he was able to share time with his brothers.

His pulse quickened at the thought of seeing his bride to be. He had thought of little else since he had last seen her. She was constantly in his thoughts, and as he had dealt with all the arrangements for the following few weeks, he could not help but do so with her at the forefront of his mind. He had been constantly on edge, afraid that she would change her mind, disappear again, or simply ask Mr Fairfax to call off the wedding. Whenever Rebecca returned from seeing her, he would grill her over Caroline's mood. Rebecca had ignored him for the most part, still furious with him over the incident, and nothing he did could seem to make it up to her.

"If Miss Lesage is willing to give me a chance, why will you not, little sister?"

"Because Caroline is too kind, and you take advantage of it. But, I have a much longer memory, and I shall not rest until you make amends for your actions, Lucian. I shall be watching your every move."

"Well, I pity the man who falls for you, dearest, he will not have an easy time of it," he had needled, trying to get her to smile. *Rebecca had looked at him for a moment, a bit wounded, before rising and walking off.*

As the carriage clattered into the courtyard, he felt his body start to hum in anticipation. Looking up at the house, he repressed a smile. Caroline was inside somewhere. They were all similarly dishevelled. He pushed his hair back off his face roughly, striding into the house, eager to start searching out the object of his affection.

"Well, I see you must have behaved yourself reasonably last night to arrive so early and in such good humour," Rebecca stated as she came to greet Wesley and Charles, wrinkling her nose a little at the state of them.

"Sister," Lucian said, smiling at her, as she swept past him with barely any acknowledgment, greeting the other two warmly. "Rebecca, the arrangements look splendid so far, you have done a wonderful job," he tried again.

"Nonsense, it is the army of servants who have worked wonderfully. Though, I do hope Caroline will be pleased."

"And me? Do you wish me to be pleased?" Lucian asked, in a teasing tone.

"I care not," Rebecca said, sniffing. "Now, first you must all go and clean yourselves up. I shall arrange for baths to be brought to each of your rooms. Then, I have organised a shooting party for the afternoon. Mr Fairfax, the Mr Taylors and Mr Tilman shall accompany you."

Wesley and Charles nodded, starting upstairs, Lucian hesitated, before starting in the direction of the drawing-room. Rebecca's voice stopped him.

"Where do you think you are going? The groom cannot see the bride before the wedding. It is tradition."

"You know I care little for such silliness. You have been less than forthcoming about my intended, despite seeing her daily, so I will go and find out for myself how she fares."

"Lucian," Rebecca's soft tone made him pause, he turned back and saw her looking at him with the gentlest expression he had seen from her in quite some time.

"She is here- that is all you need know. Treat her according to tradition, it will please her, and show your respect. Her family is all here, do not embarrass her," she said and Lucian let out a sigh. He came back toward her and smiled a little.

"Fine. I shall accede to your demands, but only if you tell me... is she dreadfully unhappy?" he asked, no longer bothering to disguise his anxiety.

"She is nervous and has many things to consider for tomorrow. But... she is not unlike other girls, on the eve of her wedding. I do not believe she is unhappy," Rebecca said, and her words cleared Lucian's troubled brow and brought a genuine smile to his eyes.

"Well then... I shall go and get cleaned up. I cannot think of a better way to spend this afternoon than around Eli Taylor with a loaded shotgun," he grinned wickedly.

❀

The dress was a pale ivory colour, with pearls sewn into the bodice and lining the sleeves. She had never considered white, being impractical to wear again as she would be wearing less of it as a married woman, however, Rebecca had insisted, claiming the beautiful contrast with her skin and hair. It was the most beautiful garment she had ever owned, and the veil, which fell over her head loosely, was as sheer as mist.

She watched nervously as the maids carefully set the dress out, hanging it properly to prevent wrinkles. The day had been spent in a flurry of wedding preparations, and she was truly exhausted by it. Her whole body ached, though her mind was alert and restless. Despite there being more to do, she had been sent to her room, for a bath and to sleep early. She was not allowed to walk around the house, now the men had arrived, as tradition dictated.

The maids brought a large copper bathtub into the room and began filling it with steaming water. Caroline took off her day gown and undergarments, wrapping her new dressing gown around her. She thought of her old ripped night dress for a moment, musing on how things had changed since then and though it had not been long ago, the time had gone slowly, and she had learned much.

Petals; rose and lavender, and others more exotic floated on the surface of the water in a lavish tide of color. Drops of water glistened like jewels against the velveteen on the petals, and she felt like a goddess from old mythology as she slipped naked into the hot water. Oil had been added, and as she sank lower into the depths, its rich smell rose in perfumed waves of honeysuckle and orange blossom.

There was a light but efficient tap on the door. She sat a little uncomfortably as the maids washed her hair. She preferred to do such things alone; but, Rebecca had advised her that the help would feel protective of their duties. Once her hair was thoroughly washed and pinned up out of the water, she sank back and closed her eyes, finally alone in her room with her thoughts. The hot water flushed her skin and soothed her tired bones. The warm copper was comforting under her back. She let her hands and mind drift.

She was getting married tomorrow, it was scarcely believable. At the beginning of the season, she had thought that there was a distinct possibility that she would never marry, whether through choice, or lack of opportunity. Besides, she would have been happy to spite that old crone of a fortune teller. She had believed herself a penniless orphan. She had heard many stories of the rich, titled Ashford family, the most celebrated, infamous, and talked about of the Bon Ton. Now, she sat on the eve of marriage to one of its sons.

She thought back to the day she had first glimpsed Lucian, through the window as he descended from his carriage, moving more like a wolf than a man with his jaded eyes, and outrageous behaviour, his uncouth drinking and insufferable manners. He had shown her sides of human nature, and Caroline had never experienced such extremes before, both good and bad, with a brutal, unflinching honesty. He was only himself and did not pretend to be anything else, as flawed and broken as that person was.

She had a moment to herself, of peace, where everything else slipped away, and her muscles relaxed. She rubbed a hand over smooth skin under the water, thinking of how the oils would scent her, and that soon Lucian would be slipping the clothes from her skin, and her wedding night would be scented with lavender, honeysuckle, orange blossom and rose. Her stomach fluttered at the thought that soon it would be his hands gliding across her body. His touch. Would these aromas forever remind her of her first night of womanhood?

Over the past week, she had imagined her wedding night time and time again, so many countless times. Sometimes her imaginings were fraught with anxiety and worry, but most of them made her toes curl in excitement, a rush of butterflies, while others were demanding and fevered, pressing her with a need that she longed to better understand.

The more she imagined, the more the images grew in vivid frequency, taking over her thoughts unbidden both night and day. She thought often of their time in Portsmouth. How he had looked as he fought for her safety, the look on his face when she ripped her ticket and told him that she would be his, and how they had held each other, raw and frightened and unencumbered for so long that she could not tell where she ended and he began. She placed herself over and over in the bed next to Lucian in that small room by the docks; thought of his breath in her hair, the smooth skin at the open neck of his shirt sleeves, of the smell of him, and how when his leg had touched hers, the shock of it had reverberated through her body, filling her with a need to be nearer, to press herself against him. What would it have felt like if only he had turned and edged his body closer to hers? What would it have felt like had she rolled herself on top of him and kissed him with a wildness she had only allowed herself in her fantasies.

Being back at Blackhill brought her fantasies to a new location and made them feel more real somehow. Now her imaginings inhabited new spaces: rooms, gardens, hallways where he might at any moment bump into her without warning, and risk a heavily-laden gaze, a discreet touch of the hand, or maybe even a stolen kiss.

Now, as her hands trailed through the warm water, and over her skin, she imagined Lucian slipping through the door, and quietly locking it behind him. He might raise a finger to his lips to quiet her, and slowly make his way over to her bath, dragging a chair across the floor over to the side of the tub. He might sit, and for a while just look at every inch of her naked body through the petals on the water, the two of them growing more excited with each passing second. Then he would slide his fingers over the surface of the water, and push the petals away from the water above her breasts, and when he could stand it no longer, piercing her with a hungry look that made her back arch in anticipation, dip his hand into the water, and brush it lightly over the raised tips of her nipples. He would use both hands, as she did now, to cup her breasts and smooth across her skin and down her belly to explore her hips and thighs. Tomorrow. Tomorrow she would no longer have to imagine.

Feeling the water begin to cool, she raised herself slowly out of the tub, stepping carefully. She dried herself and smelt the perfume of the oil lingering on her skin. Slipping her nightdress over her head, she blew the candles in her room out and wrapped a warm blanket around her shoulders. There was a fire burning in the grate and she sat before it, letting the light from the fading sunset fall over her. Staring into the depths of the fire, she thought of how her life was about to change forever in just a few hours. Closing her eyes, she let her mind take her to dreams full of smiles and laughter and family, and she drifted off to sleep.

❀

*C*aroline awoke as the wind rattled the panes of the window. It was now wholly dark, with only a luminous moon to light the room. The fire had burned low and she shivered a little at the chill in the air. It had gotten colder at some point, and she was exposed on the armchair she had fallen asleep in. She stretched, stood, and put some more logs on the fire, poking at it with a long poker, trying to stimulate some sparks to catch. She could ring for a maid, but she hated to disturb them so late in the night.

Her dreams had filled her with longing for her parents, which left her feeling unsettled. By the position of the moon, it would seem the night was deep, and the relentless ticking of time was bringing her closer to what was perhaps the most frightening prospect she had ever faced as an adult.

She went over to the window, the bows of the trees whipped in the current of the wind, and the surface of the lake, usually still as a mirror, rippled and sent moonlight shattering across the surface. The moon shone its way through a space in the clouds before the wind could cover it up again, and she felt a murmur of the breeze seep through the window, and brush against her skin.

She thought of Virginia, and the great, booming thunderstorms that would come in the summers, blackening the sky; epic rolls of thunder would shake their huge wooden house, and big fat raindrops would tap on its tin roof. She wondered if her parents were looking back down on her from those heavenly heights. She began to draw the heavy velvet drapes closed, when she felt that familiar sensation of his eyes on her, lifting the hairs on the back of her neck not unpleasantly.

Raising her eyes, ever so slowly, she met his for the first time in days. The jolt of their connection warmed the air around her suddenly. Her eyes travelled over his face, realising that she had missed it, his stubbled, strong jaw, his smile, the secret one which he only seemed to show to her. His eyes, framed by their long lashes, their endless depths, right now held hers, and she saw in his face that he had missed her also.

His mouth curved in a slash of smile, and she felt her own lips tug upwards. He raised an eyebrow at her, and she guessed he was questioning why she was awake at this time. She shrugged slightly. She saw he held his sketch pad in his hands, and curious, she inclined her head toward it. He glanced down at it, and then, with a decidedly naughty smile, gestured his head toward the door, transporting her back to the night when they had gone to the kitchen together, where he had surprised her with the warm milk, and she had surprised him with that act of trust, simply by allowing herself to be alone with him.

She nodded, not missing the slight surprise on his face, as she pulled the curtains the rest of the way shut. She slipped warm slippers on, and wrapped her heavy wrapper, and then her paisley shawl around her. Lighting a candle, she left her room, as quietly as possible and made her way along the dark hall. As she neared the stairs, he suddenly materialised out of the darkness, waiting for her, leaning against the banister, his arms folded across his chest, his loose sleeping shirt covered partially by a heavy crimson dressing coat. Mimicking their previous encounter, they started down the stairs, though, this time he put a steadying hand on her arm as they went down the dark stairs.

In the kitchen, the surfaces were covered with food, signs of preparation for tomorrow's festivities everywhere. Clearing a space, Caroline sat on the table, wrapping her feet in her thick gown and resting them on a chair. She put her chin on her knees and circled her legs with her arms, watching Lucian as he moved almost soundlessly around the kitchen. Once again setting milk to heat, he finally turned around and leant back against the range, his sketches in his hand. He smiled a warm, easy smile, one she had missed lately.

"Miss Lesage, I must say, you are certainly a sight for sore eyes," he murmured, running his eyes over her. She smiled back at him tentatively.

"You are not a wholly unwelcome sight yourself," she responded and coloured when he raised an eyebrow at her. "Well, I am sick and tired of seeing the same faces every day. Your sister has held me hostage with countless tasks at home for weeks now! A new face is welcome... even yours," she said with a smirk.

"Well, I am glad to be of service, in any way that I can," he said with a laugh, turning to stir the milk. He turned back to see Caroline holding her hand out.

"Yes dear?" he asked, deliberately misunderstanding her as he moved toward her and slipped his hand into her outstretched palm. The sudden feel of his warm flesh ran through her with a shock. She pulled her hand back and levelled an unamused look at him.

"The sketches," she said looking up at him as he finally handed them over and returned to the stove. She started to look through them. She became absorbed, her eyes following the fine details, and shading, her expression softening. She saw him glance at her out of the corner of his eye.

There were a few drawings of the moonlit lake, and she saw how he had captured the peace of the scene. Leafing through, she came to one that she could not make out. Turning it on its side, her own window took shape, and she could see it was empty. There was something lonely about it. With trepidation, she turned to the next drawing, seeing that in this one the window was now filled. She gasped quietly at her image, rendered in intricate detail. She wore her sleeping gown, white and thin, it showed her shoulders and arms. Her hair was down and her face was turned to the night sky. What took her notice, however, was how she was portrayed in the picture, it was imbued with more than a mere likeness, it held a sort of emotion, as though she was seeing herself through the artist's eyes. And she looked strong, regal almost, like a queen, or a goddess deigning to spend her time among mortals.

"It is not finished," Lucian said softly, and she realised he had finished warming the milk and now stood before her with it. Setting the drawings down she accepted the warm cup, wrapping her hands around it, enjoying the way its warmth distracted her from the enigmatic puzzle of a man who stood before her. She sipped it and made a small rumble of appreciation. He'd added a drop of honey. Lucian moved to her side and leant against the table, picking up the drawing she had been looking at.

"You say it is not yet finished?" she asked curiously, unable to see where it could be improved.

"I fear it shall never be..."

"Why not?"

"Because... you, my dear, are far too complex, nuanced and heavenly to ever really commit to paper. Though, God knows I have tried."

"You flatter me," she stated, hiding her face in the warm scent of her glass.

"Truth is not flattery," he said shortly. Caroline felt warmed by his quiet insistence and the cozy, intimate atmosphere of the darkened kitchen.

"Have you recovered?" she asked, deciding to change the subject.

"Recovered from what?"

"Whatever was ailing you when we returned from Portsmouth," he looked away at her words, studying his hands. The silence stretched out for a moment. "Lucian?" Caroline prompted.

"I fear that my terrible personality was my only ailment at that time, and unfortunately, that is not easily recovered from... though, if anyone is capable of inspiring that sort of change in a man, it is undoubtedly you," he said, glancing up at her, smiling. She smiled and sighed, but something pulled at his mouth and for a moment it thinned to a serious line.

"Lucian, there is no need to shower me with compliments so. I should think it almost impossible to catch a coach to Portsmouth from Blackhill Hall, therefore by this time tomorrow... we shall be married and..." as soon as she said it, she felt a furious blush rise at the thought that exactly this time tomorrow, they would be in bed, as man and wife. He raised his eyebrow at her, his smile maddeningly intimate.

"And?" he asked in a low tone and Caroline rushed to change the subject.

"Were you not... when we returned from the ship, were you reconsidering your desire to marry?" she said and faltered when he turned toward her, leaning in, bringing his face close to hers.

"My sweet, if there is one thing you should never doubt, it is my desire to have you by my side for the rest of my days."

"I thought perhaps you were already grieving over your freedom."

"I do not know if I would equate being wed to you with the end of my freedom," he said with a laugh and stopped when he caught the look on Caroline's face. "What is it?" Caroline opened her mouth to speak, and found no words there, snapped it shut, and then taking a grip on herself, spoke. If not now, then when?

"Well, the last time we were at Blackhill, you proposed an arrangement with me, in the advent of your marriage to Eva. I guess I am curious whether you still would seek such an arrangement. It is not unusual, I know, but we have never discussed it," she said, forcing herself to look at him, without shame or embarrassment at the question. His brows knit together as he considered his answer.

"Forgive me if I seem to be stating the obvious, but I will have little need for you to be my mistress if you are my wife..."

"Not with me - with another woman, other women," Caroline said flatly. Lucian took a step toward her, as if he might embrace her, but stopped himself.

"Caroline - no other women interest me. I was only ever interested in such an arrangement because it was a way for me to keep seeing you. Do you ask because you wish for me to take his physical needs elsewhere?" She felt her face flush hot.

"No. No, certainly not." She felt her blush spread to her neck, but carried on. "I confess, I am glad to hear you say so." A surprised smile curled up his face under a cocked eyebrow, and he moved closer still.

"Does that please you?" he asked in a whisper. She nodded, biting her lip, and then looked away.

"Darling, I am sorry if I made you doubt my feelings toward you for even a moment. Since I have met you, you have consumed my thoughts and haunted my dreams. Other women have ceased to exist for me. You are – everything.," he said simply. Her hands clutched at the table edge, and he moved a fraction closer yet again. "I know I am far from forgiven, and I fully intend to give you all the time you require to forgive me. But, on the eve of our wedding... would it be too much to ask you of your feelings?"

"What do you wish to know, my lord?" she spoke softly, meeting his gaze. He was close enough that she could feel his breath stirring the hair around her forehead and neck. She could smell the scent of his skin, sending her mind reeling to the night they had spent lying side by side in the bed in Portsmouth.

"Will you marry me tomorrow with hate in your heart?" he asked softly, his strained voice snapping her from her memories. She turned ever so slightly toward him, her teeth sinking into her full lower lip as she considered her answer, then shook her head. She gazed openly into his eyes, the air felt charged between them.

"I do not hate you, Lucian. In truth, I never did, even when you... acted as you did."

"I deserved to be hated," he said.

"Hate... I do not hate anyone. Hate is like a poison, and I would not encourage it in myself. No one is ever so lost, that they cannot be found," she said echoing the words she had spoken to him in his darkest time.

"You astound me Miss Lesage. You are an angel- a beacon in the darkness."

"The world is not so very dark."

"Mine always has been... but you show me such mercy, and I do not know why. When we were in Portsmouth, you allowed me to be close to you." He reached out very slowly and traced a soft trail down her cheek, that sent her stomach flipping. "The way you held onto me...

something broke between us, I felt. A boundary. I felt that something connected us then."

She nodded, looking up into his eyes. She could say nothing else. Her heart raced, and her body resonated with it.

"I am very much looking forward to a time when I can have you in my arms like that again- nothing between us. I have been able to think of little else this past week, in fact," he said, his voice very low, very quiet, and she felt the sound of it slide down her spine. "Perhaps... this time tomorrow... I should be that lucky man once again." Reaching out, he traced the line of her jaw.

"Lucian," she murmured

"Hmmm," he mumbled low in his chest.

"I must tell you..." She swallowed, and he moved his thumb down a path over her throat and stroked one at the hollow at the base of it. Her skin tingled, her pulse jumped. She was lightheaded. It made it easier to say the things that had worried her more and more urgently the past few days. "I am scared," she said haltingly, hoping he would understand her meaning without further elaboration, he caught her eyes and took her face in both his hands, cradling it.

"As am I," he said. He slid both hands up her neck to her jaw, and tilted it up, lowering his face toward hers. Each second stretched out like a bowstring, taught, and humming.

He stopped a hair's breadth from her lips and she could feel his warm breath brushing over the sensitive skin of her lips. He brushed one thumb softly across them, barely touching, and the sensation pulsated through her entire body. Her head spun. She could think of nothing but her lips. He lowered his mouth the final inches and met hers.

His mouth was so soft and tender on hers, his lips grazed hers gently, lighting a hungry fire within her. He took her bottom lip between his own, and she heard a soft noise rise unbidden from her throat. This was nothing like the kiss that they had shared before.

She hesitantly raised her hands to his collar, and as he broke away whispering her name. Her body ached for more of him, and she tugged at the material to bring his mouth back to hers. His hands slid through her unbound hair, moving over her cheeks and neck. She felt as though she was drugged, the heavy, euphoric sensation that passed through her like waves. His mouth fitted to hers perfectly, and they moved in harmony. As the kiss deepened and his tongue found its way inside, her body burned, hot and ignited.

Slowly standing to get closer, she found his hands moving to her back, pulling her flush against him. It felt so right, she pressed herself nearer, eager for the contact, addicted to the way it made her body feel. Suddenly, his lips were gone, and she swayed in his arms. Her heart was pounding and her breath came out heavy. She felt him stroking her hair and pressing kisses onto the top of her head. Taking a stabilising breath, she looked up at him. He was looking at her in wonder, running his thumbs across her cheekbones, his eyes intent as though he were trying to memorise her face. They stood there for several minutes before she felt it was too much and broke away to take a sip of milk.

"Well," she said, with a boldness she was surprised by. "That was my first real kiss."

His eyes crinkled when he returned her smile. "Mine too," he murmured, causing her to frown and push him back a little.

"You do not need to humour me... I am well aware of your past. Have I not seen it for myself?"

"I am not humouring you," he looked at her earnestly. "I was being honest... I have never kissed a woman like that, never been kissed like that before." She studied his face.

"Tomorrow night..." she began but had no idea how to continue.

"Tomorrow night will be as much a first for me as it will be for you. I have never cared for another person as I care for you, my dear. I am unspeakably nervous. I want to make you happy. That makes tomorrow night a new experience," he smiled. "I implore you, be gentle with me, Miss Lesage," he joked and she felt the tension ease off her shoulders. "If you are not ready, or you wish to wait until I am forgiven... I will wait. I will wait as long as I am asked to."

"You presume I intend to forgive you at some point then?"

"You are right, that was too presumptuous. I take it back," he said and she laughed.

"Are you saying that I have no choice?" she looked at him archly, teasing him. He pulled her close again, touching his forehead to hers.

"I am saying... that waiting for you... would be the sweetest agony I have ever endured. But I will endure it willingly to have you smile at me so..." he leant forward and her eyelids fluttered, but she gathered herself and raised her finger against his mouth.

"Tomorrow," she whispered. He continued to hold her near for one torturous moment where she feared her resolve would yet melt; then, growling softly, he pulled away, placing a small kiss on her forehead.

"You do me great honour," he sighed and she immediately missed his warmth as he stepped away from her. She picked her glass up again and sipped her milk, finding it had already cooled.

"You are correct," she teased.

Clearing his throat, Lucian turned away, severing the link between them. He sorted through his sketches.

"I apologise for seeming withdrawn on our return from port, I was merely preoccupied with the practicalities of the wedding and our lives together following it. I realised there are things I have not told you, not really having an opportunity to as of yet."

"Such as?"

"Such as... my father, that is, Lord Ashford, is not my father by blood," he said it so casually, she almost choked on her drink. Deciding to continue in the upfront way he seemed to be favouring to speak of the delicate subject, she spoke without emotion.

"I had heard a rumour revealing as much."

"Well, it must stay rumour, though my siblings know, of course, you are the only other person, outside my immediate family who has had it confirmed." She waited a moment, knowing that, for Lucian, this topic would be sore, the prodding of an old bruise still tender.

"Your blood father... have you ever met him?"

"No, I never had the chance. He died."

"I am sorry."

"Do not be, he was a stranger to me. Though, he did manage to make provision for me. I suppose he was the only person on this earth who hated Silus as much as I."

"How do you mean?"

"*He* was extremely wealthy and bequeathed his fortune to me, and all his estates with it. The only provision was that the money never be used to the Ashfords' gain; it had to be used solely for my personal benefit, well, me and one day, my own family. It has given Silus yet one more reason to despise me," he said without emotion.

"Lucian," she said softly, but he refused to meet her concerned gaze and continued to talk breezily.

"But it is good news for us. It means that we never need live under the rule of my father, and certainly not in any of his properties. If you want to live in the city, I shall have my townhouse opened. It has been empty for some time. If you prefer the country, then my estate, Westmere, should be to your liking. We could even go to Scotland if you wish it."

"What is your preference?" she asked, seeing he did not want to be drawn into talks of his father.

"My preference is to be by your side, wherever it may be," he said, and picked her cold hand up, and brought it to his lips, pressing a warm kiss onto it. "I have delayed you too long, you are frozen through. Time for bed. We've a big day tomorrow, Miss Lesage, and I am very much looking forward to calling you by a different name," he said, taking her cold glass from her and leading her from the kitchen and up the stairs back to the upper rooms. Caroline felt her eyes grow heavy at the thought of bed and yet felt that she would never sleep after that kiss.

"You are certainly bossy in the small hours of the morning," she complained as he walked her to her door.

"You have no idea, Miss Lesage," he put a bit of emphasis on her name. "But you will," he said with another wicked smile, opening her door and lingering on the threshold.

"Do you require any assistance?" he said, nodding toward the waiting bed. "Your sheets may be cold, for instance."

"Goodnight, my lord," she said firmly but paused as he put his hand out, stopping the door.

"A farewell kiss then?" he asked and smiled a smile to make even a nun forget herself. She considered, then leant forward, placing a soft kiss on his stubbled cheek, drawing back slowly as he turned his head with her. They stared at each other for a few scorching moments, and then she smiled,

"Sleep well, my Lord, and dream of pleasant things."

"Oh, I will. That I can guarantee," he said, wolfishly, and her stomach fluttered at the sound of it.

❦

*T*he ceremony was to take place in the charming chapel in the village, and then the wedding breakfast would be held at Blackhill Hall for those close to the family. The servants from the house were welcome to attend the ceremony, and many of them were excited. The church was over two hundred years old, and trailing ivy had begun to encroach its intricate stonework. Rebecca had seen to it that lavish arrangements of flowers and massive garlands of greenery covered every surface and corner inside, and out, making it look less like a chapel, and more like an enchanted garden with gothic windows. At the end stood tall doors that opened out onto the sweeping vista of autumnal countryside, and the blue sky was without even one cloud.

John Fairfax walked the cobbled path, holding his wife's arm. Frances Tilman was travelling slowly behind them, and they had arrived early to allow her to get settled. John knew that all the girls and the Ashfords were still at the house getting ready, and it was utter chaos there. The village was equally busy, as children in their best clothes started to line the street, some already dropping flower petals in their excitement. There was a peaceful energy today, and John hoped he had done right by Caroline, as her father would have done.

The church bells began to ring nine o'clock. One more hour and the couple would be walking down the aisle, for better or for worse.

❦

"*I*f you would stop moving, Richard might have a better chance of getting it tied," Wesley remonstrated his brother watching the valet begin his cravat again, as Lucian's agitation got the better of him.

"I'm losing patience," he growled, trying to hold still. He had so much nervous energy, he needed to pace, or run or do something. Each minute that ticked past, he became more apprehensive.

He was dressed in a cream waistcoat, over a matching shirt, a double-breasted morning jacket, with a velvet collar in a deep blue colour, and grey cashmere breeches. His silk cravat was a dove grey, matching his hat. Charles had insisted that he shave properly, and he felt as though he looked like a much younger version of himself when he looked in the mirror. His hands were sweating, and he kept resisting the urge to wipe his brow. His breath felt jittery, as though he could not get enough air. Blast all these layers of buttoned clothes! A movement from the hall distracted him, and he looked up to see his father lounging in the doorway.

"I suppose you'll do," he said rudely ignoring the looks of Charles and Wesley. "Your sister says it is past time for us to leave," Silus said, and turned away looking bored. Wesley clapped Lucian on the shoulder, smiling.

"Do you hear that, brother? That means Caroline must not have given into her better judgment and disappeared!" he joked and held his hands up in a gesture of peace as Lucian growled at him, feeling every bit as wild as he sounded. His heart felt as though it had climbed into his mouth.

He saw Silus and thought of his role in Caroline's wooing, and he pictured her, dressed and ready, innocent, willing, about to give herself to him. A choice that she had believed to be hers when she had been lied to and manipulated until the last. His stomach twisted and his throat tightened.

"Are we ready to leave?" Charles asked, collecting his hat and standing.

Lucian felt as though he couldn't breathe again, as though a vice was crushing his windpipe.

"Lucian, you look green. It is just a wedding, not a beheading," he laughed.

"What if she does not wish to marry me, Charles? What if she... might have chosen someone else."

"Brother, I believe I have seen the worst of your actions toward Miss Lesage. The very worst, and I believe she has chosen to forgive you for it. If she can forgive that, or even entertain the possibility of forgiveness, I would assume she has real feelings for you, Lucian. I have seen the way she looks at you. It is difficult to miss," Charles said slowly. Lucian shook his head,

"But you do not know what I did... what father did," Lucian muttered.

"What father did? What do you mean?" Charles looked down at his pocket watch. "That will have to wait, brother, for if we do not leave now, she will be standing at the altar alone."

The words sent a flurry of panic through Lucian. Getting a grip on himself, he nodded. It was too late for honesty- the time for chivalry and gentlemanly behaviour had passed long ago, and he had allowed it to. Now, all he could do was go ahead and accept the consequences. They started downstairs, seeing their father already in the carriage looking pleased, as black an omen as any there was one, Lucian thought.

🌼

*F*lower petals fell over the open carriage as it moved slowly along the well-lined streets. It was overwhelming. Caroline felt acutely uncomfortable at being the centre of so much attention but was comforted to be surrounded by her sisters, Rebecca happy that the village was involved, waving and calling things to families she knew by name, Katherine quietly happy to be included, and Eva smiled encouragingly to see Caroline and Katherine together for the first time since their falling out. Caroline could not help but felt a small pang of sorrow when she looked at Katherine and wished that she felt in her heart more free to share this day with her, but some matters of the heart took time, she supposed, and today, on the day of her wedding, she would neither force false feelings, nor dwell on unhappy remembrances. The girls were all dressed beautifully, and she looked between them, feeling more cherished than she could remember feeling before. She began to grow nervous though, and as the church came into view, her head starting to feel a little light. The chapel loomed overhead, and the crowd outside cheered as she arrived. She imagined Lucian for a moment, inside, his golden head lifting with the sounds of the crowd indicating her arrival. As she alighted from the carriage, Mr Fairfax was there, offering her his hand and helping her down.

"Caroline, my dear, you are a vision. I feel very proud to be here with you on this day."

299

"Thank you, Mr Fairfax. Next to my father, there is no one I would rather have at my side," she said and saw his smile deepen at her words. She stretched up and kissed him on the cheek.

"Thank you, dear. It means a lot to an old man like me, who has always looked upon you as a daughter. Now, are you ready?" She felt her friends' hands on her back and she looked around at them as Rebecca gently arranged her veil. The dress cupped her bosom snugly, with the most delicate Spanish lace for modesty framing the low bodice with its cap sleeves. Rebecca had insisted on the extravagance of silk, and it was the finest that Caroline had ever seen, shining like moonlight, and impossibly smooth to the touch, it fell gracefully straight down, showing her form to its best advantage. Intricate embroidery and beadwork in shades of white adorned the bodice modestly to mirror the bottom of the gown where it had been worked in striking, breathtaking abundance, and then crept up from the bottom hem, tendrils of vines and flowers coiling up the skirt in symmetrical peaks, leaving the plain, elegant silk of the rest of the gown to shine on its own, with no need of guilding. The veil was like a cobweb, so thin and fragile, accentuated by the deep, black velvet of Caroline's hair. Rebecca smiled at her, with such warmth Caroline could not help but return it.

"Caroline. You are the most beautiful bride I have ever seen in my life. I simply cannot find the words to tell you how happy I am to welcome you to my family," Rebecca said, kissing her on the cheek, then turning to make her way into the church. The crowd outside quieted as the organ music began inside and Caroline felt light-headed once again, but then Mr Fairfaxes hands were there, guiding her.

"Let's not keep them waiting," he said with a smile and led her toward the door. Taking a deep breath, she went from the brightness of the beautiful day, and into the candlelit, stained glass dappled interior of the church.

🦢

*L*ucian heard the music and the crowd outside. She had arrived. She had come... she had not run, and she was going to marry him. He stood, feeling Charles's hand on his shoulder, a silent show of support. He turned and waited, seeing the other ladies come in, walking down the aisle and sitting. He tried to regulate his breathing but found it impossible, it was as though all the air in the room had been sucked out.

Suddenly, he saw a movement from the brightly lit archway of a door, and then, she was there. He swallowed, trying to restore some moisture to his parched throat, as he took in the vision before him.

As an artist, he was accustomed to seeing the beauty in things and trying to capture it. The way Caroline looked at that moment, he knew he would never stop trying to recreate her on the page, the eternal muse. The sun from the opened church doors surrounded her in a halo of light. Her obsidian hair shone like polished stone and was piled up regally, with some soft curls framing her face. She walked with all the grace of a queen, her white gown showing off the beautiful golden glow of her skin. Her full, wide lips were flushed a deep rose, and she was smiling at him. But, all of this splendor paled against the artistry of her eyes. They shown, gold against the green-blue sea, and her smile crinkled them at the corners making them smaller, but all the more exquisite. She was indescribable. His world shifted then, and she was all he could see. All he would ever see.

She stopped near him, and he found himself unable to take his eyes off her, even when the people sat down, and the priest started speaking. He looked at her from the side, still a good few meters apart, and barely heard the priest's words.

"*Dearly beloved, we are gathered together here in the sight of God, and in the face of this congregation, to join together this Man and this Woman in holy Matrimony...*"

Lucian struggled to focus on the words, which seemed neverending. The warmth of the church, the glow of the candles, and soft light that fell through the many windows, even the heady smell of flowers, all colluded to make him feel dizzy with disbelief.

"*Lord Lucian Nicholas Elias Ashford, wilt thou have this woman to thy wedded wife, to live together after God's ordinance in the holy estate of Matrimony? Wilt thou love her, comfort her, honour, and keep her in sickness and in health; and, forsaking all other, keep thee only unto her, so long as ye both shall live?*"

Lucian took a steadying breath and then spoke confidently.

"I will," he saw the priest now turn to Caroline.

"Miss Caroline Elizabeth Lesage, wilt thou have this Man to thy wedded husband, to live together after God's ordinance in the holy estate of Matrimony? Wilt thou obey him, and serve him, love, honour, and keep him in sickness and in health; and, forsaking all other, keep thee only unto him, so long as ye both shall live?"

"I will," she answered, her voice was strong and clear.

"Who giveth this Woman to be married to this man?" the priest asked, and Lucian collected himself, knowing the time had come when he could look upon her, and touch her. John Fairfax gently laid Caroline's right hand in the Priest's, who in turn, placed it in Lucian's. The touch of her flesh was electric, and as soon as their hands were together, he felt hers tremble. Perhaps she was not so unaffected, he realised, and he gently applied some pressure, squeezing her hand to show his support.

He slipped a cool band of gold over her warm finger, such a tiny thing, that meant so much. They knelt down, side by side and the priest began his blessing over their lowered heads.

"Those whom God hath joined together let no man put asunder."

It was done.

They were married. Lucian couldn't quite believe it.

Outside, the village crowd cheered, and they went to the bridal carriage, pausing, Caroline turned to him, and he offered his hand and helped her into it, the picture of a loving couple. The cheering intensified as he stepped up onto the open-topped carriage, where they could be seen better by the crowd and Caroline waved and thanked everyone, though none of them could hear over the shouting. It didn't matter - her face said it all. She was radiant perfection, with the roses in her cheeks, and a decadent smile of unreserved joy on her lips. As the cheering got louder he bent his head to hers, and their lips met in a chaste kiss. The carriage started to pull away and Caroline clutched onto his shoulders to steady herself, leaning away from him with a laugh as more sugar-coated seeds and candies rained down on them and he used his hat to shield her face, and then to catch some.

For a moment, as she laughed happily into his face, and he smiled into hers, he felt as though they were all alone, and that the wide world was created for just the two of them. A tiny chalk ball bounced of Lucian's head and he turned away, spying a small child cheering, his hands full of the homemade confetti, and laughed, turning back to

Caroline, the spell broken, they settled side by side in the carriage and waved to the people all the way back to the estate.

Arriving in the courtyard of Blackhill Hall, the cheering continued as the house staff had all lined up to applaud them. Lucian jumped down from the carriage spryly and bowed to his bride as she held a hand out to descend. He slowly lowered her to the ground, her body close to his, maddeningly close, and he fought every instinct he had not to kiss her there. She rested her hands on his shoulders again, looking up into his eyes.

"Thank you, my Lord Ashford," she said

"You are quite welcome, Lady Ashford," he replied with a smile so earnest that it radiated through his body. She smiled back with her beautiful lips, and just as quickly he was struck by a longing to get her alone, to claim her as his once and for all.

His thoughts were interrupted by the arrival of the other carriages, and his brothers as they jumped down and came to them, clapping him on the back, making jokes and congratulating him. The next thing he knew, his sister had whisked Caroline away toward the house, giving the men strict instructions to be at the wedding breakfast as soon as they were able.

As Caroline let the girls pull her into the house, she looked back one more time. Lucian was standing in the courtyard, surrounded by movement, laughter and good cheer, but he was still, watching her, and the look on his face was one she had never seen before, it made her shiver in the most pleasurable way as she turned back to the happy chatter of her friends.

❦

*T*he wedding breakfast would be a relatively small and simple affair. Only the family would attend, and the servants would enjoy a special feast and cake that evening. In her room, maids helped Caroline remove her veil and fixed her hair. It had been curled with hot irons and was pinned up in all its shining glory, with seed pearls carefully strewn throughout, like stars in the night sky. They also consulted her on the arrangement of her travelling cases, as they would depart straight from Blackhill for Lucian's estate, Westmere. Rebecca arrived

303

as she was finishing at the mirror, and bade her to come to the breakfast, as everyone else was ready.

They left her rooms and met Lucian in the hallway. She smiled shyly at him, suddenly alone as Rebecca left them to go and join the family. He looked magnificent in his wedding clothes, and the blue and grey highlighted the bronze of his hair and the sapphire of his eyes. Those eyes twinkled at her now as he bowed to her, moving to her side and taking her arm, leading them downstairs.

"How are you faring, my darling? I know this must be overwhelming," he said.

"Oh? And how do you already know my feelings, husband mine?" she grinned up at him.

"Because I find myself similarly affected," he said with a smile. "In fact, it's a wonder I can still walk at all." She laughed, and rested against his arm, feeling its iron-like strength a comfort. "If you become too tired, just say the word and we shall depart."

"We cannot disappoint your sister... and anyway, it will be some time before we see our families again, and I shall miss them."

"Oh, I wouldn't worry overmuch about that. I promise to do my best to keep you entertained... when I have you all to myself," he murmured, his mouth above her ear, and she flushed, her stomach fluttering.

"Well, we are not alone yet, so I suggest you behave yourself, as I do not reward bad behaviour," she said teasingly.

"What reward is it you speak of, my Lady Ashford?" he asked, innocently, his tone contrasting with the warm look in his eye.

"Be good and perhaps you shall see," she said primly before they entered the drawing-room. Everyone was drinking champagne and talking, smiles and laughter ringing out. Caroline felt happy that her decisions had led to this day, even if much heartbreak and tears had come before it.

"Lord and Lady Ashford," a footman intoned as they stepped into the room, people leapt from their seats in another jolly boom of applause. She felt as though her face may break from smiling. The gong rang signaling the beginning of breakfast, and Lucian offered Caroline his arm and they headed the procession through to the dining room. The table was laden with food, from traditional breakfast foods to marinated oysters, various roast birds, and many exotic confectionary wonders that Caroline had never even seen before, let alone tasted. Sweets and cakes glistened in splendid sugar, coated mountains, iced with lace and roses, so beautiful that they almost looked real.

They sat and were served and the jovial talk continued in happy excitement. Caroline looked down at the beautiful food and wondered if she'd be able to eat anything at all.

"Sister," Wesley leaned in and spoke to Caroline below all of the noise. "Have I told you enough yet how very happy I am to have you join our little rag-tag gang? We shall all be the better, the brighter, and the happier for it. And Lucian looks as if he's just won England in a hand of cards." Wesley's smile was so warm and genuine that Caroline did truly feel like she had a brother for the first time.

"Thank you, brother dear," she started, leaning on the new term, and his smile broadened. "You know, you are quite the friendliest and most charming Ashford, by a country mile. When will it be your turn at the altar making some beautiful girl blissfully happy?" If Caroline was not mistaken, she thought she felt, rather than saw, a shadow cross Wesley's face for a fraction of a second.

"Oh no, dear one. I am the eternal bachelor and shall remain so for the rest of my days. You see, the women of England are like this beautiful array of cakes on a silver tray... how could I possibly choose just one?" He put a smile on his face, and lifted a large slice of cake from a nearby tower, and took an enormous bite, getting a mess of icing all over his mouth and on the tip of his nose, and sending Caroline into giggles that made her forget her confusion.

"So, no European tour?" Wesley said in mock outrage, wiping his face and changing the subject. "I had not thought you cheap, brother." Lucian smiled at him indulgently.

"You may address that question to Caroline, as I had proposed such."

"Sister, do you not wish to see the sights which Italy and France have to offer? We were so hoping that you could take our brother off our hands for a month or two, or six" he grinned, and she laughed.

"Of course, I do, very much. However, it has been such a busy few weeks, I would prefer to rest a little before we go," she said.

"I do not know who has prepared you for the first few weeks of married life, but they have been remiss if they told you it was restful!"

Virgil joked, causing the company to erupt in laughter and bawdy cheers, and Frances to groan.

❀

*C*onversation flowed freely, and Katherine took a moment to look around, never before had she been so grateful to be present at a meal. The horrible affair had been the first time she had ever really suffered for her actions. The first time something she had done had really mattered. It was a wake-up call akin to being dropped in an ice-cold lake.

She doubted that Caroline would ever truly forgive her, and the thought gnawed at her insides. At least she had not been kept from the wedding - Caroline had been too generous for that. She hesitantly raised her eyes to the man sitting on her right. A man who had not spoken to her since that awful morning, and she was sure she would never forget the look on his face when he had left her at the door. She sipped at her water, disinclined to drink champagne around him, and tensed as she heard Isaac say her name across the table.

"So, dear Katherine, you will be next, I am sure, now you have all the benefit of your mother's undivided attention," Isaac was saying with a smile. She looked down demurely and noticed the way Charles's hands tightened on his cutlery. "A girl like you will not be unwed for long, of that I am sure, don't you agree Lord Charles?" Isaac continued amiably. Katherine risked a glance at his face and blanched at the impassive stare he gave her.

"I know not. I suppose it depends on how well a gentleman is acquainted with the lady before they are married," he said, and Eli raised his eyebrows in surprise. Katherine felt her face burn red.

"Come now, my Lord, I am sure you do not mean to imply any ill feeling toward Miss Fairfax," Eli chimed in diplomatically.

"I am sure he does," Katherine said softly.

"No, you mistake me. I mean to imply *no* feeling toward Miss Fairfax," Charles said, in a grave tone, and Katherine looked at him, too cut to hide the hurt from her face. Charles met her eyes impassively.

As they glared at each other, the Taylor's caught each other's eye, saying much in a look Katherine knew well. Issac broke the tension by

306

turning the attention to Rebecca who sat at his side, across from his brother.

"You have done a wonderful job today, my lady. I know Caroline could never have dreamt of a more charming ceremony or reception. Sincere, dignified and stunningly beautiful, some would say, not unlike its creator," Isaac smoothed. Rebecca smiled back at him, raising an eyebrow.

"Why, Mr Taylor, I see getting back to London has certainly put you in good spirits. I have heard you have been quite busy, calling on acquaintances," she said archly. Isaac looked abashed.

"Well, certain society ladies are seldom home to be called on," he said, his tone making it clear of whom he spoke.

"How fortunate for your other admirers," she said pointedly.

"Indeed," Isaac said lightly, taking a drink, but he let his dark eyes hold Rebecca's captive. "I must say, I have missed your company. Most especially the constant defamation of my character," Isaac smirked.

"Well, we all have our talents."

"Oh? Well then, I will enjoy imagining what your others may be."

"So Lord Ashford, your estate, Westmere, do you visit it often?" John Fairfax asked.

"Please, now we are family, you must call me Lucian, or Lord Lucian if you must. I regret I have not been in some years, though I care for it very much. I hope that, in time, we shall host you all for a family gathering," he said.

"That will be wonderful!" Margaret exclaimed, her eyes lighting up at the thought.

"You must come also, once your lovely wife has welcomed your child into the world," Lucian said, turning to Virgil.

"Thank you for the offer. We will be here in England for quite some time, until Frances is ready to travel again, and the little one of course."

"Well, there is excellent shooting at Westmere. Mr Tilman is quite the marksman, he embarrassed us all yesterday, save Lucian," Wesley said, buzzing from the festivities.

Silus's voice called low and grave from down the table.

"When are we doing gifts, Rebecca dear?"

"Whenever you wish, father," she said, speaking up across the others.

"Very well, I have something rather special for the happy couple. It used to belong to your mother, Lucian," he said, and Lucian looked at him blankly, confused by the uncharacteristic generosity.

Once the meal was over, and the guests finished picking at all of the candied fruits, cakes and bonbons, Rebecca stood up to move through to the drawing-room and invited everyone to do the same.

Lucian took Caroline's arm and they once again headed the group, an honour accorded them that day because of their marriage. In the drawing-room, more drinks flowed and the family presented some gifts to the newlyweds. Lucian kept an eye on his father, who seemed to be all together too happy with the day, most likely at the expectation of a fortune to add to his coffers, Lucian guessed.

"Congratulations Lord Lucian, I mean it sincerely," Lucian turned to see the younger Mr Taylor before him. He smiled in return.

"Thank you, and I have been remiss to not yet congratulate *you*," he said, raising his eyebrow. Eli looked down, a slightly chagrined smile on his face.

"Well, you have hardly had the opportunity," he said with a cautious laugh that Lucian joined. He was really rather interesting, Eli Taylor. It was a bold move, approaching Lucian after stealing his betrothed.

"Shall we let bygones be bygones? It seems that everything has worked out well in the end," Lucian said magnanimously.

"I hope it did," Eli said, his eyes narrowing for a moment on Caroline and Eva, Lucian followed his gaze, and was startled to have his goodwill returned with such reluctance.

"I shouldn't worry about Caroline. She is quite content," Lucian said defensively.

"I pray she continues to be," Eli said solemnly.

Lucian opened his mouth but had time to say nothing before Charles clapped him on the back and started telling the Taylors some story of the shenanigans in their youth.

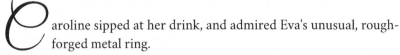

aroline sipped at her drink, and admired Eva's unusual, rough-forged metal ring.

"I do not have to wear it, but I like it. It reminds me of the ceremony," Eva said with a soft smile. Then she picked up Caroline's hand and looked at her ring.

"This is beautiful, Caroline."

"It was our mother's," Rebecca said, sitting beside them. "It is Celtic. The interwoven pattern symbolises family and infinity. Family forever."

"It is too much... shouldn't you have it?" Caroline asked.

"No, lovely. That ring is meant to be worn by someone in love, and loved in return," Rebecca said tightly, taking a gulp of champagne.

"What of your other brothers? Would they not wish to take it for their future wives?"

"Do not fret," she patted her hand. "You are more deserving of it, and it looks so well on you, shining against your skin," Rebecca said with a smile that had grown warm, and an envious tone in her compliment.

"It does, doesn't it," Silus's voice interrupted.

"Thank you, Lord Ashford," Caroline said politely.

"Please, call me Silus, or father if you wish," he said, and she forced a queasy smile, hoping Lucian could not hear his father's proprietorial tone from where he stood. He held out his hand to her, indicating that he wished her to rise. She stood slowly, feeling uncomfortable with how the man leaned in as he talked, and how his breath smelled of strong alcohol that had not been served so early in the day.

"You do remind me of her, in a way. Has Lucian ever told you the story of how I came to be married to his mother?" Caroline shook her head, searching out her husband with her eyes, seeing him talking with the Taylors and his brothers, his face uncharacteristically carefree and unguarded.

"It was not so unlike your very own story. Ask him to share it with you, perhaps you shall enjoy the similarities. Now, seeing you wearing Esther's ring, it makes me glad I have chosen the presents I have for you. They shall serve you well in my son's home," he said and gave a nod to one of the servants by the door.

The servant went to the door and opened it, stepping back to admit someone carrying the most beautiful pair of candelabras that Caroline had ever seen. They were solid gold, with precious gems around the base and they sparkled in the afternoon light. They were extremely tall, and clearly centrepiece items for a royal table, or had once belonged to a church perhaps. The room gasped and exclaimed as they were brought to her, and Caroline could hear Margaret sighing over them. As the man came toward her, carrying the exquisite items, she looked over his shoulder and saw Lucian, who was looking at his father with an inscrutable expression.

"My lady," the man said, stopping in front of her, and displaying the candlesticks with a flourish. She smiled and raised her eyes to the man's face to thank him, and in that moment, felt her world stop turning.

✿

*H*er mouth fell open a little, as she stared at him, unable to believe her eyes. Glancing down, she saw his little finger held in a splint, and as she searched his face, she saw the unmistakable flash of a white bandage under his hat.

Her mouth worked wordlessly, and a roaring filled her ears. Where was Lucian? Was he in danger? She was dimly aware that the rest of the company had continued their socialising, with no idea of her alarm. Silus had drawn her separate from the group quite effectively, and he quickly replaced his look of satisfaction, with one of concern as she tore her gaze from the man before her, up to him.

"My dear Caroline, are you well? Leave us, Harsdon," he said to the man, who turned away only after his own gratified smirk and moved toward the crowd. Caroline struggled to breathe as her mind tumbled over itself. He worked for Silus? Why had he lied? Her thoughts came too fast to comprehend.

"Who is that man?" she asked shaken, her confused eyes turning to Silus's face.

"Why, I thought you had met in Portsmouth? I was worried about your safety, knowing my son's reputation and his many enemies. He is a former bow street runner, who I retain to watch over important people for me. He's been in my service for nearly twenty years now. But I cannot understand why you have not been introduced - for he spoke of you when he returned from Portsmouth, and he had contact with my son, I know that for certain, as Lucian gave him a good deal of money as compensation for an injury he sustained on the trip... a nasty head wound."

"Lucian knows him?" she asked, feeling her breakfast threaten to return on her.

"Why, with twenty years in my service, he's known him since he was a boy. He would hardly have paid a stranger with such a great sum of money."

🏵

*T*he man had just stopped to show the rest of the group the gifts, and Lucian looked at them with a slight frown, trying to place them in his memory. Suddenly his eyes widened as he looked up and realised who was holding them. He felt the blood drain from his face. Lunging toward the man suddenly, he stopped as Charles looked at him in surprise. Collecting himself, Lucian searched for his father's face, his eyes locked on Lucian's every move through the crowd.

Silus smiled at him then, an expression of pure self-satisfied triumph. Where was Caroline? Lucian looked around wildly. Had she recognised the blackguard from the docks?

He saw her then, standing just behind his father, as he turned, leaning down to whisper something close. Her face was a mask of anguish, of horror; the lines of her body tight, her shoulders caved inwards to protect herself from the onslaught. She'd seen Lucian's recognition of the man, his knee-jerk response. There was no sense lying now. She'd seen the guilt on his face. It was too late.

"Excuse me." Lucian began to move toward them as Silus continued to murmur things to Caroline, too far away from him to hear. He dogged through the guests quickly, intent on reaching her before his father's poison did more damage. Reaching her side, he put a hand on her arm, drawing her around to face him.

"Darling," he started, seeing the dazed look and unshed tears glistening in her eyes. After an excruciating moment where her stung eyes searched the depths of his and found them wanting, she pulled her arm from his grasp.

"I am tired. I am ready to leave," she whispered and turned away from him and moved toward the door, her head bowed so that the other guests could not see her distress. He found himself alone before his father. Trembling with anger, he ached to hit him, for flesh to pound flesh until there was nothing left of the gloating smile on Silus's hateful face. He gathered himself, Silus wanted to see him break, and he would not give him the satisfaction. Besides, the arrow had already hit its mark.

"Why?" was all Lucian said, as he looked at him through narrowed eyes.

"Because you, my bastard son... you do not get to be happy," Silus said quietly, with such carelessness that Lucian's heart twisted.

"Not even for a day?" he asked hollowly.

"Not even for a moment. And if you ever forget it, I shall be here to remind you."

END OF PART 2

READ ON IN PART 3
Order now

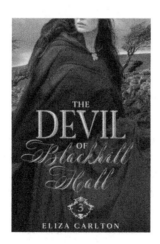

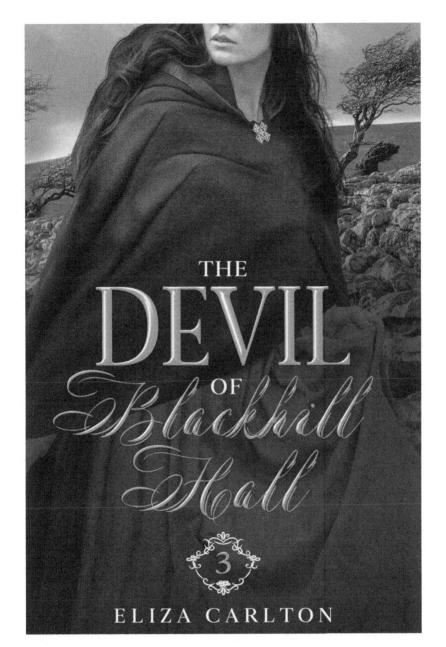

THE

DEVIL

OF

Blackhill

Hall

3

ELIZA CARLTON

CHAPTER 1

~October 1809, Wiltshire~

Silus turned before the company, flashing a bright, fatherly smile across the crowd.

"It seems we have delayed the newlyweds long enough when they are impatient to be alone." He paused a moment for people to cheer bawdily. "They will have to leave now if they are to reach Westmere by dark. Let us see them off in grand fashion, to begin their lives together," he said, and everyone cheered again, with champagne-raised voices, and started moving through the hall toward the open doors. Caroline moved along, pulled by Rebecca, in a state of shock. In the hall, she let her coat be put on numbly, and her bonnet tied. Staring at her friends, she felt tears slip from her eyes.

"Oh Caroline, we shall miss you too," Eva breathed, matching her tears and pulling her close in an embrace. Glad for an excuse, Caroline hid her face in her friend's embraces. She did not search for Lucian. She could feel him, behind her, quiet and grave. Bidding goodbye to the Fairfaxes and Frances and Virgil, she wished for nothing more than to be going home with them, safe and protected, a girl still, to sleep in her maidenly bed and dream of love and dashing knights from stories, where the men were heroic and just. Real-life seemed too cruel to face.

They went outside, the carriage was already packed for their journey, and there was no more reason to delay. The servants were gathering a large basket of old shoes ready for throwing at the departing carriage for good luck. It was Lucian's personal carriage, grander even than his family's, with its black motif and frightening wolf insignia, and six black horses ready at the front. She felt as though she were going to her own funeral in it. She stood back as he opened the door, her face averted from him as she turned back and forced a tearful smile at everyone who loved her, their happiness and well wishes gathering a lump in her throat, choking her.

She stepped into the dark interior, and sat down, leaning away as Lucian climbed in. She pushed up the window sash and looked out at the scene behind them, rendered sour now- a cruel joke- as the horses started to move. The servants started throwing the shoes, everyone cheered. She stuck her hand out and waved until the last, then they were moving down the long winding driveway and out into the country. It was finally quiet, for the first time all day, and she was acutely aware of the man sitting opposite her, who was looking at her as one might a case of dynamite. She swallowed, her eyes felt puffy and painful, and she took her gloves off, pressing her cool fingers across their lids.

She felt completely depleted by the day, and the extremes of emotions; the betrayal stinging all the more, because of her blinding happiness and foolishly trusting heart.

"Darling," his voice was a whisper, and she heard the pain in it. He should suffer, she thought coldly. She had seen his face when he looked up at the man from the docks- recognition, fear, panic, guilt. It had been all she needed to know. She shook her head, still not looking at him. She could not take his searching eyes right now. Closing her own, she laid back against the seat, letting the force of the day tempt her into oblivion.

*S*he must have been exhausted, or simply did not wish to speak to him, for Caroline did not open her eyes again until the carriage stopped. He had been watching her sleep, feeling wretched and alone, needing nothing more than her smile, or her touch, anything to show him she might learn to forgive even this. If only she'd listen, perhaps it would not be so very bad. He needed her to believe in him one last time.

He put his arms under her, meaning to carry her inside, but she stirred, sitting up and pushing him back.

"I am awake," she said, running her hands over her hair, restoring order. He watched silently as she prepared herself, then looked to him.

"Well?" she said, and he spurred himself into action. Opening the door, he stepped down, turning immediately to help her. She took his hand, but quickly let go as her feet touched the ground and she turned away to inspect the house.

It was smaller than the Ashford's estate, yet grander, which she had hardly thought possible. It looked fresher too, newer than the two-century-old Blackhill Hall, and it looked as though he had spent time improving it. The night was dark, and flaming torches lit the path to the house. The staff were all standing at attendance outside the grand entry, ready to meet their new mistress.

She waited for Lucian to take her arm and they walked along the line, she smiled at the staff, hoping to make a good first impression, wishing that her smile was not fake. Reaching the top, she was introduced to the butler and housekeeper, very capable-looking people. Next, Lucian brought her into the house. It was warm and she could see inviting fires burning large in cavernous fireplaces.

There was beautiful: coloured glass from windows and crystal chandeliers caught the candlelight. A lush, green abundance of potted plants breathed fresh new life into the cold stone. Nestled in the massive set of sweeping bay windows was a grand piano, and a gold-gilded harp. And then there was the art. Incredible, breathtaking art nearly everywhere she looked. Colours abounding, great paintings both ancient and astonishingly modern, so huge in size that Caroline could not believe they had not been painted in their exact spots. There were also artifacts of travel, Persian rugs, Indian silks, tribal masks and

Chinese lacquer. It was all so luxurious, cultured and beautiful, and yet placed with so careful a hand that it managed grace when it might have been gaudy.

She looked around, aware that as she studied the hall, Lucian studied her.

"Is it to you taste?" he asked

"You are a collector," she stated, seeing the meticulous detail and care which each of his pieces was presented and kept.

"I suppose I am."

"You like to own and collect beautiful things," she said softly.

"Darling, please-" he said, his tone tortured.

"I am tired. Please, allow me to rest," she said, quietly, not wanting the new servants to realise something was amiss between them already. He looked at her, frustration plain in his posture, then motioned for the bags to be fetched.

"Of course. I shall show you upstairs," he said, offering her his arm as she started to climb them. There were so few doors on the upper floor that she wondered at the layout of the house.

"I shall give you a tour tomorrow if you wish it. Westmere is an unusual home. My true father built it for solitude, a place to escape the city, and company, it does not accommodate many, despite its size. It has been designed to give the most space and luxury to a small number," he explained as they reached a set of double doors. Opening them, they stepped in, and she saw the staff had already lit the fire and candles, making the room warm and inviting.

It was perhaps the most beautiful room Caroline had ever seen. It had at its centre a massive half-tester bed, carved in polished mahogany, and embellished in sapphire damask, that looked as if it had been built for royalty. A fireplace dominated one wall, carved in white marble to the ceiling, while the opposite wall was almost entirely covered in windows leading out onto a splendid curved balcony. There were several areas to sit by the fire, to work at a writing desk, and many cozy cushioned corners in which to read a good book. There were two dressing rooms, leading off of the bedroom, his and hers.

Caroline walked into the room, pulling her coat from her shoulders tiredly. She felt Lucian's hands cover hers.

"Allow me," he said and she pulled away.

"I'd rather not," she said, walking away from him to inspect the dressing rooms.

"Caroline, we must talk about this," he said and she turned to face him.

"Yes. But not tonight. I cannot tonight," she said, exhaustion weighing heavily in her voice. She glanced at the bed and saw, to her horror, that the servants had spread fresh flowers across the bed, matching the enormous arrangements on the tables, mantle, and at each bedside. She stared at them and Lucian turned to look too. The romantic scene made a mockery of them.

"Are there not separate rooms? For man and wife? I thought it was the English custom," she asked.

He shook his head. "Westmere is unusual, it is a place of intimacy," he answered. "If you want... I shall sleep in one of the guest bedrooms."

"No," she said, and he looked up in surprise, his face showing a flash of hope. "I do not wish the servants to know we are at odds. On our wedding night no less," she said. His face fell for a moment before it was hidden away.

"There is a chaise in my dressing room..." he offered.

"Yes, thank you," she said, unwrapping her shawl and taking off her gloves. A knock at the door signalled that their cases had arrived. Clearing his throat, Lucian opened the door and began directing the footmen into place with them. Caroline came over to supervise the unpacking of her things with a maid. A while later when they were both growing tired, Lucian announced that the rest would have to be completed the following day so that they might rest. Closing the door behind the departing staff, he looked at Caroline who was unpinning her hair.

"Are you hungry?"

She shook her head wordlessly, and he seemed to cast about for something else to say.

"Good night," she said shortly, returning her attention to untangling the complicated intricacies of her hair, which had been so carefully styled for her wedding day.

He wanted to grab her and kiss her, remind her of their connection. He wanted to fall to his knees before her, and tell her the whole truth, in all its ugliness, and have no more secrets between them. But she had asked for some time, and the least he could do was give it to her. He hesitated, seeing her eyes find his in the mirror.

"Good night, my love," he replied simply, going to his dressing room, and shutting the door gently behind him.

❦

*T*he soft sound of skirts rustling woke Caroline from the deepest sleep she had had in weeks. The room was growing light with morning sun, and she cracked her eyes open a touch to see a maid setting the fire quietly. She sat up, noticing with relief that Lucian had brought his clothes through, making it look as though he had slept beside her.

"What time is it?" Caroline asked, and the maid jumped, turning quickly.

"It is... a little before eight, Milady," she said, bobbing into a courtesy, Caroline frowned at the new address.

"Please, just call me Caroline."

"Lady Caroline," the maid repeated, turning back to her fire. Caroline sighed and swung her legs out of bed. She pulled on her dressing gown and walked over to the curved wall of windows. Suddenly the maid appeared beside her, sweeping back the heavy floor-length drapes with a smile.

"Allow me, Lady Caroline."

"What is your name?"

"It's Sophie, milady."

"Well, Sophie, it's very nice to meet you. Thank you for looking after me."

The maid curtsied again and blushed before returning to the fireplace again. Caroline turned to look out of the windows and gasped. The panorama before her stole her breath away. There was a deep valley, with tree-covered hills on each side, a meandering river that wandered along its base, pooling in a large, natural lake, just visible in the distance between the hills. All aflame with autumn colours, it seemed too beautiful to absorb so early in the morning. She longed to step out on the balcony and turned the handle of the door, stepping out into the brisk air. It smelled clean and full of green wilderness, and she breathed deeply, closing her eyes, and let the sunshine rest on her face.

When she had had her fill, she looked to the rest of the estate, seeing a handsome-looking stable in the distance. She also saw a beautiful greenhouse, all glass and white wrought iron, and another very small but charming stone building, opulence in miniature, with carved wooden accents like an Austrian lodge, smoke curling lazily from its chimney. She heard a shout and looked toward it. It had come from the stables.

Suddenly, Lucian walked out of its huge doors, dressed in riding attire: buckskin breeches, tall brown riding boots, and overtop, a thick, dark green tailcoat. Caroline, even in her anger, could not deny they fit him well. He held in his hands the reins of a horse which he was leading out of the stable, while a groom followed them with the saddle. She could see that Lucian felt at ease here, and he ran his hands over the horse's neck gently, speaking to it. It was a dappled grey with delicate ankles and a beautiful mane; though, it hardly seemed like a man's horse. He mounted, letting the groom adjust the length of the stirrups, and then when he stepped back, the horse moved gently away.

Lucian sat the horse well and seemed to be taking it very slowly, after a while coaxing it into a trot then into a light canter. He turned toward the house, and Caroline saw him look up at her. She stiffened as their eyes met. The horse came to a stop, and still, Lucian sat looking at her. The horse, losing interest in the ride, lowered her head and began to nibble the grass, and Lucian slid off the back of the beautiful animal. His face wrung her heart, so wrapped with crushed hope. She took a last breath of the bracing air and turned back inside.

"Oh! Lady Caroline, you shouldn't go out there without any slippers on, you'll catch your death!" Sophie said as she took Caroline's robe from her and offered her some light slippers, hand-embroidered with flowers. Murmuring her thanks, she went to the last room she had not yet explored - the bathing room.

The entire room had been built around a very large tub, gleaming pink copper, which sat in the middle of the room. There was also large, matching washbowls and mirrors against one wall, and another wall of windows, offering another amazing view of the country. Marble floors shone in black and white, and above the tub hung another massive chandelier for added decadence. Caroline loved it, and she couldn't help running her hands over the cool, clean surfaces. Sophie left, closing the door behind her and Caroline went to the washbowl, poured some cool water in it, and splashed her face, properly washing off the residue of the hurtful night before.

"Darling?" his low voice startled her from behind the closed door. She reached for a cloth and patted her face with it, taking a deep breath.

"Yes? What is it?" she responded flatly.

"I was hoping that we could talk. I wish very much to explain," he said and waited for her response. She studied her face in the mirror, the dark circles under her eyes, the crease on her brow. She did not see any purpose in torturing him, but all the same, she felt weighed down. She had been manipulated. She had chosen to marry this man. And he took part in the deception, trapping her, just as he had done before. She hated herself for having thought that they were past all of that, for having believed that this was something different. But, it mattered not. They were joined now by law and under God, and she had gambled away the rest of her life with a man whom she could not trust on a gut feeling. She would have to try to make the best of it. She needed to get her head around it, think it through, prepare. She simply did not yet know how and was not ready to begin trying.

"Please," he said after a while. She opened the door and he stepped back.

"I need some time, I hope you will permit it me," she said, resisting his eyes. He moved to touch her, but then withheld himself.

"But, we must discuss this... the longer we wait..." he said, trailing off, seeming to struggle with what to say. "I don't want us to... drift apart. To make things worse."

"Time will change nothing. I ask this last thing of you. Allow me some time to understand my feelings, sort through my emotions. The last few weeks have been far from easy, and this seems to be the prover-bial straw. I wish you would try to understand."

"But, you will feel better if we talk, if you can at least see how-"

"You mean you will," she cut him off, and he frowned. She looked away. It was too much to hold his eyes. He took a deep breath and stepped back.

"Pardon?"

"You mean *you* will feel better if we talk. That is what you're concerned about, is it not?" He stood for a moment, unsure what to do.

"As you wish," he said, and bowed, turning to leave. Caroline watched him go, her heart heavy and confused. She did need some time, at least he seemed willing to give it to her. Changing into a loose informal gown, she started to sort through her possessions, hoping that some of her own things around her would give her comfort.

Sophie began to help her unpack the rest of her cases, and the day soon slipped away into a whirl or organisation. Lucian's possessions had to be put away also, and it seemed he did not have a valet present at the estate. Caroline supervised the sorting of his clothes, the task seeming too intimate considering their present relationship. His clothes smelled like him, and she left his dressing room as fast as possible.

In the evening, she took a tray in her room and then wrote to her friends and family, telling them of their safe arrival and how they were settling in. When she finished, she felt tired and decided to go straight to bed. As she lay there, about to blow out the candle, she realised that she hadn't told Lucian when they would speak. It had to be soon, that she knew, it was wrong to drag it out. Yet, there was a reluctance there, and fear. Fear of the truth. The whole situation was so confusing. How could he have done this to her after everything? It made everything that they had shared feel like a lie. She didn't really know him. Or maybe she did know him and was just too afraid to admit what he was. Closing her eyes, she pushed him from her mind and tried to sleep.

*H*ours later, after rest and sleep still continued to evade her, she heard his footsteps on the stairs. They were heavier than usual. Lucian hesitated outside the door, and then pushed it open slowly. She heard him walk through the room, heading toward the dressing room. Suddenly, he paused, and even with her eyes closed, she could sense him looming over her. She forced her breathing to sound regular and even. After a long moment, she felt the bed dip under his weight as he sat on it. She struggled to remain motionless and keep her face relaxed. Then, she felt his hand on her hair. It moved slowly, reverently, lightly brushing back the wisps that fell on her face and pulling the blanket up to her chin. Suddenly, he was leaning closer, and she felt him lightly press a kiss on her forehead. He lingered, with his nose brushing her skin, his lips pressing gently into her.

"Forgive me," his whisper was almost silent. As soon as she heard it, his touch was gone, and he was quietly standing, making his way to the dark doorway of his cold room, leaving her to lay there in the dark, her heart pounding, her face on fire from the feel of his lips.

⚘

*T*he next morning, the maid arrived with a tray for breakfast, and Caroline got up, feigning an enthusiasm for another day that she did not feel. As she sat to eat, a knock on the door startled her, and she felt her stomach jump.

"Yes?" she called through the door.

"I am sorry to interrupt your meal," came Lucian's voice. "I am only here to ask if, after breakfast, you could join me outside."

"I was planning to take a bath..." she said, quieting and waited as he shifted outside the door.

"Can I prevail upon you... just to join me for a while? You could take a bath after, I shan't disturb you." His voice was soft, and she hated to picture the expression on it. She looked at herself in the mirror, a newlywed bride, in her first week of married life. This was not how she wanted to spend it.

"Caroline... please."

"Very well. What should I wear? What are you going to do?"

"I'm going to teach you how to ride. Wear something you shant miss," he said.

⚘

*C*aroline strode out of the house, across the terrace, and through the manicured portion of the gardens. She made for the stables up ahead, seeing the dappled grey grazing, still saddled, and another horse, a magnificent black, without a spot of colour on him anywhere, at least twice the size of the grey horse tethered to a fence post. She slowed as she approached them, trying to look friendly as both horses looked up to see her approaching.

"Hello, beautiful," she said, reaching a hand out to touch the elegant grey, who snorted as she rubbed her nose. Feeling braver she ran her hand up its sweeping neck and the horse stamped its feet with pleasure, turning its head to nuzzle her. She laughed at the strange sensation, her eyes dancing with laughter as she returned her hands and continued her ministrations.

"She likes you," Caroline turned to see Lucian, leaning against the stable door watching her. He pushed off and started toward her as she turned back to the horse. "Is there any creature you cannot tame?"

"I know of one for certain," she muttered, as his hand joined her on the horse's neck, his fingers expertly soothing it.

"I would not be so certain," he said, so close to her, that it made her skin prickle.

"Whose horse is this? Rebecca's?" she asked.

"Yours... it is my wedding present to you. In truth, it was an engagement gift, but I was forbidden from seeing you, and it never quite came to pass."

"Mine? And what have I done to merit such an extravagant gift?" she said, glancing up at him, a dry smile on her lips.

"I do not require any action from you to want to shower you with gifts," he answered. "But, in truth, the answer is... everything." She turned to him then, tilting her head to the side and looking at him speculatively.

"You cannot buy my forgiveness, you know."

"I am not trying to."

"You cannot buy my love either."

"I mean to earn both," he said determinedly.

"In that case, I am glad you have youth on your side," she said and moved off toward the other horse. He followed, suddenly looking her up and down.

"May I... ask what you are wearing?" Caroline glanced down, the riding habit that Rebecca had insisted be included in her trousseau, had not been unpacked yet and it was brand new. Instead, she had asked Sophie to fetch some of Lucian's old riding breeches and a shirt, adding her own warm, fitted jacket and black leather boots. She had seen his surprise when she had walked up, and the fact that he had managed to keep the comment in so long told her that she still held the power firmly in her grasp.

"You said to wear something I shouldn't miss," she stated, as though it were obvious. Swallowing visibly with what she was surprised to see was suppressed lust, he ran a hand over his face, composed himself, and approached.

"Lelantos is not as friendly as Theia, I am afraid- in fact, he does not take well to strangers."

"Lelantos, titan of hunters and skill, and Theia... " Caroline said

"Impressive. Titan of light." Lucian finished. Caroline held her hand out for Lelantos to smell, the massive horse looked at her a little curiously, then, all of a sudden, pushed his silken nose into her hand. Caroline laughed with surprise. She couldn't help but smile at Lucian, and he looked pleased.

"I am surprised you did not just call them Hades and Persephone," she said sarcastically and he bit back a smile.

"I cannot claim it did not cross my mind," he acknowledged and laughed at her derisive snort.

"Looks like he likes me also," she said with a self-satisfied smile, as the horse turned more toward her, nuzzling her with its nose, tucking it between her shoulder and chin.

"He is male, after all. Lucky devil," he laughed, but she did not return it. Perhaps he had hoped that horses would distract her, that it would smooth matters over until they could be forgotten about. But his easy charm rankled her. "What is it? Did I say something that upset you?" She whirled back and faced him, spurred by her sudden flash of anger.

"You let me hate him, Lucian. You let me think he was manipulating me when it was you and your father all along." Her voice was sharp, a weapon carefully polished over the past few days. She stepped closer and gave him a challenging look. He met it, without looking away, but without the challenge in his eyes.

"Yes," he admitted, and fire flared in her chest.

"Why?" she demanded.

"You already know why."

"No, I do not. I want you to tell me. That should be simple enough, should it not?" she said, folding her arms over her chest.

He looked away, abashed before his face twisted in a wry smile, and he attempted to change the subject.

"I thought we were going to ride," he gestured to the horses. "Perhaps it would do us both some good, get some fresh air in our lungs,... and then we can speak more easily when we return," he tried.

She studied his face, her eyes searching for answers that were too well concealed to find.

"Did you pay that man?"

"Yes."

"When?"

"The morning you were about to depart, when I went to get your luggage... after you had already decided to stay. He approached me and revealed his true employer. I knew none of it before, I swear it to you."

She stilled, her mind working out the new information. That was something at least. If she could trust his words, then he had not schemed and conspired to trick her yet again as he had done the first time. But, it landed on cold skin. This was not the first time he had betrayed her.

"And your payment was for what exactly?" Her voice sliced through the air. He didn't respond. He looked down and let his breath out in a long, low pained exhale. "To keep this from me?"

"Yes," he spat as if the word was bitter on his tongue.

"But the ship had not yet departed?" He nodded. "You paid that man. Paid him to keep the truth from me so that I would not go back to Mr. Lee - the man that I said I had chosen?" She could not help but add this twist of the knife.

He looked up, but his face had lost some of its pleading. "Reconsidering your lofty opinion on hate, my dear?" he asked, in a callous tone. The air cracked with the building tension.

She walked steadily in a few steps and closed the space between them. She stopped a short distance away and continued her scrutiny, seeing his discomfort grow, a pink tinge starting to warm his neck as his blue eyes fought to keep their insolent mask.

"You would like that, wouldn't you?" she asked, seeing her words hit him. "It would be so much easier for you if I hated you. You would have nothing to be held accountable for, you could hate me back and go on hating yourself." He ground his teeth at her soft words, a muscle ticking in his jaw.

"You *should* hate me," he ground out, his voice an accusation.

"Maybe, but I do not. I am disappointed in you, and that is much harder to bear," she finished, seeing his mask slip for a moment, showing his pain and bewilderment etched as clear as day for one moment. He looked lost and afraid. It wrung her heart, but she turned away from him, walking back toward the house, calling back over her shoulder.

"I do not think I am in the mood for riding after all."

⚛

*L*ucian watched the clock hand move toward midnight, taking another drink of whisky and deciding that he had stayed away long enough for her to be asleep. Her words earlier had completely thrown him. He had been expecting tears and anger, perhaps some airborne objects... not this... quiet withdrawal. Disappointment. He recalled her words... disappointment worse than hate? He thought not. But now, after a day alone, he felt very confused indeed. Hate, that could be brought around, but disappointment...how did one recover from that?

Standing, he loosened his cravat and started up the stairs. It was dark, the servants long in bed. He hesitated at the door and then opened it quietly. The room was thick black, the heavy drapes shutting out the moonlight. Walking carefully, he made his way across the room, pausing by the bed. The solid darkness made it impossible to see her, but just knowing that she was there, soft and warm, made his chest tight. Pushing on, he stripped off his clothes as he went, trying to keep up the facade that he was sleeping there. He knew it could not last long. Caroline would need a lady's maid and him, a valet if he was going to try to learn respectability at last. They would not be able to hide their sleeping arrangements then. He fumbled in the dark onto the chaise in his dressing room. It was hard and uncompromising. Closing his eyes, he willed himself into a dreamless sleep.

⚛

A scream sent him bolting upright in his bed. His heart pounding for a moment, he looked around, seeing only the darkness of his windowless room. Strangled sounds made their way through the door, and Lucian sprang out of bed and ran through to the bedroom. The room was bathed in a cold, pale light, and he could make out Caroline's form on the bed. She was contorted, her body rigid with fear, her hands clawing at the bedclothes as she turned from side to side feverishly. He looked at her in alarm, unsure of what to do, how to help.

She gasped, twisting over, almost falling from the bed. He was at her side in an instant and pulled her back onto the soft mattress. She whimpered at his touch, and her hands clasped onto him, holding on as he sat on the bed and tried to lay her head back on the pillow.

"Shhh, Caroline, I am not leaving, you are safe," he murmured, brushing her hair off her face, as it stuck with perspiration against her brow. She kept a tight hold of him, and suddenly, startled him by pulling her upper body against his. Burrowing in his shoulder with her face, she pressed into him, and he felt her tremors lessen. He kept stroking her hair and felt her start to relax.

It was miraculous that she had not woken herself up, he thought, seeing her tense face smooth out. She took a deep breath and relaxed against him with a finality that seemed to indicate that the worst had passed. His presence had helped her. He took a steadying breath, his heart beating a little strangely. He lifted his own legs onto the bed, resting back, and gathering her tightly into his chest, pulling the cover over them. He could feel her heart beating against his chest, and he closed his eyes, that small vibration bringing him such a sense of responsibility and joy. She was trusting him, whether she knew it or not. For the first time in days, he felt his face crease in a smile. She had not shut him out of her heart, all he had to do was find a way back in.

T he dream had shaken her, turning up again, refusing to diminish. She knew the feeling well enough - it had chased her her entire life, increasing in intensity and frequency in times of worry, insecurity, excitement, or great emotion. They were all coming to the surface, because of the man sleeping beside her, his strong arms holding her safe against him.

And, it did make her feel safe, and contented somehow, she knew, though it was a difficult thing to admit to. She thought back to the night in the kitchen, and how she had felt knowing that this man would be hers, and that she would be his, that they would be bound together forever. Now, lying beside him, seeing him vulnerable in sleep, she felt like reaching out and touching his face, she wanted to feel his keen blue eyes on her.

At the same time, however, she knew that would change everything. Then, things would have to be talked about, problems aired, feelings discussed, and it was all such a tangled mess that she felt weary even contemplating it. Now, here, with his closed eyes and open arms, she felt close to him, and she didn't want it to end just yet. She gently laid her head back on his solid chest and snuggled deeper into his warm embrace. Letting a deep breath out, she closed her eyes, and felt a wave of calm sweep over her, missing the small smile that appeared on the face above hers.

❀

*W*hen Sophie came in, Lucian had been awake for a while, since the moment that Caroline had woken and returned to sleep. Feeling her choose to fall back asleep in his arms, had been indescribable. It was elating and simultaneously bewildering. She had been so furious with him that afternoon, the deep type of fury that simmered hot and long, rather than explode. And yet, here she was in his arms, curling into him, seeking comfort from him, and in some small way, trusting him.

Why did she continue to tolerate him? When would she realise that he had nothing to give her in return? The maid appeared at the door, and he saw the shock of seeing them together register in her eyes, even as she bobbed and started at her work. Lucian imagined that he might have seen a small look of relief, and he was glad for it, he wanted Caroline surrounded by people who cared about her, though he knew it was next to impossible for someone not to be won over by her.

She stirred in his arms and looked up at him. Her hazel eyes were clear, and she looked much rested. They stared at each other for a few moments longer.

"Good morning, my dear," Lucian said softly.

She sat up, and slid out of bed, without a word. He held back his frown and mirrored her movements, standing beside the bed. Caroline pulled on her dressing gown and then turned to look at him. Her look was a little guarded and he knew immediately that one night of comfort was not going to erase the issues between them.

"I shall leave you," he said, turning toward his dressing room, biding his time.

"You look well this morning, milady," Sophie's voice came to him from the dressing room. "His lordship too," she said more quietly, and Lucian smirked as he did up his buttons.

When he had finished dressing for a ride, he stood in the door, and placed a hand against the frame, leaning into it, unsure.

"My dear. I..." he started, and then stopped, completely lost for words. What did he know about smoothing things over with a woman? He had no idea what to do in this situation, and it made him frustrated beyond belief. The look on her face in the mirror told him everything that she didn't have to say. He gave up, made a short, formal bow and turned on his heel, striding from the room.

He had to get outside, get on his horse, and put some distance between himself and the most complicated, confounding woman he had ever met. His breath frosted the air as he started over the dew-covered grass, he walked fast, pushing his legs, enjoying the way the muscles protested.

In the stables, he went directly to Lelantos's stall and opened it. The horse eyed him curiously, sensing his unsettled mood. He led him out and started to prepare him for riding. A groom hurried in, the man still chewing his breakfast, unused to seeing Lucian at this early hour.

"My lord! Please, let me," the man said and stopped as Lucian dismissed him with a gesture.

"I shall take care of it. Return to your breakfast, Keagan. I shall be back in an hour, or thereabouts." The saddle and bridle in place, he led Lelantanos out in the yard and swung up in the seat. He urged the horse on, already feeling its energy matching his, the powerful horse's desire to fly through fields and over fences. To feel free and unbound.

Spurring Lelantos on, he focused his mind on the movements of the graceful animal and tried to rid his mind of the feel of clutching fingers, and soft, long hair as it brushed his cheek.

He lost track of time as the lush countryside rushed past. The cool air chilled his face and his legs began to burn as he pushed on. He felt such a pent-up energy in him, a writhing mass of anger, confusion, desire and desperation. He longed to fight someone, hit something, to rut, to release himself somehow, as he was so used to. These feelings were not foreign to him individually, but with Caroline, he seemed to feel everything all at once, to exist within the ceaseless hum of intolerably heightened emotion. Caroline had gotten inside him, and like a poison working through his veins, he felt completely at her mercy and powerless, a feeling he had no idea how to handle.

The only other person who ever made him feel so lost was his father, or rather, Silus. There, a slow-burning hatred, a simmering anger, was the manifestation of his feelings toward the man who had treated him as less than human most of his life. It was the strongest emotion he had ever felt toward another person. Until now.

He felt Lelantos tire under him, and he eased off, slowing as the powerful horse dropped into a canter. Seeing the lake shining before him in the morning light, mist rising from the water, he pulled to a stop and jumped off his back and strode them both toward it so that Lelantos might drink, and he might rest. Breathing deeply, he tried to calm himself, but without success. He realised that he could not stop running things over and over in his head, could not find peace, even here. His usual method of coping was to turn to drink, or anonymous women - to lose himself in destruction, and push all rational thought from his mind. But he could no longer hide in such a way - from her, nor from himself and his own failings. It was penance, in a way, he supposed.

Reaching the water's edge, he threw off his coat, his face a deep frown of concentration. He kicked off his boots, and without another thought, walked purposefully into the ice-cold water. It stole his breath away, so sharp, it cut through his senses like a knife. When the water hit his loins, the ungodly shock of it pulled everything else from his mind. He kept walking until he had to suck in a breath as the water closed in over his head, and enveloped him into its quiet depths.

Bursting toward the surface, his head broke with a shower of glimmering droplets. Lelantos raised his head inquisitively at the noise, and then returned to his breakfast. Lucian floated on his back and regarded the sky, a pure blue, dotted with the smallest wisps of cloud. Disappointed... the word echoed in his mind once more, and he agonised over it. What did it mean? What did she want? What could he possibly do to outway entrapment and betrayal? Abruptly he turned and dove deep down again, swimming vigorously, trying to lose himself in the fresh water.

Caroline enjoyed the cool air as she stepped out into the beautiful garden and the sun warmed her cheeks. She ran her hand nervously over her plaited hair and tucked the loose strands behind her ears. Taking a deep breath, she started toward the stables, finally seeing the man she had been waiting for come into sight. Stealing herself not to seem nervous, she came closer and saw the moment when Lucian glimpsed her. He was astride Lelantos and moving at a sedate pace. He came from the direction of the lake, and she could see he had taken a swim. He was only wearing his white shirtsleeves, which clung to his body, and his breeches stretched even more tightly to his muscular thighs than usual, his hair, tousled, curling around his forehead, already drying.

She raised her chin, and walked on, seeing his surprise. His eyes swept up her body, taking in her breeches, and fitted coat.

"Does your offer still stand to teach me to ride?" she asked, and saw his smile melt over the hard lines of his features, and his blue eyes took on a certain twinkle. He lowered his hand to her and waited with bated breath as she looked at it.

"I was under the impression that I had my own horse," she said archly, raising an eyebrow at him.

"You do at that. But, for a novice rider, it may be a little overwhelming... becoming accustomed to being astride a horse, keeping one's balance and controlling it at the same time. My expert opinion as your teacher is that you get used to being up here, then you will be more confident on Theia," he reasoned with a dangerous smile. This request sounded not entirely unreasonable, though. She bit her lip, her eyes suspicious, and she narrowed them at him. He tamed his smile into a modest, innocent thing, and put a hand to his heart. "The model of gentlemanly behaviour, I vow."

She muttered a curse and reached her hand out for his, putting her foot on the stirrup as instructed. He pulled, and in a moment she was in front of him.

❀

She sat rigid, her back straight, holding herself away from him as much as possible, though he felt each line of her soft, warm body curve to fill his space. Gently, he passed his arms around her front, cautiously, gripping the reigns. She stiffened but made no comment. He carefully squeezed his thighs together, and Lelantos started forward at a lazy trot. The forward movement pressed Caroline back, her body coming into full contact with his. His mouth went dry. Her firm thighs and hips, her bottom in her snug breeches, were nestled between his thighs, her whole body cradled in his arms, her head resting just under his chin. The contact almost made him groan. He was a man who had no experience resisting carnal urges, who had always taken what he wanted, when he wanted. He had never in his life felt desire like this: it awed him, that someone could make him feel so. As the trot picked up, she gradually relaxed back, the tension leaving her body, and he heard her laugh. It was carefree and as pure as a bell.

"Would you like to go faster?" he asked and laughed when she nodded her head instantly. He clicked his heels a little, and Lelantos sped up and Lucian was glad that the huge horse was already tired from his morning, and not likely to take off and scare his tentative passenger, and bring an abrupt end to the delicious, heady thrill of it. Suddenly, he felt Caroline's hands touch his, and he let her take the reins, his own hands hovering nearby, just in case. The faster movement of the horse, and the friction between their bodies, the brush of her, over and over along the length of him, was almost making him lose himself altogether.

His senses were entirely taken over - the smell of her hair, the rhythm of the horse, the surprisingly decadent curve of her round ass, the occasional brush of her breasts, without her short stays, against his forearm. He closed his eyes for a painful moment when he imagined what it might be like if she were to spin around in the saddle to kiss him - to straddle him as they rode, the taste of her mouth of his, Caroline breathing heavy with want of him, fumbling with the buttons of his front fall, and irresistibly - hers, as he controlled the horse behind her back. He imagined the wild look in her eyes when she would sink down his hard shaft, how her breath would catch. His hands would go round her soft thighs, and pull her closer as she rode him hard, her hands on his shoulders, crying out, her soft voice breaking, again and again, saying his name. It was only a moment, but it was far, far too much.

Abruptly, he pulled Lelantos to a stop and Caroline turned in his arms and looked at him, questioningly, her laughter dying on her lips as she faced his intent expression.

"What is wrong?" she asked, his eyes on hers, burning with unspoken things. He had not prepared - he knew that riding together would bring them close, but he could never have imagined how much he would want her. He fought for control, his primitive side closer to the surface than it should be around her, closer than he could allow.

"Nothing" he muttered, thickly. His cock was as hard as a rock but had risen tidily up into the waistband of his breeches, and she seemed to be none the wiser. Her eyes scanned his face, her gaze one of innocence, and he could scarcely believe that she could not see the effect she had on him.

"Did I do something wrong?" she asked, clearly worried about her lack of riding skills. He took a sharp breath.

"Sweetheart, you did nothing. It is me," he pressed on an easy smile that he did not feel. "I am afraid if we continue... I shall be unable to keep my vow to be a gentleman," he said and saw as the realisation hit her, and her face coloured a little across her wind-brushed cheeks.

"Well." She blinked but did not rush to move away from him. "I do thank you for the warning," she said, her eyes meeting his for a moment, moving from surprise and ending with a smirk. "I shouldn't like my first time to come and go without me even knowing it.

He laughed. "My Lady Ashford," he said, his voice low. "Do not worry yourself. When it comes to our first time, you shall have..." he slowed his words, "ample warning".

"Well," she said smartly, stopping the game and turning back around. "We shall see."

He started Lelantos back toward the stable, the heat in his body starting to cool, as Caroline held herself away from him again.

Once there, he jumped off the back of the great horse and stood at Caroline's feet to help her dismount. She swung her leg over, and suddenly, overbalancing, fell forward a little. He was there, his arms already around her, lowering her slowly, pressed between his body and the saddle. Her breath caught, and as she reached the ground, she smiled with a little embarrassment.

"Perhaps I do need to get used to horses after all," she admitted, sorting her clothes, and dusting herself off.

"It would be my pleasure to be at your disposal, whenever you should choose," he said, pinning her with his gaze for just a second longer than he should have, before starting to remove the bridle from the horse.

"I do not know if a teacher is supposed to enjoy the lesson, quite so much," she said pointedly, and he barked out a laugh at her disarming candidness.

"I've missed you, Caroline," he laughed, unable to help himself, and saw how his words caused her smile to slip a little, a small frown marring her brow. He instantly regretted it.

Nodding, thoughtfully, she turned toward the house. A part of him wanted to shout at her to stop, to stay with him, spend a little longer, make his day a little more bearable, but he knew he had been lucky enough already.

"Lucian?" she called and he turned toward her.

"Tonight. Let us discuss... our situation. We will confront your deception, after which, there will be no more of it. Never again, if you wish us to have any kind of relationship," she said matter of factly, and he felt his heart clench.

"Yes. Tonight, my Lady. I shall will the hours to move more swiftly until then," he replied with a courtly bow, and she nodded, her eyes flicking briefly to his, before she went toward the house, leaving him standing, his palms sweating and his nerves humming.

*H*e had spent the remainder of the day making sure the dinner would go smoothly, as it would be their first together as a married couple in their own home.

He had been a mass of nerves, yet her words had given him hope as she had alluded to the future. He knocked gently on their bedroom door, knowing Caroline was somewhere inside. When no reply came, he entered, looking around, and realised she must be in the bathing room.

Listening carefully, he could just discern the sounds of bathing. He walked over to her dresser and pulled the jewellery pouch from his pocket, his heart racing. The piece had been his mother's and he wanted Caroline to have it. She would look beautiful in it. He looked around the room, marvelling at how the once plain, and soulless room had become full of her. Her light had seemed to diffuse the air there, her scent recognisable immediately. He breathed it in deeply and turned his eyes to her vanity. It was strikingly empty, without the many pots and potions his sister amused herself with. A hairbrush lay, a few long, dark hairs caught in its clear bristles. He lifted a bottle, a French perfume gifted at their wedding, and closed his eyes, inhaling the rich, velvet of it. He recognised it. She had worn it very sparingly, he realised, that morning for the ride. A very promising sign indeed.

There was also a pouch, containing what seemed to be a writing set. In fact, she seemed to have been in the middle of composing a letter when she had left for her bath. He looked away from her careful and elegant cursive script, not interested in violating her privacy, until a word jumped out at him, caught his eye, and practically dragged his head back around.

Joshua

Casting a glance at the door, seeing it still closed, he lifted the letter, his blood turning cold at its contents.

*D*ear Mr Lee,

Joshua– if I may still call you such, indeed, if I may still call you a friend. I am writing to express my most sincere apologies for refusing to see you on the days leading up to my wedding. I know the circumstances of my betrothal and our broken engagement are still very unclear to you, and I do not wish to rehash them with you now. I only wish to apologise and express my ardent desire to remain friends. I burn with guilt at the thought of all that has passed, and could never forgive myself if I were to let my poor behavior remain the last between us, and lose you altogether. Please tell me that there still remains a chance..."

*L*ucian let the letter drop, his blood which had been cold as ice, now raged hot. She talked of his deception, yet here she was, writing in secret to the man she had told him was her first choice over he himself, while he was shut out from her room and disgraced. Did she mean to have him? Was this her punishment - to take another man to her bed while he whimpered after her like a dog, waiting for the touch of her hand?

His fist clenched tightly and he felt the overwhelming need to rage and drink and destroy. He heard a noise from the bathroom and he turned on his heel and left the room, a maid scurrying out of his way as he stormed past her. Let them run.

✽

*C*aroline could not believe the gorgeous creations Rebecca had packed into her wedding trousseau, she feared to wear them, for danger of spoiling such exquisite chiffon, lace silks. However, she had little else that was suitable for dinner, so she dressed in her favorite. It was emerald green velvet. It had capped sleeves, and a low bodice, that gathered under her breast quite tightly before falling in a column to the ground. It had delicate black lace edging, and was by far, after her wedding dress, the most beautiful gown she had ever worn. Sophie pulled her hair loosely up, and she smiled at herself in the mirror. Lucian had given her the space she had needed, and after sharing a close and pleasant afternoon with him, she felt finally ready to hear what he had to say. Whether he would be immediately forgiven was another story; but, she did miss his company, and she was tired of the strain in their first week of marriage.

Sitting beside her perfume on the dresser, she saw a jewellery bag, and her heart leapt. She had never been given jewelry before. Anything that her mother had owned had burned in the fire and been left in the ruin. Untying the silk ribbon, she saw the most complex love knot, a necklace in pale gold. It was precious, simple, and stunningly charming, and the thought of him coming and leaving it for her spread warmth through her chest. Sophie reached to put it on her. She would wear it to show him that she was his, despite it all - that she could not help but be his.

She took a last look in the glass. He would admire her in the dress and his necklace, she knew he would. Her hands tidied the dresses clean lines. She had dabbed a little perfume on her neck. Perhaps he might kiss her tonight if things went well. She could not help but hope so. And then... perhaps in a few days when things had softened between them, they may finally grow closer and consummate their marriage, after so long a time waiting. The thought gave her a little involuntary thrill that pulsed from her legs to the pit of her stomach and collided with the memory of his body behind hers on the horse. It burned there, drawing attention to itself, unwilling to let go of her.

She made her way downstairs, nervously smoothing her gloves up her arms. Arriving at the door to the dining room, she took a deep breath and entered. Inside, the table was set for two, and candles lit the room softly. There was a roaring fire in the hearth, and the silver and crystal sparkled in the light against the crimson walls. She walked somewhat nervously into the glittering room, going to the fire, she warmed her hands and wondered where Lucian was.

"Well, I was worried you had changed your mind," she heard him say and followed his voice to see him sitting, somewhat tensely in an armchair, hidden in shadow beyond the open connecting doors of his study. Sitting there, in the half-light, his face had a forbidding look to it, and Caroline looked away, moving to the table to sit. She noticed as she turned, a whiskey decanter, much reduced, sitting beside Lucian's full glass. His cravat was slightly askew and his hair looked as though he had been running his hands through it. She waited, foreboding settling unpleasantly in her stomach as he stood slowly and came toward her.

He came to stop in front of her - close, extremely close. Caroline had to tilt her head back to look at his face, his waistcoat lightly brushing her chest. He looked down into her eyes with a brooding, intense look, and she reminded herself to breathe. He reached a hand up, and lightly touched her cheek.

"So beautiful.." he whispered, his eyes moving over her face as though he was memorising its detail. She fought down her sudden nerves, stealing herself. With his posture, she could scarcely believe that he did not mean to make her uncomfortable. Refusing to give him the satisfaction, she smiled.

"Well, are we planning to eat tonight, or merely to stand and stare at each other?" she asked and waited as he finally moved away from her, crossing into the dining room where he stood by his seat and waited for her to sit before sinking into his chair.

Servers came with food, and she helped herself, watching as Lucian waved the food away. Pausing with her knife and fork poised she waited.

"Is there something wrong? Have you eaten?"

"I find I have quite lost my appetite. I see you got my gift," he said, lifting his glass.

"I did. Thank you, Lucian. It is beautiful." She put her hand up to it, to feel it again between her fingers, and allowed a warm, tender smile to show him what the gesture meant to her. She did not know what had soured his mood, but perhaps it could still shift with a bit of softness.

"And what a lovely gown," he waved his glass in her direction. "Almost as beautiful as your blue one." Caroline set down her cutlery with a clink in the heavy silence of the room. "I know how you treasure gifts from the men in your life," he said, dryly, and she looked up at him then, anger flaring in her.

"Lucian, I am in no mood for games. What is the matter? Speak plainly."

"If you knew my mind you would not ask it," he growled, his eyes darkened.

"So, I am to guess?" she asked in frustration.

"It should not be too difficult; however, clearly I am not privy to all your... activities, so perhaps you have many to choose from." Caroline pushed her chair back, her face flushing with anger. To think, she had been ready to hear him, to forgive him. He was the most infuriating man she had ever met!

"Well, if you refuse to tell me what the issue is in a civilised manner, then I shall retire to bed. I have had quite enough of your company for tonight," she said, rising and starting toward the door.

"How long will you wait to see him? Once we return to London? Should I expect to be cuckolded within the year? Or sooner than that still? Be decent enough to give me some time to prepare," he sneered, his sad eyes at odds with his angry expression. Caroline looked around madly for servants but was relieved to see they were alone. "Perhaps I will ask my father for advice on how best to live with your wife's suitors."

"What the devil are you talking about?" she cried, angry in earnest now.

"Joshua Lee," Lucian ground out.

"What?" She was dumbstruck. Did he simply look for new things to break them? "I am not having an affair with Joshua Lee!" she said.

"Not yet, but can you deny that you have initiated contact with him?" Lucian demanded and his expression hardened as she quieted for a moment, looking for an answer, so taken off guard by his question.

"No, I do not deny it. I see no reason to," she tilted her chin up defiantly.

"You see no reason? You do not think your husband would have a problem with you being in contact with the man you were to marry?"

"No. I have no problem with you and Eva, and would be happy if you chose to become friends."

"That is entirely different, and you know it well."

"I treated Joshua horribly, because of you and your father - because of your lies! He is still my friend, one who has never betrayed me, and I shall continue my friendship with him if I choose!" she practically shouted at him. He got up, his chair scraping against the floor, and closed the space between them. Fury in his eyes, he grabbed her by her upper arms, pulling her toward him, his face inches from hers, and growled dangerously.

"You will never speak to him again. You will cease all contact. I forbid it." Caroline struggled in his arms, her anger overwhelming her. She raised her flashing eyes to his.

"Unhand me this instant! You cannot dictate to me whom I shall be friends with-"

"Oh, yes I can. And I shall, damnit!" Their heated gazes bore into each other, and Caroline felt her hopes dashed once again. Slowly shaking her head, she tried to reach him.

"Lucian, do not be a tyrant. You cannot... restrict my freedom so, you promised me... you, you-"

"What? What must I do?" he asked, shaking her a little, his eyes seeming desperate for a long moment.

"You must trust me," she said, seeing him flinch as her words penetrated. He laughed hollowly, a sound his father often made.

"Trust? How can I trust you? You have run from me at every opportunity, and only when you thought all hope to be gone, did you accept me," he said, turning away.

"You hardly gave me the opportunity to feel anything other than fear for you... your actions were abominable and horribly disappointing." Her voice was scathing. It was the slap she wanted to sting his face with.

"And nothing can reverse it, I am well aware. You will never truly forgive me, and I will never truly trust you to stay... we are at an impasse. And Joshua Lee will be a source of comfort for you," he said, letting her go with a jerk, and swallowing down more strong drink.

Caroline was silent, seeing him wrestle with himself. He was past the point of reasonable thought tonight, clearly, and she would not have any more of a scene for the servants to talk about. "You will ruin us. Piece by piece," she whispered, and searing him with a look which she meant to hurt, she turned and left without another word.

Closing the bedroom door with a snap behind her, she went to her dressing table and looked at the letter. Sinking down on the edge of her bed, tears of frustration and bitter disappointment stinging her eyes, she skimmed the contents. Could this upset him so? Why? She was begging a friend for forgiveness after mistreating him terribly and it had been his fault. It had *all* been his fault.

✿

*L*ucian heard her leave, running back upstairs, to her secret letters and dear memories of another man. Anger surged again like a wave of nausea, as he thought of her sitting, pouring her heart out to Lee, writing about her brutish husband and her need of a rescuer. His outburst would drive them closer together.

He put down his glass and started toward the door, ripping up the stairs and along the corridor. Using his foot to push open the door, he found her, standing by the window, the letter in her hand, as she spun around startled.

"Catching up on your correspondence, my dear?"

"Lucian! Do not go banging around the house so... the servants-" her voice dropped into a whisper.

He threw his head back and gave a bitter laugh.

"Sweet Caroline, do you really think they do not know the state of relations between us? They know our own lives better than us... they change our clean sheets," he said with a sneer. "Do not delude yourself."

Caroline shook her head adamantly. He stalked closer to her as she started around the bed in an effort not to be too close to him.

"Do you think they do not know the circumstances surrounding our marriage? That I ruined you? Though, I am sure that continues to confuse the downstairs gossip... that I do not bed you, despite our lustful history," he said, his eyes sliding over her body as he spoke.

"It is none of their business," Caroline said hotly, trapped against the bed as Lucian approached.

"Of course not, but that does not prevent gossip from spreading. Spreading to ears across the country - your family's... Joshua Lee's... I am sure he would be an eager recipient of such news," he said, closing in on Caroline as she stopped running from him, and stiffened her spine.

"And why would he care to hear such news?" she asked archly. Lucian looked down on her, her resolute face, her set chin, and bold, unwavering glare, she was so magnificent.

"Surely, you know that no marriage is final, under God or the law, until it is consummated," he said and saw as pink tinged her cheeks, though her gaze did not falter.

"So, tell me, what are you planning? To force me, after all this time?" she spat, her breath coming faster.

She was so close, he burned to touch her, to possess her, to make her his. He gently ran his hands up her arms and was rewarded with a shiver which she sought to hide. She was not immune to him, she felt it too, the energy between them, like the air before a storm, heavy with anticipation and electricity. His breath became harsh as he withheld himself from her, and watched as her eyes fell to his lips then back to his eyes hotly.

"Would I be forcing you?" he asked, and she flushed redder still, her thoughts written on her face, her expression guilty. His smile deepened. "Since I first laid eyes on you... I have wanted this, wanted you..." he said, his words tense.

Caroline shook her head back and forth, shaking the thoughts from her mind, telling him no. It wasn't what she wanted. She had not yet forgiven him. It would be her first time. Of course, she would not want it to be like this.

"I have not yet forgiven you for lying to me, withholding the truth, whatever you do... shall be against my wishes, but perhaps that does not matter to you... perhaps getting what you want from me is all this is about," she challenged.

He stopped, serious.

"It is about making you mine, forever. About preventing you from ever leaving me," he said.

"I have already agreed to be your wife!"

"It is not enough... I want you - mind, body and soul."

"My body is the only thing you can force, and in doing so, you lose the other two forever," she said, her eyes beginning to fill with tears. The fighting, the arguing, the hurt he was so capable of inflicting on her and himself - it had begun to draw tears from this warrior of a woman. He was in torment. Surely this was hell. He raised his hands to her face, cradling it, and leant in so his forehead touched hers.

"You cannot be friends with Lee... I, I cannot-" he muttered brokenly.

"I will not promise that. I am sorry that you do not trust me, but I must have my freedom," she whispered back.

"Why in this? Ask me anything else!" he yelled.

"It is for *that* reason that it *must* be this," she replied and met his eyes as he leaned away from her, scrutinising her face.

"What do you want from me?" he asked, his voice lost.

"I do not know... but it's not this. I need you to trust me, to give away your control. I am not your doll to maneuver. I cannot live a life like this," she replied gently. She glowed, standing before him, full of light and hope, and he was reminded of a young bird he had found in the garden when he was a boy. In an effort to keep it to himself, he had run from Wesley and held it tightly, not realising until it was too late that he had crushed it.

Taking a steadying breath, he pushed away from her. Her eyes on him were too much, he felt naked under her honest gaze and he couldn't stand it.

"Lucian?" she called, her voice uncertain as he hesitated on his way to the door. He faltered a moment, wanting nothing more than to return to her side and tell her of all the demons that prevented him from trust, that chased him to the edges of his sanity. But she was pure, untainted by the sort of darkness he had found comprised the majority of his soul.

Without a backward glance, he muttered, "Forgive me," and strode out the room.

Calling on his horse to be brought round, he waited impatiently in the hall, and seeing Lelantos finally led by a groom, he left the house, the gravel crunching underfoot. He mounted and caught a last glimpse of his wife standing by the window in the hall, looking down on the courtyard, a hand to her face. Another dagger of guilt dug between his ribs as he tipped his hat at her grimly, and then, took off into the night.

CHAPTER 2

"How are you feeling this morning, brother?" Charles asked as he accepted tea at breakfast and looked over at his younger brother, slumped in his chair. Lucian gripped his head, pounding for lack of sleep rather than too much drink for once. Caroline haunted his dreams, and he found night the most unrestful time. Charles gave up waiting and turned to his food.

"Have you decided when to depart? I am sure your dear wife will be worried over your absence."

"I would not be too sure," Lucian muttered with a grim smile. Charles studied Lucian's face for a moment, then set his cup down.

"Lucian, you know you are always welcome as my guest, however, I cannot condone this... this hiding from your marriage any longer. You must address the issues between Caroline and yourself, and resolve them. Do not forget brother, you promised to make her happy, and you are far from that at present," Charles finished and Lucian clenched his eyes shut, rubbing a hand over his face. "As it is, I'm afraid I will not be home much longer to host you"

"Why? Where are you going?"

"Europe, on business. I leave tomorrow."

"And you did not think to tell me this before?" Lucian asked irritably.

"I saw no need, I had assumed you would have found the courage to return home by now," Charles said, raising an eyebrow at him, trying to hide his smile as Lucian's eyes narrowed in annoyance. "Lucian, you cannot stay here, snapping at everyone, and staring at walls like a man haunted when there is a very real woman who is waiting for you at home."

"Again, you misinterpret. I am quite sure she is relishing each and every day without me."

"Well, that may be the case, but you will not know until you go home," Charles said with a stern sense of finality. Lucian grunted.

As he wiped his mouth a servant entered, carrying a message on a tray, he quickly turned it over.

"It is from Rebecca. Mrs Frances Tilman has been secluded for the birth of her child. It should come quickly, God willing," he surmised, scanning the contents. "Lucian," he pinned him down with a look, and raised the letter in illustration. "You must return home, and escort Caroline to London. She will want to be present. They are family to her," Charles said firmly. Lucian was already standing.

"Of course. I shall depart immediately."

✿

*L*ucian's mind raced ahead to Caroline and her reaction, to how long it would take to get to Westmere, and then to reach the capital. A small voice whispered in his ear, that now, she would be going back to the city, with all its temptations, he would have no chance to win her over, unlike at his isolated estate, where the deck was as stacked in his favour as it ever would be. Yet, the more reasonable voice knew he must take her, and that Caroline would not want to miss such an important event for her family, and he could no longer be selfish where she was concerned. He had been foolish, hiding from her. Now he must do whatever he could to show her that he would try to be there for her when she needed him.

✿

*W*hen Lucian had ridden away, Caroline had watched him go, tears falling, and then she had gone to bed with her heartbreak and bitter disappointment and slept for two days. Now, eating breakfast on the terrace, her eyes kept going to the stables and she quickly averted them, when she realised who she was waiting to see. She was tired of feeling sad and hiding in her room. If the servants had opinions about her and Lucian, they could keep them to themselves, she thought. She would investigate the estate and tried to make herself feel more at home.

She visited the stables often, trying to build trust with Theia, whom she had fallen in love with, unashamedly. As she stroked the delicate grey mare, she realised that she had never thanked Lucian for the horse. He had chosen a horse so kind and patient. Maybe she would have the chance, if he ever came back, she thought wryly.

Often she stopped in front of the small building that she looked upon often from her balcony: the small, charming one with a chimney and a large expanse of windows that was on the way to the stables. She realised it was the only place in the estate she had not yet been inside of, and she suspected Lucian had spent his time there in their first week at the estate. Deciding to investigate finally, she tried the door and found it locked. Resigned, she turned back to the house. It was just one more place where she could not reach him.

After a morning of cajoling, Caroline had managed to get out of Sophie that there was a spare key for the building outside, which the housekeeper held on to. Her next mission was to wrestle it away from her, though Caroline knew how seriously the woman took her responsibilities.

She stated her case in the plainest and most appealing way she could and waited to see if it would be enough.

"Milady, his Lordship does not like people entering his private space," she said cryptically.

"Well, I am hardly any person. I am his wife," Caroline said with a forced smile and felt embarrassed at the skeptical look the older woman gave her. She scrutinised the tightly laced woman and suspected that she would harden if pushed, so she tried a different tactic. "Mrs Willis, it has been no secret that my husband and I are struggling to find common ground... please. I think that only by eliminating the secrets between us can we truly begin to grow closer," Caroline urged softly, and she saw the housekeeper's eyes soften a touch.

"Is it not better to simply wait until he returns? And you may explore it together?"

Caroline shook her head, frustrated, unsure how much to share with this woman, yet in desperate need of an ally.

"He... he does not share... willingly," she said haltingly, and Mrs Willis frowned a little. She reached for the keys at her waist.

"If his Lordship finds out-"

"Nothing will happen, do not worry. I am practically forcing you. And besides, I have more of a say in staff and household matters than he," Caroline said confidently grasping the key she held out, barely containing her smile. The woman looked uncomfortable. Wanting to speak, it seemed, but hesitant. Caroline tilted her head slightly in entreaty.

"If I may say so, my lady, I am happy that you are in his Lordship's life. He has been waiting for you... a very long time, I dare say." Caroline smiled warmly and thanked her, for her key, for her trust and for her sympathy before marching outside with purpose drawing her brow.

Feeling triumphant, she reached the door and inserted the key. The wind had picked up, and her dress blew around her, lifting and falling in the harsh breeze. She cast her eyes over to the valley and saw dark storm clouds gathering there. Turning back to the door, she gently turned the key, her heart suddenly pounding in nerves of what might be found there, pushed it open, and stepped inside.

The room was warm and dry and smelled of oils and turpentine. The whole space was dedicated to art, and she gasped as she saw an entire wall covered in oil paintings, jostling for space. They were breathtaking, capturing the valley and its abundant beauty perfectly. They were from different seasons, different weathers, a wide array showcasing all the times he had stood by these windows and spread his talent over a canvas. She ran her hands over them, the hard oil brush strokes under her fingertips, making the same lines he had. She continued around the room, seeing yet more paintings stacked against a wall.

Feeling slightly like an intruder she went to them. They were portraits, some of them, and she was shocked at the fine detail in which he had caught his siblings. There was a niggling feeling as she looked through them, one after another, so very many, and she suddenly realised what it was that bothered her- he was not in any of them. Perhaps it was not so strange that an artist not paint themselves, but some were clearly family portraits, with his mother, Silus, Charles, Rebecca, and Wesley. But he was nowhere. She frowned, continuing through another huge pile leaning against the wall.

Finally, she came across one of him, he had captured himself honestly, without a hint of flattery, if anything, a little deprecatingly, as though he could not see what others did when they looked at him. There was something else about it that disturbed her. Where his sister and brothers were surrounded in light, their eyes warm and alive, sunshine falling on them, his picture was dark. His eyes were like those of a dead man, and all around him, a void, so dark and lonely. To be that man - she shivered as she looked away. This is what awaited him in his mind, not part of his family, but something that belonged in the dark, alone. Her heart felt heavy and pained.

She understood now his desire for privacy in his studio. She checked that nothing was disturbed and turned toward the last easel. On it was a simple charcoal sketch of her. It surprised her, though she did not know why, seeing as they had been at Westmere for a week, and he had had more free time than other men on their honeymoon. It was simple and beautiful, and she looked closely at her hair and realised it must be her wedding day. Sketched from memory, it included every twist of her hair, every fall of curl and placement of pin. He had been remembering that day, in here, alone, and recreating the Caroline that had smiled at him, taken strength from him, and agreed to be his wife.

A thought struck her then. He had given her what she needed, wanted. But, now, in his absence, standing in his quiet studio, she began to see the things he had needed from her, that she had withheld. It had hardly occurred to her, hardly been allowed to, that he needed some-thing more than simply her acceptance and presence- that he needed her company, a companion against the darkness if she could be- strength, calm, and reassurance.

She slipped from the studio and locked the door behind her. A wave of raindrops swept up the garden and she ran quickly back to the house, the weather seemed to threaten more, and closed the door behind her, glad for the warmth and protection it gave. She sent instructions for a light dinner to be brought to her room and told the servants she would retire early, knowing how it was a relief for them to have time to themselves.

❀

A while later, as she turned in bed, hearing the storm beat harder against the pane, she struggled to sleep. This type of weather always unsettled her and she watched the rain rush to meet the moonlit hills. Suddenly, a clicking sound came from the door, and she sat upright in surprise. It swung open, and she could see a familiar messy head outlined in the dark. She held the blanket to her and watched him with wide eyes as he slowly entered the room. Her heart started to beat faster and faster still. He had returned. And she had not realised until this very moment, how afraid she had been that he would not.

"Lucian?" she said, hesitantly, seeing him pause in the dark.

"Caroline? I had thought you would be asleep," he murmured and the familiar sound of his low, gravelly voice sent shivers up her arms.

"The thunder... I could not," she explained, shifting back on the bed, she silently invited him to sit.

He came over and perched on the edge, and she could feel his heat, the smell of the storm on him.

"You came back," she whispered softly and saw him nod wordlessly, silhouetted against the lightning outside the window.

"Would you have rather that I had stayed away?"

"No. I mean, it is your house, is it not?" she said lightly and saw him turn his head away from her, staring into the darkness.

"Ours," she heard, so softly, she doubted he had said it at all.

"I had thought to wait until morning, but I have news of Frances Tilman. She is ready to deliver her child. I have returned to escort you to London, to be there with the Fairfaxes, if you wish it," he said, standing up. Caroline leapt up to follow.

"I do wish it! I wish to go at once... a baby..." she said beside herself with new excitement. Caroline went to the window and looked out.

"I do not suppose we could leave tonight... with the hour and the storm?" she said, disappointed.

"I came in Charles' carriage. We had no issue - the roads were passable. I do not see the storm getting much worse," he said evenly. She rewarded him with a warm, genuine smile, as excited as a child on their birthday.

"Then, we may leave tonight?"

"We may leave now if you wish."

"I do!" she said, already turning to the candle and lighting it, thinking how to pack as quickly as possible. As she started hurrying around the room, throwing open a case she realised Lucian was still standing there. She looked at him questioningly, he seemed as though he were about to speak, but instead, he turned on his heel and went to pack his belongings.

Caroline rang for Sophie, unhappy to wake her, but unwilling to wait until morning. She grew more and more excited as she began to select her items for her trunk, taking only the essentials. Next, she shimmied into her drawers and chemise and pulled a thick travelling dress on, and sturdy boots.

A while later, her trunk packed with Sophie's help, they went downstairs together, quietly, and Lucian explained everything to the footman who had opened the door at the late hour. He took the cases and directed the stable boy to attach them to the roof of the carriage. She hated to see the sleep on their faces as they worked through the rain for her when they might have stayed warm in their beds, but she found that she was far too excited to go to London to dwell on anything else. She had felt so alone, and now she was going to the Fairfaxes, to be embraced back into the bosom of her family when she needed it most, and there was to be a baby!

"Danbury, is it?" Lucian shouted to the coachman over the sound of the wind.

"Digby, sir," he nodded, sleep still heavy on his weathered features. "Digby, of course. I am sorry to drag you from your bed at such an hour, but we wish to make all haste to London. Do you think it possible, Digby, or will the storm prevent us? It does seem to be slowing."

Digby looked up at the wind and the clouds, the older man's mouth drawing down at the corners as he narrowed his eyes and considered.

"Yessir, I reckon we can make it," he said with a nod. "We may need to take some of the more sheltered side roads."

"Good man! I shall see that you are compensated for your lost night's sleep, and the wretched weather, of course."

"No need, sir. No need." He drew his wide-brimmed hat down lower over his eyes, and pulled his collar and scarf higher, double-checking the reins and harness with a practiced hand before he climbed up into the box. He was soft of step, and voice, and eyes, Caroline thought: a kind man perhaps, but he also looked capable, and as if he had done the job for many, many years. Lightning cracked in the far distance, and she felt a surge of trepidation, glad that such a reliable-looking man would drive them.

The velvet interior of the carriage was slightly damp and cool, and the rain seemed to be lessening as they started forward into the night. Caroline caught Lucian's eye, but he seemed preoccupied and looked away, grim-faced out of the window as they went.

Feeling a yawn threaten, Caroline was surprised to find herself feeling safe and protected for the first time in days, her mind straying to the man opposite her for a moment, before shying away from the realisation that it was him - that she felt safe because he was there. She let her eyes close and the motion of the swaying carriage take her to sleep for the first time that long night.

❀

*T*he carriage rocked, and a deafening roar of thunder boomed, directly over their heads. Caroline sat up in alarm, as the seat shook under her. She was disorientated and confused for a moment, and then remembered Frances and the baby. They were going to London. She saw Lucian twisting around in front of her, pulling back the curtains and looking into the wild night, his face serious.

"What's happening?" Caroline asked.

"We are caught in the storm. I do not recognise this road, Digby must have had to detour," he answered, as he pulled the curtains back and turned to her. He gave her an assessing look and took her hands. Sitting across from her, holding her hands tightly, he squeezed them until she looked at him.

"I thought the storm was passing?" she asked

"Unfortunately, I may have underestimated its strength."

"What about the coachman- Digby?"

"We will all be well when we are out of this. No doubt he'll be taking us somewhere safe where we can wait out the worst of it."

Caroline nodded, trying to silence her gasp as they hit a hole in the road and dipped dangerously.

"Caroline, everything will be well. I will take care of you." But Caroline saw the worry in his eyes. She started to reply, and suddenly, so quickly, she wasn't able to comprehend it, the carriage was flying, a loud rumbling noise, layered with a high screech ripped through the air. She was suspended, her body flying out of the seat. She tried to grip on to Lucian's hands, but they were gone, his body tossed backward, away from hers. It all happened in an instant, and then they were rolling and rolling. The carriage picking up speed as it tumbled. She could not stop herself from falling with it and bashing against the walls of the carriage, until she hit the door, feeling it open beneath her, and the hard crash of the land coming to meet her.

When she came to, she was wandering in the blackness of the storm, screaming his name, and then she was gone again, and the last thing she felt was tripping, tumbling, the stinging shock of cold water surrounding her body, searing pain, going under, and breathing in a lung full of water as the utter blackness held her down.

❀

*L*ucian came to as the freezing rain whipped his face. Groaning, he turned over, finding himself face down, halfway down a steep embankment, where he could just make out the road above, or what had been the road. Now, all that remained was the mud and rubble of a landslide.

Realising he could not see the carriage, he tried to pull himself up, the sharp shale and rocks digging into his flesh as he twisted around. It was dark, with barely a hint of moon to help. The storm was so loud, he could not hear anything else. Suddenly, a jagged bolt of lightning illuminated the destroyed landscape and he spied the carriage. It was lying some distance off, at the bottom of the embankment, half in, half out of a rapidly swelling river. The horses were churning at the ground, still tied, their harnesses broken and twisted, he could not see Caroline anywhere, nor Digby. Pushing himself to his feet, and ignoring the sharp pain in his body he staggered toward the carriage, sliding down the rest of the shale slope. He could hardly breathe, his heart was pounding so loudly.

"Caroline!" It beat, again and again... like a war drum. He struggled on. He had to find her. Reaching the carriage he tried to open the door, but it was pinned against the ground. He climbed up the wrecked box and flung open the other door. Empty. Panic clutched at him as he fell back to the ground. Where was she?

Another flash of lightning illuminated the scene and he searched desperately for some sign of her. There was nothing. Turning back to the carriage, he waded into the river, meaning to go around the other side and look there. Even in the relative shallows, he could feel the strong undercurrents grabbing at his legs, nearly sweeping them out from under him. Reaching the other side, he looked for her, in vain. There was no sign.

"Caroline!" he started shouting, against the wind, again and again, his throat raw and ragged. A flash of lightning lit the river, and suddenly, from the corner of his eye, he saw something pale, too pale to belong to this dark night.

Turning toward it, he saw a place in the water, where trees and rocks had fallen, created a sort of dam, and snagged against it, a ghostly white shape. Without further thought he dove into the icy water, heading toward it as fast as he could. The water rushed him, fed by the flood, stinging his multiple cuts and abrasions, he felt nothing as he pushed on, letting the powerful flow carry him forward.

Approaching the fallen tree, he had no way of slowing his momentum, and gritting his teeth, he slammed hard into the splintered wreckage of the wood, feeling his breath forced painfully from his lungs. Pulling himself along, he was finally close enough to reach out to Caroline. She was floating, pushed against the barrier by the water, her wool dress and cape dragging her down. Thankfully her face was managing to stay above the tide. He reached her, and pulled her body to his, tilting her face back, making sure she had air. She was limp and unresponsive in his arms. He tasted blood in his mouth as he clenched his teeth.

He fought against the water, its many hungry arms wrapping around their limbs and trying to bring them down as he began to swim them toward the shore. Her skirts and dragging cape were trapping the current, pulling her away from him, her ragdoll body entirely at the mercy of the swirling water. His hands went to his boot, supporting her with his other arm, and still leaning against the barrier, he finally found his knife. Turning Caroline around, he cut the clasp of the cape open, and carefully slid the knife down the back of her heavy travelling gown, lacerating the back, laces and sleeves, any fabric he could until the heavy weight suddenly dropped away and she bobbed in his arms. Thrusting his knife back in his boot, he started towing them toward the shore. It seemed so far with the river working against them. Debris hit them, sweeping them back to the dam, time and time again.

But Lucian fought back, his head down, using all his strength, they began to gain ground. Suddenly, he felt rocks under his feet, and then he was making his way into the shallows of the river. Holding Caroline carefully, he laid her down as soon as he cleared the river bank and immediately thrust his fingers into her mouth, to check for debris. Lowering his head, he listened, his hands on her chest, and felt relief echo through him as he heard the faintest breath. She was breathing, she was alive, for now, he reminded himself grimly as he picked her up and started further up the shore. Reaching the carriage again, he carefully laid her down and went to search for Digby.

It wasn't long before he came across him, his skull dashed on the rocks: blood like ribbons winding trails into the water.

Swallowing painfully, Lucian turned away, going to the horses, the horror of the night making him shake with guilt, bile rising in his throat.

He could see now that one of the horses was dead. Its neck had been twisted and broken by the fall, as it was caught now, its head suspended by the bridle a foot above the ground, its eyes wide, and tongue lolling out of its open mouth, in a mask of terror. At least it would have been quick, Lucian told himself. The second horse thrashed, and whinnied, its eyes as wide and bulging as its partners, trying without hope, to right itself. Lucian tried to soothe it with small noises as he worked as quickly as he might to release it from the rigging, ice-cold fingers stiff and fumbling at the buckles, though he knew that he would not be heard over the rush of the wind, like the crashing waves of the sea.

Hope, some small ember on a cold and bitter night, glowed for a moment in Lucian's chest as the horse rose on its own, delicate legs unbroken, and soft flanks intact. He was just as relieved that the poor beast had survived as he was that they would have a way to escape as soon as he could get Caroline on the creature's back. He could strap her to his chest if he could not rouse her - it would warm her at least until they made it to the next village.

Lucian began to lead the horse carefully over the slick, muddy rocks. The dragging need to run to Caroline's side, barely controlled by the fear that the frightened horse might still break its leg. The wind picked up, tossing the horse's mane. A nearby tree gave way and split in two with a crack as loud as thunder, and the horse reared with a scream, pulling on the reins, and yanking Lucian back. Pain shot through his body like a bullet, and he gripped his side and fell to his knees on the rocks, unable to breathe as the reins were ripped from his hand, and the horse bolted, running over the rubble of the road, jumping over the bodies of trees, and into the night.

Lucian fell on his hands, and his fingers dug into the mud as he screamed, the low, helpless sound of fear from a wounded animal. He pushed himself up, and the pain made him dizzy, and he stumbled and ran to Caroline, rain in his eyes, he slipped and fell, crawling over the bits where he could not run.

She seemed to have gotten even paler, her face a porcelain mask, her lips tinged blue. He hurried along the shale, grabbing what he could of the bags and cases that had fallen off the carriage. Slinging them across his body, and praying there would be something warm for Caroline inside, he reached down and picked her up. She murmured against his chest and his heart contracted painfully at the mewling sound.

He started up the embankment, his load threatening to topple him backward at every second. Dropping to his knees more than once, as fresh mud and rock slid under his feet, he battled upward to higher ground, and finally, reached the road. The path was barely discernible, and he pushed on across it, wanting to get out of the exposed areas, where more landslides were a real possibility, and into more sheltered areas where he hoped tree roots would hold fast. The rain continued to lash down on them, as he started through the forest near the road. Here the trees were packed tightly together, big, old trees, with deep roots, and foliage that provided a little protection from the pounding rain.

He trudged on, upward, into the trees. He wasn't sure how much time passed, but finally, at the corner of his vision, he glimpsed something that was not swaying with the wind, that was hard stone and solid angles. A hunter's cabin. He struggled toward it, the lightning flashing, showing him the structure, as he scrambled over tree roots and fallen trunks, each step uphill feeling like a herculean feat.

Exhausted, and shaking with the last of his adrenaline, he reached the door. It was slightly open, so uninhabited, which was a blow, but it was shelter and would be dry and somewhat warmer than in the torrent outside. He pushed it open with his foot, to his relief, it swung inwards easily and he stumbled into the dark interior, shuffling carefully with his numb feet, afraid that he would fall with Caroline in his arms. Inside was cool and damp and seemed like it hadn't been used in a while, drips making their way through the broken slates of the roof. There was a covering of dust over what little was there. But, it had a grate, and chimney for a fire, and a roof over their heads. Everything else was unimportant. He spied a cot against the wall near the fireplace and he went to lay Caroline on it, still, in her clinging wet chemise and drawers, he sat her on the floor, and went to one of the bags he had salvaged.

The cabin was dark and he cursed as he fell over crates and chairs. Locating the bag, he pulled it open and roughly yanked the garments out. He found a shirt of his, worn and thick, and a pair of breeches, and another shirt, this one soft. Turning back to her, he felt his way toward the cot and found she had fallen sideways against the cold ground. Gently pulling her up, he started to strip the cold, tight cotton off her limp body. He worked to get her arms out of the thin, wet sleeves, feeling frustration overwhelm him, he again reached for his knife. Carefully, he sliced the clothes clean though at each side, and pulled them away. They peeled back slowly, having been pressed hard into her white skin, leaving marks behind. The only color on her body was her ankle, which had swollen to nearly double its size, and the dark purple stain, already spreading slowly under the skin. The rest of her was like white marble, tinged a delicate blue, her fingers and lips the bluest of all. Panic surged through him, and he swayed for a moment, suddenly lightheaded.

Leaning against the wall, he gathered himself and pushed on. He picked her slight body up and gently laid her on the cot, and with the soft shirt, started to wipe the clinging river water from her skin. He scrubbed up and down her arms and legs, desperately trying to summon some colour. When she was dry, he slipped her arms through his heavy, warm shirt, lifting her gently to tug down the back and then slid the breeches up over her thighs. Going back to his bag, he found a heavy coat and covered her with it, pulling her wet hair up and off her skin, wrapping it in the shirt he'd used to dry her.

His mind was strangely empty during his ministrations, so focused was he. The adrenaline pumped through his veins, and he moved with ruthless efficiency. Next, he went to the fire, relieved beyond words that there remained some dry wood in the basket beside it. He quickly set the fire with what he found nearby, casting his mind back to years before when a lonely boy would help the footmen, just for the company. The tinder had been carefully kept dry, and he kindled the fire as best he could, struck the flint to steel, blew, and felt elation at the sparks and smoke that grew.

A noise from the cot broke through his concentration, and at an instant, he was at Caroline's side. She was murmuring again, her eyes fluttering, her teeth chattering.

"Cold," she gasped, her eyes clenching shut, her forehead wrinkled. He stroked her face, checking that she was fully covered. Relief surged through him. She was hardly conscious, but she was still with him, and she was strong, he reminded himself.

"Rest my love, you will be warm soon," he murmured, about to stand up, when she suddenly opened her eyes and caught him in her stare.

"Don't leave me again," she pleaded, and he felt his heart break a little, that she would think him capable of leaving her, perhaps that she had suspected he would not come back to her... as though he had any choice, as though his fate to remain beside her had not been decided almost from the first moment she had bestowed a smile on him. He gripped her hand hard and her eyes widened.

"Caroline, I am here, and I am not leaving," he said, his voice determined, and she slowly let her eyes close again, shuddering with chill.

He stood, about to go back to the fire, when the blood rushed from his head, and he swayed again, his head dizzy, and his knees suddenly buckled. He knelt before the fire and took a deep breath.

Outside the wind and rain were lashing the cabin, and lightning and thunder singing the fury of the storm. But for now, they were safe, and Caroline was getting warm. The orange firelight was growing around the room, and he could see her, bundled up, warming slowly.

He tried again to stand and found it too difficult. Looking down in confusion, he realised his own clothes were still soaking wet, and his limbs so cold that he could no longer feel them. He must need the warmth as much as she did. He began to strip off his shirt and breeches, one of his boots already long lost on to the river, leaving his foot slashed by stones and wood, and blue with cold. As he carelessly pulled his shirt off, he groaned as it stuck fast to his abdomen, and came away painfully. Glancing down, he felt his blood run cold as he saw his shirt, with a seeping dark stain marring his whole left side.

Another wave of dizziness came over him, nausea rising in his throat, and he looked to the ground, realising that he had left a trail of blood around the cabin- a good deal of blood. It was hard to comprehend at first, the dripping blood, and jagged hole, dark and muddy. He gingerly lowered his hand to it and hissed as touching it drew more blood. There was something there- a piece of something, a foreign object stuck in his body, speared through by something black and twisted.

It was a tree branch, probably from when he was thrown against the branches in the water. It was embedded in him, and he had no idea how deep, but he was losing blood, too much, that was clear. He couldn't leave it in there for it to rot and fester and turn his blood to poison, but he feared pulling it out, knowing that more blood would fall, perhaps in a glut he would not be able to stem.

Touching around the wound, he tried to get an idea of how deep it was. He swayed again, falling back off his knees. The impact jolting his side, he cursed.

"Lucian..." a quiet, distant voice came from the cot, and he turned to see Caroline barely conscious, still shivering, eyes closed. Caroline needed him, he had to make haste. Turning back around, reaching for his knife, he bit carefully down on the wooden hilt, and then, bracing himself against the fireplace, without another thought, ripped the branch free.

As it came out, he sagged forward, feeling his blood fall on the floor, a wave of breathlessness washing through him.

He rose, holding onto the walls and chairs as he went. He took the soft shirt he had dried Caroline with and wrapped it around his middle, tying the sleeves tight around a bundle of fabric. He groaned, pulling it tighter against the wound, trying to slow the dripping blood.

He struggled to resist the heavy pull of oblivion tugging at him, staggering to the cot, falling on its edge. Lifting his legs, he turned toward Caroline with the last of his strength, and pulled her tight against his chest, he held her there, clasping her back tightly to him, their bodies moulded together as one. His eyelids dropped shut and he hoped that any warmth he had would be hers.

CHAPTER 3

*T*he storm was the worst of the year, in fact, the worst in living memory. In London, Frances delivered a healthy baby girl, surrounded by friends and family. Eli and Eva shared a look over Virgil's joy when he became a father, an unspoken desire passing between them. Charles delayed his departure for his investment interests in Europe, as several ships and ports had sustained damages in the storm, and the storm itself battered still on, diminished now, though not yet tiring of its destruction. Rebecca met with her father's acquaintances in dinner after dinner. Isaac kept himself occupied and waited for a dinner invitation from Silus Ashford that never came. Katherine threw herself into myriad social obligations in the effort to establish herself in society, and perhaps find a husband; though, Margaret Fairfax, however pleased with her daughter's compliance, could not help but notice that some of Katherine's glittering impish charm had dimmed.

❀

*M*iles away, in a dark, swaying forest, trees slick with the rain that never seemed to stop falling, a small cabin stood in a clearing, smoke puffing from its chimney.

When Caroline had woken, she had been clutched with fear. She sat up gasping for breath, feeling the cold water close over her head once more. Slowly her senses adjusted and she realised she was mostly dry and warm, and lying on something soft. She looked down, her hands going to her body, patting herself, checking over. What had happened? She wondered. She remembered being in the carriage and going into the water, and then it all stopped. She jumped as she looked to the side and saw Lucian's back facing her. He was lying on his side, away from her, right on the edge of the cot. He seemed to be asleep. She gingerly pushed herself to the bottom of the cot, and slid to the edge, careful not to wake him.

"Caroline?" his dry voice came from behind her. Twisting around she saw him looking at her, over his shoulder, his blue eyes tired, and his face unusually pale.

"Are you alright?" he asked anxiously, his eyes running over her. She looked down, realising she no longer wore her gown.

"I am... well... I think. I do not know, I can remember nothing after the water, and before that..." she shook her head.

"Believe me, it is better to forget," he said.

She sucked in air through her teeth as she moved her leg and pain from her ankle flooded through her body. She moved the ankle by a tiny increment and she hissed again but was pleased to find that the foot moved, and she did not think it broken. She saw the relief in his eyes at her words. He closed them and leaned back, the effort of sitting forward up seemed to exhaust him.

Wondering now where they were, she turned her attention to the cabin. It was cold, and the roof dripped, things were dusty, furniture was sparse and the entire house was just this one room. She did not know how they had come to be there, but was overcome with gratitude that Lucian had found it, for, without it, they would surely be mired in the storm, if they were lucky enough to still be alive at all. It was dim, they seemed to have slept the whole day through, and night had once again fallen, though it could very well have been the storm stealing the light.

"And you? Are you well?" she said in a worried tone, and at her words, his mouth turned up wryly in the corners.

"Unfortunately for you my dear, I believe I shall not make a merry widow of you just yet," he mocked gently, but Caroline did not feel much in the mood for levity.

Her hand flew to her mouth.

"The coachman? Digby?" Her eyes grew wide. "Where is he?" Lucian's eyebrows drew together, but he just shook his head quietly. "Oh, Lucian." Tears pricked her eyes and she struggled with a deep ragged breath in. He grabbed her hand, but she noticed that he did not rise to hold her. Tears slipped down her cheeks. "This is my fault," she said, nearly a whisper, her breath forming a white wraith in the cold, dark room. "Had I not pushed to leave in the middle of the night when it was unsafe, he would still be warm in his bed."

"No, Caroline. The fault is mine. I was sure the storm had passed. Arrogant." He closed his eyes, and his face tightened. "I was so eager to please you after my bad behaviour, that nothing else mattered. I took a risk, and I put us all in danger."

She felt more tears come at the sound of pain in his voice. She lay back down gingerly, tucked herself into his back, settled the coat over the two of them, and cried quietly. He did not turn, there was hardly room, but he backed against her gently, getting closer, grabbed her hand, and held tight.

ours later she woke, the fire having burned down. She didn't want to wake Lucian, but they could not simply stay in bed until they froze to death, as much as she might have liked to. He had dressed her in his shirt and breeches, she noticed, and she was grateful that they were dry and warm.

She moved each muscle slowly, peeling herself away from Lucian, and up from the bed. Her ankle pulsed with radiating pain that shook her body. It was her weak ankle from her attack, but her previous injury was nothing compared to this. The pain had been a small thing then, manageable, bothersome when she moved it. Now it burned red hot with pain that drummed through her in waves.

At the edge of the bed, she lowered her legs down but left one foot above the ground, afraid to move the angle of her ankle. She braced one hand on the cot, and the other on the wall, and pulled herself up. She would hop. She had to find a way to cope there. There may be no one looking for them, perhaps not for several days, and who knew how far away the next village might be. It was dark, but if she was careful, she could manage.

Slowly, she hopped her way across the small room, the rough floor cold against one bare foot, she kept the other up and grabbed whatever she could for support on the way. The rain still beat the slates overhead, but it seemed to have slowed somewhat. She made her way to the door, resting a hand on the cold knob, and pulled. A strong wind blew in immediately, and shoved her back, sending her swinging with the door, as she clutched to the handle to keep her upright. Shocked, the freezing rain fell on her, and she struggled against the wood to push it closed again, having to use both legs as agony scorched through her. Finally, she heard the click of the latch, and leaned against it, breathing hard, the scene outside playing in her mind: the darkness, the whipping rain, the wind tearing along the hillside, howling.

She looked to Lucian, who had sat up, his head down, his posture looking pained, but his face was hidden from her view.

"We'll be needing more wood soon," she said. "And everything will be wet outside." He said nothing. "And food. We'll be needing food."

Silent, he stood up also, and whipped a shirt quickly over his head, turning away from her, being careful to hide himself.

"I had not expected such modesty from you," she made an attempt at lightness, hoping to get some response. She hopped toward her own clothes to look for a pair of boots, though how she would pull it over her ankle, she did not know.

"Well, I am shy, I confess," he said, matching her false jocundity, and she noted that did not quite reach his voice. He moved slowly to the fire, and added the last three logs, taking up a long stick and poking the red embers.

"I wish I had had that luxury last night," she teased, a slight twinge of embarrassment prickling her neck.

"My darling, if the choice comes between your modesty and your life... it will always be an easy choice to make." He walked slowly toward her, emotion painted across his face. "Caroline, I feared for your life last night... " he said, and she saw the worry in his eyes. Softening, she gave him a joyless smile of consolation.

"I know, forgive me my poor attempt at humor. I don't know what else to do with myself," she took a step toward him and searched his eyes. "Lucian... you saved my life," she said and the moment between them drew out. He raised a hand to stroke a thumb across her cheekbone, and she turned into his hand without a thought, like a cat desperate for affection, and she realised how close he stood beside her, how warm his hand on her face, and how terribly blue his eyes were. She closed her eyes, as he brought his other hand up moving her head to tuck under his chin, kissing the top of her head. "You saved my life at the docks. It was my turn," he said quietly, the joke losing its humor.

"What shall we do?" she asked, after a moment, and he guided her to a stool by the fire where she could take the weight off her leg.

"I am not yet sure, my love, but we are here, and we are together, and that is enough for now."

Lucian moved to start investigating the contents of the cabin. He seemed to be moving stiffly, a little slower than usual.

"There must be somewhere, perhaps not too far, where we can go for help..." she offered, with more hope than she felt.

"No one will discover us while the storm keeps up, of that I am sure. We are also not on a main road, and the road, when I saw it last, was quite destroyed," he said, rummaging through a collection of pots and pans he had found.

"The road was destroyed..." Caroline repeated slowly, the realisation of the hopelessness of their situation setting in.

"We may be here a while," he surmised, as he leant down to pull on his boots. As he bent over, he suddenly gasped and fell down on one knee.

"Lucian! What is wrong?" Caroline rushed to his side as he gripped onto a chair. "Are you injured?"

"I told you I was fine," he muttered. She turned to help him stand up again, and he pushed her away a little as he gained his feet and turned his face away from her, but not before she saw his face - he had grown pale and sweat dotted his brow. He pulled his boots on quickly and seemed to sway on his feet for a moment before he pulled on a coat and started toward the door.

"Where are you going?" Caroline cried, following him.

"We need to see if we can find water, or we must collect the rain

THE DEVIL OF BLACKHILL HALL 3

water, and something to eat," he said, as he opened the door, casting a glance back over his shoulder as he started out into the wild rain.

"You stay here, keep warm. I shall return as soon as I can."

"Lucian!" she called after him, in protest, but he was already gone, then the door shut firmly behind him, and she left standing in the middle of the cabin staring after him. Perhaps it was nothing, perhaps it was merely hunger and exhaustion, she thought, but worry pulled at her stomach when she remembered the look on his face. Going after him would be useless in this storm, and he would only be angry that she had come out in the rain and the cold after he had worked so hard to get her dry and warm.

Slowly she turned her attention to the single room they were sharing, and its meagre contents. Deciding to tidy the cases at least, she started to shift through the clothes on the floor. She picked up her own underclothes cut into ribbons, dried stiffly with brown river water. She didn't see her travel dress or cloak anywhere. She still could not remember much, but the feeling of intense, deathly cold was unforgettable.

She put them in the log basket, deeming the rags not worth saving. The rest of the things she sorted into piles and looked around for anything she had missed. She saw the edge of a shirt poking out under the bag and pulled it. It was dirty, damp, ripped, and covered with stiffening blood. She put a hand to her open mouth.

He *was* hurt, badly by the looks of it. How could he conceal it? He didn't want her more worried than she already was. He was a damn, heroic fool, and now he was outside, battling through dangerous weather, with what must be a sizable wound in his side.

The bleeding had to be stopped, not merely ignored, and she thought that there was the probability that the wound might be unclean, in which case poisoning of the blood could occur. If it did, it would kill him. He needed a doctor. What could she possibly do for him? Both injured, they were unlikely to be able to make it any distance in search of help. How long could they survive here? She was so tired. She needed to think, but her head swam. She sank to her knees before the fire, feeling tears begin, and allowing herself the indulgence of letting go while Lucian was not there to be disheartened by it.

Lucian could not die - it was unthinkable. He was too strong and tough, he was too powerful and vital. Myriad other reasons rushed through her, but she knew the truth, the stark truth of it was, that he could, and probably would die, judging by the blood loss, unless they could find help. She looked at the floor of the cabin and saw blood dotted around it: his blood, as he had saved her, helped her, before succumbing to his own, far more grave injury. And now, he was out, in the storm, hurt, trying to provide them food and water.

Well, she thought, standing purposefully, she could prepare for what must be done in other ways. She had to keep him warm, cleanse the wound. The fabric scraps could be boiled and used for bandages. And then she would just have to wait and see if a fever took hold.

Turning back to their small collection of garments and rifling through, she found a fine, Parisian chemise. She ruthlessly rent it into small strips and folded them carefully to keep them clean. With delight, she discovered an old cane by the fire and found that it served well enough as a replacement leg so that she could keep her ankle off the ground. She moved quicker with the cane, picking up speed as she went about her preparations. She picked up the knife she had found lying by the fire and went back to the flames, thrusting the blade into the heat of them, hissing as the metal heated up and seared her fingertips, even as they held the wooden handle. She set it with the strips and used one of them to tie her heavy hair back.

Suddenly the door opened, blowing in rain and freezing air, and thankfully, Lucian. He came in and stood for a moment before her. He held one of the buckets he had taken with him, now full of water, and a fist full of vines, attached to something heavy.

"Marrow," he said shortly at her inquisitive gaze. "There is an old garden out the back. Not much there, in fact, this may be the lot, but I can have a dig tomorrow." She took it from his hands and saw him sway a little, the exertion of his journey taking him over. He set down the water and leant against the table, bracing his hands there, catching his breath for a moment, his eyes closed. She fought down her panic at his pasty complexion and laboured breathing. Coming behind him, she carefully started to ease his soaking coat off his shoulders. He tensed at her touch, and then lifted his arms carefully to allow her access. As she hopped away, putting his coat near the fire to dry it, he collapsed into a chair, his eyes watching Caroline as she turned around on him and put her hands to her hips.

"Well. Let me see it," she ordered calmly.

"There is a well, not too far from here," he said, trying to ignore her.

"Lucian. Where are you injured?" she asked firmly, running out of patience. He opened his mouth to respond, to deny he was, the denial dying on his lips at her expression. She knew, there was no doubting it.

"My side. But it is nothing to worry over," he said shortly, looking away toward the fire.

"Nothing to worry over? If this shirt is anything to go by, it is miraculous you are walking about. I would not believe it if I did not know how headstrong and foolhardy you are," she said derisively. "Why would you keep it from me?"

"If I had known this was the lovely bedside manner I was to receive, I certainly would not have," he said, still evading her serious expression.

"Let me see it," she said briskly, standing up and rolling the sleeves of his shirt up to her elbows. He glanced at her.

"I certainly shall not," he said, crossing his arms over his chest.

"You certainly shall," she said determinedly, kneeling by his side as he attempted to twist away from her. He gasped as the movement clearly hurt him, and stood abruptly. Caroline followed suit and they stood before each other, stubborn expressions clashing.

"It is not for a lady's eyes," he ground out, and she rolled her eyes.

"You chose now to treat me like a lady," she said with annoyance, reaching out for his shirt, gasping the bottom, even as he pulled back, backing away from her.

"Caroline, please, it is fine." He backed into the cot and sat suddenly as it pressed against his knees. Caroline smiled grimly at the reverse situation, thinking of all the times he had backed her into a corner, or onto a bed.

"I shall judge the state of your condition. Now, remove your shirt and lie back please," she said authoritatively. His eyes flashed, wary and guarded, but seeing her expression, he raised himself and pulled his shirt off, biting back a groan as he did so. He fell back on the bed, and she advanced with a frown, taking in the blood-crusted fabric, so dark that it was almost black in places. She persisted, and finally, the knot loosened and she peeled away the garment, almost retching at the way it was stuck with dried blood.

It came away, and she stared at the wound. It was roughly cut, with torn edges and ringed in black blood. Forcing a blank expression, aware of Lucian's eyes on her face, she assessed the wound, her hands gently pressing its edges, as he gasped, and blood began to drip down his side.

"That bad?" he muttered at her expression.

"No. It is not so bad. It will be fine," she said, trying to reassure herself as much as him, she took a steadying breath and spoke gently. "Lucian. I must cleanse it. It might hurt." She replaced the bloody shirt and nodded for him to hold it while she hobbled to the fire and placed two deep pots by the flames and filled them with water from the bucket Lucian had brought in from the well, yelping as she singed her soft hands again.

"A lady should not spoil her hands," he said lightly, starting to sit up in order to help.

"Lay back. Today I am not a lady. Today I am a warrior." Caroline said, drawing a chuckle from Lucian as he returned to the cot. She then went to her collection of fabric strips and dropped some in the heating water. He tilted his head to the side, watching her closely.

"I may have no claim to being a chef but I do not think they will make much of an addition to marrow soup," he said, with a smile, as she came to stand over him, he fell silent at her serious look. She took in his pallor, the tightness around his mouth and eyes, his shallow breathing, he looked moments away from dropping.

"I shall attempt to bear this warrior doctoring like a gentleman, failing that, you have my permission to knock me unconscious," he said and she smirked and turned her attention to the wound. It was still bleeding, and she could see pieces of debris against the pink of muscle.

"Is that wood?"

"You've done this before, haven't you?" he teased, but she would not be distracted.

"How did this happen?"

"I am not entirely sure, but at some point, a tree tried to run me through. There is a good chunk of it that I pulled out somewhere around here."

She went to the pot on the fire with a bowl and spoon fishing out some strips of cloth and returned to his side. Holding the strip above the wound, she gently squeezed the hot water into it. Lucian moved under her, growing low in his throat.

"Don't move," she commanded and saw him move his hands to the edges of the cot and grip on. Grimly she pushed on, her stomach heaving, as she cleared away the dried blood and caught a glimpse of a long piece of bark embedded in the wound. Fighting down a wave of nausea she looked away, finding his eyes on her again.

"What is it?" he asked

"It's dirty, and there are remnants of the branch. I must..." she trailed off

"Remove them," he finished, his eyes concerned. "Caroline, you do not have to do this... you do not look well," he said and she felt her heart break a little. He was worried about her sensibilities, her delicate female nature at having to dig through a man. She picked up the knife, and looked back at him, trying to look formidable.

"Do not worry about me. warriors do this sort of thing all the time," she said, giving him a reassuring smile. "I honestly do not mind the blood. It is more the..."

"The what?"

"It's going to hurt. It is not easy... to cause you pain," she said honestly and saw how her words surprised him.

"And, yet, you are so very good at it," he quipped.

"I think you'll find I've only just begun."

He smiled, but it faltered as she picked up the knife and moved to the wound, looking at him for a sign that he was ready. He nodded gravely.

"Go ahead, doctor."

A long time later she was using the last of the strips to bind the seeping wound as tightly as she dared. Lucian had lost consciousness sometime before she had finished and now lay still. She had managed to make him drink some water before he had, and now he was quiet. She finished binding it, and then covered him with the coat, almost in a daze herself. She scratched at an itch on her cheek and felt the slick slide of her finger. She swallowed. Her hands were covered in blood nearly to the elbows. It splattered her white shirt sleeves and dried in her hair. His blood. She started to shake, as she went to the door once again, and opened it, feeling the cold air sweep over her, and held her hands out, letting the driving rain wash the last hours of horror from her skin.

Finally spent, and washed nearly clean, she closed the door and went to the fire, pouring herself some warm water to drink. It burned down her throat, and she went back to the bed and carefully climbed in, settling herself again against Lucian's back. She was hungry, and the water did little to take the edge off, but it was ignorable for now. Tomorrow, she would reassess, maybe the weather would be better, she hoped. She drifted into a restless sleep, waking many times to check on the man beside her, feeling his forehead, terrified a fever may yet set in.

⚘

"Caroline," his voice pulled her awake and she blinked in the half-light of dawn. Turning over she suddenly became aware of Lucian's arms around her, and her back pressing against him. At his sharp intake of breath, she realised she must have just elbowed him in his side. Pulling herself away from him as much as possible on the narrow cot, she shuffled around, finding herself mere inches from him. He was cold, too cold, while her own skin was warm from the coats and the close proximity. She peeled their cover of coats away and put her hand on his side. Blood. He was wet with it. He had bled through all his bandages, and into the thin hay mattress below them.

Caroline's heart stopped as she raised her bloody hand and stared at it in the half-light cast by the dimming fire.

"Lucian," she tried to wake him, shaking him softly at first and then more vigorously. He mumbled in response. At least it was something.

"Lucian, wake up. You're still bleeding. Can you wake up for me? I need you to put some pressure on this while I go get more bandages. Please. Lucian, please wake up."

His eyes opened, and she saw a slit of blue, but they rolled around and didn't seem to be able to focus on her face. He closed them, and mumbled again, putting a hand across his body to hold his wound. She put her hand on top of his and pressed down.

"Hold this tight, Lucian. I'll be right back."

She made her way as quickly as possible with her cane, cursing as it stuck on a flagstone, and she lost her balance, having to put her bad leg down to catch herself. Molten fire burned up her leg with a fury, and she gasped, unable to breathe for the pain of it before she gathered herself and pushed on. The fire was dying, but the pot in it was still warm in the coals. She got more hot water and rags from the pot, then grabbed an armload of fabric and the knife for more bandages.

The wound was much cleaner than before, and while some of it seemed to have started healing, it had not dried completely, and blood was still oozing from the area where the gash was deepest. She washed and dried the wound again of blood, both dried and fresh. She should have woken sooner, she should have noticed. Then she wadded the bandages, ripping new strips from a clean nightdress, and retied as tight as she could. She watched the bandages closely for a few moments, but the pressure seemed to stop the worst of the bleeding, at least for the time being.

Getting up, she rinsed the old bloodied bandages as best she could, and returned them to the hot water. She'd need to have them boiled and dried as soon as possible.

She looked to the small window and saw that the sun was starting to rise outside. She would need wood for the fire. If she didn't get something soon, it would die, and she wasn't sure that she would know how to light it again without Lucian's help.

Listening for the rain on the slates, it seemed to have slowed almost to a stop, though Caroline didn't think that the reprieve would last long. The wind still howled like a hungry wolf, finding its way under the door and through cracks in the windows of the cabin. Everything outside would be drenched- probably for several days.

Making a hasty decision, she grabbed one of the two low stools in the cabin, and taking it by the legs, she swung it against the stone wall, splintering it, and breaking a leg off. She swung it again until the seat fell off, and then she gathered the pieces and hopped back to the fire to throw them in. They wouldn't last long, but it would at least keep the fire alive until she could find something else. Lucian didn't stir much but murmured something about her being alright, and Caroline confirmed that she was fine before his eyes closed again. His lack of response to the crashing of furniture against walls scared her almost as much as the blood had.

She checked the bandages again. She could see a bit of blood that had come round the edges, but most of the flow that had drained him in the night had been staunched, and she was weak with gratitude. She stroked his forehead with a soothing hand and rearranged the coats to make sure that he was tucked in.

"Alright. I need you to stay here while I go look for some firewood. I'll be right back. If you start to bleed again, apply pressure, and wait for me." He nodded without stirring and went back to sleep immediately.

Outside, the rain had slowed and now seemed to be mostly fat drops that fell lazily from the thick clouds which darkened the sky. The wind was a wild thing, rushing then retreating, whipping through the trees violently enough to fill the air with the sound of splintering wood, breaking branches, and ripping out trees by the roots in some other part of the wood, before rushing back to the cottage.

Caroline found a small stack of old wood by the side of the house. It had been stacked many years ago, and generations of mice and insects had made their homes in it, and later abandoned them. While the lower logs were mostly soft with rot, the top logs might be salvaged, if they could be dried out. She'd need to get them indoors before the rain returned, but she would need both hands to carry the big things, and wouldn't be able to use her cane.

It took longer than she would like to remember hopping back and forth between the woodpile and the fire, taking short breaks when she could no longer handle the strain, or when she accidentally jarred her ankle or knocked into something; but, by the time she finally lowered her tired body on to the one remaining stool, she had a decent number of logs lined on end like a row of columns near the fire to dry, she had emptied and broken a crate for the fire to join the remnants of the stool, and had put another pot of water on to boil- this time for food. She had checked on Lucian periodically, and he had rested, his temperature warming slightly, and the bleeding having slowed significantly, which was a blessed relief to her; but, he was worryingly weak, and his face was a greyish pale that frightened her. He would need whatever strength she could give, even if all she had to offer was boiled marrow soup.

By the time the sun had set, the rain was back and raging against the cabin from all sides, but still, Lucian did not stir.

❀

*J*n the morning, she was woken by Lucian, much to her surprise and gratitude that he had not faded away quietly into the night as he had in so many nightmares that kept waking her.

He had turned from lying on his back and was facing her on his right side. She had gone to bed sleeping snugly between the wall and his shoulder and had woken with his eyes on hers. She searched his face languidly in her half-sleep for signs of pain or distress, but when she found none, she simply gave a small sleepy smile. His stockinged feet brushed against her bare one gently, and she was quite startled to find that the warm, tender gesture sent a little thrill of excitement racing to her stomach.

"Hello," Caroline said softly.

"Hello." His eyes crinkled at the edges.

"You seem to be a bit better. Why did you not wake me?" She stretched her legs, careful with her ankle, and could not help but notice how her legs brushed in places against his legs on their small cot. The sensation made her skin prickle all over, and she hoped that he would not notice the goosebumps on her arms.

"What - and ruin this? I have dreamed many times of the mornings when I might wake next to you as man and wife, and be able to look my fill at your perfect face. Though, I confess, I did not quite imagine *this* scenario, in my romantic fantasies," he smirked "what with the being stranded, wounded, and starving bits. Although, I am growing ever more fond of this little cot and shall see that the entire house at Westmere is kitted out with them, and the old French four-posters chopped for firewood." She snorted and then broke into a yawn and another stretch, covering her mouth, with a belated hope that her breath would not be too bad after a long sleep. "Besides, my dear, you are so much sweeter when you're soundly asleep. I was in no rush to rupture the peace."

She wiggled her body in a quick bump against his so that he almost lost his balance and toppled onto the floor, and she laughed when his arm pinwheeled for balance.

"Well, I guess you cannot be on death's door with such an abundance of bad attitude at the ready," Caroline countered with narrowed eyes.

"What can you mean? This is my very best behaviour," he smiled beautifully, and Caroline felt something coil in her belly.

"Well, let the Devil take you then. I've no idea why I've been working so hard to keep you alive."

"Nor do I, frankly. I scarce deserve it." His grin held its place, but she felt the emotion that tinted his words. They sat for a moment longer, staring at one another, and the knuckles of his hand gently brushed the knuckles of hers, and she brushed them back.

She closed her eyes with a deep slow inhale and pushed herself up to sit. The sun had risen and was streaming into the cabin in sharp shafts, bringing a little warmth with it, though the rain still pattered busily on the glass of the window panes.

Getting up, careful not to bump either of their injuries, she hopped over and filled a large glass with what was left of the fresh water and brought it back to sit on the edge of the bed where he had shifted to make some room for her. She held it out, and he worked at sitting up, a wince pulling his mouth and shutting his eyes. She hated to see it. She'd seen the wound itself rather closer than she would have liked to, and could only imagine vaguely at how such a horrible gash would feel in such a delicate part of the body.

"Is this the last of the water then?" he asked, bringing it to his lips. She nodded. "Well, looks like I'll be going on a little adventure today," he said.

"Why don't you tell me where the well is, and then I will find it while you stay here and rest?" she asked, but her voice was all statement and no question.

"Oh no, then what's to stop you from smothering me in the night once you know how to find it?"

"Oh, I can't imagine that such a small thing as a well could ever stop me from smothering you in the night." His eyes sparkled. He really was feeling tremendously improved from yesterday, she thought with a smile. After all that had happened, his gentle teasing felt like an anchor in the storm. It held them both together - if they could pretend now to be fine, maybe someday soon they would be again.

"Well, how about we limp our way over together, in that case?" he offered with a smile. "A promenade. What a pair we shall make."

She took the water from him and had a deep, refreshing gulp or two before handing it back.

"Fine then. But, no heroics, mind," she warned.

"What a ridiculous thing to ask of me. What if I need to save you from a wild bear, or a burning building, or a band of dangerous rogues?" She took another drink.

"Well, last time you saved me, you brought me here, and it has been a complete disaster, so I think I'd prefer it if you didn't bother, actually."

He laughed at that, bringing a hand to his side where it must have hurt him, and then sighed contentedly.

"Oh, Lady Ashford. Whatever would I do without you?"

❀

*T*hey walked in the rain, but the cold bite from the air had been warmed by the sun, and after adjusting, Lucian thought it felt quite pleasant, really.

"Quite refreshing, this little shower, do you not think?" he said amiably as they trundled along at the speed of a pair of tortoises.

"You know... it is. The cottage has grown a little bit stuffy. It is pleasant to stretch my legs... or leg, as it were." He smiled at her, a warm happy smile that animated his whole face.

The path had been ragged, unkempt, and washed away, and he was relieved to find it again without any trouble or wrong turns. They were lucky that it was not too far up the hill from the cottage, at the speed that they could manage. They put their collection of pots and buckets down to fill. They had set another bucket to catch the rain, but had found the rainwater that had filtered through the leaves was not quite as clean, and they would both need to know where to find freshwater when the rain finally stopped. If ever it would.

He reached for the rope to haul the bucket up, but she swatted his hand away with an exasperated sigh and did it herself.

She looked so achingly beautiful in the rain. She had left her heavy hair loose, which she would never have done at Westmere, nor Blackhill, where others might see her, and she looked somehow wilder, and more at home, as the wet locks hung in her face, tempting little wisps to stick to her forehead, or swing across her cheek, and stay there.

They had both worn as few layers as possible, in an effort not to soak through a heap of clothes that would then need to be hung and dried; they both wore plain shirt sleeves and his britches. He found that he could not help but notice the way that his white linen shirt clung to her skin- no short stays to bind her, nothing but smooth skin, and the wet outline of sumptuous curves.

She had absolutely no idea how remarkable she was. Not only for her breath-taking beauty but also for her rare strength. How many ladies of the Ton might have been able to survive such a trauma, and keep them fed and warm, and bind his wounds, and all with an intelligent smile on her face, and a ready joke on her lips? He had known, of course, that she was strong before, but he could never have imagined such stoic calm in the face of death, danger and hopelessness.

"You seem to be able to do everything on your own, Lady Ashford. I might well dismiss the staff when we get home, and save the coin." She laughed.

"Well then, you had better get used to the taste of boiled marrow," she smiled, focused on her task.

On the way home, they broke through the trees and saw a rainbow, and so decided to sit in the rain and take a break while they gazed at it, and he thought himself a very lucky man indeed.

🐚

When they returned home, they stoked a fire with a small table broken into pieces, and a large, damp log after Lucian had carved away the wetter outer layers. It took its time to catch, hissing and billowing smoke at first, but with the help of the table, they had a fire that would last them the entire night.

They ate the second half of the marrow, though they were both starving after their trip to fetch water on an empty stomach, and it did little to stop the rumbling. The cabin, when they arrived, seemed cozy and welcoming after their hour or two in the fresh air, and Lucian was relieved to sit still and eat a bowl of warm anything after the exercise.

"Well, my fearless warrior-woman," Lucian said, standing up slowly from the floor, and brushing off his breeches, "I think I'd like nothing better than a quick afternoon nap to fortify me for attacking the garden. Would you care to join me?" He held out a hand to her in an invitation that he hoped would sway her. She looked at his hand, and at his face, and then at the cot, thinking it over.

"Well. Yes. I suppose I am rather tired, now that you say so." As she put her small hand in his, he felt a tightening in his chest, and he knew that his whole face would be lit with a smile as bright as the flames. He lifted her gently to her feet, and played the role of her cane, placing her arm around his shoulder, and stooping so that they could both reach, he put an arm around her waist, glad of the excuse.

They settled on the cot together, a slow and awkward ballet to minimise pain, and fit themselves into the angles of the other neatly, to conserve space, and, he hoped, because it made her feel as he did - comforted, happy, excited.

"Well, good napping then," she said, her nose a mere inch from his own, and then closed her hazel eyes.

"Good napping, my love," he said softly but kept his eyes open to look at her. After several minutes, her eyes snapped open and narrowed accusingly, and he chucked. She looked like an angry kitten, precious and beautiful, but with sharp little claws.

"How am I ever to get to sleep with your big owl eyes staring at me?" He laughed again. "Turn over," she demanded, and she pushed his shoulder and settled him on his back. He was broad and took up more room this way, so he sidled over closer to her, still chuckling softly, and they readjusted their positions, fitting their bodies together tightly from top to bottom.

His heart ached with the sweetness of it when she reached her arm across him and, avoiding his wound, nestled it high across his chest, settling her hand over his heart with a soft sigh that made his eyes close, and stirred the embers of his soul.

$\mathcal{T}$he 'garden' was mostly an abandoned mud patch, around the side of the cottage, and while neither of them had any experience in gardening, cooking, or even looking at vegetables in any raw and unbuttered state, they lowered themselves to their hands and knees in the rain and looked for anything at all that they might be able to eat. Kneeling proved tricky for Caroline, who found that she could not position her leg or feet at the correct angle to avoid teeth-gritting pain.

"Come on then," he lifted her up, "it is my turn to be doctor." He attempted to pick her up and carry her into the house, but thinking of his wound, she slapped his hand and scolded his recklessness, which made him laugh, which in turn, made him clutch at his side.

"See," she scolded, feeling every bit a wife. But, she grabbed his hand with a grin and followed him back into the cabin when he sat her on the stool by the fire.

"Wait here," he said and left to find bandages, which did not take long, as his old ones had been washed and hung to dry nearby.

He knelt at her feet in what she thought to herself was a very chivalrous manner, then ever so carefully lifted her foot to his muscular thigh. He rolled up the hem of her breeches slowly, his fingers tickling her skin as he went. Then, ever so gently, he touched the skin there and took a good look at the bruising and swelling on either side.

"Is it getting any better?" he asked.

"Not much. Sometimes I do not notice it so much, but then I move it or bump it on something and it's just as sore as it was days ago."

"Well, perhaps some light pressure will help the swelling, and a bit of structure will keep it still and supported. That sounds fairly medical, do you not think?" She scoffed by way of reply. "Perhaps I should give up being a gentleman, and become a doctor instead."

"You are lucky I'm too sore to kick you," she grumbled.

"Well, we'll need to get you all healed up, in that case, so that you can punish me as you see fit." He cocked an eyebrow, then took the opportunity to put both of his hands at the base of her calves, and glided his fingers very slowly up the curve of her calf, pushing the hem of her breeches all the way up to the knee. On hand lingered, stroking ever so slightly at the soft cleft behind her bent knee.

She had never been touched like that in her life. She had never exposed her legs in the presence of a man since she was a little girl, and she felt her face burn with bashfulness, while in her belly, a fire had been stoked, and the flames licked and spread across her body, while the skin that he had grazed his fingertips over, burned hot and prickled with sensation.

"Well, I do not see how that is necessary!" she scolded.

"Shhhh. Do not interrupt my very skillful medical ministrations," he tutted and carried right on leisurely sliding his hands back down her leg. He then very slowly and carefully wrapped her ankle with enough fabric to double its size, but keep the angle firm and secure, just as he'd said. Then he looked up at her with a wolfish grin.

"Capital. Now I must inspect the rest of the leg for any further damage."

"You're about to get further damage if you don't unhand me, you charlatan," she tried to sound stern, but she couldn't help the smile from creeping into her voice.

"Oh, alright. I suppose we must dig for our suppers then. Come along, my lady," he said rather charmingly, and she hoped to keep the flush out of her cheeks as he helped her back up and out into the garden.

This time her ankle *did* give her less trouble, but things were gnarled and overgrown in the garden, and they really did not have a clue what to look for, or how long they would need to live on what they could find.

Lucian found an old scraggly bramble full of long dried pods. Lucian took a pod and split the seam with a wide thumb.

"Well, it's a bean of some kind. Looks edible," he said, and before she could stop him, he had popped the four or five beans into his mouth, chewed, and swallowed.

"Lucian!" she yelled, but it was too late.

"There. Now, we can boil those for a few hours, and if I have not yet died by then, I say we eat them. They'll need a good while to soften anyway," he said with a comical choke that made her laugh despite her outrage.

They did not find much else, though they dug with their cold hands through the mud, in case there should be some potatoes or carrots, or anything else hiding underground. They did pluck a large patch of greens which might have been anything, Caroline said, but Lucian seemed to think they were worth trying, as they were all growing in one patch, and looked as if they might have been planted. Without permission, he folded a large leaf and popped that into his mouth as well, telling her that they could go in with the beans.

"Now if you die, we won't know if it was the beans or the greens that were poison."

"That is very true, my love. But if I should die tonight, I should think you will be far too distraught with grief to have an appetite anyway."

"Doubt it," she said, and he chuckled, and then winced in pain.

To Caroline's horror, Lucian had found some large snails on the greens and held out a handful to her.

"Look!" he said, pleased with himself. "These would fetch a pretty penny in Paris."

"You cannot be serious!" she said, disbelieving.

"Oh, I am. I have had them there with garlic and parsley and a nice glass of wine."

"You have not!" she scoffed. "I won't fall for this nonsense."

"Would I lie to you?" he said, raising his eyebrows.

"Yes," she said firmly.

"Well, perhaps," he admitted. "But I swear to you that I speak the truth. They eat snails throughout France. It is a delicacy. They're quite delicious."

"Well, I might believe you, and I might not, but either way the French can keep them! Now, put those poor slimy things down. Even as hungry as I am, I am not desperate enough to eat snails!"

He looked disappointed as he reached down and put them back on the soil.

"Are you quite sure?" he asked. But by then, she was back down with her hands in the mud, this time for support as she laughed the big gulps of laughter that shook her body - the type when pain and exhaustion and hunger and desperation had so overcome her that all she could do was laugh. Lucian joined her, holding his side, and they were still smiling as they gathered up their findings and ran back to the house, clothes, and hair dripping, and limbs covered in mud.

*T*hey took turns washing, and while there was no screen, or nowhere to go for privacy, Lucian turned his back, and busied himself with his chores, keeping his head down and turned away, so that Caroline could feel more comfortable.

He cooked, and she washed the clothes in a wide basin which they filled with rainwater. They were very happy to find an old, cracked cake of soap had been left by a previous occupant. And from where he knelt by the fire, stirring the pot and poking the logs, he turned to watch her washing the clothes, her sleeves rolled up, her wet hair tied up with a strip of cloth, looking for all the world the very image of domestic bliss. He hated to break it.

"Tomorrow..." he said softly, "I must go and find Digby."

She stilled, her hands in the water, paused in their work, and just breathed for a moment, then, without looking up at him, she nodded slightly, enough for him to see it. Enough for him to feel the same sickening thud in the pit of his stomach that she must be feeling.

*T*hey had washed in warm water, they had dined on a truly terrible supper, that to Caroline's thinking had tasted better by the end of the bowl once one had gotten used to the shock of it. In any case, they were both far too hungry to complain about anything warm that they could eat, and swallowed it down with smiles on their faces. Afterward, they had both sat tired on the floor by the fire, which Caroline had swept, and they talked.

They talked about things at home in Westmere, and at Blackhill and how and when it might be discovered that they were missing. They talked of Lelantanos and Theia and guessed what they would be doing at that very moment. They talked about the new baby and voiced their hopes into the night that all had gone well with the delivery. They talked of Eva and Eli, of Rebecca, Westly and Charles, Isaac, and even of Katherine, and made wild guesses and giddy, laughing speculations at who had an eye for whom and which of them would be married before the year was over. They talked of Virginia. They talked of his father. They spoke of poor Digby and made plans for the next day.

But, they neither of them talked about any of the troubles which they had had before the crash, or of all of their arguments left unfinished. All of it seemed so trivial now, and not worth the time and heartache of tying each other up in guilt and old grievances when they might instead take great comfort and pleasure from each other's company. Here with him by the glow of the fire, Caroline felt stripped down and bared, and perhaps more open than she had been with anyone in a long time.

She noticed him gazing at her with a warm, tired expression.

"Shall we to bed, my love?" he said, raising a hand in invitation. She put her hand in his and he rose and helped her up along with him. He stood stretching by the fire for a moment and then tucked a stray lock of hair behind her ear with a tender stroke as she looked up at him.

They fitted themselves back into the cot, growing familiar now with each other's curves and angles, and how they fit most comfortably together. The knowing of this information, and the natural settling into place like clockwork, seemed so intimate to Caroline, as if they had been wed for years, and spent every night curled tightly together in the same bed.

The room was dark but for the dim fire that glowed from the other side of Lucian and outlined his face, like the sun behind the clouds, his stubble glinting golden in the low light. Tentatively she raised her hand and stroked a long path along the line of his profile. He closed his eyes, his lashes fluttering, and when she got to his lips, he placed a very small kiss upon her fingertips, that sent a shock right through her arm into her chest.

She felt drunk, emboldened, listening to the beating of the wings in her stomach, she lifted herself on one elbow, and lowered her face, slowly to his. She stopped there for a tense moment, and his eyes flew open and stared at hers, their breath stirring the inch of air between them. When she closed her eyes and lowered herself down to kiss him, it was slow, soft, and passionate - exploratory, not taking anything for granted, learning each other anew, for surely now they were very different people since last they had kissed one another.

His stubble had grown longer, and softer, not quite a beard, and she found that she not only liked the rugged look of it on her square jaw, but she liked the feel of it on her cheeks and chin when they kissed, liked the scratch of it when he had grabbed her palm earlier to kiss its soft middle. His hands came up to her hair and stroked her gently, but he did not pull her down to him, he did not press his body to hers.

She inhaled him and tasted him, and she grew dizzy from the feel of it, as it seeped into all of her breaks and cuts of the days before: the fear, the hardship, the grief and guilt of Digby's death, the worries of what would become of them both- she did not forget these things in the kiss, but rather, they came clearer to the surface, and she felt whole in spite of them, supported. She was half of a team that was surviving together, and she was stronger in herself for having Lucian beside her.

They kissed, comforting each other, making wordless promises, tears slipping down her cheeks adding salt to his lips, for how long she did not know. Then they held each other until they fell asleep in each other's arms.

CHAPTER 4

*C*aroline slept heavily, and dreamlessly, and when she stirred the next morning, Lucian was already up and getting dressed for a day outside. She sat up slowly, rested her head on one bent knee, and sighed with the weight of the day ahead.

"So, what is our plan, Lucian? How will we find him? Do you think you'll remember?" she asked, sleep still clinging to her.

Lucian stopped dressing, and looked at her, cocking his head slightly to the side.

"What can you mean by 'we', my dear?" Caroline sat up straighter and met his look with a stern one of her own.

"I mean the two of us together, as you are well aware." His eyes softened along with his voice.

"No, my sweet. This is a job I will have done on my own."

"Do not be ridiculous. Have you forgotten that you have a hole in the side of your body? You are still fragile, still healing - it's going to be very physically demanding. Surely you cannot mean to deal with this all on your own..."

"I do," he said softly. "I will, Caroline."

She stood up and made to dress.

"No." she said, "You won't." She hoped that her voice made it clear that she would entertain no further argument. In response, he grabbed her hand gently and led her back to the cot to sit next to him.

"Sweetheart," he started, a sincere look in his eyes. "This will be..." he breathed in, "a most unpleasant task-" She did not let him finish.

"Do not treat me as a child, Lucian, I know what awaits us. You will injure yourself further with your foolish attempts at chivalry. We are stronger together."

"Yes, we are, my darling, I know it well. I probably would not be living and breathing here today without you. But, Caroline... it has been four long days and nights since the poor man's death. Nature will not have been kind, it will not have been gentle. It will have begun to claim him back to the earth in a hundred small ways."

"And so, you are strong enough to endure such a thing, and I am not? Why? Because I am a woman?"

"You are every bit as strong and as brave as I..." he shook his head. "No, that is not true. You have always been stronger, from the very beginning."

"Well, then I will help. We have both killed the poor man with our foolishness, may God forgive us, and we will both be responsible for what little there is left that we might do for him. And you will not reopen your wound in digging his grave so that you might bleed out alone in the rain while I sit here by the fire shelling beans." Her voice had risen with indignation, and the more they spoke about it, the more upset she was becoming.

"Please, Caroline... I have been in battle. I have seen gruesome, unspeakable horrors, and I see them still sometimes when I close my eyes, when I dream. They are burned forever in my memory. I am prisoner to my own mind, seeing them again and again, unbidden. Please. I would spare you this, my love. It is a small thing, I will take care of it, and I will be back in a few hours. Please, do not argue."

She opened her mouth but closed it again. She was taken back by the look on his face: not righteousness, but pain and worry. Arguing more would not bring any resolution, she felt. He had decided this, and it was important to him. She sat silent for a moment, thinking it over, before taking a deep breath, and finally nodding.

"Alright. Please, Lucian, be careful. Do not hurry. Do not take too much on. Be conscious of your wound, and if it opens again, promise me that you will stop what you are doing and come back to me at once. Swear it."

"Yes. I promise, sweetheart."

"Digby is gone now, and I am quite sure that he would not have you risk your life to look after his body."

"Of course, my love. I will be careful. I will come back to you," he said, catching her eyes. "I would never do anything that meant that I could not come back to you."

❀

*C*aroline's day was a painfully long and restless one. She did not eat, as there was little to spare, and Lucian himself had left on an empty stomach. As they had found one much smaller marrow in the garden, she cooked down a few more of the beans, sparingly added half of the marrow, and some wild chives - or at least that's what Lucian had said they were, and they did smell oniony, and Caroline decided that it would be worth the risk of potential death by poisoning to add a bit of flavour to the meal.

The meal was cooked and ready by the time the sun was high on its path, but though she waited, Lucian did not come home. He said that he did not want to leave poor Digby out to be eaten by foxes and crows when he deserved to be laid to rest in his home rather than in this place of mud and rain that had taken him. The soil would be soft, and the plan was to bury him in a shallow grave, and whenever they would return home, he would return to dig him up and transport him back to be buried in a proper grave, where family might visit if he had any.

He had asked Caroline to make some marker so that the grave might be found when Lucian returned, and she sent him off with a cross she made by binding two branches together with a strip of fabric. He smiled when he saw that she had added a small posy of wildflowers, tucked in between the layers of cloth at its center.

But, though Lucian had promised that the journey would not be a long one, he still was not home. Caroline herself had been unconscious when Lucian had carried her from the site of the carriage crash up the hill to the cabin, so she could not gauge for herself how long it might take, and that extra element of uncertainty over something that she could not control bit at her. She busied herself with small chores, and heavy sighs, looking out the window often, and sometimes standing in the open doorway, scanning the wood, and listening closely for anything that might be footfall.

When it looked as if sunset was drawing near, she had given in to her panic and had just begun to dress in something more sturdy to go out to find him, when she heard the door scrape against the floor.

He let himself in, and stood for a moment near the open door, face sallow, near drowned, and covered in mud. He looked as if he had just crawled from the grave himself.

Caroline rushed to him and helped to take his sticking coat from his wet body. When he sat finally on the stool, she noticed that it was a collapse, as if all the strength had gone out of him.

"Lucian, what happened? You are back so late. Are you alright?" He nodded and took a cup of warm water from her to sip and warm himself. "Let us get you up and out of those wet clothes before you catch a chill."

"A moment, please, Caroline," he said, exhausted. She looked down at his middle, but saw no signs of blood there, to her relief, but his pallor was greenish, and it worried her.

"Do you feel poorly, Lucian?" she said, stooping to look into his eyes, cupping his chin in her hand, and tilting his face gently up so that she might inspect it. He only closed his eyes and leaned against her hand.

His skin was warm, despite the hours he had spent in the wind and the rain.

She tried to warm him with some hot food, but he would eat little, and she found that she had finished two bowls before he had eaten more than a few spoons. He spoke little and swayed gently on the stool with exhaustion.

When she finally coaxed him up, she peeled his wet shirt away, and unwrapped his bandages, to find that while the bandages were largely clean of any blood, something else had seeped through a few of the layers, a yellowy-brown color, and she had to wet the last bandage to prise it away from his skin. The skin around the wound was an angry red, and it was sticky with an oozing opaque substance that she feared was a sign that it was not healing well.

She changed him into dry clothes, and he did not argue, then she washed the wound again with hot water, as best she could, and rewrapped him. By the time she was finished, he was asleep, and when she finally laid down next to him, she did so restless and fraught.

❀

*C*aroline woke in a suffocating heat, far too hot under the coats, and sweating unpleasantly; she flipped them away from both of them to cool down. Blinking into the darkness, she lifted her hand to Lucian's forehead, and panic shot through her at the hot, clammy touch of his skin. The fever had taken hold of him. She brought over a cool cloth to mop his brow and chest. She tried to get him to drink, but he would not. She felt horribly helpless and alone. She knew that a fever could be dangerous, fatal even, but with no doctors or medicines at hand, Caroline also knew that all she could do was try to keep him comfortable and wait. Wait to see if it would take him.

"Caroline," he murmured, and Caroline answered, but saw that it was in his sleep he was talking to her. The lines of his face were tight with discomfort, and as she looked at the etched frown and unhealthy pallor, her heart squeezed in her chest, and her nose prickled with the start of new tears. She stayed awake to watch him, unsure what she could do, but not feeling as if she could leave him unattended, so she watched and waited, her mind wandering into the night.

Raising her hand to his cheek, she gently traced the strong line of his jaw, rasping against his stubble. Her hand dropped to his neck, where her fingers worked over the tensed muscles there, down still to his strong shoulders. His skin was surprisingly soft, and she ran her fingertips over the bunched muscle.

How strange, she mused as she moved her fingers over him gently, how strange to think that she was once afraid of him. He would give his life for her if only she asked it - she was sure of that. Just as she was sure that he would have died in the storm outside before he would have ever considered leaving without her.

There was something between them, no ordinary thing... something she had never felt before, it terrified her as it lured her in. She had been fighting herself as she fought him at every turn and she was so very tired of it. Even the last deception, she knew that the whole truth was that if he had told her about his father's plan before the ship had left, it would have changed nothing, except given her ability to laugh in Silus's face when he thought he was tearing them apart.

She needed him, she loved him, and it was no longer possible to fight it. How cruel that fate might take him from her now, just as she had learned it.

Her hands stilled as Lucian's eyes fluttered open briefly, fixing on hers, and she saw their usual beautiful blue colour had clouded and dimmed, shot through with red.

"Caroline..." he muttered, shuddering with his fever. She felt a sob rise in her throat. She pulled herself closer to him and pressed a soft kiss onto his hot forehead.

"Do not talk. Rest," she whispered, feeling her tears run down her cheeks onto his face.

"Caroline, listen to me. There is likely a village nearby. Leave this place when the storm passes. Walk until you find it, you can do it, you are strong," he muttered.

"I am not leaving you," she whispered, the words hurting her throat as she held back her tears.

"Sweetheart, you may not have a choice. I cannot make the same promise, I am afraid."

"No, you are coming with me. We will leave here together," she said, her voice laced with panic. He smiled against her throat.

"Thank you," he said softly, and she pulled back to look at him.

"For what?"

"For... taking care of me. For sending me happily into whatever darkness surely awaits a man such as I."

"The darkness cannot have you, you cannot leave me... I need you," she whispered, her sobs unable to be held back now.

"You will reach a village before long, I am sure of it," he said reassuringly, as her thin body shook against him. She shook her head vehemently.

"Why are you saying this? You are willing to give up so easily? Do I mean so little to you?" she asked, accusingly, her eyes leaking tears as she stared hard at his ashen face. Her irrational anger was overwhelming, her need to shake him and slap him, and make him stop, make him fight.

"Caroline-" he started, and she fixed him with the sternest look she could manage, despite her red cheeks and tear-stained eyes, and saw that his eyes struggled to focus.

"You cannot... die, do you hear me?" Her voice was filled with tears now, and she started to sob. Lucian gently put his arms around her and she pushed them off roughly. She was angry, and upset, and gripped with helplessness. "No! Stop it, stop comforting me, as though you were already dead, as though it were already too late. You did this to me. You made me love you... trust you, depend on you, and now you are just going to leave me... as they did. Are you going to give up and leave me all alone?"

"Sweetheart, I am not sure I have a choice in the matter."

"Of course you do.., you have a choice. You can choose me. You can fight harder," she whispered. She saw him muster what strength he had to answer her.

"I would choose you with my dying breath, Caroline. Knowing you... made every miserable day I have lived up until I met you have meaning, have worth, and I would repeat them all for the chance to know you again, to stand beside you at the altar... to have you smile at me, cry for me. To have you mourn me, would mean I am glad I lived to be your husband, even if it was only for mere weeks... it is enough. You have made it enough." She pulled her face out of her arms at his words.

"It is not enough... it is not enough for me... I need you. I need to be good to you, I need that chance to make you happy - there's so much more to know. To be by your side, to have your children, to grow old with you..." she whispered. He turned his face away, coughing, and grasping his side at the pain it caused.

"Lucian," she cried out, putting her hands to his shoulders and clutching them tightly. He put his arms around her, pulling her gently down, her head resting on his chest.

"If you love me, do not leave me. I shall never forgive you," she vowed solemnly and he smiled against her hair.

"I shall do my best, my dear. But know this, in case time robs us later. I love you, Caroline Ashford. I love you, as no man has ever loved. I shall never be far from your side. In this life, or the next. If my heart continues beating through this night, it is because of you. And every day afterward, it shall only be because you will it."

"I'm listening to it. It is not allowed to stop," she said from his chest and he relaxed, feeling her settle with her ear over his heart.

He closed his eyes, feeling the darkness being kept at bay by her light, her blinding light, as she lay awake, watching the shadows dancing on the walls and listening to his steady heartbeat.

❀

*L*ucian didn't wake up the next day, nor the day after, but continued to sleep, except during the times when she changed his dressing, when he mostly woke enough to swear at her, in his stupor. It was reassuring and she welcomed his crude words, anything to know he was holding on.

Caroline lost count of the number of times she felt his pulse and listened for his breath. She fell into a routine, collecting water, heating it, changing his bandages, rooting for food in the muddy earth outside.

She had boiled the last of the greens from outside. They were bitter, but she made herself eat a few spoons just to keep her going. The little bit of food wakened her hunger and it burned inside of her, fierce and demanding, but she saved what was left and brought a chair over to Lucian's bedside. Quickly feeling his forehead, she thought she felt a slight reduction in his fever, and she replaced the wet cloth she was keeping there.

"Lucian," she spoke softly, touching his shoulder. He tossed his head to the side, away from her. "Dinner." Tilting his head up, she attempted to open his mouth and pour in some of the green soup. His lips remained closed and she huffed frustrated. She pushed more and more clothes under his upper body, until he was sitting reasonably upright, and then, pinched his nose. She held it relentlessly as his head started to turn from side to side. Suddenly, his eyes flew open at the same time as his mouth did. She immediately popped a spoonful of greens in, smiling in satisfaction. He coughed, his eyes alarmed, and then finally, recovering himself, started to swallow them. He opened his mouth to speak and she spooned in more. He chewed, rolling his eyes in frustration, but she hardly let him take a break, knowing it could only be minutes before he succumbed to sleep again. After he had managed a decent amount, she set the bowl down and he relaxed back, his breath laboured. His eyes shut and he coughed again.

"What day is it?" His voice came out dry and sore, and foreign.

"I am not sure... I think it has been about six days, maybe more" she said, as she spoke, her stomach growled. His eyes fluttered and he turned his head toward her.

"Caroline, you must eat something. You must be starving," he muttered. She shook her head stubbornly.

"I'm fine, I have been eating," she lied.

"You haven't. Did you think I did not notice?" She harrumphed.

"Caroline," he said, a warning.

"Well," she answered petulantly. "If you want me to eat something, you had better hurry up and recover and take us home," she said firmly.

"And I thought I was stubborn," he murmured, a small smile playing at the corners of his bloodless lips.

"You are. Go to sleep"

❀

She did not wake Lucian to tell him that she was going to look for help. It was better that he rested, and did not tire himself with worry. Every time the rain had let up, she had thought of making it to the road and seeing if she could find a village or house, but she battled with herself, weighing up the risks of going on without food and medical attention, for how many more days or weeks she did not know, against the risk that Lucian might worsen while she was away, or the very real risk that for any number of reasons she might hurt herself further, or not manage to return to him at all.

She had tried the day before to forage in the woods for anything edible, and though she found several varieties of mushrooms and some berries, none of them looked familiar to her, and she knew that any of them could be deadly, though she was sorely tempted all the same. England was a new land but, she scolded herself, she was gently bred and ignorant; even in Virginia, she would still not know where to find food. So, many hours later, she had returned home empty-handed, wet, and cold, her ankle worse and more swollen from her efforts.

The forest was damp, dripping, and heavy was the air as she made her way down the sloping, tree-covered hillside toward where she thought the road would likely be found. It was not so far, as Lucian had said, though getting down a muddy hill with one leg and a cane was about as quick and enjoyable as she had imagined it to be.

She had not truly prepared herself for the extent of the damage. The road had once curved along the path of the river, nestled in the wooded hills, but now it was destroyed. Large chunks of road had torn away, leaving an impassable hole in its path, and with a sense of dread, Caroline turned and saw that most of the road in the other direction had also been devoured. Up ahead, there was a tangled mess of a massive fallen tree which had collapsed across the road, one of many, she was sure, and everywhere she looked was torn and littered with rocks and trees and fallen branches, as well as huge flats of mud and soil that had been lifted by the flood. She saw where the carriage had gone off, and down below, the carriage itself lay on its side near the river, broken and tattered. It looked as if it had been there many years, fading in the sun and the rain, and she turned away from it, hating the sight.

They were fenced in, no carriage or rider would be coming along this section of road anytime soon. The breathy rush of the river hurried and crashed below, dangerously high, sweeping along furiously; brown with dirt, and frothing with thirst.

Far in the distance, something rumbled, and above the clouds were brewing a deep grey. Caroline wondered if it might yet rain more, though she could not see how there could be any more rain left to fall. Would it ever be over? She felt totally unmoored in time and place, and the storm seemed biblical in magnitude. They were trapped in this no man's land, in purgatory.

She would have to follow in the direction of the ravaged road, going into the wood in the places where she could not pass. But, which direction? For a long, breathless moment, the decision of which way: one which would ultimately determine her success, and she knew, perhaps even mean the difference between keeping her husband alive or losing him, felt an utterly impossible choice.

But then, there was absolutely nothing that she could do about that, so she simply chose one over the other, and started slowly down it.

✿

*C*aroline breathed deeply and evenly- in through her nose- and out through her mouth. She was losing hope, and images of what she might find when she got home began to pollute her mind with their venom relentlessly. The journey was strenuous and slow, and while her mind betrayed her, her leg cried out in pain with the jolt of each step she made, even suspended as it was. She had had to use her hands, she had had to get down on the ground and crawl, and she had almost lost her cane once, as it too needed to be moved where the terrain was too rugged for her to use it, and she'd wished she had used something to tie it to her wrist.

When she had to leave the path to get around a hole, or a tree, or a large piece of the land that had been uprooted and thrown across the road; thorns, and nettles and jagged, clutching branches scraped and slashed and clawed at her, catching her clothes and hair, trying to drag her down.

It had been hours already. It must have been, the sun was high in the sky, and she was exhausted. She had had nothing in which to carry water, and of course, there had been no food. In desperation, she leaned down and scooped the brown water from the puddles, cupping it in her hands, and gagging as she swallowed the grit of it, but she would be a fool to trust that river again, and the time it would take to get to it and back would cost her dearly - in any case, it looked no cleaner.

She cleared her head, focused on her breathing, and tried to ignore the pain and discomfort as best she could.

✿

*T*he sun had started its cruel descent, and Caroline knew that she should turn back now - it would be safest, but she hadn't seen anything but road and ruin since she left, and while the road twisted and turned, she had wondered if a small village or a house might be right around the next bend, steps away and only just out of sight. What if she gave up just as she was about to find help? It was a scratching, insidious thought that she couldn't push from her mind.

She would carry on until sunset, she decided. It would be risky to go home in the dark, but the moon would be bright and big in a cloudless sky, and if she kept to the road, as much as she could, she reasoned that she could just go back the way that she had come, this time knowing what to expect.

Sometime later she came across a massive oak, centuries-old, that had given way in the storm. A pity, Caroline thought bitterly: another casualty to feed the storm's insatiable lust for destruction. The girth of the tree on its side was taller than Caroline was, and it was tall enough to reach the river, with its multitude of long, winding limbs. She would have to go up the hill and around it.

The roots had held to the soil, and a tremendous crater, now filled with water, formed at the base of the tree, driving her even further up the hill to skirt around it. She hit a small stream flowing down to join the river and had to follow it uphill to find a shallow place where she could cross, and once over, feet wet, she worked her way back to the road.

What she found was more and more forest. She carried on, thinking it was sure to be just ahead, listening for the sound of the river, but all she found, as the air grew colder around her, and the sun dipped low and dim, was ever more forest. The road must have taken a turn, or she had. She tried not to panic, and to keep walking in the same direction where she thought she was sure to run into the river.

The light of the moon, she soon found out, was not strong enough to light her way with a thick canopy of foliage blocking its path. She clambered through the dark, her clothes wet to the skin, and heavy with water and mud. She had to use both feet now, despite the teeth-grinding pain, and use her cane to balance the weight, anything else was too unsteady, and had grown too sore.

When suddenly she heard the rush of water in the distance, Caroline's heart leapt, and she felt fresh tears of relief prickle her eyes. It could be something other than the river that she was looking for, of course, another stream perhaps, but it was the only beacon in an otherwise dark, treacherous expanse, and the best chance she had. If she could find the river, she would find the road, she hoped, and if she was very careful, she would have a chance of making it back to the cabin by morning.

When she came across the steep drop of the ravine, she never even saw it, for what chance had she to see a black lack of ground in front of her in a dark wasteland of twisted shadows; the only light, devious and shifting, its fractures blowing in the wind, skittering across leaves and stone, twisting around crags and roots, reshaping itself, before disappearing altogether and reappearing elsewhere.

She put her good foot down, and the sickening drop in her stomach happened immediately and she tumbled down into the darkness, her scream ripping through the trees.

"*C*harles," Rebecca's voice reached him just before she materialised in the doorway, a look of concerned confusion across her face. In her hand, she held a message aloft, as if pointing a pistol at him, her other hand lifting her skirts to aid her hurried pace.

"Yes?" he tilted his head, ready for a distraction from his ledgers. "What is that in your little hand, dear sister?"

"Charles," she said again dramatically, and his brow creased at her tone. "This is a letter from Mrs Willis at Westmere." Her eyes held him a moment. "It is addressed to Lucian and Caroline. What do you make of that?" she went on without waiting. "Well, I opened it, of course, why I couldn't see any reason not to, and what do you suppose it says?" he opened his mouth, but she went on, marching to his desk, "It says that she was sorry to have not been roused at their departure, and as they had packed in haste, would they be needing any additional trunks," she leaned in toward him, eyes wide, "*for the duration of their stay in London.*"

"In London?" Charles repeated.

"London! Whatever are they doing here? Are they staying somewhere else, do you think? Would they have the audacity not to call on us, or at least notify us of their arrival?"

"It is peculiar, I admit. When last I saw Lucian, he left in a hurry to pick up Caroline in the hopes of making it to London for the birth of baby Mable." Rebecca's brow furrowed like his own. "I must admit, I was a little surprised that they were not here when I arrived days later, but then things have been… turbulent between them, and would not be unusual to imagine that their plans might have changed because of it.

Though... I have written Lucian to inquire after the two of them, and have received no reply."

"Well, that is because they are not at home, *evidently*," Rebecca said smartly, her voice rising.

"Evidently."

☙

*W*hat a stupid little fool she had been. If she was going to die, she wanted to be next to Lucian, to be in his arms, to comfort him. Hot tears streaked down her cold skin. Now he would die too, helpless and alone, thinking that she had abandoned him in the end to save herself.

After the fall, Caroline had lain there, her back on the stones, eyes like saucers staring up at the swaying branches, desperately trying to suck air into her lungs, feeling like she was downing on land. When finally her lungs gave way with a deep, shuttering wheeze, she sucked in too much air too quickly and was sent into spasms of coughing, her back beating painfully against the rocks.

The ravine was a cold rocky place where once the water had sliced through the land. It was dry now, mercifully, though the storms had turned the dirt and clay to mud. But the sides were steep, and well over her hand, though she did see a dip where she thought the ground may be no higher than a hand stretched high above her. It would have been difficult to climb had she been healthy, but with only one good leg, it would surely be impossible. She might travel down the path of the ravine, but she knew not where it would take her, and to navigate over the smooth rocks and boulders underfoot, now slick with mud, would soon see her with two broken ankles, she was sure, or worse - perhaps a bashed head, like poor Digby.

After a time, she tried to move, sitting up a few inches, and hot, excruciating pain shot up her spine like a crack of lightning, and she fell back. Her cane, of course, was lost to the woods.

She heard a rustling in the bushes, the call of an owl far away, drawing nearer, chasing mice through the darkness. The American forest was full of bears, and wolves, snakes, and spiders, all of which could kill. She knew that the English forests had been tamed by man over the centuries, but she had no idea what dangers might still lie in wait.

She breathed shaky clouds into the night. She did not have the energy left to be scared for her life.

※

*H*ours later, she pushed herself up, riding the pain like a wave pushing her forward, climbed the side of the muddy ravine, found a new stick, and started back the way she had come.

Her thoughts were of Lucian. Only Lucian.

※

*M*ore nights passed, and Caroline thought Lucian seemed to be resting more peacefully, and it seemed as if his fever was reducing somewhat. She had burned nearly all the furniture in the house, as it was the only dry wood around, all the wet logs having been used, and she began to fret over what would happen when it ran out.

In the dark and the cold, and vibrating with pain, Caroline had found the river and arrived home the following afternoon, shoes filled with blood where skin had been rubbed raw, ankle, a deep, angry purple, and more painful than ever, bruised spine and ribs, cuts and scrapes, and not a single thing to show for it.

Lucian, when she arrived, was sleeping, and had not known that she had even left. She had wept by the fire in her wet clothes, loud, angry, openmouthed sobs, and a despair that she feared would break her. Lucian slept on, too far gone to hear or to care.

She began to sleep a lot, tired beyond anything she had ever experienced, knowing it was from lack of food, but unable to prevent it. Days she had spent trying to build a scheme for trapping an animal, any animal, but with the resources at hand, and her lack of any experience whatsoever, she had come up with nothing but frustration and splintered fingers.

The days began to blend together, and she found it difficult to tell what was night and what was day. She went to collect water and sometimes would realise the moon was in the sky. The only constant was changing the bandages and trying to get Lucian to eat something. When the vegetables were gone, she went out and found the snails.

She drank a lot of warm water, she drank it to fill her empty stomach and when she lay down, it moved like a wave inside her, making her feel dizzy. Her hand sought out his, and she held on, that contact once again anchoring her, as she tried to stop them from shaking.

In her dreams, they were at Westmere, riding Theia and Lelantos for hours in the sun before returning home to a feast, the food crowding the huge table. Lucian was smiling and laughing as he lifted her from her horse, his face shining with health and happiness.

Always she woke cold and hungry, turning to him instantly to check if he still breathed, her heart clambering into her mouth. Feeling his soft breath on her hand, she would drop onto his chest, which was becoming harder and more boney day by day, and stared at the ceiling, her tears all spent, listening to his heartbeat counting the seconds of their exile.

※

*T*here were two shriveled snails and a few leaves left in the pot, and none left on the ground, she had been back and forward over it, time and time again. She was looking at it, her stomach a cavern. Wondering how she could get Lucian to eat it. She had completely lost count of their time there, nights and days were unimportant. She counted time by snails now. Two snails left. She stared at them.

A sound came from the door. It sounded like a knock. Caroline stayed focused on the pot. It must be a tree branch.

Again the knock came and she slowly turned toward the door. It was swinging open slowly, water-heavy wood dragging against the floor. Caroline looked up, feeling as though all her motions were underwater. Sunlight filled the room, real sunlight, for the first time since she did not know when she could see the sun, the rain had stopped. It burned her eyes and she turned her face away.

"Caroline," she heard a concerned voice say, a man's voice, so like Lucian's.

"Lucian?" she mumbled as she felt strong arms go around her.

"No, it's Charles and Wesley. We've been looking everywhere. Thank God we found you!"

"Lucian," she said.

"We have him, we will take care of him, we will take care of both of you, we are taking you home," Charles's voice was so warm, she felt the last of the fight leave her body as she gave in to the overwhelming tiredness.

CHAPTER 5

*W*hen Caroline next awoke, she surged upright in bed, already turning to the side to check on Lucian's pulse and breath. Her hands met cool, empty sheets and she cried out. Her eyes dazed and wild, she struggled to take in the new surroundings, a plush bed, sitting in a light and airy room. Panic shot through her, and she pushed the covers back and stood, feeling the thick, soft carpet under the sole of her foot, it was disorientating. She looked harder at the room, she was certain she had never seen it before. She suddenly felt faint and sat back down on the edge of the bed. Her whole body was limp and wrung out. She noticed a window, and pulling herself out of her daze, she limped toward it, holding on to the wall as she went.

The street below was a mix of grey pavement, white marble houses, and wrought iron fencing. Trees were lining the pavement of each side of the street, and a couple of carriages moved sedately along their way. London. She was back in London, in an unknown house, with no idea where Lucian was. Wincing that the light she pulled the curtains shut and swayed against them, trying to calm her pounding heart. Charles, and Wesley... they had come for them. She had thought them the fever dreams of a dying woman. She remembered nothing of the ride back to London, or even how they had gotten from the cabin onto a more stable road.

Lucian. His name a whisper of worry behind every heartbeat. Where was he? Was he recovering? Had he eaten? Was someone taking care of him? The questions bombarded her and she groaned covering her face with her hands. What if he had not been able to be saved? What if she hadn't had a chance to say goodbye? The thoughts drove her to a warm-looking dressing gown, lying by the bed. She quickly put it on, the heavy fabric settling on her diminished frame like a weight, slipped her feet into slippers, and grabbed a cane that had been left for her by the bed. She started toward the door, and then stopped in shock, as she caught a glimpse of herself in the mirror. A stranger stared back.

She turned away from the mirror and left the room, coming into a wide and gracious hallway, decorated in light tones, full of plants and art. She thought how it reminded her of Westmere, and she realised how much she missed that secluded place, how much it had come to feel like home.

She stayed close to the wall, limping and hopping with the aid of the cane. She found herself at the end of a corridor and started in the direction of more doors. The house was quiet: a heavy, expectant sort of quiet, only interrupted by the calm ticking of an enormous clock halfway along the hall. She came to another door, and gently turned the handle, peaking in. It was a lady's dressing room, complete with a bathtub. She brought her head out, and closed the door, and kept on going. Suddenly, she heard voices downstairs, they seemed to come from directly below her, and she froze, straining to hear.

"He sustained a serious injury. It is a miracle they survived as long as they did. Nearly a fortnight, it is an impressive feat. That young woman is battered to a pulp, she must have worked herself to the bone to see them through it."

"Will they recover?"

"Lady Ashford should make a full recovery, she is suffering from an aggravated ankle sprain, some bruising about the spine and ribs, lack of food, and prolonged strain. She needs rest, for her mind and her body. She is very frail at present - if she were to catch an illness... I could not guarantee her health."

"And Lord Lucian?" the voices moved away, and Caroline recognised Charles's soft timbre. She moved to the railing at the top of the stairs in an effort to hear.

"His recovery is less certain. He has been fighting infection, that much is clear. He is very weak, the conditions and lack of food hardly aiding his body in the fight. He seems to be hanging on through sheer will, and there is a lot to be said for that..." The doctor hesitated, and Caroline dug her fingers into the bannister, listening intently.

"What can we do for him?"

"I have him on laudanum now, and I would suggest that you keep him on a steady dosage of it. We need him to rest, his body should not be taxed further for any reason. I would also keep him from any visitors, as not to tempt the risk of illness. Furthermore, I would strongly recommend that he and Lady Ashford apart to rest in isolation, for both their sakes, until such a time that they are both strong enough."

"Well, I thank you, doctor. We shall have our staff heed your instructions most carefully until your return."

Charles led the man out the door, and Caroline shrank back, scared to be seen. Nothing would stop her from reaching her destination now. She turned back to the hallway, gripping the wall, and started forward again. Checking rooms as she went, she finally came to the one furthest away, and leant against the doorway for a moment, gathering her strength. Her hand went to the door handle, and she pressed down, her heart beating in her ears suddenly, nerves making her fingers shake.

The room was dark, with the curtains drawn tightly closed. It was chokingly warm, and she took a minute to let her eyes adjust, eventually distinguishing the bed in the darkness. Tiptoeing over to it, she hesitated as she got near, seeing his dark outline. She heard a ragged breath. He was lying so still. Hovering over him, she lapsed into her routine. She held her fingers just under his nose, feeling the breath, and relieved when it came. Next, stepping closer, she put her hand on his chest, just above his heart. Its beat was strong, certain, and pulsed under her hand, making her smile. He was alive and quite asleep. She stood up and started back toward the door. He shouldn't be disturbed, she reasoned, as she left the room, and made back toward her own.

She remembered all the things they had talked of, in the dark, howling nights, when it felt as though the whole world had become an ocean of rain, and they the very last people afloat. She shouldn't risk his health, that was all. Leaving had nothing to do with her fear of looking in his eyes, and confronting how much the man had really come to mean to her.

❀

"*C*aroline?" She heard a soft voice beside her and felt a hand on her hair. She forced her eyes a little open, the sunlight stinging. Finally, the white light faded away and she saw Eva, sitting on the edge of her chair, a book falling from her hands, her warm smile so full of happiness that Caroline felt warmed by the glow of her.

"Eva-" she said and started coughing, her throat dry. Suddenly, a glass was pressed to her mouth and she turned her head to see Katherine standing over her, her face a mixture of relief and joyful tears. She lifted her head and drank, and the cool water slid down her throat like a balm. She sighed as she settled back. Her eyes adjusting to the light, she looked around the room, taking in the unfamiliar surroundings. The room was decorated in a pale yellow, duck egg blue, and ivory motif, and it was calming.

"Where is this?"

"Your home... well, yours and Lucian's... in London. It's his townhouse," Eva explained.

"And it's *extremely* pleasing, as mother would say," Katherine said, imitating her mother's voice, making the other girls smile, but Caroline could not help but notice that her own smile did not reach her eyes.

"How is Lucian?" Caroline suddenly asked, sitting upright.

"Do not be alarmed, he is well. The doctor has been here every day, and the staff watch him round the clock. He is well taken care of."

"How long has passed? I find it difficult to keep track of days just now."

"Charles found you more than two days ago," Katherine said, looking out the window, studying the street outside.

"They saved us," she said far away. "How did they know where to find us?"

"They didn't. It was Charles and Rebecca who realised that you should have reached London, after a note from Westmere. We all started to worry, sending messengers out to all the houses in town and in the country, not finding you in any of them, and knowing the storm would make the country roads dangerous, they began to search for you. Eventually, they came upon the crashed carriage, I believe. All I know is that they left several days ago, and did not come back until they had found you. I am only sorry it took so long."

Caroline shook her head in amazement. Leaning back against the pillows she mused on how close they had come to never being found, of dying together on that narrow cot in that lonely cabin.

"What now?" she asked with a small laugh, as tears started falling again, she felt overcome.

"Now, you have to regain your strength. You might do well to avoid the looking glass in the meantime," Katherine said with characteristic bluntness and Caroline laughed through her tears, touching the scratches still scabbed across her face. Eva tutted at her sister.

"I have missed you all so much. I thought I was going to lose everything," she said with a half-smile.

"And Lucian?" Eva prompted, and Caroline dipped her head.

"I *did* almost lose him, and I cannot live without him," she said simply, her words stunning everyone in the room into silence.

"Huh. Mother was right, there really is someone for everyone... maybe I won't end up a shriveled old maid after all," Katherine said grimly and Eva tutted.

"You're tiring poor Caroline with your nonsense," she said softly with a little smile. "We'll leave you now, dearest, to get some rest, or Dr Harris will have our hides." Eva kissed her on the cheek, but Katherine hung back, looking abashed, busying herself with tidying the vanity, and then they turned to leave.

"Eva," Caroline said. "Would you mind... if Katherine and I had just a moment alone?" Both their eyes grew large, but while Eva looked pleased and eager, Katherine looked nervous, like a deer ready to bolt.

"Yes, yes of course! I'll be downstairs in the parlour. Take your time," Eva said, and hurried out, closing the door softly behind her.

Katherine's eyes shifted around the room, and her fingers fiddled together, clearly unsure what to do with herself. Caroline scooted over on the bed, and patted it, in case there was any uncertainty, and a look of relieved gratitude crossed Katherine's face as she settled in next to Caroline as they used to do.

"Caroline... I..." Katherine stumbled before Caroline held her hand up to quiet her.

"When Lucian and I were in that cottage, we had a lot of time," Caroline started softly. "We had a lot of time to talk. We had a lot of time to think. He and I talked of... well, just about everything. We talked about that night." Katherine's eyes grew wide with fear, and she drew a shaky hand to her mouth. "I had already known how desperate you were, but Lucian told me that he had been cruel to you. He told me that he had manipulated you, threatened you with warnings of how his father's vengeance would destroy us all when you would not yield. He told me that you were a broken woman that night and that you wept and mourned for me. He also told me that you had believed us to already have been... entangled in some way or another, and that he did not relieve you of this misconception."

Katherine was crying by then, big tears falling freely, as she hiccuped air into her lungs.

"He asked me to forgive you. I love my husband more than I can say, but I would not forgive you simply because he asked it of me." Katherine sobbed at that and covered her mouth to try to hold the sound in, and Caroline noticed that her eyes too were beginning to cloud with emotion. "I forgive you, Katherine," she went on softly, "because even though I hate what you did to me, I love you too much to let it spoil one more minute that we have together. One thing that I learned for certain, is that life is far too short and uncertain to let bad memories keep you from the people that you love. Can we be friends again? Can we be sisters?"

Katherine tried to speak but couldn't, her voice was stolen and her body shook with sobs that she couldn't control. Caroline felt tears begin to slip down her cheeks, and she held her arms out from where she sat, and Katherine threw herself into them.

❀

*L*ucian pushed his eyes open a crack, seeing a high ornate ceiling above him, and a cool, dry room. He tried to move, and felt pain lance his side. He felt better, however - cooler, in less pain. The fevered delirium had lifted, but been replaced by a slow, quiet sluggish muddling in which memories collided: Caroline in the water, he raced to save her, and she floated away. Was it a memory or a dream? He could not distinguish. They slipped through his fingers like sand as he tightened his fist around them. Caroline in breeches, with soot on her face. Caroline closing her eyes over a bite of wilted greens, making it last as long as his much larger bowl did. Her body pressed against his, counting his heartbeats. Her tear-stained eyes demanding that he not leave her. He felt as though he had battled hell in those days, fighting through the delirium, the nightmares, closing his eyes to a constant war not to slip away, not to leave her alone; her words his only tether. She needed him. She wanted him alive. There was a sound in the room and he turned his head, too quickly, feeling dizziness descend on him for a moment.

"Ah, my Lord Lucian, you are awake. I was just informing your brother of your progress. You are very lucky indeed."

"Caroline?" he croaked, his throat as dry as a desert.

"Now, your wife is fine, she too is recovering."

"See her-" he rasped out, trying to make himself understood.

"You will see her soon enough. For now, you need to rest. I am just going to give you something to help," the doctor said, in an authoritative voice. Lucian shook his head, trying to resist. He wanted to see Caroline, he did not want to sleep anymore, he had to see with his own eyes that she was alright. But the doctor was not to be put off, and soon Lucian felt the heavy tug of drug-induced sleep overtake him, and fell back into vivid dreams.

❀

Katherine hummed as she arranged flowers in the drawing-room. The morning was bright, her best friend was alive and safe, better still, happy that her family was together. The day was full of promise, and only one regret remained, and he had just entered the room.

Greeting his sister, Charles cast his eyes in Katherine's direction and then surprised her by coming over to speak with her. They had barely exchanged a word in weeks, and Katherine had given up hope of his forgiveness. It seemed Charles' good opinion was not casually bestowed.

"Miss Fairfax," he said, friendly enough.

"Lord Charles. To what do I owe this pleasure?"

"What pleasure may that be?"

"Why, you are deigning to speak to me, of course," she said a little tersely, her inner voice shouting at her to bite her tongue and be civil.

"I see your manners have not improved," he remarked lightly, looking over her flowers.

"If I displease you so, why initiate conversation?"

"Because, I find myself... missing your company as of late," he said lightly, and she turned her surprised eyes to his. She frowned a little, looking away. She felt vulnerable around Charles. She was afraid of being rejected by him again, pushed away, afraid she was destined to disappoint him. He had certain expectations of a woman, and it was clear to them both that she would never meet them.

"Are you not leaving for Europe shortly?" she asked, making sure to stay away from his probing eyes.

"I am. Tomorrow in fact, now that the storm has passed, and my brother and Caroline are recovering and out of harm's way."

"I see. Well, I wish you a pleasant trip," she said, forcing her voice to sound carefree. He studied her, his head to the side a little, his face inscrutable.

"I thought... I had hoped... that perhaps I might write to you if you wished. Indeed, if we could be friends again, for the sake of our families," he said softly, and she glanced at him, from the corner of her eye. Her heart constricted painfully at his words. For the sake of their families, to ease social interaction. Ever the polite and dutiful brother-in-law.

"I suppose I shall be awfully busy with my social engagements. My mother is determined to end up with two married daughters by year's end," she said with a bitter laugh. Charles's face closed at her words.

"Of course." He bowed. "If you will excuse me, I must prepare for my departure."

*L*ucian was sweating, the effort of moving was making his muscles tremble. He was thin and weak, and it was driving him mad with frustration. He needed to be back on his feet, needed to go and find Caroline. In the deep of the night, sometimes he woke from his endless dreams of her and could smell her in the room, her sweet scent around him. Had those revealing words been in the heat of desperation, a desperation born out of jeopardy. Did she mean it when she had told him she loved him, that she needed him?

Rebecca was keeping him updated on Caroline's progress, that she was growing stronger each day, and soon the doctor would be willing to 'risk agitating their nerves' with exercise and excitement. Would she come to him? Did she blame him as he blamed himself? He felt the doubt and uncertainty flow through him and longed to stride down the hall, fling open her door, and take her in his arms.

✿

"*Y*ou have a visitor," Rebecca said, hovering in the doorway. Caroline sat up straighter, feeling her heartbeat kick, she pulled her dressing robe over her more tightly, and smiled nervously, admitting the figure.

"There are my two favourite sisters!" Wesley's happy voice came into the room, as he beamed at them.

"Wesley!" Rebecca exclaimed happily and ran to embrace him. Caroline smiled and wished that she could run to embrace him also. He came to her side, taking both her hands in his.

"Caroline, I must say, you are already looking better," he said optimistically.

"Really, you needn't flatter me, I am well aware of how unpleasant I am to look at," she laughed. She had learned that she had earned herself a blackened bruise just under the eye during her time in the forest to go with her scratches and scrapes. She fell quiet when Wesley's gaze turned serious, and he tipped his head to the side.

"I know of one who would give anything to look at you in any case, and he certainly would not find you unpleasant," he murmured softly.

"How is he?" she asked.

"Why do you not tell me? You visit him each night do you not?" Caroline looked at him in surprise.

"How-"

"I have my ways..." he said elusively.

"Does he know?" she asked simply, her heart pounding as she waited for his answer. Wesley regarded her a little, then shook his head.

"I don't believe so... but I think it may be time to tell him yourself. He is waiting for you, Caroline."

"But how... the doctor-"

"I have just dismissed Dr Harris," he said smartly, in a hint of agitation, as he neatly removed his gloves with one sharp movement per finger. "I have come here to find my brother forcibly drugged and in a perpetual stupor, and the lady of the house essentially treated like a prisoner, having to risk her own health to sneak by night to check on the health of her husband in secret? What kind of medicine do you call that?" he said, his voice rising. "Well, I simply won't have it. Dr Harris is lucky if I do not go to the doctors' board about this. I have engaged a new doctor myself, Dr Gladstone, and he shall be in directly. In the meantime, after surviving that ordeal together and battling death, as you two have done, I shall be damned if you are to be kept apart."

❀

*R*ebecca left her room and started back to the drawing-room where she had left Katherine a while ago. A ring on the doorbell stopped her in the hall. She saw a doorman rushing to answer and then the door was opening. Eva came through it, already smiling at Rebecca warmly, stripping her gloves off.

"Eva, welcome. Caroline is sleeping, but should wake soon," Rebecca said, suddenly distracted by the figure of Eli appearing behind Eva.

"Lady Rebecca," he greeted her, bowing and Rebecca smiled at his impeccable manners.

"I am sorry if we are intruding at a difficult time," Eli was saying.

"Of course not, it does you credit to worry after a friend," she was saying when once again she noticed the doorway was not yet empty. Her heart leapt to her mouth as she saw Isaac's broad shoulders, dressed soberly in dark colours, emphasising the piercing light of his eyes and dark hair. He bowed to her and then approached. She had not seen him in weeks, not since the wedding when they had hardly had any time to talk. Bowing before her, he gently picked her hand up and pressed his lips to the back.

"Lady Rebecca, it has been far too long," he murmured, raising his eyes to hers. She was vaguely aware of Katherine calling Eva and Eli into the drawing-room, leaving the two of them alone in the hall.

She opened her mouth to speak but found her mind empty of words. She had been enduring an endless parade of men her father had presented her with, and she had agreed to consider them, after all. But now, standing before Isaac Taylor, she realised how she had missed him, and how she dreamed of their wild adventure to Gretna Green.

"Mr Taylor," she finally said, pulling her hand away from him, as he held it a little too long.

"We are very formal today, are we not!" he teased, taking her arm in his and starting toward the drawing-room. "Considering we are now family, we shall have to become more... familiar," he said, casting a sideways glance at her which made her cheeks heat up.

"I suppose we are family, a slight bond only, however. Hardly even worth mentioning," she played.

"Would you prefer a closer one?" he asked suddenly, turning to face her outside the drawing-room, and she flushed, her stomach flipping at his tone as much as his words. She swallowed hard and took a moment to answer. She could hear the others voices' inside chatting happily.

"Closer to me, Mr Taylor? Do you mean to move into my stables? I hear that you are quite at home in them," she said tartly, seeing Isaac's eyes crinkle with amusement and something else. He had not called on her, or written to her in weeks, it was fairly obvious he did not think of her as anything more than an acquaintance, but she enjoyed the candid and frank relationship they had developed, and especially enjoyed teasing him.

He studied her silently, his eyes frankly moving over her face, and he looked about to speak, but withheld it, seeming to change his mind.

"How does your reconciliation with your father go?"

"He shall forgive me when I make the amends he is waiting for," she said, with a bitter smile.

He continued to look at her for a moment. Then slowly reached out toward her face. She froze. His hand brushed her cheek, and she almost closed her eyes and leaned against it, but before she knew it, his hand was before her face, holding the violet she had tucked into her hair.

"You, my lady, have no need of adornment. You put this poor flower to shame, and it is to be pitied. Its life has been wasted," he teased

"One may sympathise," Rebecca said, caught in his words. She realised how close his hand was, and suddenly felt foolish. "I - I must return home. I have an engagement tonight," she said, turning away from him and brushing past to enter the drawing-room and say her goodbyes to the company there, knowing that after an encounter with Isaac Tayler, dinner tonight would be all the more unbearable.

❁

That night, Caroline bathed for the first time in, well, she didn't like to remember. They had thought her too weak before, but now she was allowed, and it was the most exquisite thing she had ever felt. The hot water enveloped her body, warming her through, chasing away the memories of the icy river, and having to huddle against Lucian's burning, feverish body for warmth. Though she mused, as she lay her head back against the lip of the copper tub, there were worse places to find warmth. She used a lavender-scented soap and scrubbed at her skin until it was pink and tingling. It felt unspeakably decadent to be clean again, after an eternity of mud and ash and brown, dried blood.

After a while, she rose and returned to her room. The place was quiet, as everyone left for their own homes in the evening, save the servants. They were quite alone for the first time since their arrival. It had been days, and she had seen him every night, checking on him sometimes more than once, but he had never woken. He was awake now, and coherent, Wesley had said, he would know her face.

She missed him, madly, if truth be told. A bond had been forged in those days of terror and hunger, and it was not easily pushed aside. She did not know what to say to him, how to act with him, after everything they had shared. They had brushed death together, faced down the spectre side by side, with only each other to turn to. To say it changed their relationship seemed too weak a statement. She had been so close to him, no secrets, no physical boundaries, for a while she had known his body better than her own. Now, in this setting, she was not sure how things would look once they had readjusted.

She entered quietly, with any luck he would be asleep and she would have time to gather herself before waking him. His room was warm and bright, the curtains drawn on the windows and the bed, the fire banked. She sat at the mirror and combed out her hair. It fell in waves and tumbled across her shoulders and down her back. She looked at her reflection and felt a strange feeling of nervousness.

She had chosen a lace-edged nightgown, wrapping an equally thin silk dressing gown around her shoulders, tying the sash. The last time she had seen him, she had been in his clothes, covered in mud and blood - she longed to be beautiful for him again. She was nervous, and she stalled, absently tidying the brushes in front of the mirror.

"Surely the prospect of seeing me is not so bad..."

His warm voice sent heat rushing through her, into her ears and her heart contracted painfully. She turned to the bed, seeing the curtain had now been drawn back, and he was watching her.

He was sitting, propped up against the pillows, a loose white shirt, unlaced around his chest, his arms at his sides, one side, bulky with bandages. She allowed her eyes to drift slowly to his face.

They looked at each other, as though from a great distance, their connected gazes pulling them together. He was thin, and still pale, but his smile consumed his face, his stubbled jaw, recently shaved, and as strong as ever, his blue eyes as deep and soft as she had ever seen them.

Her chest started to heave and then tears were falling, her face twisting, feeling weak with relief, yet, her eyes never left his. Suddenly she was moving, and she barely gave him time to brace himself before she threw herself into his arms. He pulled her fast against him. She cried, clasped tight, and felt the last vestiges of anxiety fade. She felt his hands on her hair, stroking it gently, and abandoned herself. The horror of their experience and the absolute reality of what might have happened pressed down on her. Now he was sitting here, alive, holding her.

It felt like coming home.

She did not know how long passed in that embrace, lost in their shared celebration of life. Pulling away finally, she looked up into his face, so close to hers.

"Caroline," he murmured, his lips quirking into a smile, one that turned into a look of amazement as she reached for his cheek with her hand. She ran her palm over his stubbled cheek, tracing the hollows of his face. "Are you well?" he asked, a little breathlessly, she nodded, intent on the feel of his warm skin, just the right temperature, under her fingers. . "I - I am so sorry I could not take care of you," he muttered.

"You are the reason I am still here," she argued softly, and he turned his eyes to hers.

"How could that be true?"

"You promised not to leave me, I could hardly fail to make the same promise, could I?"

He pulled her close to him again and captured her lips in his, this first kiss since the night in bed, the night before he buried Digby, the night before the fever set in. She melted, feeling whole again, winding her arms around his neck and pulling him closer.

Their kiss was not soft. It was not gentle. It was hot and hard, and proof of life. They kissed until they were breathless, her hands pulling him closer, his hands in her hair, capturing her jaw and taking her deeper and deeper. Until she could feel her heart pounding against his chest, her breath harsh, and her body on fire, his own body mirroring it.

Feeling lightheaded, Caroline broke away, leaning her head against his chest, breathing deeply, her head swimming. She felt his fingers on her back, clutching her thin gown, his chest falling rapidly. Slowly she sat up and he moved his eyes over her, drinking her in.

"Caroline," he said, his face crumpling with some memory, some worry. "Before the crash... I never said how sorry-" She put her finger against his lips, stilling him.

"No, let us not talk of it. The people who fought and lied to each other, who hurt each other at every turn, they never left that cabin, they died one of those dark nights, and the rain bore them away. We are different. We are..." she struggled for the words

"A young wedded couple..." he offered.

"In love," she finished.

"In love?" he asked, a smile forming on his lips.

"In love," she confirmed, matter of factly, and sighed as he dropped his head to her neck and started to gently kiss the virgin skin there.

"Show me..." he whispered, his stubble rasping against her, and her hands fluttered to his shoulders and then made him groan as she shifted away from him. "Where are you going?" he complained, as she wiggled over to the other side of the bed.

"Do you really think I can have forgotten the position of your wound? It is safer for me to be over here to sleep..."

"I was not, in fact, planning on letting you sleep for a while," he growled and she laughed, her cheeks colouring by his hooded look.

"I did not play nursemaid for so long to watch you hurt yourself before you are fully healed. The doctor should have my head. I think not... there will be time for... everything else... soon enough" she said in a tone broking no-nonsense.

He groaned, but submitted to her demands to lie back, and watched as she arranged the bedclothes over him, and blew out the candle. In the dark, she stretched a hand out on the cool cover, and with surprise, found his, already there, open, waiting for hers. He threaded his fingers through hers and squeezed, and she felt complete; like she had a home again and a family again, inside of just one man.

CHAPTER 6

*C*aroline slept well, for the first time in weeks. It was not the deep slumber of the starving, or the restless sleep of the scared, or the waking nightmare of checking on the man beside her every few minutes to see if he still lived. It was the sleep of someone who feels safe, after a long time, and she revelled in it.

Waking slowly, she registered the morning light filtering into the room first, and then the warm, hard arms around her. She smiled a little, pushing herself against him, enjoying the comforting feel of him at her back, warm and getting well. She found the pressing of something firm against her back as she pushed closer. That was new.

Still, old habits die hard, and she still turned over gently, careful not to touch his wound, and stared at him. In the morning light, he was all golden stubble and tawny eyelashes. His eyes opened then, and she realised he was also awake, enjoying their closeness. His eyes were blue and clear, and she rejoiced to see them, she had feared for him when the darkness seemed to have crowded in on him.

He trailed a hand down her arm, above the covers, slowly, and goosebumps chased his fingers. She felt locked in his gaze, stray shafts of sunlight, falling in patches over them. Neither spoke, but she felt as though her eyes held a constant stream of conversation with his. His hand continued its lazy motions, moving up to her hair, running his fingers through it, and she smiled slightly, at the pleasurable sensation. His fingers then made it to her cheek, where they stroked her skin, his touch reverent.

Suddenly, she caught his fingers and moved them to her mouth, where she placed a soft kiss on the smooth back of his hand. His smile curved irrepressibly, and he mirrored her gesture, pulling her hand to his mouth, though, he turned hers over and pressed a light kiss into the palm. He glanced down at it. A slight frown marred his brow as he took in her fingers, still rough and burnt from her days at the cabin. Breaking firewood, carrying buckets to and from the well, cooking over the fire, pulling herself through the thorns and brambles, had all taken their toll on her fingers, and he now raised each one, and pressed a kiss to the tip, as though he could erase the marks.

He moved closer, placing her hand against his heart. She could feel its beat, now so strong, and gripped the laces of his shirt slightly, and tugged him forward. He came willingly, his expression a mixture of intensity and tenderness. He cradled her face between both his hands, marvelling.

Then he lowered his mouth to hers, and she sighed softly as their lips met. The kiss was gentle, a light grazing, to begin with, then he dipped his mouth, tasting her, savouring her, and she responded, lifting her head to press more firmly against him. She gasped as he moved his mouth to her jaw and started kissing along it. Her hands clutched at his shoulders, her body was a stranger to her now, the sensations so foreign. He reached her ear and softly drew her lobe into his mouth, and she jerked at the sudden sting of pleasure. Smiling against her neck, he continued his journey downwards, his hands pulling her closer to him, easing the straps of her lacy gown from her shoulders. Her breath hitched, leaning back a little he met her eyes, and stilled, waiting for her to guide him.

She swallowed, her lips tingling from their kisses, watching him intently, seeing the questioning look. Her body was on fire, and she fought to keep her head. All she could think of was his hands on her body, and what would happen next, and how it could possibly feel. It scared her, as it thrilled her. Making a decision, she steeled herself and then dropped her shoulder deliberately, letting the strap of her gown slip further down her arm.

They both watched its descent, and then his mouth was back on hers. She let herself melt under his sensuous movements, willing herself to relax, though every touch of his fingers made her heart race. His fingers dragged the strap down, and she untangled her arm from the silky fabric. She felt the cool air against her skin and looked up to see Lucian gently peeling the silk and lace away from her chest. His expression was one of wonder, and she smiled at it. He made her feel like a goddess made flesh.

He stared down, before lowering his face, pressing a kiss onto her breast, his hand coming to cup it, rolling his thumb over her nipple, then sucking it into his mouth, hot and wet. At the sensation, Caroline moaned, a sound unbidden from the depths of her, her hands automatically going to his head, holding it against her, and he growled with satisfaction, smiling against her breast, his hands slipping around her back, pulling her to him as her head fell backward, riding the waves of sensations rushing over her, as his tongue swirled.

"Caroline, the doctor has come for Lucian, but we cannot find-" Rebecca had already started opening the door. Caroline gasped, pushing Lucian's head from her, and diving under the covers. Horrified, and her face scorched with shame as she burrowed into the bedclothes. Lucian rumbled with laughter.

"Oh! Well, I suppose I may call the search off," Rebecca said, seeing her brother reclining against the pillows, a bemused look on his face, his hands behind his head.

"Rebecca, my dear. Of course. Perfect timing, as always," he said, laughing again as he heard Caroline squeak with embarrassment.

"Well! How was I supposed to know... I thought Caroline had better taste than this," Rebecca said with a smirk, which grew at Lucian's scowl. Rebecca went to the window and flung open the curtains. Lucian turned his face away from the bright light and rested his hand on the cover lightly.

"Caroline, dearest, I believe my sister is already aware of your presence. You may reveal yourself," he said, humour thick in his voice. She peeked above the covers, and closed her eyes again, wishing it away. Rebecca fought down a smile and turned to Lucian, her arms folded, treating him to her no-nonsense look.

"Doctor Gladstone has arrived," she said, and Lucian tore his attention from coaxing Caroline out of her hiding place and glanced at his sister.

"I shall join you presently," he said.

"He is waiting now," she insisted and Lucian shot her a look of annoyance.

"I shall come along in a moment. Have him wait in my study," Rebecca rolled her eyes and went to the door.

"Well, it would be very rude to keep him waiting, when I'm sure that he has other patients to call on," she said, shutting the door behind her.

"Caroline," Lucian said in a low tone, caressing her name. Caroline threw the heavy blankets back, desperate for air. She sat up and her gown fell open again, taking Lucian's attention with it immediately. He smirked and leaned forward toward her, but she was too fast for him. Scooting off the bed, she stood one-legged, and pulled the sleeve back up, flipping her hair back, she slipped her silk dressing gown around her shoulders and belted it tightly. Lucian watched with a pout.

"The doctor," was all she said as she used her cane expertly to limp around to his side of the bed and pull the covers back off him, taking him under the arm to help him stand. He let out a long sigh of frustration and let her help him upright. Once he was standing before her, he passed both arms around her and pulled her in for a long and lingering kiss. Pressed against her body, she almost dragged him back to bed. His smell drove her wild, and as he kissed her deeply she felt him harden against her stomach, and she found that the knowledge made her grow warm and tingling in answer.

"I feel like I have been waiting my whole life for you," he murmured.

"In that case, a little while longer will not kill you," she said innocently, with only a slightly wicked glint to her eye that acknowledged the effect she was having on him.

"I would wait forever for you... if you wanted," he said softly.

"I know," she said with a smile and then lowered her gaze a little, before looking back at him through her lashes. "But, you do not have to... I am yours." He pulled her to him, holding her hard against him, ignoring the pain he must be feeling in his side, her head fitting perfectly under his chin, his hands spanned her back, and she linked her arms around him.

"If I did not make it out of the woods, if I died there, if I never woke, please never tell me... and allow me to live in this dream forever," he said roughly.

She smiled and pulled back from him.

"Try and keep that in mind when the doctor is examining you, it might not be so agreeable," she said teasingly, patting his back, and turning him to the door. As she reached for the door handle, he stayed her hand and she turned back, looking at him in surprise. His eyes were serious and intent on her face, and once again she felt their unspoken depths. His eyes held a hope, a need... a longing so deep it was dizzying.

"Tonight," she whispered, with a small smile, secret and intimate on her lips. Lucian, looking thoroughly drunk on his desire, let her tug him toward the door, supporting him.

He stopped on the threshold.

"I shall proceed from here, thank you, my darling," he said.

"I can help you," she said, going to place her arm under his again.

"Caroline!" he smiled, exasperated. "Look at yourself. You have only one good leg, as opposed to my two, and you are not suitably dressed to be wandering the halls," his eyes swept over her gown and exposed skin, and he turned and cleared his throat to break the stare.

"I hardly need be embarrassed in front of a doctor, or your brothers," at the last, Lucian lowered his eyebrows in a scowl and she laughed at his obvious discomfort.

"Lady Ashford, will you ever concede an inch to me? At least to make me feel like I have just a little bit of control occasionally, even if it is just a farce?"

"Fine, I will humour an injured man. But do not think for one moment, that I am giving any control to you permanently - just until you feel a little better," she warned and he smiled at her, shaking his head a little.

"I would never wish for that, my love. Your great stubbornness and world-renowned obstinacy are some of your most endearing qualities," he teased, and Caroline smiled sweetly back at him.

"Would that I could say the same of you," she said, pushing him a little out of the door, so she could close it, leaving him with a last glimpse of her smile and flushed cheeks.

----

*D*ear Miss Fairfax,
    I confess I have started this letter many times; however, what I might say and the words to say it, have eluded me. Now, the hour grows near that procrastination is folly, if the words are to be said at all. And I believe they must be. In fact, I need them to be said, for the sake of my sanity.

From the first moment of our acquaintance, you have captivated me, enthralled me, and bewitched me well beyond my wits. I am afraid that has prevented me from acting in the gentlemanly way I should have toward you.

The feelings I have for you have made it difficult for me to act so, and I apologise for it. While I maintain that the mistreatment of Caroline, is not something that I could ever forget, of my brother or of you, distance has helped me to understand that you did it for fear of your sister's health, and your family's well being, and more importantly, you did it in the belief that Caroline cared deeply for my brother. I see now that I should have discussed it with you, and given you the chance to explain your intentions, and perhaps would not have acted quite so severely.

I am aware that you now feel uncomfortable around me, and I truly do feel sorry for that, as I would have you enjoy times when our families will come together. I write to assure you that I shall never make you feel so again and that I regret my actions.

I hope, someday in the future, we shall be able to spend time together again, and that I may make amends. I wish you luck in the coming season and hope you fulfil your mother's expectations to your own satisfaction also.

I hope you shall save me a dance when I return from Europe, whenever that may be.

Your brother and friend,
Charles

Katherine stared at the letter, the words almost memorised at this point. He was gone, Rebecca had confirmed his departure that morning, leaving only this in his wake. What did it mean? She agonised over it. He had feelings for her, he was apologising, when it was she who should. He was so frustrating, she had countless questions to ask, and now he was gone, to return at some unknown point in the future. She carefully folded the paper, and slipped into her bodice, feeling his words warm there. He thought about her, enough to write her... she was not so forgotten then. For the rest of the day, the slight crinkle of paper made her smile.

❀

*C*aroline spent the day with the Fairfaxes, finally well enough to leave the house and visit their townhouse. She cooed over Frances's tiny babe, its precious weight in her arms, its soft skin, and its smell tugging her heartstrings. For a moment, she found herself wishing Lucian was with her, and then she grinned at the thought of him holding the little one, his face alarmed and unsure, suspicious over every gurgle and hiccup the baby made, not trusting himself for a moment.

Eli and Isaac were there with Eva, and Caroline talked with her friends, thankful for every moment. Eva and Eli were the pictures of happiness, and from the look on Eva's face and her inability to leave Frances's side for long, Caroline thought maybe this baby was only the first for the Fairfaxes. The thought warmed her heart, Eva and Eli would make kind, compassionate parents. Isaac looked a little forlorn, sitting in the corner, watching them. She sat beside him and smiled, seeing his eyes far off.

"You are awfully melancholy today. Have you no jokes to get us all laughing as you usually do?" Caroline prompted. He blew out his breath and turned his grey gaze on her.

"*M*y jokes are all spent, sadly. I cannot seem to see anything to laugh about anymore," he muttered, pinching the bridge of his nose between his fingers.

"I have not seen you at our house often... we have missed your company. Perhaps friends might cheer you," she said lightly, watching as his fingers tightened into a fist. He looked about to talk and then looked away.

"I have been no company lately, I confess..." he trailed off, and then turned to her, as though suddenly remembering something.

"How are you feeling?"

"I am much recovered, thank you."

"And your husband? Lord Lucian? I believe he has been well taken care of by his family."

"Yes, they dote on each other. Wesley and Charles have been to keep him company every day, though Charles is now away. Perhaps you might-"

"And Lady Rebecca? Does she visit often?" There was something in the studied casualness of his tone that made Caroline glance at his face, which was also carefully blank.

"Every day and often at night... she has been running the house for us," she said, and Isaac nodded, crossing his arms and falling silent, lost in his thoughts. Caroline watched his profile, and then reached for tea, giving him time.

"You are close with her, are you not?" he asked and Caroline nodded.

"Has she spoken to you of her father?"

"Not recently. Though I know him to be very disagreeable and tremendously unlikable," Caroline said quietly.

"Yes, he does seem to be. Even to his children," Isaac said, frowning.

"Especially to his children!" Caroline emphasised, thinking of Silus's face when revealing Lucian's deception. "He has not yet been to see Lucian," she confided, and Isaac raised his eyebrows at the news. "He claims he is too occupied with business, and with Rebecca, though with what, I cannot say," Caroline continued, suddenly aware of Isaac's attention. "Do you know what busies them?" she asked suddenly, yet saw a guard fly up over his expression.

"No, sadly not," he muttered, abruptly standing, and Caroline leaned away alarmed, catching her teacup.

"Forgive me, I must go," he said, and quickly took leave of everyone, exiting the room so quickly that Caroline wondered what she had said. She caught Eli staring after his brother with concern, and Eva lowered her hand to his to comfort him. They shared a look, a look so close, and so full of shared secrets that, in an instant, she missed her husband. To know his thoughts, with only a look, to feel his emotions as though they were her own.

*E*li and Eva escorted Caroline back to Lucian's townhouse. It was close, with all the fashionable streets of London set within the same area. Lucian's was in the heart of one of the oldest and grandest, and she wondered if his father had lived if he would have visited him there, gotten to know him, maybe he would have benefitted from having a father figure who was not as cruel and sadistic as Silus. They travelled by carriage as the weather was very cold, and before Caroline had realised it, the short Autumn had quickly turned into Winter. Despite the cold, Caroline was disappointed that she could not walk the short distance for the sake of the stretch and the fresh air, but her ankle was still much too sore to wander about the streets, not to mention her bruises and scratches which would be seen and remarked upon, and no doubt the streets of London would be ringing with the gossip that Lucian had brutalised her for some reason or another. At the house, she bid Eva goodbye and grasped Eli's arm as he helped her to walk to the door.

"Thank you. It has been so wonderful to leave the house today, and I have missed you all so very much," she said, her breath puffing in the air in front of her.

"We have missed you as well, dear Caroline," he said, helping her carefully up the steps.

"I do worry Isaac seems less than happy lately," she said, looking up to Eli's face as they climbed. He was quiet and they arrived before the door, a footman already opening it for her.

"I believe that dreaded malady, which my dear brother has managed to avoid for so long, has finally struck him... he is heartsick," Eli said with a wry smile. Caroline studied his expression, seeing his worry lying under the light smile.

"Caroline! You are home. Good, it is far too cold for you to be out, and if Lucian calls me upstairs to inform me of it one more time..." Rebecca complained coming to the door, holding Caroline's Kashmir shawl in her hands. Eli looked to Rebecca for a moment.

"Lady Ashford," he said, bowing formally.

"I asked you to call me Rebecca," she persisted with a mock scold.

"Perhaps I shall just call you Mistress Lion Tamer, as you seem to have all the Ashford men in hand..."

"I would answer to it!" They laughed, and Caroline joined them, thinking how strange a feeling that not long ago she had resigned herself to death, and now she was on an impeccably beautiful crescent in London, in an elegant gown, laughing easily with her friends.

"I must take Eva home," Eli said, breaking her away from her mind's wanderings. "Goodnight Caroline. Thank you for today, and for your concern for Isaac. He would be touched to know it."

"But we will not tell him."

"No, we will not tell him," Eli confirmed with a smile and bowed to both women and left, going down the stairs and into the waiting carriage.

"Come inside!" Rebecca said, exasperated, pulling Caroline in and wrapping the shawl around her shoulders. It was already starting to get dark, despite it only being late afternoon and Caroline felt the weariness of her first full day up and about settling on her.

They went to the drawing-room, to sit by the fire and Rebecca rang for tea to warm them up. They chatted comfortably of Frances's child, Mable, replacing Caroline's trousseau and the Winter activities in London.

"It is the biggest ball of the Winter months. It will also be your first debut as a married couple in society, and finally, a chance for all the Ton to see the truth behind the scandal Lucian caused."

"I thought the point of our marrying was to *avoid* scandal," Caroline said.

"Caroline, society loves to gossip, and there are few they love to talk of more than those who care nothing for their actions or consequences... and Luke is that man. You should never hear some of the stories that have been spread about him throughout the years," Rebecca said with a shudder.

"I might have already heard some of them," she admitted and then continued under Rebecca's look. "Are any true?" she asked.

"That depends entirely on what you have heard. Though you do know my brother, I am sure you may guess which ones hold a grain of truth."

"I have heard... tales of illegitimate children..." Caroline said, trailing off, and Rebecca's face softened as she looked at her friend.

"If he has any, he does not know of it. It is his greatest fear, or one of them anyway, to father a child and forget them - to condemn them to the life he has led, to grow up without a father... it is the most groundless of accusations you may make of him," Rebecca said, and Caroline felt quietly relieved.

"He told me once he had killed a man... more than one..." she said, looking to Rebecca, her insecurity and worry present in her eyes.

"You know little about my brother's past it seems, though it is hardly surprising, knowing his tendency to keep his guard up."

"Please tell me... I wish to understand him better," she said. Rebecca considered it.

"I do not wish to share more than he would want me to, but I suppose facts are facts. He purchased his own commission to the navy when he was sixteen years old. Our mother had already been dead six years, and my brother's relationship with Silus was only getting worse. Lucian longed to be away from him, to make his own life. He knew his own father was dead, but that he wouldn't inherit his estates or fortune until his twentieth year. Father was intent on making every day a living hell for him, and so, he left. He told no one, but left us each a letter, Charles, Wesley and I."

"Where did he go?"

"Egypt, to begin with. He once mentioned the Battle of the Nile, though he has never spoken in detail about it. He started at a basic rank but soon progressed. I once saw a rather infamous captain saluting him, and of course, he counts Admiral Lord Nelson as a friend."

Caroline looked at her with widened eyes, her mind reeling, trying to take in the new information, and fit it to the man she already knew.

"After Egypt? I do not know," Rebecca went on. "He does not often speak of it. Perhaps Ceylon, the Dutch East Indies, as he has mentioned places I would not have thought possible to know unless you have witnessed them. He returned in 1805 after the battle of Trafalgar, claimed his inheritance and separated himself from Silus as much as possible. But, you see, once he was back, he never really stopped trying to gain his acceptance, win his approval... our father has always known how to manipulate him and that has never changed." Rebecca seemed to be speaking to herself, so focused was she on past memories. Collecting herself, she suddenly turned back to Caroline.

"So you see, he must have killed men, I would be more doubtful if he claimed not to have."

"He made it sound as though it were through duelling," Caroline said, her mind whirling at all the information. Rebecca laughed.

"Caroline, there may be no man in London who has been more challenged by jilted lovers or jealous husbands. There was a man once. He came home... earlier than expected and found Lucian at home with his wife. He went raving mad and pulled a pistol on them both. I am not sure exactly how it came to pass, but the man ended up dead. Four years ago now. Father only just managed to keep him from the noose, with some connections he has in the police force, though Lucian seemed to wish for his own arrest. He tortured himself afterward - punished and haunted by his mistakes. Though, when the darkness lifted, he was not interested in reform, instead, it got worse. That is the only death I am aware of. Though, I believe he might have killed Joshua Lee if he had threatened his claim to you..." Rebecca said seriously, seeing the somber look on Caroline's face. Caroline shivered, and wrapped herself more tightly, suddenly cold through the warm shawl.

"He has been to war. He has fought and loved and killed, seen places I can only dream of, it is... strange, to find out about a whole life someone lived before you."

"War, and travel and death, perhaps... but not love, not for a woman at least. I can promise you that Luke has never before loved any woman," she said, pinning Caroline in a serious gaze. "Until you."

It was a bond they shared, to love such a complicated and troubled man. Rebecca then steered the conversation back toward gowns for the upcoming festivities and Caroline joined in the talk wholeheartedly, relieved to move back to light topics, her mind overloaded by her revelations. The hour grew later, and Caroline started to feel tired as Rebecca spoke of leaving and they were both surprised when the footman entered to announce a visitor

"Lord Silus Ashford," the footman announced, and Caroline felt a shot of panic run through her, closely followed by loathing. It was as though talking of him had lured him.

"Father! You did not tell me you were coming to visit today," Rebecca exclaimed.

"Must I tell you my every plan, even before I have made them, daughter? And I am surprised to find you still here," Silus said, and Rebecca looked down. Silus entered the room with a swagger and came to stand before Caroline, running his eyes over her critically.

"Lady Caroline," he said, picking her hand up and pressing his lips to the back. Caroline resisted the urge to snatch her hand back.

"My lord," she said, bobbing respectfully. Rebecca started to sit, and Caroline gratefully sank into a chair.

"I apologise for my absence, I have been quite occupied with business as of late."

"Of course."

"I am glad to see you well, and I hope you shall fully recover soon. I had worried about you - you seemed quite shaken when last I saw you," he said with a barely concealed smirk.

"I am quite recovered, thank you," she said shortly, wishing Rebecca would make some conversation.

"My first thought upon hearing the awful news of your carriage accident was for you, my dear."

"And your son... of course," Caroline could not help her biting tone.

"Of course, though, I know his tenaciousness, and as with so many stubborn creatures, I doubted that he would die so easily," Silus said with a laugh, as though he had made a joke. "However you, my dear, are altogether more delicate and... vulnerable... than he." There was something to Silus's tone and look as he glanced over her. She felt a sense of unease growing in her stomach. It was almost a threat, the way he spoke those words.

"Father, do you not wish to visit Lucian?" Rebecca asked to break the silence. Silus continued to look at Caroline, seeming annoyed that she was failing to respond to him. He blew his breath out.

"I suppose I should, as I am here."

Rebecca stood, and they followed suit. Caroline decided to accompany them, and slowly ascended the stairs, Silus offering her a supporting arm. She stiffened at the contact but knew there was little she could do to shrug it off. They went down the hall, and Rebecca knocked, then opened the door first, Caroline heard her telling Lucian that his father was here. She hung back, hoping Silus would remove his arm from her, but he merely pulled her forward with him, pulling her in snugly to his body. Entering, she saw Lucian sitting up in his bed, his drawing implements cast aside, his face already set hard. She saw his blue gaze flick over her in surprise, instantly dropping to his father's arm, and her expression. If it was possible, his gaze hardened further.

Silus strolled to Lucian's side and clapped him harshly on the shoulder of his bad side.

"Well, son, you do not look too worse for the wear. Indeed, no worse than you usually look after a bout of drinking and whoring," he boomed, and Caroline saw some colour drain from Lucian's face at his father's heavy hand. Yet, he did not flinch, and sat, staring resolutely ahead at the wall, his face blank.

"I thank you for your concern, father," he ground out. Silus turned aside and suddenly pulled at one of Lucian's sketches, holding it to the light. Again, no reaction from Lucian, except for the way his fists tightened.

"Good God, man, do not let your bride see this! She will think you soft in the head."

"Father!" Rebecca exclaimed. Caroline felt her frustration mount, and she hated the powerless way Rebecca and she stood by, mere witnesses.

Suddenly, without thought, Caroline was moving. She rounded the other side of the bed, and sat beside Lucian, taking his clenched fist between her hands. He flinched at the contact, turning to her, meeting her eyes for the first time since she had entered the room. She saw in his eyes his hatred of the man standing over him, his hatred of his own powerlessness. She squeezed his hand steadily and smiled at him, hoping that her eyes would be reassuring to him, comforting him. In that instant, the room fell away, and they were alone, there was only she and him.

"Well, I see your forgiving wife has forgotten your sins, Lucian... if she knows them all, that is..."

"Luckily for me, she is an angel."

"To your devil, I suppose. Though, who knows if hell would have you," Silus laughed charmingly.

"Father, Caroline is tired, we should leave them," Rebecca inter- rupted suddenly, and Silus started for the door nodding.

"Rest well, boy, I am sure you shall need your strength soon enough. Lady Caroline, a pleasure as always, I look forward to spending more time with you in future, and to welcoming you into our family properly. No need to see me out," he said to Lucian with an almost malicious smile as he strode away.

Lucian tore his eyes from Caroline as she turned to look at his sister. The three of them shared silent looks, unsure of what to say after the unsettling and unpleasant encounter.

"Time for a rest, I think. Caroline should return to her own chamber."

"Why?" Lucian asked agitatedly.

"Because the doctor orders rest, she is weak, and you need to rest your wound as much as possible," Rebecca said tersely. Lucian let out a sigh.

"Dr Gladstone has said that we need not be kept apart."

"That is true, but he most certainly did not condone any sort of... vigorous activity, and obviously you are not to be trusted alone with the poor girl." He smirked wickedly at that, and Caroline felt her cheeks heat as his smile.

"Shall we?" Rebecca directed, and Caroline nodded, squeezing Lucian's hand a last time before they left the room. They walked down the corridor, each lost in thought.

"You were speaking of Isaac Taylor earlier, with Eli. Forgive the intrusion, but it looked a bit serious. Is there a matter for you to be concerned over?" Rebecca asked nonchalantly.

"Not so to speak, he just seems a bit... deflated. I cannot remember a time when Isaac was not full of jokes and stories. Eli confessed he is heartsick! Though I have yet to see a woman affect Isaac..." Caroline rambled as they reached her room. She cast off the shawl, her eyes drifting to the door, taking in Rebecca's face.

"Look at you! You have tired yourself out," Rebecca fretted, changing the subject. "You must heed the doctor, it is important to build your strength gradually, and not to catch a cold or chill." She directed a maid to remove the bed warming pan and help Caroline remove her dress. Caroline's movements felt heavy, and her eyes kept closing, and then she would catch herself and open them again. She felt her hair fall and slid her arms through the soft wrapper the maid held out, smiling gratefully at her. She crawled into bed, sleepiness already washing over her as she closed her eyes. She tried to hold on, to wait for him, but the need to sleep was too strong.

Her dreams were deep and sound, though she became aware that at some point during the night, she was no longer alone. Any trace of chill that lingered from her trip outside was completely dispelled as his masculine warmth burned through her. His strong arms held her tight as he eased into the bed beside her, wrapping himself around her, stroking her hair back. She mumbled incoherently in his arms.

"Shh.. sleep, my sweetheart," he murmured, his lips close to her ear.

Lucian could no longer sleep without her by his side, and he had waited for what felt like hours until his sister had departed and the house had grown still. Holding her in his arms, the smell of her hair against his neck, the way her hands curled around his was worth his graceless stagger along the hall and the pain in his side. It was even worth a visit from his father, to see her eyes burn at him so, to feel an ally, a companion against the man who had made his life a misery. For the first time in his life, Silus had seemed small, and so very insignificant. She was only a small thing, but so powerful. He fell asleep with a smile on his lips.

CHAPTER 7

"Caroline..." Lucian's voice held a whisper of a smile as he woke to find Caroline's hand under his nose checking his breathing. She quickly dropped her hand to his cheek, feigning a caress.

"What? Can a wife not touch her husband?" she asked sleepily, trying to rearrange her features into a mask of innocence. Lucian grunted as he pulled her close, and dropped a kiss on her lips.

"Of course, it is something I greatly encourage as a matter of fact. I am delighted you brought the topic to my attention," he said in a seductive voice, dipping his mouth to kiss her neck. She allowed him for a moment unwilling to put a stop to the delicious sensation that melted across her body, but then, head winning the battle, she pulled away, her hands firmly pushing him back. Knowing better than to fight her, he fell back, frustrated, with another grunt of pain as the weight came off his side.

"Don't think I do not see how your wound still pains you, and is still bleeding occasionally. I will not have the wretched thing reopened after all we have been through because we could not wait just a little while longer. The doctor said-"

"Believe me, I know well what the doctor said, I am beginning to think he takes a sick, perverse pleasure in denying a man his conjugal rights." Caroline leant over him, biting her lip to repress her smile.

"How you must suffer," she teased, his jaw ticked as he lowered his arm and looked into her eyes with a narrowed look.

"You have no idea." She swallowed a little the intensity of his gaze, then let her hand wander across the expanse of his neck. "Caroline... it is time to realise you have little chance of being rid of me. I am not going to die... Stop checking that I am breathing. Stop worrying about the hole in my side. I am here to stay, my love. I might not be strong right now, but I soon will be... and then... you will be fresh out of excuses," he said, and her cheeks glowed at his smile, so sinful. He took the opportunity, and his mouth went again to her neck, as he rested his weight gently on top of her, slow hot kisses trailed across sensitive skin - warm breath, soft lips, scratching stubble mixing sensations until she began to feel dizzy with need. The smell of his was like a draft, pulling her under against her will. He shifted again, pressing closer to her, and she heard him suck in a pained breath.

Caroline shot him a look of disapproval and then pulled herself away from him, as he moaned in quiet frustration. Reaching out for the bell-pull near the bed, she got up to dress. Their fateful and much delayed 'wedding night' would still have to wait. Limiting his physical exertions was the only way she could think to help, to have a small fraction of control over her constant worries that he was not healing quickly enough, or thoroughly enough. It was too much of a risk. She could imagine that he would not heed his body's protests or even pain if in the heat of the moment. She could imagine it very well, in fact.

He watched her with dark eyes, full of want as she moved around her room, preparing for the maid to enter.

A knock at the door surprised them both, and Caroline broke off the searing eye contact with a laugh.

"I suppose it is time to start the day," he groaned as if he could imagine nothing worse.

She smiled at him, a little indulgently, without comment, calling to the door. As it opened and Wesley peered in from the hall.

"I thought you were up! Good heavens, brother, you look a shambles. The doctor shall be here any moment. Why don't I tidy you up and help you back to your room," he said in cheerful scorn, taking Lucian under the arm and starting away much faster than Lucian would have liked.

"Is this breakneck speed really necessary?" he growled.

"Speed! We are barely moving, really, it is beyond time you recover your strength, it is wholly unattractive... this weakness in a man," Wesley goaded.

"I thank you for the kind reminder," Lucian ground out.

"You are most welcome."

Back in his room, Lucian sat on the edge of his bed, gritting his teeth as he started to peel off the muslin plaster. It was time for a discussion with the doctor.

🙊

*C*aroline winced at the jumble of the carriage over the cobbles as it set out toward the Taylors' house. Eva had written, telling them that she had big news to share, and Caroline was anxious to find out what it could be, hoping excitedly for news of a baby on the way.

Both ladies and gentlemen sat and had tea, talking about inconsequential things, with Katherine, who had received the same letter, until Isaac and Eli were summoned by their father to discuss business. Once Eva was alone, the girls turned their excited looks to her, and waited for an explanation. Eva looked away, seeming a little unsure how to proceed. Eventually, she was drawn out, however, and her news was far from what either of the girls had hoped to hear.

"I cannot believe it! Virginia! For how long?"

"I confess I do not know... but I believe it will be for a long time, perhaps forever. Mr Taylor never considered staying in England, and certainly not for his sons to build their lives here. They were only here for the season, and the travel," Eva explained gently.

Caroline felt a wave of sadness sweep over her. Her family, as small and unusual as it was, was breaking up. The Fairfaxes, the Taylors, and the Ashfords were the only family she had left, and she had imagined many happy days of them all together, having children and sharing their lives together.

"Are you happy?" Caroline asked, finally realising the look on Eva's face as one of apprehension. Her friend's face softened, and Caroline remembered Eva's words about missing Virginia. A smile broke across her light features and she dipped her head, nodding slowly, and Caroline grasped her hands, squeezing them tightly.

"Then I am happy for you, my dear sweet sister," Caroline whispered and felt a lump gather in her throat.

"Well, I am not! How can you think to leave us, Eva? How am I ever to choose a husband without your confidence?" Katherine cried, teary-eyed, but with a slight smile that belied her recognition of the look on Eva's face.

"Will Isaac go with you?" Caroline asked, sudden concern crossing her features. Eva nodded.

"He must return also, our time here is finished. Though...I cannot imagine living so far from you all," she said, gripping Caroline's hands.

"Shh, do not fret. We are all family, are we not? And family is never separated long by distance," Caroline said brightly, though she could not shake the feeling of loss that descended on her shoulders.

"I see you have heard the news," Eli's voice came from the doorway, and the ladies stood up, to speak with them.

"Girls, it is wonderful to see you," Mr Calvin Taylor said as he came in, bringing with him his business partner. Caroline stiffened with surprise as she saw who it was.

Isaac entered the room with his father, followed by someone dark and lithe."Mr Lee!" Caroline said, feeling unease grow in her stomach. She felt her palms grow a little damp. She had not thought about writing to Joshua again since the night Lucian found her letter, and she had admitted to herself it was a dangerous game to play. This was not to say that she would let her husband control her, however, there was no need to add fuel to the fire of Lucian's jealousy and insecurity.

"Miss F- I mean, Lady Ashford, forgive me," Joshua corrected himself, bowing as he saw her, a smile springing up on his tanned face. She bobbed to him and forced a smile as he came instantly to her side. As the rest of the people in the room fell into easy conversations, Joshua sat down beside her and gave her his undivided attention.

Caroline was grateful Rebecca was not present, she did not want the news filtering back to Lucian if it could be helped.

"I was so worried when I heard of your carriage accident. Why it's been the talk of the city... it was miraculous that you were both rescued unscathed."

"Well, unscathed might be too generous a term, however, my husband and I are still recovering," she said and felt a blush threatened as his eyes ran over her, drinking her in.

"You look quite well to me," he said quietly, and Caroline took a breath.

"Well, married life seems to suit me," she countered pointedly with an uncomfortable smile.

"I am happy to hear it, as I confess to hearing something rather different in the beginning." Caroline's back stiffened.

"Mr Lee, I do not think my marriage a suitable topic for you to be discussing with me or anyone else for that matter," she said quietly, but with an edge that even she could hear in her voice. He looked away, his hands tightening on his hat.

"I apologise. I was just worried about you... your betrothal was so quick, and do not forget, I was present at the Ashford estate for your... courtship," he said and Caroline was interrupted from speaking as Katherine stood up, indicating to Caroline that it was time to leave. As she bid her goodbye to Joshua, she hesitated as he reached for her hand to kiss it.

"Now I have returned to London, I look forward to seeing more of you, Lady Caroline," he said softly, and Caroline forced a smile at him, before turning and starting down the steps with Katherine.

"Well, well, it seems Joshua Lee has lost none of his confidence," Katherine remarked as the carriages pulled into view.

"Indeed. Let us hope it does not begin to cause us all trouble," Caroline muttered.

❧

*H*e burned for her, though he still woke every morning and expected her to be gone. Yet, each morning she was there. Her soft, gold-touched skin, glistening raven hair over smooth neck and shoulders in the cool winter light.

He turned from his reverie as his sister knocked on the door, and came in to sit in the window, gazing out at the London street, lost in private thoughts when Lucian joined her. She had been melancholy for weeks, and he was not sure why.

438

"Are you not excited for the ball, sister?" he remarked.

"I suppose," Rebecca said shortly, her head leaning against the window ledge.

"Becca..." he called. She turned to him, her head still back, and smiled a little at his inquisitive gaze.

"Yes, Luke. It shall be thrilling, no doubt."

"It shall be a nice diversion, I think. I find that even I am looking eagerly to the date."

"Surely you cannot mean to go! Don't be silly, it is far too dangerous. You and Caroline both are still decrepit!" He barked with laughter at the insult.

"A ball? Dangerous? Let us not sensationalise, little one. It is still over a week away yet, and I am sure with our swift progress, we shall be able to swan in and give you young things a run for your money." She scoffed. "Besides, look at me. Aren't I the very image of manly strength and vigor?"

"You look like an old apple that someone has dropped down the stairs."

"Becca!" Lucian laughed. "This is a rare mood, even for you. What is amiss? You have still not found anyone to your liking amongst father acquaintances? You know my offer stands, dearest... to come and live with us, forget Silus and marry who you wish... someone with whom you have a real affection," he said seriously. Rebecca looked at him with shining eyes, before turning them away, and back to the street.

"Luke, I know that would cost you too much... your relationship with our father need not be complicated further. Anyway, this is the consequence I accepted," she said, her voice steely. He stared at her, his emotions confused, wanting so much to protect his younger sister, yet unsure how. "You know, I am not so sad, I am sure I shall make a pleasant match. I am sadder that our company is being reduced so dramatically... first Charles, now Eva and Eli..." Rebecca trailed off, and Lucian narrowed his eyes at her omission.

"And Isaac Taylor. I admit that the Taylor's have turned out to be better company than I had anticipated, especially Eli. We might have been better friends, under different circumstances," he mused.

"As it is, the whole of London watches the two of you interact with bated breath."

"Which amuses us both no end," Lucian said with a smirk as he took a seat at the window opposite his sister. "Perhaps I should challenge him to pistols just for the sport." Rebecca slapped his arm surprisingly hard, but as a sting arose on his skin, so too did a soft smile on his sister's lips.

espite the very vocal protestations of both women of the house, Lucian had insisted that he accompany a few men to find Digby's grave so that he could be returned home to Westmere. He discussed this with the doctor, who had conceded, to the fury of Caroline and Rebecca, that if Lucian did not do any actual exercise, and if he was careful for the duration of the journey, rode in a carriage instead of on horseback, and did not walk far, that he would be safe enough for travel, as his wound had stopped bleeding entirely, and healing well on its way. Lucian would then part from the men as they brought Digby to Westmere, and he would return home to London, to cut his trip short and perhaps save himself a little of Caroline's displeasure.

There was the ball to look forward to, and the imminent departure of Eva and Eli to plan for, so Lucian was glad that Caroline would be kept busy for the days that he would be away. As upset and worried as she was with him for leaving, he was all the more upset to be gone from her side, for after their time in the cottage, he felt that to be apart from her for any duration was a torture, and to spend a whole night without his arms around her, her warm skin next to his, was an anguish that he could no longer bear.

But, this one small task was all that they could do for Digby, and Lucian would not overlook it. He was to be buried at Westmere, and when the Lord and Lady returned from London, they planned to have a small service with the staff, and any family that they might be able to find. Digby's wife had passed away years before, but Lucian had sent several letters and discovered that he had a grown daughter living in Devon, who had her own family and three small children. Lucian had written to her quite a sincere and heartfelt letter voicing his sorrow, and had sent with it, enough money to see her and her children fed well for several years, saying that it was the money that Digby had been owed for the journey. Lucian had not included it in the letter, but he would make sure that Digby's daughter was well provided for for the rest of her life.

🕸

*T*he evening of the ball was filled with preparations. Lucian dressed in proper white tie for the first time in too long, and almost welcomed the tight, form-fitting garments. He had spent so long, thin and weak, and he felt a tug of vanity as he looked in the mirror. He wanted his wife to be pleased with his appearance. In a somewhat unorthodox manner, they would be meeting at the ball instead of arriving together, as Lucian had only just returned to London, and as this would be Eva's last evening in London and Caroline wanted to dress and prepare with her sisters as she used to.

His large house seemed too empty without her. He trotted down the stairs meeting Wesley, whose emerald green velvet coat and gold paisley waistcoat made him even more dashing than usual.

"Brother! You do scrub up well," Wesley grinned, taking in Lucian's lean frame, tailcoat, and white cravat. His hair had been cut and the unruliness restrained somewhat, and his face, despite being cleanly shaven only that morning, had a glow of golden stubble, catching the lamplight. He smiled and clapped him gently on the shoulder.

"I am sure you are quite pretty as well, Wesley. You'll make all the ladies terribly jealous, I should think," Lucian said with a smirk as the brother started for the door.

"Ha! And so they should be. Not everyone could suit a green such as this one!"

The street outside was dusted with snow, and there was a distinct nip in the air. It would soon be Christmas, a time of year Lucian had barely noticed before. But this year, he planned to celebrate it, surrounded by family and friends. As Lucian swung into the carriage after Wesley, he mused on how his life had changed so dramatically in such a short time, gone the barren wasteland it had once resembled.

"Come. Let us not keep your beautiful wife waiting. I'm sure that she will be most anxious to see that you did not choose to stay at your little cabin in the woods for another extended holiday," Wesley said and

441

Lucian laughed and shoved his shoulder as the coachman called to the horses and they jolted forward.

✿

*C*aroline's head spun a little with the champagne she had consumed as they dressed. She alternated between happiness to be with her sisters, and sadness, with the thought it might well be the last time together. She was wearing a dress that she had recently had made with Rebecca's help. It was deep red velvet, quite suited for the season, and now that she was a married woman, she could begin to wear the darker colors that she had always thought suited her coloring. The dress was edged with gold. Gold lace and scrolling, pale gold gloves finished the beautiful garment, and her hair was pinned with gold pins and deep red roses. She had not dressed up to such an extent since her wedding, and she marvelled at how long ago it was. Soon they would start a new year, throwing the differences of her life to the previous year into harsh relief.

When they arrived at the ball, with the Taylors as their escorts, Caroline looked around the beautiful ballroom, still a society ingenue, impressed and awestruck by the high, ornate ceilings, grand columns, and intricate colourfully tiled floors. Christmas greenery hung heavy in vast evergreen boughs, where clusters of red-berried holy shone like little rubies against their waxen leaves. Mirrors lined the ballroom, huge and gilded, competing with the light of the candles, magnifying the golden splendor of the evening indefinitely. In contrast to the light, white muslins of the summer, dancers wore richer darker colors, in velvets, silks, and shimmering brocades, and the scent of warm, spiced fruit cakes soaked in brandy filled the air with the irresistible allure of sugar.

When they entered, Caroline suddenly got the distinct impression that people were looking at her. Rebecca had warned her that as their first social engagement since the scandal and the wedding, and of course, the elopement, with the added excitement of their recent brush with death, that the whole group of them would no doubt attract attention - Eva and Eli, Lucian and Caroline. There was even speculation over Rebecca and Isaac's involvement, though Silus had managed to stem the worst of it, which might have tarnished Rebecca's reputation beyond the mending that great wealth could provide.

A dozen whispers echoed after them as they walked into the huge hall going down the grand curved staircase, as people moved out of their way drawing back to speak to others. Caroline caught Katherine's eye and stifled a laugh at the twinkle there. Katherine turned to the small group they made and announced dramatically.

"Well, I propose we get some champagne before Lord Lucian shows up and ruins the fun with pistols at dawn," she said, whispers whipping into a frenzy at her words. Caroline resisted the urge to roll her eyes, and Eva looked positively horrified, as Eli only chuckled. Isaac, on the other hand, smirked and offered Katherine his arm, joining in loudly.

"I agree, I am far too young to lose my dear brother...whilst sober at any rate," and they started through to the refreshment room. Caroline slipped her arm through Eli's and he led both her and Eva after their siblings, causing the gossips to explode with speculation.

"Rebecca shall have our heads," Caroline murmured as she kept a light smile on her face. They reached the refreshment room, and the men procured drinks for their companions. They chatted and joked, enjoying the looks from the gossips.

Caroline's eyes searched, still not seeing the one face she was searching for in the throng.

"What say you, Isaac? Shall we dance before it becomes intolerably crowded?" Katherine was saying, setting down her flute and looking around a little. When she received no reply, Caroline looked up and saw that Isaac's attention had drifted away, and he was now looking to his left, with an intensity she had rarely seen from him. His eyes were trained as a hawk's, his face devoid of all humour and joking, and reflected a stark admiration, his mouth slightly open.

"Isaac?" she prompted, turning to see what held his attention so.

"Forgive me, dear Katherine, I shall have to claim that dance later," he murmured as he already started away, walking slowly toward whatever had caught his attention so thoroughly.

"Oh! Rebecca has arrived!" Caroline said suddenly, and they all turned along with the heads of the crowd at large. She saw Silus Ashford's tall head coming through the crowd, accompanied by Rebecca, who did indeed look stunning, in a deep green ball gown, her chestnut hair caught up in an intricate knot, holding her father's arm as they entered the refreshment area.

Caroline saw Isaac's tall stride taking him toward them, and she envied him his courage, throwing himself in the path of the patriarch of the Ashfords so fearlessly. Rebecca's blank expression, occasionally smiling, an easy falseness which suddenly melted into one of genuine pleasure when her eyes met Isaac's.

"With Silus," Eva observed, casting a look to Caroline, whose own smile had slipped at the sight of the man. Caroline had told Eva everything that had happened, and Eva had told Katherine, and they knew well that Caroline did not relish his company.

"I do not suppose I shall be able to keep Lucian and him apart," Caroline fretted, her eyes once again searching the crowd for her husband.

"Eli Taylor! A last taste of high society before you leave for the rugged homeland?" an inquisitive voice asked brightly and Caroline cringed, hearing the familiar accent. Between Silus, and now Joshua, she hoped Lucian was delayed.

"Lady Caroline, Mrs Taylor," Joshua said, bowing to them as they turned.

"Mr Lee," she said, her grip tightening on her champagne flute, trying to communicate that he was not to attempt to kiss her hand. Lucian could be anywhere in the crowd, and she feared his reaction a little, not for herself, but for Joshua, and Lucian's healing wound, which did not need aggravation.

"Please, call me Joshua, we were friends were we not?" he said lightly and Caroline averted her eyes from his warm gaze.

"Of course, yet I am not sure my husband would approve of such informality between us, and in mixed company."

"Ah, and I remember a young lady who did not wish to be controlled, who longed for equal partnership in marriage," he said, with a laugh at the end which brought a stinging retort to Caroline's lips. She was no meek, obedient wife, scared of her controlling husband. She fought down the retort, rationalising that anger might only confirm his condescending assumptions.

"Will you leave soon for America also?" she asked abruptly, changing the subject.

❀

"*L*ord Ashford," Isaac said, bowing low before the imposing man, trying to keep his eyes off the vision in green standing beside him.

"Mr Taylor, is it not?"

Isaac nodded and looked to Rebecca who was smiling at him. "Lady Ashford," he greeted her, his eyes locking with hers.

"Mr Taylor," she said with a slight dip of a curtsy, and they stared at each other for a few moments. Suddenly, Silus cleared his throat and brought them both back to the present.

"Well, I think I shall go and see about a hand of poker... I see Lady Caroline and her sister over there, no doubt Rebecca wants to join them. May I entrust my daughter into your capable hands?" Silus asked, raising an eyebrow at Isaac.

"I would be honoured, my lord," Isaac said, holding out an arm for her. Silus narrowed his eyes at the pair, turning away to go upstairs.

Isaac started to walk toward their assembled company slowly, longing for a little more time alone with Rebecca.

"You look stunning tonight, my lady."

"For tonight, let us be familiar... Isaac. For I fear this shall be our last chance," she said, and her voice was so sad, so resolved for a moment, he longed to turn to her, and take her in his arms and press her - did she want him to stay? Was she as indifferent to him as she always seemed? Instead, he took a deep breath and forced his signature smirk.

"Yes, it seems the society of London has quite overwhelmed us... how will we cope with the social scene of Virginia once we return?"

"I am sure you shall manage," Rebecca said, her tone teasing. "Is it very different?" she asked.

"Yes, very... the rules and etiquette for one. Do not mistake me, we have rules, and propriety; however, after visiting here, I see that Virginia is somewhat more relaxed. The balls are a little wilder, perhaps, the music a little more vivacious."

"And the girls more beautiful, I suppose. I am surprised you have waited so long to return!" Isaac stopped, drawing her around to face him, taking in her bright expression.

"No, that is where I must admit that London has no parallel."

Rebecca met his eyes for a moment, and he swept his gaze deliberately down her, seeing her cheeks flush in response felt like a reward, and the proof that she was affected by him made his pulse race.

"Be careful Isaac, I might mistake you for giving me a compliment," she said.

"It would be no mistake, Rebecca," his voice was soft as it whispered her name, and her brow creased in a slight frown as she looked at him, tilting her head to the side.

"You are too kind. The incurable charmer," she said but he shook his head.

"No, I am not, and you know it well," he said. Rebecca's gaze suddenly shifted over his shoulder.

"Ah! Luke is here."

They turned to see Caroline standing speaking with Joshua Lee. Rebecca's eyes widened as she turned back to Isaac, her expression prompting Isaac to take her arm again, and start toward the group, hoping that a peacekeeper would not be needed.

⚅

*L*ucian moved through the crowd sinuously. He had observed the room from the top of the stairs, instantly picking out Caroline. She stole his breath away, her delectable body wrapped snuggly in crimson velvet, which practically cried out for his hands to run over it. The delicate column of her neck was flushed slightly pink, from the heat of the room, or champagne, he did not know, but he longed to put his lips to it. He felt an almost animal sense of possession as he watched her, smile, and laugh, her beautiful face captivating and expressive. She drew looks from every man in the room, but she was his, and his alone. Tonight, every moment would be a struggle to maintain a civilized facade when he wanted nothing more than to whisk her home and kiss her deeply until she begged for him.

"Do not act rashly brother, but I see Joshua Lee has returned from Europe," Wesley said in a light voice, laced with worry.

It was then that Lucian was able to tear his eyes from the ravishing vision of his wife and focus on who she was speaking to. The surge of anger that hit him in the stomach was overwhelming, and he was breathless for a moment. His jealousy, he knew, was one of his worst traits, though he had never felt it quite so keenly before. It was irrational, yes, he knew now that she was his, but she had once felt something for this man, once had imagined a life with him, and he simply did not like having the man anywhere near.

Lowering his head, he started through the crowd. As he weaved in and out of people, he suddenly realised that charging over to them and making a scene might not be the best way to approach the situation. His face lowered, he circled them, concealed by pillars and couples, and observed her. She smiled at Lee, but it seemed a little strained. They did not touch, he noticed with satisfaction, but Lee was grinning at her, inappropriately, he thought sourly. Lee suddenly gestured to the dance floor, and Lucian felt his stomach tighten. Caroline looked around then, glancing at the stairs, and he wondered if she was looking for him. Did she wish for him to arrive, or want to dance with Joshua before he did?

He hated himself even as the thoughts formed, she had not done anything to deserve his distrust, yet he was unable to stop them. His father's voice, as always, taunted him, toyed with him, pulled his weaknesses out into the harsh light, and he felt the shame of them, even as they tormented him. He saw his brother approach them, and be welcomed into the group. Caroline asked him a question and Wesley replied, his answer sending Caroline's eyes back to the crowd.

He felt a sudden shock as she saw him, her piercing bright eyes on his.

Her expression pulled him, her smile tentative and she turned to him as he started toward them. He suddenly became aware of the quietness in the room and the fact that all eyes seemed to be trained on them. He realised that the scene was practically every gossiping matron of the Ton's dream, he was about to approach his new bride, as she stood with her previous fiance, as well as his former betrothed and the man she had eloped with. He could practically feel the nervous energy emanating off the crowd, and the lust for blood, violence, or at least a spectacle of some sort.

Arriving before them, he had still not taken his eyes off Caroline, and hers, green like jade tonight, burned into his as he stopped before her. She suddenly placed her hand on his, and with a smirk, he raised it to his lips.

"My love," he murmured, pressing a kiss onto her glove, and was rewarded with her impish smile. She inclined her head a touch, and looked up at him, through her dark lashes.

"My lord," she whispered and he felt his breath leave his chest once again. Without taking his eyes from Caroline he murmured.

"You must excuse us," nodding politely and tucking Caroline's hand into the crook of his arm, starting through the crowd to the dance floor.

❀

*H*eads turned to watch them go, and they shared a smile. On the dance floor, a slow song was playing, with couples forming into sets. As they reached the polished dancing area, Caroline realised that their friends had followed. They formed a set, Isaac and Rebecca, Eva and Eli, and Caroline frowned to see Katherine and Joshua together. If he was in the set, she could not avoid dancing with him.

Caroline became aware of Lucian's eyes, which had still not moved from her. She smiled ruefully at him and realised how devastatingly handsome he looked. Once again strong and broad, his form fitted perfectly into the broad-shouldered coat, with its narrow waist. His hair caught the light and looked like spun gold for a moment, and his blue eyes blazed at her. His gaze was intense, yet, there was a touch of humour under it, a pleasure he was taking in showing the whole of London that they were together, united, unbreakable.

The music started and they moved toward each other. Caroline hoped that they would both be recuperated enough to keep up, but felt the music and the life in Lucian's eyes feeding her excitement. Coming close, her chest brushed his, his face so close for a moment, and then she whirled away and he was gone. Soon she was face to face with him again, and she raised her hand to meet his, carefully keeping the few inches of air between them for propriety's sake.

"You look utterly bewitching," he murmured in her ear as she slowly circled him.

"You make a pleasant prospect also," she replied, tingling as one of his fingers broke the rules of the dance, and gently glided a line down her hand.

"Thank you. I am feeling more myself," he said softly, and his breath against her ear caused a ripple to descend her arm.

The music changed and she suddenly found herself facing Isaac's warm smile.

"Caroline, I am very glad to see you tonight. I was hoping that we could speak later... there is something of great importance I wish to ask your opinion on," he said.

"Of course," she replied, glancing up at him.

"Are you well?" she asked, suddenly concerned by his serious look. Before he could answer, she was once again swept away and faced with Eli. They danced, and he made a joke that had her laughing before she changed partners again and donned a more guarded smile for Joshua.

"This reminds me of the ball where we met," he was saying and she nodded noncommittally. As she spun, she caught Lucian's eye and saw how he was watching them with an unreadable expression.

"I wish I had had the courage to follow my instincts then, instead of dallying and losing... everything I wanted."

"Yes, well, timing is very important," Caroline replied automatically, not paying much attention to his soft words.

"It is, is it not? It seems there, Lucian truly bested me," he said and Caroline suddenly turned her face to his, uncomfortable at his words.

"Mr Lee... please... I-" she started, going through the motions of the dance without thought, feeling her cheeks heat up under two men's scrutiny.

"Yes?" Joshua asked eagerly.

"I love my husband," she blurted tactlessly. His face hardened for a moment, and suddenly a warm hand was on her waist, pulling her back into the moves of the dance. She met blue eyes as they looked at her seriously, they circled each other.

"You look shaken... what has Lee been saying to you?" Lucian asked darkly. Caroline shook her head, relaxing her face into a smile.

"Nothing of importance," she murmured, coming close to him again, and seeing the possessive gleam in his eyes as he looked over at her, giving her a little thrill of being desired. Their hands wavered in the air before Lucian's closed the gap and gripped hers. She gasped, hoping no one was watching, and looked at him in askance.

"What is this about, Caroline?" he demanded, and her heart twisted as she saw that lonely, lost boy look that Lucian lapsed into sometimes when his fears were laid before him.

She sighed and as the music ended, squeezed his hand back, tugging him toward her. He came willingly and still held her hand against his side, his other reaching up for her cheek, where he gently stroked it, before placing a gentle kiss on her lips. She looked up at him, her eyes too blue to be real, as her smile softened them.

"I am yours... as you are mine," she said, gazing earnestly up at him. His eyes grew warm, and he lowered his mouth to kiss the top of her head.

"Do not forget it," he said, smiling as she muffled her response into his chest.

"Impossible."

✹

*W*esley watched couples moving on the dance floor, becoming bored and already checking the clock to see when he might leave. Katherine shifted impatiently at his side.

"We could dance," he suggested and seeing her distracted look in response, continued, "But we both know... your restless heart would not be in it."

"What do you mean?" Katherine asked, feigning an innocent expression.

"We might be dancing together, but, I daresay it would be wasted, what with your hoping that I was...another," he waggled his eyebrows playfully needling her.

"What fresh gossip is this, Lord Wesley? I haven't the slightest idea what you speak of," she said determinedly. Wesley smiled and shot her a glance of disbelief.

"Come now, we are friends, are we not? You miss my brother," he stated matter of factly, and Katherine fanned her face and looked away, visibly ruffled.

"And why would you possibly think that?"

"Because he misses you... and I have noticed your distinct lack of interest in husband finding," Wesley said, and Katherine gasped, shocked. She studied his profile for a moment, before turning back to the dance floor.

"What can you mean, he misses me?" she asked, striving for a nonchalant tone.

"Because he writes to me on a regular basis. Charles is even-handed in his manners, he enquires after everyone... health, happiness, any news really... except you. He never asks about you," Wesley said. She looked down into her glass where her heart had fallen.

"That would seem to indicate the opposite, Lord Wesley," she observed grimly.

"You do not know my brother enough...yet. He cannot bear to know about you - if you are well or not, if you are engaged - he cannot stand the thought of it, so he does not ask. He attempts to put you from his mind, or else go mad," Wesley explained.

"When will he return?" Katherine asked, suddenly. She was never one any good at disguising her emotions, and he heard the vulnerability in her voice.

"I do not know, I'm afraid to say."

Katherine nodded, and abruptly set her glass down. "Will you please excuse me, I must check on Eva," she said hurriedly, already moving away from his sympathetic eyes.

⚘

"*R*ebecca, would you do me the honour of another dance?" Isaac asked, his eyes fixed on the perfect beauty before him, who had been busy dancing with an array of other acquaintances. It seemed now that after the scandal that had been whispered about her family, she was not as unreachable a prospect as she had once been. As she was turned and whirled around the dance floor, however, her eyes were never far from his. He hoped he was not wrong.

"Why not? I hate to be the exception," Rebecca teased as he led her out into the crowd, her eyes sweeping over the other women in the room. Isaac smiled at her, pulling her closer for a waltz.

"Yet, you are," he stated as they began to dance. She swayed against him, and he felt his heartbeat strangely at the thought that he might yet lose her.

"Tell me what it is like... your home," she said softly and he leaned back, surprised by her question.

"It is... a climate of extremes. Our winters are blanketed in snow past the knees, while our summers are warmer than you could even imagine. In the summer the heat settles on the waving golden fields and shimmers. The cicadas sing into the nights, fireflies rise from the green grass like dancing stars, and the sky is the blue of a cornflower. Horses roam in free pastures and mountains are vast, untamed, dangerous" he murmured, "full of life."

"It sounds incredibly beautiful. Free," she said, her eyes meeting his.

"That is just the word for it," he replied and they danced silently for a while. She was lost in her thoughts, and when Isaac spoke, she brought her attention back to him.

"How does it go with your father?" Isaac asked lightly, seeing a shadow cross her features at his question. She tossed her head and shrugged.

"Well, I am not yet engaged."

"I have noticed. May I ask why?"

"I have not yet found someone whom I could consider."

"I see, and so your father gives you a choice in the matter?" Isaac asked, his heartbeat picking up as he waited for her answer.

"Yes, I was quite surprised myself, but he consults me... I do not think he will force me unless I take too long over it," she said, with a bitter laugh at the end. "Why do you ask?" she inquired, her voice becoming soft. They swayed to the music, him leading her through the steps easily, and he caught her in an intent look as he stared down into her face.

"To be quite honest, I cannot stop thinking about it," he confessed and Rebecca's colour rose, but she kept her gaze steady on him. Her face was a question, and Isaac struggled with how to answer it. He was unsure. He only seemed able to dance around the subject. He knew he was not good enough to marry her, she would need a titled, landed man. He should not even suggest it, it would be an impertinence, but if he did, would she laugh at him? Would she be insulted? Would she be lost forever as a friend to him and that playful bond which had grown between them on the road to Gretna Green be severed forever? The music came to a close, yet, he did not release her, he held her arms and swallowed, feeling nerves tighten his throat.

"Why is that, Mr Taylor?" she asked again, and her beautiful eyes were so honest and open, he could not help but respond honestly. She was his friend, a companion, someone he had grown comfortable with, yet been drawn to - her delicacy, her strength, her commitment to her family, and her wit and grace.

"Because... I wish that you might consider me," he answered, pulling her a fraction closer, his heart in his mouth. "I wish that you would choose me."

She stared at him, shocked into silence. They continued to stare at one another, his heart thudding in his chest, their gaze unbroken as a new dance started and couples started to brush against them.

"Lady Rebecca, may I have the pleasure?" A young man said, bowing to her, coming between her and Isaac. She pushed him to the side as quickly as she could without being terribly impolite, and saw Isaac's back, moving away from her, through the moving bodies of the dance floor. Her stomach in knots, she watched him go, confusion and elation beating through her every vein.

❀

Silus watched the young couples on the dance floor. He saw Wesley standing off to the side, surveying the dancers, Katherine Fairfax at his side. Useless boy, he had not yet stood up once with any of the countless ladies of fortune. He too would need to step up soon and marry advantageously, no matter what his tastes. Perhaps Katherine Fairfax was a viable prospect for Wesley, despite her low birth. After all, no one else had come forth, he did not think Wesley would fight it as much as he would any of the other good matches that his father could make for him, and Fairfax business had been good of late, and it would be difficult to turn down the dowery that came with a Fairfax daughter. A tall head with blonde hair swept past and he felt his speculative smile drop as he recognised Caroline and his bastard.

Lucian thought he had bested him because he had managed to trick the young woman into believing him a worthy man. How foolish she was. Yet, Silus did not underestimate the cunning of his son. In that respect, he had taught him well. In that respect, he seemed more of his blood than any other of his children. He was ruthless and immoral, much like Silus himself. How different would he have been if he had grown up with his father by blood, he wondered.

Something needed to be done about the small matter of Caroline's inheritance, which Silus had not yet received even one penny of. It frustrated him no end that Lucian's fortune was untouchable, but he contented himself with the thought that taking Caroline's would be more satisfying as she seemed to mean something to his son.

He wondered idly if she was a whore, such as Lucian's mother had been, but he thought not. No, there was something strong about this girl, something that would have to be handled carefully.

He turned back to the poker table, already regretting his heavy losses. Well, no matter, soon the Lesage fortune would stem the flow.

"*J*ust because I must rest my ankle does not mean you must miss a fun evening to play nursemaid," Caroline smiled. "Should you not wish to dance and converse with others? We have been stuck together, without other company for quite a while," she teased, as Lucian helped her off the dance floor, a supportive arm around her waist most scandalously.

She could feel the heat of his body, close to hers, and her gown started to feel unbearably hot and constricted. She imagined for a moment what his arms would feel like around her, without the gown, and felt her face grow hot at the thought.

"If you are too warm, we might stroll outside... I know a lovely little spot," he remarked and laughed as she hit his chest lightly.

"Do not joke of it... it was awful. You truly frightened me," at her words, his face sobered.

"I apologise, really, I hate myself when I remember how I treated you when I was little more than a stranger to you." They continued, weaving in and out of the couples still dancing.

"You were a stranger then, so I forgive you, though, I must confess the circumstances I found you in... still frightens me," she said with honesty. His face looked surprised for a moment, before shifting into a concerned look.

"What do you mean?" The music stopped and Caroline felt nervousness rise at the turn of the conversation. The room was hot and his eyes on her face were demanding. He wanted her to explain, and he would not wait.

"Let us find somewhere cooler," she suggested, and he looked in annoyance around the room, before turning back to her, with a small smile.

"I have a better proposition. Let us return home. We can talk, resolve this matter. And then I can show you how much I love you, and how recovered I am," he said. Her face flushed, and she bit her lip. She had spent her entire evening wishing for that very thing. She looked around to find her friends, wondering if she should stay. Then, she reached a decision, her tone was resolute, her chin set and determined.

"Yes. Let us go home."

His smile was irrepressible, and she found that her own smile was widening to meet it. He raised her hands to his mouth and gently kissed them. He tucked her hands into the crook of his arm and started off toward the doors. Caroline tugged his arm as they passed the refreshment room.

"I must say goodbye to Eva... they leave tomorrow," she said, his face dropping. He worked visibly to control his impatience and gave her a strained smile.

"Of course. Let us find them now, shall we?" he ground out, already hurrying her comically through the room. She laughed at his determination, as she struggled to keep up with him.

CHAPTER 8

*L*ucian watched from the upper balcony as Caroline and Eva embraced another time, and tried to quiet his need to be on their way. Of course, she required time to bid farewell to her sister, and he had removed himself, to allow her some privacy. That did not mean he couldn't watch from a discreet distance, he reasoned to himself.

"You are not playing tonight?" Silus's voice slid from behind him, and he stiffened, keeping his eyes on Caroline, his source of calm. He moved his shoulders noncommittally.

"Perhaps it is for the best. You never have had the best luck," Silus chuckled darkly, coming to lean against the bannister. Lucian grit his teeth and longed for one of his brothers to show up and relieve him from the torment of having to speak to his father.

"Things change," Lucian muttered, watching as Isaac Taylor approached Caroline, and they fell into conversation.

"Ah, I suppose you mean Caroline, your loving little wife. I wonder if I was ever as naïve as you, boy, I cannot recall. Let me give you some advice, from father to son, as it were," Silus said with a smirk. "She will use you up, and move on when it suits her, it is in their nature. Women are distractions, temptations, and that is all. If you care too deeply for them, you only open yourself up to humiliation and ridicule," Silus said, in a low voice, his gaze lost in the distance. Lucian glanced at him, surprised by his earnest tone. Silus gestured down to the dance floor, where Caroline and Isaac were talking, quietly, off to the side, though still within full view.

"Looks like it has already started, my boy. Once she has made you care for her, once she has blinded you with lust and affection... then it really begins. The lingering looks, and dances, the private conversations and clandestine encounters. Soon, before you quite realise it... you will be looking at your child across the dinner table, and wondering if your blood runs in his veins," Silus finished maliciously. Lucian clenched his jaw.

"Caroline is not that sort of woman."

"And you think your own mother was? They are all the same, and the sooner you learn it the better. I cared for your mother, once. Before she destroyed our family and my reputation and pride along with it," Silus said quietly, and Lucian looked at him, shocked by the suddenly vulnerable tone to his voice. Meeting his son's eyes, Silus's face hardened. He cleared his throat and turned to leave.

"At least you, my bastard, having nothing of the sort to lose," he muttered and strode off, leaving Lucian gripping the balustrade.

❀

"*Y*ou see, the situation is really quite difficult. I do not think her indifferent to me, not wholly, yet I do think I might be far from winning her affections," Isaac said.

"I think you might not be so far as you imagine," Caroline replied, smiling at him. Rebecca and Isaac, she could not think of anything better.

"Well, in any case, I wanted your opinion, being the closest thing to a sister she has now... with no mother, and a father such as hers..."

"She is sorely in need of someone to represent her," Caroline agreed. "You may always speak to Lucian."

"He may be gentle around you, sweet friend, but he is hardly easier to approach than Silus, for us mere mortals," Isaac said.

"What then will you do?" Caroline asked, looking at him speculatively.

"I do not know," Isaac admitted in a heavy gust from his lungs, his eyes following Rebecca as she returned from the dance floor on another man's arm.

"Whatever you decide, do not dally, or she may end up engaged to someone whom she cannot care for, and we will find ourselves mired in very familiar difficulty once again," Caroline warned, reaching out to touch him with a rye grin.

From the corner of her eye, she saw Lucian descending the stairs toward them. His face looked a little dark, his expression careful as he focused on Caroline's hand on Isaac's arm. He approached and Caroline pulled away, Isaac forced a lazy smile, and the time for secrets and confessions was over.

"My dear," Lucian said, stopping before them, looking between them pointedly.

"If you will excuse me," Isaac said, visibly preoccupied and troubled, he left and Caroline turned her full attention to her husband, who had proved himself to be terrible at waiting and completely without patience.

"Come to take me home, like a badly behaved debutante and her maiden aunt?" Caroline teased and was relieved to see a lighter look appear on Lucian's lowered brow.

"Ah, and I suppose I am the maiden aunt in this tale?" he asked with a raised eyebrow.

"Certainly... you are of more advanced years, and the one who is desperate to return home so early, though we rarely go out."

"I had hoped you might be looking forward to returning home early also," he said, suddenly serious. She stepped closer, her expression softening into a genuine smile as she placed her hands on his chest and leaned close, meeting his eyes with hers.

"I have no concept of what awaits me, so I suggest you take me now, and show me," she murmured and his eyes flashed.

"I should like very much to kiss you thoroughly right here and now, and then pick you up and carry you home. Sadly, I am aware of the scene which we're already making, and the gossips will be at it like chickens. I am only glad Charles was not here to bother me about it." His sapphire eyes glowed, and his voice was a low, dark rumble, drawn through a wicked smile.

Before she knew it, Lucian's hand was on her waist, another on her arm, guiding her forward. She laughed at his haste, and barely concealed impatience with anyone who dared delay them as they collected their coats and the carriage was brought round. She felt a fizzle of nerves and anticipation climbing up from her stomach.

🞉

*T*hey climbed into the crimson velvet of the carriage's interior, and Lucian chose to sit across from her. He tapped on the roof to signal the coachman, and then taking off his gloves, leaned forward and held his hands out to her to take.

"Let's speak of your concerns... before I am no longer able," he murmured, taking a deep breath. Caroline nodded and her brow creased, awkward and unsure how to speak the things she needed to ask.

"You are right, it is important," she said and blinked uncomfortably.

"You spoke of the night in the maze, how it frightens you... in what way?" he prompted. Caroline dropped his gaze, and her eyes searched out of the window for a distraction, before setting her shoulders and turning back to him.

"Well, suffice to say, it was a shock to come across any couple in such a compromising position, in public, no less... and a couple who are not even betrothed," she said.

"It was quite a shock to be disturbed in such a position, with a rock to the head, I assure you." Caroline laughed at his tone and returned her eyes to his, the laugher in them relaxing her. She tilted her head to the side, and asked more seriously,

"Was it... a common occurrence? I do not imagine that the time I came across you, was the first..." she picked her way carefully through.

"You imagine correctly," he said. Her mouth set at his words.

"Well, how common?" she challenged.

"I do not care to assign it a number. You need only know it is finished forever, and that I do not miss it."

"Did you love them?" she asked.

"No. I have never loved anyone until you," he said quietly, and her heart squeezed in her chest. "I love you, Caroline, in case I have not yet told you so," he teased, his words bringing an involuntary smile to her lips, even as she pushed it aside and fixed him with a serious look, not to be deterred from her line of questioning.

"Why would you... be intimate with them, if you did not care for them?"

"Sadly, my dear, physical intimacy need not be linked with affection or even more than the barest of tolerance." The idea at first confused her then saddened her. "Caroline, the man you saw... he did not feel, did not care... he was incapable of love. He threw himself into mindless distractions, otherwise to live each day fully conscious, would be to know what it was to live an empty, and useless life." She saw the way the words had cost him. His face was a portrait of casualness, yet his eyes showed a depth and shame he did not hide.

"Well... in that case, I cannot hate them. The women who gave you comfort... when you were so lost."

"You always surprise," he said at her words. "My lioness. My warrior." She looked away again, but his hands squeezed hers gently in encouragement. "Caroline, my love, tell me," he commanded softly.

"You were hurting her," she said simply. He sighed, moved to slide in beside her, keeping hold of her hands.

"Caroline... there are things I do not wish to explain to you... only because I do not wish it to colour your discovery of intimacy, of me, of yourself."

"You mean that I am too young and naïve?" she said feeling a flare of indignant embarrassment, but he caught her chin with his hand, pulling her face around to him, his blue eyes intense on hers.

"No... I mean only... I want us to discover each other together, both with fresh eyes."

"But, if it is what you like, I fear that I will not suit your tastes."

Lucian let out a breath. "Caroline, the actions of a man, desperate to feel something, anything, after so long... they are not the actions of his heart. Those women... I was who they wanted me to be."

"Why would they want that?"

"Because, my love, unhappiness lives in many a home. Some women dreamt of a young, rough, demanding lover, instead of the old, tired man their father chose for them. And I was a man without a heart, with a driving desire to lose myself in destruction and distraction."

"But if it did not make you happy..."

"Then it made me numb, which was better than the alternative. *You* made me feel again. I only wish to give you a fraction of the happiness which you bring to me."

She turned to him, her eyes searching his, and her heart leapt. She did not have to consider whether or not she forgave him, it had been done long ago, but having aired the worries that had gnawed at her so long, and hearing the sincerity in Lucian's voice, the warm support in his hands, she knew she could let go of it.

"In that case, my lord... I find that I am quite impatient to arrive home."

He moved closer, and her breath hitched as she took in the darkened look in his eyes. He swept the loose hair from her shoulder, and leant in, pressing feather-light kisses onto her neck. She let her head fall to the other side, allowing him greater access. A roiling surge of want tugged at her insistently. His lips, soft against her skin, and the rough scrape of his stubble made her shiver. His breath was warm, as his mouth moved up to her ear, she felt her skin tingle with heat. Her breath came faster as the air warmed.

Suddenly, in one sweeping motion, his strong arms came around her and he scooped her smoothly from the seat, to sit across him from the side. Even sitting on his lap, he was still a few inches taller than her, and it made her feel small and dainty in his strong arms. Protected.

"In that case... we need not be *overly* patient," he said through a wolfish smile. Taking her chin, he lifted her mouth to his and kissed gently at first, breathing her in, his tongue flitting across her closed lips before he kissed her more deeply, more passionately, reminding her body what it had been in anticipation of for so long. He kissed her, so hot and demanding until she squirmed, restless with the growing need of her body, and she felt under her the length of him harden, ready for her, impatient.

She broke away, hungry to taste his skin, and moved her mouth to his neck, tasting with her lips and tongue, her eyes fluttering closed at the smell of his hair. He let out a growl, clutched his hands around her hips, and pulled her in tighter, giving her a little thrill of fear and excitement. She nipped at his neck with her teeth lightly, experimentally, and he let out a low moan, so rewarding. She moved back to his mouth, kissing him deeply, herself completely forgotten, and he trailed a slow hand up the side of her waist to her breast, where he stroked the skin that pressed against the top of her bodice in long gentle strokes with his thumb before cupping her and squeezing her in a way that made her stomach flutter and her heart thud against him.

A jolt of the carriage nearly sent her flying, and he caught her tightly in his arms before putting her back in her seat, so that they might appear somewhat less licentious when the coachman opened the door for them. One look at Lucian's face, and she knew that there would be no hiding it.

⊛

*T*he house was warm when they returned, and snow was falling quietly outside. Candles lit the windows and Caroline thought how wonderful it was to feel as though somewhere was your home.

They entered, greeting the servants, and taking off their heavy winter coats and cloaks. Their hair mussed, and their cheeks and lips flushed in a way that Caroline hoped may look like the result of cold air and a night spent dancing. Now, standing in the hall, Caroline fought down her nerves. She could feel the expectation of the man next to her, and how he wanted her, how he controlled himself now, not to pick her up and spirit her upstairs. She smiled at him, seeing his eyes darken to the colour of the evening sky.

"I shall go to my rooms and change. You may wait down here. I will call for you," she said firmly and hid her smile as his impatient, relenting agreement. His eyes followed her as she ascended the stairs.

"It is rude to stare, my lord," she called down.

"Have a little mercy, my lady," he growled.

⊛

*H*e had never been a patient man. To *almost* have something that he had wanted with a blinding desire for longer than he had thought possible to survive, and then still have to wait just a little while longer, was excruciating and exhilarating beyond reason. He moved quickly to his study and poured himself a modest drink. His throat was dry, yet he did not want anything to affect his mind tonight. He sat in front of the fire, and waited, wondering how long it would take for her to change, his foot tapping impatiently.

He spent an unknowable time there, his mind lost in thoughts of her, and bitterly of Silus; the man's words whirling in his mind, like poison through the veins. Everything that Silus did was to hurt him, to sabotage his happiness; therefore, not a word he said was to be trusted. Yet, he had seemed almost genuine when he spoke of his mother. Lucian pushed the thoughts away. Caroline was not his mother and he was not Silus. They would not go down the same dark path that they had.

"Milord, Lady Ashford has sent for you," the maid's voice came from the door, and Lucian felt as though his heart had stopped for a moment, before it resumed beating, with a painful thump. He breathed evenly and thanked her, standing, he started slowly toward the stair. He realised he was already breathless as he started up the steps. He felt as though he was very far outside of his body, and it was continuing without him, the magnitude of the moment unfathomable.

🐚

*C*aroline sat in front of her dressing mirror, staring at her reflection. She was still a little thin, but the cuts and bruises had faded, and she felt her face was pink with youth and life again. She had dressed in a French lace peignoir over a matching nightgown which she felt was almost scandalously innocent looking. She had brushed aside the black laces, and deep crimsons, choosing instead one of ice blue silk, edged in delicate white. Her thick, black hair, free and unbound, fell around her shoulders, its thick, soft waves catching the lamplight. She heard a soft tap at the door and took a deep breath. She stood up, smoothing her gown, her hands feeling damp and unsteady.

"Come in," she called and felt her heart pound as the door slowly swung inward. Lucian stood in the doorway, his eyes on her, surveying her slowly, the way he did as he sketched her. Without a word, he came forward, pushing the door shut behind him without a glance. He walked slowly over, deliberately, his eyes on hers.

"Caroline," he breathed as he came close enough to touch her. She smiled at him and saw in his smile both awe and disbelief. He stood before her, and then reached out. She gasped at the contact, his skin was so hot, it seemed to burn. He ran his hands gently up her arms, slowly, finally reaching her neck, where they slid up either side of her face and he came in close, touching his lips to hers.

The kiss was soft and she melted into it. The dizzying sensations that his soft lips sent through her made her forget to breathe for a moment, and she clung to him, breaking away to catch her breath. She gripped his jacket tightly, her head buried in his chest as her heart pounded almost painfully. She felt his hands on her hair, they stroked and smoothed it, before moving down, his fingertips trailing over her shoulders and upper back, so lightly as to cause her flesh to tingle in their wake. They dipped lower still, sending the trembling sensation to her lower back, and then to her waist. He held her by her waist and gently pulled back, leaning forward again to kiss her. She was entirely consumed by the kiss, feeling a feverish sensation travel over her, prompting her to put her hands on Lucian's broad shoulders, pull him closer, hold him to her as she trembled slightly with nervousness.

"I am sorry, my darling. Being near you overcomes me. I do not wish to rush you. Shall we sit by the fire a moment and talk? Have a glass of wine perhaps?"

In response, she grabbed his lapels, and pulled him to her, he growled a soft noise of appreciation, and she felt an immediate answer in the warmth between her legs. Slowly, she felt his weight shift and realised they were moving backward, his hands under her, lowering her gently, and soon she felt the soft bed under her back. She raised her head and watched as he stood at the end of the bed, his hands going to his jacket, which fell to the floor, soon joined by his cravat and waistcoat. She watched his every movement, his eyes on her all the while with mounting tension that she could feel in her fingertips. She bit her lip as his clothing fell, and saw his eyes only grow more intent as he watched her mouth. She had seen his body before, many times when he was close to death, but never like this. This was new. This was different.

Then he was kneeling on the bed, slowly prowling upwards, over her body, like that great, lithe predatory cat she had always thought him to be. All strength and power, barely leashed. His eyes on her were like a touch, making her burn in the places they fell. Her skin felt tight like a glove. She couldn't hold herself still. She felt wild with nerves and anticipation when he finally arrived face to face, staring down at her intensely. His arms were braced on either side of her head, his body weight off her. She lay under him, feeling strangely powerful under his hot gaze, as he scrutinized her with palpable lust, his eyes falling over her shoulders, throat, lips, and back to her eyes. He swallowed thickly as she tentatively raised her fingers to his mouth, which looked so pink and full to her, she wished to touch it. She gently ran her finger over the sensitive skin, and gasped as his mouth suddenly opened a little, and his tongue rasped against the pad of her finger for a moment, before his mouth was on hers again. His kiss was drugging, powerful, addicting. His tongue swiped strongly over her lips and delved inside, stroking along her own, sucking her lower lip between his, and moving with such carnal rhythm that she ached to be devoured by him.

His hands framed her face, tilted her head, got lost in her hair. He wrapped a fist around the long silk of her hair and used it to tip her head right back, holding her a willing captive to his mouth, as it slowly kissed downwards over the stretched length of exposed neck, his stubble and tongue dragging against her skin in hot, wet, open-mouthed kisses. She couldn't stop herself pushing forward, wanton, helpless with desire, her hands holding him to her, as her brain became slow, languid. She watched in a dream as his golden head moved lower still, reaching the tops of her breasts, her nipples straining hard against the fabric of her gown.

Her gown slipped lower, and lower still, as Lucian tugged it effortlessly down, spilling her bare breasts to his eyes at last. He raised up on an elbow to look over the sight she made: helpless with want, spread before his hot gaze.

"Incredible. You were made by the angels themselves. I have never in my life seen anything more beautiful," he said, the words reverent as her breath quickened, but then his voice took on a lower throaty tone than she'd ever heard before, "I have never craved anything before the way my body cries out for yours," he confessed, and she felt her body respond to the sound of those dark words from his lips. "I thirst for you, Caroline, to madness." The words were pulled from him, rugged and raw, just on the civilised side of feral, a line Lucian toed constantly, and tonight, she wondered what it would take to tip him over it.

"Well then do not keep me waiting, my lord," she said, feeling her nerves and arousal collide with a flip of her stomach, pushing her to boldness.

He smiled, and it was a wicked thing to match her tone. He cocked an eyebrow and locking her in his eyes possessively, lowered his mouth to her bared bosom which now heaved in short, excited breaths. His mouth latched around a soft, pink peak, sending a blinding flash of electricity burning through her at the new sensation. He pulled it ruthlessly into the warm cavern of his mouth and set his tongue to it in a tantalising motion that made Caroline's toes curl. She had not imagined that a man might put his mouth to her nipples, and she could never have dreamed of the way it felt, the way it made her yearn almost painfully. His fingers sank into the soft, fleshy globes of her breasts, caressing and kneading in a way that ripped a cry from her lips.

"Yes, sweetheart. What a beautiful sound. I want to wring every drop of pleasure from this body, and hear every single moment of it." She caught her breath. His coarse words only served to inflame her further, for reasons that her addled brain could hardly understand. There was something incredibly intimate about that moment, nothing held back, no vulnerability hidden, no secrets remaining; the two of them, closer now than ever they had been. Making their love real and physical in a way that they had both waited for for an eternity.

His mouth released her nipples only after both were sucked pink, and left swollen by his touch. Her breasts ached for more, and the rest of her body had melted into a liquid warmth she had never felt before. Between her legs, that most private place, felt wet and empty, and in desperate need of filling.

His hot kisses trailed across her ribs, heading lower with every moment, and her centre clenched as she realised where he was going with his mouth.

"Lucian," she gasped, when he sank back on his heels and peeled away the layer of her nightgown, a garment surely only made for this very plundering, and tossed the garment carelessly aside, never removing his eyes from hers. She moved to close her bare thighs, modesty making her blush hot for a moment until Lucian tutted quietly.

"Do not hide from me now, my love," he said. His gaze was darker than she'd ever seen it. Wild. Possessive.

"Lucian," she protested again, but it was weak this time, for she couldn't tear her eyes from the look of worship on her husband's face. He slid his large warm hands over her round hips and down her thighs slowly and back again, oozing his palms over her newly touched skin like warm honey.

"Do you want me to stop, my darling?" he asked, his voice hot and low and patient. For a moment she could not think, could not speak as his hands glided over her skin.

"No," she rasped, hoarse and breathless before she could even think of how to answer. "Please," she pleaded, her body begging unbidden.

"Caroline, you are every bit as exquisite as I knew you would be. The smell of your body is enough to make me lose myself before we have even begun. I am already insatiable for the taste of your pleasure. I want to taste you, all of you, my sweet wife, and I plan to do so now, and whenever and wherever I might get the chance in the future." She nodded fervently. Drunk on desire as she was, she would agree to anything he asked. Yes, she wanted it.

She wanted him with all her heart and body and would hold nothing back. He slid his hands up her legs to her knees and pressed them as wide apart as they could go. Stroking his hands down her tender inner thighs, he lowered a hand to the nest of curls, the only thing hiding her quim from her husband now.

She watched him, almost in slow motion, lower one hand between her legs, using the tips of his fingers to glide gently over the lips there, that gentle touch, barely there at first, sent jolts of lightning fizzling up her spine, pushing away all thoughts of anything else but the place on her quim where his fingers met her skin. She was quivering with need for him, shaking now, her excitement obvious, and Lucian smiled as his fingers parted her, and began to slide through her wet folds.

"Dear God," he gasped, looking up at her, with his wickedness falling away, and only a tender pained look remained a moment. She had never heard anything so beautiful. It was like a prayer, and she the goddess, feeling more powerful than she ever had, seeing how the mere touch of her had reduced this big strong man to a thing helpless with hunger for her.

Lucian leaned down, lunging with that wolfish grace, and licked a long, hot stripe up the centre of her cunny. She cried out, a garbled, graceless exclamation, and let her head fall back, when her husband's long, and clever tongue set to work on her core. He licked up and down her slit, sinking his tongue just inside her entrance, and then up, to suck on the pearl of nerves that sat at the apex, a place that made her dizzy with pleasure. Her world was set spinning, and she reached out for more of him, grabbing his hair, tugging at it, directing his head, taking him where she wanted him.

A feeling was building in her like nothing she had ever felt before. She shied away from it, even as she rushed toward it, carried on a river of Lucian's attentive, persistent touch. His blunt-tipped fingers played with her entrance, dipping in and out, touching her most private place. His tongue worked on that num of pleasure, sucking it into his mouth, flicking it and rolling it between his teeth. She found her hips rising and falling to meet the thrusts of his fingers and roll of his tongue, rubbing against his face in a lewd way that she had no way of controlling. She was beyond that now. Her fingers sank into his hair, and pulled him closer, she could feel his grin against the inside of her thigh as he turned his face to speak as in a rough rumble.

"My God, Caroline. You are delicious," he breathed, and then returned to her with new determination to push her over that peak of feeling. His tongue worked her faster, his fingers spread her wider and she grew only more frantic as the wall of pleasure Lucian had been leading her toward hit her fully, and she cried out his name, as her body tensed around him. Her thighs clenched tightly on his broad, muscled shoulders, and her cunny clenched hard, issuing forth only more wetness and pleasure like nothing she'd ever imagined before. Lucian gave her no mercy, continuing to suck and lick at her until she was twitching with the last pulses of her climax and her muscles were slack and pliant.

He dragged kisses up her stomach, finally returning to her mouth, kissing her with renewed vigour, his smile practically debaucherous as she stared dazedly up at him. He leaned in to kiss her, and she could taste the slight musk of her own pleasure on his lips. It felt unbearably

carnal at that moment, as though he was branding her with his owner-
ship and mastery of her body, just as she was branding him with her
scent, with the taste of her. She had never in her wildest imaginings
known that any woman could feel the way she did then. Every part of
her at once vibrating with desire, and also perfectly whole, relaxed and
at peace. It was transcendent. She was totally lost. More his now than
she ever was her own. She closed her eyes, and let the word swim
behind them, breathing hard, her mind and body reeling, pulse thudding in her ears, as she slowly came back to herself.

She opened her eyes to find him drinking in the sight of his handiwork. Suddenly, it felt unbearable to be naked and so filled with joy
while Lucian was dressed and full of need. Her hands went to the hem
of his shirt. He rocked back as she leant forward, pulling the garment
off, and throwing it to the floor, her eyes already fastened on his chest.
She placed her hands on the expanse of flesh, and he groaned at the
feeling. She gently slid her hands up over his shoulders, and down, her
fingers tracing the hollows of his ribs, his sinewy muscles, and outlined
the shape of his nipples. He clenched his teeth, allowing her time to
explore.

Suddenly, she had turned her attention to his wound. The skin there
was pink but covered over. The new skin was still healing, and she
gently ran her fingertips over it. She was frowning at it, and she leant
forward and pressed a soft kiss there. He held his breath, and in his
eyes, a look so full of emotion that she felt her own eyes prickle. Caroline kissed the jagged scar, thinking how close she had come to losing
him, how close this had come to taking him from her, and yet, how it
had also brought her to him. She wondered if everything that mattered
in life was a balance of pain and happiness.

She felt Lucian's warm hands on her shoulders, and she met his eyes.
They were looking at her with such affection, such... love, wholly and
completely, she felt entirely happy, and protected for the first time in a
very long time. He laid next to her, his eyes sweeping down her, from
head to toe, his eyes mirroring those of an artist taking in the most
exquisite work of art he had ever witnessed. She sensed a reluctance in
him, as though she was glass that could break.

"Now, I am new to these types of activities, but I am a firm believer
that everyone should have their turn...and it is yours now, is it not,

husband?" she murmured to him, goading him on. She wanted his weight on her and his brutal possession. She wanted him wild and unreserved. She wanted him to lose control because of her.

"I don't want to hurt you," he replied hoarsely, and she couldn't help but let a small laugh escape her at that. She brought her hand to cup his cheek and gave him a tender smile.

"I believe we are quite past all that, are we not? I want you, Lucian, every single part. Hold nothing back, for that is the way of it between us now. You told me that I am yours. Now, show me," she said, her voice dropping to a whisper, and then leaned up and brought her hands to the fastening of his breeches. She could see his manhood, it was straining against the material of his hose, a long, thick hardness that made her mouth dry with anticipation and nerves as well. Bravely, she stroked her fingers down it and Lucian muttered a curse, his hands fisting to white in the sheets beside her.

Her fingers started to pluck at the buttons and laces of his breeches. She tugged at them impatiently as they did not fall, and he smiled, moving to help her. She watched him with wide eyes, her face fascinated as more of his body was revealed to her, his desire for her evident. His cock was flushed a dark red, marbled with thick veins, and it jutted out from at a hard angle. She lowered a finger to touch the velvety skin, fascinated by its alien appearance. Lucian let loose a strangled laugh that was part curse and part moan, and she slid her fingers to grasp around the girth of him as far as they would go, which wasn't very far at all. She tested, caressing the impossibly smooth lines, the taught, swollen skin of his head, her thumb rubbing over the bead of wetness there, sliding her head down the shaft of him, using the slow and steady movements that he had used on her.

"I bid you stop, sweetheart. I cannot take anymore," he said thickly, as he bore her slowly back on the bed, interrupting her curious exploration before she might continue.

Caroline sighed with satisfaction as she felt his body settle over hers, his hands back to her face, holding it as though it were a precious thing. His eyes bore into hers, and she could see that not only the sensations but emotions were overwhelming for him. She smiled and kissed him, lowering her hands to his back, she slowly raised her legs on either side of him, arching her back slightly, nervous, so nervous, but wanting him all the more for it. She could feel his heart beating with force against her chest as strong as her own, but he still held back.

"Lucian... make me yours," she whispered and saw the last of his strength flee his expression. Suddenly she felt his arms tighten around her, and he moved between her legs. His cock pushed gently against her entrance, now so impossibly sensitive and swollen from his mouth, and slid in the slickness there up and down for a moment, and then fraction by fraction, slowly inside, her skin stretching to accommodate him. Lucian's face was pained, a mask of control and self-discipline. A mask she longed to shatter. As he pushed a little further, pain blossomed, a sharp twinge that quickly receded. She gasped at the feeling, biting her lip.

"Does it hurt you?" Lucian's voice was all concern, and she found her head shaking immediately.

"No, not overly much, just... well, I did not expect it to be so big," she complained quickly, and Lucian laughed into her shoulder as he stopped his progression.

"We do not have to-" he began, when she stopped him by wrapping her legs around him and pulling him further into her. He gasped, his eyes dark with surprise and pleasure, and his mouth came down on hers hungrily, his tongue stroking, his teeth tugging at her lips. His hips started to nudge in and out in short, pleasurable bursts, allowing her time to adjust to his intrusion.

"Caroline," he exhaled her name, "I think I might die of pleasure," he murmured, trailing kisses from her ear to her mouth, as he moved slowly and carefully, capturing her lips in a blistering kiss. Her hands glided across the smooth skin of his broad back, exploring the feel of him, his shifting of muscles as he moved. Those small, nudging movements slid ever more easily into her body, chasing away the pain, and replacing it with growing pleasure. Unfurling like a flower from deep within, twinges and ripples of pure sensation washed through her, as Lucian's movements became longer, deeper, more satisfying. Her eyes flew open wide, and she stared up into the darkness, feeling something awaken within her. She called his name, her voice barely her own anymore, and moved her hands down his back to the solid mussels of his backside, pulling him in tighter, her body pleading now for his. He groaned, a deep animalistic noise that made her shutter with longing.

Soon, he was inside her to the hilt, pushed as deep as could be and they were completely one, their bodies pressed tight to each other. And for the moment, he stayed perfectly still and rose to look at her in the eyes. She clutched at him, enjoying the musky scent of him, the weight of him, the feeling of his heart beating against hers. She raised her hips and ground herself against him, telling him with her body that she wanted more. She wanted faster, harder, more. She wanted it all.

With a groan of surrender, Lucian's last shred of restraint broke, and he began to move in earnest. Caroline cried out, at the loss of him and then return, undone by the new sliding feeling. He was slow and steady, gentle with her, and she soon began to move with him, pulling him closer, raising her hips, needing more, searching with her mouth, kissing his neck and face, panting moans of pleasure. He began to move faster, as her legs moved higher, wrapping around his hips instinctively. The rhythm sent waves of pleasure through her, and she threw her head back, her voice low and throaty as she urged him on, calling his name, calling for more.

He growled, his intensity building as he pushed in and out of her in a languid, determined pace. He pulled her face back to his, forcing her eyes open and she saw his intent expression, his forehead beaded with sweat, his neck flushed. He was thrusting hard into her now, his cock rubbing against all the tender and delicious places inside her that she had never known existed until this night, and she felt a shivery feeling build in her. He was moving her toward it, with a relentless pace, and she ground her hips against him, trying to catch hold of that elusive sensation.

She chased after that feeling from before, the one his mouth had wrung from her. A blinding pleasure unlike anything else. This time, it felt different. She could tell another climax was approaching, but it felt even deeper, this time building inside her core, sucking into it every ounce of energy from her body. He grunted at her desperate, writhing movement, slipped his hand between them, and found that pleasurable pearl at the top of her cunny. He rubbed slow silky circles, increasing his rhythm, drawing her out as his cock continued to thrust into her, nearly all the way out and back in again. Her moans were loud and ragged now, scratching out of her with each exhalation until she saw stars behind her eyes.

Lucian leaned in over her and pulled her tighter, grinding into her, impossibly deep, her mouth, wanting more of him, sucking the salt from the skin of his neck. He reached back and slid both hands under her backside, lifting her to him, and she bit her teeth hard into his shoulder, muffling her screams when the feeling she had been chasing finally crashed down on her. It swept over her, like a relentless tide pulling her under again and again in rolling waves. Every cell of her body contracted at the same moment with an explosion as bright and flaring as the death of a star.

Lucian buried himself deep within her. He strained and jerked, filling her with his spend. She could feel the blossoming of that warmth deep inside her, his seed pouring from him and into her, marking her as his, maybe even planting the seed of a child. The thought made Caroline tremble, caught in the throes of her own quaking, while a smile stretched across her face.

They breathed together, the same hot air, in hungry gulps. He stayed pressed deeply inside her until his cock stopped pulsing within her, and the last of him had entered her. Then and only then, he slid out of her, and moved carefully to her side, as Caroline's hand trailed down his shoulder and back wanting more of his skin, unwilling to part from him.

This. This is what she had been waiting for for so long. This is what he had promised her with his every move, his every look, his soft caresses, with the taste of his mouth, with the stroke of his tongue against hers. He looked at her, emotion, tender and raw, stretching out between them in a wordless exchange that she could feel in her chest, and it stole her breath away.

⬡

*L*etting out a deep sigh, Lucian pressed his forehead to hers and was surprised to find it was not only his forehead that was wet but his eyes. Suddenly, Caroline's sweet kisses were pressing into the corners of his eyes, her face happy and full of emotion.

"I love you, Caroline," he said simply. "So much that it destroys me and makes me new again."

"I love you too," she sighed and murmured softly, a heavy weariness seeming to overtake her as she settled her head on his chest, her arm around his torso, and her small hand instinctively, protectively, over the place where his wound was. Her naked body fit against him as she drifted away, and he stroked her thick hair, musing over what had just happened, of his impossible good fortune. Surely, in all the history of the world, no luckier man had yet breathed.

In the end, it was him who was overcome, him who was not prepared for the onslaught of emotion that making love to someone brings. Someone who loves you in return. Making love to Caroline. He felt as though she had looked into his very soul, and given herself to it. She had given him the gift of her trust, her love, and it had moved him, he could not deny it. He felt changed and was not sure what was harder to understand, the effect she had on his body or his heart. Both were powerful beyond measure and had thrown his life before this night into a hard comparison. His life had been black and white and now he saw colour for the very first time.

He felt her heartbeat against his chest, and he closed his eyes, treasuring that vibration. That small patter, so tiny, yet vital, it was what made his world turn, his everything, and he would do whatever he had to to keep it safe, to show her how very cherished she was.

Please consider leaving me a review or some stars!
It makes the world of difference to new authors

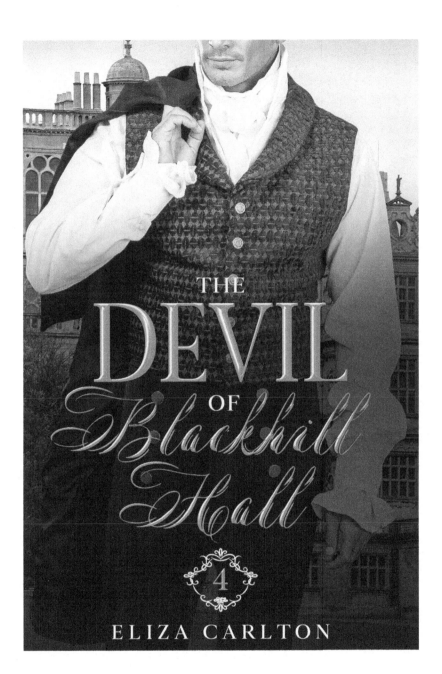

THE
DEVIL
OF
Blackhill
Hall

4

ELIZA CARLTON

CHAPTER 1

~January 1810~
Hampshire

*T*he Ton talked for weeks of the Lord and Lady Lucian Ashford, who danced every dance together, whose eyes were never far from meeting, whose smiles seemed reserved only for each other. In the flurry of the Christmas festivities, social obligations, and heavy snow, no one quite realised that the infamous couple had retired to their country estate. With Eva and Eli returned to America, Caroline found little reason to stay in London, especially with the weather. She held an image of the snowy valley of Westmere in her heart and longed to return to it. Unable to deny his wife anything. Lucian swept her home. They were not to be isolated for long, however, as Katherine, Rebecca and Wesley soon came to stay with them for a winter house-gathering. It was a quiet, intimate time: music was played, songs were sung, and memories made.

Christmas came and went, as did the New Year, and soon another year was upon them all. Rebecca had been granted a reprieve from her father's matchmaking, yet remained mystified as to Isaac Taylor's sudden deceleration at the winter ball. They'd had no further contact, and her heart ached uncomfortably when she thought of him, which she found most bothersome. Katherine watched the frozen lake from the window of the library, thinking about lands far away, and the men who travelled them, each day perhaps bringing them closer to home or taking them further away. Wesley spent a great deal of time keeping the girls merry company, and never once complained about the lack of gentlemen at the party, despite Lucian being too taken with Caroline to provide any diverting male company to speak of.

They were a lively group, with Katherine providing the outrageous commentary, Rebecca the witty cynicism, and Wesley the light-hearted cheer. Caroline and Lucian, they provided the heart - a young couple, so in love.

They ate together each night, though the days were their own. Wesley tirelessly played music to the group's neverending requests, playing violin sometimes so beautiful that it made Caroline cry, and sometimes so quickly that they all had to get up and dance. He played piano as well, sometimes with Rebecca at his side, who played just as well as he, if not even more masterfully. Rebecca also played often at the big beautiful golden harp that Caroline had first spied when she had first come to Westmere, and wondered to whom it had belonged. They all sang together, often with Katherine at the helm, and even Lucian joined in when he was in the right sort of mood. Sometimes they all hushed reverently as Caroline sang low, sad songs that she had learned from the mountains in her home far away.

Caroline could not help but notice that the music played at Westmere was happier and freer than it had ever been at Blackhill Hall. In the snowy darkness, they talked and dreamed, laughed and became a family of sorts, and it was a time Caroline would forever cherish.

Caroline dearly missed riding, with the ground too icy for Theia to risk. She still visited her stable, and fed her treats, and talked to her daily, however. Lelantos demanded her attention also, and Caroline smiled as she thought of how he reminded her of her husband.

Lucian was busy at this time seeing to his estate responsibilities, especially as the winter grew colder and harsher, and the village more desperate. Caroline was touched to see his even-handed and thoughtful dealings with the local community, and how he supported the people, making sure none went cold or hungry in that icy, hard winter. The people of the town had always been fairly treated, yet they had never seen much of the landowner. Now, with him in residence with his kind and compassionate wife, a new energy settled over the village. The family was spoken well of, and Lucian was greeted in the street with smiles and small gifts. Caroline had even begun to visit the homes of many of their tenant farmers, bringing baskets, quietly checking that all was well, and finding her way into the hearts of many.

🦋

"*I*t is not fair, Luke – Wesley is cheating again!" Rebecca whined, throwing her cards to the table. Wesley laughed, pushing his chair back with a scrape.

"You impinge my honour, dear sister, I would never stoop so low!" he said, barely able to keep the smile off his face for more than a moment. Caroline levelled a look at Wesley, and he looked wounded, still playing the victim.

"Rebecca, you chose to play with him. On your head be it," Lucian muttered as he read by the fire. He seemed to have no interest in the card game, though Caroline could not help but notice that this particular card game made him look up and over the top of his book with telling regularity. Caroline evaded his gaze, heat seeping into her cheeks as she realised she had lost, and she realised that Lucian had noticed. Wesley had cheated, she was sure of it, yet being sure would not release her from the wager she had placed with the rogue reading calmly by the fire.

Caroline raised her cards to her face and used them as a fan, the breeze lifting the black tendrils of hair that always seemed prone to escape her bun. She could feel Lucian's eyes burrowing into her, and as always, the heat in her face magnified, her skin prickled and her breath grew short. Damn Wesley and his cheating - if he knew what he had condemned her to: a reckless gamble lost, and a debt collector, who would never forget what was owed to him.

She caught Lucian's stare, and it seemed to burn through her, full of unspoken intentions and dark desires. He cocked an eyebrow, and she turned away abruptly.

"Caroline, are you well? You seemed flushed," Katherine observed as she helped Wesley, her partner in the game, rake in their winnings.

Caroline smiled meekly, knowing she must make an excuse to leave, yet dreading it. It would seem too obvious, too circumspect. Yet, it was agreed in the wager, and she hated to back down or to be punished relentlessly for failing to face the consequences of her loss. She let an expression of pain flash across her brow, aware of Katherine's scrutiny, and raised a hand to her temple.

"I must confess... my head... perhaps it is a headache," she murmured, feeling guilty as the assembled company expressed their concern. She shook it off, standing slowly, she spoke quietly, still clutching her head.

"If you will excuse me. I believe I must to bed."

"My dear, do you require my assistance?" Lucian enquired politely, already standing, Caroline shot him a glance before smiling a little wickedly.

"No, of course not. In fact, nothing would make me happier than if you would take my place at the card table, so the game may continue without me," she said too innocently and saw Lucian's eyes narrow, just a touch.

"As you wish my dear," he said, his smile slow and lazy and heavy with the promise of payback. Caroline swallowed nervously, as she exited the room and ascended the stairs quickly. She reasoned she had about an hour, maybe less, before the wager was collected. She was learning new things about the enigmatic man she had married each day, and one of them was that Lucian was not a man who easily forgot a promise.

֍

*M*aking every effort not to look too hurried as he finally escaped the drawing-room, Lucian quashed the teasing comment which Wesley held on his lips with a look. His younger brother turned his amused face back to his cards, as the women bid Lucian goodnight.

Once in the cool, warmly lit hallway, Lucian dropped the pretence and started toward the stairs, taking them two at a time. Anticipation pooled in his belly at the thought of what awaited him. He wondered briefly if she would refuse to honour their bet, however, he thought it unlikely. Caroline's word was her bond. As he reached the landing, he slowed, his heart starting to beat quickly. He bypassed the door to their room, and stopped briefly in a room he used as a studio, gathering up his tools, his fingers already itching for their task.

Returning to his room, he knocked softly and smiled at her slight delay, before she called to enter. He pushed the door open and his breath caught in his chest, before he stepped inside quickly, shutting the door to hide the sight in front of him.

The room flickered with candlelight, the heavy drapes pulled shut. It was warm, and the air smelled faintly of her sweet perfume. Caroline was standing in the centre of the room, her hair unbound, falling to the middle of her back in gentle waves, the creamy golden skin of her arms and shoulders looked as smooth as amber in the light. She held a sheet, tightly wrapped around her, held in place by her hand. Her eyes met his, and she looked up through her dark lashes, as she slowly raised her hand from where it clutched the sheet and slid it up to her neck. The sheet fell from her breasts to the floor, making her a living statue, a breathing embodiment of beauty.

Lucian's heart kicked in his chest, but he did not rush to her as his body cried out to. Instead, he smiled at her slowly, like a lion who would play with his supper before he ate it. Caroline narrowed her eyes in return.

"Lady Ashford, I half expected you to attempt to wriggle out of our wager," he murmured, very slowly beginning to circle her, so that he could enjoy the lavish view from all angles.

"I am a woman of my word, my Lord."

"As I see. You look positively ravishing, my dear. Just as you looked when you realised that you had lost your hand at the card table," he said, chuckling as a blush threatened her smooth cheek, and she pushed it down, and raised her chin, giving him a haughty look. Taking his time with a slow pace, he circled around back to the front and came closer to her, only stopping when he was within touching distance.

"I might have known you would insist on this... debauched desire," she said, her voice growing low and scratchy. He rumbled deep in his chest, deciding he had waited long enough. Caroline's eyes widened as his hands moved forward and began to slide smoothly over each warm, perfect breast reverently, taking particular time over each nipple. She gasped in pleasure, making something writhe in his stomach before she dodged out of his grasp.

"*That* was not part of the wager! You are utterly incorrigible," she ground out, running away. Lucian kept his eyes on her face, unable to hide his grin.

"That is certainly true, and yet, you love me."

"Also certainly true," she said in a matter-of-fact, and his heart beat faster in a way that had nothing to do with her state of undress.

She turned from him and made her way slowly to the divan, the decadent fullness of her bottom taunting him. Lucian admired her confidence, she was utter perfection, and he had spent the last months making sure she knew it. He was glad to see that his words and actions were not unnoticed. Some men preferred meek, shy things, who waited quietly in bed, and worried that pleasure was sinful; but, watching Caroline blossom into a sexual creature, ever freer with her body and her appetites, was beautiful, and intoxicating. It made him hunger for her all the more - perpetual, unsatable. She lowered herself primly on the edge of the divan and glanced up at him from under her thick black lashes.

"So, how shall I pose?" she asked and Lucian felt the moment when his desire took a momentary back-seat to the artist within. He set his things down, stripping off his jacket and cravat, loosening his waistcoat as well. He strode over to her, looking critically at the light, and turning the divan slightly. Then, his hands were on her warm skin, and he was urging her backwards so she was lying along it, he kept returning to his seat, and judging the pose, before coming back and changing her position. Finally satisfied, he placed her arm above her head, in a posture of complete ease and unselfconsciousness, and turned her face toward his chair, brushing her hair back, so it fell in waves across her naked chest.

"Is that all?" she asked.

"Not quite," he said, and suddenly pressed a hot, slow kiss on her lips, which sent a visible flush of heat running over her skin, and made her nipples rise in answer. She inhaled deeply as his kiss intensified, and then he suddenly pulled back, standing over her with a wicked grin.

"Perfection," he breathed as she gasped in indignation, picking up his parchment and pencil, settling into his chair.

"Contemptible cheat!" she cursed him, and his mouth curled in self-satisfaction.

⚜

*C*aroline lost track of how long she stayed in that prone position. The room was warm, thankfully, so she did not get chilled; however, there was little to distract herself after a while. Watching Lucian draw was as enthralling as ever. He always started feverishly, ripping through parchment with distraction and frustration, desperate to capture everything his wide, blue eyes took in.

The next stage usually involved him setting down his tools, pushing his shirt sleeves back, and starting again - slower, more intently. This would continue for an unknowable amount of time until a break would come for a drink or to stretch. Caroline realised, slightly alarmingly, that he had not progressed in his usual fashion. He was utterly absorbed, and the outside world had fallen away from him so completely, he had no concept of time. He was quiet, and she had soon dropped any attempt at conversation. He seemed determined to draw her in silence, half madness, half obsession and he could not be pulled away from it. She heard the clock in the hall chime midnight and her eyebrows shot up, unnoticed by her husband, whose attention was elsewhere.

She moved her hand slightly and was instantly met with a censuring look. He turned his attention back to his paper.

"My love, I think you may have used up your time... let us retire to bed," Caroline tried.

"I believe there was no time limit set," he said adamantly, not looking up as he reached for another pencil. Frustrated, Caroline searched for a way to bring the evening to an end. In all honesty, she was not sure she could lie one minute longer, naked, in front of the man she desired near constantly. There was something strangely erotic about lying so vulnerable in front of him, fully dressed, as his eyes lingered intently on every part of her. That he seemed to be having no such trouble, was irritating, to say the least.

Slowly, she returned her arm from over her head and laid her hand on her chest.

"Caroline, I thought I asked you not..."

Ever so slowly, her face flushing with embarrassment as she did, she began to trace lazy circles on her chest. She felt her nipples respond and gently brought both hands up to trace them.

"...to move," he finished in a whisper as he finally raised his eyes and took in the whole picture she made in front of him.

Lucian set down his papers and sat frozen in place. Caroline arched her back, and slid her legs against each other, letting out a low noise. She turned her head and looked at him, sliding her eyes up and down him, and then slowly, deliberately, sucked her full bottom lip into her mouth. Lucian made an involuntary growl and she smiled at him, holding her hand out. He watched her closely, then, surprising her, slid back in the chair, settling more firmly in place.

Feeling emboldened and excited, Caroline closed her eyes and continued to explore her own body. It had felt strange since she had lost her maidenhood, her body was almost like that of a stranger's. It did not feel the same, it was new and exciting, full of desires she had never fully understood before. Her body had never been familiar to her, and she was rarely naked when growing up, even bathing in a gown or under a sheet most times. Lucian had encouraged in her all sorts of primitive behaviour. As a man with hardly any inhibitions to speak off, Lucian's relaxed comfort with her body, and his own, had been a revelation to her. If she had tried to imagine her actions at that moment, the year previous, it would have been impossible.

Her breath caught, as her fingers trailed lower, reaching the apex of her thighs. She saw Lucian had sat forward, his arms braced on his knees, his face intense, full of longing and want. As he watched her, the apparent need for him to join her making him fidget in his chair.

She closed her eyes again, and stroked a finger along the wet seam of her sex, and let the sliding sensation wash over her. Suddenly, she felt his hands closing over hers, drawing one to his lips and kissing each finger passionately, gently sucking the tip of some, while he held on to her lower hand moving his fingers with hers encouragingly.

She writhed beneath them, and soon he let out a low growl and put his hot mouth to her, and pressed hot kisses into her burning flesh, starting first with a nipple, his teeth grazing and nipping maddeningly as his soft tongue caressed her. Then he caught her eye with a fevered glare and smiled before slowly tracing the line of her body with his soft lips, and his scratching stubble, and his wet tongue, tasting her skin as he went. Then she felt his hot breath between her legs, and he waited for a moment, as she arched her back and writhed uncomfortably with need and demand. As he slowly lowed his warm lips to her, she gasped and jolted, and he hummed with the enjoyment of watching her. Soft moans escaped her as he used his tongue to slide up and down her until she saw stars behind her eyes, and then it sank inside of her until she cried out so loudly that she feared the staff might hear her.

"I must make a point of betting with you more often, my dear," he mumbled deeply, his stubble scratching against her inner thigh, making her gasp. She swallowed hard and wet her dry mouth, and replied after a moment, her voice hoarse.

"I must make a point of losing more often," she said, while she was still able, before he moved his mouth slightly, and she lost the ability to speak.

❀

*I*n a study far away in the capital, Silus Ashford stared at the hark-haired man sitting before him, shifting nervously in his seat.

"I am still not clear on what you would have me do? My father is not easily swayed, and he almost always puts business first when it comes to matters of money," Isaac stated.

"A sentiment I understand well, which is why I am sure you cannot fail to recognise that in her marriage, my daughter must bring some sort of advantage to her family."

"I do understand; however, what you ask is excessive... father feels," Isaac said, hopelessness beginning to bleed into his businesslike tone.

"Well, Mr Taylor. In that case, I am afraid our dealings here are at an end," Silus said, sitting back in his leather chair, watching defeat weigh down on the younger man's shoulders. Isaac stood stiffly and began to make his way toward the door hesitantly, as though he wished to make another appeal, but was fighting himself. He reached the door and waited for a fraction of a second. "I hear that your brother is off to the Americas, and you are soon to follow." The boy turned back with some-

485

thing in his eyes which Silus very much hoped was optimism. "Have a pleasant trip."

🦁

"*N*o, this is quite wrong. The head should not be bigger than the body, simple logic should tell us that much," Rebecca argued as she pushed at the massive ball of snow she had been gathering in the garden, rolling it patiently until it gained a respectable size.

"But, he would be so much more interesting with a massive head!" Wesley argued.

"Please, my lovely Caroline, settle this for us, will you?"

"Well, it all depends... is it a male or female you plan on making?"

"Male," Westly said confidently.

"Female," Rebecca at the same time, making Caroline laugh.

Katherine walked out toward them, carrying a collection of clothes that Caroline had helped her raid from Lucian's dressing room. The snow was deep underfoot, but they had wrapped themselves in countless layers for the outing. At Wesley's insistence, they had decided to make a snowman, and Caroline had to admit it had been a wonderful idea. The sky was bright, and the sun reflected off the snow in a bright glistening sheen that lifted the heart. It was beautiful and a much-needed escape from the house. She only wished she could have enticed her husband from his study to join them. He was worried about something, letters were arriving with increasing frequency, and Lucian often disappeared with them into his study for hours. She wished he would allow her to know his worries, so that she may ease his burden, yet he had remained stubbornly determined that she should have a carefree Christmas.

They continued rolling the snow into balls, and the Ashford siblings continued to argue the finer points of snowmanship. Caroline and Katherine, deciding to leave them to it, started to make a pile of much smaller balls with mischief in their eyes, which, had the other two not been so busy with their bickering, might just have been noticed.

As the snowman finally came to completion, Katherine made the first move.

"Is he not handsome?" Wesley smiled boyishly, topping the snow-

486

man's fat head with a hat at a jaunty angle. "Perhaps we could roll up a husband for you, Becca. This one is far prettier than the men that father has been offering," Wesley laughed, delighted with himself.

"Well, allowing that it is a female, I think it looks an awful lot more like the round widow Wagner that father mentioned just the other day would make a fine wife for you, Wes," Rebecca said scathingly, wiping the smile off Wesley's face. As he opened his mouth in horror, he was suddenly hit in the mouth with a snowball. It exploded over the side of his face, and he turned, sputtering out the snow from his mouth, his face a mask of shock, in the direction of Caroline and Katherine, who were already gathering up more ammunition, nearly out of breath with laughter.

"Traitors!" Wesley yelled, immediately running for Katherine. She screamed and Caroline and Rebecca ran after them, throwing snowballs at Wesley, some hitting at extremely close range. After Rebecca caught him full in the face, and another was pushed down his collar Wesley started calling for reinforcements.

*L*ucian! Lucian! Come to my aid! I have been attacked by hellions!"

Caroline doubled over, hands on her knees, drawing a breath as she struggled to stop laughing. Sharing a look with Rebecca, they surprised Wesley by pushing him into a snowdrift together, as Wesley continued to call for his older brother.

"Well well, I see you have the men in this battle quite outnumbered, hardly fair, seeing as one of them is made of snow, though I must say he is sharply dressed," Lucian said as he started toward them, eyebrow cocked at the sight of the snowman's familiar-looking silk cravat tied in a bow. Caroline felt her stomach flutter at the sight of him, and she wondered if he would always cause this reaction in her.

"It is a snowwoman!" Rebecca demanded, annoyed, before grabbing up some snowballs and aiming them at her brother. Lucian laughed and dodged them effortlessly. He ducked in front of Rebecca and twirled her around, landing her in a bank of fluffy snow. Caroline laughed as Rebecca screeched her snowy protestations. Lucian caught Caroline's gaze and flashed her scorching look.

"Laugh while you may, sweetheart, for I am coming for you next."

Wesley was chasing Katherine around who was cursing at him like a sailor in his cups, and Rebecca was stuck in the drift, throwing handfuls of snow at her older brother, until he dunked her head in the powdery whiteness. Outraged, Caroline risked running closer, her feet almost soundless on the snow, holding a snowball in each hand, and brought her hands together smartly, on either side of Lucian's head.

Whirling away, hearing Rebecca cackle, Caroline ran to a safe distance and then dared to turn back. She felt a jolt of excitement shoot through her as Lucian turned to her, slowly, deliberately, lowering his head, shaking it, sending snowflakes and water droplets flashing through the air, a grin playing around his lips, he called her name like a chant, making the hair on her arms stand up.

"Caroline..."

She twisted away and started gathering up snowballs, backing away at the same time.

"You know you cannot escape me," he threatened, darkly.

She threw a few more and then screamed as he lunged closer suddenly. She turned and ran as fast as she could, knowing it was futile, but unable to stop herself. She was not surprised when she felt his arms go around her middle and pull her up short. He held her against his chest and she squirmed as she saw that both his hands held huge piles of fresh snow.

"No!" she shrieked, laughing so hard that she shook in his arms, shaking her head as he brought his hands inexorably closer. Her feet, as they scrambled for purchase on the slippery ground, suddenly gave way, and Lucian ended up in the snow right along with her, with Caroline held firmly against his chest. He groaned as the cold seeped through their clothes, and Caroline heard the air whoosh satisfyingly from his chest as she twisted around so she was looking down on him. They gazed at each other, suddenly so close, winded with laughter and running, breathing harshly. She leant forward and placed a soft kiss on his lips. He tasted like cinnamon and sugar.

"What have I done to be deserving of that?" he asked playfully.

"That – is for joining us, and smiling. You have been working too hard lately," she chastised lightly.

"Worry not, dear one. I shall soon conclude this... business, and I will be able to join you so often that you shall be quite sick of the sight of me."

"Impossible," she murmured and leant to kiss him again, trailing her mouth to his ear where she whispered very softly, "Especially, when you look like this." As he opened his mouth for a kiss, he was met with a double handful of snow. It slid down his collar and into his ears, into his mouth as he laughed, trying to catch her as she wriggled off him.

"Minx!" he railed as he shook his head, and stood up stiffly from the prolonged cold. By the time she dared to look back again, she was already at the entrance to the house.

"I wish you better luck next time, my love," she sang provocatively as she sailed into the house, and out of his reach.

He stood for a long moment afterward, shaking his head, the smile, which had never been far from his face in recent weeks, lingering still. He cast a quick glance skywards as he started back to the house, the snow crunching satisfyingly underfoot, already imagining the ways he would take his revenge.

🎏

*W*hen Katherine returned, she found that a letter had arrived for her. These days, when a letter came, she immediately sat down and read it, devoting the afternoon to memorising its every word, admiring every elegant turn of phrase, the bold, swooping hand, and searching out hidden meanings in its determinedly proper tone.

She eventually sat to write a reply, her quill posed, yet unable to think up anything witty enough, or pretty enough or remarkable enough. She sighed, returning to her window seat and picked up the letter again. Charles was in Italy, and the manners there shocked him sometimes, though he did imply she might have enjoyed it. She giggled at that, he still found her so impertinent. Little did he know what a well-behaved young lady she had become in his absence... well, some of the time, at least, which was an improvement.

The season had begun again, and Margaret would be pushing her into the paths of eligible men just as soon as she could get her back to London. The thought made her feel slightly nauseous. She did not want any titled man that her mother would scrape up: some fool to fawn over her and rub his fingers in private over her inheritance. She wanted someone noble, above such things. A perfect fit - someone whose strengths matched her weaknesses, and vice versa. Someone she could respect and strive to be better for.

She hugged the letter to her chest and sighed again, thinking how only one man she had ever met could meet that description, and he was a world away.

🌸

~March 1810~
Hampshire

*T*he days began to grow longer in that newly hatched spring, and with Wesley and Katherine returned to London, and Rebecca wishing more and more to withdraw to her own company, Lucian and Caroline found quiet delight in spending time companionably in the library after they had dined, on the evenings when they were not busily abed. Reading was a hobby that they both held a love for and sharing it was a secret joy that Caroline had not expected.

The library at Westmere would have been a sumptuous pleasure for any book lover, but to Caroline, it was nothing short of heaven. A massive, two-story bay window commanded one entire wall, flooding the room with the capricious whims of mother nature, changing the scene daily, and spurring Caroline on to read for the changing mood, from bright pooling sun on glistening snow, to lush verdant green valley, to colourful, cosy autumnal greys and reds, to dark, brooding thunderstorms that shook the floor beneath her feet.

All other walls were covered in carved dark oak and row upon row upon lavish row of books. The ceiling was domed and painted with a scene of the heavens, and around the room ran a balcony, spiralling down in grand wooden staircases in two matching corners. The only thing to match the windows was the fireplace, the marble carved with Greek gods, and its mouth nearly large enough to swallow room whole.

There was, everywhere she looked, a comfortable and hidden place to sit and read, just as it should be.

*T*hat particular night, Caroline had climbed midway up one of the sliding ladders to reach a tantalising selection of French novels from a higher shelf, when Lucian returned from his study.

"Hello, my heart," he called to her as he walked in and closed the door, but she had begun to read the first few pages of her new selection, and found herself altogether too captivated to answer. He walked quietly over and placed a large, warm hand on her bottom, cupping it tenderly. "What has gripped you so, my darling?" he asked, and she heard the smile in his voice.

"Mmm. Laclos. *Les Liaisons Dangereuses....*" she said, without looking up. "I have never been allowed to read it."

"Dangerous Liaisons? Well, I myself am delighted that you are interested in such licentious pursuits, more and more delighted each day, I might add. Pry, read to me a bit, darling. I do so love to listen." She turned around on the ladder and settled back against it, book in hand.

"Your wish is my command, as always, dear husband," she teased with a smirk and found an answering one under his raised eyebrow. She began to read as he stood nearby, starting again at the beginning, in case they should like to read the whole book together in pieces, as they often did. As she got lost in the story, she found an interested hand gliding down her leg, and then to her surprise, rising very slowly up her skirts, taking its time over the rim of each of her stockings. She stopped for a moment as a finger ran itself along the seam where her stocking ended and her skin began.

"Oh, please do not let me stop you, sweetheart. I adore your passion for reading, in fact, I find it most rousing the way your voice caresses each word with such... unbridled ardour. In French, it is a decadence I cannot resist." He stopped. His hand stilled until, with a smile, she began again. Under her layers of skirts, she could see nothing, but she felt him pull the bow of her garter ribbon very slowly until, with a little tug, it gave way, and his fingers dipped lower still under her stockings, at the newly found skin there.

His other arm came up and clasped casually onto the ladder by her waist, pinning her in, as his lower hand moved inch by inch further up. By the time he began delicate strokes along the curls at the apex of her thighs, she had lost all sense of the words she was saying, her mind on the centre of her, and the promise of his hand. He dipped his fingers between her closed thighs and ran a finger smoothly along her seam back and forth, ever so slowly before finally splitting her and running his finger between the folds of her. She gasped, and her knees went slack, as he moved his body in to keep her steady.

"Please remember the rules, my love. Need I remind you? I will pleasure you, most obligingly, so long as you continue to read to me that filthy story in your beautiful French," he smiled like a beast, and Caroline could not help but swallow hard, and nod, and taking a breath, begin again.

His finger glided slickly in her growing wetness, and he rumbled an answering sound that made her breath hitch. But, Caroline kept reading, trying her best not to stumble over the words as his finger toyed at her opening. He spent a few languid moments there, softly and delicately stroking her. Then, to her shock, he removed his hand altogether, pulling it from her skirts, and bringing it to his lips where he licked her wetness from his fingers, then slid his long middle finger into his mouth, wetting it to the base, before grinning, cocking an expectant eyebrow pushing her to read on, and when finally she did, returning his hand to her skirts.

Moving her eyes back to her book, she began again, forgetting quite where she had left off. This time he moved his finger up into her, pausing at her opening, taking time with the sensitive area there, rolling his finger around in small, slow circles, and stroking the rough patch just inside of her that began to make her tremble slightly.

She heard her voice grow thick and husky, but she kept on, maddeningly trying her best to keep her voice still and reading steadily. His finger moved up slowly, all the way inside of her, his palm cupping her as he moved. He pulled his hand slowly out and slid it back in, so slowly that she longed to throw him to the floor and straddle him and take him hard for the satisfaction of finally scratching the frustrated want that he was building inside of her. Slowly, gently, he moved, and she felt herself swelling around him, her wetness on his hand as he cupped her, grinding against her with his palm, as his finger stroked the inside of her.

A hot jolt of lust shot through her body, and she heard her reading broken by a needy moan. She swallowed, and kept on, as he toyed with her relentlessly. He pressed his face to the place on her skirts where his hand was, and she felt the breath of his kisses make their way through the layers of her muslin.

"Don't you dare stop," he warned, and suddenly she was off of her feet, swung into his arms, as he moved her to the leather wingback by the fire where he often sat. She laughed, reading on, and he lifted her, pulling her skirts up and placing her bare bottom on the leather of the chair. Slowly he removed each of her stockings, and began pressing hot kisses into her skin, first on the soft arch of her foot, and then moving up to the inside of her ankle, and making his way further up, until he grabbed her firmly behind each knee, spread her legs wide, and pulled her quickly towards him, sitting just on the edge, where nothing obstructed his waiting mouth, herself entirely bared to him, he flashed the wickedest of grins, that made her stomach flip.

"Tell me what happens next, sweetheart," he purred darkly.

Closing her eyes and breathing in a shuddering breath, she took but a moment to regain her composure, and then lifted the book and read again. His hot mouth was on her in a flash, kissing her, warm breath stirring the winding excitement in her stomach. He spread her legs a little further, pulling her nearer still, and licked up her centre, flooding her with a liquid heat sensation that made her cry out quietly. He licked her this way several times, splitting her a little more with his tongue each time, driving her wild with need for more, until he raised his hand and parted her with his fingers, and his tongue lapped at her, sucking, entering her.

Her voice, as she read, was coming out now between pants and moans, but he did not complain and doubled his attentions when she cried out more loudly. Caroline knew that he loved to hear her like this, and knew that the purpose of forcing her to read aloud was so that he might hear all the more clearly each hitch in her voice, each scratch in her throat, each sigh, each moan, each curse she muttered, and he made his own sounds of pleasure into her quim, aroused and ever more hungry as he pleasured her.

She tried very hard to focus on the words, though they started to swirl in front of her, and found that the distraction of the reading was keeping her from her climax in the most incredible way, building more slowly than her usual quick eagerness, growing into something stronger, bigger. She held the book a little closer, and ploughed on, her mind in a battle with her body, and felt him grin into her at the sound of her struggle. Caroline was determined not to let him win too easily.

She had no way of knowing how much time passed, but the thing that had been slowly building at her core was pushing her into insanity, when he finally put her knees over each of his broad shoulders, wrapped an arm around her hips, and pressed her hard against his mouth, his stubble scratching as he held her tight, sliding two fingers into her, in and out, so wet now with his saliva and her desire, increasing his pace as he licked relentlessly at the pearl of nerves at the top of her.

Her eyes fluttered back behind her head as she finally lost all control. She heard the book hit the ground as she grabbed at his head with one hand, trying to muffle her screams with the other, as wave after wave of climax took hold of her, shaking her legs and jerking her body with such force that she would have fallen from the chair had he not held on to her tightly. It was searing, blistering, delicious euphoria.

For minutes afterwards she continued to moan quietly and to pant, as the blinding sensation finally abated. When she came to, blinking, the ridiculousness of the situation took hold of her suddenly, and she surprised herself with a loud peel of laughter that she could not stop as the joy of the climax collided with the hilarity of what had just occurred, and the fun and excitement of this new game he had devised. Lucian laughed with her, with rather a smug smile on his face.

"That, my gorgeous darling, was a spectacular performance," he said, his eyes dark and intense on hers. "I am quite sure that is how French is meant to be spoken, in fact. Laclos himself would have approved."

He came to kiss her, and she kissed him back, still floating on the decadent flood of her climax, and found that she wanted more of him.

"Oh, the performance is not yet over, Lucian. This is only the inter-mission," she said with a smug smirk of her own as she stood up and pushed him slowly, kissing him deeply, as she led him backwards. When they had reached the sofa, she pushed him down to sit with a harsh shove, and he let out a dark laugh. She knew he liked it when she took control.

She straddled him, and kissed him hungrily, grinding herself against his trousers, until his breaths and heartbeat became faster. Then she stood up and kneeled in front of him. Looking up, and locking her eyes with his, she slowly unbuttoned his fall front where his rigid cock pushed forward, and folding the fabric down but leaving the rest of him fully clothed, his top buttons closed while just this one part of him was fully exposed.

He gasped and moaned when she wasted no time licking the tip of him, and then, putting her hands around his shaft, took him into her mouth, tasting him, gliding over his smooth skin with her tongue, and sucking lightly while her hands began to glide back and forth and she took him deeper. He cursed, and his hand tightened in her hair almost painfully, but he did not guide her head but instead let her do as she pleased, and she enjoyed herself, taking time over each area of him, listening to his breath and his sounds to figure out which movement and rhythms he liked best. She had been learning more and more lately, and had discovered that it flamed her own arousal to solicit such a response, to put him entirely at the mercy of her mouth.

He was panting heavily now and she could tell from the sound that he was growing close to losing himself, so she slowly pulled away from him, inch by inch, making him groan in pleasurable frustration. Then, she lifted her skirts, and straddled him again, this time using her hand to position his wet cock carefully at her opening. She too was wet and swollen with lust and his earlier attentions, and they glided together easily, as she took him in very slowly, kissing him deeply as she pushed down, his member sliding inside of her, pulling a moan from her own mouth, muffled as it was by his.

She slid down, giving herself time to adjust, and making him wait, until finally he was completely sheathed, her legs wide on either side of him, and he cried out, grabbing her backside with each hand, as she rocked back and forth, moaning a little with each moment, as he moved inside of her. She began to sit up slowly, and then press back down, moving along the length of him.

"Christ, Caroline," Lucian breathed into her hair. "Don't stop." She moved faster then, pushing her hands against his shoulders, as he pulled her bodice down roughly and took a nipple in his mouth, teasing her, scraping her gently with his teeth. She began to ride him, coming down harder and harder, no longer caring that the noise that they were making might be overheard. His hands on her thighs, he called her name, and she crashed down on him, again and again, harder than she had before, enjoying the roughness of the new sensation, a tiny bit of pain to lace the unbearable sweetness of pleasure.

He grabbed her thighs so hard on each side that his fingers dug into her flesh and would leave bruises, and she felt herself shatter in his arms, pulling him close to her, spasming around his cock. He tightened and held her down hard as he pulsed into her, climaxing together in a fit of sound and flesh.

Afterwards, she stayed there for some time on his lap, joined as they were, her forehead pressed against his, as they rode out their bliss together. Slowly, they returned to earth in one another's arms - connected, one, whole.

Later, as they collected their things, Lucian grinned at her devilishly.

"This has been a most… educational evening, for the both of us, I believe. I think we should return to our studies often, and more diligently in future, would you not agree?" She smiled at him, taking his hand in hers, and twining their fingers together as they set off back to their rooms.

"Oh yes, most assuredly. Only, tomorrow, my Lord, it shall be you who will read us chapter two."

*ebecca had known full well what would happen when she had made that decision, so many months ago now, to plot for the union of Eli and Eva. She had said that she was contented to sacrifice her own happiness and inflame her father's ire for the sake of liberating Lucian and bringing about the happy marriage of two people, new to her then, but who had since grown to become dear friends. When she looked at the two adoring couples; Eli and Eva, Luke and Caroline, she swelled with pride, and also a little grain of bittersweet jealousy, for the love and happiness that they all had. But she had not known when she had schemed and plotted and set her mind on noble sacrifice, that it would be Isaac she would be sacrificing.

He had confessed some feeling for her at the ball, but though her heart had soared then to heights she had not known before, they had soon crashed back down when he had disappeared almost entirely from her company or that of any of her family. She had begun even, when her mind was dark and clouded with unhappy thoughts, to think that he had since regretted the sudden fancy, or that perhaps, flirt that he was, he had promised his heart to many of the women of London, and while her heart knew it not to be true, her head tortured her with scenes of his lovemaking with every young lady of the Ton.

But, as her despair had begun to drag and pull her down, a letter had arrived.

A letter for her scrawled in a hurried hand.

*L*ady Rebecca,

I write to you to atone. I must apologise for hoisting my feelings upon you in such a way on that dreamlike night, so long ago now, at the ball. It was the behavior of a cad. I knew that you were too far above me, but arrogantly I had hoped that I might yet reach for you and that if you cared for me too, even a little, that the heavens would take pity, and smile upon us some bountiful measure of luck that I did not deserve. They were the dreams of a fool. I know that now.

I will not trouble you to endure my delusions any longer. I will know you now, only as a friend, if you will have me, but, I do have a request. I have heard you speak disparagingly of your marriage prospects in the past, and I wish to make one last appeal to you -

Please, whatever you do, do not simply settle for any man who does not deserve you, any man that you do not care for. You are not a commodity for your father to sell. You are a most remarkable woman. I did not know that there were women like you in all the world. I could not have dreamt it. Your strength, your intelligence and blinding wit, the depth of your heart, your boundless generosity and self-sacrificing nature, your undying loyalty to your family, the joy you breathe into my life and all those around you, and yes, by God, your beauty, which has no parallel in the mortal realm.

Do not merely accept any suitor that your father brings forth. You do not owe him this. Fight for your own happiness with the same unflinching bravery that you fought for your brother's.

I will soon be rejoining my family in America, but know that wherever I am, I am your friend, and you are always in my heart and in my thoughts.

I love you.

Forgive me.

I love you.

*S*he wrote to him. She knew that he was right, that it could never be, but yet she wrote to him, and she sent a man on horseback to ride through the night.

CHAPTER 2

~April 1810~
London

*C*aroline linked her arm through Katherine's as they made their way along the busy London street. It was all abustle as carriages rattled past, and sellers cried their ware. As the girls passed by stalls, the smell of hot pies was almost too good to forgo.

The Taylors had stayed near to Lucian's exclusive address, and Isaac had convinced his father that it would be advantageous for him to stay on there to keep an eye on a mining operation which they had recently invested in, even though he was the only Taylor remaining in England. The situation with Isaac and Rebecca confused Caroline to no end. She saw the way they each yearned for the other and yet were powerless to move forward, though Caroline did have her suspicions as to who might be responsible for whatever obstacle hindered them, and she decided to investigate further when she returned to Hampshire. In the meantime, to Caroline and Lucian's surprise, Silus had begun sending suitors to Westmere to dine with Rebecca, with Lucian as chaperone, and visit a few days before Lucian well and truly scared them off again. It was an arrangement which, if Lucian's letters were anything to go by, was seriously unpleasant for everyone involved. Caroline had laughed at his letters, she worried for Rebecca and sympathised with Lucian, but most of all, she pitied the men who had come to call on an eligible maiden, and found that a beast prowled the castle.

Frances and Virgil would soon be leaving for America, having decided to settle there, with their most recent addition. Katherine had entered the season once more, and she had asked Caroline to come to London to help her endure the endless monotony of dress fittings and social calls in preparation. For the season proper, Lucian would join her, and they would escort both Rebecca and Katherine to functions and events, along with Mr and Mrs Fairfax.

Caroline pulled at Katherine's arm as they passed by another stall, the smell making Caroline's mouth water.

"Wait," Caroline said, looking at the glistening food. Katherine rolled her eyes and pulled her on.

"Caroline, you'll be as big as a house if you are not careful. Anyway, mama warned you against street food," Katherine said blithely, seeing the Taylor's house come into view, and narrowing her eyes at the sight of a familiar carriage sat in front of it.

Caroline nodded reluctantly and allowed herself to be moved along. There was another reason for her visit to London, more specifically for a doctor's appointment, one which her husband was entirely unaware of.

She was with child. His child. The prospect was still terrifying. Caroline was overjoyed, and yet, terribly frightened. It was common knowledge to her that her mother's pregnancy had been fraught with difficulties, and apparently, the women in her family had not become mothers easily. She had intended to tell Lucian, before anyone else, yet she had not allowed for Katherine's eavesdropping.

As they arrived at the door, it opened before them, and they were escorted into the drawing-room, where Caroline immediately saw that Isaac already had a caller.

"Lady Ashford! What a pleasure." Joshua Lee's voice was warm and his smile seemed genuine as the men stood to greet them. Caroline smiled demurely, and sat down, as far away as possible from him, while Katherine and Isaac started a lively conversation. Caroline was glad the group was small, so more private conversation was not possible. After a short while, Joshua took his leave and she watched him go gladly. While he was the model of good behaviour, she still felt uncomfortable around him, given what had transpired.

Alone with Isaac at last, Caroline fixed him with a disapproving look.

"Alas, something tells me I will feel the loss of the company of Mr Lee quite keenly," he mused, his tone light as he settled back in his chair.

"Isaac, why have you not visited us at Westmere?"

"I have been engaged in rather tricky business matters, which, sadly, have kept me to London," he said stiffly.

"And why have we not had so much as a letter to that effect?" Caroline continued.

"Too busy with your... social obligations?" Katherine asked, a little too sweetly, a hint of steel in her gaze.

"I have barely been out over this doorstep, except to... It matters not. I have not called on anyone else socially, and I shall not before I call on you. You know this."

"Maybe so, but does Rebecca?" Katherine challenged.

"She must," he said, his confidence draining visibly at the looks on their faces. Caroline noted then, his pale complexion, and nervous eyes.

"Isaac, be frank with us... what is going on? Have you been meeting Lord Ashford?" Caroline asked. Isaac gave a short laugh and looked away.

"I suppose you could say that," he bit out, running a hand through his hair, a move uncharacteristically flustered for him. Caroline studied him a moment before she decided to cut to the heart of the matter.

"What does he want?"

"The better question might be, what doesn't he want? It would be shorter in the telling," he muttered.

"Isaac... tell me," Caroline insisted. Isaac finally stopped looking around, and brought his face back to hers, his expression defeated and sad.

"He wants vast sums to be moved to his accounts for the privilege of asking for Rebecca's hand. She is worth it, of course, but it is more than I would ever have access to before my fortieth year," he said, and Caroline and Katherine sat back, stunned.

"But, I don't understand. You are the man. It is for Lord Silus to supply a dowry to the marriage, not you. You will be providing the upkeep for Rebecca for the rest of her days, which will be rather a remarkable feat, I am quite sure!" Katherine said with a scoff.

"He knows I have lost my heart completely to her and would do anything in my power. He wants money. It is all he thinks about. And if I cannot purchase her hand, he will simply find someone else who can."

"That tyrant," Caroline spat, unable to comprehend how a man such as Silus Ashford had produced the children that she had become so fond of. "Tell me everything, from the beginning, let us find a way out of this mess," Caroline said.

"There is no way out! He controls Rebecca, and she fears for my safety if we were to defy him as Eli and Eva did. I would risk anything to be with her, but she says that she will not risk my life for it."

"Can we go to Charles with this?" Caroline asked, and Katherine visibly brightened. "He is the only one who might hold some sway."

"He is too far away," Isaac huffed. "What could he possibly do from Europe, when his father has already begun the process of finding a match? There is no time."

"Why not run off to the continent, or America, or... India!" Katherine said, eyes wide and alive with excitement. Isaac shook his head.

"Silus Ashford had made it his business to collect souls, people in his debt, people with secrets, people whose entire livelihoods are poised under his thumb, under the threat of his whims. That is his real business, and he has spent his lifetime tirelessly amassing desperate people, rich and poor alike, all over the world, as much for monetary gain, as for the sheer joy of it. Rebecca assures me that there is no place where we could run that is far enough out of his reach."

"Well..." Caroline's brow creased as thoughts raced. "If you cannot elope, and you cannot run, we will have to get you the money somehow. Lucian and I have more than we will ever need. I'm sure if I spoke to him that he would be willing to make over a portion of that to secure his sister's happiness." Isaac's face crumpled, looking ever more desperate.

"Are you sure about that? I hear that Lucian has worked very hard to keep your fortunes out of the hands of his father. What you ask is no small thing. It might seem small to you, yet, to your husband, he would again be undermined and controlled, and manipulated by his father..."

something he has fought to change his entire life, from what Rebecca has told me. To your husband, there is no worse demon in all of hell than Silus Ashford. What might it do to him to ask him this?" He shook his head again. "No. No, there is no way out of this. I have considered it from every angle."

Caroline was silent as she thought over the situation. Isaac was right about their relationship, obviously, she had seen first-hand the emotional scars left on Lucian from that man. How she hated him. It made her seeth to think of him, manipulating them all, manoeuvring them into position. He may have even suspected that Rebecca would go to her protective brother Lucian, the only Ashford with an independent income, to beg for her one chance at happiness.

Silus may yet have been planning this for some time. No doubt he had boiled with fury when he had discovered the prenuptial marriage settlement which Lucian and Mr Fairfax had carefully put in place to keep the totality of Caroline's fortunes from Silus's grasp. Perhaps this was his revenge, his way to beat Lucian down yet again and make himself richer in the process. Perhaps that was even why he was sending suitors to Westmere, it occurred to her belatedly, rather than bring Rebecca to London where they might easily access her - he wanted Lucian to witness every minute of her torment, trying to keep her suitors at bay as more and more circled ever nearer, and the fight became more hopeless.

She put a hand to her belly, thinking of the child that grew there, one that needed two whole parents, one that she determined would not grow older under the villainy of such a sick and malignant grandfather. She thought for a few moments more, before turning back to Isaac, renewed conviction on her face.

"I am certain that if we put our heads together, there is a way forward. You are going to marry Rebecca, Silus is not going to get his hands on our money, and Lucian is not going to know about any of this."

"How do you really mean to accomplish all that?" Katherine scoffed but leaned in closer, sitting on the very edge of the divan. Caroline took a deep breath and set her shoulders.

"I confess, I haven't a clue. But, we will formulate a plan, one which does not leave the sanctity of this circle. Do you understand?" she asked, looking around at their faces for agreement. "First of all, I believe it is time for me to become more acquainted with my dear father-in-law."

🏵

"**C**aroline, my dear, what an unexpected surprise." Silus's voice was as thick as honey, as she was led through to his opulent drawing-room. The sound of his endearments lingered on her skin like flies. She sat and waited as he did. Lounging back in his chair, he regarded her curiously at the irregular visit.

"I happened to be in London, with Miss Fairfax. She is preparing for the spring balls," Caroline explained.

"Ah yes. The Fairfaxes are well, I take it?" he asked, though Caroline suspected that he knew more about the Fairfax family's well-being than even she did.

"Yes, very well. In fact, we have just gotten news that Mrs Taylor, formerly Fairfax, is expecting a child."

"Ah, well good. A child of the new world, for they left for America, did they not?"

"They did," Caroline confirmed, smiling politely at the maid as she poured her a cup of tea.

"I admit, I have often hungered to see it, though I don't believe I ever shall. Europe, I know well, but the Americas... I imagine them to be intoxicating, and rather exotic... if you are any evidence, that is," Silus said, watching her as she took a sip from her cup. She wasn't sure if it was meant to be lecherous or insulting - perhaps both.

"Have you had the opportunity to call on many acquaintances in town?" he asked, studying her reaction carefully.

"I have been lucky enough to spend a great deal of time with Mr Taylor, as he is a great friend of the Fairfaxes," Caroline said, her eyes fast on Silus in return. They locked eyes for a long moment, each guessing at the extent of the other's knowledge.

"I suppose you must have been spending time with your Mr Lee then, as he is never far from Isaac's side."

"I believe when money and friendship become tangled, it is difficult to separate them," Caroline said evenly.

"It does seem so," Silus murmured, smiling at their smooth exchange,

504

carefully skirting over the real issues. The silence held for a moment more before Caroline eventually broke it.

"Lady Rebecca remains at Blackhill?" she said.

"She does. But do not worry over her solitude. She is kept quite busy, I assure you, with entertaining so very many of my friends. Besides, it does her good, I think, to be out of the hustle and bustle of town."

"And away from Mr Taylor."

"I suppose that too might also be seen as an advantage. There are so many ways for a well-meaning, proper and exemplary woman to be ruined these days, and I am sure I need not tell you, *Lady Ashford*, that I quite worry for my daughter in town at times." He smirked, and she felt vomit threaten.

"Your ability to skirt the issue is quite impressive, my Lord," Caroline said bluntly, and saw Silus's eyebrow twitch in surprise before he threw his head back and let out a laugh.

"So ruthlessly bold. Why I do believe I am starting to understand why you drive my son to distraction. You remind me of his mother," he stated, settling back further in his leather chair and scrutinizing every inch of her in a way that was, no doubt, meant to make Caroline feel every bit as uncomfortable as she did. "So, what do you presume is the issue?"

"My fortune," she stated calmly and could see, with a little satisfaction, that she had surprised him. "It is why you are forbidding Lady Rebecca and Mr Taylor their happiness, is it not? Because you expected it, and Lucian bested you, and you know that his sister is a weak spot for both of us." He took a moment, surprised perhaps, but not unfooted.

"It need not be your fortune. If Mr Tayler is capable of coming up with the sum on his own, I will be quite happy to accept it."

"Yes, but then you could not torture Lucian with it, and I believe that is probably more enticing to you than a sum of money to an already rich man." A smile coiled across his lips.

"Ahh, you are smarter than you appear, I see. Shrewder, too. How very American. Are you here as a mediator between my son and me, then?"

"No, I come alone. In fact, let us be clear, Lord Ashford. I do not wish for my husband to know of what we speak, or even that we are speaking at all." She said sternly, steeling herself for battle with the dragon.

"Oh, I am not surprised to hear it, dearest. I suspect you keep many a secret from my son," he said, his eyes dipping to her bodice. "So you have come here to bargain, then? Alone? But, surely you are aware that nothing but the copper of your pin money can be spent without your husband's direct consent."

"That is true. But perhaps you are unaware that my lands are still held in Mr Fairfax's name as guardian, as he has not yet set about the process of making them over to Lucian." Silus's eyes sparkled and narrowed at that, with an interest that he could not hide from her.

"Ah," he frowned. "I am afraid that it is not much to bargain with. I mean to use your dowry to invest in a little speculative pet project of mine. I need money, not some fallow farmland in Lord knows where."

"My parents' land is rather vast, as I'm sure that you are well aware. Mr Fairfax's lawyer assures us that, if sold, they could attract quite a healthy sum, significantly larger, in fact, than what you have asked of Mr Taylor. As it is one of the largest estates in the Shenandoah Valley left intact, our lawyers get frequent enquiries. You would not have to wait long for a buyer." He inhaled deeply, taking a moment's pause, steepling his fingers, and taping them thoughtfully together. He levelled her in an uncomfortable glare.

"And you? You would just give me your family land... the land of your departed parents, and *their people*," he said the term as if it were a degradation, "so that I could gamble it on some enterprise or other?"

"It is the land on which my parents burned," she said, tasting ash in her mouth at the sacrilege.

"And you care not for their legacy?"

"Their true wishes were for my happiness... I shall not disrespect them by putting money over that," she said honestly, and Silus suppressed his look of triumph.

"And you wish for your husband to know nothing whatever about losing your inheritance and his rightful property?"

"I wish to see Lady Rebecca happy, and my husband also. It is a fair exchange, I believe."

"Oh, I doubt very much that this will make your husband happy," Silus said critically, with a little tick of his lips. Caroline ignored it.

"I wish to propose a deal, and the deal shall be as follows," she went on quickly, trying to gain the upper hand while he still visibly hungered for her offer. "In exchange for my lands, you will allow Rebecca to marry as she chooses. You will stay out of my life, and more importantly, out of Lucian's. On this, I will not negotiate. We will not hear from you again. You will initiate no contact with him." Caroline said boldly, lifting her chin.

"So, I am to be estranged from a son that I despise. Anything else?"

"Let me be clear. If you should see us in a crowded street, or ballroom, you shall give the barest acknowledgement, and a wide berth. You will stop torturing my husband, and making it your life's work to ruin his happiness," she finished, her tone unyielding, not betraying the nerves she felt in the pit of her stomach. Silus looked at her sharply, calculatingly.

"Lucian will learn of this eventually, my darling. You will not be able to keep it from him forever."

"Perhaps not, but we have no plans to journey to that part of the world, and if he should ever hear of it, by that time it will be done, and Lady Rebecca happy and with family, and he will not lament the loss of something that he has never seen."

"Oh, if you so say, my dear. I'm sure you must be right." His voice was oily. He would tell Lucian himself one way or another, she was sure of it, but he would be cautious and wait until he had the money in his hand so that there could be no dispute, and if all went according to plan, it would all be too late, and Rebecca safely married.

"Well, you have surprised me, Caroline. You are even more artful in your deceit than I had imagined." He smiled as if paying her a compliment, and she flashed with anger. Even in her deception of Silus, which hopefully he would not realise for some time to come, he had manipulated her too, of course. He had forged this lie between her and Lucian with his own hands, and already it gave him joy. A lie, a wedge, that they both had sworn would never again happen. His duplicity was like a sickness, spreading and growing, and in one way or another, infecting everyone around him with its insidious poison, even Caroline herself.

"I must say, you have given me quite a deal to think about. I will consider your offer. You may go," he said rather rudely, standing and turning his back to her to pour himself a brandy, no doubt in self-congratulation.

☙

*T*he crunch of gravel signalled the arrival of another carriage. Looking up from his ledgers, Lucian felt a wave of frustration well up at the sound. They no longer had any notice anymore of which of their father's friends would be calling, when they would arrive, nor how long they might stay. It kept them in a constant state of unease. Lucian was taken with the idea of his sister finding a husband whom she could care for, and might have been patient with his chaperoning duties, but for the fact that Becca had despised every one of them with increasing fervour. It was abundantly clear to everyone that Silus had chosen each for their wealth or connections, with no thought whatever for their age, temperament, looks, or suitability. At the first sign on Rebecca's distaste, Lucian did his best to chase them back home again, but some combination of the long journey back to London, tenacity, and desperation for money, made a few of the men surprisingly persistent, even in the face of Lucian's gruff incivility. He was unsure why his father had not himself entertained his business partners at their London townhouse, or even at Blackhill Hall; however, though it was agonising, he was glad that he could still protect Rebecca somewhat, when Silus may have forced a coupling more aggressively.

He reluctantly put his work down and made his way to the door to greet the man. The carriage was very expensive indeed, and as the gentleman swung down from its plush interior, Lucian could see that he was older, perhaps closer to their father's age, but he was strong and lithe, and despite the greying at his temples, he wore his age well. Perhaps this one would be different, he hoped, for Rebecca's sake, and for his own sanity.

"Captain Shaw," the man said, striding toward Lucian after a quick tip of his hat. "No doubt you expected me," he added before Lucian could respond.

"No doubt we did," Lucian answered grimly. "Ashford," he said in response and tipped his own hat.

"I am aware. And where is the girl?" he asked, straightening his waistcoat and jacket, not out of nervousness, Lucian thought, but out of a need for everything to be orderly, like the rest of his person. Lucian sneered at the casual address of his sister.

"*Lady Ashford* is indisposed at present, and shall not be available until dinner." Shaw's mouth tightened in displeasure, which pleased Lucian somewhat. This one, he regretted, would not be the one.

"I will show you to your rooms."

After a stiff walk to the guest quarters, Lucian made his way over to his sister's rooms where he found her reading by the window, looking as dreary as the grey sky outside.

"I love *A Midsummer Night's Dream,*" he said. "I always carried a bit of a torch for Titania," he smiled, "So strong, and powerful," he joked, but her answering smirk was more wry than amused.

"Who's here, Lucian? Another of father's suitors, no doubt. It's not Oberon come for me this time either, is it? It's Bottom." He barked a laugh at that. How she managed to hold on to her good humour when clearly so downcast was a mystery.

"I will not make your decisions for you, little one, but I will say that he looks more an Oberon than he looks like a Bottom," they both laughed and Lucian was pleased to see it on her face. "He has a not-unpleasant face and form, though it might have been around for a little bit longer than your own."

"Ah. Another ancient Mathusala then?"

"Wrong book, cricket," he tsked, and she shot him a scolding look. "No, he's no Methuselah like that last one. Poor dear, you have had to endure an entire parade of the most unsavoury dregs that England has to offer, haven't you?"

"Don't forget the Scot," she said, and Lucian laughed.

"Ah yes, The Soup-Sucker."

"And the German..."

"The... Belcher, if I remember correctly."

"You do," she answered tartly, clearly beginning to enjoy this little game of theirs.

"Who else?" Lucian began listing on his fingers. "Let's see... there was Saggy Stockings, Methuselah of the Watery Eyes, of course. Uhhh... oh yes, the one who brought his whiskery sister, whom I still very much believe him to be in love with. He stayed the longest. We couldn't get rid of the two! Like they were on a little honeymoon together, and loathe to leave it." She laughed at that, screwing up her face in disgust.

"Oh, we mustn't forget the pincher!" Rebecca chimed in and Lucian frowned.

"No, we will not! Although I daresay he won't be pinching anything with that hand for a good few months, the bastard."

"Serves him right, I'd say. Let it be a warning to the unsuspecting ladies of London. There was also the Handsome Hair-Flipper, who did nothing but talk about his mother the entire time."

"Oh! And the Food-Spitter, with the donkey laugh," they both did an impersonation, and then collapsed in fits of laughter at the ridiculous faces the other made.

Once Lucian had collected himself, he grabbed her head to his chest and kissed the top of it, holding her tight.

"I must say, it does me good to hear your beautiful laugh, Becca."

"What? This one?" she asked, and did another donkey laugh imper- sonation, making his chest shake with laughter again.

"Yes, of course, that one. Like music to my ears," he laughed. "I told Captain Shaw that you will not be free until dinner. That should give you some time. Maybe you could like this one," he said. "Maybe this one will be different."

"None of them will be different, Luke." And with that sentence, all the joviality dissipated like so much smoke, and despair had returned to her voice, and Lucian's heart dropped at the sound of it.

❀

*R*ebecca walked into the dining room, resplendent in ashen pink silks, and Lucian smiled with pride. She looked more and more like their mother every day. She had continued to make an effort despite her repeated disappointment, and Lucian wondered if perhaps she still held out hope for some decent match herself, though the beautiful glow of her appearance had never once extended to her eyes.

"Captain Shaw," Shaw announced himself as the men both stood, and he clicked his heels in a tight bow.

"May I introduce Lady Rebecca Ashford," Lucian said, and she made an elegant curtsy before walking to her seat across from Shaw, which Lucian held out for her.

"Charmed," Shaw said, and Rebecca conceded a small, polite smile.

Dinner proceeded uncomfortably, though the food, as always at Westmere, was delicious. Shaw spoke mostly *at* them, rather than to them, and did not bother to try to find a topic which Rebecca might find the least bit interesting. When he was not speaking about his own estate or his time at the Navy, he ate silently, as the siblings filled in the silence with polite conversation, Shaw not bothering to participate in any way. Lucian had grown well past the point of tiredness and his thoughts had strayed to Caroline, as they always did when suddenly his mind snagged on a change in tone.

"...And that is where we shall move as soon as we are married," Shaw said unfalteringly, cutting his lamb into tiny squares.

"Pardon?" Rebecca said, clearly as stunned as Lucian.

"When we are wed, I shall bring you to my estate in Holland. You will be quite comfortable there."

"But..." she spluttered, "I thought you were English," Rebecca said lamely, and Shaw shot her the disapproving look of a headmaster.

"I am, but as I have said, I live primarily in Holland, and you shall join me there. Perhaps you did not hear it."

"But my family is here. I have no wish to move to Holland or anywhere else, Captain Shaw. Please do not speak, sir, as if the matter is done."

"Oh, it is quite done, I assure you. The matter has been settled with your father. I must say that I am surprised that he did not bother to inform you."

"I'm afraid you are mistaken," Lucian sat straighter and put a note of severity into his voice. "Nothing will be decided before Lady Rebecca has made a choice which she is certain of."

"Her father made out to me that it was quite decided, and indeed, I shall continue with that understanding until it is contradicted by he himself."

"I am sure he did, however, Lady Rebecca is not to be bartered for," Lucian said, beginning to grow angry at Shaw's tone.

"Is that so? She is a woman very singular in England, in that case, for it is my understanding that all unmarried ladies can be bartered for by persons with enough capital to do so, and I assure you that I am quite up to the task," he said, putting his cutlery down neatly, pinning Lucian with a challenging look.

"Captain Shaw, you forget yourself," Lucian said slowly, and dangerously, trying not to lose a temper he may not be able to rein in. "You are a guest here at Westmere, Lady Rebecca's guest and my own. We, neither of us, shall be bullied, nor insulted, by the likes of you. You will apologise to the lady, sir, and school your attitude while you remain in this house, unless you care to leave it," Lucian said, raising an eyebrow in entreaty, and waited for Shaw's answer.

"Yes, I believe I shall," he said, wiping his mouth neatly with his napkin and folding it carefully before placing it on the table. "You and your sister are children, and it seems you will behave as such. Your notions of her marriage prospects are fanciful at best. Her father will decide, as is right, and has already done so. You seem to forget, Lord Ashford, that despite her beauty, she is not untouched by scandal, and if she is to be bartered for, then the bidding will start appropriately low. I myself have struck a deal with your father simply due to the convenience of marrying next month, and leaving for Holland immediately afterwards." Shaw stood then and turned to Rebecca then with a stern look. "This is what has been decided. Best you reconcile yourself to it now." Before Lucian could get out the curse on his lips, Shaw went on. "I will ride now to London to discuss this with your father in person, and I shall return next month to collect my bride."

Lucian stood as well, placing both balled fists on the table and leaning toward the man as he made his way to the door, needing to put the solid stretch of mahogany between Shaw and his fists.

"You will never come back here again, do you hear me? And if you do, I shall see to it myself that you leave in pieces." Lucian's voice was filled with every bit of menace that now surged through his veins, and his hands had begun to shake with fury. He held himself back only for Rebecca's sake, who was now in tears, hand to her mouth, trying to hold them back. But, rather the scurry off, as the others had done, Shaw left just as confident and unhurried as he had been since his arrival, unfrightened by Lucian, just as sure that he would claim Rebecca despite her lack of consent, and it was all Lucian could do not to lunge for the man and bloody him mercilessly until red splattered the walls and he exhausted himself.

Caroline skipped dinner that evening. She had spent a very long afternoon with Mr Fairfax and his lawyer, and though it had gone as well as it could, she was left drained, nauseous, and with a sick trepidation building in her stomach like the writhing of worms, eating her from the inside out. What had she done? The minute she had engaged Silus Ashford, she had started something, and she was not sure where it would carry her, carry them all. Katherine and Isaac had helped in the planning, but it had been Caroline who had pushed for this when they had refused. It had been her idea, she had fought hard to persuade the others, and the result of it would be on her head alone.

Mr Fairfax had taken a week of convincing, and though she had not told him the whole of it, he had eventually decided that as she was a grown woman, and this was her birthright, he would do as she asked, provided she listened to his lengthy concerns on the matter. She had shocked him, she saw, when she explained that her husband was not to be notified of any of this business; but, despite his apprehension, Mr Fairfaix had always remained somewhat suspicious of Lucian, and in the end, he had relented.

They had begun the process of making over her parents' lands to Lord Silus, not as a sale, but rather, as something passed from the name of one family member into the name of another. The piece of the puzzle which she had kept from Silus was that the land, which had belonged to her grandmother, was native land. Some twenty years hence, it had been proclaimed by Congress that native lands could not be sold without a public treaty and executed under the authority of the United States government. It would be a lengthy process, and Silus would need to be present; he might call for the public treaty and grow old waiting for it. Silus would never leave his interests in England long enough to make the six-week journey to America and back, especially when some ships had been known to get caught in unfavourable winds and drag the journey to three or four months, or in a storm and perish altogether.

In the meantime, the land would be his, and he might still profit from it with crops and harvesting timber, but that too would take time and patience, and many years before any return was made.

And, when Silus never managed to sell the land, it would pass down his line, to Charles first, of course, but Caroline knew, without doubt, that if Charles, or any other of the Ashfords, should come into possession of Caroline's family lands, that they would soon make it back over to her or to her children. She stroked her smooth belly, thinking of the tiny life she carried. It broke her heart to sign the papers, to sign away the last real thing she had of her mother and father, but she knew that with patience it would be hers again and that sooner or later, it would belong to her children, and perhaps they might live there and prosper on the land of her family and their family before them.

If it worked, she would have sold a fish on a line, that she could slowly reel back. If it worked, Rebecca and Isaac would have their wedding. If it worked, Lucian might finally get out from under the noxious influence of his father. If it worked, she would have used a regulation created to oppress her grandmother's people, to trick a wealthy white Englishman, an oppressor in his own right, to liberate them all from his tyranny.

If it worked. What would happen if it didn't, she did not dare to think.

ucian watched the cool spring light filter through sparse clouds, so light and delicate outside the window of his study. It had no earthly concerns to weigh it down, to send it plummeting to the ground, it floated, gracing the earth, and reminded him of her. It had only been a short time, yet the hollowness of her absence was unimaginable. He thought about her constantly and cursed himself for ever agreeing that it was a good idea for her to visit Katherine in London. Though, how could he have denied her, when she smiled at him so, kissed him and assured him that they would be reunited quickly?

He glanced again at the letter, crumpled in his hand. Silus's had been demanding Caroline's fortune since their wedding. He felt he was owed it, and he also felt it was time to hand it over. Lucian massaged his temples with his fingers and tried to shed the nagging weight of messy and complicated decisions. What his father sent most often were reminders of how the family needed the money, how his siblings were dependent on it for financial security, that it was a duty, expected of the son, to hold the family up through an advantageous marriage. He held the family welfare over Lucian's head, appealing to his love for them and his protective nature to try to force Lucian to sacrifice everything Caroline's parents had provided for her.

It was all a manipulation, of course, but one thing he knew was true, Silus had lost a good deal of money on a poor speculation, and with the way the man haemorrhaged money just as quickly as he could make it, Lucian knew that he could bring them all crashing down with a few false steps. This new investment opportunity was a sound one, Lucian had looked into it himself. He closed his eyes, the pristine greenness of the season on the other side of the window hurting his head even more.

Behind Lucian's closed eyes, a familiar scene began to play, a fever dream he had experienced frequently whilst injured at the cabin with Caroline. In the dream, his parents are arguing over money, and other things. He watches them and is unable to speak, unable to move. Caroline's dreams send her bolting awake, screaming for her parents, yet, this nightmare, he always wakes from slowly, clutched with unease, silent and choked with unsounded words.

He had been exceedingly quick and careful to keep Caroline's fortunes from Silus in their marriage settlement, long hours spent with John Fairfax and their lawyers. Her fortune had been the only reason that Silus had allowed the marriage in the first place, yet the idea of him profiteering from their marriage, or having any hold over them or their coffers, made Lucian cold with apprehension, like a hand that would hold him under the surface of the lake. He wished he could just break ties with his father forever, and never feel the sickening dread of his presence again; yet, there were always untold punishments where Silus was concerned. Any cause for his displeasure, real or imagined, and there was always sure to be some recompense, sometimes it was immediate, more often it was long waited for, stewed over and plotted by Silus in his study - a machinist, pulling strings, and setting events in motion. But that was not the whole of it, he knew. Yes, he hated his father with bitter violence, but there was something there, some inexplicable part of him that could not quite let go - the boy inside, still frightened and alone, who could not let go of his father's hand.

Worse than all of it was how he struggled to tell Caroline. He dreaded her knowing of the power his father still had over him. If he could not himself explain it, how might he hope that she could understand? But when she looked at him, with those astute eyes, he knew it was only a matter of time until his confessions spilt forth.

A knock at the door shook him from his thoughts, and he called for the visitor to enter. Another letter, Lucian scowled as he saw it, however, as soon as he saw the writing, he knew it was not from Silus. Reaching for a silver letter opener he quickly ripped it open, intrigue piquing at its contents. He stared at it while, and then rose, knowing there was someone he had to speak to before he replied.

🦪

*R*ebecca sighed as she trailed her hands over the books in the library. The spines were worn and supple, and she cast her eyes over the huge collection her brother had inherited from his father and had added to himself. The room was full of warm, afternoon firelight, giving heat to the cold sunshine falling through the windows from outside. She selected a book, *Evelina*, delighted that her brother had so many novels and did not see them as beneath him as other men did, and settled into a comfortable armchair to read it. Lately, when music failed her, her chief escape from the utter disappointing nature of reality had been through literature. Luke had always spoken of a good book's transportive powers, and she knew that he had clung to them in his youth. She had never needed escape more, she had never been so trapped.

Lately, Rebecca chose to lose herself in romantic tales, noble heroes and beautiful heroines. She read so as not to think, and tried her best to detain her mind from wandering onto treacherous ground, where a certain man was sure to appear.

Her father had confirmed, of course, that he had arranged for her to marry Captain Shaw, and Lucian was doing his best to appeal to her father's care for her, and explain how very unsuitable he believed Shaw to be, but while Lucian held little sway with her father, he had been surprisingly silent on the matter as of late. His silence had let in enough light for one small seed of hope to sprout, and if anything, Rebecca knew that that was far more dangerous than despair.

She looked up as footfalls disturbed the silence, and saw her brother coming toward her, a letter in his hand. He smiled at her as he neared, and sank beside her on the window seat, tilting the book she was reading to inspect the title. Nodding his approval, he stared at her a while, as she waited patiently for him to speak, then, he placed the letter on her open page, leaning back, looking away and allowing her privacy to read it. Rebecca was curious and read eagerly, her heart pounding at the contents.

She read it three times through before she slowly closed the book on it, preserving its precious words between the pages. Lucian looked to her, his expression gentle.

"Quite an unexpected visit from Mr Taylor, wouldn't you say? What would you have me reply?" he asked.

"It is your home... it is not my decision," Rebecca stalled.

"Come along, Becca, I do not kid myself that he travels so far for my pleasant company."

"But, I am no longer free to accept callers. Captain Shaw-"

"It is not over yet, Becca. I am doing everything I can. Do not give up." His voice softened then, and he reached his hand out to hers. "The question remains, little one, what am I to answer? How do you feel about the man?"

Rebecca opened her mouth to speak, and found no words. There were no words for how she felt about Isaac Taylor. He puzzled her and annoyed her no end. He was insolent and frustrating, and she could not stop thinking of him, and the last time they had danced together, his hands resting lightly on her, his smiling mouth so close, his eyes looking into hers. The letters which they had sent each other spoke of a poet's love, colourful and everlasting, but that love did not have a place in the world yet, only on paper carried on the backs of horses through the night. What was their love when it was made flesh? The notion frightened her, mostly because she worried that her tiny heart, so long neglected, would not be able to survive such joy. She blushed slightly, dropping her brother's frank gaze.

"I believe I understand," he said, placing his hand atop hers for a moment, before standing. Lucian looked down at her with a soft, protective look across his face. "I will tell him to make haste."

🦪

*C*aroline groaned as the light increased the pain in her temples. She leant away from the side of the bed and sighed as she dropped back against the pillows, weak with effort. Katherine wordlessly removed the porcelain bowl, and Caroline grimaced.

"Sorry," she muttered as Katherine handed it to a maid.

"Nonsense," Katherine said brusquely as she paid a cool cloth across Caroline's brow and felt her temperature. "Lord knows, I'm happy and lucky to spend any time with you that I can, even if it involves holding your hair back." Katherine said with a wry smile, "But, my lovely little patient, how long do you think you're going to keep this a secret? Whatever your husband may be, he's no fool." Caroline felt nerves tightening her stomach again, sending another ripple of nausea over her.

"Kitty, please, I know that. I do. Yet, you know what Mrs Fairfax has told us about my own mother's pregnancy... how difficult she said it is for the women in my family to carry children. I do not want... to disappoint anyone."

"And, you think your husband would approve of not being told?" Katherine asked scepticism heavy in her tone.

"Of course not, he would be quite livid, I am sure. But, the longer we wait, the more certain we may be, so... please... just a while longer. Anyway, he must stay at Westmere for the moment, and I will not tell him by letter," Caroline insisted. Katherine looked at her narrowly, then sighed reluctantly.

"Ah well. Far be it from me to encourage people not to make stupid choices."

Caroline relaxed, feeling her apprehension melt away. She missed Lucian desperately, but life in the city, the pregnancy and trying to stay ahead of Silus was taking up all her time at present. She had been to see him several more times. She had played the game hard, and well, she hoped, even appealing to the humanity which she thought might yet lay somewhere inside, and he had eventually given permission for Isaac to travel to Westmere to ask for Rebecca's hand. The deal they had struck was that he could propose as soon as Caroline began the legal process of making her land over to Silus, and when he had the deed in his name, and not before, then Rebecca and Isaac could marry.

He was not a good man, but the more time she spent with him, the more she could see that perhaps he had had some goodness in him once, before life had beat it out of him. Caroline noticed that with each meeting, Silus had grown a little more talkative, strangely; seeming, if she wasn't mistaken, almost as if he was enjoying her company. She had decided to treat him like a human, and he was beginning to behave like one. He was not uncharming. Charm was a tool he had honed, no doubt, for his arsenal, and it sat easily upon him, despite all Caroline knew, like another persona, so easily donned. Both perhaps existed in the same mercurial man. She had seen him be loving with Rebecca, and on occasion, even with Wesley, and there were times, in that dark study, that she felt that he was showing her something of the same. It was an odd feeling which confused her. Sometimes she caught herself thinking that some familial bond might yet be salvaged, and at other times it crept through her like rot, the guilt that she was winning him over only to more easily deceive him, and the fear that the betrayal would be all the more brutal for it.

She sighed tiredly, the effort of plotting and scheming quite beyond her, and not natural for her. The Spring balls would start soon, and she would be expected to go with Katherine. Rebecca need not return for it, as she was about to receive a proposal, yet Katherine, poor Katherine would most definitely be in attendance, a fact which Margaret made sure everyone in London knew. These things all conspired to weigh her down, yet more than anything, she missed her husband, and that was an aching, emptiness inside that would not subside.

⁂

*R*ebecca was sitting in the library when he arrived. She heard the footsteps and assumed it was her brother, roaming the halls, as he had taken to doing, no doubt imagining he might find Caroline there, not stopping his haunting until he found her. He was bordering on insufferable without Caroline. Rebecca would insist they left for London as soon as it was possible, just to save Lucian from madness and herself from murder.

The footsteps approached and then paused. Rebecca, not bothering to glance up, remarked dryly.

"Please, Luke, do not wear down the floorboards any longer. Why don't you channel your frustration into your correspondence, as I am sure Caroline will be happy to read it."

"A letter is a poor substitute for seeing the object of your affection in the flesh," Isaac Taylor's voice came to her, and she froze, suddenly aware of everything, her appearance, her posture, the book she was reading, and the tick of the clock in the distance. She slowly raised her head and met his eyes as he stood in the open doorway, a smile on his face that made her heart kick in her chest.

"And yet... you seem quite able to abstain," she said, and Isaac smiled at the attack.

"Ah, well that is only because I firmly believe that my extended absence from your company is the very thing that might endear me to you. I am told I am much preferred at a great distance. In fact, I'm considering a trip to Scotland next, to put as much distance between us as possible before I ask for your hand."

Rebecca inhaled a sharp quiet breath, and it burned in her chest. She stared at him, unable to think of a single word in the English language. Isaac smiled a soft, sentimental smile, full of unspoken dreams, and walked slowly toward her.

"I've missed you every single moment when I was not by your side. I could never have stayed away, never endured it, had not my every waking moment been devoted to trying to carve out some path for us, some possible future... together."

Rebecca swallowed a hard lump in her throat, her eyes prickling with tears. Each inch that he drew nearer, her heart raced faster. She was holding her breath as he came then, so impossibly close that she could smell the sweet bay spice of soap on his skin. Isaac reached out gently and took her face in his palms, and at the touch of his skin to hers, her stomach flipped, and the world swirled around her as he softly grazed a thumb across her cheek, feather-light, and looked into her eyes as he would stare into her soul. She feared he might see all her hopes there, all her fears, all her desperate longing, hopelessly wanting him for a year or more, for an eternity. They stood for a moment locked in each other's gaze, until Rebecca, dizzy with the gravity of it, closed her eyes.

"But... there is no path," she whispered, afraid to speak the words into the air between them. "Father has already made a match for me, and apparently it has been settled. Isaac, I love you, but-"

Suddenly, she felt his lips soft and warm on hers. Something exploded inside of her, relief, fear, blinding, unutterable joy, and flames of red hot wanting that licked up her body and engulfed her. He kissed her, slowly and sweetly, and her heart, if there was anything left of it that was not already so, became his in its entirety.

"Be mine, Rebecca... be my wife, my partner," he whispered, and she felt her heart swell to the point of breaking. She felt she had wings.

"Yes," she breathed. "I am yours already. I have always been." Her tears began to spill. "But, I cannot. My father-" she started.

"He gives his consent," Isaac stopped her, and Rebecca's eyes shot to his.

"How is it possible? It can't be."

"Because you are loved... that is how," Isaac said, kissing her again, more deeply, and more fully than the first, now that he knew that she was his. And, in that kiss, Rebecca's world changed forever.

~April 1810~
London

*T*he night was so familiar that Caroline kept expecting to see Eva and Eli dance past them. The first Spring ball, according to tradition, was being held in the same place as last year, a place marked with many memories for her. She stood with Katherine and Mrs Fairfax, smiling politely, being introduced to new debutantes, for whom she was surely thought of as a cautionary tale, excepting those such as Margaret, who only saw now a rich girl, who had become a Lady of English society, and therefore had fulfilled her life's purpose.

Katherine was swept away to dance, misery plain across her face, as

Caroline went to the terrace for air. The night was cool still, yet inside was stifling, and she enjoyed the breeze. Staying on the terrace, she looked to the maze, in the distance, and thought how much had changed. Creeping through that maze, finding Lucian with that girl, her nieve, him jaded. It seemed like a different man from the one who stroked her hair as she fell asleep, who dreamt up little surprises for her, who left hidden notes among her things and wrote her poetry in French, and never could be near without twining her hand in his. Seeing him then, through her present eyes, she only wished to put her arms around him, and told him that one day he would be loved, one day, he would be needed.

"Caroline, you are a sight for sore eyes," Wesley's voice drew her attention back and she smiled at him.

"As are you, I know almost no one here, and care to speak to less than that," she muttered, drawing a laugh from him.

"I see you have spent too much time with my brother. Lucian's attitude toward society has become contagious."

"Perhaps this is true," she admitted, looking inside and seeing Katherine back by Margaret's side.

"Why don't you ask Katherine to dance? She's in need of respite from her mother, and her mother's suitors."

"Ah, Mrs Fairfax is displaying her wares?" Wesley dodged as Caroline hit him lightly on the arm with her fan.

"Ouch! Sister, stop. When did you get so strong? I have a secret, and will never tell it you if you do not behave yourself."

'Why? What do you know, Wesley?"

"Only that Mrs Fairfax needn't be quite so diligent this evening. In fact, I'm going to recommend that she enjoy the punch," Wesley said mysteriously with a wink and went inside to ask Katherine to dance. Caroline frowned, trying to puzzle out what it might mean.

A low voice interrupted her thoughts once more.

"Caroline, I saw you out here, and thought I might offer you a drink." Silus's voice came from behind her, and she summoned a smile before she turned.

"You are too kind, my Lord," she said, taking the champagne, her stomach turning at the thought of the bubbles. Her constitution had been delicate lately.

"I believe it was at this very ball, you first made the acquaintance of my son, if rumour is any indicator of truth," Silus said, in a conversational tone.

"Well, rumour rarely is. I had met him before when he came to introduce himself at the Fairfaxes. "

"Yes, but this is where you truly discovered the measure of him."

"There I would disagree. That might have been the kind of man he was once; however, I assure you, he is much changed," she said shortly.

"You cannot change a man, and when you think you have, after time, you realise it was you who has changed," Silus said, following it with a quiet voice. "It was a favourite saying of Esther's, and I am sad to say, I only proved her correct."

"Perhaps she was right... and I misspoke. Lucian is the same man he has always been, but now he no longer hides it."

"Whatever did my son do, to deserve you?" Silus said, his voice soft and Caroline glanced at him quickly. He was studying the moon, a pale circle hanging over the garden.

"He tries," Caroline answered honestly. "For me, he tries. He has not always gotten it right, but he tries with every ounce of his being to be the best version of himself. We all do, do we not? I am sure it is how you won your wife," she said and was surprised as his eyes hardened, and he smirked a lopsided grimace.

"Perhaps one day I shall tell you the story. But, not tonight. Farewell, Caroline. Enjoy your dance," he said, and strode away, leaving Caroline to puzzle over it.

❀

"So, do you not detest it already? The ball, the people, the polite conversation, the monotonous dancing?" Wesley was asking as he and Katherine circled each other on the floor.

"Of course I do, yet, I am surprised that you do also. You have been at Westmere for months, do you not long for the company available in the city?" Katherine asked lightly, yet as she met Wesleys' eyes, hers softened with sympathy. "I know this is tedious for you, dodging through eager mothers and daughters, with their nets and hooks at the ready. I am amazed that you have managed to evade them for so long," she said, turning under his arm and following the complicated steps. "Has there never been... someone? Someone who might seek to deserve you..." Her voice was soft and affectionate, even to her own ears. His eyes left hers and looked around the other couples as they danced, and Katherine resigned herself that he would not answer.

"Yes. There was once. But it could never have been, and they are gone now, and it was quite so long ago that I have taught my heart the lesson of it, and am now content to be alone." His voice was soft. The hint of raw emotion that scratched at it hardened and smoothed over quickly to match his sideways grin. "Besides, when I have all of you scoundrels and your shenanigans to shepherd, who has any time left over for indulgences of the heart?" Katherine felt her heart squeeze at the practised nonchalance in his tone, when she had seen so much more beneath it, and let the topic go.

"Well, we are all of us the better for it. You are our peacekeeper. Our Benvolio."

"Hmm. I quite like that. You know, my sweet friend, you are a very different girl, to the one I met last year."

"We are all changed... whether for the better or not, who knows," she murmured.

"It is for the better, certainly, and we all see it. You care more for others, for your sisters, and for Rebecca. You have discovered more room in your heart, Katherine."

"Well, perhaps I realised I did not need quite so much for myself," she said with a self-deprecating laugh.

"Or perhaps someone else has caused you to examine it...?" he asked pointedly and she sighed.

"Let us not share the hopelessness of our situations Wesley. For we are too young, and a good deal too attractive to be so miserable," she said, a bittersweet tone. "Let us think of pleasant things, and salvage what we can from our respective prospects of a lifetime's disappointment. Or, perhaps we should marry each other, and spend our days providing endless sympathy and cakes for each other." Wesley threw his head back with a laugh.

"I am sure we should want something more than sympathy from a partner in life, not to mention the profound expanse of our waistlines at a lifetime filled with nothing but cake, despite its obvious attractions.

And, as to us marrying from common cause, there is one, at least, who might raise objection to the prospect."

"Oh? You surprise me, my Lord. And who would that be?"

Wesley smiled at her, rather devilishly then, and spun her around, under his arm, quite out of sequence with the dance, and let go, sending her spinning away into the hard chest of a man standing behind her.

"Miss Fairfax," he bowed.

"Lord Ashford," she stammered, her face flushed and heart beginning to pound.

"Please, I believe it is past time you called me Charles," he said smoothly, taking his hand in hers, and lightly kissing the back.

CHAPTER 3

"*L*ord Charles... what are you doing here?" she stammered, still trying to catch her breath. He smiled at her, stepping closer and pulling her tightly into a dance. Katherine barely noticed they were moving, so absorbed was she in the man before her. He looked the same, yet different. His skin was tanned, his hair longer, yet his broad frame and dark eyes, mercifully unchanged. His smell was familiar, but also somehow wilder and more exotic - salt, storm, and spice. It swirled around her as they spun, and she felt drunk and windswept and hungry with longing. The look he gave her now, the warm smile, the intent expression, so different from what she had experienced from him recently, yet so similar to how he used to look at her.

She took a deep breath to calm her nerves and glanced away, thinking only of escaping from that face, otherwise she would never stand a chance of carrying out a coherent conversation.

"I have been travelling for quite some time, and my foreign interests are concluded at present, so I thought to return home. There is something about London that has occupied my mind, in my absence."

"Really? I am quite surprised, my Lord, to hear that you have thoughts of anything at all save business, when it has never seemed so to me. Pray, tell me what so occupies your mind." He smirked a crooked smile at her, which sent her heart thumping.

"It is terribly impolite to ask a man to confess the thoughts which keep him from his work during the day, and from his sleep in the night. Though, I cannot imagine that such a little thing as impropriety might stop you," he said playfully, his roguish smile quite taking the sting out of the words.

"Ah, well you see, then you have been away too long. You will find me quite reformed - a living monument to good behaviour."

"If that were true, I should be most aggrieved to hear it."

He spun her then, and when she returned to him, the look he levelled her with was so searing, so intimate, that she lost her words entirely.

"I myself am working on my own reform, you will find," he went on.

"Surely not, my Lord, for you are much too good already, and canonisation seems like it would be such a bother." His eyes sparkled, and her stomach filled with butterflies.

"My reform is rather different. I wish to be more like you, Miss Fairfax," he answered, and she laughed at him.

"Never! Certainly, one Katherine is already far too much for this family."

"Indeed, I speak true. You see, I seldom directly say the things I mean," he said, drawing her a fraction closer, "or ask for the things I want." She caught her breath at his tone and flustered a moment before she replied.

"It's true then. I have never suffered from that particular affliction. If you should ever require a teacher..."

"Oh, I know just who to go to," Charles agreed, with the dance ending, he bowed low to place a kiss on her hand.

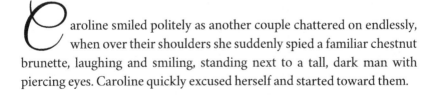

*C*aroline smiled politely as another couple chattered on endlessly, when over their shoulders she suddenly spied a familiar chestnut brunette, laughing and smiling, standing next to a tall, dark man with piercing eyes. Caroline quickly excused herself and started toward them.

"Rebecca!" she exclaimed. As she neared, she saw Rebecca's eyes were large and smiling, her hand was tucked into the crook of Isaac's arm.

"Caroline," Rebecca greeted her warmly and immediately hugged her close. Caroline looked at Isaac's face, over her shoulder and caught a moment of immense gratitude.

"I did not know you would be back tonight! I am so happy to see you," Caroline went on, a thought suddenly tickling the back of her mind.

"You did not know? I would have expected Luke would have told you," Rebecca said, nose wrinkling for a moment in confusion before she pushed it aside and focused on more important things.

"I have so much to tell you. Isaac, we need some privacy," she said imperiously, flashing him a look, with Isaac took in his stride, a grin playing around his lips.

"My dear, as you wish. But I shall find you soon enough, for tonight, all your dances are mine," he smiled, warm and open, bowing and sauntering off into the crowd.

"Come, let us find somewhere private," Rebecca said, pulling Caroline's arm, she held back.

"Wait, did your brother come with you?" Caroline asked, seeing a familiar impatient look on Rebecca's face.

"Yes, of course. He has been insufferable since you left. He jumped at the chance to stop playing chaperon and return to you."

"Where is he?"

"I'm sure I don't know, he came with us, however, so he is around here somewhere; no doubt lurking in the shadows, avoiding society as much as possible and keeping his eye on you."

At her words, she felt as if his eyes were on her, though she glanced around and could see no sign of him.

"Very well, let us go," Caroline finally agreed, starting forward with a new lightness in her step.

***

*L*ucian looked down on the two, heads close in each other's confidence, as they started away to the refreshment area. He recalled the night, a year ago, when he had found himself watching Caroline, drawn to her even then. As other girls rushed around, giggling and gossiping, she had been an oasis of calm, a repose for the eye. He had raised a toast to her, and she had stared right back. It had intrigued him, her fearlessness, though now he knew her, he knew it was that very attribute that had lured him in. Her strength. It was strength that gave her the stillness, that self-containment, that independence; for she had faced loss and tragedy in her past, and risen from them, as a phoenix from the ashes. How his life had changed, how she had changed it, he mused as he watched Rebecca pulling Caroline excitedly, every bit as part of his family now, as he was.

His sister was struggling to contain her enthusiasm, all her masks of cool indifference dropped for once, and it made him happy to see her so excited. One of the hardest burdens to bear had been knowing Rebecca's sacrifice for him, and he had dreaded finding out who her betrothed would be. But, unexpectedly, Silus had allowed Isaac Taylor to ask for her hand. It puzzled Lucian, though, he supposed that the Taylors had tied themselves up financially with his father to achieve it, which they would surely regret in the future, and his father had always had an uncharacteristic soft spot for Rebecca.

His father. The thought of him caused him to raise his glass back to his lips and gulp down a little more stinging brandy. When he arrived at the ball, his eyes immediately seeking out Caroline, he had seen them together, on the terrace. His impulse had been to approach them, take Caroline away, yet he had stopped himself. She was not in need of his protection, it seemed, in fact, Silus looked more disturbed by their conversation than Caroline did. Of course, he did, for it was what she excelled at, disarming people, stripping apart defences.

Now, he watched the two women disappear and reasoned that he could wait for his reunion with his wife, for surely after he made his presence known, they would not stay long at the ball, and Rebecca deserved to share her happy news with someone.

He spied Wesley, far below, and raised his hand. His younger brother seemed agitated and excited, and Lucian followed his gaze to a handsome couple on the dance floor. Charles and Katherine Fairfax. His elder brother had returned as he had hoped, and Lucian could see his genuine expression of pleasure at being reunited. Lucian cast a last glance down at the seething floor and checked his pocket watch. He could barely hold off going to find his wife and gave his sister thirty minutes more to herself, then, he would not wait a moment longer.

❀

*C*aroline watched as Isaac swept Rebecca onto the dance floor, and was happy that, whatever the outcome of her plan, that she had helped to make at least that moment happen. Rebecca was happier than she had ever seen her. Katherine also seemed to bound with joy, though she was working to conceal it. Caroline was not surprised by it - Charles had finally returned to her side. Charles was more difficult to read, ever the gentleman, and not one to display emotion freely, he was a closed book to her. As she watched Wesley ask Katherine to dance, and they looked to her for permission to abandon her alone on the sidelines, she felt warm hands slide up her arms from behind. The person said nothing, only leant in, bringing their body fully against her back.

"If you are not my husband... I fear for your life, sir," she teased and felt the way Lucian smiled into her hair.

"Happily for me, my lady, I happen to be the lucky mongrel," he murmured, moving to the dance floor and taking her hand. "I am glad to see that my reputation precedes me, even in my absence," he noted, pulling her into his arms and joining the waltz.

"Meaning?"

"It is the only reason a woman as ravishing as you could possibly stand by the edge, partnerless," he said with a grin, and she smiled up at him. They danced in silence for a while, their eyes unwavering from each other's, and Caroline felt her cheeks begin to ache from the smile she could hardly keep from her lips.

"I missed you," she said simply.

"As I did you. In the future, I forbid you from travelling without me. Anywhere. Ever."

"Well, then you must stay close at my heels, my Lord, like a well-trained puppy." He roared at that, and his eyes softened.

"I am so relieved to see you well and happy," he said before something pulled at his brow. "What was my father bothering you about earlier?" he asked suddenly, studying her face. She stared at him, trying to smooth her features, and hoping that he did not see the guilt and worry that settled there.

"Oh, nothing of importance."

Lucian stared back looking uneasy.

"Care to elaborate?"

"It is of no consequence, I'd much rather hear about Westmere, I miss it so."

He studied her a while longer, and then pulled her close again.

"I will not press you. Nothing matters more than that you are back by my side, and all is well in the world again."

"Lucian? I wish to go home soon," she said suddenly, looking up at him.

"Are you feeling unwell?" he asked, worried. She smiled reassuringly and shook her head.

"Not at all, I have just missed you too much to share you with all of these people," she murmured softly, and a smile crept across his face.

"Then let us leave at once, for if you have missed me, think of a man in a hot, sandy desert, wishing for water, and you begin to have some inkling of how I have missed you, my love."

*Silus watched them go, an unpleasant feeling forming in his stomach. Lucian looked happy, could hardly contain his smile, like a simpering fool. The girl glided beside him, lighting up the room as she passed. He had loved Esther, loved her desperately, yet she had never once looked at him with the love and acceptance that Lucian's wife regarded him with. Was there anyone less deserving in the world of such devotion? He thought not. This thorn in his side, this child, this man, whose very existence was the living proof that Silus had never himself been loved, that even his beloved Esther had never once been his, though he had worked so hard to bend her to him, her heart and her body had always belonged to another, and now that they were both long dead and buried, it did not give him a moment's satisfaction, any peace. Instead, it continued to fester in his stomach and rot him from the inside, without even a woman to strike for it, or her lover to run through with his sword. And, every time he saw Lucian's face, his eyes so much like his father's, or his smile, ever more frequent now, so very much like his dear mother's; sick, hot hatred, self-loathing, and loss, threatened to drag him down into that dark abyss. He hated that weakness in himself, and he had tried now for two decades to cut it from him in whatever way possible, but it had succeeded in nothing but a family who feared and hated him every bit as much as their mother had in the end.

He had not planned for her, he had not thought for even a moment that someone as strong as Caroline could love his son. Love him and his family enough to give away her fortune and sell her birthright to see them happy. Silus had become the villain in the piece, yet again, when it should have been Lucian. She was unfathomable. Her unflappable steadiness, holding Silus in the unflinching gaze of those wide, almond, uncanny eyes, made him say things that he should not: slipping, showing his hand, his weaknesses.

He growled and resisted the urge to throw his glass onto the dance floor below. He had wanted tears and desperation. He had wanted Lucian's fury. He thought the acquisition of her parent's lands, an estate that rightfully belonged to Lucian, would grieve her, and with any hope, part the two lovers, but she had not batted even an eyelid. She seemed altogether too content with the negotiations. He had not anticipated such selflessness, such goodness. He did not know it existed.

🌺

*T*he room was dimly lit, only a few candles burned low. Caroline relaxed back against Lucian's chest, the warm water of the bath swirling around them.

"I suppose something may be said for your penchant for indulgence," she mumbled low with eyes closed, admiring the consuming warmth of the bathtub. She was sitting between his legs, both of them submerged in hot water, and she could not remember a more decadent feeling. She felt relaxed and strangely whole again, now that he was with her. There had been such a heavy, nagging exhaustion weighing her down of late, and whilst some was surely due to her condition, the absence of him had also contributed. He had become her closest friend and most devoted ally, her lover and her partner, the laughter in her day, and lately, when she was without him, a physical ache seemed to pervade each moment.

She leant forward, reaching for the cake of soap, and he grumbled a complaint as her body lost contact with his. She passed him the bar and settled back.

"You may as well be of use back there," she teased him, as he lathered the cake between his hands, filling the air with the smell of lavender.

"Oh, I plan to be," he growled suggestively as he placed his foaming hands on her shoulders, starting to knead the muscles there. Caroline sighed and slipped more against him, her naked hips coming into contact with his. Lucian murmured his approval into her hair, as his hands continued their soapy path down her arms, to her hands, and then back up. Caroline felt dizzy with anticipation as his hands once again reached her shoulders and then started down toward her chest. As they neared her breasts, suddenly, they were removed, and she almost cried out at the loss.

"All in good time," he said softly into her hair, sending prickles spreading out from his warm breath against her wet skin. He lathered his hands once more, and she bit her lip, waiting as patiently as she could. When it seemed he was deliberately making her wait, she started to shift round a little, between his legs, bringing both her hands under the water, to rest on the tops of his thighs. The movements caused him to still instantly, and he placed the soap back down, and then his hands were on her breasts. They massaged them, gently squeezing them, rubbing his soapy thumbs over her nipples, again and again, making her arch her back with pleasure.

"Have you missed me, Caroline?" he whispered into her ear and his breath once again made her flush. She nodded.

"Tell me, my love."

"I have longed for you every day," she admitted, feeling one of his hands start to descend to her stomach. She responded by running her hands up and down his inner thighs under the water.

"Missing you has nearly driven me mad with longing. I cannot be without you, Caroline," he murmured, his hand making circles on her abdomen, and Caroline thought wildly of the secret she was holding from him.

"You never shall be," she promised, all thoughts flying from her head as he pressed lower still. When he finally touched her, it was enough to make her head spin. He held her back against him, using his feet to draw her legs open, exposing her completely to his fingers.

"You are mine, my love, as I am yours, without exception. When you sleep in an empty bed, you will hunger for me beside you, as I do you. When your body aches and skin is hot, you will wish for my touch upon you, as I long for yours." Her body had been changing so much in the past two months, that she had not noticed that this part of her too, her desire, was changing as well. She was needier than ever. His touch was already sending her spiralling out of control, and Lucian, recognising the signs, pulled her tightly to him, cradling her tenderly as she was dragged over the edge and lost all control, clinging onto his arms and calling out his name in hoarse gasps. She didn't try to hide it or quiet herself. She knew that he felt the most primal sense of pride, of possession, watching her come undone under his touch. Her body knew his, and his hers and there would never be any other touch they would tolerate. Love on his lips, he whispered vows into her hair, wet against her neck as he kissed her.

"I cannot tell you how good it feels to have you in my arms again," he said, tucking her hair behind her ear. "The water has lost its warmth, unfortunately, despite our best efforts to heat it up." Standing, he got out and went for the towels, and as he did, Caroline savoured the long-missed view, admiring his beautiful form: thick, muscled shoulders, beautiful broad chest, narrow hips, strong, thick legs, and superbly firm buttocks. He was a statue in marble, perfect to her in every way. Turning back to her, he picked her up out of the water, gave her a last kiss and lowered her to the ground. She loved when he picked her up as if she was nothing. Bending down, he picked up a towel and started to dry her. She went to take it off him, but with a smile, he pulled it away from her and continued his attentive drying. He walked around her, kneeling to dry her legs and feet, bringing his hands slowly over her form, appreciating every curve and hollow on the way.

"Perfection," he said, raking her naked skin with his hot gaze before leading her to the bed. Her nightgown was already laid out for her. It was high-necked and prim, falling to her feet and made of thick white fabric. He lowered it over her head and raised an eyebrow at her.

"I did not know I would be receiving visitors this evening, much less my husband," she replied and laughed as his expression darkened. He grabbed the towel from his waist and rubbed his hair dry, and Caroline crawled up the high bed and slid under the covers, unable to keep her eyes from the naked form of him. He was glorious, undeniably male, his hard, uncompromising body made her mouth dry. As he turned back, a grin suggesting that he knew he had been holding her attention, she looked away and feigned absorption with fixing her hair. She undid the pins and let the heavy curtain fall down her back. Lucian picked her hairbrush up on his way to the bed and slid naked under the covers. He sat back and held his arms open, and she snuggled into her place, enjoying their routine. Leaning forward she closed her eyes as the hairbrush began to move through her hair, firmly, easing out knots and tangles, pulling pleasurably on her scalp.

"Charles has returned, you did not give me any warning," Caroline said.

"He wanted to surprise Katherine, and the date had not been decided. Was she happy to see him, do you think?"

"Of course, what woman could fail to be?" The brush stopped for a moment, before continuing and Caroline hid her smile.

"I did not know you found my brother... so attractive."

"Well, I do have eyes, and he is just such a splendid specimen of a man."

"Caroline-" he grumbled.

"I jest! Silly, man," she laughed. "Truthfully, I have never had a brother before, and Charles and Wesley feel every day more like my own flesh and blood. It's a nice, cosy feeling, to have a family of my own."

"It does my heart good to hear you say so." He brushed her hair with tender fingers, and it made Caroline feel safe, treasured and wrapped up. "I am greatly relieved that Rebecca is getting the gentleman she cares for," Lucian said, changing the subject, "though I confess, the whole thing took me rather by surprise."

"Hmm," Caroline agreed, a little noncommittally.

"I do wonder how Isaac Taylor has managed it, however, as I know Silus too well to believe he is doing it purely for love of his daughter."

"Perhaps he has had a change of heart..." Caroline said. Lucian's hands forgot their work as he drifted off, pensive and silent. She took the brush from his hand and put it down on the table. Leaning away, she quickly tied her hair into a thick plait, which lay over her shoulder as she snuggled down under the covers and faced him, their poses mirroring each other. He looked tired and peaceful, and she thought that perhaps her news should wait until morning. As her hand moved unconsciously to her stomach, however, she realised she could wait no longer.

His eyes had drifted shut and his breath was even. She gathered her courage.

"Lucian," she whispered, softly, seeing his eyes flutter at the sound of his name, yet remain closed.

"Yes, my love," he replied and she bit her lip, unsure how to tell him.

"I have a present for you," she said, nerves building in her as she watched a smile spread over his full lips.

"And what would that be?" he murmured.

Hesitantly she reached out for his hand, and then slowly, deliberately, brought it to her stomach. She spread his fingers out and pressed his splayed palm to her. His eyes slowly opened, and looked at her, a hint of confusion, then dropped to his hand on her stomach. He sucked in a gasp, his eyes were round with shock.

"Good God. Is it true? Am I to be a father?" Caroline scanned his face and saw that it was awash with conflicting emotions, moving like ripples across the top of the water. She nodded slowly and grasped his hand tightly against her.

Lucian looked back to Caroline then, and she saw the moment where fear slipped away. Tears began to glisten at the corners of his eyes, and he let out a laugh, overcome, and smiled so joyfully, that she felt all of her own fear fall away with his. He leant forward and pressed a kiss on her lips, softly, like a prayer.

"Thank you," he whispered against her lips and followed it with another sweet kiss. He then pulled away and dropped his head to her stomach, where he began to press soft kisses on the taut flesh there, feeling her hands come to rest on his hair, cradling his head to her.

"Thank you," he whispered after each kiss, and Caroline felt the words echo through her very bones.

She brought him back to her, and cradled his face in her hands, and she kissed him, tears clouding her eyes, grateful and relieved that this secret between them was no more, and she felt perhaps closer to him than she'd ever done, now that they shared this thing so much bigger than the both of them. She felt they were in the cottage, confessing all their secrets into the cold night air and unfurling together, pressing ever closer, binding themselves as one. Reaching down, Caroline pulled at her nightdress, bringing it over her head and escaping from it, so that her skin could press against Lucian's, and then fit herself to him in the way that they used to in that old hay cot in the woods.

His skin was so warm, so smooth, and she ran her hands along it, feeding from the feel of it under her fingers. He held her so tightly that she knew he'd never let her go. Another long, languid kiss stirred him against her belly, and she could not help the answer in her own body, reaching out for him.

"You have given me life, Caroline, in so many ways. When I was swallowed by darkness, you breathed your light into me, when I nearly died, you saved me, and now this, it is too much to bear," he kissed her face in reverent praise. "New life, a child, a family. You are a wonder."

He kissed every part of her body, every inch of her stomach, her hips, her thighs, speaking his promises into her skin, up her ribs, to her sensitive breasts, and she threaded her fingers through his hair, pulling him tighter, as need pooled in her belly.

When they finally came together, it pulled a sigh of contented relief from Caroline's lips, that she was whole again after so long apart. They moved together tenderly, caressing, as they did, every inch of exposed skin in gentle devotion, holding each other close, their kisses forging this new bond, and they entered together into this new stage of their life. Caroline's body too, was new, and she yearned for him in a new way, as he stroked the inside of her, sliding to his hilt, every bit of him hers, gently pulling from her love, and lust, and satisfaction.

Tears slipped down her cheeks, and Caroline realised that never in her whole life had she ever felt so loved, so adored, so cherished. He kissed the salt tears from her cheeks, and they held tight to each other as they tumbled together into blissful oblivion.

CHAPTER 4

~August 1810~
London

"*T*hank you so much for this, Mr Fairfax. I cannot tell you how much I appreciate it."

"Humph. I still do not understand why you would have any dealings at all with that *odious* man, but I will leave off lecturing you further, as the thing is quite done and dotted now, and there is nothing for it but to sigh." Caroline smiled and kissed him on the cheek.

They stepped out onto the leafy pavement, the trees of London thick with lush foliage and a warm, lively sun making the pale sandstone and marble of the streets glow. They got into the waiting carriage and started away from his lawyer's office and back to the Fairfax's townhouse. Caroline had told Lucian she would be spending the entire day there with Katherine. She had indeed gone there first, before making this trip with Mr Fairfax to finalise the transfer of the deed, and now they were returning home.

The thought of double-crossing Lord Silus had been even more uncomfortable than she had expected, when it came to signing the papers; however, she had gone through with it. She could see no other way for Rebecca and Isaac. What surprised her most was that it wasn't just the fear of the consequences of duping Silus that made her nervous, but the feeling of guilt for betraying someone with whom she had begun to forge a connection, however small and tenuous it may have been. She felt that the interest and consideration that he had been beginning to show her lately was clearly unusual for the man, and try though she might, she could not ignore it. On long sleepless nights, when her belly pressed on her and her worries taunted her awake, she wondered if things could have been different. If she could have appealed to the man, and made her way slowly into his heart with a patience and kindness that he was probably unaccustomed to being shown, rather than with this lie on her lips and betrayal in her heart.

Caroline knew she was soft-hearted, too softhearted most of the time, yet, when it came to family or someone she loved, she could be as fierce as a lioness. She knew that she could not let the fact that Silus had shown her a softer side of himself in recent months sway her. Too many tears had fallen, too many hopes and dreams dashed for that man to succeed in his plots to keep his children from happiness, either for his own gain or simply for the desire to make them unhappy. She reminded herself often of Lucian's rough-healed heart, and dark childhood, and it helped to strengthen her reserve.

Now that the deed was officially made over, the wedding could go ahead, and hopefully, Lucian would never know what had happened.

They arrived at the Fairfax's and entered, finding a company already assembled in the drawing-room. Upon entering, Caroline felt her stomach drop seeing Charles standing to greet them, Katherine by his side, a look of pure happiness on her face. She hoped Charles would not mention to her husband that she had been out, as Lucian was sure to ask why and where she had gone with Mr Fairfax. She forced a smile at Charles, one which quickly became a look of alarm, as a throat-clearing across the room pulled her attention, and she forgot about Charles letting her secret out.

He was also standing, his golden hair glowing in the light thrown from the window, his blue eyes slightly narrowed, and he missed not one moment of her discomfort as she smiled at him, a beat too slowly.

"My lady," Lucian said, bowing to her, his smirk already indicating that she had some explaining to do.

"My Lord, I thought you were engaged at home?" Caroline said, trying to sound light and nonchalant.

"I was, but when Charles expressed his intentions to call, I thought... why not visit my lovely wife?" he said, and Caroline could swear he was enjoying her discomfort.

"Hmm," she said, turning away from him, flashing a desperate look at Katherine.

"Capital. I shall leave you young people to it then," John said from the door, disappearing to his study, the door closing behind him.

"Caroline, I am so glad you are back, and I am sure my father is very grateful for your assistance," Katherine said, sitting down slowly, her face the picture of innocence. Caroline felt relief flow through her. If she had to lie, at least she had a master at her call, she thought.

"And what would the nature of this assistance be?" Lucian enquired from his chair, where he was sitting, his casual pose fragile, though it did not fool Caroline, who sat fidgeting, and avoiding his eyes. He had been growing increasingly suspicious of her secrets.

"Please, Lord Lucian, it is not polite to enquire so," Katherine said, imperiously, shooting a smug smile at Charles as she did so. As Charles and Katherine locked eyes with a crackling tension, Caroline grew aware she could no longer stare at them, pretending to be engrossed in their conversation, as they had lapsed into silence.

"Caroline," the way Lucian called her name, as always, gave her chills. However, this time there was something altogether more challenging and dark in his tone. She stood up and moved to the divan where her husband sat, steeling herself to lie more effectively.

"Come along, my love, we both know you are going to tell me where you were..." he said in a teasing tone, yet she could hear a hint of vulnerability underneath. "No more secrets...did we not pledge?" he said softly, and she raised her eyes to his face. His playful mask had dropped and she could see how puzzled he was that she was keeping things from him.

"I am sorry I did not tell you before... I was going to the doctor, and I wanted Mr Fairfax to take me. He is still the closest I have to a father. As for not taking you, I am already nervous, women in my family do not carry children easily, and I did not want to worry you," she said and held her breath, guilt thudding now through her belly. She felt the poisoned words settle over her as her husband regarded her, and she waited. When she felt sure that he would not speak, he finally broke his silence.

"I am sorry you felt you had to bear that burden alone. In the future, I would far rather carry it than have you do so alone... please, involve me, Caroline," he said and she smiled, tears prickling her nose. She felt wretched. At least it was done, she reminded herself, the papers signed, the wedding could go ahead, and soon this would all be over. She could only grip his hands tightly, turning her face away, sure he would see her deception. But he said nothing, only put his arm around her, and called for tea to be brought, insisting on extra biscuits, worrying that Caroline had over-exerted herself.

❀

*L*ucian put on a brave face, in public and with Caroline; however, the truth was that in his worst moments, the thought of his impending fatherhood made it difficult to breathe. The fear and anxiety of Caroline's condition hounded him, suffocating his every waking hour with hideous, apocalyptic visions of a world without her. And, he was having recurring dreams of his own childhood, the most memorable parts, not usually the most pleasant parts. He had awoken one night from such a dream to find Caroline watching him.

"What do you dream of when you wake so?" she asked curiously. He sighed, gathering her to his chest.

"I am dreaming of when I was a child. When I knew nothing of the world, or my place in it. I knew only that my father did not love me as he loved my siblings. Lately, I have also been dreaming of my mother."

"Really? I thought you could not recall her,"

"I was old enough when she died that I should recall her... it is strange. Lately, I have been recalling her with child, I think. Perhaps it is your lovely silhouette that has reminded me. I seem to remember her with child, and I was afraid for her. In my recollections she seems not calm or peaceful, as you do, my dear, she seems vulnerable, and scared," he answered, focusing on the hazy memory of a woman, her face hidden in shadow, flinching every time a door slammed. He turned his attention to Caroline and looked at her through the dark of the room.

"I cannot fail to notice that your own dreams, terrors, have abated."

"Yes, they seem to have... I do not miss them."

"Do you feel, perhaps, a bit freer now to tell me more about them?"

She was quiet, her fingers interlacing with his; playing with them. Finally, she spoke.

"I awoke to a world aflame. My father came for me, he carried me out. I can still remember the smoke, and the fire, the way it dripped down from the ceiling, devouring the walls. He carried me outside and put me down. He went to leave me, and I begged him to stay. The house was a ball of fire. No one was coming out of that house again. A neighbour tried to prevent him, pleaded with him not to leave me parentless, not to sacrifice himself... but he couldn't. He looked at me and said he was sorry... he was sorry he couldn't stay with me, but he couldn't live without my mother, and he couldn't leave her in there to die alone. He kissed me, and he was gone. I hope he found her, somehow, before the entire place crashed down, I hope he found her, and they were together," she finished, feeling choked by her memories.

Lucian was quiet and simply held her closer. No wonder she feared losing control. Her father had been selfish in the end, and loved his wife more than his daughter... and it had touched Caroline in every part of herself. He pulled away and looked down into her face, gently wiping away the stray tears that had fallen.

"You will never be alone again, I will always choose you, my love, my life... for there is nothing other than you."

"And if you had to choose? Between me or our child?" she asked, quietly.

"It shall never happen."

"If it did..." she insisted. He sighed and looked away from her, unable to take her the intensity of her eyes.

"What would you have me do?" he asked looking back, his voice quiet.

"You already know, my love." He hesitated, stroked her hair back from her forehead, before lowering his mouth to press a kiss there.

"Then I would do what you ask, for I only ever want to make you happy... I will choose to keep our little one safe, no matter the cost to either of us, even if just to say such a thing is unfathomable... a blasphemy that rips at my heart. I am sure I would never be faced with such an ungodly decision; but nevertheless, you have my word."

"Thank you," she whispered, and smiled at him, a smile so pure as to chase away the ghouls of such morbid thoughts, and he brought his mouth to hers, hoping to capture it, hoping that the warmth of it could drive the cold from his bones and doubts and insecurities from his heart.

🍂

The weeks passed in London, and the season bore relentlessly onward as the temperature soared. The Fairfaxes and Caroline found it amusing, the way the English sweated out their mild summer, complaining at every opportunity as a great national pastime, while Caroline herself longed for the searing heat of Virginia, and the great, breathtaking expanse of sharp wooded mountains which came to life under the warmth of that golden sun.

Caroline's legal arrangement was finalised, and her pregnancy continued to progress, without incident. Katherine and Rebecca remained in London, the former driving the wedding speculators wild with curiosity, and the latter eagerly planning her wedding in a radiant bliss with the help of both Caroline and Katherine, all of whom continued to forge a stronger bond, and allow to fade away those painful memories of the summer before.

Lucian found himself at leisure, as Silus had ceased his incessant demands for Caroline's fortune, inexplicably. Lucian instead spent all of his time with his beautiful wife, her skin growing even more luminous, her smile ever ready, her appetite for chocolates increased, watching her grow, their time together seeming even sweeter, getting used to the idea that soon, it would no longer be the two of them.

🍂

The wedding had come before Caroline could even have a dress made that would fit properly. It seemed to Caroline that both Rebecca and Isaac were in a hurry, not only to be man and wife, but also for fear that Silus might change his mind, and withdraw his consent. Caroline was glad of their haste to the alter, as it was a fear that she also shared.

Though the crowd was small, and the notice short, Rebecca, who had spent much of her youth dreaming of the day, and had been well prepared to whip up a breathtaking wedding in no time at all.

When Caroline had looked up from her chapel pew, and saw Rebecca walking down the aisle, her heart had stopped and her breath caught, and the sweet pain in her chest bloomed and brought tears to her eyes. Then Rebecca smiled at Isaac, and it was the most radiant, most unguarded, unbridled, earnest joy that she had ever seen on Rebecca's face, perhaps that she had ever seen anywhere - it was a living breathing thing, it flew to him. When she looked to Issac, and he smiled back at her, dumbstruck with true love, Caroline had hiccuped, and floods of tears began to stream down her cheeks, in such a well of emotion that Caroline hadn't the strength to hold back. Her beloved sister-in-law and her childhood playmate, they had found love here, across an ocean, and across the gulf of their class divide, despite Silus, despite, or maybe because of, their constant bickering, it was love, and it was all too much for Caroline to handle.

She wept in that pew, she made a scene of herself, and it was a blessed relief. From the first day that she had begun to plot against Silus, worry and fear had seeded and gown each day, and with demanding speed. It was a thing that chased her, that she could never escape from, even for a moment, even in sleep. But there, watching Rebecca and Isaac commit to a lifetime of loving one another, she knew she had been right. She had managed it, and it was worth every moment of planning, every minute of anxiety, every nightmare, it had been worth signing over her parents' land to someone like Silus, it had been worth it all, and she would have done it all over again, for a moment such as this.

Lucian had put his arm around her, and squeezed her close, handing her his hankey. Blowing her nose, both arms now around her round belly, Caroline looked up through her tears at Lucian, and there she saw an emotion in his eyes that she had not seen since their own wedding day, and she could not help but be proud of what she had wrought.

⊛

A week after the wedding, Lucian had planned an outing with his sister, for a very expensive luncheon where they would discuss her upcoming journey to the continent, and shop for any last-minute things that she might need for her travels. Isaac had moved into the Ashford townhouse, rather than Rebecca move into his, as it was far larger, and it would not be long before Isaac had something more suitable secured.

Lucian waited uncomfortably in the house of his youth, whilst his sister dallied upstairs. Rebecca had wanted to include Caroline in their plans, yet Caroline was growing more and more exhausted by the pregnancy. The afternoon would be a pleasant one, nonetheless, and he was happy at least for the quality time that he would spend with his sister when he knew that it would be in shorter supply now that she was a married woman. As he waited, however, those warm feelings grew stale, and he was beginning to regret it, as she took an absurd amount of time preparing. How could any woman need so much time? He heard the door opening behind him, and was met with the very face he had hoped to avoid.

"Ah, Lucian, you are still here I see. If past experience is any measure, Rebecca will not reemerge anytime soon. Join me in my study for a drink," he commanded and left without a response. Lucian stood, with his fists clenched, cursing his sister for a moment, before moving after Silus.

The room was dark and smelled of cigars and brandy. His father was already settled behind the desk, a glass in hand. As Lucian entered slowly, he noted that he had not been poured one, and chose to sit, rather than taking one himself. He stared at Silus, wondering what game he might be playing. Silus looked at him with a merry twinkle in his eye.

"Your little wife looked fit to burst at the wedding, and I realised that I had never properly congratulated you," Silus smiled lazily. Lucian remained still, not giving anything away. "Though, perhaps I should warn you... children are not always a blessing," Silus said with a little frown.

"Is there a point to this conversation?"

"Can a man not congratulate another on their good fortune?"

"Some can. Can you, father?" Lucian ground out. Silus merely chuckled, raising his glass in acknowledgement of the barb.

"That wife of yours. I have not seen her of late. Is she much affected by the pregnancy? Is she properly seen to? Which doctor do you have on call?"

"Why do you ask?"

"Merely passing the time, boy." Silus took a deep breath and adopted a more pacifying tone. "Your mother had no problem bearing children, but many of her friends perished."

"She is strong. She stays at home, mostly, and we have Doctor Keeble to attend her."

"Keep her contained inside. Women should not be out and about in this heat and rabble, especially when with child," Silus muttered, looking into his glass.

"If I didn't know better, I would think you worried after Caroline's health, father," Lucian said, his tone slightly mocking, unable to believe the show of concern that the older man was putting on. Silus cared little enough for any of them, and nothing at all for Lucian, and that would never change.

"Well, luckily, you know better, don't you, boy. I suspect, out of our whole family, only you truly understand me."

"I would not claim that."

"Oh, I would not be too sure... you understand me because you are me. We are the same, Lucian, it is why we cannot stand each other."

"I cannot stand you because you have made my misery your life's purpose."

"Perhaps... as one might destroy a reflection they hated in the mirror. Perhaps I think that the world only needs one of me..."

"It has only one."

"That is where you are wrong, my dear boy, you are me, and everyone knows it, even your dear, sweet wife," Silus said, and Lucian swallowed at the tone that entered Silus's voice as he spoke of Caroline. He was drunk, Lucian knew, though with Silus, it was not always easy to tell.

"Stay away from Caroline. You have no business with her," he said.

"Don't I? There is much you don't know of your innocent, honest wife. I suppose she is an expert at deception, women such as her always are. I pity you, my son, for you know not what is coming for you."

"Do not speak of her. You are not worthy even to say her name," Lucian said, standing, his fists clenched, his rage building. His father spoke of Caroline intimately, almost possessively, and it made him mad with rage. Silus stood suddenly, his face twisted in fury, he leant across his desk.

"I remember well when I was just as you are now... married to a deceitful siren, growing ripe with child... who even knows if it is truly yours. God's teeth, Lucian, she almost married another man mere months ago! Have you learned nothing from my mistakes?"

Lucian took a deep breath, drew it in and out evenly, forcing the anger from his face. He spoke quietly, calmly.

"I have indeed learned from your example, father, and I will not be a man like you, and I will not treat my wife as you did yours, nor my children."

"How about a bastard?" Silus mocked.

"My child will not be a bastard. And even if they were, they would still be a child, innocent, and in need of love. I would not condemn them to this..." he waved his hand in Silus's direction, "mockery of parenthood."

"I wonder if your wife knows your liberal policy on adultery, perhaps I shall take advantage of it for your next born... why wouldn't she prefer a version of her husband with more experience?" Silus had moved around his desk now and was standing close to Lucian. Lucian barely restrained himself from attacking the older man. His words caused a red haze to descend over him, and he could barely think straight. He was grinding his teeth so hard he tasted blood.

"All these little chats we've been having. She's been begging me for a little attention," Silus whispered, and Lucian lost his remaining restraint. His punch took Silus on the left side of his face and sent him sprawling across the desk. Lucian was on him in an instant, hauling him up again, and pulling his arm back to send another blow across his jaw.

"Luke! Father! Stop this! What is happening?" Rebecca screamed from the doorway, running to Lucian's side. She pulled at his arm, and he paused in his blow, still standing toe to toe with Silus, still itching to remove the smile from the twisted man's lips. They stared each other down, Silus looked to the side and spat out a long stream of blood.

"So sensitive... Perhaps you trust our wife less than you think," Silus said, pushing Lucian away and staggering back against the desk. Rebecca was crying now, and Lucian put his arms slowly around her, his eyes not leaving Silus.

"Luke, come on, let us leave. Neither of you will speak sense at this moment," Rebecca implored him, yet he could not tear his eyes from his father, lounging so confidently against his desk, his face the picture of arrogance.

"Lucian!" Rebecca begged once more, tugging at his arm, and eventually, he let himself be led away. He felt numb and overwhelmed by the words of that hateful man. This is what he did best, Lucian knew that; yet, there was something in his manner, in his very tone, that hinted that he was privy to something that Lucian was not, and it had given him the confidence to taunt him.

He shuddered as he thought of how he had spoken of Caroline, of lying with her. He desired her. The thought turned his stomach, bile rising in his throat. He remembered them together at the ball. She probably had no notion of her effect on him, of the thoughts that were running through his mind when he looked at her. To imply that Caroline's child was not his was ridiculous, and Lucian did not believe it for a moment.

However, there was no denying that Silus had taken an interest in Caroline, one he had not had before she came to London without him. There had been something off in her manner: a hesitation, unexplained outings or simply an avoidance of his eyes. Though, he could not see how it could possibly be connected to his father. It was a twisted game of Silus's, to torment him, he was sure of it, yet he wondered what truth hid behind the lies.

⊛

*C*aroline kissed her sister goodbye and watched as Charles and led her down the stairs and escorted her to her carriage. Caroline was glad so many of her acquaintances were coming to call on her at home, as she would be lost without their company. The growing child, and the tiredness and fear that came with it, could not be borne without distraction. Her husband was providing one of course, but she had found herself wanting to confide in him about Silus far too much. He was suspicious, she could tell. She had never excelled at deception, and they were altogether too close for any lie to go long undiscovered.

She felt wretched about it and reminded herself often why it was necessary. Perhaps if she had gone to him in the beginning, then it would have been discussed. Yet, he had been in Westmere, she in London, when the issue had presented itself. Whatsmore, there was no predicting how Lucian would have reacted. Silus ignited in him a torrent of dark and unpredictable emotions which were far too twisted to be trusted in such delicate matters. She had taken the steps that she had thought best for them all. She hoped when, if ever, he found out, he would remember that he had always said he valued her strength and independence.

The one element she had not accounted for was Lord Silus himself. He was as hard to predict as Lucian, and he had been a constant drain on her of late. He wrote frequently, with questions about the land and her lawyers. As her visitors disappeared into their carriage, Caroline caught sight of another message boy making their way to her door. She felt the ever more familiar worry grip her stomach at the sight of the Ashford crest on the seal as she bid the footman to pay the boy, and clutched the letter.

"A little late for mail, is it not?" Lucian's voice came from the top of the stairs and she froze as she fixed a calm expression on her face. She slipped the letter into a pocket of her gown and turned around, smiling at him. He was leaning on the balustrade and watching her carefully, a little too carefully. Caroline smiled up at him, and then started forward, slowly climbing the stairs, leaning on the railing as she went.

"Quite. I refuse to read a letter delivered so late, it is rude, is it not?" she said lightly as she drew level with him on the stairs, pausing only a moment before starting upward. Lucian's hand suddenly shot out and rested gently on her arm.

"I could read it for you," he said, his tone matching hers for lightness, yet there was something far sterner just underneath. Caroline stilled, and then slowly, raised her hand and covered his.

"I am too tired. It must wait until morning, I'm afraid," she said and tried to ignore the flash of worry she saw in his eyes. She moved forward again. "Come, will you not join me in bed, husband?" she asked, reaching the top of the stairs, and realising he had not yet moved, only stood staring at the space she had occupied.

"I cannot tonight, sadly. I have promised Wesley I would keep him company at the club..." he said somewhat stiffly. "Unless you ask me not to, I should go," he finished, meeting her eyes for the first time in their exchange. Caroline thought of the letter in her pocket, and how she might possibly obtain the time alone to read it.

"Go, keep Wesley company. I have kept you to myself too much of late - he must miss you." Lucian narrowed his eyes at her slightly and then looked away, his gaze a little distant.

"Very well. Do not stay awake for me, for you know how Wesley likes to see the morning in."

Caroline watched him go, her heart throbbing painfully. She had practically just pushed him away, and it was awful to watch him leave so obviously dejected. She realised it might be the very first time since they were married that he had left her side without a kiss. Her empty cheek seemed a recrimination as she watched him gather his things, and bow to her, his eyes down, and stride out into the night, the door closing with a hollow bang.

Caroline sighed, and turned, walking slowly, she reached her room and sat heavily down on the edge of her bed. She pulled the letter from her pocket, cracked the seal, and opened it slowly, already dreading its contents. She immediately noted that his usual elegant penmanship seemed sloppy and blurred, and the ink not properly blotted.

Dear Caroline,

It pains me to say it, however, I believe I owe you an apology. In recent weeks, I have seen my daughter blossom and flourish under Mr Taylor's attentions. It is you I have to thank for this. It was the condition of our agreement, yet it seems to have benefitted me far more than you.

I fought with Lucian today, and I must admit I came close to confessing our entire arrangement to him. After he left, I have been overcome with memories of his dear sweet mother, and even as I write this, I struggle to remember why I was not to tell him... to reveal the time we have spent together, to reveal the kindness you have shown me, our growing friendship. He should know... I believe he meets Wesley tonight, and I shall finish some business here, and then meet them also, glad of heart...

The rest of the letter was too blurred to read, yet the words she had taken in were alarming enough to send Caroline to her feet and hurrying for her outside wrap. Silus had clearly drunk too much and was now about to stagger to Lucian's gentleman's club and confess everything, perhaps gloat that he had gotten to the Lesage fortune after all. There was no telling what Lucian might do. He would feel as if he had been made a fool, and angry and bitter that his father had succeeded, but most of all, he would be cut to the bone that she had gone behind his back. He would feel she had betrayed him.

She hurried gingerly down the stairs and informed the footman that she needed the second carriage brought round. If he was surprised that she was going out alone so late, he did an admirable job of hiding it, Caroline thought, as she stuffed the letter into her pocket and went out the door into a warm evening. She accepted help into the carriage and then sat back and gave instructions to the coachman. As the carriage lurched forward, she fell back against the seat and wrapped her arms around her middle. What she could do, or say to the man, she was not sure, but she had to try. If Lucian was to hear the whole sordid story, it had to be from her first, of that she was certain, or she risked destroying completely the bond of trust they had so painstakingly built.

❀

*L*ucian watched as she left the house, her face white and worried. He felt the strangeness of the situation; the stark reality of seeing his wife sneaking out of their home in the night, settling like a ball of ice in his stomach. He leant forward and tapped on the carriage, and they began to follow her at a discreet distance. The carriage bounced over the cobbles yet he sat unmoving as a stone, his eyes fixed straight ahead his mind racing. Tonight, he would have answers.

❀

$\mathcal{T}$he patriarch of the Ashford family sat in the shadows of his study, watching the clock tick lazily. Would she come? He wondered. He glanced at the glass in front of him, not nearly as empty as he had feigned. He needed his wits about him, not clouded with alcohol. He picked up the letter from his solicitor he had received that afternoon, just after Lucian had left. As his eyes followed the words he felt a surge of rage well up. She thought she could trick him? This tiny little slip of a girl, barely a woman, of savage blood, matched her wits against his and aimed to rob him of what was rightfully his, of what had been promised to him. She had looked him in the eye, and lied, so earnestly, so believably, so sweetly, that he had loved her for it. He ground his teeth and breathed deeply to calm himself. He had to wait, had to be patient. A knock suddenly sounded at the door, and his bloodied lips turned up into a smile.

"Come in," he called softly.

CHAPTER 5

"*L*ord Ashford, are you well?" Caroline asked hesitantly as she sat down opposite the forbidding looking man behind the desk. His face startled her - battered, his lip cracked by a fist presumably, and intent. The study was dark, long shadows dancing over the bookshelves, licking up the walls and brushing the high ceilings. It choked her.

"Quite well, my dear. You got my letter..." he said, watching as she pulled it from her pocket.

"I did, and I thank you for the kind words, however, I still would have it that my husband was not made aware of our arrangement," she said, watching for a hint of an emotion from Silus, yet there was nothing, he kept his face carefully blank.

"Because of your clever little mind, my daughter Rebecca is very happy, very happy indeed, and we should not have you go unthanked," he said, and Caroline wondered how much he had actually drunk, as he seemed more lucid than she had imagined. "I suppose you are my daughter too now, though I struggle to think of you as one," he said, and his eyes trailed over her for a long moment. Caroline shifted uncomfortably, suddenly aware of her own vulnerability before this man. She swallowed and smiled.

"That shall come, I imagine, given time," she said lightly, adjusting her skirts uncomfortably.

"Ah yes, time. Perhaps with time, I shall see you less as a woman, a temptation, and more as a daughter. Time softens and smooths many things. Perhaps... given time, perhaps, I shall forget how you have tricked me," he said, and at his casual words and studied indifference, she froze. Fear ran like ice up her spine as she sat rigidly, her hands going to cradle her swollen belly.

"What can you mean-" she started, only to be shocked into silence as Silus slammed his fist onto his desk, drumming his violence into the room so loud that it made her jump.

"Lie to me no more, or I swear you shall pay for it!" He roared, rage bulging his eyes like a wild thing. Caroline rushed to her feet and started to back toward the door, but he was faster than her, already rounding his desk, his face already suffused with an eerie calm, he stalked her back toward her chair until she was forced to sit down. "Make yourself comfortable, Lady Ashford, for I have not given you permission to leave," he said darkly, and braced his arms on her chair, leaning forward as he spoke.

"I do not need your permission to leave, and I shan't ask for it," she said forcefully as she went to stand, and gasped as his tight grip descended on her arms, and he squeezed her, hard, pulling her closer to him, and closer still, until only a hair's breadth was left between them. Her heart was pounding, her palms slick with fear, yet, as always, she raised her chin and met his gaze steadily.

"You shall abide me, girl, I have broken stronger women than you before, and they were not in such a... delicate position as you," he said, and suddenly threw her back into the chair. The wooden back jarred her and she fell silent as his voice lowered so deep and dangerous that she had to strain to hear it.

"You gave me..." he said so slowly, each word a threat, "garbage. Useless garbage."

"I gave you thousands of desirable acres, just as we agreed."

"But it cannot be sold, can it? It is Indian land, savage land, and no sale would be valid unless made and duly executed at some blasted public treaty, but you already know all of this, I am quite sure."

"Those lands are yours now. They are forested, the game is abundant, the soil is rich, it can be made quite profitable, with time."

"Ah, and there is that word again," his lips coiled unpleasantly. "I do not have time. If I didn't need the money now, I would never have let my son marry a savage slut like you. And what have I earned with my generosity, huh? Not a farthing. And you coming here all this time, batting your big eyes, saying every little thing I wanted to hear, playing me like a fiddle all along, making me into a fool."

Her heart began to pick up at the look on his face, at the menace in his voice, as she watched him walk back around to his side of the desk, where he sat down, a little too calmly and steepled his fingers, looking at her over the top of them.

"So, now that all our cards are on the table... what am I going to do with you?" he mused.

※

*L*ucian felt his hands tremor, the pressure of being tensed so long grating on his muscles. He sighed and pushed himself out the carriage, where he had been sitting, his gaze fixed on his former home, barely blinking. He walked slowly into the small park that sat just in front. He had come here often as a boy, to escape Silus, and he saw it had changed little. He sat on a bench and covered his face with his hands. His mind was whirling, and he could hardly bring it together. He felt as though all parts of him were disconnected and he had forgotten how to join them together in movement.

Perhaps she was visiting his sister, he thought sourly, as even as the thought formed, he knew it to be untrue, she was out with Isaac that evening at a party. No, there was no denying it, he knew the truth in his bones, she was visiting his father. For what reason, he could hardly guess, yet he had known something was amiss since the night he had seen them together at the ball. His father had hinted as much earlier, and now here was the proof. What business they might have together, he found impossible to imagine, unless his father had lured Caroline in with promises of reconciling the family, or other such nonsense, and Caroline would believe him, for she always looked for the best in people, for a way to forgive what should be unforgivable.

Perhaps it was to do with money, it would certainly explain why Silus had stopped demanding her fortune. Whatever it was, he trusted Caroline. And yet, she had lied to him. She had withheld it from him, whatever it was, and their newfound trust had been secondary, dispensable. It hurt. It seared through him like alcohol on an open wound. He felt shame almost immediately, for he was no paragon of virtue, and he had let her down more times than he could count. But, Caroline was better than him, she always would be, and he wondered what could have motivated her to do this, whatever it was, in secret.

He glanced at the warm lit windows, seeing nothing inside, and clenched his fists again, trying to calm himself, and let the urge to spill Silus's blood retreat.

❀

*C*aroline clasped her hands together to stop her fingers from shaking. He knew the truth, her deception was out. Now, all she could do was get out of this house as fast as possible.

"Did Lucian ever tell you how I courted his mother?" Silus asked suddenly, idly. Caroline shook her head, her eyes darting to the door, wondering how long he planned to keep her here. If she tried to run again, he would get violent, she felt sure.

"I saw her once, at a ball. One look was all it took. I asked her to dance, and she refused me, said she had her dance card all filled up. I saw it later, and it was not full, she just didn't want to dance with me," he said with a bitter laugh.

"She was betrothed, you see, everyone knew of it. He was a Count, or a Duke, or something of the sort, and they were to be married. It was a love match, or so I was told, yet, I have never taken no for an answer when I truly want something. I was persistent, and in the end, I did dance with her. On our wedding day."

"She broke off her engagement?"

"She had no choice. After what happened, her fiance's family disapproved, and their betrothal was broken."

"What happened?"

"Why, I ruined her, of course, much like Lucian did you... however, I was not so shy about it. Charles was born seven months after our wedding," he said, so utterly nonchalantly, she wondered if she had heard him correctly.

"You ruined her?" Caroline said, horror creeping into her tone as she said it.

"Oh, I ruined her in many ways, over the years, but, yes, this was the first time I ruined her... destroyed her reputation, ripped away her dreams, her love..."

"Why?"

"Because I wanted her." Caroline looked away, repulsed.

"Now, do not judge me too harshly, for you forgave my son the same crime."

"I am tired, I wish to leave, Lord Ashford," Caroline announced abruptly, sickened by the story, feeling vomit burn at the back of her throat, and desperate to return home.

"You have not been listening, my darling. Tonight you do what I want." She shot him a look at the false endearments.

"Oh, such fight, such fire... Esther had the same, you know, in the beginning. It was so much more entertaining, watching someone so strong, bend to my will. Later, when the fight was gone, she was much more tedious," he chuckled.

"You cannot keep me here indefinitely," Caroline said.

"Of course not, but I've never needed much time, to get my point across, to teach a lesson, I should have been quite the effective teacher if I had been lowborn," he mused, casually. This was your choice, Caroline. All of this could have been avoided, if only you hadn't tried to cross me," Silus said quietly, his eyes searching hers. "Was anything you said to me real? Or merely a game... how deep does your treachery go?" he asked, and Caroline, seeing the threat in his face, decided to stay silent. He suddenly got up and moved toward her, she gripped the arms of the chair and braced herself. She would not run, show him her fear so he could feed off it.

"How can you forgive Lucian for the things he has done to you?" Silus said as he crouched beside her chair.

"Because I love him. Because I saw the good in him," she said simply and saw Silus's eyes narrow at her. He silently contemplated her, raising a hand to her hair, he tucked it behind her ear.

"Could you see the good in me?" he asked, his voice vulnerable for an instant. She jolted at the contact and made to move, yet his other hand clamped down on her arm.

"Don't move, my dear... don't... make me hurt you," his words held a chilling certainty.

"You don't have to hurt me. You could just allow me to leave. I have given you what you asked, the marriage is done, our business is quite over," she said as calmly as she could. He turned his attention to her arm, where he ran his finger gently down it.

"Quite over, is it? Oh, I don't think so, my dear," he murmured, his eyes intent on his fingers path down her arm, over her trembling hands.

"What do you mean to do?" she demanded. She was not in control, but nor would she allow herself to be toyed with. He ignored her.

"Everyone is happy, aren't they? Rebecca got her marriage, that Taylor got my girl, Lucian his happy wife and growing baby, and you... well, you win, don't you?" She stared at him, fear choking her, her eyes wild for a moment. "I have been your little plaything, haven't I? It was not enough to trick me, to make me a fool. You wanted me to grow to trust you, to learn to... care for you-"

"Lucian knows I am here, he will come for me," she said, struggling to keep her voice calm. Silus looked at her pityingly.

"I highly doubt that. Though, if he should, I have prepared for that eventuality. You see, you were not the only person to receive a letter tonight... I happen to have several close friends in the city's legal system. One in particular who is *quite* devoted. I might have mentioned to him... how my bastard has become increasingly erratic and volatile toward me, and even his young wife..."

"No. You can't do this," Caroline whispered as she felt her pounding heart almost make her swoon. His hand moved now to her round belly.

"Ah, and this is the next one, isn't it. The next deceitful, lying bastard in line. Sure to turn out just like his father. Although, now I wonder if that isn't better than the alternative."

The horror of the situation overwhelmed her as she sat there, but his hand, touching her, touching her child was enough to send her from her terror. She lashed out suddenly, surprising Silus, her hand reaching to his face, her fingernails met his skin, and she sank them in as deep as she could manage, scraping a line across his cheek, peeling a curl of flesh away under her fingernails. He swayed backwards as she made it around the desk.

"You bitch," he spat, grabbing his face as he lunged for her.

She bolted toward the door, but his hand suddenly clamped around her arm. She screamed as loudly as she could, as he whipped her around, pushing her against a table, with him before her. He pushed his whole body against hers, and she winced, caving her back in an effort to keep her stomach from the close contact.

He bent her backwards until her spine protested sharply, and she gasped with the pain. His face was in hers, his hot breath crawling down her collar. He leaned in and put his lips to her ear.

"You should not have toyed with me, Caroline. I am not a man to take your little games lightly," he murmured as his teeth scraped her skin. Caroline forced her panic from her mind and twisted her head to the left, looking for something, anything. Her hand closed on a heavy ink blotter, and without a second thought, she brought it down on the back of his head as hard as she could, aiming for the juncture between his head and neck. He cursed and she pushed him away as he fell backwards. She ran around the other side of the table and saw a silver object glittering, and snatched at it. She ran toward the door as fast as she could, glancing back to see that he was still gathering himself, trying to go for her, but stumbling.

She reached the door and breathlessly turned the knob. It didn't move. She tried again, shaking it, and still, it remained closed fast. It was locked, the realisation dawning on her slowly. She was trapped there, at his mercy. Silus, no longer in a hurry, walked toward her. Her back was spasming, and the ripples were reaching her abdomen. She clutched one hand around it for support, hiding the other in her skirts, the silver object gripped hard.

He reached her at the door and raised a hand to her. But he didn't strike her. Instead, he stroked her hair again, slowly, and then wrapped the silky ends of her loosened braid around his fist, pulling her head back, deliberately, until she was arched against him. "Come, dear girl, you must have known what would happen."

Caroline bit her tongue as he moved close behind her, leading her back, from an increasing pressure on her hair, until she was once again against the desk. He turned her to face him, and she saw his eyes were wild, dark and dilated, barely recognisable. He was panting, his face smeared in blood from the deep furrows of her nails. He was enjoying it, she realised with terror.

He smiled at her, and leant forward, burrowing his face in the hair by her neck, breathing in deeply.

"I wish it could have been another way. But, you have brought this on yourself, you must know that," he murmured as his hands moved lower to her stomach. One palm pushed hard against her and channelling her fear and rage into something keener, something sharper and more urgent. She twisted away, and drove the silver object, a letter opener, into him. He bellowed in pain, and hit her hard, across the face, sending her sprawling to the floor. She shook the tears from her eyes and tried to focus them. Her hands were bloody, and she saw him struggling with the sharp object, embedded in him. She had aimed for his heart, and her own sank as she watched him pull the opener free, seeing she had only damaged his shoulder.

"A mistake, little savage!" he growled as he came closer. He then took her hair and started to drag her toward the study door. She opened her mouth then and started screaming as if her life depended on it. It did, she realised.

"Scream all you want, my dear, no one would dare interfere, though there is hardly anyone to hear you tonight," he said as he pulled her along. Caroline used her feet to propel her, lessening the dreadful ripping of her hair.

They approached the stairs. He started to haul her up them. She opened her mouth and screamed again, as loud as she could, crying for help, for Lucian, for someone to hear her. She was suddenly let go, and fell to the marble stair, panting, blood dripping from her ripped scalp. Pain rang through her body. Silus gave her no respite, however, and gripped her by the jaw, lifting her slightly only to slam her body against the wall. She looked up and caught his eyes. They were lit with some kind of madness. It bored into her, this wild, twisted beast, and she could see its blood lust, she could see how it licked its lips at her fear.

"If you kill me, hurt me... everyone will know. Lucian will kill you." She was crying but tried to keep it as much as she could from her voice. Trying to sound strong and commanding. Trying still to reason with him, knowing that anything else, save a miracle, was lost to her.

"I will deal with the bastard, and as for the others... why, I'm not going to hurt you, I will simply find you, after your terrible fall, and weep for you, and people shall console my broken heart. No one would dare question me, I own every rich man in this town. Anyway, my simpering police dog shall make sure I am not troubled by inconvenient questions or false accusations. He continued to drag her up one step at a time, speaking slowly. Her body jarred at each step as bone met marble, carpet, and metal. "That's bastards for you, isn't it? Some turn out to be useful, while others just need to be broken."

Caroline squeezed her eyes shut, afraid to glance at how high up the perilous stairs they were. She screamed again for help, and desperation ripped at her throat, as her fingernails dug into his hands, scratching, scraping, yet he gave not an inch. She realised he had stilled, and gone very quiet. She risked opening her eyes again and saw he was indeed lost in contemplation, staring at her.

"Ester. You're so like Ester. History plays out again and again, and we are so helpless to stop it. I am just the pawn of fate, you see. I will break you and Lucian, just as Ester and I were broken."

"What are you talking about?" She cried. "You are mad," she wept, seeing that nothing she said registered at all, certain he had fallen into some kind of delirium.

"Shh, my love, it will be over soon." He was going to kill her and the baby. Though the thought for her own life was not a concern - if he made her lose the baby by force, she hoped that he would kill her as well, because she wasn't sure that she was strong enough to survive the loss.

She had brought it on herself, he was right. She had been headstrong and foolish. So convinced of her own intelligence and daring, she had led them all down a path of destruction. Lucian. The thought of him broke the remaining pieces of her heart. Her soul, her reason, her purpose. He might never know the whole story, might think she had betrayed him, might think she did not love him as he did her. Soon he would be alone... and the darkness would close in on him again, leaving him to wander, lost in solitude and grief. If this was to be her last breath, she wished she could spend it with him, her last moments in his arms, her last glance of this world, his face. She had tried to play a dangerous game, and she had lost everything. She wanted him to be happy, she had wanted to help him get revenge on Silus, make Rebecca and Isaac happy, and punish the man who had wrought such unhappiness. And now, she would pay the price of her arrogance.

"Help! Someone! Lady Ashford has had a most awful accident!" Silus suddenly shouted, his voice booming and filled with fear and panic. Caroline saw one more flash of lucidity in his eyes before she felt his hands let her go, pushing her as she dropped. She shot her hands out to grab onto something, yet they slid, as slicked with blood as they were. Her last scream caught in her throat, and she went silent with white terror as she watched the stair rise to meet her. Her arms went around her belly, her treasure. Her thoughts of her child and Lucian, and the family they almost had. She held that image in her mind as the world went black.

CHAPTER 6

*L*ucian looked again toward the house, unsure whether he had heard a sound or not. The night was alive outside as carriages rattled past and horses clopped and neighed across the hard cobbles. People stopped and conversed in the street, and the whole of London seemed to be enjoying the warm night air. When he could stand it no more, he stood up and breathed deeply. Sure that he finally had his emotions under control, he strode toward his childhood home, ready to get the answers, and to take his wife home. He had been able to see nothing from the windows, as the curtains had been drawn in the study, and from what he could tell, that's where they were. Surely by now, they would be in the middle of whatever they were up to, and he hoped to discover it all by barging in or listening in, he would play it by ear.

Caroline may have explaining to do, but they would resolve it between them, as they had every other obstacle in their path. He went up the stairs and turned the knob to enter, but found it locked. As long as he knew this door, it had never been locked. Well, so much for the element of surprise. He knocked loudly. After a few moments, and no reply, he knocked again. It was odd, the servants in the house were usually extremely punctual.

He banged a third time and suddenly heard, from the very depths of the house, a scream rise up. It was haunting and rent the air in two. It was not Caroline, Lucian was sure, but someone was screaming, and the sound chilled him to the bone. In an instant, he leaned over the railing, drew back his arm, and smashed one of the windows that framed the entry.

He pulled himself over the railing, over the steep drop down to the basement floors, and pulled himself through the broken window. He ran, blood dripping from his hand and arm onto the floor, following the sound of female shrieking. Then he stopped and felt his world stop turning.

Caroline lay at the bottom of the stairs, completely still. A maid stood over her, crying and hugging herself. Caroline's black hair was fanned out against the royal blue carpet, and all Lucian could think of was how it shone, iridescent almost, like crows feathers, in the candlelight. He moved forward, as though in a dream, and fell to his knees beside her.

She was so still, as he pulled her into his arms. He called out her name, again, and again. Her eyes were closed, and he could see bruises already formed around her mouth, and blood drying on her forehead. He cried out her name, loudly, quietly, a whisper, a scream. She would not wake. Why would she not wake, he asked himself, feeling his reason slip away. Her hands were so pale against her dark gown and so white against the blood that coloured her slender fingers. He saw how her hands still cradled her stomach and felt sick roil in his own. Her child... their child. He smoothed the hair from her face and tried to arrange her comfortably.

"Get a doctor! Go now!" he shouted at the trembling servant, who turned and disappeared in a flurry of skirts.

"Caroline, sweetheart, do you hear me? You are going to be fine, I promise you, just hold on, wait for the doctor... we have seen darker nights than this," he whispered, his words jumbled as they fell from his lips, he could feel tears on his cheeks, yet the rest of his body was cold and numb. All he knew was her fragile weight resting on his legs. So fragile, so breakable, this perfect being. He choked down hysteria as he noticed the paling of her cheeks. Her eyelids did not even flutter.

There was something so familiar about the way she lay, her small body, her risen belly, the odd angle of her leg. He felt so sure in that moment that he had seen it before, somehow, somewhere. As he sat there, cradling his wife's head in his lap, her blood staining the floor beneath them, he felt as though time slowed down, the clock seemed to allow an eternity to lapse between each tick, and he felt himself transported. Taken to another night, when he had found a woman he loved, broken and beaten on the floor. The whirling pieces of memory clicking into place suddenly, a pattern taking shape, something so clear before but never quite revealed.

"I should think it too late for a doctor, however, I am no expert, to be sure," Silus's voice floated from the top of the stairs, as he walked down them. He looked utterly composed as usual, apart from the deep scratches on his cheek, and the strange light in his eyes.

"What a terrible accident," Silus said as he came closer. Lucian felt as though he was detached from his body, as though he was looking down on the scene from a great height. He gently moved Caroline to the floor, and stood, his eyes fixing on the man he had called father once.

"Like mother's accident?" he asked, his voice hollow. Silus scrutinised him, his head to the side.

"Yes, I suppose it does strike a resemblance... how odd, it seems these stairs are quite the hazard."

"What was she doing here at this hour?" Lucian asked, his voice remote, his arms already straining with barely contained violence.

"Why, I told you we were friends, did I not? Anyway, we had some financial matters to discuss, it seems Caroline wanted her fortune to be used for the family's interests..." Silus continued, circling away from Lucian as he stood protectively over her prone form.

"I will kill you for this," Lucian said suddenly, with a deadly finality, stepping toward his father. All emotion was gone from him. He was cold. He was dead on the floor next to his love, his blood mixing with hers.

"You mean you shall try," he retorted. Father and son faced each other in the hall, both strong, both tall and straight-backed. The silence was so deep that it seemed a viscous liquid which must be waded through.

Lucian suddenly lunged forward and landed a heavy punch to the older man's jaw. He staggered backwards, and then suddenly changed direction and ploughed into Lucian, pushing him backwards, hitting the wall hard and driving his breath from him. He ducked under Silus's attack and dodged away from him, turning to deliver efficient blows to his kidneys and head. Silus staggered and went down on one knee. Lucian continued to feel nothing, his emotions unreachable, he was numb, so very cold inside, and struggled to keep the red haze from his vision as it blurred the edges. Stepping forward, he hit Silus in the face, hard, and heard the telling crack. He moved away as the older man fell backwards and hit the ground. Barely out of breath, Lucian looked down at him, as he lay, his face a mask of blood, gurgling as he choked on it. His hands were flailing around him. Lucian looked at him with disgust. The man who had hurt everyone in his life, who had hurt Caroline. He deserved so much worse than death.

A small sound made him whirl around, and he saw Caroline's eyes had now opened and she was looking around her, tears sliding down her cheeks, mixing with the blood on her face. He was at her side in an instant.

"Caroline, I'm here my love," he said, her hand found his, and he gripped it hard. Her eyes, swollen, stared into his. She moved her lips, tried to speak, but he could barely catch the words.

"I can't hear you, sweetheart," he murmured, moving closer, and realised too late what she was trying to impart to him, as her eyes widened and moved over his left shoulder. He went to dodge Silus, but he did not move fast enough. The silver letter opener was cold as it slid into his shoulder, piercing his body with blinding pain.

"I suppose it is a weakness of the men in your family... for your father displayed it also. Never turn away from an enemy, just because they have fallen, never show mercy," Silus spat as he leant against the wall. Lucian struggled to pull the object from his back, standing stiffly, his fingers trying to reach the hilt.

"Oh, I forgot you did not know... how your father met his end. A duel, with an unfortunate outcome, covered up to protect the parties involved," Silus laughed. Lucian leant against the opposite wall, watching the man, knowing that he had never met such a dark version of him before.

"You see, boy... we are not so different after all. I ruined Esther, as you ruined Caroline and I disposed of her when she tried to leave me. I got rid of your father when he became a problem, just as you would have done with Lee. We are problem solvers... the difference between us is that you are weak at heart, you show mercy, you show kindness, and you have allowed this girl to tame you. And now you will stand there and watch me end your wife, as you stood by and watched me end your mother when you were a little boy. You ruined her life, you destroyed the world of the only person who could love you," Lucian took a deep breath and allowed his rage to take over. It did so in a calm and cold fashion, and he straightened up, and ruthlessly pulled the dagger from his back.

"No, father, that is where you are wrong. I am going to kill you, and I am going to enjoy it," he said calmly and quietly, as he walked slowly toward the man he'd always called father, who was sagging now against the wall.

"Lucian-" Caroline rasped from the floor, but he was too far away to be reached, his mind too stretched, too pained.

He easily fended off Silus's blows, and threw some of his own, his callousness seeming too casual for the blood that splashed the walls. He caught both of his hands as they attempted to reach him, and bent the wrists back efficiently, swiftly, the crack of the bones so satisfying, spurring him on. Silus howled in pain, and Lucian delivered an elbow to his windpipe that silenced him, making him wheeze. He then smashed blows across his sides and stomach, kicking him until he started to cough up blood.

"Lucian! No-" Caroline tried to say. Spotting the blood-smeared letter opener, he bent over to pick it up, and then tossed it in his hand as he returned, thinking of all the times this man had hurt him when he was little, all the times he'd felt alone, felt unwanted, less than.

He advanced. Silus had stood again, and was against the wall for support. He wore his shirtsleeves, his waistcoat unbuttoned and opened in the front, exposing the soft flesh underneath. Lucian slowly slit a long line up Silus's stomach to the breastbone and smiled as blood began to seep from the cut, staining the torn white linen of his shirt.

"Lucian!" Caroline cried, but he was too far gone in vengeance to stop now.

Lucian continued to make shallow cuts all along Silus's body, slowly, so that he might feel each draw-out moment in agony writ upon his flesh. He started to sway from the loss of blood as he slowly wept red onto the floor. Lucian realising then with disappointment that his father did not have much longer to suffer, placed the letter opener over his heart, almost leisurely, and slowly started to push the blade in, inch by inch.

"This is for my father," he whispered as he dug the opener in another inch, making Silus gasp.

"This for my mother," Lucian continued, twisting as the letter opener went further, and Silus gurgled blood from his mouth that dripped onto the white of his fine lace cravat.

"And this is for Caroline... and I would do it a hundred times over if I could," he whispered, and slowly pushed the opener into the hilt. Lucian caught Silus's face in his hand and held it steady... catching his eyes, looking into them intently, he watched the light seep out of them.

"Enjoy hell, father," he whispered, his gaze locked on the man dying before him, watching the darkness take him, his eyes soaking up every second of his pain, his death.

A shattering scream sounded from the doorway, and Lucian twisted around to see the same maid, staring at him as though he were hell itself come to swallow her up.

"Where is that doctor?" he shouted at her, and she turned to flee a second time, but he wondered if this time she would return.

"Lucian?" Charles's soft voice cut through his remoteness, the red clearing slightly, as Lucian turned to see Charles and Rebecca standing in the doorway, in shock. He looked down at his hands, his arms, his clothes, standing in the half-light, painted in his father's blood. The floor was a lake of red, pooling in a slow spread around his father's white body, and Caroline lay unmoving nearby. Rebecca screamed as she saw her, and rushed to her side.

Caroline. He had almost forgotten her, in his hatred, in his need to rid the world of Silus, he had forgotten the only thing that was important to him.

"Lucian?" Charles exhaled the name, his breath barely making its way past his lips, a ghost of a word. "What is this?" Charles stood open-mouthed and unmoving, before he swallowed, made his way to his brother, and touched his arm. Lucian jolted at the light touch and resisted the urge to rip his older brother's arm off, so strong was the hate and violence that still flowed in his veins.

"Charles! She needs a doctor, now!" Rebecca cried, tears running down her face.

"I sent the maid for one... she seems to have run off now though," Lucian said, his voice dazed as he looked around. Charles shook his head as if to wake himself, and then seemed to harden, his voice coming out clear and firm now.

"Rebecca, go and find her, see if someone is coming, I shall go myself, if not," Charles commanded briskly as he strode over to Caroline. Rebecca scrambled up and ran from the hall, and Charles knelt beside Caroline and touched her gently.

"She was talking before. Her eyes were open," Lucian said, coming over to them, his head still clouded and foggy. "She must be resting now, she was well before, she spoke to me," Lucian mumbled, reassuring himself. Caroline would wake up any moment, and they would laugh at all the alarm that had been caused.

"Lucian," Charles said in a serious tone, pulling Lucian's attention to Caroline. "She needs a doctor now."

"I told you, brother, she was awake, she is going to be fine," Lucian said. The dried blood on her hands was flaking off onto the carpet, and he became absorbed with brushing it away from her, certain Caroline would not want it on her dress.

"Lucian..." Charles said again, this time, his tone was so sad, and solemn that Lucian glanced up. Charles was holding Caroline to her side. Lucian saw the dark stain spreading on her skirt, yet could not understand what it meant. Lucian looked to his brother in confusion, his mind unable to accept the image.

"Charles, we have another problem," Rebecca said breathlessly as she ran back into the room. There was something different in her voice this time.

"The maid, she called on the Watch. She told them that she saw Lucian murder father in cold blood. They are on their way here," Rebecca said, looking at the brothers as they all sat surrounded in blood and ruin.

"Idiot girl," Charles swore as he stood up, going to Rebecca he took her hands in his and held them close.

"You must take the carriage, go find a doctor, bring him here. Go now, alone, it will be faster."

"What about Caroline?" Rebecca cried, "I cannot leave her."

"All we can do is get help, as fast as possible. Do this now Rebecca... if you want her to live," Charles said, and as she nodded to leave, her eyes straying to her father where he lay. A sob escaped her lips. Charles suddenly pulled her close and pressed a kiss to her forehead.

"Run, sister," he whispered, and she was gone. Lucian had regained his senses somewhat and was now gripping Caroline's hands, stroking the backs of them and whispering to her. Everything felt surreal to him, a dark dream that he could not wake from, but hearing the concern in his brother's voice, he tried to focus, tried to pull himself together.

"Lucian, the police are on their way here. Given the maid's testimony, and seeing father, I think it best you are not here when they arrive," he said, pulling Lucian upright by the shoulders.

"I'm not leaving her. I will not leave her side," he swore as he pulled away, back to Caroline.

"You must, if you ever wish to see her again. You know of father's friends in the law. You *will* hang for this, Lucian, if we do not act fast."

"But he tried to kill her," Lucian spat.

"Until Caroline wakes, it is easy to prove otherwise, based on what the maid witnessed, and the state of... the body. These are not honest men. One, in particular, was father's friend, an unscrupulous, sharp-witted terrier of a man. He could manipulate evidence, even with Caroline's story. Go now. Hide. I will take care of Caroline, and I will find you when we know more."

"I cannot leave her," he demanded.

"You would have her wake to find you hanged when her testimony might have prevented it?" Charles challenged, shaking Lucian by the shoulders. Lucian looked away numbly, overwhelmed by the spiral of destruction that had suddenly come crashing down onto their lives.

"The baby... the child," he suddenly said, his throat squeezed with emotion. He turned back to Charles for answers.

"The doctor shall do everything he can.. for Caroline and the babe," Charles said. A sudden banging resounded through the house.

"Open up. It's the Watch," a gruff voice called. Charles gripped Lucian by the shoulders hard.

"Go now! You must!"

Lucian looked at Caroline, agonisingly torn, and then back at his brother. He made to leave, and suddenly turned back, looking Charles right in the eye, he said earnestly.

"If it comes to a choice... between the child or her... it has to be her... she cannot die... if you must make a choice, it must be her, Charles, promise me... chose Caroline," Lucian was lost, alone, and utterly mad with grief as he stared at his brother wide-eyed, he could not believe the words that were coming from his own mouth. Charles, caught by his intensity nodded slowly. Then, with a crash, the Watch began to break through the door.

"I promise... now go! Go! I shall find you," Charles said, pushing him toward the door toward the kitchens and the warren of back exits. Lucian looked once more to Caroline, split in half by the agony of leaving her there, and finally moved toward the door. As he slipped out, into the night, his heart remained inside by her side, while the numb, empty husk of him slipped down dark alleyways, blood-soaked and shaking.

CHAPTER 7

*C*harles closed the door and poured water into a basin, finally washing the blood from his hands. Hours had passed since he had come across the scene which would haunt him for eternity. The Watch had entered and begun their questioning. They had brought a doctor at least, he thought wryly, as he remembered the fusing of the old man they had dragged from his bed. A second doctor, this one younger, arrived with Rebecca. He had been proud of his sister, the way she held together and presented a united front to the curious Watchmen, as they surveyed the scene, despite the way her eyes drifted often to her father, now covered by a blood spotted sheet.

Caroline had been moved carefully to a bed and Charles planned to go to her side, as soon as the detectives allowed him to do so. He braced his newly washed hands on either side of the washstand and stared at himself in the looking glass.

His father was dead. He could scarcely believe it. There had been no affection between them, yet, he had been a part of his life for so long, he could not escape a certain magnitude of feeling. What had he done in his final moments? What had he done to Caroline? The thought was unbearable, and Charles gripped the washstand to steady himself. Now his brother ran from the law, ran from the hangman's noose, and from his father's friends and influence, which already extended from his grave.

Sighing, he turned back to the door, readying himself to step out, preparing himself to answer the Watch's questions another time.

The hallway was crowded, and Charles pushed through the throng to find Rebecca. She was sitting, pale and trembling by the door. He crouched beside her and took her hands in his.

"Come, we shall go and see Caroline if they permit us to leave," he murmured, pulling her to her feet.

"Lord Ashford," a rough voice called, and Charles turned around slowly.

"We have not been introduced. My name is Jack Hughes. I'm a Bow Street Runner, and a very close friend to your father, may he rest," the man said with a grim face, tipping his hat with the barest of politeness.

"If you do not mind, I need to escort my sister from here, this is all too much for her," Charles said stiffly, noting the way the detective was looking around the room, at the blood on Charle's sleeves and Rebecca's hands, he seemed to be missing nothing. He had seen the man before, though he couldn't place where, but had never spoken to him. All the same, his reputation was that of a hard, efficient and ruthless man who, like many of the Watch, was quite corrupt.

"Of course, you may leave at once, we have had a witness come forward, claims she saw the whole crime, so we won't be needing you again until tomorrow," the man said as he scanned Charles's face carefully in a way that made Charles want to turn from him.

"I am sure our version differs from hers dramatically," Charles said evenly, standing his ground.

"Naturally, because she saw it happen, and you didn't," Hughes said with a squint, and Charles felt fear flicker through him.

"My brother was only defending his wife."

"Oh, I think those are hardly the wounds of self-defence. It's a bloodbath, isn't it? Let's discuss it tomorrow, shall we? Where can you be reached?"

"We shall be staying at his home, just a block from here, where my sister in law now recovers after our father attacked her," Charles said pointedly.

"So you've said," Hughes remarked, eyeing Charles's reaction. Not wanting to appear ruffled, Charles stared the man down, and inclined his head slightly, acknowledging the comment.

"You are free to go, and don't concern yourself, we shall get to the bottom of the matter, make sure the guilty are brought to justice. It will be my own personal mission, and I won't know a moment's peace until it's done," Hughes said. He then caught Charles in a heavy stare, and in what was surely meant to sound more of a threat than a reassurance, he added, "You can be sure of that."

🦁

"*L*ucian," Caroline called into the darkness of the room, the sounds of busy ministrations and the feel of strange hands on her body.

"Lucian..." Caroline moaned again, as she attempted to open her eyes, yet found the same scene playing continuously. Lucian killing his father, blood splattered across his face, all light gone from his eyes. She tried to bring his attention to her, but he couldn't hear, wouldn't listen.

"Shh, Caroline my love, you must rest now, you are weak," she heard Katherine's voice, gentle and worried. A spoon was pressed to Caroline's lips. Caroline went to call out for Lucian again but found the spoon in her mouth before she could muster her voice. It was sharp and foul, medicinal. Most ran down her face, but she managed to swallow some, hoping the liquid would make her voice strong enough that he might hear her.

She heard a male voice, unfamiliar to her. "The is not look good for the child, as you can see, but I am told the mother is strong. The sheets will have to be changed often. Burn them."

🦁

A light drizzle fell that day, the first time in weeks. The summer had been pleasant and fair, but today the sky clouded over, and the sun hid its face, as though it too were afraid to face the morning. Lucian did not feel the rain, he did not see the clouds. In front of his eyes was only darkness, around him nothing. He could feel nothing. He sat in the light rain, dazed, watching the house from afar. He had seen the doctor leave with Caroline to carry her to their townhouse. He had followed them, where he now sat, hiding, waiting across the lane, watching people go and come with drawn faces. Charles and Rebecca had arrived, the Fairfaxes too, both Mr and Mrs as well as a frantic Katherine. Isaac Taylor had called, and Rebecca had cried in his arms by the window. Lucian was glad there was someone to put their arms around her for comfort. Glad she was loved. If Caroline died, there would be no consolation for him, no living, no tomorrow. At another window, he saw Katherine speaking at length to Charles, and his brother seemed upset. He had seen the men of the Watch arrive too, and Bow Street Runners, casually taking up residence in the street, waiting for him, he supposed.

He watched them all, as though it were a play, and he a spectator. All these good, honest people, allowed their grief, innocent and blameless. He did not belong among them. He was to blame. Since he had come into Caroline's life, she had known misery and pain, fear and betrayal, death and violence. It was his curse, his legacy, to inflict pain on those he loved. He had cost her her child and probably her life. Loving him had cost her everything. Loving him had killed her. Silus was right, they were the same.

A person passed close by his hiding spot, and he stared at them, watching them until they disappeared. Should it even matter if he was discovered? Would it matter if he hanged? Would it hurt? Would he see her again? Would she hate him in the afterlife? He was not sure. The only thing he knew without a shadow of doubt was that if Caroline died, nothing would ever matter again.

🍥

*C*harles sat at his brother's desk, staring at the wall, the dreadful events of the last hour replaying in his head. Katherine had explained the plot, of which she had known, and Isaac Taylor as well. It explained why Caroline had been there, and why Silus had lost his reason, perhaps. Charles could see all too clearly what had happened, and knew his brother was... if not faultless, at least driven to extremes to protect the life of his wife and child. However, he struggled to see how to present it to the law, in a way that favoured Lucian and showed his innocence without Caroline's testimony.

That was not the worst of the news, however. The doctor had been most discouraging about Caroline's chances and had notified them promptly not to waste prayers over the baby. The taste of the conversation was bitter ash in his mouth, and he cradled his head in his hands, a sharp pain piercing his skull.

He knew his brother was waiting for him, even had a good idea of where he might be found, yet his heart broke at the thought of going to him. He must, though - he could not imagine Lucian's torment at not knowing the outcome, held away from his love, when she needed him the most. They could not meet here, they were watched. He only hoped Lucian would see him leave and follow, and together they might be able to evade their trackers and find a moment alone. Charles dreaded that the most - to look in his brother's face, and tell him all that he had lost.

۞

*T*he London docks were as busy as always, despite the rain. The backdrop as grey and filthy as old dishwater and the relentless rain that fell felt fitting as Charles ducked into a bawdy house, and watched the last man who had been following him give up and turn back toward the road. He watched in silence for a while longer before handing the mistress a coin and leaving through a back entrance. Turning back to the ramshackle buildings that lined the port he walked in the shadows toward one and did not need to glance back to tell who now followed him. He slipped inside and shook the rain off his coat. It smelled damp, and the store was full of lumber, which smelled like trees rotting in the heavy air. The floor was downtrodden mud, which had grown wet and marshy at the edges of the room.

The door opened briefly behind him, and he turned around, preparing himself for the sight that met him. And it was quite a sight. His brother looked as he had never seen him before. He was still, silent, a controlled terror that permitted him to function, yet his eyes were tortured, open caves of despair. His hollow cheeks and stained clothing made him look like a sick and starving urchin. Perhaps at least it would serve as some sort of disguise if the grief did not kill him first.

"Brother," Charles whispered and went forward to embrace him. He wrapped his arms around him and was met with a body of stone. Lucian, unmoved, stood unyielding.

"Tell me," was all he said, as Charles pulled back and composed himself.

"She lives... for now. The doctor has been and Katherine and Rebecca are tending to her night and day, never leaving her side," Charles said, trying to sound more confident than he felt.

"Our... the child?" Lucian asked, his voice a dirge. Charles felt his own voice die, his throat closed, and he could only look away, could not look his brother in the eye.

"It...the doctor warned us not to hold much hope." Lucian's face hardened into something even colder if it was possible, jaw clenched, eyes empty.

"It's my fault. I was just outside. If only I'd-"

"You cannot blame yourself. The only one to blame is father, you know that."

"And what good does it do for me to blame him now? His blame is mine now to punish myself with every day, but little good it will do any of us. I don't deserve to be here breathing when they are fading away."

"Lucian, please do not speak so. Both their lives still hang in the balance. Katherine says she is speaking- it is a good sign. I believe she will recover. I must believe it."

"You have more faith than I do, brother," Lucian said, still turned away, as his face stretched and twisted under the burden of his grief.

"What of father, and The Watch? I wish to see Caroline, even if for one last time."

"They are looking for you. I have met father's friend, his name is Hughes. He seems... persistent. I think it best you stay out of sight for the time being," Lucian turned back to his brother, saw his exhaustion, his sadness written plain across his face.

"I killed your father, Charles... you must hate me," Lucian suddenly said, regarding Charles from across the room. Charles looked away and took a moment.

"He might have been my father, but he was not a good man. After what he has done to Caroline... I would have done the same"

"No, brother you would not have. You might have beat him, maybe even killed him. But you would not have enjoyed it as I did, you would not have tortured him as I did. It is my nature. For that, for your sake, and Rebecca's and Wesley's, I apologise," Lucian said, his voice raw. He turned to go then, and Charles watched his hunched shoulders, his body seemed to be caving inwards, unable to bear the weight of his burdens.

"If she dies... I shall let the Watch take me. I will not live in this world without her." Lucian said coldly.

"Lucian-"

"No, do not try to dissuade me. If she dies, I am only a dead body walking."

"And if she lives?"

"I shall run from the Watch, for I will not have her know of my fate. I will not have her carry that burden."

"We'll find a way to clear your name. You were only defending her."

"His body will tell a different story."

"No. We will figure something out. Do not lose faith, brother." Lucian shook his head.

"Cleared name or not, I have brought nothing but misery to her, to you, to everyone. It would be best if I went away, somewhere I can never harm you again, never hurt her again. I heard her voice, Charles. I heard it, but I was blind with rage, all I could see was my need to hurt him. If only I'd stayed with her..."

"So... you would desert her now, after all she has been through? You would leave her alone?" Charles cried.

"I promised her I would do the best for her, even if it costs me. Look at me, Charles. I am not the best thing for her, I might very well be the worst. She will have a better life without me."

"She would not agree."

"You think so? Ask her again when she has lost our child, and his blood is on my hands."

CHAPTER 8

"*L*ucian," Caroline called, her dreams filled with fire again, after so long. She ran in her dreams, though this time she held a baby, their baby, in her arms, protecting it from the fire.

"Lucian!" she screamed, she could not find him in the blazing house. The baby began to cry, and she looked at it, seeing soot and fallen ashes streak its face. She had to get out, had to leave him there, or risk the child.

"Lucian!" she screamed.

Caroline opened her eyes, her throat raw and dry, her whole body hurt. Her eyelids protested against the light, she squeezed them shut again. She made a noise and felt a warm hand cover hers. "Shh, it's alright, we are all here." Katherine, it sounded like Katherine's voice.

"Lucian?" Caroline whispered but was met with silence as she slipped back into her drug-addled dreams.

❀

*J*t took him hours to evade the men watching the house, to wait for a gap in their routine. He had been watching the house and them for more than a day now, however, so he knew the best time to enter unseen.

He had met Charles again and spoken about Caroline. It seemed she would survive, though she would always bear the scars of that night. He had heard the news silently, and sat numbly, taking it in. Charles held him to his promise, that he would not let The Watch take him, should she survive. Charles had made secret preparations for a boat to France. He would leave the next day. They did not speak of the child again. There were no words to fill that silence, no way to convey the depth of that despair.

His name was far from clear, as the letters his father had written came to light, throwing Silus into the role of a concerned old man, scared for the health and safety of his daughter-in-law and grandchild, and for himself against his impulsive, violent son. The maid's testimony was equally damning, as she described in detail the slow, inhuman way Lucian had killed Silus. She had been outside, in the privy before she had heard Silus's shouting that Lady Ashford had fallen. As the staff's usual monthly night of personal leave, she was the only one who had remained at home on that balmy summer night, too young to venture out with the others. The scratches on Silus's face were brushed away, mainly by Hughes, as an injury caused by the grapple with Lucian, despite Caroline's hands being streaked with his father's blood.

Lucian soundlessly made his way up the back stairs. The house was utterly silent and black. He knew the way to come in undetected and his light footsteps disturbed no one, not even a cat that had lain sleeping in the kitchen. He reached the hall, and slowly started toward the door of the room they had shared together.

Pausing only a moment to look around, he pushed it open and stepped inside. The air was heavy with the smell of medicines, herbs and the tangy scent of blood. His nose rebelled against it, knowing it was Caroline's. He took a moment to adjust to the velvet, copper-tinged darkness, and then made his way to the bed.

Charles said she had still not fully regained consciousness. She lay still, her hair spilled over the pillow, her face as white as the moon in the black night. He drank her in, starved for her. He knelt beside her and after a moment dropped his face to the pillow beside her.

"Forgive me, Caroline, my love, please forgive me..." he whispered reverently. He was afraid to touch her, to feel that soft skin, as though the memory of it would burn him in years to come, the reminder of all he could never have.

"I was so selfish, so, so selfish... I should have left you alone, let you live the life you dreamed of, the life you wanted. I only thought of myself and how I needed you... I was wrong, so wrong," he muttered, feeling his eyes sting, his voice hurt. "If only I'd been there sooner, I might have stopped it all. I waited outside like a fool searching for secrets while you were nearly killed! While he..." His voice cracked and he choked on a sob, unable to go on. "I know you will hate me for leaving when you finally wake. I will take your blame, I will take your hatred. But, I will not be selfish again. You cannot build your life with a wanted man, or be there to watch me hang. You could not live in a house with a man whose face reminds you of all he has cost you, of who you have lost.

"When you wake, I shall be gone, and you can start again. Start a new life, and forget about me. I shall atone with my absence. I'll give you your freedom, for it is what I should have done long ago." He stood to leave, his face now wet, his heart twisted and a physical ache crushing his chest.

"I... I will always love you, Caroline. I will spend my life loving you... and it will be the most meaningful thing I shall ever do," he whispered as he pulled himself away from the bed, not being able to resist leaning forward first and pressing a final kiss onto her dry lips.

"Goodbye, my love," he murmured. As he closed the door behind him, he felt as though he was closing the door on the best part of his life. In silence he made his way out the house, and back into the streets, hiding, keeping out of sight, heading toward the docks again. The light in his life had gone out, and only the cold, empty darkness remained.

✿

"*I* told you what happened, yet you seem determined not to listen," Charles said irritably as Hughes asked him the same question again.

"And you mean to tell me that you have no idea where your brother may be?" Hughes asked, his tone making it clear he did not believe him for a moment.

"None whatsoever," Charles said calmly, presenting the low-rent-detective with his best defensive veneer of upper-class arrogance and supremacy. Inside he was shaken. The evidence against his brother kept mounting, and Caroline was not yet awake enough to discuss it.

"I must speak to your sister again," the detective announced.

"Someone shall need to be present with her, myself or her husband," Charles stated. Hughes allowed it with a wave of his hand, and Charles gritted his teeth, the man's manners were abominable, his familiar sneer repellent. He strode out of the room and indicated to Isaac that he should take Rebecca in. Rebecca was very quiet and pale as she sat staring out the window. She was not handling it well.

Charles sighed as he sat down in Lucian's study, needing solitude for a moment. He looked up as the door opened.

"Here, I thought you might need this," Katherine said as she carried in a cup of strong tea. She set it down and leant against the desk, looking at him in concern. He looked at the tea and realised he lacked the strength to remind her of her place in the house. What did it matter? What did any of it matter?

"Thank you, it is kind of you," he muttered.

"No comment about my maid's skills?" she teased with an arched eyebrow and he leaned back, surprised enough to smile for a moment.

"I wasn't going to mention it," he said and saw her shake her head, a smile of her own on her lips. They gazed at each other, their smiles dissolving into shared worry and understanding.

"Are you well?" she asked suddenly, and he bit off a bitter laugh.

"I might never be well again," he said, massaging his temples with his fingers.

"Allow me," she said softly, moving behind him and placing her cool fingers on his head. She deftly pressed the source of the pain, and he fought a moan.

"We shouldn't..." he muttered and heard her exasperated sigh.

"Because it is not proper?" she enquired irritatedly.

"No, because the tea is growing cold," he said with a slight smile. She laughed a little and sat down opposite him, and he sipped his tea in the comfortable silence

"Well, what are we going to do?" she asked.

"We are going to wait for Caroline to get better, for her to wake up.

Pray for it, hope for it, do everything we can. Once she does, we hope beyond hope that her testimony might just save Lucian from the noose."

❀

*I*saac led Rebecca from the room and helped her upstairs. She was shaking. He opened the door to the room she had been sleeping in and brought her to the edge of the bed. She sank down, her eyes fixed far away.

"Rebecca, why don't you rest?"

"I should check on Caroline," she said.

"Check on her later, you must lie down and relax awhile. Katherine is there." Isaac insisted, coaxing her backward onto the soft blankets and pulling her slippers from her feet. Rebecca remained quiet, staring at the ceiling. He covered her with a blanket and kissed her forehead.

"Stay with me?" she asked quietly.

"Of course I will, my darling. Anything you need, only say the word and I am here." She nodded.

"My family is diminishing... no mother, no father... now my brother too disappears."

"Lucian is not dead, he is in hiding. He will come back as soon as this is all resolved."

"And what if it is never resolved?"

"Do not speak so, it shall be. Of course, it shall." He laid down next to her and over the covers, held her close. Rebecca was quiet again and then, after a while, turned around so she was facing Isaac. He saw tears running down her cheeks, and pulled her in to his chest.

"Sweetheart," he said as he stroked her soft hair. "It's okay. It's all going to be fine, you'll see." She shook her head as her shoulders began to shake, continuing to cry in silence a moment more, and then finally spoke, her eyes downcast.

"I know he was not a good man... and I know he hurt Caroline and he deserved to die... but-" she broke off, her eyes brimming with fresh tears.

"He was still your father, my love, and you can mourn him. Please, make no apologies." Isaac said, holding her closer and feeling her restraint break, as she started to cry in earnest against him.

She cried for her mother, who she had never truly known, for her father, who had let his greed and weaknesses rule his life and for her brother, who had seen the only happiness he'd ever known spectacularly ripped away from him. She cried for the family that they once were, or might have been if they had all been a little different, a little better.

⁂

𝒲hen Caroline opened her eyes, she recognised the room straight away. The fog that had plagued her, the endless dreams had faded and she sat up and looked around. The room was the same as always, comforting, it felt like home and she wondered where the one thing that was missing was.

"Caroline?" a voice said beside her, and she saw Katherine had fallen asleep in a nearby chair, book on her knee, and had just begun to stir.

"Kitty," Caroline, said smiling as Katherine flung her book to the floor, and ran over to Caroline's bed, tripping a little on her skirts. "God's breath, Caroline, are you awake?" She felt Caroline's forehead and pulled down her eyelids to look into her eyes for what signs, Caroline wasn't sure.

"Kitty, stop, I am well!" she laughed, "Thank you, for staying with me." She was puzzled when Katherine's excitement faded into a solemn expression. "What's the matter? Where is Lucian?" Caroline asked, and felt a tremor of unease at the way Katherine's eyes slid to the door, a brief moment of panic before she smiled.

"Everyone is waiting to see you, we have worried so.. let me fetch them," she said and was gone before she could be stopped. Caroline looked around bemused, and stretched, she felt a twinge in her back and stomach and gasped at the strange sensation. In fact, her whole body felt a little worse for wear, she realised, as she attempted to stand up.

"Caroline! You have to rest," a shrill voice came from the door heralding the arrival of Mrs Fairfax. Caroline smiled, surprised to see her, yet glad. Katherine also returned, but seemed to busy herself needlessly tidying things by the bedside.

"The doctor is on his way," Margaret said, with a pat on the hand.

Caroline sat back amongst the pillows her brow furrowed. "Caroline, my dear, what do you remember?" Margaret asked gently. Caroline stared at them, trying to piece together the hazy memories that lay in the recesses of her mind. She felt like she had slept so long, and dreamt so vividly that it was difficult to separate those dreams from reality.

"I went to the Ashfords'," she started, and as she spoke, memories descended on her. They were vague and misshapen. "I– I was discussing a deal with Lord Silus. I didn't want him to have my parents' land," she said, sorting through the images trying to make sense of it. "I was going to leave it to..." her voice broke off suddenly as she looked down, and pulled the blanket off of her stomach. Her eyes went to the distended swell of her belly and she laid both hands on it. Margaret suddenly got up and went to the window, wringing her hands. Katherine's eyes were bright, too bright, shiny almost, with unshed tears.

"What is it? What has happened?" Caroline asked, her palms pressing into the taut wall of her womb.

"Caroline, the doctor is here, I think we should give you some privacy," Margaret said from the doorway, and Katherine and her mother left quickly. The doctor entered - a small, kindly-looking man. He sat down beside her and checked a few things, then patted her hand.

"You had a terrible accident. Do you remember it at all?" he asked.

"I – I remember being at the Ashfords' house. I remember talking to Lord Silus. I... I can't quite recall... Lucian was there, he was angry. His father and he quarrelled. I think they might have fought, I can't recall clearly. Why can I not recall?"

"You had a terrible fall, you hit your head very hard, and it has taken weeks for the swelling to go down enough for you to wake up... your memory should come back, given time."

"I fell? What about the baby... is the baby well?" Caroline asked suddenly. The old doctor fell silent and looked down, he patted her hand again.

"Sometimes there is no understanding the ways of God-" he started, and Caroline felt her panic flash into anger.

"Do not speak to me of God, tell me the truth!"

"There is no hope for the baby."

"But, I felt him moving, in my dreams, he was moving, I felt it, it woke me up," the man's eyes shone with pity and Caroline turned away from them.

"My dear, we could do nothing to stop the bleeding. It is a miracle that you survived at all, but I'm afraid that the baby could not have survived it." Caroline began to shake. The doctor reached out to pat her hand again, and she snatched it back before he could touch her. Her breath was coming fast and shaky.

"Leave me. I have no more need of you," she dismissed him curtly, working hard to control herself, and he leaned away in surprise.

"Lady Ashford, I am sorry if the truth is hard to hear, but it remains the truth nonetheless."

"Get out. Send me my husband," she ordered, sitting back on the pillows, looking away from him and placing her hands gently over her swollen belly protectively.

The doctor stood, flustered, putting his hat back on. He looked as though he were about to speak, but then thought better of it, and turned and left the room. Caroline looked down at her stomach, tears clouding her eyes now, nausea rising in her throat. He could not be right, it could not be correct. She pressed gently with her palms, waiting for some sign, something to give her hope. There was nothing. The door opened and she looked up, tears already spilling from her eyes. Rebecca stood in the doorway, with Isaac and Katherine. Behind them, she could see the tall upright figure of Charles.

"What is happening? Please, tell me what is going on," she cried as the girls entered the room. Rebecca hugged her, her own tears falling.

"Oh Caroline," she said as held her close. "Do you remember anything?"

"Pieces... only fragments," Caroline admitted in shaky breaths. "You must tell me what happened... and where is Lucian?" she cried again, frustrated and helpless. Rebecca looked to Charles, her expression pained. He came into the room and sat on a chair by the bed.

"Caroline, first, let me tell you what a relief it is to see you awake. We have sat here, day in and day out, waiting for you; Katherine more than anyone. You were never alone." He broke eye contact and looked down, his hand searching his pocket. "He left me this for you," he began, holding out a letter.

"Charles," Caroline interrupted unable to bear it one moment more.

"Where is my husband?" she asked and felt the silence surge in after the question. Even the birds in the trees outside seemed to hold their breaths.

"I am afraid... I do not know"

⁂

*W*eeks passed. Caroline's memory came back slowly, little by little each day. Unfortunately, it seemed Hughes had questioned the doctor, after Caroline's retelling of her memories, adding more fuel to the fire. She cursed herself for her stupidity.

She rested, she slept, ate what she was given, yet she found it increasingly impossible to hold out any hope whatsoever. She stopped asking about Lucian, stopped sleeping with his letter under her pillow. She stopped laughing entirely, and smiles, even sad, quiet ones made as a reassurance, were increasingly rare to come by. She didn't care enough to pretend.

Her family and friends watched this decline, with increasing worry, but the extra attention only angered her. She lay and watched the sun move along the walls of her room, her arms cradling her midsection. Sometimes she hummed a lullaby, sometimes she muttered stories to herself. But she did not cry, not once. When Katherine asked her about it, she told her all her tears were spent, and she had spent a lifetime crying over one man, and it was time to stop.

She tried to give an official testimony of her version of events, with Charles' help, but no one seemed interested in hearing it, let alone recording it. They would have to wait until the hearing, inspector Hughes, had insisted dismissively. He had been gruff and distasteful, and she had hated him instantly and hoped that she would not have to see him again.

Caroline asked if she might return to Westmere, only to be told it had been seized by the crown, pending her husband's capture and trial. Her house in London was also to be seized. She elected to move back in with the Fairfaxes over the Ashfords' townhouse. She lay each day in her old bedroom and tried to remember the girl who had laughed in there, wished and dreamed. She had not opened the letter, just looked at it. She had stopped even that and tucked it away in some drawer or other. Katherine became her constant companion, and she tried desperately to pull Caroline from her darkness, but Caroline found that she could not muster enough interest to try. She could see that she was breaking Katherine's heart, and not just hers - Rebecca cried every time she visited, which was frequently.

One afternoon with Katherine, Caroline cut her finger on a knife that she played with from the sewing basket. She made no sound, only gazed at the blood. Watched it well up, and run down her hand, and then watching it with fascination as it spread between all the small lines of her hand. Katherine threw down her things with a huff and stood up.

"Shall you clean that, or shall I?" she demanded in frustration. Caroline only shrugged, sending Katherine over the edge.

"Caroline! This is enough, it must stop! You cannot go on like this, none of us can. Yes– Lucian is gone, he is a wanted criminal, and he cannot come back anytime soon. So... you must go on... you must wake up! Start to live again." Katherine shouted, and Caroline looked at her, taken aback by her anger. "Who are you? You are not Caroline, I know that. Caroline was stronger and braver than anyone I knew. She was my rock." Katherine demanded, leaning forward and looking into Caroline's eyes. She stared blankly back at her. Katherine looking like she might scream instead whirled around and dug through Caroline's drawers. Caroline watched passively, until Katherine rose back up, brandishing Lucian's letter in her hand.

"If you never plan on reading this, let us just be rid of it, shall we?" Katherine said as she strode to a candle and deftly lit it.

"Shall I, or do you wish to?" Katherine asked, her eyes scrutinising Caroline's. There was something, a flicker, like the flutter of a trapped bird caged inside. Katherine dipped the paper toward the flame, and finally, Caroline moved.

"Don't!" she cried suddenly, sitting upright and watching Katherine with fear.

"Oh! You care about this letter? Why don't we read it then?" Katherine continued as she slit open the top. Caroline surprised her then, by lunging forward and grabbing the envelope. Katherine backed away, holding her hands up in surrender. Caroline held the opened letter in her hands, the spidery script already calling to her from inside.

🐚

*T*hat night Caroline watched the moon rise and fall from the view of her window. She sat still, unmoving as day became night, soon to become day again. She held in her hands a letter, with familiar writing on it, her name scrawled across it.

His last letter to her, the last words they would exchange would have nothing from her. She could only receive the words, not respond to them.

She had been holding it for hours, unable to put it away, afraid to read the last thing he would ever say to her. Afraid to cut off that contact forever. As the moon began to fall, just before the predawn light lit the room, she finally unfolded it. This was their time, their time of hot milk in cold kitchens, of whispered affections, in the stillness before morning, when nightmares woke them; their time of togetherness, in the dark before dawn.

Dear Caroline,

If you are reading this, then I have been a luckier man than I deserve to be. I failed you, time and time again, but this last failure, cannot be atoned for. I understand now what you tried to do, and I thank you for it. No one has ever loved me, as you did, and I will never love another as I do you. I am a selfish man, a flawed man, and sadly these traits outweigh my better ones, those that would not exist if not for you. I was dead long before I met you, and you restored me to life; and that time, brief as it was, was worth an eternity of suffering. I have known you, and it is enough. I am sorry for all the pain that I have brought you. You had such a bright, happy life when I first met you.

I should try to keep my promise to keep you safe, and that is why I shan't return. A wanted man, a murderer- I cannot make you a good husband. I never have. I have failed you, in every conceivable way. I have thrown you into jeopardy and broken your heart too many times. I will not force you to look at my face every day and see what I have cost you, cost us. You deserve the world, Caroline, and I will only bring you darkness... it is my nature, and I am bound to it. So, I release you, as I should have done so long ago. I set you free to love and live as you desire, to make your own choices and to be happy. You will be well looked after - everything I have left is yours. If I know that somewhere in the world, you are happy, it is enough.

As for me, forget me. Or, if you should remember, remember me as a man who loved you, a man who tried to be better, who fought his basic nature, to be worthy. I will continue to strive to be that man for you. If ever I do something good, it is for you, and in your name.

I wish you happiness, health and above all, love. Know that someone, some-where in this world loves you.

Forever yours,

L

Her tears fell on the page, running the ink, as she moved it away out of reach. She took in the words and stared again out the window. Picking up the letter again, she moved it to her stomach and pressed it against her. The love in the letter, so real, so full... she held it to her and imagined her family together. They should be together. None of this should have happened, it was not the way it was supposed to be. Love, their love, was not some ordinary thing. She was sure of it. It was special, transcendent. She fell asleep finally holding the letter to her, her tears wetting the pillow.

In her dreams the house was no longer on fire, it was gone, burned down. The damage was done. She walked through the ruins and all she saw were blackened remains of her life. It was silent, too silent. She felt a pressing on her stomach and looked down, seeing the letter still pressed there. It fluttered in the wind, the sensation sending chills over her skin.

CHAPTER 9

~November 1812~
Wiltshire

*I*t was the type of Autumnal day that was written of in storybooks. The leaves were orange and red, crisp in the slight breeze. The sky, a beautiful blue, cloudless, and though the air held a nip in it, it was welcome so late in the year.

Caroline strode to the stables and readied her treats as she went. As she came closer, the sound of Lelantos and Theia, greeting her made her smile. She went to each one, stroking them, speaking to them and feeding them their daily treats. Theia was her treasure, and she rode her almost every day. Lelantos, she had more trouble with; it was difficult finding someone who could keep their seat on him. If he missed his master, however, he did not show it, instead showering his hard-won affection on Caroline. She had thought about selling him, but could never bring herself to do so. She reasoned that she would be depriving herself of seeing Wesley attempt to ride him sporadically and unsuccessfully, which was worth the cost of the upkeep alone. She thought a lot of bills and upkeep these days. Whilst she lived inexpensively, a

591

virtual recluse from society, she did not like to be a burden on her family. The remaining Ashfords had become brothers and sisters to her, and Katherine had chosen to stay in England, even after the Fairfaxes had been called home.

She left the stables and followed her usual route, down to the river along it, and back toward the main house. It was so imposing, Blackhill Hall, with far more land than any of them ever needed, unlike Westmere, her mind shied away from the thought. She never thought of Westmere anymore, it was too painful. The intimate house, the cosy grounds, she wished to forget it, forget all of it... to suffer less the pangs of nostalgia that sometimes crippled her.

As she came closer to the house, she saw Rebecca waving on the terrace. She strode faster.

"Charles has arrived, he has news!" Rebecca called and Caroline pulled off her hat and gloves as she went. Stopping inside the house, she pulled off her riding boots, now caked in mud, slid on slippers, and then hurried through the house to the drawing-room.

Entering she saw that Katherine and Wesley had already gathered, and were waiting impatiently. Rebecca appeared behind her, and they sat down together, Isaac arriving a moment later, standing in the doorway. Charles smiled at Caroline tiredly as she came in. He too was a changed man in the time since his father's death. Running the estate, and managing the family's accounts, whilst trying to clear his brother's name had left him little time for anything else. Caroline glanced at Katherine, who was pouring him tea, and thought how she had changed. Seemingly content with waiting for a proposal, Katherine had committed her life to the Ashfords and Caroline and spent all her time with them. How long would Charles continue neglecting his own happiness? How long would Katherine let him? At least, after everything, Isaac and Rebecca still had each other, and were more in love then than they were on the day of their wedding.

"Thank you, my dear," he murmured to Katherine, pressing a kiss on her departing hand as she set the tea in front of him. He sat back and looked at the assembled group.

"Well, do not keep us in suspense!" Rebecca whined.

"Of course sister, allow a man to catch his breath," Charles said, massaging his brow. "I have spoken with the magistrate and the chief of the Bow Street runners, they have agreed to let us present our own evidence as well as re-examine that produced by former runner, Mr Hughes."

"Excellent news, is it not!" Wesley exclaimed, beaming. Charles nodded carefully and looked to Caroline.

"It certainly is; however, the next stage, our key defence will rest on you, Caroline. Will you make your testimonial in person?"

Caroline fought down a wave of anxiety and nodded.

"Of course, anything I can do," she murmured.

"We also have the witnesses who saw the scratches on his face, and the doctor who examined Caroline, and can attest to her injuries, to her hands, nails and the bruising on her face and neck," Charles continued dispassionately. Caroline gulped, hearing her injuries listed so and took a mouthful of hot tea. I believe with some monetary persuasion, the doctor may yet change his mind and be willing to testify about Caroline's... condition after the fall."

The group went on discussing the technicalities of their defence and Caroline drifted away.

Jack Hughes had been implicated in a massive bribery scandal shortly after he finished gathering evidence for the case against Lucian. When a guilty judgement had been pending, and about to be passed, the scandal had broken, calling into question the lead detective's credibility. Caroline suspected Wesley had more to do with it than he let on, seeing as Hughes was caught red-handed at Wesley's gentleman's club, Wesley had been present for the takedown and was rather smug upon repeated retellings of the story. Either way, it had been enough to strip Hughes of his title, allowing Charles to ask for the case to be re-examined.

"At this rate, you'll be back at Westmere before Christmas," Charles was saying to Caroline. She turned back to them, a sad smile playing around her lips.

"To be honest, I am not sure I will return... I thought about selling it... that way the money is at our disposal," she said, stunning everyone into silence. They stared at her.

"I mean, I am not sure what we would do there alone... and there are so many memories."

"You will make new ones, when Luke returns," Rebecca said softly, and was silenced by a look from Charles. Caroline turned her face back to her tea, and took a sip, letting scalding liquid steady her, buying her time.

"Of course, it is merely an idea. I just thought, well, if any of you needed it, say for Blackhill... or, think of what good we might do with it, a school or hospital might be built with such a sum," she said, smiling at Wesley who smiled back in return. The Ashford's business interests had changed quite dramatically in the two years that had passed. Rather than gambling on wild speculation, the Ashfords had become a name synonymous with philanthropy.

"There is one last thing I have from London," Charles intoned, pulling a large square object from his bag. They gathered around and looked at it.

"Well, what is it?" Wesley insisted.

"A gift, a very special one," Charles said, his eyes met Caroline's and twinkled for a moment.

"For me?"

"No, not for you, Wesley... it's for the birthday girl," Charles said, turning to the doorway, which he had noticed from the corner of his eye had creaked open.

"Me birday!" a small voice exclaimed and everyone in the room turned to the doorway. Caroline smiled as she stood up, going to the door. Caroline laughed at the flour and sugar that decorated her little dress and apron. Then she bent and picked up her daughter, the last part of Lucian that remained in their lives.

"We made a birthday cake, didn't we Elspeth," the nanny said. "It was a mess! I think Elspeth is a better baker than I, even with cook's help."

"Cake," the little girl replied promptly, her eyes already trained on the present.

"Sounds delicious, may I have some?" Wesley asked.

"Me cake," Elspeth said haughtily, drawing a laugh from the group. At two years old, Elspeth was the image of both her parents. Light brown soft curls, full, cupid's lips, and big blue eyes, she was Caroline's heart. She lifted her easily and balanced her on her hip, bringing her to the divan, where her family stood around watching her. Charles rounded his desk and crouched down beside her. He passed her the wrapped parcel.

"Happy birthday Ellie," he murmured, stroking the curls back from the little girl's smooth forehead. She tried to pull the thick paper off, grunting with determination, Caroline helped her a little, and soon the present was sliding out. It was a paint set on a beautiful wooden palette. Watercolours, Caroline noted. She felt her eyes sting as she watched Charles explain how she could make pictures with it and her fingers. Caroline wondered if he had ever explained it to another fatherless child, many years ago.

"Can you say thank you to our Uncle Charles, pumpkin?"

"Actually, it is not from me... And do you know who sent you such a nice birthday gift?"

"Who?" she demanded. Charles glanced at Caroline before he spoke.

"It's from your daddy..." Elspeth looked immediately at Caroline upon his words, a frown on her curious brow. Caroline swallowed down her panic, and smiled, kneeling beside her, she looked at the gift.

"How beautiful it is! Lucky little lady," she whispered. Her smile felt forced and she felt for a moment, a trembling in her very heart as her daughter looked at her with such clarity, as though she saw straight through her defences.

"Wow, I must say, that is a very pretty painting set Ellie, can I use it too? Can we paint together?" Wesley asked, suddenly moving toward them and breaking the stare between mother and daughter. Elspeth, looking at him, considered and then nodded decisively.

"Right oh, let's go and set up some pleasing prospect, shall we?" Wesley said, picking her up as she held her little arms out to him. He carried her from the room, and Caroline heard their conversation as they went.

"Daddy..." Ellie was saying, pointing at the paint set as Wesley nodded.

"I know, I heard, you are such a lucky girl, I don't know any other little girls who get such special painting sets," they went out into the hall and the rest of the group relaxed. Caroline shot a scathing look at Charles. He had the grace to look embarrassed.

"I apologise, Caroline, I should not have startled you with that."

"The gift is thoughtful Charles, but the sender... why not tell the truth, that is from her loving uncle, she would love it just as much."

"Children need to feel connected to their parents, even if it is a facade, a small white lie, to spare their feelings. Moreover, I wish to represent him... somehow, in some small way," Charles said and Caroline felt her anger drop away. None of this was easy, for any of them.

"I know you do. And I know that your heart was in the right place. Thank you," she said, and then forced a bright smile.

"Now, I have a long list of demands for the birthday feast, there are lists for food, drinks, entertainment."

"Do not worry about the entertainment. We are all prepared," Katherine announced, smiling conspiratorial at Rebecca. Caroline laughed, knowing they had been setting a small stage up in the other drawing-room. There was nothing Elspeth loved more than music and dancing, well, perhaps finding a way to involve her family in it. They were an unorthodox group who had all taken increasingly less interest in their part in society, shunning all others now for their tight, insular group. Her daughter was probably spoiled for all decent society, yet, Caroline could not care less. She was surrounded by love, and that was all that mattered. This ragged group had held her together, when she had thought all was lost, and they continued to fight for her future, her happiness. She owed them everything. And sometimes, when they were all together, lost in laughter and companionship, she almost forgot the gaping hole in her heart, the one that sometimes threatened to swallow her whole. She forgot that there should be another chair around the table, she forgot what the bed felt like then there was another person in it, how warm it was.

Talk had turned to the birthday feast and she listened along, swept up in the excitement of the shared celebration. Two years, the age of her daughter would forever mark the length of her loneliness and his exile, but she could not lament it, or anything else that had brought Ellie into her life. Her constant reminder of how her world had ended and started all at the same time.

"Caroline, we cannot have three puddings, I have been letting out my dresses more and more lately - soon they'll be nothing but tatters left," Rebecca was complaining.

"**B**ходить" the old lady unbolted the door, and reluctantly let him enter.

"спасибо" he murmured as he strode up the stairs. In his sloping attic room, he pulled his case from under the bed and opened it. Means of communication were too dangerous at present, and it was about time he got out of here. He packed his travel documents, some money and started to slip other things into his pockets, adding layers for travelling. St Petersburg would not be breached, he was willing to bet his life on it. Soon the French would be in retreat, and Napoleon vulnerable, fleeing back toward Paris. The Russians were regrouping and would plan to follow, and he was sure Prussia, Austria and at least Sweden would also be planning on seizing this opportunity. The information was worth something, and it would be worth the most to the first people to hear it.

Slipping down the stairs, he crept out the back door, and onto the canal-lined streets of St. Petersburg. He was heading South West and he needed a horse, and some supplies before he could be on his way.

That night he slept off the road a little way. The summer had been warm in Russia, but winter had begun creeping her long fingers down from the North, another reason to get South as quickly as possible. The ground was hard, yet it was quiet, the darkness crept in, as the last of cool nights in the turn toward Winter. He had built a small fire to keep warm and huddled close to it now. He was far enough off the road to be safe, or so he hoped, if not, there was the knife in his boot. He ate in silence with the wind for company, sipped some water, rationing his supplies, then stretched out and looked into the fire. The flames moved sinuously against their black backdrop, coaxed by the wind. It never changed, the flames, the fire. He had stared into it in many a place in the last few years, in army encampments, banquet halls, military hospitals, in the street, huddled with other men for warmth, for survival. It cut a stark difference to his years of drawing rooms and aged whiskey in cut crystal. Of family, and friendship, of love... of her.

As always, when night fell, and the darkness crowded in, she came to him. Her smell, her laugh, the way her obsidian hair moved across her shoulders as she shook it free at the end of a long day. He closed his eyes and imagined the warmth that moved over his face was her fingers. He fell asleep, as always with her voice ringing in his ears, memories that had become more real to him than his actual life. He passed his days delighting over which tales to tell himself by night. She was in each one, the times they had spent together his lullaby, and each night she sent him to sleep, which he hated to wake from, and hastened to return to.

✿

*T*he chamber where Caroline had been seated to speak to the judge was small and oppressive: dimly light, and choking dusty air. She felt her heart clamber into her mouth as she sat, and her breath grew short. The questions were mercifully quick and to the point. This judge was not a man to deliberate, overly long, and he let her leave quickly. He had seemed honest and fair if looks were any measure, which she was sure they weren't, but at any rate, it was over and she was able to return to the country. Being in London was dizzying, not only because she was the source of gossip wherever she went.

If the tales of Lord Lucian Ashford were romantic and exaggerated before, they had since become things of legend, and she found girls throwing envying looks at her, and sighing over the utterly romantic and dramatic state of her relationship with her husband. They would be disappointed to know the truth, she thought bitterly. There was no relationship, no contact, no idea or notion of where he was, and what he was doing. If he was even still alive, she had no idea.

Elspeth asked her, from time to time, and she always gave a suitably honest, yet vague answer. Once his name was cleared, he may well return, so she did not wish to tell Elspeth that he wouldn't, however, the letter stuck in her mind, and his vow to save her from the harm he would cause. The words stoked anger in her now, anger that he stayed away, though she knew he must at present. But anger that he was capable of it, of shutting her so wholly out of his heart when hers remained a mess of broken dreams and longing.

She planned to spend that night at the Fairfax's old townhouse in London before she travelled with Charles and Katherine back to Blackhill Hall the next day. They had bought the house, and it was a useful base in London. Caroline had never set foot inside the Ashfords' London home since that night, and she never would again.

Charles took his leave of the two women early, to attend to matters relating to the courts. As the ladies sat in the parlour, chatting, reminiscing, a caller was announced. It was unusual as they were seldom at home here in town, so they straightened themselves and waited for the person.

"Mr Lee ma'am," the footman intoned, and Caroline hid the look of surprise from her face.

"Why, Mr Lee, you look utterly unchanged in the years since last we saw you," Katherine waded in.

"I may say the same for you both, ladies. It is so refreshing to see your house open, I admit I was only passing when I noticed and wondered who might be in attendance."

"Well, your curiosity is our gain," Katherine said politely.

"No, the gain is all mine," he murmured, turning his attention to Caroline, who was quiet.

"Lady Ashford, may I enquire after your daughter?"

"She is very well, I thank you. She remained in the country," Caroline said.

"Ah, yes, well, I have always thought London a poor location to raise children, the country is much better. I wouldn't have got into half the scrapes I did if it weren't for the rambling fields of home, nor had half as much fun," Joshua said.

"I agree, Mr Lee. I miss it sometimes," Katherine said with a palpable wistfulness in her tone.

"And your sister, I trust," Joshua prompted.

"Yes, of course, I miss her every moment of the day."

"Well, I am very happy to tell you that both Mrs Taylor and her husband are well, and..." he leaned on the edge of his seat, "expecting their second child."

"No! My goodness, how can this knowledge not have reached me yet! That is wonderful. This war is not doing anything to improve the relations between common people, that is sure."

"Did you have much opportunity to call on the Taylors in Virginia?" Caroline asked suddenly, deciding to join the conversation a little abruptly.

"Not as much as I would have liked, but, yes, some," Joshua said smoothly, smiling at her.

Caroline nodded, feeling better she had participated, yet completely unsure how to carry on the discussion. This is what happened when your usual conversation partner was two years old: adult conversation becomes something foreign. Katherine and Joshua chatted on and after a short while, he made his excuses to leave. The visit was pleasant, and Caroline realised that she had missed the varied company, occasionally. She spent so much time with her friends and family, they ran out of things to talk about, and sometimes caught themselves rehashing the same old stories.

After he left, they went to bed, and Caroline lay in that familiar pose and stared at the moon out the window. Sometimes she wondered if he looked at the same moon if he thought of her when he did. She wondered if thoughts of her made him sad or happy. As the full moon rose, she drifted off to sleep, dreaming of a man who moved like a wolf, somewhere out there in the night.

~*February 1813*~
Wiltshire

*T*here was some kind of commotion going on at the house, Caroline could see it: yet, there were only a few times she had the chance to go riding of late, and she longed to make it last. She decided it could wait and finished her ride, going far and wide, pushing Theia when she felt she wanted it. They had been lucky to avoid snow so far this Winter and wrapped up, she found the cold air refreshing. She had never stopped riding astride and put her strong body down to the countless hours she spent riding or running after her squealing human ball of energy.

Finally returning to the stables, out of breath and tired she handed her horse over to be groomed and pulled off her riding hat. She walked toward the house, slowly, catching her breath. Walking in, and shedding her boots, as always, she wandered through the huge house until she heard voices coming from the study.

"How long?" Katherine's voice asked quietly.

"That I do not know... but I must do this. I cannot rest until I have."

"I know how important it is to you, of course, it is to me as well... I just..." she trailed off, and Caroline heard Charles moving about in the study.

"When I return, we shall be married, the biggest, most extravagant wedding your heart desires"

"My heart only desires you," Katherine insisted and Caroline backed away slowly, not wanting to interrupt their privacy. Her heart sank. Even through the closed doors, she had heard the pain ringing in Katherine's uncharacteristically quiet voice. She could only imagine how Katherine must be feeling - after all this time, growing softly older and less marriageable by the day within arm's reach of the man who held her heart, always in limbo, always a bit uncertain. As time ambled by, each day must rub at her like tight leather against a blister, niggling at first, but growing more raw and bloody with each step.

✿

"*K*atherine, you know I want nothing more than to be with you, and never parted from your side; but, I must do this."

She heard the immovable note in his tone under the softness of his guilt for leaving, like granite wrapped in velvet, and knew that he could not stop himself from going, any more than she could stop herself from asking him to stay with her.

"Let me come with you," Katherine tried again, not letting him pull away from her as he stood by the door, his case packed. The house was asleep, and only they remained awake.

"You, my love, are too precious to risk... and what of Rebecca, Caroline and Ellie, they need you here."

"Wesley is here, and Issac."

"Please, Katherine. I will be home before you know it, and I will reunite our family. I would not leave you for anything less vital to this family's happiness."

"What if something happens to you?" Katherine said desperately, pain gathering at her forehead, and drumming down her spine. They walked slowly together, their bodies pulling in opposite directions, a subtle ballet of body language that Charles was winning.

"Nothing bad shall befall me, I promise you."

"How can you promise such a thing?"

"Because, our love story has barely begun, and nothing can prevent true love. Delay it, perhaps, not stop it... this is merely a delay," Charles murmured, pulling her in for another soul-searing kiss that gilded her pain and worry with bittersweetness.

"Be careful," she whispered against his lips, and before her tears could fall from her eyes, he was gone. The carriage moved away down the winding driveway and she watched the moonlight glint off the horses' harnesses until they were out of sight. She wrapped her arms around the hollow coldness in her stomach and looked up to the sky. The night was clear and cold, winter upon them in earnest. Sighing she turned back to the house, going into the bright warmth, though it failed to chase the chill from her bones. She had a feeling she would not be warm again for a long while.

⚙

"I don't understand," Caroline repeated. Wesley paused as he spooned up his breakfast.

"They ruled in our favour Caroline, Lucian is a free man in England. His name is clear, as is yours. Your property is reinstated, you are a rich woman once more," he joked, and put his fork down as he saw she was stricken by the news. She stared at him, her mouth slightly ajar, her heart seemed to have stopped beating in her chest.

"I am sorry I mentioned it so casually," he said, shock written across his face, "I thought you had already been told..."

"Why wasn't I?" she asked suddenly, wondering how such news could have gone undisclosed in such a small group.

"Well, Charles was preparing yesterday, and left late last night, and I can only assume Katherine is not in a fit state to attend breakfast this morning. I'm sorry, my dear, but I supposed we all just assumed that someone else had-"

"Left for where?" she asked, her stomach feeling hollow at Wesley's words.

"He has gone to find Lucian, he has gone to bring him home... for you... for us, for Ellie..." Wesley said. Caroline stared at him, a tear ran from her eye and dropped to the table.

"Home?" her voice wavered as she spoke. Wesley stood up, moving to go to her, but Caroline suddenly pushed her chair back from the table. She went to the door of the room,

"Thank you for telling me," she called back as she left the room and gathered her heavy winter skirts, and ran upstairs.

She hastened down the hall and came to a door, where she knocked briefly before pushing it open. It was dark, the curtains still drawn, but Caroline could make out the bed well enough. She moved toward it, and without hesitation, climbed in. She pulled the covers around her and opened her arms. Katherine's tear-stained face came willingly to her shoulder, and she sobbed her heartbreak and worry into her sister's embrace. Caroline stroked her head and held her tightly.

CHAPTER 10

~September 1813~
Ménéham

*C*harles walked home from the common room, returning to his rented bed. The tiny town in France he had followed signs of his brother to, was turning out to be slightly too small to hide the fact he was an Englishman in. He did his best to blend in, and his French was more than adequate, yet still, some of the looks he had gotten over dinner, made him a little apprehensive.

There was only one last place to check, tomorrow morning and then he would be on his way from here.

The next morning dawned brightly, and he collected his things and left the inn. The town sat on the water and was quite picturesque, with its small boats moored and clusters of local business ringing the harbour. He walked along the cobbled street, enjoying the smells of the local food; keeping his head down among the locals. He walked to the church and glanced all around. There was no one watching him as far as he could see, so he went to the rough wooden board outside, where sheaves of white paper had been tacked up. He started to search through them. It was the same in every town.

Hearing a rumour of an Englishman who spoke French like a local, with burnished golden hair, who should not be crossed in a fight. Then, checking the lists, which was the most disheartening part of the search. So many dead men, most little more than boys. He ran a finger down the page, trying to decipher the tiny script, so cramped as to fit too many names on one page. His finger kept on running, faster than his eye. Suddenly, something jumped out at him, an L. A. He skimmed back up with his finger, finding the initial, and following the line along to the full name.

L.A. – Lucian Ashford – January 9th 1813 – disease

It was like a punch to the stomach. Charles closed his eyes, and counted slowly, bracing an arm against the wall to hold himself up. It was a dream he had, often, that he found his brother's name on one of these abominable lists, when now Lucian was free and could return home - always, in his dreams, he found him too late. He opened his eyes again, checking the name once more, his heart quaking. It had not changed, it was there, in ink, scratched on the parchment. The record of his death.

A commotion to the left of the square pulled his attention around and he saw a group of local men speaking together and gesturing to him. Looking one last time at the list, he turned and walked away. One last place he needed to visit before he left. If Lucian had died of disease, he had probably done so at the local hospital, or on the battlefield, in which case he would have no way of knowing for sure. Charles prayed for the latter. Anything that left room for hope.

He made his way to the hospital, which also had a large military medical area. He spoke to a few people, and finally tracked down the person in charge of records. The man grumbled and complained, but after Charles greased his palm, he was more obliging. He went off with the name written down. Charles looked around the hospital, the beds were full. It was quiet and peaceful there. Nuns drifted between the beds, softly rustling as they soothed and calmed their patients.

Without warning, the man returned, and dropped a canvas bag at his feet, before turning away to deal with other matters. Charles's heart was pounding. He pulled open the bag and reached inside. The identity papers were worn, damaged by sun and water. He pulled it out and held it up to the light. The world around him seemed to slow down then, and his heart beat strangely. It was so familiar and so foreign at the same time, as though it were happening to someone else, though he had lived it many times in his worst fears.

The papers were difficult to make out. It was not definitive, he decided. There were a few other things which might have belonged to anyone: shoes, a snuff-box, a tinderbox- he forced his shoulders to relax an inch, it probably wasn't him, these could have belonged to any soldier. There was a last object in the bag, and Charles pulled it out. It was a letter... he turned it over in his hands, his fingers practically trembling as he unfolded it.

Dear Caroline

Charles's throat closed. It was like a physical blow, a fist to the heart, he coughed and slid from the edge of the empty bed where he had perched.

"Monsieur, êtes-vous bien?" a nurse rushed to his side, as he coughed again and again, unable to drag air into his lungs. His eyes were dripping, unable to contain his emotion, as it exploded like lit gunpowder, incinerating everything inside of him. The nurse fussed around him, as he sat hugging his knees to his chest, he could not tear his eyes from the paper lying on the floor.

Dear Caroline

It was the end of everything, his search, their hope, the legal case... all for nothing. Caroline would remain alone, Ellie fatherless and their family reduced again, Katherine abandoned for a foolish dream. The fuss was growing around him, and he struggled to his feet, reaching down for the letter, he folded it carefully and put it into his pocket. Grabbing the identity papers, he left the hospital, the nurse and doctor staring after him.

~January 1814~
Wiltshire

*C*hristmas had been an intimate affair at the Blackhill Hall. Ellie had loved it, though she missed her uncle Charles, as they all did. News from abroad worried them all, especially that pertaining to France.

When word reached them from Charles that he would be home soon, the house was thrown into disarray. There was no word on how his search had gone, or if he was returning alone. Caroline watched the road each day, her heart pounding. Elspeth asked constantly why everyone was nervous, yet they had no reply for her. Caroline rehearsed what she would say to Lucian, how she would introduce their daughter, one that everyone had believed would die, her miracle.

There had been no way to tell Lucian that he had become a father despite the accident. No way to bring him back. With the court deciding against him, and the madness of birth, realising that Caroline's arrangement had come to fruition, making her fortune practically untouchable, and leaving her the wife of a wanted man, penniless and dependent on her family, there had been no time to search for him then.

Once that had passed, and a routine established, they had turned their attention to the legal problems. Caroline's memory had finally been fully restored, but whilst it had brought Lucian's freedom, privately it had brought other things. Did he blame her? Her memories were painful of the events leading up to Silus's death. She had been so naïve, so incredibly idealistic and foolish. She remembered the look on Lucian's face, the way he had watched the life leave Silus's eyes. It had scared her, such darkness, she wondered if it had overcome him now that he was alone, or if it was better without her.

How would she explain it all to Ellie, his sudden presence in their lives again? Would Caroline recognise him? After so long apart... Where had he been, what had he done? What sights had he witnessed? Who was he now? What if he had changed beyond recognition, what if he had met someone else, fallen in love with some sweet, honest girl from an exotic land. She then wondered how she had changed, and how he would perceive her. She was stronger, more independent. She had gotten that which was so important to her once, and the irony was, all she wanted was to be by his side.

Over two years, and nothing from him... not even a letter to inform her that he was still alive. It broke her heart. He had decided to stay away, for her good, a sentiment that she would argue heartily against, yet she had not had that choice, and he had decided for both of them.

She was pulled from her thoughts as she saw a cloud of dust hover above the rise. A carriage approached. She smoothed her perspiring palms against her skirts and wasn't sure what to pray for.

✿

*T*hey gathered in the courtyard, and Rebecca gripped Caroline's hand as the carriage drew nearer. It finally stopped and Caroline tried not to peek into the dark interior. She felt as though her heart was beating twice, three times as fast as usual, and all her senses were trained on the carriage. The door opened and a figure stepped down, it took her a moment to realise it was Charles. He stepped away and turned to the group. Caroline could not prevent her eyes from returning to the carriage, willing the door to open again. Yet, it did not, it remained shut, and she felt Rebecca squeeze her hand as if to break bones. Katherine moved to her other side, gripping her around the waist.

"No, Charles, no," Rebecca whispered, and Caroline turned her attention to Charles as he walked toward her, his face serious.

"What? Tell me, what is it? You couldn't find him?" Caroline demanded.

Charles swallowed hard and looked down.

"I... found him."

"He doesn't want to come home..." she said in a whisper. Charles was reaching into his coat pocket, and handing her something. Papers. Rebecca let out a loud sob and threw herself into Isaac's arms. Caroline stared wordlessly down at the papers in her hand. Her brain could not reconcile it. She watched Katherine reach for Charles with her free hand, unwiped tears now sliding down her face, and Caroline realised what it meant.

She turned away from the courtyard and silently walked through the Hall. The house that held so many memories. She saw him sketching her through the window as she climbed the stairs steadily. She saw him waiting in the hall for her after their wedding, to escort her to the breakfast. She saw him waiting for her at the top of the stairs for their kitchen excursions, felt him gripping her elbow as she descended the stairs in the dark.

She walked numbly along the hall, the very one where the Fairfaxes voices had drifted to them on the floor, and she had tried to escape, terror flooding her veins, and he had gently but firmly betrayed her and changed her life forever. She reached the playroom and walked straight inside, dropping to the floor beside her daughter, their daughter. She pulled her tightly to her, dropping kisses on her head and face. Elspeth wriggled and complained for a moment, before looking up and seeing the tears on her mother's face.

"Mummy" she whispered as Caroline buried her face in her hair, and for once Ellie allowed it.

~November 1814~
Wiltshire

"*L*et us not forget, one last present," Katherine said brightly as she handed a package over to Ellie. Ellie clapped her hands in delight. Grabbing it, and causing laughter, she sank back and looked around at everyone in attendance.

"I guess what this one is," she announced, feeling it carefully through the paper. "A book?" she guessed confused, finally ripping the paper off. It was indeed a book, coloured and beautiful. "What's it about?" she asked. Rebecca leaned forward and flicked it open.

"It's about America, the new world... that's where your mummy is from, that's why she talks funny," Rebecca laughed. Ellie giggled in response, turning the pages innocently, before dropping her final prediction.

"This one is from daddy?" the silence that fell after her light words made her face fall, and lip quiver. Caroline was paralysed at the comment, and completely unsure how to respond. Wesley jumped in and tried to divert her attention, but Caroline's own reaction had not gone unnoticed by her astute daughter.

It was hours later, as Caroline tucked her into bed, singing a lullaby, and stroking her smooth cheek that she brought it up again.

"Does my daddy live in America?" she asked. Caroline bit her lip and shook her head.

"No, sweetheart, he doesn't."

"Where does he live?" She pressed. Caroline kissed her on the cheek and smiled down at her.

"It is too late to talk about that tonight, let's talk about it another time."

"When?"

"Another time."

"Tomorrow?"

"If you wish," Caroline said with an internal sigh. She had to tell her sometime, explain everything, but she didn't know where to start. She wished her daughter goodnight and went downstairs.

"Did you tell her?" Rebecca asked. Caroline shook her head.

"She was asking about her father, not your book, sadly."

"Did you tell her about Lu- her father?"

Caroline shook her head again, sinking into a chair by the fire, and staring into the flames.

"I'll try and get her to read the book again tomorrow, get her interested in it," Rebecca offered.

"Do hurry, dear sister, not long now, and we'll all be Americans," Wesley said, waggling his eyebrows.

"I shall never be an American. I shall always be English, thank goodness. I just don't think it would suit me. Seems rather taxing on the lungs," Rebecca said, and Katherine shot her a sideways smirk before she went on.

"Well, I don't know about Caroline, but I can't wait to go home. What about you, Isaac?"

"Mmm-" Isaac agreed. not looking up from his paper. "I'm looking forward to some bourbon and some proper mountains."

"Charles darling, you are going to die at the wild manners there, but I cannot wait to see Eva and Eli, and mother, father and Frances too."

The decision to move to America had come suddenly. Isaac suggested it one evening when they'd all been sharing some brandy, and the notion seemed to have taken the room by storm. It seemed to Caroline that they had all been going through so much, all waiting for Lucian, all waiting for their lives to go back to normal. After the last few years, England itself felt stuffy and restrictive to them, holding them tight and fast to painful memories. No more waiting. It took little more than an evening discussing by the fire for them all to decide that they wanted nothing more than to set out to a new land for a new life. They could all have their fresh start in Virginia.

After Charles's careful management of the coffers, focusing less on speculating, and more on crops, mines, fair rents, and the procurement of the newest technology in harvesters; the family's fortune was now steady and sustainable, and left quite enough for them to be generous with causes that were dear to their heart. Blackhill Hall was in good repair, and could be let, if they decided that they needed the extra income. Between them there were also several more homes and town-houses that might be let or sold, and with Caroline's fortune and lands still untouched and intact, even Charles saw no reason why money concerns need worry them for a very long time.

Isaac could return to his family, and Rebecca has begun to hint at starting a new one. Katherine would be close to her parents again and her sister, she and Charles would marry, and free of English social restraints, Charles might even try his hand at business. Wesley was giddy at the notion of an adventure, and though it was never said, Caroline suspected that he was also hopeful at the notion of escaping from under London's choking social censure, where anonymity might afford him certain freedoms. And Caroline, Caroline could raise her child in the new world, free from the shadows of her father, in the country of Caroline's birth and heritage. At the thought of it, her heart lifted and soared like a bird on the wing.

There was nothing but painful memories left in England. She needed a clean start, a chance to heal her broken heart, which would not happen living in her dead husband's home, haunted by the persistent ghost of his memories, a man she missed so much at times it was hard to remember to breathe.

One more month, and they would be on their way. She had not told Elspeth yet. She worried for a moment over what to tell her about her father, then pushed it away. Caroline would tell her just as soon as she could speak the words.

⁂

Francois Dubois enjoyed the hard work of his farm. The political situation in France was uncertain, yet he enjoyed the simple lifestyle of his day to day. He tended the animals and the crops, picked vegetables, and watched the boats coming and going from the small village in which he lived.

Some days, the widow Rochelle would come with a pot of her home-cooked soup, and coax him to rest in the shade of a hazelnut tree and eat with her. They would sit and eat, she would chatter on about the village and the town, people they both knew. He would smile and nod, enjoying the company for a while. Once when a storm suddenly hit, they had taken shelter in his house. Her wet dress clinging to her body, she had asked if she might stay, and he had responded that it was indeed too dangerous to go out in the storm. As they sat together before the fire later that evening, she had lightly touched his sleeve, and then slid her hand up his arm, squeezing the farm-forged muscles on the way. He had allowed it for a moment, his body sighing at a touch, any touch, before he gently took her hands in his and dropped them to her knee.

"I am sorry," he whispered, her rejection clear on her face.

"What is the matter? I thought you liked me?"

"I like you well enough, you are a lovely woman," he replied, staring back at the flames, and her.

"So, what is the problem?"

"I am not a whole man," he said, and she frowned at him, looking him up and down, wondering where he hid his deficiencies.

"You appear whole to me," she whispered.

"No, I am not."

"Well, what are you missing?" she asked, growing offended.

"A heart," he had said simply, unable to tear his gaze from the flames.

�❀

*W*hen Joshua Lee arrived at Blackhill Hall, Caroline stayed away from him. Her heart was a waste ground and she trod a delicate balance each day, interaction with someone such as Joshua, a reminder of her past, a reminder that she would one day need to move on, made it harder sometimes. He was helping Charles to prepare for their journey to America, and would in fact be accompanying them, as their trip happily coincided with his return home.

Caroline spent her time preparing for the trip in her own fashion. She walked the house where she had been a girl, pulled into womanhood so suddenly. The place where she had found a new family and become a mother. She committed the gentle hills and valleys of England to memory, the greens and purples. The lake with its herons and glimmering reflections. Sometimes she sat at her old window, and stared out of it, at another window, memories taking her far away. Sometimes, as the night became morning, she fancied she could see him there, sketching with feverish intensity, his face catching the beams of moonlight that shone off the water of the lake. Yet, when the moon sank and the sun took its place, the window became empty again, always empty. She would not forget it, every small detail, for it was where their love had lived, had grown. The story of her great love lived in these walls, in this land, and when she left it, she would not forget one detail of it.

One morning, she dressed Ellie warmly and took her out through the extensive gardens, each one different, some formal, some for the kitchens, some kept carefully in a way that made them look wild, like a tumble of wildflowers which had all just chosen to bloom there. They walked for a long time, skirts dragging through the wild grasses that had grown near the river bank. After a while, they came to a tree that grew some distance from the lake. The lush green mop of leaves had turned to spun gold in the crisp Autumn air, and it looked even more magical than before.

Ellie watched as her mother tied her skirts up and off her legs, and then lifted the hanging curtain of branches, exposing a tunnel into the cool, golden darkness. Ellie squealed and clung on tightly as Caroline started to walk through, and reached her hand out for her daughter to join her. Ellie gasped when she found that there was a room under there, where the generous tree's limbs and leaves could block out the world, for a few more days at least before winter winds would whisk them away.

"Who's she, mummy?"

"She's the fairy queen." Ellie gasped again, blue eyes round and shining. "Isn't she beautiful?" Caroline smiled sadly.

"What's her name?"

"I don't know, pumpkin. Why don't you ask her?" In the shadows, the sculpture gazed down with hooded eyes and looked almost as if she might turn her face up to her guests at any moment. Ellie kept hold of Caroline's hand, and took a few steps closer, reaching her hand out to touch the smooth green stone of the hem of her gown reverently.

"Is it magic?"

"It is a magical place. This is a very special tree where a little boy, a very special one, used to come all the time. He used to play under here, and talk to the fairy queen, and he started to draw pictures here like you do. Sometimes when he ran away from scary things, and came here to feel safe and be protected by her," she continued.

"If she's a fairy, can she give wishes, mummy?" Ellie whispered.

"Maybe, sweetheart. Maybe she can. What will you wish for?" Ellie's little face screwed up, not one to make a wish in haste.

Caroline sat down on the soft carpet of moss and laid back as she had once done, watching the fading golden sun shine through the leaves, like gold leaf on the arching dome of a cathedral. She had not been there even once since Lucian had left. Her chest felt so tight that she thought her ribs might crack under the weight.

"I will wish for a sister!" Ellie said decidedly, reaching out for the hand of the queen, squeezing her eyes closed tight, and biting her lip.

Caroline closed her eyes and hoped that her daughter would be too distracted to see the tears which slipped from them and slid into the hair at her temples.

They were quiet for a while, until Ellie started to wander around, petting the moss, looking for snails, collecting sticks to build a fairy house.

"Are there trees like this in America?" she asked.

"No, darling, this is the only tree just like this in the whole world, and it belongs to you now. But, in America, there are lots of beautiful trees, magical trees, trees that you can climb and look out over the fields from, like a bird high in the clouds, trees much much bigger than you can even imagine." Caroline gripped Ellie's small hand and pulled her down on the moss next to her where once her father had lain.

614

"Ellie, I want to tell you about your father." The little girl's eyes lit up at her words and Caroline took a deep breath and started to explain the things that should never have to be told to a little girl who had never met her father.

Afterwards, Caroline finally conceded to her daughter's demand for stories of him. Ellie, who clearly did not truly understand, but was glad that she was finally able to hear stories, laughed and listened raptly with wonder and love lighting up her blue eyes for a man whom she would never know. It shattered the broken pieces of Caroline's ruined heart.

When the light faded away, and the air grew cold, they gathered up their skirts, brushed the leaves off, and made to go.

"Wait, mummy. Make a wish," Ellie demanded, pulling her with both hands back to the statue. Caroline began to shake her head but gave in at the look on her daughter's stubborn face. She took in the woman's beautiful features: soft, peaceful, a world away, and Caroline's heart shuddered as she closed her eyes, reached out, and let out a long, slow lung-full of breath; each painful beat of her splintered heart wishing for the same thing.

A dead wish that could never come true.

"*A*llow me," Joshua Lee said as he pulled Caroline's chair out at dinner. She sat down and turned a hesitant smile toward him.

"Thank you. We are so informal here at Blackhill, it is sometimes difficult to remember how one is supposed to act."

"Do not worry on my account. I have always been a little too lax in matters of etiquette for England," he said with a warm laugh.

"So, you leave tomorrow?" she asked as dinner was served.

"Yes, I will go and procure the tickets, finalise some business and wait for your arrival in two weeks, before we depart for home. I must admit I am looking forward to company on this voyage, it is certainly a long time to be alone."

"Less than two months? Why, Mr Lee, that is no time at all to be alone, believe me," she said with a small smile.

*T*he simple farm life was wonderful while it lasted, but eventually, it was time to move on. Another man called Francois Dubois came back from war and was sad to hear of his father's death, yet happy to find his father's legacy still intact, held together by a stranger with his name, with blond hair and an accent that was hard to place.

Napoleon had surrendered and was now imprisoned on Elba. The war was over, and a new time of peace was beginning. Time to rebuild and live again. Francois took over the farm, tried to pay the blond stranger, but he would not hear of it, and simply left one day, walked off out of the village with nothing more than the clothes on his back. The man set off toward the coast, having said that he had a hankering to see England. Francois had wished him well, and he was gone.

CHAPTER 11

~*November 1814*~
Portsmouth

*P*ortsmouth was as chaotic and dishevelled as she remembered it. The smells and sounds of gulls made the city clamorous and overwhelming after so long in the peace of the country at Blackhill. As they made their way to an inn to wait for their things to be transferred to the ship, Caroline urged them away from an all too familiar building that lined the waterfront. They ended up in a warm, dry, if slightly shabby, common room very close to their ship's dock, which Joshua had recommended. Charles, Isaac and Joshua were occupied outside, and Wesley remained with the women, given the unsavoury reputation of the area.

They ordered lunch and ate leisurely. The group was in high spirits that day, none more than Ellie, their adventure starting. Caroline was nervous, worried about the crossing, so close to Winter. At least money could afford them as much comfort as could be had, a world away from the poor wretched souls who ran for a new land with nothing left in their purse. She found that she was apprehensive to see the home of her youth. She also felt a heavy sort of sadness at leaving England, one which she pushed to the side, yet could not quite forget.

"You know, one of the best meals I have ever eaten was very similar to this, on the road to Gretna Green. We had been travelling for so long without pause, that the unmoving seat and dinner was quite the best thing I can remember."

"I am sure the company had nothing at all to do with it," Katherine waggled her eyebrows, not finding the food as appealing as Rebecca.

"Where is Gretna Green?" Ellie asked.

"In Scotland," Rebecca told her.

"Why did you go there?" Rebecca did not rush to answer.

"That, my love, is a long story...it involves my sister, whom you will soon meet, and she is very, very beautiful," Katherine began, settling back to tell it.

❀

*C*harles finished his tour of what would be the family's accommodation on the ship. He nodded to the captain and climbed up the steep steps to the deck.

"How do you find it? Not the most comfortable, I know," Joshua said, coming to find him.

"It is more than adequate, thank you, Mr Lee, for helping us so much with this," Charles said, pulling on his gloves and hat, the brisk wind of the high upper deck chilling him.

"Please, no thanks are necessary. Knowing that you sail with three women and a child, I could hardly stand by and not help to make you all more comfortable, and safe. I am only sorry it is the best the ship can offer."

"Worry not, Mr Lee, those three women are hardier than you might expect," Charles said with a laugh as they made their way down the gangplank and toward the inn where the rest of them waited. Seeing their things by the hold, they veered off and watched their heavy trunks being boarded.

"You seem to have brought surprisingly little, given that you will remain there for an extended amount of time."

"We plan to remain there indefinitely. We have family there, and there is little point holding onto things of... the past," Charles stated emotionlessly.

"Of course, and you will find the climate and lifestyle different perhaps," Joshua went on conversationally, highlighting the differences he always found the most striking when he travelled between the two countries. Charles listened politely, his eyes watching the cases, then drifting over the docks.

As they finished with the luggage, Joshua excused himself to check out of his boarding house and disappeared down the dock. Charles looked at the place where the remaining members of his family awaited him. He was finding it harder than he had expected, leaving England. A knot sat in his throat, unmoving, despite his attempts to swallow it. He thought of how their bright conversation would pull him from his melancholia, and realised he was not quite ready for it.

He turned and walked along the busy waterfront. Business, from inns to pubs and brothels spilt their wares out, the smells not something he would forget in a hurry. He chose a decent looking pub and entered. The common room was quiet, and he sat at one of the roughshod tables and asked for a strong drink from a surly-looking server. As his drink came, he sipped it, grimacing at the taste. Still, it was slightly numbing, and left him alone with his thoughts.

They had not sold any of their properties in the end, and had decided to keep them just in case they needed to return at any point, but had let the townhouses for extra income. The war of 1812 was fresh in everyone's mind, though Mr Lee assured them all that it had ushered in an era of peaceful trade and negotiation. Charles had combed through his ledgers, settled things with estate managers and tenant farmers, notified banks of their plans, before checking it all over again. He hoped it would be enough.

"Now, now, wot's a high and lofty gentleman like yourself doing, drinking in ere then?" a rough voice pulled him from his thoughts, and Charles tensed, turning to see two men standing beside him.

"Minding my own business is all," he muttered and froze at the glimpse of a knife one of the dirty looking men flashed.

"I wouldn't mind takin some o yer business myself. How much do men like you carry on you anyway? Let's go outside and have a talk about it," a quieter man said, and Charles looked around the room for anyone who might be of aid. It was dark, and there were few patrons, none of them sober. He met the eye of the barkeep, who looked down guiltily and scrubbed at the bar busily, not looking back up. He felt the sharp point of the blade bite into his side, dulled through his wool jacket, at least until pressed harder, as he knew it eventually would be if he argued. His whole family were waiting on him. They relied on him. It was not a risk worth taking, his pride be damned. He set his face in stone and stood up, as the man with the knife urged him toward the back. Charles mentally took inventory of his possessions and hoped that if he was quick-witted enough, he might escape with his life after they took his purse.

He had some money on him, not a lot, but the thing he worried the most over, were the tickets. He had the tickets on him.

They pushed him through a door and he found himself in the alleyway behind the inn. It was stinking with piss, and refuse buckets and slops poured from the kitchen windows. The floor underfoot sank as they walked through it, and the air was filled with shouts from the buildings that towered over the narrow walkway on each side, the screaming of the gulls deafening overhead.

"Stop ere, it's good enuff," one man said as he started to dig through Charles's pockets. He held his arms out and tried to reason with them, which was thoroughly ignored.

"Ere! Wot's this?" the man asked, as he pulled the tickets from his pocket. The two men poured over them. They couldn't read them, but could obviously recognise them, and Charles wondered how many innocent passengers had lost their tickets at the inn.

"I never seen one wif this paper before," one said, rubbing the fine paper between his fingers.

"Must be first class and all that. They'll fetch a pretty penny" he said, smiling, and shoving the white papers into his filthy pocket. Charles sighed and started to unbutton his heavy overcoat.

"I am afraid I cannot allow you to take those," he announced as he took off his coat and threw it over a barrel.

With his body less encumbered now, he squared himself to endure their attack. He had never been in the military, yet had been trained in fencing and other physical pursuits from a young age, and he had always been strong, tall and broad. More importantly, from the breath of his adversaries, it seemed they might have overindulged already today. They wouldn't take much to drop.

One came at him, swinging slowly, he ducked quickly under his arm, and used the man's momentum to smash him into the wall behind, where he crumpled to the floor. The other, the quiet one, narrowed his eyes in anger and produced another knife, this one long and thin from his sleeve. He was the bigger threat, and he started forward, not attacking, but baiting. Charles held back, keeping his defensive pose.

Suddenly the man swung a punch which Charles went to dodge, realising almost too late that the other hand held the knife. He twisted away and barely escaped a stab to the neck. He stepped away warily, watching the other man. As he backed away from another lunge, his foot suddenly slipped on the muddy ground and he felt himself falling backwards. He landed hard on his back, and felt his breath leave his body.

The man was over him in an instant, raising the knife up to plunge it into his chest. Charles watched it, its delicate arch, the way it shone as it rushed to meet him.

Time seemed to slow for a moment, as the man's face twisted with hatred, his arm descending, unstoppable. Charles squeezed his eyes shut, not wanting that thief's face to be the last image he saw. He conjured another: blond curls, laughing eyes and a wicked smile. He waited. And waited. He heard a noise, a man gasping, wheezing and the gurgle of blood. He opened his eyes, trying to understand what had happened.

His attacker lay beside him, his neck a bloody scarf, as red liquid poured from a huge gash. He struggled for breath, his hands flailing against the ground beside him, his eyes finally glazing shut, and Charles wondered what he saw, as terror lit his eyes, and life left them.

His heart pounding, Charles slowly sat up, wiped the splattered blood from his face, the stinking mud already permeating his clothes, making him shiver with cold. Suddenly, a hand appeared before him offering him help. He went to take it, and looked up into the face of his saviour, dull grey light glinting through blond hair.

Then he was sure.

His heart stopped.

"You always were a clumsy fighter, brother."

End of Part 4

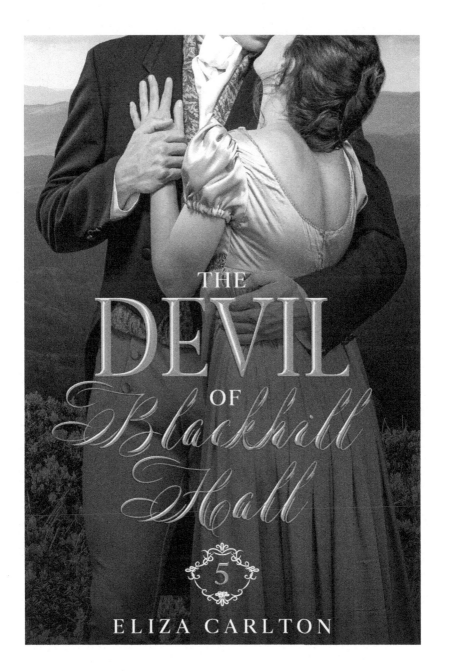

THE
DEVIL
OF
Blackhill
Hall

5

ELIZA CARLTON

CHAPTER 1

~November 1814~
Portsmouth

*C*harles let go his hand, as though it were scorched, and stepped back, his face draining of colour.

"How is it possible... it cannot be..." he muttered.

The figure standing over him was thin and weatherbeaten, his threadbare clothes blowing in the wind. His face was far from clean, his blonde thatch longer, loose strips framing his hard cheekbones, the rest pulled back and tied by a piece of string. His face was partially concealed by a thick beard that nearly hid the hollowness of his jaw. The blue of his eyes, once so vibrant, seemed dimmed - a watercolour brush dipped in murky water.

Lucian watched Charles curiously, his head to the side. Charles stared back, his mind spinning. He reached out an unsteady hand and touched his brother hesitantly on the arm. Lucian's brow crinkled as he watched the movement, yet he remained silent. His face was set, expressionless, and Charles wondered at the man before him. A spectre he was not, yet he was not his brother either.

"You... you are dead," Charles whispered. Lucian frowned at him.

"Most days, I am sure I would agree with you," Lucian said quietly, stepping back as Charles stood briefly, then sank down onto a wooden crate, unable to tear his eyes from the ghost before him. The sounds and smells around them had faded away, and the two men could not drag their eyes from each other. Charles was struck by the difference in his brother. Gone was the confident grin, the wicked mischievousness that Lucian had always radiated, drawing men and women alike. In its place was a vacancy, a hollow quality that Charles longed to shake off. His blue eyes were clouded and without expression, his face hardened by the time, the lines more clear, even his form seemed stripped of any softness or comfort.

"I came to find you, in France, I searched for months... I found your name on a list of the deceased. It said you had died of disease. I... I took your personal possessions back to England." Charles schooled his voice and spoke into the charged silence. Lucian leant back against the wall of the alley, his eyes drifting occasionally to its mouth, always watchful. He nodded slightly, before speaking.

"I met an old man in that village... he was dying, and was afraid that his family land would be seized by the state without a son present to inherit them. With most of France's sons at war, nothing has been secure. We swapped identities so that it would not be revealed that he had died before his son came home..."

"So, you were there? In Ménéham?"

"I believe so, I was there for a while. I told him my identity was more of a burden than a gift, but he was grateful for it at any rate," Lucian said.

"We got your personal possessions...a letter..." At these words, Charles saw a muscle tick in his brother's jaw, a flash of a memory came over his face before the blankness returned.

"There have been a great many letters over the years, more than I can count, to be honest."

"Why did you not send any?" Lucian looked at Charles steadily, unblinking, and Charles saw it then, the chasm of emptiness that yawned there, in those eyes.

"But..." Charles struggled. "How came you to be here now? I cannot understand it."

"Coincidence," Lucian sighed as if he were too tired to bother explaining. "I've been working the docks, there is always work to be found for men with no past, who want no questions asked of them. Safe enough if you keep moving. I was in Bournemouth last week, and Liverpool before that," he shrugged.

"Why did you not you come to us - send word?"

"Why did you come to France to find me?" Lucian's voice, sounding almost like a stranger in its tone, cold and accusing, it pulled Charles back as his hollow eyes searched his.

"Because you are a free man. Your name is clear," Charles said, clearing his throat, and his eyes absorbed with this Lucian, this new man who seemed achingly familiar, yet so changed at the same instant.

Lucian took the news quietly, showing barely a sign of the significance of the news, and Charles was unable to tell if it meant anything at all to him.

"In that case, why are we sitting in this alley? Let us go and have a drink somewhere a little nicer, at your expense of course," Lucian joked, his laugh bitter and devoid of emotion as he went to one of the bodies, pulling Charles's money and other stolen pieces from his pocket, scraping the filthiness off them.

"I cannot," Charles said, getting to his feet, and attempting to restore order to his clothes. He felt his reason start to return. His brother was not dead. It was real. Charles swung his coat over his soiled clothes, feeling chilled to the bone. Lucian straightened out the papers in his hand and glanced at his brother.

"Why not? Sick of my company already, dear brother?" he teased, cocking an eyebrow at him. Charles hesitated uncomfortably for a moment. He wondered how to tell him, how to break the news, that at this moment he was closer to his wife than he had been for years. His former wife, he corrected himself. Charles had reported his death to the English authorities.

"Lucian... Caroline is here." At his words, Lucian froze. His whole body tensed as if awaiting an attack.

"Why?" he asked, and even as he did, he looked down the paper in his hands. For a moment, Charles caught something in Lucian's face, a raw pain, for a flash, unable to be controlled. He stared at the tickets blankly for a moment that stretched out. Charles watched as Lucian struggled with something that he could not see. Then, he sniffed, and ran a hand through his hair, shaking off whatever had possessed him. He held the tickets in his hand and separated them out. Seven tickets.

"You are going to America?" he asked, raising his eyes slowly. Charles nodded. His mind was already racing to Lucian's next question. Ellie. What could he say? He wondered madly. It was not his news to tell, it was Caroline's. He did not wish to take it from her. How would Lucian react, to finding out he had missed the first four years of his daughter's life?

"Who goes on this trip?" Lucian asked, leaning back against the wall, folding his arms over his chest, his nonchalance heartbreaking.

"Caroline, Katherine - we are engaged, Wesley, and Rebecca goes with her husband Isaac Taylor. We have no plans of returning, Lucian." Charles saw the indifference in Lucian's face and wondered how he could keep his reactions so hidden.

"That is only six," he said, his voice hard, uncaring, casual almost.

"Joshua Lee travels with us." Charles made a decision, and he did not know if it was the right one, only it was the one that felt right at that moment. Elspeth was between Caroline and Lucian, and he could not involve himself. The only reaction from his brother was a tensing of his shoulders, yet his eyes told Charles that it was not heard easily. Then Lucian smirked, his smile too knowing.

"It is not in the capacity you think, however. Joshua Lee just happens to be returning to America. He travels with us coincidentally." Lucian laughed hollowly.

"I am sure," he snorted, looking down, and shaking his head slightly.

"What I mean to say... is that they are not together. Caroline and he. There is no one in her life. No one since you. She is alone. She has mourned for you these long years, Lucian." Lucian suddenly turned away from him, pushing off the wall.

"Stop, tell me no more. It is not a subject I wish to discuss. You know what I promised."

"A promise made in the heat of desperation and heartbreak. Surely now, you can see more clearly. She loves you still, Lucian. She doesn't blame you," Charles stepped closer, trying to reach him, this forbidding man before him.

"Stop," Lucian warned, his voice threatening silkily.

"Come with us. Start again in the new world with us. We leave this very hour. This meeting is meant to be, brother, though I have never before believed in fate, I cannot help but see the hand of it now." Lucian turned away, and Charles saw for a moment, a slight tremble in his hand as he held it up, a plea for silence.

Lucian stood, presenting his indifferent back for a while, before turning, his smirk back in place.

"Don't, brother, I know you mean well, and I thank you for it. But, I have made my peace with my decision... long ago. I am not the man you knew. I cannot go back, and pretend as though the last four years have not happened."

As his last word was spoken, a loud blast shook the dock, and Charles glanced toward the mouth of the alley. It was their ship, the long process of boarding had begun and everyone would be waiting for him, beginning to worry. He turned back to Lucian.

"I cannot leave you here, I cannot walk away from you. You are alive, it is a miracle. We cannot part again. I do not want to live a life without you. I cannot return to Caroline without you, when you are mere metres away..." Charles pleaded, yet even as he did he could see the resolve forming in Lucian's blue eyes.

"That part of my life is over. It is finished. Let her believe me to be dead. Let her forget me. And you should forget me too," Lucian said, his voice remote, and Charles had never quite heard such finality before.

"Why?" Charles asked, suddenly angry, furious at this unreachable stranger with his brother's eyes.

"Because... I made a promise, the only one I've ever kept, the only one that has ever mattered..." he trailed off, and for a fraction of a second, Charles saw him, his brother, more lost and broken than he had ever been. "Nothing has changed. Her life will be better without me. I vowed to protect her, even against myself, if need be. I will not break it now out of selfishness and weakness. It is all I have..." Lucian finished.

"Not true, you have us, your family... you have her."

"I lost you all years ago... when I ran, when I didn't come back, when father..." he drifted off again, before turning toward the mouth of the alley. "It looks like our reunion will be cut short, brother, your ship is preparing to depart," he said, his tone once again ice cold.

Charles felt frustration and anger rise up in him, and prompted by another blast from the ship, he turned and started toward the entrance of the alleyway. Seeing the ship before him, people swarming up the gangplank, already waving down to loved ones on the dock, he turned back briefly.

"If it is over, then why are you here? Why not stay away? Why come to England at all?" he demanded, as hurt burned up his face. Lucian looked at him, his features twisted with such sadness. Their eyes held for a long moment.

"Charles! Where have you been, come, let us not miss the boat as we stand beside it," Wesley's voice called, and Lucian looked eagerly, before he caught himself, and stepped back into the shadow. Charles lingered a moment more, unable to accept that he must leave him behind.

"Take care, brother," Lucian said with a grey finality, and turned and stepped out into the sunshine beyond the alley.

❀

*T*he fire of the inn was warm, and Lucian drank deeply. It was quiet inside, while outside the sound of the nearby ship loading was deafening. Charles would be on it by now, no doubt. He couldn't stand and watch them depart. He watched the flames weaving in and out, and he comforted himself that he had done the right thing, kept his promise. He was no longer the sort of man who had a family. He shifted his back against the rough-hewn pillar he sat behind, the instinct to stay hidden too ingrained to change now. It was getting colder, and he wondered where he might go next. Somewhere warm maybe, to wait out the Winter. He thought of the warm halls of Westmere, huge fireplaces and soft beds. Empty now, always empty...

'We will not return,' Charles's voice haunted him, ringing in his ears. He pushed it from his mind and focused back on his surroundings, the present.

He pondered his status as a free man, realising what it meant. He was free. He could go home. He could go back to Westmere, though, even as the thought occurred, he knew he never would. There was only so much pain one soul could take.

In the time he had been away, his intentions to stay away from Caroline for her own benefit had never been tested, because he could not return no matter how much he had wished it. Now though, now... only his will to do right by her remained. The resolve to keep his promise had been his only protection over the years, the only thing to cling on to, the certainty that his exile was giving her a better life. He was a darker man now than he had ever been. The loneliness and pain of separation had hardened around his heart, the knowledge that she must hate him, for breaking all his promises, for leaving her alone, emptiness - a wall that made his heart unreachable, untouchable, and after long enough, unfeeling. He would not shackle Caroline to such a man. The man who watched her bleed alone on the floor, their unborn child dying in her belly, while he instead took his revenge and murdered a man in front of her eyes.

"I am not sure where it might be, she probably dropped it in the sea," an irritated voice came from behind him, so painfully familiar, he couldn't move, as all his attention leapt to it.

"I am sure she didn't, it is her favourite," the next voice spun his world off its axis. It was soft, calm, and beautifully melodic. It was the voice he'd heard in dreams every living day for four years now. He held his breath.

"Well, we can buy her a new one, in New York, they have horses there, do they not?" a light tinkling sound, her laugh. His heart twisted painfully, stinging the backs of his eyes.

"Yes, of course, but this one is special. Go, I shall only be a moment, I want to check properly," Caroline said, waving Rebecca away with her hand. Lucian turned his head slightly to the side, from behind his hiding place. He saw her, his beautiful sister, her head held high, sweeping out of the inn. Suddenly, from directly behind him, he heard the scrape of a chair on the wooden floorboards. He slowly stood, hiding his body behind the wide pillar, waiting with bated breath.

"Excuse me, sir," Caroline suddenly said, right beside him. His heart pounded wildly, and he prepared to speak.

"Yes, ma'am, can I help you?" another man said, the innkeeper.

"I seem to have misplaced a small wooden horse, a child's toy," Caroline was saying, as Lucian steadied his trembling hands against the splintered wood of the pillar.

"I'm afraid I've not seen it," the man was saying, and before he knew it, Caroline was thanking him kindly, and rushing away again. As she passed, he could swear he could breathe the smell of her. She passed by and he turned his head, his eyes burned, itching for a glimpse of her. She started to move into his line of sight when he was suddenly knocked hard from behind. Turning he saw a man had bumped against him whilst trying to pass. He stepped away to allow him to pass09 and turned back around his eyes going to the door, but it was too late, she was gone.

He sat down again slowly, his mind far away. He shifted uncomfortably on the bench and heard a scraping sound. Lifting his foot, he saw the object that had fallen, caught between his foot and the wall, and doubtlessly the object they had been searching for.

Before he even had the chance to think, he was up and moving toward the doorway. He didn't stop to question the instinct, all he knew was that his body moved of its own volition. If he could see her, perhaps he could replace the last image he had of her, lying in a room scented by her blood. Afterwards, he could fulfil his promise, he told himself as he slowly, cautiously walked toward the docks in front of the ship.

He looked around and saw her nowhere. Just as well, he told himself, shading his eyes against the murky sun, and starting to turn back to the inn, glancing down at the object he held.

Suddenly, his eyes were drawn to a bonnet, holding a bundle of black silk hair in place, while whisps escaped in the wind, and blew across her neck. She was walking up the gangplank of the ship. He moved closer, as though lured by a spell. Her back moved steadily upwards, and he longed for her face, if only she would turn for a moment. As she reached the top, he saw her join his sister. Rebecca, he swallowed hard. They moved away, her back still to him. He watched until the very top of their heads disappeared.

The boat let off further blasts. The dock started to clear out, as people waved goodbye and then drifted away. The gangplank was removed and stowed. Lucian stood as still as a statue, rooted to the spot, held in place by some force he could not understand. He watched as families and couples moved away from the railings, going to the front of the ship to watch the waves break.

That ship held everything that had ever mattered to him in the world, everything that had been good, and watching it start to sail away he felt a pressure against the wall inside. Years in building, years of loneliness and solitude, years of torturous memories and dashed dreams, years of overwhelming pain, and in mere moments, it was shaken.

He slowly shook himself, looking down, moved his feet. It was painful. He had finally let her go, like he should have years before in this very same spot.

He was about to turn away, to go back to his drink, and many, many more before his cold empty bed, when a glimmer of sun on shining hair pulled him. He shaded his eyes again and looked up.

Her bonnet had flown off in the wind and she was laughing and grabbing it. Her figure was thinner than before, as her pale dress flew out in all directions. She faced the wind and let her hair fly out behind her, her body pressed into the rail for balance. Katherine was behind her, gathering up the heavy obsidian mass and pulling the bonnet back on. Their lips were moving, and they were smiling, he could almost imagine their jokes. Katherine finished tying it and moved away. Caroline remained at the rail, and leant her arms over it, looking down at the dock.

He froze, unable to move, unable to take his eyes off her. She was everything he remembered and more, standing in the wind and the last rays of light. She spread her fingers, and he watched her letting them trail through the air, the fine sea spray. Her gaze seemed to linger on the dock, and he wondered if she was standing there, alone, thinking of him, as he was of her. Remembering that fateful day when she had decided to stay with him when she had ripped her ticket and chosen him. He wondered if it made her sad, if it was the most regrettable decision she had ever made.

Suddenly, as relentlessly as magnets pulling together, her eyes found his. He stepped back a step, feeling as though lightning had struck him, the force of that impact was so great. The boat started to move away, and she gripped the railing for support. She stared at him, and he stared right back, moving toward the boat as it left the dock, maintaining the distance between them. Her face was confused, and her aquamarine eyes wide as they moved over his face, his body, up and down, over and over, unable to believe he was truly there.

The boat let off further bursts of horn and he reached the edge of the land. He looked up, unable to tear his eyes away. She moved a hand to her cheek, and he realised she must be crying. Caroline continued to watch him, and he continued to watch her back. Her face was less distinct now, he could see less. Her features disappeared and became a blur. The ship was moving out into the open sea. He stayed there, until the end when the vessel was only a small dot on the horizon. He stayed there even after darkness had fallen, and the waves were glimmering under the moon.

❀

"*W*here were you?" Caroline cried as she sat on a chair in Katherine's room. Her eyes were swollen and red, her cheeks pale, her lips still bloodless. Charles paced in front of her, his expression tight and withdrawn. He came to a stop before her and sighed, his eyes already pained at the news he had to impart. "Did... did you see him?" Caroline whispered, her hands trembling as she accepted a glass of brandy from Wesley.

"I did," Charles confirmed, drawing shocked looks from the entire company.

"You saw Luke? He is alive?" Rebecca breathed, sinking onto the bed, looking shaken to her core as Isaac put his arms around her, his face like thunder as he waited for Charles to supply an explanation.

"Tell us, Charles," Caroline said quietly. She waited, her heart quaking. She had seen him, standing on the dock, and her entire world had fallen apart in a single moment. At first, as she gazed at the place where she had taken the greatest leap of faith in her life. She had almost been able to see them there, standing in the blowing wind, her torn ticket fluttering around them, the way he had gripped her hand to his heart, and promised to become a better man for her. The moment where she had stopped fighting. Her eyes had seen her memories of herself, young and scared, gradually fade, as the shore started to move away, yet, he remained. His tall form, his serious gaze, ice blue eyes, they stayed. As the ship moved under her, she saw that he was no memory. He was truly standing before her, older, more worn, sadder... real.

"I was involved in an altercation, at a common room, which explains the sad state of my attire. Lucian, stepped in, when I was bested,"

Katherine made a noise of alarm, looking over his uncharacteristically dishevelled fiance.

"You spoke to him?" Caroline said slowly, the truth of the whole situation sinking in. Charles looked away from her pained face and nodded. Wesley made a noise of exclamation.

"I did, but please, believe me, it was as much a surprise to me that it is to you."

"Well, brother, surely you told him that his name is cleared. That he did not have to run any longer," Wesley said, confusion and desperation in his voice. Hurt was painted across his face.

"I did." Charles dropped his head in the silence that fell in the aftermath of that news.

"Well, he must not have understood you properly. He must have been in shock," Rebecca said weakly, quieting as Charles simply looked at her, his face blank, and Isaac squeezed her to his chest.

"He heard... he understood," Charles whispered. Caroline listened, her face emotionless, though inside her it felt as though a storm was crashing and bruising her from the inside out, she wrapped her arms around herself, as though to stave off a sudden cold.

"But, did you tell him where we were going?" Wesley said adamantly, unable to accept that Lucian would not seize the first opportunity to come home to them.

"I did, Wesley. He knows we will not return from America," Charles said. The tension in the room was punctuated with such sadness, that Caroline could not stand it. It was directed at her, their sympathy, their guilt over their own brother's actions. She stood up, and straightened her dress, feeling a calmness creep over her. Aware that every eye was on her, she turned to Charles.

"Does he know... about Ellie?" She asked.

"No, Ellie was not my news to tell. I did not want to overstep my bounds," Charles said quietly. "I hope that was right." Caroline nodded.

"Thank you. I am relieved," she said. As she started toward the door.

"Caroline? Where are you going?" Rebecca called, still in shock.

"To prepare my daughter for dinner," Caroline said calmly and stilled only when she saw the tear run down her sister's cheek. Of course, for he was their brother. She was not the only one whom the news affected so.

"Rebecca... Lucian is alive... it is a happy day," she said slowly.

"But-" Wesley began.

"Wesley, make no excuses for him. He has lived another life since we saw him last, and we cannot begin to imagine it. If he doesn't want me anymore... if he does not want this life, then no amount of tears can change that," she said, the words like a bitter draft sliding down her throat. Charles stood up and walked to her.

"Caroline, you cannot mean that... he loves you still, I saw it. Nothing has ever been more evident. He is doing what he thinks is best-"

"And taking my choices from me, once again. Leaving me alone, as he promised he never would. Charles, please, do not – I am so... incredibly tired of crying over one man. He is alive, and it is enough," she murmured.

"Is it truly enough?" Wesley called out to her, making her pause on the threshold.

"Perhaps not today... or tomorrow... but it shall be... one day," she said, her mask of calm slipping for a moment, before she turned and left the room.

"Why did you not tell Luke about Ellie?" Rebecca demanded angrily as she watched the door close.

"Because, dear one, Caroline needs to feel that he came for her... not for any other reason," Charles said quietly.

"But... he did not come!" Katherine shouted.

"Exactly," Charles said, softly, his heart breaking anew for the woman who had become a sister to him, who had lost too much and waited too long for the man she loved to return to her. A man who never would.

※

The endless sea, the certainty of the sunrises and sunsets, and the colours they painted on the water became a way for Caroline to block out the pain in her heart. And Elspeth, of course, her soft curly head, her easy smile, reminding Caroline that she did not live for herself, reminding her to be strong and steady. It took a few days for her family to return to normal around her. Eventually, the dark cloud passed from overhead, and they laughed again, and joked, played together, not wanting to dwell again on the pain of losing a brother a second time. But they never mentioned his name, it was as though he had died all over again.

Caroline did not allow herself to think about him, except at night, when the heavy moon hung low over the shining water, and the blackness all around threatened to swallow her whole, she let her mind linger over him. He was alive, it should be enough. He was alive, somewhere in the world... it should be enough. If his heart was empty of her, after all the suffering that it had endured, perhaps it was the price she had to pay, to know he was well. Love like theirs cost too much. She reached into the drawer beside her bed. Quietly, so as not to wake Ellie, she withdrew a worn letter, holes along the creases, practically falling apart with age.

Dear Caroline,
Sometimes, in the night, when the stars shine at me so innocently, I dream of you, I long for you, I burn for you... yet, the morning always comes, and with it, the realisation that love like ours... cannot exist in this world. Together, we burn too brightly. I was never fated to be happy, to be whole, and you were punished for it, my sweetheart.

The letter was left unfinished there, and Caroline had carried it with her, since the day Charles had returned with the news of his death, his last words to her. Whether he had expected her to read it, was unlikely, yet she gripped those words to her, cherished them. Now, however, she saw in them the resolve to stay away more clearly than ever. He had made a decision, he thought it was right. He was blind. She pushed down the small voice in her mind that whispered that he would come, that he could not stay away forever, that he would join them, that he could not forget their love so easily.

But, she knew that he wouldn't. He had made this choice, and he was so resolute that he had stood motionless and watched his entire family sail to a new country, with no plans of return. He had made another life, and his old one, the one he had shared with her, was over. She heard his words in her dreams, promises to stay by her side, promises that she would never be alone again. They felt like poison to her now. He had always taken away her choices, and she had always forgiven him, blinded by love. She could not forgive him in this though... for because of his choice, his decision, her daughter would never know her father. Caroline lay, pierced and tortured as fresh pain blossomed a deeper red with each thought, yet her eyes stayed dry. She had been earnest with Charles before, that she was finished crying for him, finished mourning him, finished missing him. She had to be, or risk losing what was left of her.

🩸

*I*t had been a surprise as he strolled the docks that morning, deciding where the wind should blow him next, resisting the urge to travel to the capital. The tall stride, upright carriage had caught his eye and he had felt something there was so familiar, he had been drawn to seeing the man's face. He had followed him into the common room, and kept to the shadows, now as natural a habit as breathing. The man had ordered and his voice had sent Lucian back, years into his past. Charles. His older brother. His family. It was unmistakably him, yet his face seemed different. Older, more serious, if that was possible. Lucian realised that they must have all changed, himself included, but to see the evidence of it there before him, made him feel in parts of himself that had long been forgotten.

He had been about to leave. It was too dangerous. Despite the fact he might endanger Charles by approaching him and risking being caught together - they were not in London, but the news of a young Earl brutally murdering his father as his wife nearly died on the floor beside them, would have swept through the country as fast as horses could carry it, and there was an award for his capture that some would not soon forget.

There was also the danger of news; of not being able to resist knowing about all of them, his family... and about her. Yet to know, was to want, and he could hardly stop himself from travelling to London or Westmere to see her... in secret, from the shadows, winning a few more images to replace the tattered ones in his memory.

Then the two men had approached Charles, and Lucian had had no choice. He had tried to hold back from the fight, but in the end, stepped in.

After watching Caroline leave, after seeing her again, after so long, it had awoken something inside him. He had thought he had been too broken, his heart too hardened by utter loneliness and despair. At first, it felt akin to an attack of some sort. A curious dizziness, a rush of blood to his head.

He had staggered off the docks and back to his inn, the wooden toy in his hands gripped fast. Falling onto his bed, he had gasped for breath and felt his entire being shudder. His throat closed, making the passage of air difficult, his hands trembled. His head spun, and behind his closed eyes, she was all he could see, the disbelief, the pain in her eyes, powerful enough for him to see it even from the shore.

She had believed him to be dead. He felt the impact of that, as an accusation. He had not thought when he gave up his identity, that Charles would find a record of his death. Even in his absence, he continued to hurt her.

'There is no one in her life. No one since you. She is alone,' Charles had said.

The words were insidious, they wriggled inside his heart, as a maggot in an apple, and destroyed his resolve. She was alone, she had not married again, had not fallen in love again. Perhaps she loved him still, though he wondered how it could be possible, after everything he had cost her.

The questions kept him awake each night and hounded him all day.

It drove him to drink and ultimately must have contributed to what happened next.

Perhaps it was fate intervening, he could not say for sure. The sailors he had met, at first it had been fun to discuss his various sea adventures with them, lose himself in the memories of simpler days, settling at the fire most evenings, not able to leave Portsmouth quite yet for some reason, he had enjoyed his captive audience, he who had been alone for so long. His first mistake was telling of his former navy debacles, the second had been brash and drunk - telling them his real name.

Could he have fought harder, he wondered, escaped in the night, for no one would come after him, that he knew. He had served his time in the Navy, surely no one would argue that. But with the unfinished unease in Europe and the War with America dragging on, Britain needed men and somehow he had ended up on board before he had even realised it.

Well, he rationalised, what was one more battle? Once more to the guns and the canons. Once more into the breach.

It mattered not that it would take him across the sea, far from home, for he had none. He was a feather blown in the wind, and he would follow that breeze, and not look back. He ignored the voice that whispered that the only home he'd ever known was somewhere on this sea, moving closer each day. He ignored the voice that whispered, "There is no one in her life. No one since you. She is alone." He ignored the way the words made that wall around his heart crack slightly, more and more each day. He ignored the way the child's toy in his pack called to him, as he spent the long hours of the voyage turning it over in his hands, staring at it. He stood on the deck, most nights, listening to the sea, the air freezing, and he welcomed it, he needed it, to feel cold and remote, to keep his heart frozen. He looked ahead, into the darkness, as his destination drew closer. *America.*

CHAPTER 2

~January 1815~
Richmond

"*M*r Lee, you have done us a great service, I cannot thank you enough," Charles said as he walked up the broad stairs of the Taylors' generous townhouse in Richmond.

"Please, call me Joshua, I believe we may be passed such formality by now," Joshua said. Charles considered it, before inclining his head briefly, allowing it with a smile. Joshua had helped them to procure a large townhouse, close to the Taylors, where they would all stay together, as a family, excepting Katherine, who would remain at Eva's house until she and Charles could be married.

At the end of a long journey, they were all glad to be settling at last. Charles had known as soon as their ship had landed in New York - they could be happy there.

"*T*omorrow. You shall see them tomorrow darling, but you must sleep now."

"But I'm not tired," Elspeth said as her eyes struggled to stay open.

Caroline smiled, stroking her soft hair back, perched on the edge of her daughter's bed. Elspeth had finally met her cousins, and the three were a force to be reckoned with. Hearing her tiny breaths even out, her little mouth dropping slightly open as sleep took her. Caroline stood up as quietly as possible, went out into the hall and drew the door closed behind her. Reaching the stairs, she saw Eva come out of a neighbouring room, holding her skirts close to quiet them. They quietly descended the stairs together.

"I see you have not trusted their care to anyone else? Though, I might have expected as much. Does society not think it terribly outmoded, caring for one's own children?" Caroline teased as they entered the drawing-room.

"Why, yes of course, though I am yet to care," Eva rejoined with a laugh. Caroline might have guessed that Eva would be a devoted mother, much like Caroline was herself. The drawing-room was full of her family, and Caroline knew without a doubt that she was glad to be home. It was so comforting, strangely, and she had not expected that. Perhaps it was because there were no memories of him here, nothing to remind her or perhaps she had grown accustomed to the realisation that he was alive, and had chosen a different life. Either way, she felt more at peace than she had in a long time.

"Caroline, Joshua Lee just left, he wished for me to express his desire to call tomorrow. I told him that it would be fine," Charles said from where he sat before the fire. Caroline felt for a moment that everyone was watching her, and holding their breaths.

"Joshua? That is a little informal is it not?" Katherine teased.

"I believe it is time, the man has been a great friend to us," Charles announced, watching Caroline's reaction closely.

"Yes, I believe he has. I would be happy to receive him tomorrow," Caroline said with a yawn. "Now I know it's early yet, but I am fit to drop with exhaustion, and little monsters will be awake as mercilessly early as usual come morning. Goodnight, my dears," Caroline said with a sleepy smile, rising and leaving the room to their goodnights, but not before hearing a whisper of Mr Lee's name, and catching in the mirror the looks that the others shared together, impish smiles from the less discrete members of the group.

~January 1815~
New Orleans

"*H*ere, take mine," Lucian muttered, shoving his grey bread at the young boy shaking beside him. William eyed it for a moment, about to refuse, when hunger overcame him, and he grabbed at it, stuffing it into his mouth gratefully. The boy was hungry, with little on his bones but cold, pale skin, and Lucian had been longer without food before. Lucian crouched down beside the water bucket, and dipped his hands in it, bringing the stale water up to his mouth, drinking deeply. They had been on the move all night, moving into one bad position after another, and there was no doubt that they had incurred heavy losses. The number of men the Americans had mustered outnumbered them, and the British were cold, wet, unused to the mud, the humid, sticky air, or the mosquitos, mud and rain weighing their uniforms down, and rotting their feet in their boots, they barely had the strength to do anything but lay down and die.

Lucian was hidden behind a low-lying hill with the ragged remnants of his brigade, and the grey, pre-dawn light was gradually revealing the desperate situation they were in. Americans were closing in, their position was vulnerable, their backup scattered or killed. William coughed quietly as he forced the last of the dry bread down his raw throat, and Lucian moved to the side to allow him access to their dwindling water supply.

He couldn't quite remember when William had become his shadow, or indeed if he had ever actually been introduced to him formally. He had broken up a fight onboard the boat, two weeks into the journey down from Philadelphia. The men were bored and restless for battle, and the long voyage had done nothing to quell their bloodlust. Skinny and young, William and his Scottish accent had been ripe for torment, and the men aboard had laughed to see the boy, barely a man, with his nose stuck in a book, while they sailed to fight. Lucian had no interest in becoming a protector of the defenceless, however, their cackling and bullying disturbed his solitude too often, and he was forced to step in. Perhaps he might have left it at that, and the men would have carried on their torture more quietly, but for the look in the lad's eyes. It had been so terribly reminiscent of another boy, young and scared, that he had taken care of when he was not that much older himself, protected from harm, made hot milk for in the night after children had been cruel, after insecure boys had become bullies. So, he had warned the men to keep their distance, and they had, without question. The next morning, William had popped up at his elbow and had hardly left it for a moment since.

"So, what do you say? I shall take the fifty on the left, you the fifty on the right," William whispered, and Lucian gave him a smile in return. He was afraid, it radiated off him, and why shouldn't he be? Lucian reasoned it was normal to fear death, to want to live. He tried to remember when he had been as young as William, in the Navy, facing foreign shores and bloody battle sites. Had he feared death? He couldn't recall. There was only one thing he could remember fearing the loss of, and it was not his life.

"I prefer the left," Lucian muttered, seeing the young man's need to distract himself. William laughed, pressing his trembling hands together.

"Very well, you chose first, you are the veteran," William chattered on, and Lucian nodded occasionally, his mind going to the battlefield. They would not win, he was sure of it, how many would die was the only question that remained.

"Should you fall... I will find her, your Caroline, and-" William was saying, snapping Lucian back to reality suddenly. He turned to him.

"What?" he asked roughly. William gulped, seeing the fierceness come to his mentor's eyes.

"I will find her... your lady, and tell her about your braveness, and courage...speak of your love for her," William said hesitantly.

Lucian recalled the first night he had spoken of Caroline to his new friend. They had been aboard the ship, and William had been talking about his past with wide dark eyes. He had signed up to fight for the money, but before he had left he had met a girl, a local girl from Lanark. A shy girl that seemed to love William instantly, though he could not say why. She clung to him, and in that short time before he left for war, he had clung back, and she had soon been with child. She travelled too to America and had settled in Durham, North Carolina, where they had been told there was a community of other Scots, and there she waited for William, ready to start their new life as a family when he could return to marry her and meet his son and give him a name.

Lucian had been quiet, listening to the boy's hopeful plans, when suddenly, without warning, his mouth opened and he started to speak of Caroline. It had begun innocently enough, just a mention of family who were settling in America, but before he'd realised it, he had become absorbed with telling William all about her, the woman he would hold his heart forever. Speaking about her, sharing his memories, made them fresh again for him, and he felt as though he had relived each one during that long sea journey.

"There is no need... she would not believe it," Lucian said, coming back to the present.

"I would make her believe," William said with a set jaw, just beginning to grow wisps of blond whiskers. Lucian chuckled and dropped his head.

"Some things are beyond even you. Now, are you going to be quiet, and help me plan how we are to get out of this mess?" Lucian said, seeing a messenger running along the lines.

🐾

"We cannot know for sure. We need a scout," the officer muttered, looking at his bedraggled band of men. Shots were being fired all over, gun smoke lay thick in the air, shrouding the tall grass, even the frogs and cicadas had grown quiet, imminent death heavy as a mantle.

"I'll go," Lucian said, standing up in a crouch.

"No, I should go," the officer started, but Lucian cut him off with a gesture.

"Not necessary. I will gather information and return presently," Lucian said, his tone brooking no disagreement. He had thrown himself into the path of bullets often enough, and half suspected that it was his destiny to live forever, unscathed, desperate for release from the emptiness of existence.

The young officer finally nodded, his relief palpable. Lucian took the opportunity to go, seeing William engaged elsewhere, cleaning his gun. No need for the young boy to die too, he thought. He used the tall grass, keeping low, and crouched; he travelled far in that way, always out of sight. Dropping to his stomach and remaining unmoving for long periods, sometimes hearing American voices pass him by. They reminded him of the Taylors and Joshua Lee. As he lay flat at one point, listening with interest to a soldier describing the American defensive positions, a sudden hand on his arm prompted him to pull his knife, never far from his hand, and roll over aggressively. With a snarl already on his lips, the knife bore down on his attacker's neck, his young body already crushed beneath Lucian's, he realised his identity only moments before it was too late.

"William, what the bloody hell are you doing? I could have killed you," Lucian whispered angrily.

William's eyes were wide, terrified.

"They told me you went to scout..." William stammered, and Lucian resisted the urge to drop his head in his hands. He rolled away from him and started back.

"Where are we going?" William asked, once again at his elbow.

"We are going back... you will be killed out here," Lucian muttered, making sure they stayed down. It took longer than before to reach their position again, as Lucian waited more, hesitated more, knowing that the young man behind him would not take as many precautions as he should, but would follow him blindly. Finally, a familiar rise came into view, and they made their way toward it. As they came closer, Lucian felt his skin prickle. Something did not feel right.

They approached slowly. Lucian gestured for William to stay behind him, and on his stomach, crawled around the hill. The sight that greeted him almost made this empty stomach heave. The men's bodies were lying in disarray, a mass of twisted limbs, glazed eyes and drying blood: twenty, maybe more, shot down, the bodies peppered with the spray of grapeshot.

Lucian felt William come up behind him and wished he could spare the boy what he was about to see. He moved forward, rising to a crouch, as he shuffled amongst the bodies, looking for unspent gunpowder. He heard William emptying his stomach of his meagre breakfast behind him, and did not look back, did not shame him. He picked the weapons from some of the bodies too, unwrapping fingers tight as claws. He suddenly realised that one body amid the others wore a different uniform, American. He glanced down at the soldier, little more than William's sixteen years, before turning away. So many lost, for nothing.

He did not feel the man move, did not hear it, his ears too stunned from the prolonged booming of the cannons and muskets. He did not feel how close the musket's blade came to his back. All he heard was William's shout of warning, and then he was falling forward. He landed hard on the bodies of dead men, instantly rolling over to defend himself. He saw the American soldier, risen up on one knee, his musket buried deep in another.

"No!" Lucian shouted as he started forward, his hands going to the American's neck, as he twisted it violently, a crack sounding, before the man fell backwards, drawing his musket, and William with it. Lucian took William's shoulders, and turned him over, as he slid off the blade, seeing the blood come coursing from his chest. William coughed and wheezed, his hands going to Lucian's shoulders, clutching at them.

"What were you thinking? You damn fool!" Lucian demanded, pressing his hands over the hole in the boy's chest.

"Not thinking..." William spluttered, blood welling out his mouth.

"William... no, it should be me... I should be the one..." Lucian muttered, tearing a strip from his shirt to tie around the wound. William's fingers stopped him, and Lucian forced himself to look at the young man's face.

"Stop... leave it... it is done. It is a good day to die, is it not?"

"No, it is not. You shouldn't die... you have a life ahead of you... people waiting for you," Lucian choked on the words, a knot in his throat.

"As do you..." William said. Lucian shook his head slowly, grief drowning him.

"Promise me... something..."

"Anything... my friend, anything," Lucian said, and saw how his words warmed William's eyes.

"*F*riend," he whispered, closing his eyes briefly, before opening them again and looking at Lucian.

"There is a letter... in my pack... for Annie. Please give it to her... please, and my purse, there are... a few coins..."

"Of course," Lucian murmured, squeezing his hand as tremors shook his thin body. William tried to take a breath and coughed again, it sounded wetter and more gruesome by the moment.

"Ashford-"

"Luke."

"Luke," William said, with a ghost of a smile.

"Promise me... don't wait until it is too late," William said thickly. Lucian couldn't speak, as he felt tears well in his eyes. He nodded silently, seeing William's eyes begin to lose their focus. He started to mumble incoherently, gripping onto Lucian's hands. Lucian watched him, was there with him, supporting him, until the strength of William's hands faded, and the light in his eyes went out. Lucian slid down in the mud and blood that had collected in the grass. He gently closed his friend's eyes, making a silent promise to deliver his letter to his cousin, to help someone remember him. He did not know how long he sat there, his eyes blank and empty, as all that filled them was death and destruction.

An unknowable time later, he numbly rose, cold and wet, and went to William's pack, digging through it, he came to the parchment and purse. He stuffed it safely into his pack, and turned, casting a last glance at the brave boy that had delivered him, unworthy, from harm. What a waste, he thought as he started over the hill.

~February 1815~
Richmond

*T*hey had dined on bison that night, an exotic rarity for the Ashfords, and bottles of delicious red wine soon turned into a bottle of port over which the family chatted, cheeks warmed by drink, and discussed their great adventure.

"So," Isaac stood up with a smirk and pointed his glass to each of them. "Charles shall become a cigar-smoking American tycoon, Wesley is already halfway to becoming a cowboy with that hat of his, my beautiful wife... shall begin a society news rag where she can funnel all of her talent for snarky quips, and Miss Katherine over there will... hmm, run a wedding-planning service for hire, where she can order people about and get fat tasting cakes all day long!" he laughed to the growing jeers and heckles of the others and a cushion to the face from his doting wife.

Caroline smiled a warm glow of a smile that radiated over her skin. She loved them all so much, perhaps most when they were drunk and boisterous.

"And what of you, Lady Caroline? You shall not escape our plans to industriously take America by storm! So, what will it be? Gold prospecting? Railways? Cattle rustler?"

"I should become a governess so that I might teach you some manners, young master Taylor," Caroline shot back.

"Good luck to you," Rebecca said. "Some people are simply beyond teaching."

"Oh, I'm always grateful of your lessons, Mrs Taylor. In fact, I hope to receive another later tonight."

"You lout!" Rebecca gasped and hit him again with the pillow.

"It is a good question though," Caroline went on a little more pensively once some of the noise had died down, feeling the wine swim lazily through her veins. "To be honest, I've been contemplating my time as of late. I seem to have so very much of it, and, if I'm honest, with my rents and my parent's fortune still untouched, I'm quite a bit more comfortable than anyone ought to have any right to be. I've been thinking... well... why couldn't I use it to do some good?"

Wesley sat up, his eyes wide and shiny and mouth ajar. "You must! Oh, Caroline, you must!"

"I don't know, perhaps it's a silly notion."

"Not only is it not the least bit silly, I think it's quite marvellous! I confess, I myself have been missing our London causes. In fact, why can we not all contribute? Surely we are in a position to, are we not, Charles?"

"Well..." Charles said, drawing his brow together. "Yes, we certainly could. We are new to the community, and as we intend to make it our home, I think it would be a fine beginning to contribute in some way. What had you in mind, Caroline?"

"Oh, I don't know. Let us all put our heads together–"

"Caroline," Wesley broke in, narrowing his eyes suspiciously at her. "I know you have some shining plan, so don't let's be bashful."

"Well, I was thinking... that I have had cause many times over these past years to learn the value of good health. I have always counted myself lucky to have had access to doctors when I needed them, indeed, I do not think I would be here today, nor Ellie, had not Dr Keeble acted quickly to keep us both alive." Rebecca reached out and grabbed Caroline's hand and gave it a squeeze. Caroline squeezed back and went on while she had everyone's attention. "I think often of other people, other women, who need help and cannot secure it. To be afraid that you are dying, and have no one to help you, simply because you lack the means, would be a terror which no one should have to suffer."

Wesley sighed, as if he had just heard something beautiful, and leaned back against the sofa, eyes to the ceiling.

"Could we not invest in a local hospital? Or even fund the building of a new one?" he asked to the rafters.

"It's a wonderful idea," Katherine said, "isn't it, Charles? The hospital here is small, and people often travel to Philadelphia for better care."

"Yes, my love. I think I could put the word out and see what we might do."

"I don't know how, but I'd like it to be a support for all sorts of local families, whatever the size of their purse, or the colour of their skin," Caroline said, blushing a bit, hoping that the wine would disguise it.

"Hmm..." Wesley considered, his slurring voice doing nothing to diminish Caroline's hopes. "Yes. We could not build one of those horrible charity hospitals, either, where medical students cut people up for practice, and illness hops from one bed to another. What about... well, It would take some doing, but we could perhaps set up a board who can use the profits from the wealthier Richmond families to fund the care for needy families, rather than just donations that come in in drips and drabs. We could ensure the same doctors, and the same conditions no matter who the patient." He hiccupped as he stood up and raised his glass. "We shall build... a Utopia!"

Caroline had smiled then as they went back and forth fleshing out new ideas, and the smile was something earnest and strong and genuine, and much later Rebecca had told her that it was the first time in years that she felt she had her sister back.

~July 1815~
Richmond

"*I*t must be perfect. Goodness knows I have waited long enough," Katherine exclaimed as they walked to the dressmaker.

Richmond was a charming town. Much smaller than London, of course, but that suited everyone just fine, save perhaps Wesley, who had mentioned the possibility of buying a townhouse in New York City for the occasional jaunt into society. The streets were wide, clean and uncluttered, red-bricked and white-columned, and the city arched to follow the graceful curve of the James River, where they had found a townhouse that overlooked the water. It was much greener than London, with large parks and tree-lined streets, the air was fresh and crisp, and no matter where they went, they were never very far from the vast, breathtaking, purple mountains which left the Ashford's speechless, and reminded Caroline of her childhood.

Caroline sighed internally as they navigated the busy shopping streets before coming to the best dressmaker in Richmond, indeed, one of the very best in the South, Katherine had reminded her. Katherine was proving exhaustingly eager in her preparations, and Caroline was starting to feel the strain of it.

Inside the exclusive boutique was surprisingly bare and free of adornments. One thing that the small city had was a lot of banks, and another was a great deal of money. It was reserved for only ladies of the highest class, and Madam Toulouse made only one gown at a time, leaving the boutique bare of anything but tidy samples of fabric and lace, and books with all of the newest designs from New York and Europe. Caroline settled in to watch and give her opinions to Katherine, letting her mind wander slightly.

Elspeth was enjoying their new city, her new cousins to play with, which quieted her constant demands for a little sibling, one which, Caroline thought, would probably never come. Though comfortable and happy, things had been far from settled. Rebecca and Isaac were something out of a fairytale, and Caroline wondered how she might ever have imagined them as two complete people when clearly they had spent their whole lives waiting to be one. They would have their own place soon and move out of the Ashford townhouse, and Wesley was starting to talk about a bachelor pad of his own. Katherine, who was presently staying with her sister, would soon move in with Charles at the townhouse, following their wedding, but she and Charles had begun to talk of something larger, an estate perhaps, closer to her parents. With so much happiness everywhere she turned, it was hard for Caroline to be anything but happy herself, and she was, in a way, but she found herself fretting often over the fragile happiness of the house, cosy and busy now, but soon to be emptying out, leaving her to her charming rooms and beautiful terrace where at least she could enjoy sitting to watch the world pass by, the river flowing and babbling on its way elsewhere.

Joshua Lee called on her with increasing frequency, and she allowed him, with the family's encouragement. Legally, Lucian was a dead man and provided he stayed that way, Caroline would be free to marry again if she wished. Lucian had made himself a new life, and even after he was able to come back, after he had been begged by Charles to join them in America, he had refused. There could be no plainer terms.

She reminded herself of that at times when Joshua sat close to her, or his hand brushed hers as she passed him tea. She fought down her reaction. She would learn. She was a free woman now. She would not allow the past to consume her future.

*A*nnie Paterson had been lovelier than Lucian had expected, large dark eyes, milk-white skin, and shining black hair, and he had felt once again, a push against his dead heart, as he had hand-delivered the letter in his care. Seeing her read the last lines William would say to her, Lucian had been reminded with force, the power of love, how it healed and how it tore. Somewhere in another room, he heard a baby wake and begin to cry, a strained, tinny sound, but Annie did not get up to go to it. Instead, he saw her disappear before his eyes, and go to where William was, and say goodbye. He felt humbled by the experience.

The journey north to the Carolinas had been arduous, and he could not escape the words of William, his final words. He was right of course, and Lucian had made a promise, and he hated to break his word. Before going to see Annie, he had found a guest house along the way and cleaned up, so as not to shame William. He looked at his face in the mirror, revealed to him in its entirety for the first time in so long that he could not remember. Who was that calm and remote man, he wondered? He looked like a man who had seen much and lived to tell of it. He looked like a man who had nothing to lose and had made his peace with that.

He knew where he would go next. He couldn't escape the feeling of her, as he drew nearer and nearer to Virginia, as though she were a beckon that he was inescapably drawn to. As he walked under the night sky, he wondered where she was, if she was awake, or asleep, if she was happy.

As he left the modest common room at Annie's boarding house, he turned northward. It would be a few days' ride, but his promise weighed heavily on him, and he wished to see it fulfilled for William's sake.

⚜

*L*ucian made it to Richmond, and walked under the same clouds that shielded Caroline from the sun, his hair tossed by the very same breeze that tugged at her bonnet. He found himself a guest house in the poorest part of town, thinking that he might remain hidden longer there. One day became two, and two became many, yet he could not bring himself to go to her. The thing scratched at him relentlessly in the day and gnawed at him in the night, teeth growing ever sharper, but torture was not new - he had known it well these five long years.

The humble little place, small room and sparse furnishings, were what he needed after so long lost, so long tumbling in the wind. He got used to shaving each day, to changing his clothes, and sleeping on a bed, though there were some nights where he could not sleep, and he moved to the cold hard floorboards. Sometimes he made conversation about the weather with the proprietor, forcing himself to ease back into being someone who could talk to others, even socialise. He tried to remember how people spoke, how people made light remarks that meant little or nothing at all and laughed at polite jokes whether they found them funny or no. He tried to sleep without his knife by his hand. It was a time of adjustment, and often he felt he was playing the role of a man, rehearsing his manners, walking upright, like a beast who imitates that which he can never be.

There was another place he wanted to visit. He had heard tell of a new hospital, being built by generous new benefactors who had moved here from London. He wished to see it, to find out what Charles had made of the Ashford name after the ruin that was his father's legacy. If the Ashford fortune had been built on the backs of the desperate, perhaps this hospital, made of his fortune, might provide a shelter for other desperate souls. Lucian found beauty in that.

As he approached the site, he could see the work was in full swing. People were coming and going, dust filled the street and Lucian could see it was to be a grand site indeed. He stayed a while, leaning against another building, watching the work, his mind lost in the past.

A carriage drew up, and Luvian saw none other than his elder brother step down from it. Charles walked onto the worksite, confident and sure of himself, and Lucian envied him in that moment. He had a place, he had a life. Turning away, he returned to the damp boarding house, bitterness in his throat.

~August 1815~
Richmond

"*J*f you know he is there, why do you not speak to him?" Katherine demanded angrily of Charles as she piled the handwritten invitations to her engagement party to one side. Her hand cramped from the calligraphy, and she wondered why Charles insisted she do it herself. He was still controlling, and she enjoyed every moment she got to fight him on it - it had become a game, an intimate language, for both of them. She turned to see her fiance leaning back in an armchair, his look contemplative. She sighed and went to him, sitting on his lap, and pulling his chin to tilt his face toward hers. Her position pulled him from his thoughts.

"Katherine, you mustn't," he scolded, trying to move her, as she held on.

"Oh, it is only Eva and Eli..." she said, wriggling more securely into his embrace. He gave up fighting and rested his arms around her.

"I am starting to see that America is undoing all the good influence that England ever had on your manners," he rumbled wryly.

"Aren't you glad? You have so many more things to chastise me for," Katherine teased, biting her lip slowly, suggestively, holding Charles's gaze captive. As he leant forward to meet her lips, Katherine suddenly stood, moving away from him and his groan of frustration.

"So, tell me... what are you going to do about your no-good brother?" she asked.

"What is there to do? He will come when he is ready..."

"And Caroline can wait without end totally unaware? That is ridiculous! They are supposed to be together..."

"She is too hurt, and he is too broken. He could not make a good husband for her, or a father. Let Caroline move on."

"With Joshua Lee?" Katherine said with a sneer.

"Perhaps..."

"When I did what I did years ago, I thought she loved him. And I was right! I don't know that I've ever seen two people more in love than they were at Westmere. How can you now wish for her to end up with someone she doesn't love?"

"Please, Katherine, do not talk to me about your misguided ideas of grand love and mad plans." Katherine scowled at him and tested again.

"But if Lucian is alive then they are married still, in law and under God..." she narrowed her eyes, studying him carefully.

"Yes, I do admit that that has given my conscience some grief. However, despite right and wrong, my loyalty is to Caroline and her protection, and I find that I would not have her shackled to a man who would make her life a misery. I saw him in the alley, I spoke to him - he is not the Lucian anymore that you knew once. We are in a new world now, and especially with my brother's habit of keeping to the shadows, and most of the world believing that he is dead, I think Caroline could move on to a new life provided that she does not return to England where there may still be some danger. I have thought it over carefully, and I believe the only way is to leave Caroline in the dark about his presence in Virginia so that she might free herself from him. I think even God would not want any more pain to befall that woman."

Katherine looked away toward her engagement invitations, thoughts and questions whirling like an electrical storm. Slowly she turned back to her fiance, a smile played around her lips, one which she knew usually made Charles nervous.

"I suppose you must be right, my love, though... I should suspect the shock of running into Lucian in the street, or at a party, or even just hearing that he is here from another, would be quite terrible," Katherine continued, and Charles nodded slowly.

"I must admit, that has worried me. What would you have me do?"

"Well, you might prepare her for the possibility, at least. Then she will be better able to decide what she would say, how she would act... what if Ellie were with her?" Katherine said, her tone so reasonable that she could see Charles's reserve wavering. He let out a big sigh.

"You are right, my dear. It would be a most terrible shock, and hurtful. Though the hurt I cannot spare her, I'm afraid, the shock is something that I could take the sting out of. I will tell her. I must admit to being more than a little concerned that he has not yet moved on - if he does not stay hidden and unnamed, then he will jeopardise Caroline's freedom once again. I suppose it is too precarious. You are right," he said again, a phrase she never tired of hearing, "I shall speak to them both."

"I think it for the best, dear," Katherine said, turning away, her fatigue forgotten, as the wheels of her brain began to turn.

✿

*I*t became his routine, after writing to Annie Paterson, checking on the progress of the building, watching Charles work, and Wesley sometimes, when he came along to organise people and show investors around the site. His desire to go to them and speak with them, go home with them, sometimes was overwhelming, yet he resisted.

He was not sure how long it had been exactly before he received the handwritten invitation. Lord Charles Ashford and Miss Katherine Fairfax invite you to their engagement celebration. He sat and stared at it for a long time. Before folding it up and placing it in a drawer. Inside the drawer was one other object, the child's toy. He had stared at it and pondered over it day in and day out since that fateful meeting in Portsmouth.

Who was the toy for? He had wondered, to begin with, and then remembered that Eva Taylor had a child, probably more than one by now, and of course, there was Frances Tilman, the birth of whose child had set off that chain of events that had finally brought Caroline and him together. Each day afterwards, he drew the letter and stared at it, before hiding it again.

Dear Lucian,

Brother, I do not pretend to know why you are here in Virginia, nor what brought you. I suspect it is not your desire to see your family again, as you have not made your presence known, and yet you come to observe us anyway. Family is inescapable in that respect, I suppose.

I am writing to ask for your attendance at my engagement party. Five long years I have waited to marry Katherine Fairfax, and I would have my brother there to share with him such a meaningful event in my life.

I ask you because it is a costume party, and I think you might easily attend without risking your anonymity here. Indeed, I'm afraid I must request that you remain a man unknown in Richmond, or else steal away the fragile independence and security which Caroline has found here.

If you worry over seeing Caroline at the party, fear not. She knows of your intentions to stay by your word and has accepted it. In fact, she has grown close to Joshua Lee of late, and we do our best to encourage her in this, according to your very own wishes, brother, for you have said time and time again that she should move on to have a new life without you, and we must assume that you did not mean for her to spend the rest of her life alone. I can only guess that this is why you have taken on an assumed name, and have not come forth. You were right - Caroline is someone who deserves to be made to feel safe and secure after the life that she has led. It is what she needs.

The last years have left a bitter mark on our family's history, and I long to put it behind us. Why not come and pay your respects to those who love you, those who never stopped caring for you, those who mourned your passing with such heartache, and let us all begin to heal.

I include details of the venue and dress code. I hope to see you there, for all that we once were, and in the name of the family we used to be.

Your brother,

Charles

*H*e knew what it would mean, seeing Caroline again. He could hardly avoid her at the engagement party. It was folly to even consider, yet his brother's words were like a spell that lured him in, whilst it shamed him. Five long years - everyone's lives had been on hold because of him, trying to free him from the murder of their father. To see them all again, to speak to his family, to her. That wall that he held onto so desperately seemed to have developed chinks in it lately, and a raw, unmistakable yearning oozed through. He read the description of the dress code, snorting, thinking Katherine had surely had a hand in it. It wouldn't be so difficult to procure, he supposed, if he were to go. Not that he was going. But if he were...

🐚

"*W*hy? Why now? Why did he come?" Caroline asked, proud that her voice did not shake.

"I admit I do not know," Charles said, leaning forward, his elbows to his knees, watching her. Caroline sighed and fell backwards in the chair. She looked at Charles and they shared a long moment before she spoke.

"He is going to find out about Ellie," she said, her heart beating strangely at it.

"Yes, I suspect he shall, there is no preventing it."

Caroline nodded, her mind already drifting to that confrontation. It had almost been a year, a year of knowing he was alive, a year of unconscious waiting. But there was no point in waiting. He had made his choice, and she had spent that last year chewing over what decisions he had left her, scraps that they were. If he did not want to be in her life, then she would not force his hand with unexpected fatherhood. He did not deserve to know about Ellie. No, she knew that that wasn't right, but it did not stop her from feeling so in her bones.

She thought of Joshua. Of course she did, Charles had been his advocate for so many months, and though it was painful, she could not help but take the advice to heart. He was a good man, a steady one, and she did not doubt that he would make an excellent husband and father. She wanted security and safety for Ellie, and peace for herself. What would it mean with Lucian now in Richmond?

"I should tell him about her myself, except, I am afraid he would run from me before I had the opportunity," Caroline said with a bitter laugh. It hurt, of course, but less like a fresh wound, and more like an old, ugly scar that was sometimes sensitive to the touch. Charles looked away, anger pulling his lips into a line.

"You should know..." he hesitated, clearly finding something difficult, "that I have invited him to our engagement party, though I have heard no response, and do not believe that he will attend."

Another small cliff to fall off of.

Her heart twisted, as did her face before she hurried to smooth it over.

"I am sorry. I can only guess how that must feel to you, but I believe we should all begin the business of moving on from this tragedy. But, it need not change your life, Caroline. He is a changed man. I felt it when I spoke to him. He is... a broken vessel, empty and hollow inside, though it pains me to say it."

"Aren't we all?" Caroline replied.

CHAPTER 3

~October 1815~
Richmond, Virginia

"𝒦atherine, I must have my costume, Joshua will arrive any moment."

"I cannot believe you are allowing him to escort you to my engagement party," Katherine huffed as she pulled a shockingly long box from under her bed. Eva laughed at her sister in the mirror.

"Well, I remember a day when you thought Mr Lee quite the appropriate suitor for Caroline, Kitty. Am I not right, Rebecca?"

"Well, that day is not today, and I do not approve," Katherine interrupted. "This is my night, and I do not think a date is necessary. I demand that all my guests are at their most beautiful, and when Joshua Lee is around, Caroline's eyes go as dull as dishwater," she let the jibe sail into the room with a wicked smirk and Caroline rolled her eyes before grabbing the box from her and pulling it open.

"I must admit that, though it is a very rare occurrence, and I am shocked even to utter such a thing... I do agree with Katherine for once," Rebecca announced breezily from the mirror with a wink in Katherine's direction.

Caroline sorted through the garments in the box, her focus more carefully trained on trying to make sense of the costume than on her sisters' unsolicited opinions.

"I did not know that you do not care for Mr Lee, Rebecca. May I ask why not?" Eva asked.

"It's not that I dislike him...simply he is not..." Rebecca trailed off, catching Caroline's eye in the mirror, and the girls fell silent as they were always apt to do, whenever he came into the conversation. She was tired of all of it, in fact, it barely pulled a rise in her at all. Caroline looked down into the massive box, and gasped, pulling from the bottom a large pair of feather-covered wings.

"Katherine, these are beautiful!"

"I know," Katherine said with a self-satisfied smirk.

Caroline pulled out the long gauzy white gown, and gold mask, touching them gently, as though afraid of breaking them.

"Well, no matter. Nothing spurs a man on faster than competition," Katherine said in a low voice as if to herself. And Caroline gave her a calculating look.

"Don't you meddle, Kitty," Caroline warned.

"Me? When did I ever?" Katherine scoffed. "I'm wounded to the core, Caroline, truly I am!"

"You're worse than Ellie on a bad day - far worse," Caroline said with a grin, thinking of the pixie smile that her daughter got when she suspected that she was doing something that she shouldn't. "Heaven protect us all if you should ever have any daughters."

"Well, I for one, hope to have two girls, as we certainly don't need any more Ashford men, I should say!" Rebecca said. "I swear, this family is going to grow so big we will need the entire row of townhouses to accommodate us."

"That doesn't dissuade me one bit. I plan on having many more, to fill up all those houses," Eva added with a blush. "Katherine, how about you?"

"I think three is a good number, four at most."

"Four! That sounds altogether too tiring," Rebecca joined, and almost naturally the conversation lulled as it moved to Caroline who was caught between a laugh and a sigh for a moment.

"I think one is the perfect number... for me," she said quietly, pushing her chin out, straightening her shoulders against their sympathetic gazes.

"Right, well, will you not dress, Caroline? We do not want to keep your admirer waiting, dull though he may be," Katherine said quickly, Caroline suspected because she knew how it irked Caroline to be seen as pitiful or sad.

"Yes, yes. I'm hurrying, I'm hurrying." Caroline said, moving behind the screen to change.

❀

*T*he venue was beautiful, hung heavy with stretching bows of coloured leaves in golds and reds instead of flowers, to celebrate the changing season with a glorious flush of colour as only America knew how. They had spared no expense on candles, and they glittered off of cut crystal and shining silver, and glistening silks, and flickered in the Autumn breeze which whispered through the opened windows. The night smelled of burnt sugar, and the punch was served hot, made of tart apples, honey, and bourbon, and spices that scented the air like a freshly baked pie.

The walls were painted with a breathtaking expanse of murals - forests, mountains, fields, and great beasts, men on horseback in pursuit. With the fresh air stirring, the room did its best to trick its guests into thinking that they were in the wild, magnificient outdoors. The costumes heightened the otherworldly feeling of the night, like a swarm of beautiful, impish ghouls and fairy folk dancing around a campfire.

Joshua dressed as a black horse, his beautifully made mask, suiting his broad build and shining black mane of hair. They went first to the refreshment area. He handed Caroline a glass of Punch and she accepted with a smile. With magic such as this, it would be impossible not to enjoy the evening, Caroline reminded herself.

"I swear, the town will talk of this party for months to come. The Ashford's have arrived, and doesn't everyone know it?" he said with a smile.

"Well, Katherine is hardly one to shy away from attention. Though I am surprised at Charles, he usually prefers a more quiet atmosphere," she said.

"Perhaps he has waited too long for that which matters to him the most, and now, he would do anything to make her happy," Joshua suggested and Caroline gulped her punch, as his dark eyes searched hers.

"Why! Mr Lee, how wonderful to see you." Margaret Fairfax's voice had not softened with age, rather the opposite in fact, and Caroline smiled to see her and Mr Fairfax again. They had travelled up from Charlottesville and were now staying in the city. Suffice it to say, Margaret, having long ago given up hope that her daughter would ever marry, was beside herself with happiness at the upcoming nuptials.

"Caroline, my dear. You look splendid," Mr Fairfax said, kissing her on the cheek. "We always knew you to be an angel, you never had us fooled for a moment."

"You are far too kind, Mr Fairfax! Though, even you are not generous enough to forget the years of trouble I caused with muddy cheeks and your fair daughters in tow," she replied, smiling warmly at the sound of his laugh.

"You must make time for us to drop by this week, I have a little something for Ellie," he whispered with a wink, and Caroline could not prevent the surge of affection for her would-be parents. As Joshua and Margaret conversed, Caroline talked with Mr Fairfax of the hospital plans.

"I am pleased to see you here with Mr Lee, my dear. When I heard he had returned and was very much alive, I must admit I expected a reconciliation long before now." Caroline forced a neutral expression to her face.

"You speak of my... former husband?" she said.

"Who else, dearest? Of course I do, that scoundrel. For he was a scoundrel even then, and I had many misgivings about allowing the match, yet, there was a certain something in his demeanour when he spoke of you that led me to believe in an earnest depth of feeling for you. Well, what do I know? I am just a foolish old man... but I am glad to see that you have laid these issues to rest, and made peace between yourselves. I do not begin to understand how you have agreed to all of this," he said waving his hand in the direction of Joshua's turned back, "but I am glad of it. How did Lord Lucian take the news of Ellie?" John asked as Caroline frowned at him slightly.

"He does not know," Caroline answered carefully, swallowing hard. "I have not yet had the opportunity to tell him." John raised his eyebrows at this. "What is it?" she asked.

"You cannot be serious! Oh my, well, I would be quick about it, my dear, lest he find out from another, there are some here tonight who might mention the newly returned Lady Caroline and her beautiful daughter, I think."

"Here tonight?" Caroline echoed, confusion colouring her voice. John suddenly understood her and touched her shoulder gently.

"Caroline. Lord Lucian is here tonight. I have seen him with my own eyes."

At his words, Caroline felt her heart turn inside out in her chest and her mouth dry up. Here. Caroline had no words, she felt an escalating panic build in her stomach, and making a rapid excuse, she turned and went toward the powder room. She kept her head down, suddenly afraid of seeing that face, amidst the crowd.

The powder room was cool and quiet, and she sank down onto one of the divans and closed her eyes. He was here, he had finally come. Since Charles had told her that Lucian was in the city, she had known it was only a matter of time until they met. Fate had set them on colliding paths from the start, and all they could do was follow them, as much as they tried to avoid it.

"Caroline?" A voice asked from the door, and she looked up to see Rebecca entering the room. "What is it?" she asked, sitting beside her.

"It's... Lucian. He is here," she whispered. She saw the news hit Rebecca, causing her face to lose its colour, the laughter dim from her eyes. Rebecca reached her hand out and squeezed Caroline's.

"Luke is here?" Rebecca repeated shakily, before standing slowly.

"Where are you going?" Caroline asked, already knowing the answer.

"I – he is my brother," Rebecca said, as explanation. "I'm going to hold him in my arms, as I thought I would never do again," she said, emotion rawer than Caroline had seen for many years. "And then I'm going to beat him to a bloody pulp," she finished, her voice hardening into ice. Caroline merely closed her eyes again, resting her head on the back of the divan.

❀

*L*ucian moved through the crowd silently, the happiness of the guests, the excitement and anticipation rolling off him, and leaving him unscathed. He thanked Katherine for the theme, a masquerade, at least he avoided new introductions to this Virginian society he had little interest in. It was madness to come. He knew it, yet, he could not avoid it, could not stay away.

He had seen John Fairfax, the man's hard gaze on him, yet ignored it. He kept moving, kept his mask in place. He told himself he was not looking for her, as he stalked the perimeter of the hall. He told himself it was not the very reason he had come.

He accepted a glass of champagne and sipped it, his eyes searching the ballroom, before turning to one of the open terrace doors and stepping out. He walked to the iron railing and set his glass down, looking out over the torch-lit garden. It was quiet, peaceful even, out there, and as he let the cold air cool his skin, he tried to ignore his burning desire to return inside. He felt as though he did not belong here. He hadn't felt as though he belonged anywhere for a long time.

He felt the solitude of the terrace change for a moment before the wind brought a familiar perfume, one he could never forget. His dead heart lurched in his chest, as he spoke her name quietly.

"Rebecca," he said, still not facing her, unsure if he could take the sight of her. He heard her move closer, until she stood at his side, leaning on the rail, looking out into the night.

"Who invited you?" she asked.

"Katherine, I suspect."

"Of course," Rebecca murmured wryly, before turning to face him. She looked at him. The last time she had seen him, he had just killed her father and stood covered in his blood. He finally turned to face her, and their eyes met and held. Rebecca reached a hand up to his cheek, and touched his tough expression, melting it with her fingers. His jaw relaxed, his eyes closed, and he seemed at that instant to be her brother again.

"I've missed you," she whispered.

"Becca-" he started but she stopped him.

"I've missed you, and I've hated you. I've been so angry with you, and I have cried and been bed-bound with grief over you. I have mourned your death, deeply, unrelentingly, and then mourned your estrangement - your *choice* to keep yourself away. How could you not come with us, Luke? How could you leave us? Forget us?"

"I have never forgotten you, Rebecca, you are my life. But, I promised-"

"Your promise has brought nothing but pain, and anger and hate. Your promise was folly, selfish stupidity," she spat, and as she spoke the words, in his heart of hearts, Lucian knew them to be true. Even as he knew it, he shook his head. There was so much he wanted to say, to tell her, to explain, but he found that no words would come - they were far too heavy and important, and sat in his stomach, refusing to make their way up his tight, choked throat.

"You do not understand, sister... the things I caused... to you... to..." he trailed off, unable to say her name.

"Caroline? To Caroline? She is here you know. Of course you do... and you are here to see her, on your little sight-seeing tour, from behind your mask like a coward." Lucian shook his head.

"I am here to pay my respects to-"

"Come now, Lucian Ashford, do not lie to yourself, or me, it does us a disservice. You are here to see Caroline, for ever since you met Charles in Portsmouth, she has consumed your every thought." Lucian gripped the bannister tightly. A moment of silence followed before he replied.

"I see you still know me better than I know myself."

"Well, men do not tend to be that complicated," Rebecca said with a frown.

"Rebecca-"

"I must return inside. I find that I cannot look at you just now." She surprised him then when she swept him up into her arms and held him for so long that tears came to his eyes, and he felt her little body shaking with sobs so silent that even he could not hear them. The music swelled through the night air, and they stayed that way for some time clenched together before she broke off suddenly, wiping her eyes, and tidying her shining pile of braided and beaded chestnut hair. She moved toward the door, before stopping and speaking once again. "Where are you staying?"

"Not far. A boarding house. I suspect Katherine knows," Lucian muttered grimly, wondering, not for the first time how she did. Rebecca nodded, her face still hard despite her large tear-washed eyes.

"Caroline is here with Joshua Lee," Rebecca said smartly, at last. His head grew heavy and bowed lower, his hands white on the railing as she turned and went inside, leaving him to his grief and silence alone.

🙼

*T*he band struck up a waltz, and the familiar strains wound around her, threatening to pull her back to her memories. She had finally ventured from the powder room and could find no one of her party who was not dancing.

The ballroom was crowded: the expensive dresses swishing, jewels glittering in the light of the chandeliers. Her eyes sought out her sister, happily dancing with her fiance, clearly in love, and in anticipation of their wedding. How she envied them their bright, shining future, their safe, unbroken hearts.

Both wore masks, as everyone did. Some very vividly coloured, others with swirling gold and silver. Some covered their wearers face entirely, disguising all but their voices, whilst many revealed a whole lot more and just disguised the eyes coquettishly.

Hers was gold, an intricate fan of sculpted lace that framed her features, like a veil, tracing her eyes, which shone green against the gold of her mask. Her dress was simple, white, the soft empire waist draping closely down her body, with layer upon layer of gossamer white fabric, trailing long and romantically behind her. Upon her back, the feathered wings Katherine had given her, large and beautifully dramatic.

Standing by the edge, she saw Julius Caesar approach and smiled at him.

"Lady Caroline, may I have the pleasure of this dance?" he asked, holding his hand out to her. She was just about to extend her own when a familiar voice cut in; and, in that blinding instant, shattered her heart like teeth through spun sugar.

"I'm sorry to be the bearer of bad news... but this dance has been promised to me," his voice was light, but there was steel just underneath, and her new dance partner did not seem the type to argue, accepting his rejection with a smile, he bowed, and departed swiftly. Caroline breathed deeply and prepared herself to turn around, glad for the first time for the mask that shielded her feelings from him.

Turning slowly, she crossed her arms over her chest and found herself face to face with the devil. All in black, his breeches and fitted coat were dark midnight, his boots gleaming. His coat fitted him high to the neck, then tight across his broad shoulders, tapering down to his narrow waist. His mask was also black, without detail, and covered the top portion of his face, more black against his burnished golden hair and bronze stubble. There were gleaming back horns, large and curling, which looked as though they were carved from bone. Though, knowing him, she wouldn't have been surprised if they were. His mouth was the same, full, pink smile, that knew too much about her.

His eyes, she looked in them last, as she knew how difficult it would be: they glittered at her, blue diamonds, and in them, she tried to ignore the look that penetrated her to her core. He had always been able to look at her, and make her feel naked under his gaze, as though they were the only two people in the room... in the world.

He extended his hand to her, and she knew she shouldn't accept. It was too dangerous, it was bad enough that he was here, never mind having time to speak to her alone. He would hurt her again. She wanted to hate him, to slap him, to ignore and hurt him, but she moved to him against her will, as if in a trance. Their fingers touched and she felt his energy course through her skin. Leading her slowly onto the dance floor, he gently pulled her close and they began to dance, their eyes never leaving each others.

"I thought all your dances were mine," he murmured as she finally dropped his gaze, noticing Katherine over his shoulder, and knowing immediately why her friend had chosen her costume. She kept silent, not trusting her treacherous heart to speak. All her dances had been his, for as long as she could remember, and he had walked away from her.

They continued to dance, and she felt her heart start to beat in an even tempo again.

"You planned this?" Caroline asked, trying to break the painful silence that had fallen.

"You've always been the saint to my sinner... it seemed appropriate," he murmured, pulling her a little closer. The draw of him, his smell, his hands on her, they drew her in like a moth to the fire. The song came to an end, yet they remained close. He held her tightly, and she tried to build up the will to leave. Suddenly, he captured her gaze and spoke.

"Caroline... I-"

Stepping back suddenly, Caroline pulled herself out of his arms. She couldn't listen to him say her name anymore. He was so close, too close. The pull of him, the ease with which she could curl into his arms, finally home again after so long. It was confusing, her heart and her head conflicting, yet the truth remained. He was here for his brother, not for her.

With a little distance between them, she felt her courage returning: her resolve to never let him hurt her again, her determination to never allow him to hold her happiness in his hands. They were strangers to each other now, too much time had passed, too much pain had occurred, too much had been lost.

Taking another step, she raised her eyes to his, watching him, and he gently took her hand, his fingers caressing hers through silk gloves, his face creasing with sadness.

"Your ring," he remarked, looking back at her, and she felt heat rise in her cheeks.

"I am a widow. Or didn't you know?" she said softly as she felt his hands tighten on hers, but he didn't say anything, his eyes reflecting an emptiness she'd never seen before. It was fathomless.

"Caroline?" she heard a voice at her side and pulled her hand out of his soft grasp. Backing away, she started shaking,

"Please excuse me," she said, hurrying through the crush of people. She felt tears stinging, and she prayed to keep her composure long enough to get out of the crowd. Rushing up the stairs, she almost tripped and regaining her balance, stopped, feeling the slow fading of his presence like a wound that refused to close, a throb, each step more painful. Taking a deep breath, she continued slower, until she reached the top.

Turning on the top step, she couldn't help but look back down at the ballroom: the dance floor, a riot of colour and sound, of joy and laughter she felt so far from.

And, as though she had imagined him, he was gone.

※

*L*ucian slipped out into the warm night. His heart was racing, and his head dizzy. He had faced down death many times over the last five years, yet nothing had made him feel more frightened nor more alive as the moment he had taken Caroline's hand, her eyes on his. He leant against the wall of the building at the back, breathing deeply, trying to strengthen his heart. He could barely catch his breath. Suddenly, without warning, he was thrown away from the wall, and a solid punch landed on his chin. He staggered backwards, and looked up, catching his attacker's face in the light of a street lamp.

"Wesley!" he exclaimed, as he dropped his hands from his instinctive defensive position. His little brother threw another punch that fell heavily in his gut and forced his breath out. Coughing he held his hands up in surrender.

"Wesley! Stop! What are you doing?" Isaac Taylor's voice came from behind them, and suddenly, Wesley was being pulled back. Lucian rested his hands on his knees a moment, before standing upright. He saw his younger brother pinned back by Isaac, with a look more fierce than any he had ever seen on his face.

"He shouldn't be here... this is for family," Wesley snapped as if his voice were a sabre.

"Wesley, calm down. He's still your brother..."

"Not anymore he isn't. He stopped being my brother, or having the right to come here, the moment he heard he was a free man and elected not to join us. When he chose to leave us, forget us." Lucian felt each word like a blow to the chest.

"Wesley-" he started.

"Please, I have no interest in your pathetic excuses, Lucian. You have no idea what we have been through, what Caroline has been through," Wesley spat each word like acid.

"Wesley," Isaac said, trying to soothe him, as he continued to hold him back.

"No, Isaac! You cannot dissuade me. A coward stands before me... a deserter. He must leave." Isaac looked to Lucian, a helpless expression on his face. Lucian took a deep breath and nodded.

"You are right, brother. I shall leave. I should never have come. I don't belong here anymore."

✿

"Wesley! How could you? You've spoiled all my careful planning," Katherine scolded.

"Why, Katherine? How can you have invited him?" Wesley demanded, flinching as Rebecca rubbed a herbal ointment on his cut knuckles. Katherine sighed.

"Wesley, he still loves her, she still loves him, they have a child... do I need more of a reason to wish to see them reconcile?" Katherine demanded. Wesley snorted at her words, his eyes still flashing with anger.

"He walked away from her, he broke her heart... he doesn't deserve a second chance, with her, or with any of us. Hell, he doesn't even want one!"

"Of course he does. Think about your brother for one moment... he has been alone for five years, alone, completely, homeless and without any news of the people he loves. What kind of toll does that take on a man's soul?"

Rebecca spoke up, her voice tight, her face torn and confused.

"He chose to stay away... in Portsmouth."

"Because he thought he was making a necessary sacrifice," Katherine argued.

"When has Lucian ever sacrificed anything for anyone?" Wesley demanded and quieted as Rebecca shushed him. "Exactly. When? Never, that's when. He's not human. He rejected us all - his family, his wife, his daughter." Wesley cried, and dropped his face into his hand.

"Love clouds our judgements, as does pain and grief. You know how

671

our poor brother has always been quick to descend into blackness," Rebecca said, seeming unsure which side of the argument she wanted to take. "And..." she added, "he does not know that Ellie survived."

Wesley calmed after a while, composing himself. He was passionate, and he felt things keenly, but Katherine had never seen Wesley stay angry for long - he was too generous, and his heart too large. He stood up, pain written across his face, and strode out of the room.

✿

*C*aroline tucked a strand of hair up into her bonnet and looked out of the window as the site of the hospital drew closer. 'There,' she told herself, 'you see, Caroline, the world has gone on spinning just as before, and nothing at all has changed... just as it should be.' She put her hand to her chest for a moment to ease the pain, then she took a deep breath and let it out slowly. Katherine and Rebecca were chattering about something wedding related, which was all they seemed to do of late. Not that Caroline could blame them, they deserved their happiness and more. They deserved everything, this surrogate family that had made her part of their lives so determinedly. Joshua Lee was looking politely on as they spoke, feigning interest, and as she caught his eye, she hid her smile. His expression revealed his torment for an instant.

She smiled at Wesley as he looked out the window. He was excited, she could tell, and she knew he was looking forward to the morning. The newly hired Dr Lombardi, chief doctor in charge of patient care, had called another meeting with the architect and the other head physicians and had asked Wesley to join to represent the Ashfords.

When the carriage stopped, Wesley opened the door first and jumped out. The warm air hit Caroline, as well as the lingering dust and overwhelming yellowness of the light around the construction. Wesley's hand reached back in, and she took his hand, climbing carefully down. The site was chaos, with men milling everywhere, some directing interested glances over at the newly arrived carriage. Caroline gingerly walked over the crunching rubble, waiting as Rebecca and Katherine climbed down behind her.

672

"Well! I see it still has far to go," Katherine said with her typical bluntness, looking around.

"Yes, indeed, one can hardly envisage how it will ever become a building, never mind a hospital," Rebecca said. "Wesley, explain it to us... we are part of this too," Rebecca demanded from her brother.

"Very well, sister, yet, there is someone who might help better than I, the foreman. I see him over there. Let's ask for a tour," Wesley said, leading them toward a man in the distance. The three walked off gaily, and Caroline followed slowly, waiting until Joshua approached her and walked at her side. She coughed for a moment, the cloud of dust moved in the wind over them. He stopped them and turned to her. Reaching into his pocket, he removed a crisply folded white handkerchief. He handed it to her, and she pressed it over her nose and mouth.

"Thank you, the air is awfully thick here, is it not?" she said as they started walking again.

"I suppose it must be, especially for you. The air of the English countryside is all you have breathed these past years. Cities are dirty, unclean places."

"Yes, you are right. I cannot imagine again smelling the scent of the air of Wiltshire, so fresh you might say it actually smelled green," she said with a laugh, feeling herself suddenly blush as she stumbled over a rough stone, and felt his warm hand enclose her elbow. They stopped there, her leaning against his chest, her balance caught, yet unable to move away. His face was close to hers, and his expression so painfully ardent, that Caroline wished to break their gazes, hide her embarrassment.

"There is another place where the air is as clean and fresh... in Tennessee," he said softly, and Caroline knew what he was implying. She met his gaze the best she could, yet was speechless. The last days had upset the delicate balance she had thought she had found in herself, the harmony and acceptance of her life.

Seeing Lucian again, the memory sent a lurch through her stomach, it had undone so many resolutions she had made, opened so many wounds she had thought long healed. The stray lock of hair escaped again in the wind, and she watched as Joshua reached out and caught it, tucking it slowly behind her ear. She was frozen in that instant, at such intimacy. She had no response for him, she had no words to say to him.

A sudden clanging pulled their attention, and Caroline saw all at once the work on the site halt abruptly. The men around them were running toward the noise, and she cast her eyes ahead and saw that a beam had fallen on a man, pinning him to the ground. She threw her hand over her mouth, gasping at the sight, as the men tried to lift it from him. She saw Joshua strip his jacket off, turning to her, urgency in his eyes.

"Wait here. Do not watch, Caroline. We shall do what we can," he said, already moving toward the crowd. Caroline saw Wesley, in the distance, also dashing in, and the pair joining the straining men around the beam. Her heart was pounding in her ears as she watched. She was so lost in the scene that she jumped when a low voice spoke quietly beside her.

"He is a good man," it said, and she stiffened, feeling her palms dampen in her gloves. She screwed her eyes against the dust and put a hand over them, trying to keep her eyes on the accident.

❀

*L*ucian had watched her arrive, saw her emerge from the carriage with the others, a strange feeling going through him as he saw Joshua Lee join them. It was what he had wanted for her, what he had urged Charles to encourage, so why did it make him feel physically sick? When they stopped and Lee had given her his handkerchief, the discomfort only increased, and when she had stumbled, reaching for him to support herself, he had had to turn away, unable to stomach it.

He told himself that it was foolishness to return to the site each day, and he wondered why he did it. Was it to feel a part of her world for a moment? To imagine he was still a part of that family once again. It was weak, and he had thought that any weakness in him had long ago died, along with any hope of seeing his family again. He had made peace with it, with himself, somewhere in the deserted lands he had travelled, in the warm nights under the stars, in the knowledge that finally he had done something right, by letting her go.

He too regarded the scene in front of him, considering helping, but knowing that there was no more space for help, he would only be in the way. Besides, it would have been impossible for him to drag his blood-less body anywhere but closer to her. Just there, so near, he saw the wind stir the loose strands just under her bonnet at the nape of her neck, and the thought of how she smelled there, honey, soap, salt, Caroline. It made him close his eyes as the feeling took him over. She was not something that he was capable of resisting.

Weakness. Unutterable, intolerable weakness. So, he walked over to her side, and said the very last thing in all the world that he wanted to, and felt the cold wash over him, and soothe his thudding heart. He thought she might not reply, so long was her silence. He felt comfortable in it, just being close to her, made him calm, even as it tore his chest open.

"Yes. I suppose he is, after all..." Caroline said finally. "Why are you here?" she continued, without even a glance in his direction.

"I confess, I do not rightly know. I am curious, perhaps. I wish to see what you have made of my family legacy... how you have changed it from waste and greed, into something with worth."

"It is still a project and not an easy one."

"I do not imagine it is. I do not believe any part of the last years have been for anyone. Especially you."

"Or you," she murmured, and he wondered if he did not mistake the note of compassion in her voice - surely even she could never be capable of such a thing.

"I should leave you, Lee may not take my presence well."

"Yes, I suppose you are good at that," she said. He dropped her gaze at the words and made to leave. It had been a horrible exchange, painful and cold, but even still he could not regret it.

"Lucian! Wait... I need to speak with you. It is important," she said. He turned back slowly, looking at her with his head to the side. Her expression was unfathomable, and he was surprised to see her colour under his scrutiny.

"It does not concern me... or us," she added harshly. "There is... something else." He continued to look at her, for a long moment, before nodding. He could hear Wesley calling her name, as the group approached, and Lucian decided that he was in no hurry to repeat their performance of the other night. A last shared look, and then he was walking away, one step in front of the other, his worn clothes flapping in the dusty breeze, hatless, his long hair being tossed loose of its binding.

He moved out of sight, and Caroline turned to face the others, ignoring her racing heart, and the overwhelming fear of what she had done, and the consequences it may yet hold.

CHAPTER 4

*C*aroline was tugged awake, her dreams falling away as small hands pulled at her face, and arms. She kept her eyes closed a minute more, hearing Ellie's huff of frustration. Without warning, she lunged forward, grabbing the squealing child in her arms, and dragging her onto the bed, and under the covers. Ellie giggled, wriggling into her mother's embrace, happy in their cocoon.

"Why are you so sleepy, mummy?" Ellie asked at Caroline's yawn.

"I don't know, sweetheart, the last few days have been very tiring I suppose."

"Because Auntie Katherine is getting married?" Ellie asked.

"Yes... that is why, and so we all have to work very hard until after the wedding."

"Can I come to the wedding?" Ellie asked.

"Of course you can, but you have to be very good, and quiet."

"Who else is coming?"

"Lots of people, your whole family!" Caroline answered, taking a deep breath at the thought. Ellie was looking at her shrewdly, and Caroline realised her mistake too late.

"Not my whole family... not my daddy," Ellie said. She was so prepared for disappointment. Caroline debated with herself, aware that her daughter was watching each emotion flit across her features.

677

The image of the day at the building site clouded her mind once again, a frequent ghost in her every waking moment since. Standing so close to Lucian, despite her overwhelming anger and frustration at him, her hate for how he made her feel, there was only one thought running through her mind. Elspeth. Ellie. She had to tell him. She had to give her daughter a chance of having a father. Yet, she was afraid, more afraid than she could ever remember being. If he walked away and returned to the life he had chosen over them, she was not sure how Ellie would recover. Yet, if he stayed, it was almost more frightening. How could he be in their lives again, yet separate, how could she see him and stop her heart from breaking with each visit?

She was angry with him, so angry, but would it fade in the years to come? She wondered. Could a love like theirs ever be mere friendship? Or was she destined to love him forever, even as their lives took them away from each other into the arms of others, as the pain and hurt of the past between them proved too much to ever forget?

"Mummy?" Ellie prompted, and Caroline suddenly realised that she hadn't answered.

"Well, since it is Uncle Charles's wedding, maybe your father will come... he is his brother." Ellie sat up immediately, making a tent with the covers and her head.

"You said daddy could never come home," Ellie said, her eyes wide.

"I know, my love. I thought that before, I didn't know... if he could come. But now, I think he can," Ellie looked away, processing the news, and Caroline wondered what she was thinking. She was surprised when she turned back with a sudden subject change.

"Does this mean I can have a brother?"

"What! Why?"

"You said before I couldn't, just like you said daddy could never come back. You changed your mind about it... can you change your mind about my brother?"

"Oh Ellie," Caroline laughed, pulling her closer, her hands going around her waist and tickling her. Ellie laughed, trying to twist away from her mother's nimble fingers, the conversation forgotten for the moment.

*C*aroline had collected herself as best she could. She had rehearsed what she would say, and how to say it. There was no way to postpone it further. The wedding was less than two weeks away. The family would want their brother there. Elspeth would be there. There was no mistaking her parentage, and Lucian could no more doubt it than he could his own reflection. It was a miracle he had not already found out, she guessed he must have become even more formidable to talk to, and more of a recluse than ever to still not know.

She smoothed down her pale green gown. It was the colour of jade, not unlike the outer rings of her irises, and it was embellished with fine scalloped lace edging. Her hair was caught up in silver combs, a blue ribbon at her neck. She caught sight of herself in the reflection of the window and blushed.

What was she doing? Why did she care how she looked? She was vain and silly, and she felt ashamed of herself. Had all the pain of his abandonment, and the nights she had cried, more heartbroken at the cruellest truth, that he did not want her, been for nothing? Had she learned nothing from them, that still she looked at him with love in her heart? Her reckless heart that had always loved too readily, forgiven too easily and remained too loyal when all hope was lost.

A sound from the street drew her attention. She looked out. Carriages passed, and couples promenading, still wearing summer clothes, with delicate parasols held up. It was warm again, unseasonably late, the whims of the weather proving fickle this time of year, and such a welcome change after years of grey England. The park opposite the townhouse was still golden and beautiful, and she could see children playing, their governesses keeping a watchful eye. She sighed, turning around restlessly, and returning to her chair and book.

He must be told. That was the only reason why she waited for him now. Not to see him, not to be close to him - only to deliver the news.

❀

*L*ucian paid the young messenger, seeing him sprint off with his precious cargo. He had written to tell Caroline that he would call later in the day when he hoped they might have some privacy. He smoothed down his clothes, feeling ashamed for their condition for once when another man had arrived with a letter for him in an unfamiliar hand.

He had written to Annie Paterson regularly but had received few responses, each shorter and more bleak than the last. He did not know when his promise to William would be fulfilled, had not yet figured out how he might help William's widow in all but name. He had tried to send her money, but she had returned it. She was destitute and stranded now, an unwed mother of a fatherless child in a foreign land without friends or family, waiting, no doubt, for a lover that would never return to her. Lucian was responsible for her. It had been his life for William's, though the sacrifice had been one that left black ash in his lungs, to choke him whenever he thought on it.

The young girl had been so devastated by the news, and in her reaction he had seen a different woman, in a far off country, realising that the man she waited for would never return. It was a guilt, a weight, that he could never quite shed. He had been to visit her in Durham once more, bringing her food and sugary cakes in the hopes of fattening her up, but she barely raised an eye to them. She had said that hearing about William had helped her, so Lucian had continued to write to her, and, in turn, it had helped him somewhat to swallow the guilt he felt, over both William and Caroline, two people he had failed so utterly. He was too late to comfort Caroline, she had already suffered through losing him, yet it was not too late to comfort someone whom William had loved. He hoped with time that he could help her to make a home in this new land somehow, or if she preferred, to return her and her baby home to Scotland.

Lucian ripped open the letter, keen to see some indication that she was brightening slowly, healing for herself and the child.

My Lord Ashford,

I write to you this final time to ask for help. I know I have no right to ask you for any favour, but I do not have another to ask. And you see, it is not for myself, but for my boy, for Callen, that I swallow my pride and ask now for your charity.

Callen will need some place, and I have seen too many die in the workhouse or sallow and parish in some cold orphanage. You have always been so kind, to me and to William, and I ask for your kindness again to find him a home, with a family, or to work, but someplace safe where he can grow up off of the streets and one day, perhaps, have the opportunity to make a life for himself.

William wrote of you. He loved you. I have enclosed his few letters here for you to keep, my only items of any value, and I believe he would be happy to see them now in your hands.

forever yours,
Annie Paterson Campbell

*L*ucian did stop to find his coat, he did not pack a breakfast, nor fill his canteen. He got on his horse and he rode.

❀

*C*aroline clutched the letter, before folding it, before dropping it, sighing. She waited still, shifting in her uncomfortable dress, thinking how it made a mockery of her. His letter had told her to expect him that afternoon. Like a fool, she had gotten ready far too early, and sat and waited in the drawing-room, unable to do anything else. The hours had ticked by, with nothing; her dress tight and scratchy, and missing Ellie, who had gone to the Taylors to be looked after by Eva. She had been quite alone, with the others engaged in some form of business, wedding or otherwise. The tick of the clock mocked her also, reminding her of all the time she had waited for him, this man, to whom her time was worthless.

The noise of a door slamming sounded through the house, and she froze, listening, waiting for footsteps in the hall, waiting for Lucian to appear at the door, but he did not. The caller seemed to have come for Charles, and she could hear male voices in his study.

She went to the window to look for signs of a carriage, wondering who it was, and what their business could be with Charles. She jumped as the door slammed again. A movement below caught her eye, and she stiffened, seeing Lucian suddenly stride out of the door, swing up onto the back of a horse, and ride away. She stared after him, shocked. He had come, and left, without seeing her after all.

"Charles?" she asked, as she knocked and opened the door at the same time. Charles straightened up from his position in front of the safe in his study. He looked as weary as she had ever seen him.

"What did Lucian want?" she asked directly. Charles pushed the heavy metal door shut, and then sat in his chair, cradling his tired face in his hands. He looked reluctant to answer.

"Please – tell me," she urged, sitting across from him.

"He came for money. He barely had time to explain," he said, glancing up at Caroline before his eyes flicked away.

"Money for what?"

"He did not say."

"Well, what did he say?"

"Something about a woman... a Miss Paterson." His face was worried, hurt, sympathetic, and Caroline did not mistake the significance of it. Her eyes widened as she inhaled the news.

"And what else, Charles?"

"And something," he continued painfully, "something about being responsible for a baby."

"A baby..." she said, her words cold in her mouth.

"He did not have time to explain. I'm sure that things are not as they-" Charles broke off as Caroline suddenly stood up, and walked toward the door. "Wait, Caroline – we know nothing about this woman."

"I know all I need to. Lucian has another life now. Another... another family. Either way, nothing has changed. He has not come home to us, that much is clear. He has barely even seen us. I will not live like this. I want confirmation that he shall leave me alone, or I want a divorce, Charles." He lifted his eyes and pinned her with a startled look.

"Caroline, please. Do not even speak the word. I'm sure that-"

"No!" she almost shouted, her rough tone startling Charles. She shook her head, taking a grip of herself. "No," she whispered. "Do you know what I did today? I waited for him... I waited for him each second feeling like another year, and here he has come and gone, making clear what is important to him. A baby. A baby, Charles! I have been waiting for him for so long, I have forgotten that I was supposed to have a life also, I have forgotten how to live. I cannot wait for him anymore. I will not."

🌸

*I*n her room, Caroline threw off her itchy dress, cursing it. She had never needed proof of his disregard of her, yet he gave it her so generously. She was embarrassed and pained, all the past hurt and anger flooding her, burning hotter than ever before.

She yanked out the pins from her hair, so carefully placed, pulling strands of hair out with them. She cursed her naivety. A woman. A baby. A baby he had been responsible for. A woman he had lain with, probably loved. He had a baby with someone else. She pulled the basin to her and was sick. Wiping her mouth with a shaking hand, she refused her tears to drop. Damn him. She'd be damned if she'd shed one more tear for that man.

Tugging a brush through her hair in long, sharp strokes, she looked into the mirror and the woman who stared back - she wasn't free. She was married to a dead man that no longer wanted her, who had moved on. She knew she must end all ties between them. And if any remained, let it be between Ellie and her father. He must act just as he said that he would - to leave and allow her a new life without him. He did not want her. The man could not possibly have been clearer.

She grabbed Lucian's note from the dresser, promising he would call that afternoon. She held the tip to the flame and enjoyed watching it burn. Her rage was still not sated as she brushed the ashes to the floor, her hand suddenly went to a small drawer. She pulled it out and grabbed a couple of faded letters, his letters to her, from long ago. One by one she held them to the flame and watched as the fire ate the last remaining words of affection between them, the last evidence of his love. As they curled and melted away, she felt a serene sense of catharsis.

Tomorrow, she would see to her separation, or even divorce if it came to that, and if such a thing brought shame upon the family, then that was Lucian's fault, not hers, and soon she could forget about Lucian Ashford, as he had so clearly forgotten her.

🌸

*C*aroline was amazed by the resilience of the human heart. How, broken and dead and burned to cinder, how somehow it could still hurt. She was angry with herself mostly. What a little fool she had been, curling her hair and waiting prettily on the divan for him to return. She had told herself that it was only for Ellie, but just as Lucian lived and breathed and walked the streets, she knew her heart still beat his name.

She could not open herself up to this again, she would need to be stronger.

When it was clear to both of them that Lucian had gone, and would probably not return, Caroline and Charles had spoken. He had asked her to his study, he had handed her a drink, and she knew that it would not be pleasant.

"Caroline, my dear," he started, clearly wishing that he did not have to. "I do not claim to know why Lucian has come to Virginia after all this time, but it seems that he has left it again."

"Yes," she said. "It does." She blinked and held her head up. She would not put poor Charles through another scene like last time.

"I do not know where he is, or if he means to return," he went on, "but I have given this some thought, and I do not believe that you should have to live at the mercy of his whims. You are aware, I'm sure, that for things to continue as they are, he must remain hidden, a dead man in the eyes of the law. It would be a dishonesty, plain and simple, but if Lucian agrees, if he can be relied upon to carry on as he has been, discrete and unnoticed, then he may move on with his life, and you, Caroline, can move on with yours, just as we have discussed before, just as I have encouraged you to do. No one need know that he is your husband, no one need know that you are not a widow. I believe that you... might even marry again if you wish it."

Her mind drifted again, carried away to her youth, sitting in front of the haggard fortune teller when she got a faraway look in her eye and told Caroline of great love and sorrow, that she would twice be a bride.

Caroline blinked hard and opened her eyes to catch an unmistakable flash of regret touch Charles's brown eyes.

"And if he returns?" she asked. "What then would you have me do, Charles?" Caroline noticed a note of frustration in her voice. He was her

protector and ally, and she loved him, but she could not help but be annoyed at the situation.

"If he returns, then we will go on with our lives, just as I have said..."

"Or..." she prompted.

"Or... I am sorry, Caroline, but I must ask it. Is there yet somewhere, in your heart, the same one that has impressed me with its compassion and wisdom, its strength, since you were little more than a girl... that could find itself capable of once again loving my brother? Your souls were once melded as one, and everyone who looked upon you saw it. Caroline, I know it is much to ask... too much. Yet, if there remains even the smallest shred of love for him in your heart, perhaps you might try..."

"Charles, please... stop," Caroline said, feeling tears sting her nose. "I doubt I shall ever stop loving your brother," she began and felt guilty as she saw the hope light up his eyes. "He has given me Ellie, and all of you... and for that, and more, I will always love him. But... and it breaks my heart to say it, for me, Lucian died years ago. He died in France when you came home carrying his possessions and I mourned him. And then, he died all over again when he stood on the dock and watched me leave, sail to a new life without him. The man here, now, who comes and goes as he pleases, he is not the man I loved. Not anymore. He is not the man who held me at night and promised to never leave me, to be by my side always, to keep me safe. And I am not the girl that he loved. We are changed, both of us. We are strangers now."

Charles looked away briefly, his hand going to his face, where he scrubbed it over his features roughly.

"So will you then... move on? Try to build a home with someone else? Joshua Lee, perhaps?"

"Perhaps," she answered. It did not begin to explain her heart. Somehow he had returned, and yet, nothing in her life was any different than it was before.

"Could you care for Lee?"

"I am not without feeling toward him. And as for love? All I have ever learned from love was how to cry. I will not cry anymore," she said, feeling more resolute as she said it. Speaking through her feelings made her see the sense of it. It was true. The emotional wreckage of her past was unspeakably awful, and it was best to leave it there, in the past, and let it burn. There was no use waiting for him when she did not know where he would disappear to tomorrow, or if he would even say goodbye before he left. "He might never come back, Charles."

"Yes, quite. Well, let us think further on the trajectory of this course of action. We will need to be prepared for any possibility."

Caroline felt an anxiety grip at her stomach.

"What possibility?"

"We must manage this all very carefully. I am sure you can see the predicament we find ourselves in, should you wish to marry again. Or should he return and be reluctant to leave. If he stays in Richmond we cannot hide him forever. What if he changes his mind? What happens when he finds out he has a daughter?" He sighed forcefully and ran a hand through his hair.

"He has promised that he would stay away." Caroline felt a flash of anger, knowing that Charles was not wrong. *"He has had plenty of time to come back to me, yet he has not. Why should he now, when he has a new lover and a new child of their own?"*

"He is a man tormented, Caroline. We cannot rule out the possibility that he may yet break his promise and try to claim you."

❦

*T*he early morning sun seemed at odds with the heavy exhaustion Lucian felt settle on his shoulders as he slowly climbed the stairs of the Ashford's home. He had been gone for longer than he could remember, three weeks, four perhaps, and had slept little.

Annie Paterson had been hanging when the matron had found her the week before Lucian had arrived. The baby had been tucked into a basket in another room, crying, a few coins wrapped with his name, Callen Paterson Campbell, along with Lucian's name.

"How was I supposed to know what to do with the waling babe? I never had one of my own, and the poor thing needed a wet nurse as soon as he could get one, so I had him picked up," the thin matron had told him. She had handed half the coins over and kept the other half for unpaid rent, and she said she didn't know where the baby had gone after that. Lucian had spent weeks looking for a baby and had only returned home when he had run out of money, and out of leads.

He knocked on the door, hearing a footman already approaching. He had left, left her waiting for him - disappeared again for weeks. How could he possibly explain? Would she even listen?

"I am afraid she is not receiving callers," the footman announced.

Lucian rocked back a little, his face blank as he tried to come up with another way to ask to be admitted. She did not want to see him, hardly surprising, yet he wished he might at least offer some sort of explanation.

"She is not at home," a voice called along the hall, and he saw Wesley walking toward him. Lucian stiffened, and stepped back, making to leave.

"You can wait inside if you must. It matters not to me," Wesley said, gesturing inside with a dismissive hand. Lucian nodded slowly and stepped in.

"Very well. Thank you," he said quietly, seeing the narrowed look on his younger brother's face.

"I suppose you should wait in the drawing-room, we mustn't let strangers snoop around the house unattended... one cannot be too careful in a new city," Wesley drawled, leading the way to the drawing-room. Lucian fought down an angry retort and merely nodded. His brother held every right to talk down to him. They entered the drawing-room, and Lucian sat, watching as Wesley poured himself a drink, and sat too, offering him nothing.

"So, I am curious... why are you here? Have you not yet inflicted enough damage?"

"I am here because I must speak to Caroline," Lucian said, his exhaustion robbing him of any ability to explain more clearly.

"Oh. Of course! How kind of you to turn up. Probably just a little late though, I'd wager?" Wesley said, his voice mocking. "How much is it this time? Three weeks? Five years? Lucian looked away, ignoring the baiting his brother excelled at. "I must admit, you had me fooled, Lucian. I always looked to you with such... admiration, and your relationship with Caroline... I truly thought I had never seen two people more suited to bring out the best in each other than you two. I thought I'd never again see a more devoted husband. You had us all fooled to help us forget your disgusting behaviour. And we forgave you. But you had plenty more to offer. So, cheers to you, I take my hat off to you! Well played."

"Shut up, Wesley. Of course I love her, you fool. You cannot believe otherwise," Lucian growled, giving into anger finally, his nerves worn thin.

"How could she, or anyone else, really still believe that?" Wesley said curtly, and Lucian felt the statement sink through him. Caroline doubted his love. He didn't want to believe it. Surely she knew that he had done it all for her? She had his letter. She knew that he had stayed away, every blindingly painful second, because he loved her. Of course she must.

"Wesley, I love her with everything I have ever been. I always have. Do not speak of what you do not know," Lucian warned low, feeling wound tight, and as if he may spring.

"No brother, it is you who know nothing. You know nothing of the woman you married, the woman you claim to love, how she has changed, how she has lived, how she has cried for you. You know nothing of her dreams now, her hopes... you cannot love a woman you do not know. I wonder now if you ever did. You have no idea how to love, do you, brother?"

Lucian stood, his anger boiling, his fists clenched, as he tried to speak calmly.

"I will not sit here and listen to this-"

"You turn up here just to upset us all, and then you just disappear again! Where were you?" Wesley shouted. "Nevermind. Why do I even bother asking?"

The front door slammed, then, breaking the tension that was swiftly mounting between them. Snapped out of their linked stare, they both turned, Wesley coming to his feet as people entered the room. First Rebecca and Katherine, both falling silent as they saw Lucian standing there. Next, like a knife in the gut, was Joshua Lee, with Caroline on his arm.

Lee's face was a picture of shock, and then anger, and Lucian saw his grip tighten on Caroline before he schooled his features. The group stood, frozen in awkwardness for a long moment, before Katherine moved forward into the room, and offered him a tentative smile.

"Why! Lord Ashford, you have returned. How lovely to see you."

"Please, do not call me that, Katherine. Am I not still...your friend?" he asked, tearing his eyes away from the sight of Caroline and Joshua, focusing on Katherine and her overly bright smile, and trying to push the image of Caroline's dainty, be-gloved hand nestled in the crook of Lee's arm.

"Of course, Lucian. And I suppose we shall finally be family soon enough," Katherine said, ushering everyone into the room with an impatient air. Rebecca relaxed somewhat and came to greet him, pressing her cheek against his.

"We are already family," he ground out to no one, fists clenched.

"Lord Ashford... come back to life, I see," Lee said, clearing his throat, his tone making it abundantly clear that he much prefered the dead version of him. "So, when do you plan to leave again?" Joshua asked pointedly. Lucian forced himself to calm the flash of temper that burned up his neck. He would not give them a show and act like a wild beast who had stumbled into their sitting room to smash the china.

"I do not yet know," Lucian answered carefully, his eyes unable to stop returning every few moments to Caroline, whose looks simmered with hatred. "Caroline, I must speak with you. I see that... I have called at an inopportune time. Please notify me when I should call back," he bowed. He was at an impasse. He could not talk to her here, and he doubted that she would listen if she would even grant him an audience. He would come back when she was alone. If she would not speak to him, he would write her a letter. If she did not read it, he would sleep in the hall if he must, sleep in the road, and wait. "Please excuse me. I will find Charles," Lucian said finally, moving for the door.

CHAPTER 5

*C*aroline leaned her head against the glass, watching Joshua's broad shoulders disappear down the street. What the hell was Lucian doing here? She thought he had gone again. This time for good, maybe.

The footman standing beside her offered her a small smile as she leaned back.

"When did everything become so complicated, Henry?" she asked him, and he smiled at her question.

"For me, it always was, ma'am."

She turned away and started back toward the drawing-room, and then stopped herself.

"Tell my family I have retired, if they should ask. And please send Ellie to me when the other Lord Ashford leaves. Please ask Nanny to keep her busy in the nursery until then"

"Very good, ma'am," Henry replied and Caroline slowly started upstairs to her room. She did not wish to see Lucian, nor to hear his excuses. She did not wish to hear even one word about his woman or his baby. Charles had promised to communicate with him if he returned, and that should be enough. Caroline did not wish to further engage. She reached the landing, and walked along it, to her room, thankful once again that Ellie had remained out of sight.

Lucian heard her leave the others, heard her steps on the stair overhead. She had been spending time with Lee. Of course she had. At the thought of them together, pain seared through his chest like he was being flayed open. He was not surprised, but that did nothing to lessen the pain. So that was all, she would refuse to speak to him, and no doubt she would be remarried before he even realised, with Charles's help.

Charles had been busy with a contractor from the hospital and asked Lucian to wait. He was caught there, indecision freezing him. He could return to the drawing-room and demand more information from Katherine and Rebecca, or he could simply leave... or... as the thought occurred to him, he was already moving.

He climbed the stairs two at a time and went to where he guessed Caroline's footsteps had taken her. He paused outside the door and extended his hand. He saw to his horror, that his fingers trembled slightly. He gripped them hard and took a breath. He could not breathe properly, his heart was squirming in his chest and he felt almost dizzy. Composing himself, he knocked gently.

"Come in, Ellie" he heard Caroline's voice call back, and holding his breath, he turned the knob and opened the door. At first, he did not see anyone. The room was bright and airy, and the scent of her struck him like a hammer.

In his mind's eye he was home again in Westmere, their sunlit bedroom, with its generous bed, never empty for long. He was lost in her smell, and he could almost feel the skin of her bronzed shoulder, or the hair at the nape of her neck tickling his nose as he breathed it in.

"I shall bathe, if you wouldn't mind preparing, Mary," Caroline's voice said, and he was struck dumb, suddenly seeing through, into her dressing room. She sat at a low stool, her gown cast off, onto the chair behind, her chemise was thin, almost translucent, and it hung off one shoulder, the other shoulder covered by her curtain of hair as it fell down her back, a cascade in waves of draped black velvet.

He swallowed hard, his mouth dry, and he knew he had lived without colour or beauty in his life for so long, until this moment. After so many years, the memories had dulled, become worn and tattered. Now though, she was more magnificent than ever. In five years, he had not looked at a woman as an object of desire... they were only people like any other, and there had been nothing to spark his interest or ignite his passion.

But suddenly, in that instant, it flooded back to him, and his body, not so old after all, responded forcefully. He realised her eyes were on him, in the mirror, and he stared unashamedly back, his expression one of shock, and pure, unadulterated desire. Stark, plain want was written across his eyes, and he knew he should look away, but could not bring himself to.

The prickling over her arms, the flush of heat that travelled down her back, it was so incredibly familiar, so familiar, in fact, that seeing him there, was not a surprise. She stood up slowly, grabbing her robe, as she quickly threw it over her barely concealed form. She turned back, seeing his eyes fill with some kind of emotion as they roamed over her and she walked toward him, stopping just in front. Silence filled the tension charged air. Suddenly, she raised her hand and slapped him, hard.

The crack punctuated the silence, and he dropped his head as she saw her red handprint blossom on his cheek. He was silent. No retaliation, no retort. He merely turned back to her, his eyes inscrutable.

"Get out," she ground out, raising her chin defiantly, crossing her arms.

"We must talk."

"I said leave. At once!" she shouted suddenly, and he flinched back, before shaking his head slowly.

"Not before we speak."

"We have nothing to speak of."

"We have everything to speak of."

"No – you do not get to tell me what to do. Not anymore, and never again."

"Caroline, please-" he said, touching her arm. She jerked it away and saw his face crumple.

"No! Do not touch me! You do not get to touch me, do not get to speak to me... do not get to look at me so... ever again," she cried, standing her ground as he suddenly stepped closer.

"Look at you how?"

"Like... that. How dare you? You have no right," she said with contempt thick in her voice, her face tilted upwards to his in defiance.

She hoped that he would shrink away, but instead he leaned closer still, testing her, pushing her. She did not sway, did not show weakness.

"I have every right, sweetheart... I am your husband," he murmured softly, reminding her, cruelly, that they were still bound together, and that she was not free, no matter how she wished to be.

"You are no such thing. Why did you come back here? You do not want to be here, so go!" Caroline raised her arms and shoved him hard, though he barely budged his face tightening.

"You seem awfully agitated, for someone who longs to be rid of me," he murmured coming closer.

"Do not flatter yourself. I despise you more now than I ever did before!"

He stayed before her, uncomfortably close for a long moment, his eyes flooded with emotion. Time played out, and Caroline felt his eyes sink into hers, his will battle hers, as she tried to remain strong, righteous, to take shelter in her well-deserved hate.

She held onto her anger, her only defence, and waited. Her eyes could not move from his. Suddenly, he lifted his hand, ever so gently, cautiously, waiting to see if she would stop him, raised it to her cheek, and the tips of his fingers, rough and calloused, gently caressed her skin for a moment. She closed her eyes, feeling a surge of emotion, more overpowering than anything she had felt in years.

"If that is true... then why do you tremble so?" he asked, so softly, she had to lean into him to hear.

"Where were you? Why did you never come?" her voice came out smaller than she had hoped, her eyes still closed. She felt his hand pause.

"Believe me, I wanted to come, I was called away, on something very important."

"A woman?"

"A friend."

"A baby?"

"Yes, a baby. But-"

"Lucian," Charles's voice came from the door, shaking them both out of their spell. "Come downstairs. We must talk," Charles said, turning away and leaving.

"Go on," she said. "I do not wish to listen to your stories."

"Caroline. It's not what-"

"Go!" she screamed. "If you do not go now I will ask Wesley and Charles to remove you."

He walked to the door slowly, an internal battle seeming to war inside of him.

"What did you want to speak to me about... before I was called away?" he asked, pausing on the threshold. Caroline studied him a long moment, her eyes narrowed, biting her bottom lip until it hurt.

"Nothing," she said, seeing his face close. He nodded and left, walking out into the hall and down the stairs, no doubt to speak to Charles about the mess of the marriage. Caroline sighed and turned away, Ellie filling her mind. She would tell him, of course she would. But when she told him was up to her.

CHAPTER 6

"$\mathcal{L}$ucian, I do not expect to come home, and find out that you are upstairs with Caroline, in her room, and compromising her once again."

"How can a man compromise his wife?"

Charles looked at him, his eyes blinking. He raised an eyebrow in askance and Lucian laughed humourlessly.

He muttered something that Lucian couldn't hear, pouring two large drinks. Lucian accepted his and sat down. He felt strange, dizzy almost, dead on his feet. This might all be a dream, and he still on the road.

"Lucian. We must talk of how this is to proceed" Charles was saying warily before him, yet Lucian found it hard to focus on his words. His mind was still in Caroline's room, surrounded by her sweet scent, his eyes full of her golden skin and shimmering hair, of her striking features, sensual, so painfully beautiful, and her skin, creamier than he could have imagined beneath his fingers.

"Lucian!"

Lucian snapped his attention back to his brother and tried to focus on his words.

"Brother, she has said that she will ask for a divorce if this cannot be settled amicably. You do not want that for us, do you? For her? For..." he trailed off, closing his eyes and scrubbing his hand through his hair in much the same way that Lucian knew that he did.

"I am sorry... I wasn't listening."

"Divorce, Lucian! Divorce," he said more quietly, settling on the word with a soft finality. "She would have that right, I believe, as you have knowingly abandoned her for several years," Charles said, and Lucian suddenly felt the words settle like a stone in his stomach. Divorce. It was extreme. Nearly unheard of. It would drag the whole family down into the mud. Would she really risk the life that they were all building in this new land just to be rid of him and marry another? Lucian kneaded his temples, his tiredness over the past days making it impossible to focus. He was aware that Charles had ceased talking, and was now regarding him over his glass. He met his gaze. There was no sound but the clinking of ice.

"A penny for your thoughts brother," Charles said grimly.

"I – I do not know... I am stunned, perhaps," Lucian said, sipping his drink, hiding his true feelings.

"She does not want to remain married to you."

Lucian swallowed, the starkness of the statement too hurtful to ignore.

"I have enquired. I even made it known that if she could find, even a shred of feeling left for you... that she not decide straight away... but wait."

"She refused?"

"She did. She implied that she felt your feelings would not be positive toward a reconciliation, that you would not be capable of such a thing, and that she did not know when you would leave again. And indeed, you left for weeks Lord knows where, and we did not think you would return." Lucian bowed his head, trying to clear the scent of her hair from his nostrils. "I beg you, brother. Do not push yourself on her. Submit to stay in the shadows for all our sakes. With a bit of sleight of hand, this might all be quietly arranged, and Caroline remarried before the season is over. Then you may build your own life, just as she can build hers."

"And if I... didn't. If I wanted to stay?" Lucian asked, and braced himself for his brother's words. Every instinct he had was screaming at him, telling him to keep his promise, to let her go, to do it for her sake.

But then, his heart... his heart whispered of the way she leaned into his hand, of how her hands trembled when he touched her, and how she pushed him away, with eyes that begged him to stay. If she still loved him... despite everything... it was too much to dare hope.

"Lucian, she has already begun to move on."

"I noticed as much," Lucian said, gulping his drink, and all of the swirling confusion to the rocks. "Charles. I cannot live without her one more day. I cannot... I... cannot simply walk away again from her and survive it."

Charles paused, deliberated once more, let out a long sigh, and then made a decision.

"There is more here than you know, brother. Do not be hasty. Do not leave again just yet. Let us proceed with caution, and we will see if there is somewhere some shred of hope that still lives."

❦

That night, Lucian walked the city the long way home, letting the cold air sober him. They were still married. She still belonged to him, as he did to her. She could not push him from her life at present, she was forced to interact with him to resolve the issue. And him? He should be leaving, listening to her request that he leave them, and giving it to her without reservation, just as he'd promised her... and yet, if he had ever known anyone, he knew her, and he knew that her heart was not indifferent to him quite yet. He had hurt her and damaged her, and nevertheless, Caroline still cared for him, despite herself. Could he use that to his advantage? Bend her to his will, use her feelings against her, to break down the walls she had built against him? Did he have the right?

He knew he did not. He knew that he should go - back to Europe perhaps, or maybe even further east. But he could not go. Could not leave her. And what was to become of William's poor baby? He could not give up. The thought of him out there alone, lanced through him again and again, the sound of crying in his ears.

He walked on through the shadows of the night, chased and torn in two by the hounds of his own thoughts.

🐚

*T*he next day was crisp and sunny, and Caroline felt irritable, disappointed with herself, yet determined to put aside her feelings of the previous night. She had hardly slept, tossing and turning, thoughts of Lucian, his voice, his hands on her, his eyes, tormenting her well into the night.

Today, she would not be so weak, she told herself as she dressed. She should never have allowed him to touch her, to speak so intimately with her. She had to go to the dressmaker that morning for her gown to wear to the wedding. As she joined Rebecca walking to the tailor, she was quiet and pensive, Rebecca's light conversation rolling off her.

"Caroline? Are you listening to me?" Rebecca demanded.

"Yes, of course..." Caroline murmured, forcing Lucian from her mind. They continued on in silence, and Caroline realised that Rebecca was mulling over something too.

"Is something bothering you?" she asked.

"You have not told Luke about Ellie?" Rebecca asked bluntly, and Caroline swallowed, suddenly nervous. She shook her head, as she kept on walking.

"And you really think it is right to keep it from him?"

"Do you propose that I tell him and have him stay... because he feels responsible toward me? Guilty? Should I force his hand?" Caroline asked, her voice coming out a little sharper than she had intended. Rebecca stopped in the street and turned to her.

"He deserves to know, Caroline."

"Of course he does! Do you really think that I do not see that?" Caroline said, exasperated.

"Then, why do you not tell him?"

"When, Rebecca? I saw him a month ago and spoke to him for the first time in five years! Since then, we have either been constantly in mixed company, fighting, he has failed to arrive to an agreed visit, or has disappeared for weeks on end without word." Rebecca looked unconvinced.

"What are you so afraid of?" Rebecca asked, showing a bit of fight of her own, and Caroline opened her mouth instinctively to respond and felt a loss of words there. There was nothing she could say, and Rebecca's words felt like a slap in the face. She felt tears suddenly rear up, and the emotions of the past week swamp her.

Caroline blinked back the tears, yet they still threatened, and so she turned and started walking again, her face down, attempting to regain her composure. Rebecca was right, she was terrified. The things she had said were true. What if she told him? What if he left anyway? What if he stayed? If he stayed she would never know if he stayed out of love for her... or out of a sense of obligation. It was selfish and wrong, yet she could not help it. After the hurt of finding out that he had chosen not to join her, not to be her husband again when nothing stood in his way, the betrayal had sunk into her very core, and she could not shake it.

"We shall be late," she muttered simply, continuing on.

"*O*h, Caroline. Perhaps it is too cold for this. What if they take a chill?"

"Eva, dear, it is only cream and sugar. I daresay that the children will survive it."

"But it is *iced* cream. Will it be very cold, do you think?"

"I think it will be marvellous," Caroline laughed.

There had been an ad that morning in the paper that a local shop had acquired the newest technology in iceboxes and was now offering ice cream, a rare and decadent treat, available 'almost every day', the ad had proclaimed. Caroline had never had ice cream. She didn't know anyone who had, but president George Washington was said to have spent two hundred dollars on ice cream in one summer, and if it was good enough for him, it was good enough for her.

She was simply desperate to distract her racing mind and drumming heart, and the feel of his touch on her cheek which still lingered on her skin, and the torment of imagining Lucian's face when he discovered that he was a father, when he discovered that Caroline had kept it from him. She had grown withdrawn and snappish the past two days, and it was not fair to anyone, least of all Ellie. Trying to right herself, she had cajoled Eva into the outing, their three little ones in tow.

If there was anything in the world that might have distracted Caroline from her anguish, it was the taste of that ice cream. Even Eva had loved it, and ceased her worrying, as her eyes fluttered closed and she took every moment she could to savour the heavenly ambrosia. The children went wild with delight, squealing and giggling as they ran around the park to warm up. Caroline was congratulating herself on an excellent decision and found that even when it began to rain and they had to run for shelter, it did not dampen her spirits.

They ran for the nearest familiar shop, Pendragon's Book Sellers, and all crowded in, shaking the raindrops off onto the wooden floorboards.

"Thank you so much, Mr St John, you have saved us all from being swept away in the deluge. We shall all be very careful and quiet, won't we, children?" Caroline said pointedly, catching the eye of each of the three children, her own little one in particular, as she was a known mischief-maker among them.

As the children scurried off with Eva to wrangle them, Caroline sighed contentedly and ran her finger along the gilded spines, taking her time over the quiet joy of it. Eventually, she picked up Mansfield Park, a new novel by an anonymous author whom she had heard might be a lady novelist, and as Caroline cracked upon the spine and caught the smell of leather and paper, she felt that the day was getting better and better with each passing moment.

'About thirty years ago Miss Maria Ward, of Huntingdon, with only seven thousand pounds, had the good luck to captivate Sir Thomas Bertram, of Mansfield Park, in the county of Northampton, and to be thereby raised to the rank of a baronet's lady, with all the comforts and consequences of an handsome house and large income.'

And that's as far as Caroline got before a crash sounded, like the world was caving in around their ears. Caroline ran from her cosy corner to find Elspeth holding a book in her hand next to a large pile of books which had clearly once been a display, probably one which had taken some time to build and balance, and now lay strewn messily across the floor, next to Sophie who was wailing loudly from the fright of it.

"Oh no, Elspeth! What have you done?" Caroline hurried over and tried to begin stacking the books while Eva soothed her screaming toddler. "Mister St John, I am so sorry. I will pay for anything that's been damaged. How did this happen, Ellie?" Ellie held the book out to her mom, her eyes round and lip quivering.

"I just wanted to look at the book on the bottom," she said sweetly, her voice shaking.

Footsteps could be heard approaching from another room, and Caroline bent down quickly to scoop Ellie up to her hip before she too could start wailing and further rupture the peace of the formerly quiet little bookshop.

"Might I be of service?" she heard a deep voice ask, and ice suddenly poured down her spine. She looked up and saw that it was just as she had feared. Lucian Ashford, in all his imposing air, was standing in the doorway, a book in hand, come to assist with whatever calamity had struck. He had a lopsided smirk on his face as he recognised who it was. But then, Caroline saw the exact moment when he saw what she cradled in her arms, and his smile dropped slightly, a frown furrowing between his brows, and Caroline's world spun off its axis.

"Caroline... who..." he started, before his frown deepened, looking more closely at the face of his daughter. Caroline felt her face flush hot with anger and shame, a change that her daughter could not help but notice.

"Mummy?" Ellie said. "Are you mad at me mummy?"

"Mummy," Lucian repeated slowly, his voice like cold steel.

"Who's that man, mama?" Ellie asked, sounding unsure. The look on Lucian's face was terrifying, and Caroline's heart raced and thudded in her ears before she closed her eyes for a moment and took a deep breath.

"Eva," she called out in an even tone. "Can you take Ellie, please? I need to step outside for a moment."

Eva walked up without a word and took Ellie from her arms. Caroline turned on her heel, and without so much as a glance, marched straight out of the front door, bell chiming, and stood under the striped awning to await her doom while the rain splashed at her ankles.

She heard the bell jingle again, and the door snap shut, but she didn't turn away from the falling rain, too afraid to see the look in his eyes.

"Caroline..." he called to her but she didn't answer, just crossed her arms in front of her, trying very hard to decide what to say. Lucian gripped her elbow and spun her around to face him.

"Caroline, look at me," he demanded, gripping both elbows, caging her in. "Is that your daughter? Is she mine? Do I have a daughter, Caroline?"

"I tried to tell you the other day when you never tuned up. When you took off for weeks, and then I assumed I wouldn't have to anymore because we thought we'd never see you again, Lucian."

"I had to go. It was... Why did you not try again? How was this not the very first thing that you said to me?" he demanded.

"When? When should I have told you, Lucian?" Carline shot back, stepping in to him to be heard over the driving rain, "When I gave birth scared and injured, calling your name? When I waited for word from you while you had fallen off the ends of the earth? Or should I have told you when you were a dead man, and I cried myself to sleep every night grieving the loss of you. Should I have shouted it to you, Lucian," her voice began to rise in indignation, "as the ship pulled away in Portsmouth, and left you standing on the dock, denying me and your entire family?" she shouted, her voice beginning to crack and he suddenly shook her by the arms in frustration.

"Caroline! I have spent five years, thinking that our child was lost... that our baby had died, and your heart with it, and that it was my fault," he said, and Caroline heard a roughness in his voice, a breaking that called tears to cloud her eyes. "If I had known, I would have... done things differently."

"You... you didn't want me, Lucian. And I do not want your duty, your obligation. It is not what I wanted for me or my daughter."

"I have never not wanted you. How could you even speak it!"

"You left me, Lucian. You left me!" Caroline felt long-held tears finally break and run down her face, and it made her all the angrier. "Even after you promised that I would never be alone again, you left me to mourn your death, just as surely as my father did. I loved you," she jerked out of his arms, and she shoved him, furious with herself for losing control. "I loved you more than anything-"

Lucian suddenly grabbed her and pulled her in to him, pressing his hot mouth to hers, kissing her forcefully, angry and hurt, in the first kiss Caroline had had in five years. She felt her head spin, her heart wrenched painfully, the ground began to open up to swallow her whole. But, before she could lose herself completely, she pushed him away, and struck his face with a stinging crack, the pain to her hand waking her from the spell just as surely as it did him.

"Stop! I am not a doll that you may pick up and discard at will! You cannot just come and go, and destroy me at every turn. I was just learning how to live again. Do you not see... I cannot survive you again. I want to move on with my life," she pleaded. "Please, please do what you promised and leave me alone." The wind whipped rain into Caroline's face, mixing cold raindrops with salt tears.

"I cannot," his voice scraped over the words, over the lump in his throat, his blue eyes more wounded than she had ever seen them.

"Please," she said, pushing the tears angrily from her face with a cold, shaking hand, and taking a moment to calm herself. She inhaled a shuddering breath. "I want you to be part of your daughter's life, if you wish to be, she needs you, but, Lucian, please, leave me out of it, leave our marriage be." She pulled her hand from his tight grip and turned away, closing in on herself. They stood side by side, and the rain thundered against the tight drum of the awning, amplifying every drop, making them feel like they were at the centre of a great storm that was about to consume them.

"Tell me... tell me about her," he murmured softly, his voice vulnerable. She waited a while, to steady her voice, to breathe, to calm her pulse, and hold together the pieces of her shattered heart. And when, as she had always done, she collected herself and regained control, she answered.

"Her name is Elspeth, and she will be five next month."

Lucian closed his eyes, and after a pause nodded slightly. Caroline took hold of one shaking hand and steadied it with the other, and went on.

"She is called Ellie for short, and she loves horses, painting, and dancing. She is full of trouble and so smart..." Caroline said, hearing her own voice soften and warm, a tiny ember in her heart glowing with pride.

"*Well*, are you coming?" Caroline asked, gesturing to the steps of the house. Eva had taken the children home in the carriage, and Lucian and Caroline had walked the short distance back with the rain drumming their sorrows into them as they made their way back in silence. Trying to breathe deeply, to keep calm, she walked up the stairs, before he answered, the door already opening as they approached. She could feel Lucian at her elbow, feel his nerves, his anticipation and impatience. The footman took their hats and gloves and brought towels to dry the worst of it.

"Henry, where is Ellie?" she asked.

"I believe she is in the nursery, my lady," Henry replied. Caroline thanked him and started up the stairs, Lucian following silently. As they walked along the hall toward the room, Caroline could hear Ellie and Nanny Lehmann laughing. She suddenly realised that Lucian had stopped, and was no longer beside her. She turned back and saw him, standing still, a tall statue in the hall. His face was trained forward, staring at the doorway at the end.

"Come," she said, walking a little back to him. Seeing his fixed stare, she steeled herself and lay a hand atop his, causing his eyes to finally drift to her, fiercely blue and tormented. "Do not be afraid," she whispered, as he looked at her, still unmoving. His eyes communicated his pain, his worry, his nerves. Slowly, she slid her hand into his, deliberately, interlacing their fingers as he watched her, his face frightened and confused. She started forward, tugging him gently behind her, feeling relieved when he came hesitantly forward. They approached the door, and Caroline fixed a bright smile to her face.

Ellie was sitting in the middle of the room, serving tea to her dolls. Nanny was sitting in one of the chairs beside the small table, knitting, and occasionally sipping her imaginary drink. They both looked up to see the visitors at the door. Ellie waved happily, before Nanny collected her needles, made her excuses and left them to their privacy.

"Mummy, you have returned just in time for tea. Madam Sally rarely receives callers," Ellie chirped, her attention suddenly shifting to the stranger standing behind her mother, and the way their hands were intertwined. Her little head tilted and she stared at them curiously.

Caroline came a little further into the room, drawing Lucian with her. Ellie stood up and came over to them. She looked at them both, seriously, studying their expressions, and joined hands.

She then reached out, and grasped Caroline's hand, and pulled it from Lucian's, and turned away pulling Caroline to the small table. She pulled her down into the chair Nanny had vacated and then set about pouring her tea. Lucian watched them, his empty hand clenched tight. Ellie leaned in and whispered to her.

"Who is that, mummy? Does he want to come in?"

"Why do you not invite him?"

"We haven't been introduced," Ellie said.

"Of course, I'm remiss in my duties," Caroline teased and turned her smiling face to Lucian.

"Lord Ashford, may I present to you, Miss Elspeth Ashford. She would like to invite you to take tea with us," Caroline said seriously, and Lucian bowed deeply, making Ellie giggle.

"Miss Elspeth, how charming it is to meet you. I graciously accept your invitation," he said grandly, and came forward uncertainly, looking for a seat. Ellie looked around her crowded dining table, and with all the finesse of her Aunt Katherine when deciding wedding seating, abruptly pushed a large bear off a chair, letting it fall rather unceremoniously to the floor. Lucian and Caroline looked at it, and Ellie shrugged.

"Mr Thomas eats too much," she said crossly, waiting for Lucian to sit down. Caroline laughed, and Lucian merely looked surprised.

"But of course he does. Thank you." He bent and sat in the chair, folding his legs up as much as possible, though they still threatened to push the table over. He avoided Caroline's gaze, no doubt seeing the laughter hovering on her lips, as Ellie presented him with a teacup the size of a thimble to drink.

"Delicious!" he pronounced as he sipped at it. For a few moments, they sat, while Ellie watched them both through her lashes. Lucian could not stop looking at her, and Caroline watched his eyes as they traced her little hands, and perfect fingers, the way the light from the window shone through her curls, making a halo around her little head.

"Why is your name like mine?" she asked suddenly. Caroline took a deep breath, and reached out and took her daughter's hand. She was not sure if this was the best way to do this, there was no guide, she supposed, and pushed on.

"Ellie, remember how I told you that your father might come to Aunt Katherine's wedding?" Ellie nodded, and Caroline felt her heart tremble a little at the look in her daughter's eyes. She turned to Lucian then and saw how his hands were tense, his shoulders hunched and realised how incredibly nervous he must be. "Lord Ashford is your father," she said, her voice wavering as she spoke. "His name is Lucian." Ellie continued in her food preparation for a moment, her face serious and set. She pulled her hand from her mother's hand and turned to study Lucian. Caroline saw him swallow, his tanned skin turning pink at the cheeks and unguarded joy and heartbreak in his blue eyes. He smiled nervously at Ellie, waited for her to speak. Ellie continued to look shyly at Lucian, finally speaking.

"If you are my father... does that mean you can give me a brother?" she asked suddenly, and the breath that Lucian had been holding in, rushed out, and he laughed, his face creasing into a breathtaking smile.

"Well, that's really up to your mother..." Caroline narrowed her eyes at him for a moment as he grinned at her. Ellie leaned closer to him, her little blue eyes round.

"She is terribly difficult to convince of things, but maybe if you try..."

"We can try together," he whispered back, and watched as Ellie bit her lip, and then nodded decisively. Caroline bit down a scold at his words, giving his daughter false hope that she would not soon forget.

🍥

*E*llie allocated jobs for each of them, and time passed, as the sunlight from the window moved across the sky.

"Ellie it is time for our nap," Caroline said, and Ellie scowled.

"I am not tired today."

"You must have your nap, sweetheart."

"No," she said, crossing her arms over her chest and turning away. Caroline sighed and smiled apologetically at Lucian, and something warm unfurled in his chest. Ellie was perhaps the most beautiful thing he had ever seen, her unruly brown curls with wisps of gold, and bright blue eyes, searching his face, her smile, a ray of pure sunshine. He watched them together, mother and daughter, the feeling of it, inde-scribable.

"If you do not have a nap now, you will be too tired to play with Jeremy and Sophie when Auntie Eva comes for dinner," Caroline said, and the little girl frowned at her words. Ellie turned back to the table, looking between her parents. Lucian kept quiet, watching the way Caroline reasoned with her daughter, did not push her.

"I will take my nap," Ellie announced suddenly, and Caroline smiled at her, already standing to prepare her. "If he tells me a story," she finished, looking slyly at Lucian. Lucian was taken aback.

"Agreed," Caroline was already saying, picking the little girl off the floor and leading her to the bed. Lucian started to clear up the chairs and tea things, feeling nervous. He had rarely interacted with children, and he had no idea how to tell a children's story. He searched his brain for one, as he heard Caroline getting Ellie into bed. He finally turned, seeing the woman he loved, and his daughter, *his* daughter, sitting on the bed together. Caroline smiled at him, and he drew a chair over to the edge of the bed.

"I am afraid I do not know many good stories," he said. Caroline reached out and picked up a book, handing it to him. He looked at the brightly coloured cover, feeling relieved as he opened it.

"Which story would you like?" he asked, and Caroline stood up slowly, and moved toward the door.

"Mummy, where are you going?" Ellie suddenly asked, and they both turned to her.

"I thought I would go and help Auntie Rebecca. She's been so busy lately. Would that be alright, pumpkin?" Ellie considered this, looking at Lucian, and then nodded.

"Just one story," Caroline told Lucian, with a soft smile as she left the room.

"She means two, or three at most," Ellie corrected.

"Does she really?" Lucian murmured softly back.

Caroline would not keep the smile from her lips as she walked the hall and reached the stairs, denying herself the pleasure of looking back. There was only so much a heart could take in one day.

CHAPTER 7

*L*ucian, done finally with putting Ellie to bed, stormed into the drawing-room, and saw its sole occupant, Caroline, sitting tensely on the edge of her chair.

"I want to see her... every day," he said suddenly.

"She is usually busy with lessons, and sometimes she goes..."

"I don't care what time it is, morning, evening, night... I wish to see her every day, to become a presence in her life, and you will not keep me from her," he said quietly.

Caroline nodded slightly, opening her mouth to speak, then thought better of it, and closed it, a slight feeling of fear spiking through her.

"Speak your mind, Caroline, you have never held back before, let us not now begin," he said, and she glanced at his back, seeing his blue eyes on her in the mirror over the mantlepiece.

"It is not so simple, Lucian. No, I will not keep you from her, but we have much to discuss, much to arrange."

"Yes, there are a great many things. But they can wait, I... I was not prepared for this." Caroline nodded, thankful for the reprieve.

"Now, I must take my leave, there is... very important business which cannot wait."

"Yes, you mustn't keep her waiting," Caroline bit out before she could stop herself and felt embarrassment beat her cheeks at the look he shot her.

"I shall call tomorrow," he said curtly, and left, without a backward glance.

Jealousy was a bitter draft, a rush of white-hot anger. Yet, it was hardly her right. He had not seemed angry... not as angry as she expected, yet it was still fresh. In time, his anger would come. Along with the hate, and the blame. She gripped her arms tighter around herself and watched the street, until the passers-by cast long shadows and the sun dipped below the horizon.

❀

*L*ucian had spent the days since his return writing letter after letter, so many that his hand cramped and ink ran dry, enquiring, hiring help to track the baby, sending funds to multiple people, not knowing where they would end up, or who was trustworthy. It was too much for one man alone, he had discovered in those weeks of searching. Unwanted babies were often acquired by people who wished for the baby's parentage to remain unknown, childless couples who wanted children to be thought of as their own, or busy, crowded orphanages who neither kept records, nor cared, but also villains, who acquired babies for nefarious purposes, to sell, to trade to brothels, and other schemes that Lucian heard whispered, but dared not think of.

On the ground, he was slow and cumbersome, following trails that went cold, riding his horse through unused paths from city to city through thick wood, and steep, rocky Appalachian mountains. Letters were faster, and while he itched to return to his search, he knew that more could be done through careful planning and organisation than through tireless pounding on doors. Yet, it did not allow him any peace, any respite. Each day that passed, the trail grew colder. Each day was one more that secured William's baby more tightly to the shadows. Lucian's only hope was money. It was the only thing he had left in his arsenal.

Besides, he could never have left, he knew, when fate had just dealt him a new hand, ripped away everything that he knew, everything that he had been sure of, and replaced it with hope, with another chance, with a daughter, a daughter so beautiful that he broke his heart just to look at her.

He spied a familiar tailor's ahead and entered. After a brief conversation with the proprietor, he was measured, and a glass of sherry placed in his hand. The tailors were professional, and did not ask too many questions; but, the warm room, with its leather furniture, and crackling fire, the tidy rows of neatly folded fabrics, all conspired to whisk him back to another life when he was another man.

"And what do you wish to do with these?" someone asked, holding his former clothes gingerly.

"Dispose of them," he ordered, his gaze turning back to the fire. Now that he had a daughter whom he fully intended to charm, he could no longer look like a street urchin. He was not yet sure how, but he would be Ellie's father and Caroline's husband again just as soon as he could manage it.

Caroline, he had discovered, was not responding well to being pushed. He could force her, of course, as he once did; force his way back into their home, demand the right to everything he had given up. But, she was so hurt, so angry, if he forced her now, she might never forgive him, or she might demand a divorce, that granted or not, would disgrace them all. His life was changing so rapidly, barreling forward without allowing him even a moment to get his bearings. It was too much for a man who had thought of nothing but putting one foot in front of the other for years now, but he would not run from it again. All he could do was try his best to adapt.

First, he just had to get closer.

Whether or not Lee would be a better husband and father than he mattered not, for seeing Caroline, the light of his life, sitting by his daughter, he knew he would do anything to be in their lives, to belong to them, to never be parted. And no matter how Caroline denied her heart and denied him... he had seen it in her eyes, her love for him, so undiminished after all this time. He could use that, exploit it, draw it out. He would not fail. She might have been happy with Lee, peaceful and serene, but she would never love him as she did Lucian, he was sure of it, and for a woman like Caroline, a life without love would never be enough.

As he was fitted and finished his sherry, it was all too familiar, the life he had thought he would never return to again. He could have lived forever without returning to society, the shallowness of the company, and frivolous nature of the events, the fine clothes and inane small talk. But, he would endure it, he would embrace it even. For he was still Lord Lucian Ashford, married to Caroline, with a daughter. It was stunning, unbelievable, yet there it was, and if he was to be accepted back into that life, if he was to ward away potential threats, such as Lee, he would have to play the part, he would have to return to the man he once was.

She'd need to be persuaded, seduced, won over slowly. And now Lucian knew, that he would do whatever it took, with every beat his heart had left to give him. Suddenly, he had so much to lose again, so very much, and he knew he could not survive the second loss of it.

"*W*ell. I suppose you're all wondering why I've asked you to be here…" Lucian said and paced nervously, wishing that he had practised a bit beforehand.

"Or why you're even at our home in the first place," Wesley said into his teacup. Lucian looked at his family, all seated, straight-spined and wondering what was coming their way: Rebecca and Isaac, Charles and Katherine, Wesley and, of course, Caroline, so beautiful that it made his chest ache and fortified his nerve. Caroline was taking his sudden appearance with her usual calm grace, but also a slight tightness in her mouth that belied her discomfort.

"So," Lucian tried again. "I know that I am not in a position to ask for any favours…" Wesley scoffed and Lucian shot him a censuring look. "But I find I must ask for one all the same."

"Oh, *quelle surprise!*" Wesley said.

"Wesley, would you kindly shut up long enough to allow me to get this out."

"Well, spit it out then," Wesley said more quietly.

"I want to move in," Lucian blurted and then cursed himself for not first delivering a charismatic and stirring speech. There were not the shouts and mumbles that he had expected. Instead, there was something worse - dead, deafening silence, so full of friction as to raise that hair on one's arms. All eyes were on Caroline, and she blinked a few times, tightening the grip of her hands in her lap, but said nothing.

"I know that I do not deserve a second chance as part of this family, but I... I love... I love you all. I never stopped," he exhaled forcefully and tried to ease the knot in his chest. "And I do not think now that I can live another day without you," Lucian said more easily, truthfully, with a soft sentimentality encroaching in his voice that even he could not fail to notice. He cleared his throat. "I miss you. All of you," he said, looking squarely at Caroline. He caught himself and went on quickly before anyone might raise any objections.

"Yesterday, I became a father, in the most literal sense," Lucian saw some of their faces soften at that, and Caroline looked down at her hands for a moment before looking back up to meet his eye, "and I find that after just a few hours in Elspeth's company, I am already so much in love with her, that my feet have not touched the ground since, I could not sleep, my heart is so big and full that I feel it may burst from my chest," Lucian began pacing again, too eager to keep still.

"Oh, Luke..." Rebecca breathed. "Of course you are."

"If I lived here, I thought... I want to be with Ellie every moment that I can. I want to be with all of you every moment that I can. I have languished in a prison of my own making now for so long that I lost myself along the way, but now... now I see how selfish that was, how foolish. I thought I was doing what was best for you all, please believe me. But, now that there is a little life in this world because of me, Caroline has given me reason to live again, to wake me from the nightmare of my misguided choices. She has given me a reason to live.

"What I'd like to propose is a two-month trial, whereby I live here, as much a part of the family as you can bring yourselves to allow. After this, at two months to the day, we shall reconvene, and you will let me know your decision. If after two months, we find that we cannot live as a family anymore, I will find a house of my own outside of the city, and I will keep our interactions to a minimum, solely in the context of being

Ellie's father." He could not help but his eyes flash to Caroline's, but her expression gave nothing away.

"No," Wesley said finally. "You cannot swan into this family as if nothing has happened. You have broken ties with us all. You have thrown us all away, and we have all grieved bitterly for you, most of all, your wife, Lucian. You just suddenly want us back now, and we are all supposed to greet you with open arms? This is so typical. It's horse shit, is what it is!"

"Wes," Rebecca said. "What about Ellie?"

"Exactly! What about Ellie? You think she deserves such a heartless, unreliable, inconstant father, to come and go as he pleases?" Wesley's voice was raised and hurt, and Katherine talked over him.

"Wesley, he's your own brother! He loves you, did you not just hear him say so? A child should have a father, Wesley. He's standing right here, he wants to be part of her life."

"She *will* have a father. Joshua Lee will do a very good job of it!"

"It is just two months," Rebecca said.

"It is an eternity," Wesley shouted.

They began to shout and bicker among themselves, and Lucian stood silently, his eyes locked on Caroline's, trying his hardest to speak to her the way they used to, to show her how he felt about her. He could not come here and ask for her love again, though the need was strong enough to tear his soul to pieces. He must wait. He must win it. He must earn it. She stared back at him, and try though he might, Lucian could not read her. Angry perhaps? Hurt? But also something softer. Compassion? Feeling, he dared to hope.

"I am not sure about this," Charles finally broke in on the others, his brow pinched and voice tight. "I understand your desire to be part of your daughter's life, but where does this leave Caroline? She has begun to make herself a new life here after a very long period of grief, brother. You have walked away from this life, and she deserves a chance to make her life as she would wish it, and not be strong-armed again into a marriage that she no longer wants." Charle's voice was calm but firm. He was protective. Protecting Caroline from the destruction that Lucian brought into everyone's life, and though his brother was right, it twisted Lucian's stomach to hear it.

"I know this. I know that I could never ask that of her, and have thought of a possible option to move forward without jeopardising Caroline's stability here, without breaking my promise. I will go by my second name, Nicholas, for the duration of the trial period, should anyone ask it. I will interact with Richmond as little as possible, and Lucian Ashford shall remain legally dead. If this trial does not work, then I shall give up that name forever, and never speak of it again. I shall be a cousin perhaps... cousin Nicholas. Caroline can remain a widow... she can... she could remarry if she wishes, without complication, without my interference, without the need for a divorce, or the scandal of it tarnishing the whole family."

They all sat in a silence so tense and fragile that Lucian worried he had failed.

"I will leave now. Please think on it. I am sure that it will take some adjustment, but... I want to be part of this family again. Please. Please consider giving me a chance."

It was just as Caroline feared, and she felt petty, and small and selfish. This was not for her. He was not asking for her. In the great tapestry of her life's hopes, most now long since unravelled and torn asunder, the very last little thread of hope for Lucian snapped with an almost audible tear. This was for Ellie, and she would not keep them apart any longer. She could survive anything for her daughter. Even this.

"Two months," Caroline said, the first words she'd spoken in that room, and everyone quieted. She looked at them all steadily, voice and face calm and still as glass, locking eyes with them each, one at a time, and with a final nod, she looked back to Lucian. "Two months," she agreed. "For Ellie."

❀

*C*aroline held a candle aloft, cupping the delicate flame with the curve of her hand, as it flickered its light against the walls. She made her way, on soft, stockinged feet to Wesley's room. He had not joined them for dinner. She tapped, opened the door, and found him sitting at his window, looking out into the darkness at what would have been the water several hours ago when the sun had been obliging. He held a glass of bourbon, and as Caroline came into the room, he looked up with eyes round and dark and pained, at once, so much a man, and also a boy.

Caroline walked over quietly and sat down next to him at the window. He looked away, hiding from her the red eyes that she had already seen, and Caroline reached out, and grasped his hand in hers, and squeezed, and when she did so, Wesley could be stoic no more. A shuddering gasp burst from his lips, and tears poured down his face, and a loud, gulping sob escaped him. She grabbed him to her and held on while he cried into her shoulder, and brought tears to her own eyes.

She was not the only one grieving, had not been the only one torn apart by all of this, and she had been so focused on holding tightly to the fragile facade of her own self-control, while also trying to protect the tender beating heart of her little girl so that it did not break as her own had done, that Caroline had forgotten to show her family the same love, consideration, and protection that they had been showing her for five years.

"I still love him," Wesley sobbed, his voice cracking as his chest shook, "God help me, I cannot stop."

"Shhhh. I know," Caroline said, her own tears falling onto his linen shirt. "I know."

🌸

*T*he next day arrived as if the world intended to go on just as it had every day before. Wesley and Rebecca had been busily planning a ball to raise funds for the hospital, and the dressmakers arrived and fitted all the ladies for their gowns a final time. Ellie was also fitted, which she was very excited about, and Caroline was glad of the distraction.

When Lucian arrived, only a small bag with his possessions, and followed Charles upstairs, her heart thudded uncomfortably. Ellie noticed the commotion in the hall and wandered out to see. Caroline followed her, escaping notice for a moment, as the tailor tried once again to meet Rebecca's specifications.

"Whose bag is that?" Ellie asked, hanging onto her Uncle Wesley's hand, and pointing at Lucian's army issue pack on the floor. She looked at it with wide eyes.

"It is your father's," Wesley said, bending down to lift her up. She squealed as he threw her in the air a moment. "Oof! You are getting too big, soon you will be bigger than me, and I will never be able to lift you," Wesley teased her, and laughed as she hit his chest with her fists.

"No matter, my daddy can lift me, he is very strong," she said.

"Is he really?" Wesley teased, making a doubtful face at her, making Ellie giggle. "Strong smelling, perhaps!"

"I see my sister is making it as difficult as she can for the seamstress," Lucian's voice came from behind Caroline, and she whirled around, clutching her robe around her. He was walking slowly up the hall, clearly watching her, watching Wesley and Ellie.

"Well... that's why she is always the most striking of all of us," Caroline said, giving him a tight smile. Her eyes moved over him, suddenly seeing the change in his appearance. He looked so achingly familiar at that moment, as though he had stepped from her memories. His breeches were tight, the muscles in his legs only more defined. His narrow waist emphasised by his nipped-in tailcoat, dark green, his shining boots, a deep mahogany. His face was slightly stubbled, and his hair, still as golden, but clipped shorter now than it had been since he had returned, yet slightly longer than he used to wear it, and unruly as ever, like he'd just come from his bed. She realised she was staring and looked away.

"Caroline! I need you," Rebecca suddenly called from along the hall, and Caroline nodded, moving away swiftly past Lucian, who merely stood in the middle of the hall, watching her.

"I shall see you later, Caroline," Lucian murmured softly so that just she could hear it. Caroline paused a moment, drawing level with him.

"If you are lucky, my Lord."

✿

"*W*esley, if I have to hear one more story that begins: 'In the lost years of exile' – I shall have to shut your mouth for good," Lucian growled as he swayed against his younger brother. They walked along the street, following Charles's upright walk ahead as he talked with the Taylors. Wesley bumped against his shoulder and laughed. They were deep in their cups, that much was clear.

He drank at first to blur the pain he felt of feeling separate from his brothers, removed by the unspoken things between them. Gradually, they had relaxed into an uneasy truce, and the night had progressed. After their disagreement, Charles had forgiven him, it seemed, largely at least, and was civil, and seemed also to be relieved at having the family together again. Wesley was altogether a different story. He looked at him through slitted eyes, made constant remarks, and cutting comments, forcing Lucian to bite down his temper, but the venom seemed to have gone from his voice.

They reached the house, and went inside, as quietly as they could, bidding the Taylors goodnight. Lucian walked in, and went to the drawing-room, pouring himself a drink as he did. He sank down in a chair and sipped his bourbon, his mind going to the woman in the room upstairs. He wondered if she was sleeping, dreaming, if she still woke with flames chasing her, or if her demons were finally laid to rest.

Lucian stood unsteadily, and started upstairs, passing by her room without pausing and making his way to the guest room. As he was about to close the door, he heard the sound of crying, lonely and desolate. It was coming from Ellie's room. His heart beat strangely, and as he was about to go to the sound, he saw Caroline's door swing open. She hurried out, blinking her eyes in the candlelight, wrapping her dressing gown around her. Her hair was loose around her shoulders, hanging almost to her waist. She hurried to the room and stepped inside. He started forward, unable to resist, crept along the hallway, and paused outside the door.

"I had a bad dream," she choked out through sobs, her little lip quivering, and Caroline put her arms around her and rocked her gently.

"Shhh shhh. It's alright darling. I'm here now. It was only a dream."

"Tell me a story."

"Of course, my darling. What kind of story would you like?"

"Tell me a story about daddy... like you used to... before."

"How about we read one of your-"

"Just one, and I will go back to sleep," Ellie insisted. Caroline sighed and settled on the bed.

"Alright then. Once, a long long time ago, your father was travelling with me, through an awful storm. The sky was very angry that night, and the rain was falling, and thunder and lightning were crashing down. Then the carriage went off the road! And it fell down a steep bank into the river. I went into the water, which was awfully cold...and your father was thrown to the rocks."

"Then what happened?" Ellie asked, listening as though she had not heard the story many times before.

"Well, I was terribly cold in the water, and just when I thought I could not stand it one more moment, your father appeared, wrapped me in his arms and carried me off to safety."

"He must be very strong."

"Yes, he is... he carried me into the woods, and to a cabin there, where we stayed for many days, with no help, and almost nothing to eat... before you uncles came to rescue us," Caroline continued.

"What about the snails?"

"Ew yes, we had to dine on yucky snails every night!"

"Was it difficult?"

"Yes, frightfully so."

"Were you very scared?"

"Yes, I was very afraid… but… at the same time, I felt very safe."

"Why?"

"Because your father was there... and he made me feel safe."

"How?"

Caroline paused, unsure what to say. She looked at her daughter, her hands tightening on the covers, her face enraptured.

"Because, I knew he would never leave me... that he would stay with me, and take care of me, as I would take of him. I trusted him, and I promised myself that if we survived that terrible storm, I would never forget that feeling."

Ellie smiled, satisfied with her story and let her eyes drift close. As Caroline pressed a kiss to her forehead, she opened her eyes a touch.

"If I need you... you will come?" she asked sleepily.

"Of course. I shall never leave you, my darling... I will always be here to take care of you."

"Like daddy is for you?" Ellie asked, so innocently that it cut Caroline's heart. She nodded silently, and waited a moment, listening to her daughter's breath even out, and sleep take her over. Quietly, she left, closing the door behind her, and starting back down the hall to her room.

"A sweet story... yet I remember it a little differently," Lucian's voice stopped her in her tracks, and made her body instantly tense. She whirled around, peering into the darkness of the hall. She swallowed.

"In what way?"

"I seem to remember you being the one who cared for me and kept us safe."

Caroline was quiet, finally making out his figure, as he sauntered slowly along the hall toward her.

"You have returned... You have been drinking?"

"Oh yes. Much," Lucian said as he stopped in front of her. Caroline looked up at him, taking in his askew attire and red-rimmed eyes. It seemed they had been indulging this evening, and she wondered if the other Ashfords were as worse for wear. He smelled like pipe smoke and bourbon, she noticed, as he came near, he also smelled the way he used to.

"Goodnight," she said suddenly, feeling too close to him, the space too confined, the hall too quiet. She turned to leave and gasped as he touched her arm.

"Stay a little... will you not?" he asked, his head to the side and she looked hard at him. It was their first contact in days, their first touch, and it lit her on fire. She shifted nervously.

"Another time, perhaps," she said, pulling her arm from his grasp.

"You mean, let us wait until we are no longer alone? You have gotten remarkably adept at making sure we never are," he murmured, still swaying slightly in front of her. She turned away from him and walked to her door, her palms damp and nerves shooting through her.

"I – I think it does not disappoint you. You do not seek me out either," she replied quickly, her feelings too close to the surface to hide, her vulnerability too close to disguise. "Goodnight," she said over her shoulder, as she pushed her door open and turned to close it. She looked back and saw him standing there, in the semi-darkness, his face unreadable in the shadows, watching her.

She slipped quickly inside, shutting it tightly behind her, and leaning against it, feeling her heart pound. It felt wretched, and she felt so very alone at that moment. He had stayed away, and saying it aloud had made it real. She felt more alone than she had felt without him even, for the loss of his regard, the loss of his love, was even harder to bear. Wrapping her arms around herself, she went back to her bed, undressing and crawling under the now cool covers. She closed her eyes tightly, and wished she could escape the confusing emotions that flowed through her, wished she could quiet her hammering heart and lecturing head, always at contrast with each other.

CHAPTER 8

*W*esley strolled across the balcony slowly, looking down at the ball with all the proprietary pride of a father. It was all going even better than he had hoped. Some were there to support the new hospital, while many from all corners of Virginia, were there to get an eye full of the new family, freshly arrived to Virginian society. They had raised far more than they had hoped, and speeches had held an audience captive while Wesley and others raised issues and brought things to light that many of the higher classes would no doubt have prefered to ignore. It was a fine night's work.

"Ah, Lord Ashford," a deep voice called from nearby. "You are a difficult man to find. I haven't seen you near the dance floor even once tonight." Doctor Lombardi moved to his side, leaning casually over the balcony next to Wesley. Wesley's stomach tightened. He was such an astonishing man, so capable, so principled, so kind. He had travelled from the west for the opportunity, and was not just an accomplished doctor, he was also an outspoken abolitionist, which, while raising many an Virginian eyebrow or nasty word, was just the type of person they needed at the helm if the hospital was to navigate the troubled waters of caring for all those who came to its doors in need, without exception. Doctor Lombardi, was calm, fair, rational, and quietly charming enough to calm even the most disgruntled patron or patient, and his speech that night had moved Wesley to tears.

"Yes, well," Wesley smoothed. "No rest for the wicked, I suppose."

The doctor caught his eye then, his messy salt and pepper waves, usually hidden under a hat, made Wesley's mouth dry.

"Well, I am very pleased to hear it, Lord Ashford."

"Wesley, please."

"Alright," he smiled, slow and warm and wide, so relaxed, so American. "Wesley then," he nodded "Mateo," he said, putting a hand to his chest. "I must congratulate you on all of this. What you've done in under a year is nothing short of a miracle," his face grew a bit more serious. "Will you have a drink with me, Wesley?"

❦

*L*ucian took in the grandeur of the ballroom and felt a swell of pride to be part of his beautiful family, growing every day, it seemed, and hoped somewhere deep in his newly beating heart that he would join them as a brother, as a father, and as a husband, with his own name. The orchestra started to play another song, and people around him excused themselves to dance. There were several single young ladies partnerless with ambitious mothers hunting for someone to display them on the floor, yet he faded into the background, as promised. There was only one woman here to attract his attention.

Caroline had taken his breath away when she'd arrived, her richly coloured gown falling close to her body, her jet hair and amber skin shining more brightly than usual against it, her eyes shining like jewels, more alive with the joy of what they had accomplished. She knew many people in attendance, he noted, as he watched her greeting people, conducting all the social niceties with a grace and elegance that he so lacked. He knew no one, and was not displeased that it remained that way. As he moved through the crowd, it parted before him, curious looks following in his wake. The silent man who sought no attention, no introductions, even from the freshest flowers of society. A man with eyes that searched for one.

He kept his distance, for the most part, played a few cautious hands of poker in the gentleman's lounge, more to pass the time than out of interest, and emerged sometime later, to find Caroline dancing with Lee. He ground his teeth as he watched them, swirling around the dance floor. Caroline smiled and laughed up at Lee's damnably handsome face as they talked with ease. Seeing them together, Lucian felt a jolt of unease atop the expected displeasure. It might not be as easy as he had thought to pull them apart a second time.

He made his way down to the lower floor, and positioned himself near the dance floor, ready to catch her as she finished. As the song came to a stop, and Lee drew away, pressing a kiss onto the back of Caroline's gloved hand, Lucian stepped forward, his smile a warning.

"Good evening, Mr Lee."

"Lord Ashford. I am surprised to see you still here," Lee said pointedly, and Lucian barely restrained himself from shoving him over. Instead, he looked to Caroline, whose face made it obvious that she wished to be anywhere but there.

"No doubt you are. Perhaps you should get used to it. May I?" he held a hand out to her and waited to see if she would accept his invitation. She hesitated a moment, and then slipped her hand onto his, looking apologetically at Lee.

"I -" she began to speak but was interrupted by him.

"Of course, my dear, worry not - you are charity itself," Lee said, flashing Caroline a smile that made Lucian's fist itch.

Lucian pulled her away, onto the dance floor, perhaps a little more strongly than necessary, causing her to look at him in askance. They took their positions, and the dance started. They circled each other, without touching.

"Where is Ellie this evening?"

"She is with Eva's brood, and will stay at the Taylors' this evening."

"Just as well I suppose. Does she often wake in the night?"

"No, well, she did not use to, but the move from London has been very traumatic and..." Caroline trailed off, as Lucian's hands went to her waist and they began the face to face portion of the dance.

"It is me, isn't it? My presence," Lucian asked then, and she looked up, finding his face so very close to hers.

"She is happy you are here."

"However..."

"She worries you will leave again, of course, now that she has become accustomed to having you around, she would not like to lose you."

"And what of you? Have you become accustomed to having me around?" he asked.

"I do not know if I ever will... I still imagine you as some spectre of my mind most of the time," Caroline joked flatly.

"As you are... to me," he said, feeling the slight shift of her body through layers of fabric. "The same one who haunted me every single day and night that I was apart from you."

"Are you here alone? Did you not bring a guest?" she suddenly asked, catching his eye in an assessing look.

"Is that jealousy I detect in your tone, my Lady?" he said, using a title that he knew she no longer used often. "I must confess that I am glad to hear it." He pulled her ever slightly closer to him and thought perhaps she was holding her breath.

"Of course not, your romantic life is none of my concern, just as mine is none of yours," she said, and stiffened.

"You are mistaken, my love. Your romantic life is very much my concern, and my interest... for you are my wife."

"Lucian, don't. Are you forgetting our agreement already? This is for Ellie, only for Ellie. I wish to separate from you. Our marriage is over. I will not be married to you, out of a sense of obligation on both our parts. A marriage must have love, it must have trust."

"And these are your feelings for Lee?" his blue eyes searching, reading as he used to every small emotion that ran through her.

"Yes, I trust him."

"And what of love? Do you love him?" he asked, and her mouth tightened, and something like anger flashed across her eyes.

"I will."

"No, sweetheart, sadly you will not, for you shall never have the chance," he breathed as they neared one another, his mouth near her ear. "I will not allow it... there is only room for one man in your heart, and it will be me."

"And what of trust? How can we ever have that again?" she demanded straight-backed, tall and proud, being protective of herself, he knew.

"It must be earned, that I know. I will not push you, but nor will I let you go willingly."

"You said that you would leave in two months."

"More than I require," he murmured suggestively, his eyes running over her face. Once again, the world contained only them.

"Of course you should want me again when you can no longer have me when someone else brings out your competitive spirit. You've come crawling out of the shadows. And I some exotic beast to be chased, shot, and hung in the hall."

"No my dear. You are my family," he said, possessively, frankly, with nothing but truth in his voice. She was intoxicating when she was like this - so strong and self-possessed.

"You can always be in Ellie's life, without me, there is no need-"

"There is every need. Just like with every breath that I have drawn into my lungs since first I met you."

"What of your promise? You promised that you would do the best thing for me."

"And all I have heard since I have returned is how wrong that promise was, and how it hurt you... so I have made a new promise." He spoke tenderly, but firmly.

"And I suppose you want to tell it me."

"I will never again be parted from you. I will always be by your side, at your elbow, on your arm, escorting you home, waiting for you at the breakfast table, tucking Ellie in at night. I promise that no matter the walls you have built, no matter the defences you have constructed, I will dismantle them brick by brick, stone by stone, until your heart is washed clean as the sandy shore, caressed by the tide. I promise I will pursue you to the ends of the earth and back again."

Caroline's eyes, if he was not mistaken, had grown a little clouded with the threat of unshed tears. She could not look at him in the eye. She was fighting it with everything that she had left, and it was a bloody battle she waged inside.

"You have gone mad," she whispered.

"Perhaps," he said.

"Why are you saying this to me?"

"Because you deserve to know my intentions. There is business to settle between us, Caroline, mistakes made on both sides, reconciliations to be had, explanations to be listened to... but ultimately, I intend to remain your husband. You should be aware of that," he said.

This close, with the smell of her hair, and the soft touch of her skin, and her delicate hand in his, he wanted to take her in his arms, to crush his mouth to hers and fill his world with her. He wanted to pick her up into his arms and take her home to bed.

The song ended, and Lee stood some distance away, his hand lifted in wait.

"My lady Ashford," Lucian murmured with a genteel bow.

"Thank you," she answered tightly, placing her hand in Joshua's, all the words she longed to say to Lucian curdling on her lips.

❀

The next day, Caroline woke to a quiet house. She came awake suddenly, from dreams filled with longing and desire. In them, her mind returned to the long nights of Westmere, a roaring fire, strong arms surrounding her, and a hard body against hers. She tumbled from those dreams to cold tangled sheets and flushed skin.

She lay in bed and listened to the quiet ticking of the clock in the hall, breathing deeply, pushing the lingering drug of her dreams aside. She let her eyes drift around the room, gliding over the pale light filtering in the windows. When she closed her eyes, memories of the night before drifted through her head, his hands on her back, his soft murmurs in her ear. Seeing him across the room, flashes of his hair, moving through the crowd, his eyes never far from hers. She indulged in those memories, longer than she cared to admit, before she heard her lady's maid knock at the door.

After dressing, she went directly to the breakfast room, where she ate lightly, alone, and then prepared to leave. She decided to walk to the Taylors' as the distance was small, and the weather pleasant enough. She strolled down the pavement, again, lost in her thoughts of the previous night.

Lucian' words followed her, tracing her steps. Her heart beat erratically at the notion that he might still love her. She would love Lucian until the day she died, but his confession changed little. Even if he did still love her, which, rather than love, may, in fact, just be a passing desire to be part of a family again - to connect with his daughter, she thought perhaps that love must be different for him than it was for her, otherwise, how could he have stayed away so long? Being so long apart would have killed Caroline - it had.

She chastised herself at the fresh memory of pain. She should not allow him the power of her happiness, and even her very sanity. She could not be a fool for love once more. She did not love Lee, she knew it well, but he was a good man, and a steady one, and as much for the sake of her broken heart, as for her daughter's stability, she knew that Lee's kindness, steadiness, and security was better for the both of them, no matter what her heart wanted.

Climbing the steps of the Taylors', she smiled pleasantly at the doorman, as he took her things and directed her to the drawing-room. She marvelled at how quiet the house seemed when it was quite the opposite when Ellie was united with her cousins at her own home.

Eva was sitting quietly in the drawing-room with her needlepoint.

"Caroline! How lovely to see you. How was the ball last night?"

"As delightful as you can imagine, though I missed you, my dear Eva. Without decent company, you cannot imagine how much small talk must be endured. Thank you so much for watching Ellie," Caroline said sitting near them.

"It was our pleasure. She has adjusted so well to her father's return. You must be proud of her."

"I am indeed."

"I was just saying to Lucian this morning, that it really is a marvel, she has accepted him so willingly, and bears the newness of your relationship so admirably," Eva said, focusing on her needlework.

"What had he to say of it?"

"He agreed, though I suspect he believes her to be quite the most gifted and special child to ever walk the earth, so he was not surprised." Caroline smiled a little before Eva's words caught her.

"This morning?" she asked, untying her bonnet with a quizzical brow.

"Yes, this morning, when he came to collect Elspeth."

"Collect her?" Caroline asked, a slight note of alarm entering her voice unbidden. Eva looked to Caroline.

"Of course, he came early, and said he was taking Ellie out for the day. We just assumed he had planned it with you," Eva said, as if it was nothing at all. Caroline fought down the sudden feeling of panic that flared in her stomach. No harm would come to her of course, it was just, perhaps the very first time that Caroline had not known her daughter's whereabouts.

"I suppose it slipped his mind," Caroline answered tightly, as she felt the stirrings of panic that she had little control over. She abruptly stood up. "Well, I better wait for them at home. No doubt they will return there soon enough."

"Is everything alright, Caroline?" Eva asked, putting down her needlework to look at her more closely.

"Of course, I... I should return home," Caroline said, pulling her gloves hurriedly on, and going to the door, making her excuses as she went.

❀

"*B*ut, why can't I ride that one?" Elspeth asked her father, pointing to a huge horse, standing to the side of the paddock.

"He is far too big for a proper little lady such as yourself," Lucian said, stroking the top of his daughter's head as it came level to the fence.

"He is not," Ellie said crossly, dodging determinedly away from him, and skirting the fence, trying to get closer to the grumpy looking beast. Lucian followed behind her, his heart swelling at the sight of her little legs moving as fast as they could, and the sneaky glances she cast over her shoulder. He smiled indulgently, and simply followed. Closer, yet still safe behind the fence, Ellie stopped and thrust her little arm through the wooden slats. Lucian moved behind her a little more quickly as he saw the horse take an interest in the waving hand and start toward it. Lucian gently pulled Ellie's arm back through the fence, and then suddenly swooped down and picked her up, so she had a good view. Ellie giggled and watched with wide eyes as Lucian ripped some grass from beside the enclosure and held it out, and the horse, its massive head dipping over the railing, gently ate it from his hand. He murmured softly to the animal, reaching to stroke its long neck and soft nose. Ellie froze, suddenly afraid of its proximity.

"Would you like to feed him?"

Ellie slowly shook her head. Lucian bent and pulled up more grass. He then arranged it flatly on his hand and put his hand atop his daughter's small one.

"Shall we do it together?" Ellie nodded, her eyes not leaving the gleaming mount before her for even a second. They held their hands out together, with Lucian rough and calloused one covering Ellie's tiny delicate one. She squealed as she felt a velvety trace of the horse's nose and lips ticking her arm.

Understanding there was no more food, the horse started off for the other side of the field, and Lucian settled Ellie more firmly on his hip as she cradled her hand against her chest, smiling.

"Have you ever ridden before?"

"No... mother said I was too young at home, and then we moved here, and we don't have any horses here. Mother used to ride every day at home."

"Did she really?" Lucian asked and Ellie nodded wisely.

"Yes, every day, for hours."

"And, would you like to start learning soon?"

"Yes! I would love to! But mummy says I am too young."

"I might happen to know a very good teacher..." Lucian tested, leaning down to drop Ellie lightly to the ground as she squirmed.

"Really?"

"Yes, really." Ellie considered him for a moment, and then a cynical tint came to her eyes.

"Mummy never does what you ask her to," Ellie said, slightly reproachfully. Her ally had turned out to be less influential than she had hoped.

"She doesn't, does she? I am glad I am not the only one who has noticed," Lucian said with a laugh.

"Maybe it is because you went away for a long time." The soft words froze him, and he looked down to see his daughter looking at him with perfect clarity, her sweet words, striking him right to the bone, cutting to the quick. Spying a nearby bench, he lead her to it, and sat, pulling Ellie up onto it and looking at her seriously.

"Elspeth, I wish you to know, I would never have left your mother, or you... if I had had any choice."

"Uncle Charles says a person always has a choice," Ellie said.

"Well, most of the time he is right, but sometimes, it can feel like you do not have a choice. If you believe you do not have a choice, truly believe it, it is the same as not having one... do you not agree?"

Ellie thought about this for a moment.

"What if you believe that you must leave again?" she suddenly asked.

"I will never leave you again, nor your mother. In that, *you* have no choice! I am here to stay, like it or no," he pushed her little nose with his finger as she giggled. "You can count on me, my sweet. Just like you can count on your friend here. He has been pestering me to see you," he said, pulling the little wooden horse from his pocket. Ellie gasped, as if it were magic.

"Carrots!" she screamed. "Where have you been?" She snatched the little horse up and hugged it to herself, cradling it, and petting its wooden head.

"Carrots was with me. He helped me return to you, all the way from England."

"Oh, thank you, Carrots! You're a very good boy. I love you," she kissed him between the ears. "I love you too, daddy," she said easily, not looking up from her horse. His chest squeezed so hard that he thought his ribs might break. He had trouble breathing and realised a lump had formed in his throat, so he cleared it, blinked, and took a big breath.

"I love you too, my little girl. More even than you can know. Now, come, we must return home, or we shall witness your mother's fiery wrath!" he said conspiratorially, standing up and taking her hand, moving toward the carriage by the road.

❀

*L*ucian ushered Ellie inside and watched as she took off upstairs immediately, looking for her mother.

"Elspeth?" Caroline's voice floated down the stairs and Lucian heard them reunited at the top of the flight. He removed his hat and gloves and wondered if it was possible to disappear before Caroline came to speak to him. He cursed himself. He should have asked, he realised, yet he was still so unused to interacting with others, of getting permission. As he went to the study, he came across Wesley leaving.

"Ah! You have returned. Well, that means that I can leave Caroline to you while I head out for a sherry with a friend from the hospital."

"Oh. I didn't realise that anyone would be waiting," Lucian said.

"No matter. I would rather like to stay and see the fireworks between you and Caroline, yet alas, I must not dally any longer," Wesley said, smiling mischievously at him as he put his gloves on.

Lucian turned into the study and poured himself a drink. Caroline was going to be angry, he thought sourly. Yet, how was he supposed to know when he was allowed to take his daughter out for the day when Caroline refused to communicate with him. This long silence had to end, this walking on eggshells. He had put his intentions out there the night before, in no uncertain terms. He had made his feelings known. Whether she could accept them or not, there was no point in waiting around.

Upstairs, he heard a door shut with a snap. Letting out the long breath he'd been holding, he started from the room.

❀

*C*aroline shut the set of drawing-room windows that overlooked the river. The wind had picked up, and it was growing ever colder at night as it whipped across the mist of the water, a preview of the long winter ahead. She had hoped that the cool air would help to soothe her temper but found it had not quite diminished it completely. Ellie and her father had had cake and candied nuts on the way home, it would seem, and Caroline had made sure that Ellie had eaten something a little more nutritious before she sleepily got ready for an early bed, having missed her afternoon nap.

It was silly to be too upset, she knew it, but it symbolised so much, so many of her fears come to reality. The loss of control, over Ellie, over her life... having to start compromising with Lucian, taking account of his opinions about their daughter in all things, it was going to be hard to relinquish.

Pausing in the hall, curiosity pulled her past it, and to the room at the end, the guest room. She put her ear to the door and listened. Nothing. He had probably gone out again, anticipating her anger, and gone to seek more pleasant company, perhaps of his new woman.

She told herself grimly that she did not care, as she walked back to her own room. She pushed open the door, and stalked inside, suddenly overcome with frustration, she whipped her shawl off and threw it on the floor, and flopped back on the covers covering her face with her hands.

"Might I ask what that poor shawl has done to receive such treatment?" Lucian's voice sent her shooting up from the bed and whirling around. He was sitting in the window, a glass in his hand, looking at her.

"What are you doing in here?" she demanded harshly.

"I have come for my requisite telling off. I thought I would save you the trouble of seeking me out."

She narrowed her eyes at him.

"How kind of you. So, you are aware then how inconsiderate your actions were this morning?"

"I am, and I have come to apologise," he stated calmly, his unruffled demeanour frustrating Caroline even more.

"You cannot just take Ellie away, anytime you feel like doing so," Caroline snapped at him.

"I apologise. I had thought you might wish to sleep late and that I was doing you a service in entertaining her for the morning."

"Why would I sleep late?"

"Well, considering the hour you returned home, I thought you might be tired."

Caroline scowled at the comment. He had disappeared shortly after their dance, and she had barely seen him again.

"It is not your business when I left the ball," she stated, and stared at him, their eye contact unwavering, her cheeks warming at the hard expression in his eyes. "You chose to disappear early... rather a trend, I'd say," she snipped.

"Quite some time before you... there is only so much a man can stomach." He looked at her menacingly.

She snorted and looked away, sitting up and sorting her dress, which had ridden up, she glanced up to find him watching her hands, his head tilted to the side.

"What brings you to my room, Lord Lucian?"

He narrowed his eyes at the cold formality. "I came to apologise for today, and also I think it is time we addressed some problems between us."

"It is hardly the time-"

"I can think of no better."

Caroline opened her mouth and found herself at a loss for words. She watched him gradually stand up, and finish his drink in one large mouthful. She was suddenly afraid of the words that might be said, that could never be taken back, and never forgotten.

"I... I do not wish to talk," she said, coming out stronger than she had anticipated. He raised an eyebrow at her.

"And what makes you think you can decide that for the both of us?" he said, maddeningly, and she felt her mouth drop open at his tone.

"Because it is as much my decision as it is yours."

"I have not been much a fan of your decisions of late," he said, and she felt her face flush, at the same time as anger swelled in her chest.

"Believe me, I am no admirer of your decisions either. Your decisions left me alone, on a boat to a different country -" she started.

"And you attempted to hide from me that I was a father," he growled, stepping forward, his chest coming up against hers. She glowered up at him, tears of anger, and something else, something darker and more unbearable gathered in her eyes. Here was the fury she had been waiting for.

"Do you really think I would relish telling you? A man who walked away from me only months before?"

"That was not your decision to make."

"I know! I know that – I have had to make a lot of decisions that I did not wish to make over the years."

"As have I. My decisions involved deciding whether to eat or not that day, whether to go on fighting, to live, to survive, or just give up... I had to decide to keep breathing, keep living with the cavernous longing in my chest every single day," as his angry words fell from his lips, so did the tears from her eyes, finally freed, and dripping down her face, as she glared balefully at him. Her head started to shake from side to side, and her shoulders caved in, making a cage around herself, trying to pull away from him with every part of herself.

"And I have spent five years... knowing that it was because of me... that my decision to keep things from you had lead us into this nightmare," her voice was hardly a whisper, breaking, saying the words that she had worked to deny in her heart for so many years of misery. She turned away from him, trying to regain control of herself before painful, chest wrenching sobs could swallow her whole.

"Caroline-" he said, softening. He reached out a hand to touch her shoulder, and she pulled away. Sympathy would only push her over the edge.

"Why are you here? Why do you care? Ellie loves you, you will never be out of her life now, so why bother with me?" she asked, hating to hear the catch in her thick, tearful voice.

"Because... I love you, I have never ceased loving you, and I never shall... I am not capable of it," he came in close behind her, putting his hands gently on her shoulders, and then slid them down her arms in a soothing caress before he gently turned her back to him. They were so close. He was so warm, and everything in her body cried out to throw her arms around him and bury her face in his chest and be held as she let go. But she did not.

"You seemed plenty capable of it in Portsmouth," her soft words flaying flesh from bone, she could see clearly, his eyes so close to hers.

"Do not suggest that it was not the hardest moment of my life. I died that day."

"As did I!" she shouted back, her voice raw, and his face looked as though she had struck him, but he merely reached out and cupped her face, running a thumb gently to dry her tears. "You should hate me," she said, with a shuddering inhale as anger, guilt and desperation collided in her chest. "You should hate me!"

"Caroline, what madness is this, what are you saying?"

"It is my fault... everything that has happened... Silus's death, Ellie's fatherless childhood. It is all because of me. You killed your father because of me, forced to run for five years. You missed your daughter's childhood... all because of my schemes and lies. My arrogant foolishness." She shook her head and brushed his hand from her face. "Why do you not hate me?" her voice rose, her face was hot. She raised her hands and pushed him, hard, once, and then twice. She pushed him backwards, her whole body driving against him. He swayed back a step before regaining his balance and pushing back against her. She tried again, but he was unmoveable, a stubborn wall of a man, his face so maddeningly understanding. Her hands balled into fists, she started to pound his chest, tears running her eyes, her mouth frozen in a wordless snarl.

His hands came to her wrists, and roughly, without care of consequence, he slammed her back against the wall.

Her breath flew from her chest and she opened her mouth to gasp, which was swallowed by his lips, hot and urgent descending on hers.

He pushed her back into the wall, his whole body in hard contact with hers. His hands held her hands still, restricting her movement. He kissed her mercilessly, with the want they had carried for each other, all these years, a cruel, demanding prison.

He kissed her with the dizzying desire that comes from so long denying the one thing you cannot live without. Gulping her down like a daft of water, to a man lost in the desert. The stubble of his cheeks cut into her skin. He bit down and she gasped, her blood a tinge on his lips. His hips ground against her, desperate for contact, needing to feel her, and for her to feel him.

When he broke away, as suddenly as he had made contact, Caroline sagged against the wall, with only his hands on her wrists to keep her up. She gulped down air, her lungs burning, her mouth of fire, hands trembling. He stayed in front of her, mere inches apart, his breathing harsh, resting his chin on the top of her bent head, as he released her hands, and they slowly fell to rest on his shoulders. Swallowing thickly, he muttered into her hair.

"Never blame yourself for Silus's evil," and heard her catch of breath. "I could never blame you. I too am at fault for all that happened. Do you not see that? I could not see past my own fury. I thought you were dying, and rather than go to you, comfort you, spend perhaps our last moments together telling you how much you were loved, all I could see was revenge. I was like an animal." She cried harder at his words, hearing them spoken aloud.

"This love... it has only destroyed us," she muttered brokenly.

"No my love... it has saved us. Over and over again. Nothing matters but our love. Let it mend our broken souls."

She looked up at him, confused, ashamed, a swirling whirlwind of emotions that she couldn't untangle. She felt a flash of what it might be like to give in and return to each other. A flash of being his Caroline, if only for a moment.

Her hands moved quickly to his jacket, and with a tug, she pulled him back to her lips. He pushed her back into the wall once more, her mouth on his, her tongue slipping against his, her teeth tugging on his bottom lip. Her hands were moving over his head, tugging on his hair, pulling him closer, harder against her, wanting to be consumed. He slammed against her with his hips, frustration between them over the layers of clothes and skirts which kept them from touching. With a growl, he bent sharply and reached for the bottom of her gown. He pulled it up, out of the way, as his hands immediately traced her burning upper thighs between the tie of her pantalettes, his hands moving underneath, to her hips, where he cupped them, and suddenly lifted her against him. She responded willingly, wrapping her legs around his waist as he returned his attention to her mouth, pushing her back against the wall once more. He moved his mouth to her neck, sucking, biting, scrapping his stubbled chin over her sensitive flesh, as she writhed against him, moving her hips against his, torturously. He held her hard against the wall, as he unbuttoned the fall front of his trousers. A hand under each cheek of her bottom, he locked eyes with her, for a drawn-out moment where Caroline's world swam, and all should could see was her own need.

"Yes, Lucian. Now," she said in a gasp. "Now. I need you."

When he pushed inside of her, it was not a gentle thing, it was strong and steady, an unrelenting advance, taking her one inch after the next until he was completely inside of her, and with the slight pain was a blinding joy and a need so strong that it pulled a scream for her lips.

"Lucian," she said, again and again. "Lucian."

He ground into her, moving, but not pulling away for even a moment, and tears slipped down her face, and she held onto his head and his shoulders, pulling him closer with her legs wrapped around his hips. This need was hungry, it was demanding, it was angry at being ignored for so long, and she moaned into his hair, a rough, rasping thing.

Suddenly he pulled her away from the wall, holding her fast against him, he turned and strode to the bed lowering them both slowly down so that they did not lose contact. His blue eyes on hers were almost black as he slowly pulled out of her. His hair a riot of lustful untidiness, he unbuttoned his jacket with haste, yanked off his cravat.

She tried to catch her breath, hopelessly caught in the torrent of desire that he alone was capable of producing in her. She rose and fell with it, tumbled toward what she longed for, craved the touch of him, the undeniable need to feel him back inside of her.

"Remove your dress," he commanded, his voice thick with desire, barely contained. His waistcoat joined his jacket on the floor, and her eyes moved over him, greedily absorbing him. "Now, Caroline."

Before he could finish his undressing, she raced to do the same. She quickly untied her pantalettes and pushed them off with her stockings. Then she sat up on her knees and began to unlace her dress, letting the gauzy muslin slip down around her shoulders.

"Take it off," he ordered, his eyes catching her every move. She slipped it off her knees and began unlacing her short stays. He kicked his boots off and unbuttoned the top of his trousers, and as he did so, her chest rose in heaves, in greedy anticipation, the feel of his length still lingering inside of her. She kneeled, her body only covered by the translucent chemise as he let his trousers drop over the muscles of his strong legs. He was completely nude, and her breath hitched in her chest as she took in the sight.

Finally, she saw his beautiful body that she had traced with her mind's eye every long night while he was away. He was harder now, leaner, his muscles nearer the surface, skin more tanned from rough days outdoors, doing what, she did not know. There were also new scars and scratches since last she saw, souvenirs of their separate lives made flesh.

As she dragged her eyes to his again, their gazes locked. She untied the lace of her chemise, gathered the length of it, and held his eyes as she slowly pulled it up, and over her body, leaving nothing now between her skin and his. He cursed, and she barely had time to breathe before he was on her again, his weight so very welcome, she wrapped her arms around his neck, moved her hands over his back. He kissed her furiously and she welcomed it, opened herself to it, the onslaught of passion.

"We have so much to make up for, my love, so much," he breathed. "And I will see to it, that you can think of no other man but me, burn for no man but me... I shall push all others from your heart, until it beats my name, as mine does yours," he promised into her neck as his mouth travelled down her skin, his hands suddenly going to hers, and pulling them tight over her head. He broke off kissing her, and leaned away, looking down at her, held prisoner beneath him, her breasts bared, her body supplicant under his. He kissed her hard again.

"You are mine. You will never doubt my love for you, because you shall know... that even in my darkest time, and my deepest despair, only the thought of you kept my heart beating," he said, his breath on her skin, as his mouth moved to her nipples, and Caroline felt entirely consumed, swallowed up by her passion, and his, and caring for nothing else.

This was no tender, sweet moment, no long and leisurely joining of two hearts. It was passion, pain and unguarded, longing and need, built to a torrent, inescapable and all-consuming. It was the physical manifestation of five years of loss and hunger, of hate and love.

She raised her hips, wrapping her legs around him, she did not wish to delay longer. She needed him, with a need unlike any she had ever felt before. Everything was moving fast, too fast to breathe. The feeling of his legs falling between hers, spreading her legs wide, and his weight shifting against the length of her body, made an animal of her, nothing but need and lust and teeth and nails, as he entered her again, her body swollen with want and slick with hunger.

Slowly, excruciatingly, inch by inch, their breath mingling, their eyes never leaving each other's, he pushed deeper inside of her. Waves of feeling rolled over her, and she pulled him closer, her hands going to the sides of his face. He moved in her, faster and faster still, building to a punishing speed. She pushed back against him, making every thrust echo through her body harder and harder still. She clenched her teeth, as his skin slid against hers, slick with sweat. She felt her unravelling, her threads being slowly unwound, being taken control over, her body overwhelmed by the feelings, and his body, so new and familiar, still fitting hers so perfectly.

Just when she felt she could withstand it no longer, he pressed his hips against her and pushed himself deeper, grinding hard against her. It tipped her over the edge, and she gasped his name, as her fingernails dug into his shoulders. He flexed and jerked and she saw her awed expression mirrored in his, as she felt him spill his hot seed inside her, his eyes never once leaving hers.

She gasped big lung-fulls of air, trying desperately to catch her breath, as he rolled aside and began to kiss her neck. Soft, tender delicate things, he moved over her skin kissing her gently, and then to her face, his soft lips on her chin, her cheeks, her nose, her eyelids, his warm breath on her forehead.

"I have missed you," he whispered. He made his way down to her mouth, and kissed her again, tenderly this time, so soft and with so much devotion, that she felt dizzied by it. He took her face in both his hands.

"I love you, Caroline," he said. "Never forget it again."

He kissed slowly down to her ear, tugging her lobe softly between his teeth, then down her neck, across her collar bone, then down the middle of her chest, between her breasts. He took his time, running his soft lips over every inch of her skin, that by the time he gently sucked the pink peek of her nipple into his warm mouth, she needed him again. He ran his tongue across her, and with his other hand, he rubbed his thumb so gently against her other hard nipple that she started to moan. And she continued to make soft, needy noises as he kissed his way over each side of her rib cage, over her navel, and to her hips.

His warm mouth made its way to her inner thigh, and he grabbed a bundle of sheets from the bed and quickly wiped his seed from her quim before he put his mouth on her.

His hot breath met her first, and then his lips brushing agonisingly against her until he gently spread her with his fingers and kissed her. So long she had spent, so long without the touch of a man, without Lucian, denying herself any release, even the touch of her own hand, for the painful memories it would bring her. The wet heat of his mouth on her cunny was more than she could take, and she threw her head back and let out a low, primal moan, as he licked her. She wound her hands in his hair and groaned louder as she started to lose control again.

"Oh, Lucian," she panted.

"Tell me," he said.

"Lucian."

"Tell me, Caroline."

"I need you."

"Uh huh," he said as he slid his finger into her.

"I need you now, Lucian," she panted. She cried out as he slid his long middle finger against her inner wall, rubbing at the top of her with his thumb the way he used to.

"Tell me, again" he said again.

"I need you," the world began to spin behind her eyes. "I need you inside of me," she writhed against his hand. "Lucian," she cried out and it was almost a scream. She was begging now, pleading with him.

He stopped then, and he moved over her. He caught her eyes, suspended above her, his cock at her opening, and for a moment he just looked at her. His eyes worshipping every part of her face, as she looked up at him.

Slowly, gently, tenderly, he slid inside of her, his forehead pressed against hers, his breath stirring the hair at her temples. How long they stayed like that, she did not know, still, joined as one, complete. A tear rolled from her eye, and he traced it with his thumb, breaking their trance, as he started to move in her.

"You are my life," he said. "You always have been. This is what I was made for." He rocked inside of her until she started to unravel. She clasped her ams around his broad back and Lucian lifted her enough to slide an arm underneath her hips, pulling her even closer to him as he gound deeper still and gently lowered his mouth to hers, kissing her tenderly as she came undone, holding her body tight against his own as they lost all sense of where they were and who they were and who they had been, and what they had done, and there was nothing in the world but their two bodies, joined and complete.

❀

*S*ilence slowly crept back into the room, with only the sounds of their hard breathing filling the air. Caroline finally let her eyes fall shut, the consequences of what she had just done, rushing down on her. What now? Who were they now? She felt Lucian press a kiss on her shoulder. She squeezed her eyes shut and curled to her side. He was there, behind her, pulling back against him, sliding an arm around her waist. She felt her tears threaten to return. She felt ashamed of herself. She had let her body's base desires, and her heart's sad desperation lead her to act impulsively. She was a fallen woman, fallen to her husband, yet fallen all the same.

Lucian could not have failed to notice her sudden stiffness, her withdrawal after they had shared something so intense, after they had bared their souls to each other.

"Caroline?" he said softly, his voice a question.

"You should go... before Ellie wakes up," she said quietly. "She often sleeps with me. This would be confusing... for her."

"For her, Caroline? Or for you?" She pressed her eyes closed and said nothing. "Do you regret it?" he asked suddenly, bracing his elbows on his knees, looking at the window over them.

"No. But I do not know what it means," she whispered.

"What do you wish it to mean?"

"I... I do not know."

Lucian sighed, and rose to his feet.

"I do not wish to leave," he said suddenly, as he collected his clothes. Her heart felt torn in two.

"Please... I just..." she trailed off, unable to vocalise her confusion. Lucian dropped his shirt over his head, and pulled his breeches on. He walked toward the door.

"When will you tell him?" Lucian asked suddenly, and she flinched, the question she had been expecting finally asked.

"Who?" she asked emotionlessly.

"Lee," Lucian replied, just as dispassionately.

"Tell him what?" she said stubbornly, tears once again gathering at the corner of her eyes.

"That whatever this is between you is over, Caroline. That you will never be his." She began to cry. It wasn't Lee, it never had been. It was the loss of her self control, her control over her life, the careful peace she had been building without him. Lucian turned to leave. "Do not make me tell him, Caroline. It would be kinder coming from you," he stated calmly, before stepping out of the room and walking the short hall to his room.

He closed the door quietly behind him and sat on the edge of the bed. She had reduced him once again to petty threats and manipulations when he'd thought himself so beyond it. Would he ever be more than a desperate man, chasing after his salvation, when it came to her?

Would there ever be anything he would not do? Would there ever be any rule he would not break for her?

His head was racing and he dropped it into his hands and schooled himself to take deep breaths, as he desperately tried to calm his pounding heart.

CHAPTER 9

*L*ucian gently closed the storybook on his lap and held his breath. The inquisitive eyes had eventually dropped closed, their heads huddled together under the makeshift fortress they had built with cushions and throws. He shifted uncomfortably, as he braced his hands on the floor to stand up. Hours of sitting had numbed his feet and legs, and he walked stiffly, trying to bring blood back to them.

It had been nearly a week since his encounter with Caroline in her room. Nearly a week since he had come back to life and died all at the same time. She had withdrawn, and he had not attempted to see her alone, remembering the way her back shook as he had left the room, her broken voice. She needed some time and he would try to give it to her, for he had also seen the love in her eyes as he made love to her, and he knew that at least echoes of him still resided in her heart.

He continued down to the kitchen waving the scullery maid to bed, and setting the milk himself to warm, recalling happier times when Caroline had perched on the table, her thick hair loose around her shoulders, swathed in a great dressing gown, watching him. Those times seemed to be very far away now, he thought as he stirred in some honey. He would do anything to return to that simple time, before the years and cruel fates had twisted them into two people who no longer knew how to love each other, yet could not stop.

❀

*T*he hospital dinner was unfortunately timed, Caroline thought as she struggled with a clasp for a necklace. She looked in the mirror with a sigh, feeling far from beautiful. The nights had been long of late, and her bed lonely, her dreams offering no rest as the battle raged on inside her between her head and her heart.

When she slept, she dreamed of him. His smell, his taste, the feel of his skin and the touch of his hands. It drove her mad. Her body was craving Lucian, and she tried her best to ignore it, but in her dreams, in the vulnerability of sleep, her desires were uncontrollable. She had barely spoken to him after their night together, and that extended time of not speaking had only heightened the tension between them. When their eyes met, her heart stopped, if their hands brushed over dinner, her skin felt singed. If she felt him pass nearby, she lost the ability to breathe.

She picked up her reticule, and cast a last look around the room, before leaving it. She walked down the stairs, and saw Charles already waiting in the hall, along with Lucian. They both looked marvellous, dressed in white tie, and as she caught Lucian's eye, the way he tilted his head slightly to the side and his eyes swept over her made her blush. It was to be a long night, she thought nervously, as he raised his arm to escort her to the carriage, and she avoided his direct gaze, staring ahead.

As she got into the carriage, she looked at the door in alarm as Lucian pulled it shut behind him.

"What of Charles?" she asked, her voice bordering on shrill. Lucian settled opposite her and looked at her with a wry smile.

"He will escort Katherine, he is taking his own carriage."

"Oh, I did not realise that... it would only be the two of us," she muttered, flustered. Lucian smirked a little mockingly at her.

"Well, try to control yourself, my dear," he teased. Smoothly he moved across the carriage and sat next to her, tensing slightly as she pulled away.

"Worry not, your virtue is to remain intact... for this carriage ride at least," he said darkly.

"How gentlemanly of you to remind me," she snapped at him.

"Remind you of what?" he asked innocently, deliberately forcing her to acknowledge their encounter.

"You are insufferable," she said, as she looked away, his teasing making her itch to retaliate.

"So I have often been told, mostly by you, my love."

"Please, do not call me that... not tonight, and not here. As you may well guess, Joshua Lee shall be here tonight, and... I do not want him to hear it."

"Will you tell him?" Lucian asked at length, as he fought down the sting that her request gave him.

"What would you have me tell him? That I laid with my husband? We are married still... it is no sin," she said, unsure what compelled her, and gasped as he suddenly gripped her fingers harder, making her look at him, taken aback by his sudden anger.

"No, the sin is pretending that you do not return my love... for allowing this farce of a relationship to continue with Lee. That is the sin. The sin is to waste one more moment apart, when we know better than others... how precious time is."

"Is it not a sin to use it against me, to force me to do what you want?" she asked, anger in her eyes.

He held her gaze and then raised one mocking eyebrow at her.

"There are no blacker sins than those I have already committed, this one is barely a blemish on my tarnished soul."

The carriage suddenly stopped, and she realised they had arrived. The door opened, and Lucian got out, turning to help her down. As she descended, she felt her body come into full contact with his, as he held her.

"Stop," she hissed near his ear as she pushed him a little further off. "Yes, Lucian. Tonight I will tell him. But I will do it my own way and in my own time, and you shall not push me.

"I think I can speak for everyone here when we welcome the addition of the Ashfords' philanthropic activities to our great city. They have come as a family and are set on making Virginia a better place. I only hope they go easy on us," the chair of the board raised his glass as the room laughed politely and drank. Caroline took another gulp of her wine, the dinner was turning into a nightmare.

Lucian was merely a few seats away, and the snippets of conversation that were drifting to her from his direction were doing nothing to calm her. Seated in between two very attractive, rich widows of New York society, who were set on finding all about the handsome Lord Nicholas from far away England. There was a lot of arm touching, throaty laughter and fanning coming from that section of the table, and Caroline pushed herself to ignore it all.

"Oh! Lord Ashford! You are such a cad... who would say such a thing!" screeched a womanly voice trying too hard to be alluring. She heard Lucian' low chuckle and gripped her knife harder than ever.

The dinner stretched on endlessly, and finally, they were released, and the women left, leaving the men to their cigars and sherry. As Caroline made her way through to the drawing-room, she was stopped by a voice coming from a dark nook in the hall.

"Caroline," Joshua said, his face smiling boyishly at his deception. Caroline looked around at him, seeing no other men.

"No one will notice my absence, come, let us get some night air, I have not spoken to you in so long alone," he murmured, and Caroline felt cold grip her spine. She nodded mutely, and let him lead her to a set of double doors that opened onto a terrace. It was not wholly private, yet quiet enough for what she had to do.

She had to let Joshua go, and leave him in no question that there might yet be a hope of some future together. Perhaps she had known it from the very start, and her head had refused her heart for as long as it was able. But it could be denied no longer. Whatever would happen between her and Lucian, she was ruined for all other men. To pretend otherwise was foolish, and she was no longer a young, naïve girl, full of dreams and hopes, she could not pretend anymore.

Joshua smiled as he pulled her close, and without warning, embraced her. She took a deep breath and steeled herself.

"Joshua, we must talk," she whispered, leaning away to see his face. He mistook her actions and moved forward to kiss her. She turned her face and felt his lips land on her cheek.

"Sorry to intrude," Caroline froze as she heard Lucian's voice, low, a growl, a tone she knew well, and one that never ended pleasantly. He stepped forward and wrenched Joshua away from her, pulling her close to him. Joshua staggered away, and turned back, seeming to gather himself before he sneered at Lucian.

"Caroline is not your property, Ashford. You abandoned her. She was alone much longer than you were ever together. If she chooses me, you will have to accept it," Joshua began but stopped his advance, arrested by the savage look on Lucian' face.

"If you touch her again, I will kill you," he said simply, his words more a quiet certainty than a warning. His words snapped Caroline from her mindless observation, and she turned to look up at her husband.

"Lucian, stop this. You are behaving like a brute. Mr Lee does not deserve this."

"Have you told him?" Lucian persisted, and Caroline felt the colour drain from her face. "Do not push me, Caroline," Lucian murmured into her ear, his hand tightening on her arm as he tried to pull her away.

"Stop it... unhand me." she snapped, as she tried to prevent his brutish manhandling. She tore her arm from his.

"Why must you keep hurting me?" she cried.

"I might ask you the same," Lucian ground out woodenly.

Joshua moved to her side protectively.

"Just because you share a house..." Joshua was saying roughly.

"We share much more than a house... we share a bed, do we not Caroline?" Caroline's eyes met Lucian's eyes and saw a small flash of victory there that disgusted her. She was betrayed, and utterly disappointed in him, and poor Joshua would be the one to suffer it.

"Caroline, is that true?" Caroline continued to stare hard at the side of Lucian's face, even after he had dropped his head. She finally turned to Joshua.

"I am afraid it is. I am sorry that I was not the one to tell you, I brought you out here specifically to do so... and I would have, if we had not been so rudely interrupted," Joshua pulled away from her, turned away, dropping his head into his hands.

"I am so sorry Joshua. You deserve so much better than I... I have done nothing but hurt you. You are a good man, a wonderful man, perhaps the best I have ever known, the kindest and most compassionate."

She tried to put a comforting hand on Joshua's shoulder, but he shrugged it off. He stared bleakly ahead, and then let out a strangled laugh.

"I should have known. Charles encouraged me, you encouraged me, but I've only myself to blame. It is my folly. I knew it was madness, but I could not help myself. I should have removed myself from you the moment we found out that this bastard was still alive," Joshua suddenly stood, and Lucian stepped closer to Caroline, watching him closely, his sudden movements making him unpredictable. "For that is the only chance I ever had... is it not? If you were honest with yourself... only if he were rotting in the ground, food for the worms, then, perhaps you would have allowed yourself to care for me." His face was red, hurt. "But... that is all. You would allow yourself to care for me, you would never love me as you love him. No matter what horrible things he does to you, you cannot let him go. Whatever tired and twisted thing exists between you, it shall never be severed in this life... you are bound together, for eternity, and damned is the man who comes between you." Joshua cast a last contemptuous glance at them as he turned and strode off the terrace.

They both watched him go in silence.

Inside, there was a commotion, as the diners started to filter out to view the gardens, and take in the night air. Katherine and Charles appeared, throwing warning glances at Lucian and Caroline where they stood, reminding them of the importance of this night.

"I hate you," Caroline whispered for only Lucian's ears, her bright smile strained.

"I know," he replied quietly, placing his hand on the small of her back as they joined in a group conversation.

"I think they will kill each other before too long," Charles murmured as he watched Lucian and Caroline moving around the party, Caroline's brittle laugh, and the way she moved out of Lucian's touch whenever possible, and how his brother moved in close at every opportunity.

Katherine smiled and touched Charles's cheek, drawing his eyes to her. She saw something entirely different when she watched them together. The way that Caroline leaned into Lucian when she wished the conversation to be taken from her, the way Lucian took the lead when Caroline signalled him. The way a slight incline of Lucian's head and Caroline's hand was reaching for his arm, as they moved around the gathering, the way sparks flew when their eyes met, joined in silent exchanges, communicated with only their eyes during mindless small talk.

"My love... you have so much to learn about affection, obsession," Katherine said, leaning in close to his ear to whisper the last words, "lust and desire." Charles stayed a moment, his mouth close to her cheek. "Those are two people, barely restraining themselves from each other, two people who can think of nothing else than devouring each other, of losing themselves, abandoning all reason, and letting their passion, their love consume them," as Katherine spoke, they saw Lucian rest a hand lightly at the base of Caroline's neck, brushing a thumb over the nape of her neck, and they saw, almost unnoticeable, Caroline shiver, before pulling away.

"And, how would you know of such things..."

"Well, I am an avid reader," Katherine said with a smile. "And I have lived it these many long years."

Of course she had. He had made her wait for him for so long, and she had borne it with grace and unwavering loyalty, and he knew he would spend the rest of his life rewarding her for it.

"Then we have much to make up for, my beloved," he promised, his lips lightly brushing her skin.

"Caroline, may I?"

"No," she hissed quietly, but he sat down anyway.

"I have a proposal for you," Lucian suddenly said. She turned to him and raised an eyebrow.

"There are card tables here, and it put me in mind... well, I was thinking, perhaps we could make a wager, as we used to," he said, and she coloured a little, thinking of some of their past bets, and shot him a narrow look. He grinned and hurried to explain. "Nothing of that sort, my dear, I was merely thinking that we play a hand of cards, a game of your choice, and if I win you will agree to spend time with me again, stop pushing me away so intently, and at least allow me the chance to win you over before our time in the house together is finished."

"And if I win?"

"I will desist in trying to get you alone constantly, trying to make you care for me again. I will be but a lodger in your home, out of sight, only there to spend time with Ellie when I can," those words lanced through Caroline, curiously hurtful.

"That is hardly any stakes to play at all. If I win... you will move out now and start your own life in your own home as you promised, and you will give up on this farcical marriage, just as surely as I have," she said searingly, anger still coursing through her, fury at what he had done not an hour before.

He cooly looked back, his eyes assessing her.

"Very well. I accept your terms... but if I win... for the remaining month of our time together, we will truly live as man and wife, no more separate rooms. We will... give this a real chance." His words took her breath away.

❀

*S*he stared at him levelly, but Lucian smiled as she could not stop her cheeks from reddening at what he was suggesting, yet, at the sight of his smile, she brought her chin up in a haughty display of the stubbornness that he had missed so much.

"Very well," she said firmly. Lucian raised an eyebrow at her, his head tilting to the side.

"Are you ready for the implications, should you lose?" he asked.

"I need not be, for I shall not lose," she said determinedly, standing, and making her way to the card table. She was remarkable. He sat still as a stone, before standing, and following her. He smiled at her as he followed her upstairs, watching her form move and sway under her dress.

He took a seat at the table leaning back confidently, trying his hardest to disguise his nerves.

"What game?"

"Fermin-de-fer. It is chance only," she said, as she sat down. His jaw tightened. What on earth had he gotten himself into? Was he about to lose the woman he loved more than life itself in a reckless hand of cards? Well, he reasoned, if they continued on the road that they were traveling on, he would lose her just as surely.

"Best of three," Lucian nodded firmly, and called a man over to deal.

The man dealt the hands expertly, and they each inspected their cards. As they played through the first two hands, a few nearby tables turned their attention to the two of them, though they had no idea the stakes, they could not fail to see the tension stretched across the table.

Finally the first two hands passed, and the score was doing nothing to ease Lucian's fears, as they had both won one hand each. He took a deep breath as he nodded to the dealer to start dealing the last hand. A lock of wavy black hair fell loose across Caroline's brow, and he longed to reach across and tuck it behind her ear, just to feel the silk of it under his fingers.

As the dealer flipped the cards over quickly, Lucian looked down to his hand, and felt his stomach drop. It was not a good hand. He clenched his teeth, and tried to give nothing away as he raised his eyes to Caroline. She was staring hard, his hand laid on the table, and then at her hand, still concealed from him.

He saw her swallow nervously, upset, and suddenly she was standing up. The table rocked back, and Lucian made to stand, but she held a hand out to him, staying him.

"Stop. I... please excuse me," she said, and whirled around, making for the door. She still held her cards in a death grip as disappeared.

"Women, huh?" said a man at the table next. "Such poor losers. My wife never fails to make a scene either," he laughed cheerfully.

Caroline closed the door of the powder room, and stared at her reflection in the looking glass. She looked pale, and her cheeks were red. Her eyes huge and round, afraid. It was madness, what had she agreed to. It was scandalous. How could they behave so foolishly? She closed her eyes, fighting a shudder of heat that went through her at the thought of sharing a bed with Lucian each night. She took a deep breath and composed herself. She tucked the cards into her reticule. She splashed some cool water over her temples and the back of her neck. Time to face her fears.

The carriage ride back was quiet, Ellie drifting in and out of sleep across Caroline's lap. They barely spoke, and she avoided his hot glances. When they stopped, Ellie awakened, and climbed sleepily down. Caroline took Ellie's hand and, without a glance at Lucian, led her upstairs, as Ellie murmured her tired goodnight to him. She tucked Ellie into her bed, and left the room. She reached her own and briefly considered running inside and locking the door. Yet, if there was anything she knew of her husband, it was that a locked door would not keep him from what was his. And she would not back down now. She would bear the consequences of her rash decision.

She swallowed, straightened her spine, and passed her door and slowly went down the stairs. She found him in the study. It was dark, with a low fire burning. They did not speak. He rose as she entered and poured her a glass of tawny port, which she took, her fingers jumping as they touched his. She sat down opposite him, regarding him as he watched her in return. In silence they sipped their drinks. Her heart was racing, her skin prickling. After a long while, once their glasses had run dry, and their eyes had spoken an eternity to each other, Lucian stood.

"Shall we?" he asked, coming to her side and taking her empty glass from her, placing it on the desk. He offered her his arm. She took it, and slowly they left the room. It was an unreal sensation, and she felt akin to one walking to meet the executioner's axe, everything heightened, too sharp.

He placed his hand on the small of her back, as they went up the stairs, she could feel the heat of his hand through the thin material of her dress. She bit her lip, trying to breathe deeply, and calm her pounding heart. They reached the door of her room and paused.

"Having second thoughts about your impulsive bet, my dear?"

"No," she said, turning to face him, her chin raised, not willing to back down.

His face was unreadable at her reply as he nodded his head at the door. She turned and placed her hand on the knob, and turned it, stepping into the room lit softly by a fire. She went in and brusquely removed her cloak, tossing it on a chair, and busied herself around the room, trying to hide shaking hands. As she went to the mirror, raising her hands to her hair, unpinning it, and then reaching for the brush, she suddenly felt his presence behind her.

"Allow me," he said softly, his hand moving over hers on the brush, and she snatched hers back, his touch as electric as ever. She felt the brush touch her head, and it was soon moving through her hair in long strokes, sending ripples of pleasure waving through her. She let her eyes drift to his in the mirror, and lock into his warm gaze.

They shared a long look, an honest look, more honest than they had, in a long time, without anger or tears. She saw the man she loved, that she had always loved, standing behind her, and her heart beat for him, even as it quaked at his intentions.

Gently, he placed the brush on the dressing table in front of her, and as his hand retraced, brushing slowly, and deliberately up her bare arm. She closed her eyes a moment, dizzy with the feeling. Next, she felt something that snapped her eyes open. His fingers on the laces of her gown. She stiffened, unsure what to do. She felt as though she could not breathe. She closed her eyes, unable to meet his, as they carefully took in her reactions. As her laces came away, exposing the skin of her back, she felt his thumbs pass over it, caressing it, sending jolts down her spine. She gulped, as she felt his lips, and stubble roughened chin brush against her in the spot where just at the nape of her neck. At length, she steadied herself, breathing deeply and turned around. He did not step back, forcing her to lean away and look up at him.

"You will not force me," she whispered confidently, watching him, as he studied her, his eyes moving over her neck and chest, her hair, her lips, her eyes. He gently ran his hands up her sides, her bare arms, reaching her shoulders. There he slowly pushed the loosened gown back, letting it slip from her shoulders, and slid down her upper body, exposing the fine, silky chemise she wore underneath. She kept her eyes on his, seeing them turn blacker by the moment.

"No... I could never force you," he answered her quietly. He stepped away then, and took her hand, inviting her to step out of the gown. She did so, her heart in her mouth. He took another step back, and then, his hands went to his own clothes. She almost forgot to breathe, as his clothes joined her gown on the chair, his coat, and waistcoat the starched cravat and his boots tossed aside. He reached forward and pulled his shirtsleeves off, casting it carelessly aside, his eyes not leaving hers. He was back before her then, shirtless, his tight breeches hugging his muscled hips, low and snug, and straining at the urgent press of his need for her.

He came to her, tilting his head to the side, looking at her with such longing, it made her breathless. Gently, he picked her hands up, and raised them over her head, her arms felt weak and quivering as the heat of his skin seared through them. Leaving them in the air, over her head, his hands dropped again, to the edge of her chemise, and slowly, relentlessly, he began to drag it up, and over her head. The cool air hit her heated skin, and she shivered. The tension between them, the air was thick with it, was heady and intoxicating. She felt the chemise clear her head, and heard it drop to the floor. Then, there was silence. Slowly, gathering her courage, she opened her eyes, and found his eyes on her face, soft, and lost looking, so unbearably like the young man she had known, the young man once moved to tears by the act of making love.

He reached out, and she registered that his hand, when it returned, held her nightgown. It was high necked, and plain, and he was dropping it over her head before she knew it. She felt it settle on her shoulders, the hem brushing her toes. He turned then, and took her hand, pulling her gently toward the bed. He pulled the covers back, and she felt her hand trembling for a moment. Then he was sliding across the sheets, pulling her after him. She felt the bed dip under their weight. He settled next to her but did not touch her, and she knew she could let out her breath.

"Why did you tell Joshua like that?" she suddenly bit out, needing to get the thing out into the open, needing to rid herself of her anger for him. "You were too cruel, and you once again forced me... you cannot force love, you cannot force affections to be returned, and you cannot control me. If I come to you, it has to be from free will. Is it possible that you *still* fail to see that?"

She still felt angry at him, for telling Joshua, yet there was part of her that was relieved. From the moment she had known Lucian was alive, she had known she could never be with another. He was part of her, as real as her blood or the veins it flowed in, her sinew and bone. But she had struggled to cut him from her heart these long years, and the pain of it still throbbed. If she were to return to him, to lose her fragile hold again, it had to be her choice.

"You still love me, I know you do," Lucian maintained, and she turned to look at him a long moment, wondering how he could know so little after all this time.

"Yes, of course I love you, Lucian, but you fail to see the point. You have been gone for five long years, you abandoned me. Did you think that just because you have decided to wander back that I would come running for you? I am not your woman anymore, Lucian, I am my own, and you must learn to understand it."

"You," he started. "You are right," he said. "I am sorry. My jealousy got the better of me, once again, I admit. There is no defence, except that the thought of you has never made me act rationally, and from almost the first moment I saw you, I knew that my rational self would never be consulted in matters concerning you. I am struggling to be patient. Forgive me, Caroline."

"Pretty words, Lucian," she said sharply, exasperated, and turned away from him to signal the end of the conversation.

"They are all true. I will do better, Caroline. Please. Trust me once more."

He settled on his side and pulled her next to him, so casually as if he had been doing so every night of their marriage. Caroline thought to push him away, but she did not, and he cradled her into his body in a posture so familiar to her that it made her chest ache, just as it had done all those years ago in a little cottage in the woods.

CHAPTER 10

*L*ucian woke early with the first rays of the sun, his heart too light to sleep. What wild luck, what foolish risk, and somehow he had spent a night with Caroline in his arms, and had woken to find her still there. She was angry with him, but things would change now, surely. Here was his chance - to be near to her, to speak with her, win her over, his chance for emotional intimacy. Things would start to change. They must.

Flowers, he thought, cakes... he would make her a tray so that they could eat breakfast in bed together, away from prying eyes. He wrapped in his robe and made for the kitchens.

"Lord Ashford," a boy said. "Man brung this for you this mornin sayin it was urgent."

Lucian took it, and walked to the study, ripping it open.

*L*ord Ashford,

I am pleased to report to you that the whereabouts of the infant you have been trying to locate, have been discovered. He is currently in Bath, North Carolina, where I can meet you to collect the remainder of my fee before I bring you to him.

I can be certain of his identity as he was apparently delivered with a note written in his mother's own hand with his name, Callen Paterson Campbell, and also your name, if I can assume your Christian name is Lucian.

Do not delay. His conditions here are not healthy for a child of his age.

V. Mesman

❀

*C*aroline had woken from a very deep sleep to find the bed empty. She bit back her disappointment, put on a plain dress, but as she sat to pin her hair up, something caught her eye.

*D*ear Caroline,

    I am sorry to leave again without so much as a warning. I am afraid I must make haste to protect a child, and will need to travel to North Carolina, which I hope shall take no more than a fortnight, provided the snows do not come early.

I will explain everything when I return home.

Forever yours,

L

She crumpled the letter and threw it into the fire, angry at herself. More waiting. More uncertainty. She pulled her hair into a tight bun and prepared herself for the day ahead. She had functioned perfectly fine without him for long enough, she would not cease now.

.

❀

.

The days passed and Caroline fell back into her old routine, reading, helping Wesley with the social aspects of the hospital business wherever she could, taking Ellie to the Taylors' to play with the other children, and helping Katherine prepare for the wedding. She did not have much time to lament her circumstances, though she found the house particularly empty with Lucian gone. Charles was away to look for estates where he and Katherine might one day call home, and Wesley had recently moved out and relocated to his own townhouse not far down the river, but closer to the hospital, claiming, with mischief in his eye, that Lucian had chased him out, but Caroline knew better.

She refused to feel lonely, but found, once again, that she was no more able to bend her heart to reason than she ever had been. She thought about Lucian often, wondering if he felt the same aching emptiness.

Ellie was upset to begin with that her father had gone, but then a letter arrived for her, from her father, and Ellie took it away with her, hugging it to her, and smiling. Caroline matched her smile, and tried to forget the sting that reminded her that there was no note in her name, no time spent committing thoughts of her to paper.

More than a week passed in this way. She kept herself busy and began to prepare for herself and Ellie to travel for the wedding. It was to be held in Charlottesville at the Fairfax estate, Katherine having decided that nothing would make her happier than to be married at her childhood home, just as she had imagined it as a girl. Christmas was always her favourite time of year, and after the wedding, the family would all stay at the estate to have a warm, snowy Christmas together, melding the two families as one into the New Year.

Caroline did not know if Lucian would travel with her. Nothing was certain anymore. She was apprehensive, the first time she would return to the place of her youth after so long, the familiar house and lawns, sights and smells, and the countryside that would, she knew, remind her of her parent's lands, quietly still, waiting not far off.

Caroline found it difficult to sleep nights and took to sitting by her window. The moonlight over the water drew a harsh parallel to her nights as Westmere. She had been so young, so full of hope and naiveté, she now realised, so happy. She remembered with astonishing clarity seeing Lucian at his window in Blackhill, his eyes taking on new life when he saw her. How young they'd been, how unspoiled, she mused, watching the street lamp flicker slightly, homesick for the people they had once been. Although she would never admit it to herself, she had started a vigil, one that she continued late into each night. She could never define what drew her to the window, some ineffable quality, some intangible need, yet it was there, and it was real.

One night, after Lucian had been gone over two weeks, she retired from the window deep into the darkest hours of the night and retreated to her bed. The sheets felt cold as she slid off her dressing robe and got in between the thick cotton. She lay in the dark, listening to the clock ticking, trying to will her mind to rest.

As she tossed and turned, she heard the rumble of a carriage outside, and flinging her heavy blankets aside, ran to the window. A large, black carriage, four horses. By the flickering light of the carriage torch, she saw the broad unmistakable form of her husband swing down from the carriage, lithe even after the journey. Then, to her horror, he reached back inside, and from the carriage's shadowy depths, another person emerged, and he carefully helped her down.

It was a woman, and she held a baby in her arms.

Caroline's heart pounded. Lightning rushed through her veins, making her light-headed as she ran to cover herself with a wrapper, slippers. He had brought her here. How could he ever do such an unspeakable thing? Hell reared up and bathed Caroline in its flames.

She heard the front door and ran to lock her own. What would she do? Would he come to her? Would he make her meet the woman, his mistress, the mother of his child? It was unthinkable.

Slow footsteps on the stairs.

And then, a soft tap on her door.

She pressed her back to it, trying to quiet her breath and squeezed her eyes closed.

"Caroline?" Lucian's voice called softly. "Caroline? May I come in? There's someone I would wish you to meet."

She gave herself a moment. A moment for searing panic. A moment for denial, for bargaining. Then, she breathed in. She straightened her back, wrapped a shawl tighter around her shoulders, tidied her hair with a few quick movements and, steeling herself, unlocked the door.

There he stood, in the near blackness of the hall. Alone. His eyes were tired. They were soft with sincerity, with guilt, with emotion, with resolve, and they reached out to her despite herself.

Then, a soft noise, a gurgle, and she realised that he wasn't alone at all. In his arms, he held a baby.

"*C*aroline," he said softly. "My love. I realise now that I should have spoken to you sooner, but I did not know then how things would happen, and we had... enough to deal with on our own without any new revelations. Forgive me, darling, for springing this on you. May we come in perhaps? And I will explain." She nodded after a moment and moved aside, following him to the fire, where she sat down in silence, wrapped her shawl more tightly around her, and waited.

"This is Callen. He is not mine, Caroline," he said, and pinned her with his eyes a beat while he let that life-altering piece of information sink into her chest. "But, he has no one in the world left for him, and I'd like to give him a name. I want to raise him as my son," he soft voice reached her, no louder than the crackling fire, "our son, if you will have us."

"Is this the child of Annie Paterson?"

"It is."

"And who is she to you?"

"She is merely an acquaintance, though one that I cared about all the same. A close friend, perhaps my only friend these years past... William Campbell..." Lucian said, the name dropping from his lips, and the sound of his voice around it tore at Caroline's heart a little. "He hoped to marry her, they were in love, at the grand age of sixteen."

He looked down, his brow crumpled, and he put his hand through the blankets, to stoke the little one's sleeping face with a finger, smoothing over the soft blond down of his head with so much tenderness and emotion that Caroline's heart kicked. This is why he left, and where he had been. This was why he had been afraid to tell her. He gazed down at the baby with soft eyes and pain on his face, and Caroline realised that he might never have held a baby in his arms before, certainly never one that he could call his own, and she knew then that no matter what happened to him, to them, that Lucian would never again be parted from that child.

"He no longer wishes it?" Caroline asked after a pause.

"He is dead. He died in the mud in New Orleans, saving my life," Lucian said quietly and turned his lost eyes back to her. Caroline looked at him, and she could not help but feel as if his sorrow were hers. She knew how much it had cost him, it was written plainly on his face. A heart that had broken too many times.

"His woman, Annie, no more than a girl herself ... she... did not wish to live any longer without him," Lucian said finally, tightening the blanket needlessly around the sleeping baby.

"Poor girl. I remember the feeling well..." Caroline murmured softly. Their eyes met, and a long moment passed. An ocean of distance between them, waves lapping, drifting them a little closer somehow. "Who is the woman downstairs?"

"A wetnurse brought with me from Bath."

She nodded, and they sat in silence for a while. Not strained, not painful, not angry or uncomfortable, but quiet, listening to the little sleeping breaths of the baby, thinking about life perhaps, humbled by the enormity of it. Caroline could not help but picture that once it had been her own future being discussed, on a night, perhaps, not unlike this one, by a young couple who were not her parents.

"He is my responsibility now, Caroline, and I will not shirk it, but you still have a choice. I will not force another child on you that is not your own. We can live separately, as I said before, and I will be father to them both."

"Well," Caroline said softly after a moment, "let me hold him then... and you can tell me more about your friend William."

🏵

"*A* baby!" Elspeth screamed. "A baby! A brother! I did not know it could happen so quickly," she panted, eyes wide as saucers, stamping her little feet with uncontainable joy. "I knew you could do it, daddy. Where is he? Can I see him? Will he play with me?"

"His name is Callen, and he is only wee," Lucian said gently, trying to soothe his daughter before she jumped out of her skin. "Right now he is having his breakfast, but I will ask Nanny to bring him down just as soon as he is done."

We shall see,' Caroline had said. 'I would not turn a baby away for anything. He can have a home here now, and always, if he needs one. As for the rest,' she said quietly, and Lucian had felt his heart strung out like yarn on a spindle, 'we shall see.'

It had been enough for him. It had been more than enough.

❀

*T*hey quickly fell into a pattern, he would breakfast very early, before Ellie and Caroline had risen, making his way to the baby, who he knew now was an early riser. Caroline had been busy, and they had spent most of their days spinning in their own orbits, from one task to another, Ellie keeping them both just as busy as the adjustment to having a new baby in the house. Lunch was seldom remembered, but dinner, dinner was something he came to treasure. Each night, after the baby went to his early bed, the three of them ate together as a family, in the otherwise empty house. Others came and went, to visit, or to see the baby, but dinner was always for them alone. Lucian was never late, usually early in fact, as that time was more precious to him than anything else.

"Ellie, listen to your mother, she sets you a perfect example," Lucian said, with a barely restrained smile as he watched his daughter squirm.

"But why can't I use *this* fork? It doesn't change the taste of the food," Ellie was observing as she mixed the order of her cutlery. Lucian caught Caroline's eye across the table.

"Because, sweetheart, it is like a dance, you must use the right steps, in the right pattern, or be out of step with everyone else," Caroline answered, as she leant forward and rearranged Ellie's cutlery.

Lucian watched them together, his heart swelling, and he could not help but hope for their future together.

He knew no more now of Caroline's feelings than he had before. He still kept his own rooms, and while they had continued to sleep next to each other, he had taken her words to heart, and he would not force her, he would not try to reach for her in bed and confuse her with passion, though he ached to do so - so much that it often kept him from sleep. He used those hours to think of her, of what she needed, of what he could bring to her life, how he might be a better man to her, and he used them, each moment passing slowly, to help slack the thirst for her, to drink his fill of the sweetness of sharing a bed with his wife. Caroline. His Caroline. So close. He watched as her eyelashes would flutter in her dreams, the halo the light cast from a heavy moon through the window and onto her shining jet black hair that framed her face. Surrounded by her, his overused memories suddenly seemed as dogeared and limited as ever, while laying holding the real object of love in his arms.

CHAPTER 11

"Ma'am" a small voice pulled Caroline from her sleep as she suddenly came awake with a start. Daylight flooded the room, and she looked around disoriented. She glanced to the other side of the bed, and saw the empty indentation where Lucian had lain.

"Yes?" Caroline managed, collapsing back and wondering suddenly what the time might be.

"Well, I did not mean to wake you... it's just I went to check on Miss Ellie, as she's usually up at this time..."

"And?"

"And, she's not there, Ma'am," the maid bit out nervously. Caroline stared at her perplexed.

"When was this?" she asked finally, her brain returning to motion.

"Just a moment ago."

"And the baby is…"

"In the nursery, ma'am"

"Is his Lordship here?"

"No, ma'am."

"Mightn't Ellie be with him?" The young girl's brows knit together as she considered it. "I am sure she is with her father, but I thank you for your concern," Caroline said, smiling brightly at the maid, touched by her worry. As the girl set to lighting the fire, Caroline rose, and pasted a pleasant smile on her face as she went about dressing. Of course Ellie was with Lucian, where else might she be? She reassured herself, yet her eyes kept straying to the street, hoping to find two messy heads making their way home.

Lucian sniffed the bouquet he had chosen for Caroline as he approached home. It was heavy with hothouse blooms in dark reds, oranges and yellows, like Autumn, he thought, and best of all, it smelled incredible and he knew Caroline favoured fragrant blossoms. He jogged up the townhouse steps and entered, seeing the drawing-room door slightly ajar, made his way to surprise his beautiful wife.

The butler passed him his mail as he passed, and he carried it with him into the drawing room. Caroline made a picture, sitting in the window at her writing desk. He crossed the room in a couple of long bounds and presented her the flowers with a flourish, taking her hand in the process and surprising her by pressing a kiss on her soft palm. She brought the flowers to her face, closed her eyes and inhaled.

"My Lady, you look as breathtaking as always this morning," he continued, moving to a nearby chair and picking up the neat, ironed newspaper.

"Lovely flowers, Lucian. Thank you," she said, still somewhat reserved as usual. He knew they still had far to go, but if flowers would help to pave the way, then he would buy all of the flowers in the South. He looked up from his paper and caught her staring at him, a faraway look in her eye.

"Is there something the matter, darling?"

"No, not really... it is only that, sometimes, you seem so changed, I struggle to find the man I once knew. Yet in other times..."

"I am right here," he finished for her, leaning forward. Their eyes held for a moment longer, until she looked away, turning her attention back to the page in front of her.

"So, has Ellie gone upstairs?"

"Perhaps. She often does, does she not?" Lucian said, opening the paper again, the thought of his daughter bringing a smile as always. He missed the way Caroline's pen paused in her hand, suddenly frozen and turned to him.

"She was with you this morning, though?"

"Sadly no. Why? What is wrong?" Lucian asked, lowering the paper seeing Caroline's face draining of blood. Caroline's mouth opened in a silent cry as she rushed to her feet and hurried out of the room. Lucian followed and ran upstairs behind her. Caroline tore down the hall and flung the door to Ellie's room open. She lifted the bedding and threw the pillows across the room, pulling open the wardrobe. Lucian stopped in the doorway, his mouth dry as he watched Caroline hunt with a manic desperation. Lucian reached out and took her by the shoulders, forced his own face into a semblance of calm.

"Caroline, calm down, tell me what is going on? Where is Ellie?" he asked, already knowing the answer.

"I - I don't know. The maid said... said that they hadn't seen her all morning. I thought, I thought she'd be with you," Caroline said, her cheek's reddening, her large eyes filling with tears.

"Well, when is the last time you saw her?" Fear coiled in his chest.

"Last night, when I put her to bed. The maid... she could ...I must look for her." Tears began to fall, as Caroline whirled toward the stair. Seeing her hysteria rising, Lucian quickly bent and scooped her up, ignoring her protests and carried her down the hall. Using his foot to push the door open, he deposited Caroline in an armchair by the window, pushing her down by the shoulder as she immediately went to rise.

"Stay there a moment," he insisted and walked across to the room to pull the bell pull several times, signalling that something was amiss. He poured her a glass of water and returned to her side. She took it after a pause, though she could barely halt her frantic breaths enough to drink any. Lucian crouched by her side and took her face between his hands. Her skin was hot, and he struggled to pull her chin to him. Once he had captured her tortured eyes, he spoke calmly and evenly.

"Sweetheart, we need to speak to the staff and find out who saw her last, what happened this morning. A little girl, especially one as beloved as Ellie, does not simply walk out of the house unnoticed. As for her room, there might be some clue there, so we should try and not disturb anything," he said, seeing reason start to come back to his wife's eyes. She gulped and after a moment nodded in agreement.

"Lucian, where is she? What is something has befallen her," she whispered, tears gathering again. Lucian felt his own throat constrict at the thought, and closed his own eyes, pulled Caroline in close to him, resting his lips against her forehead.

"It hasn't, she will be well, she must be," he murmured against her skin. Caroline's hand crept around his neck and held him close to her, seeking comfort in his sureness.

"We have to find her..." she whispered back, pressing her face into the nook of his neck and shoulder. He nodded, a wordless confirmation, holding her tight against him. Behind him, a knock at the door signalled the arrival of the servants. He cleared his throat and leant away. He looked at Caroline, her pink cheeks, stained with tears and luminous eyes, her face so clouded with emotions. He raised his hand and cupped her cheek, smoothing back her hair.

"I will find her, I promise. I will not rest until I have found her."

*Hours later, the house was filled to the brim with servants, family and police. Nanny Lehmann was away for a few days looking after a sickly brother, unfortunately, which had caused some confusion. Ellie's movements had been accounted for up until eight in the morning when she had been seen in the kitchen, looking for bread to serve at her doll's tea party. The kitchen maid nipped outside to help the grocer's delivery boy with the gate, and when she had returned, Ellie was gone. She had just assumed she had gone back into the rest of the house and thought nothing of it.

The police tried to reassure Croline that they'd find her, and she could not have gone far, probably wandered off somewhere by accident. Caroline nodded absent-mindedly, her mind barely registering the words, her eyes focused across the room on her husband. Lucian moved through the rabble purposefully, finding out everything he could from relevant people, and moving on. He spoke briefly with Wesley and Eli, before grabbing his hat and gloves and starting toward the door. Caroline rose in her seat to follow him, and he turned back and looked at her. Their eyes met, and volumes were spoken, he nodded once, twice, a grim, determined look on his face, and turned leaving the house with a slam of the door.

Caroline sank back down in her chair, and turned her dazed attention to the young detective beside her. She barely heard the words, her eyes still on the door. Damn the police, she thought, the only person with the power to find Ellie, and bring her home, had already left. Lucian would find her, she had to believe it, for if he couldn't, she did not know who could.

Lucian went directly to the places he'd had Caroline write down, places Ellie loved. He went through them methodically, searching them high and low, asking if anyone had seen a child that had matched her description. Nothing. Fighting the panic building inside, he raced to the last spot on the list and searched. A cold feeling of dread crept through him as he realised she was nowhere to be seen.

He remembered Caroline's eyes as she watched him go, as though he took all hope with him. She trusted him to find Ellie, above all others, as he did himself. He sank onto a cold iron bench and stared at the ground. Ellie was out there somewhere, in the city alone. He was working from the hope that she had ventured out on her own for some reason, as the alternative was too unbearable. It was indescribably terrifying.

Where would she go, he wondered, if not somewhere she treasured with her mother? A sudden thought flickered across his mind, and he let it pass, before dragging it back to be examined. Perhaps it was not somewhere special for her mother, he realised, standing again, he took off down the street, scattering the afternoon strollers in his wake.

❀

"*C*aroline, just try to rest. I will come and fetch you when Lucian gets home," Rebecca said gently, pressing another cup of tea on her. She shook her head, her eyes still trained forward, on the drawing-room door. The men were all out looking, along with the servants. The room fell silent again, the clock ticked, counting the moments of her agony. Perhaps Lucian would not find her, she suddenly thought wildly. The thought tore a chasm beneath her, and she realised just how very meaningless her life would be without Ellie.

There was a noise from the door, and both her and Rebecca's heads turned. The door swung open, and Caroline rose to her feet, her heart clambering into her mouth. Seconds seemed to slow, as the door revealed inch by inch Lucian walking in, Ellie in his arms.

"Ellie!" Caroline cried, her voice ugly and harsh with fear and relief. She shot over the room and put her arms around her. She could hear the sounds of relief sounding all over the house as Rebecca called off the search. Ellie wriggled their joined embrace and slid to the floor. Caroline dropped beside her, tears gathering again in her eyes as she grasped her little hands, and tugged her around to look at her.

"Ellie, where have you been? You scared mommy so much," she whispered, her eyes sliding over every detail of her daughter, checking for any injury.

Ellie avoided her glance, and looked around quietly, she seemed upset. Caroline looked up at Lucian in askance.

"Elspeth, you may go to your room now," he said firmly and Ellie nodded, more obediently than Caroline had ever seen her.

"What happened?"

"I am afraid Ellie's feeling a little guilty, for making everyone worry. I really do not think she had considered the consequences of her actions," Lucian said, approaching Caroline and holding out his hand to pull her up. She stood beside him, her tears still clouding her eyes and her immense relief making her mildly faint. Lucian gripped her arm and led her to the divan. She sank into the pillows and watched him sit beside her. He looked so tired, she realised, and worn, as though this morning had aged him.

"She was at the horse stables. I once took her there and promised to teach her how to ride. It seems she was impatient," Lucian said with a humourless laugh. They were both quiet, lost in their thoughts. "I am to blame-" Lucian began. "So much upheaval. Me, the baby…" Caroline, overcome, reached out her hand to his. He looked down as she wrapped her fingers around his and squeezed reassuringly.

"No, do not doubt that having you in her life has made our daughter more happy than I have ever seen her," Caroline said, a small smile on her lips, she continued, "The house has been in such confusion since we moved here. People coming and going, fathers showing up and staying, the staff do not know who is supposed to be here, and it is not a settled or secure environment for a child. It is not quite a family home but merely a way station at present... and that needs to change," Caroline spoke softly.

She looked down at their hands, pressed together, and he squeezed her hand back, and she felt she had roots again, holding her safely to the earth.

"I suppose I shall go and speak with her, she might be upset," Caroline said, shifting forward on the seat to stand. She hesitated a moment, and turned to him, giving him a tender smile.

"Thank you, Lucian... Luke. Thank you for bringing my daughter back to me... our daughter back to us," she said, her eyes meeting his and not flinching away from the intensity of his gaze. Time spun out between them and the air started to thicken with tension. Eventually, Caroline pulled her hand away, and stood, feeling the loss of contact as it pulled her back to him.

As Caroline walked to the door she was met by the maid.

"Mary, please see to it that Lord Ashford's belongings are moved from the guest rooms, as soon as possible," Caroline said quietly.

"Very good Ma'am, and where should they be moved to?"

"My quarters," Caroline said firmly.

❀

A long time later, Caroline still sat beside Ellie, her voice growing softer and softer still, waiting to see if she had dropped off to sleep. Ellie had lost a beloved doll and had a brief encounter with a man who had scared her, but apart from that, she had returned home to them without so much as a skinned knee or torn sleeve.

Satisfied that she now slept, Caroline rose and made her way to the hall. There was a large part of her that did not want to leave her side for the rest of the night, but she worried that it would encourage that kind of behaviour, and therefore resigned herself to a potentially sleepless night in her own quarters.

She heard a creak on the stairs that made her jump, and she saw Lucian shrouded in halflight coming toward her.

"I am told I have been moved... permanently," he remarked softly, and Caroline forced herself to meet his gaze. Her nerves dissipated as

770

she took him in, the man she loved, whom she had always loved in some way or another. He was still that man, she had seen it today. She nodded.

"And, so you are. If you behave," she said with a smile, moving ahead of him to enter the room. Inside was cosy and warm, and she could not help but glance toward the bed as she walked past it to her dressing table. Lucian paused only a moment, before starting to ready himself for sleep. It was the usual habit now, but something had changed, though Caroline could not be sure what it was, but she was sure that they both knew it. They undressed in companionable silence, punctuated only by sudden glances, followed by reddened cheeks and flashes of desire.

"Ellie is alright?"

"Yes. She endured a lecture and intensive cuddling, and is sleeping soundly now."

He smiled softly and nodded.

"And the baby?" she asked.

"Snoring soundly. He's quite loud for such a tiny, cherubic thing."

She smiled and began to undress, trying her hardest not to cast furtive glasses at him.

"Well, I suppose I shall retire," he said. Caroline took a deep breath and gathered her gall.

"Wait, can you assist me with my necklace?" she asked and turned to him. He came toward her, and she could not stop her eyes from roaming over his broad chest in only his shirtsleeves, loose enough now at the neck to glimpse enough to make her flush. She stood before him, and then lifted the heavy curtain of her hair up. He moved closer to reach the delicate clasp and she waited, the tension between them climbing to an unbearable pitch. She felt goosebumps break out from the accidental brush of his fingertips on her skin. He struggled with it, and had to lean forward, attempting to see, causing his chin and lips to touch her hair. She took a steadying breath and suddenly tilted her head up as he continued to work, not noticing the proximity of her lips. Following her instincts, she suddenly pressed forward and put her lips against the corner of his mouth. He froze in surprise and she slowly drew back, looking up into his eyes.

"Thank you again, for today... for everything," she whispered.

"There is nothing to thank me for, you do not have to... thank me," he replied, his voice hard to decipher. His back stiffened. He thought she was offering herself in gratitude, as a sacrifice, she realised. Suddenly it was important to Caroline that he understood how she felt, that her heart, so damaged by her love for him, was healing.

She spun away from him, and went quickly to her armoire. She searched for something in the drawers. Inside she reached for the bag that held her mother's perfume, and next to it, a reticule. It was a cherished place, a place to conceal secrets. She pulled open the reticule she had fetched and with sure hands, removed the hand of cards that had sealed her fate.

The decisive hand.

A final deep breath, she turned to him, and approached, fanning them out. The winning hand that she had held all along.

He took the cards and studied them. She waited, her heart pounding as she imagined all the thoughts that might be running through his head. He looked at her then and smiled - a smile that meant more than any she had seen from him. She leant forward again and placed another kiss on his face, and another until he raised a hand to her cheek, and stroked the curve of it, making heat rush through her, and she could not prevent herself from turning her face into this palm, her lips moving against the skin there in a plea of desire.

His hands, spurred on by her actions, dropped to her shoulders, where they stroked in long movements down her arms to her hands and he entwined his fingers with hers the way he used to when they had been so in love in Westmere. Something warm blossomed in Caroline's chest, an old ember, long thought dead, coaxed back into glow. She deepened her kiss, and her head began to swim. Taking his hands in hers, she moved them behind her, and placed Lucian's hands on her lower back, making hers free to wrap around the back of his neck across the warm skin and into his soft hair. She stood on her toes to bring him nearer, and he pulled her with wide-splayed hands tighter against him where she felt the hardness of his body, his chest, his hips, his cock pressing against her, and her stomach flipped.

Caroline's hands went to Lucian's shirtsleeves, brushing her hands down over the thin fabric, and to his waistline, gathering the linen in her hands, and untucking it from his breeches, first the front and then the back, freeing it before she slid her hands underneath to the heat of his smooth warm skin over solid muscle. The feel of him made her feel reckless and she pulled his shirt up quickly and over his head. He was beautiful standing there in front of her in only his snug breeches. Her eyes moved as quickly over his body as her hands did, and she found herself pushing him backwards toward the bed, fire burning in his eyes, just as it surely must be in her own.

Once they got to the footboard of the bed, Caroline made light work of the buttons of his fall front, as she undressed him completely, uncovering first the hard demanding length of him, and then his thick muscular thighs as he breathed heavier and she moved him backwards over the mattress.

The usual playfulness that she expected to see in Lucian's face when they went to bed together wasn't anywhere to be found. Instead, his face was flooded with emotion, eyes large and dark with something else... love, wonder and hope, raw and honest, simple and unguarded, not demanding anything of her, but accepting, with open arms, any part of her that she was ready to give.

He laid back in the soft amber light of the fire and she followed him onto the bed, sliding over his form, her thin shift, the only thing between their two yearing bodies.

"You've come back to me, Luke," she said softly as she brought her face up to his. "Not when you first arrived. I didn't know you then - that man was someone I had never met before, and I thought that perhaps the Lucian that I had loved so much was gone forever. But, you've come back to me, and convinced me that you're still the man who I loved, whom I will always love. Not unchanged, but nor am I." Lucian brought a hand up and stroked it through her hair, her eyes speaking to her more than his words ever could. "But you are here, and I find that love you as much as I ever have."

"My darling. I mean to stay and to earn that love." He said, as she brought her face down to kiss his lips. "Never. Never again will I leave you. No matter what happens. Not for any reason," he whispered, as she pressed kisses across his face, "I know you may not yet believe it, but you will. I promise that I will show you every day. I will make you feel safe and secure, protected. You and our little growing family." She smiled at that, the thought of their two beautiful babies - theirs - safe and sound. They had been building a new life together before she had even realised it, the family she had dreamt of since she had lost her own as a little girl.

She began to kiss down his neck and across his chest, open mouthed now to taste his skin as he whispered love into her hair. Bringing a hand down between them, she stroked him, and brought him to her center before sliding down on to him, a bit at a time, the length of their bodies in constant contact as she sheathed him.

"I was a fool to think I could live without you," she breathed, and her voice grated, more coarse now than before as she moved languidly up and down across his body, taking him in a little further with each return. "Lucian, I never lived a single day when you were not by my side," she said, as she opened her eyes, and looked up into the dark gleam of his shining eyes. "That was not life. It was just existence." A low gasp escaped him as she took him to the hilt, and he grabbed onto her hips, squeezing their round curves before moving to caress her bottom.

"Caroline," he breathed out her name in a breath so full of meaning, a call to her soul, that it sent goose bumps rippling across her flesh as she moved their bodies together, joined, inseparable. "You never stop amazing me," he said. "I did not believe that anyone could have a heart like yours. You are too good for me."

She moved then to sit up and straddle him, sitting up where she could look him in the face, and she clasped his face in both her hands, tracing the familiar shape that she had struggled to commit to memory for so long, that she had tried to remember every night, and caught his eyes with hers.

"Never," she said. "You are a good man with a kind and loyal heart. Lucian, I am not complete without you. We fit together."

She started to move again, riding him, coming down on the length of him, moving against him as his hands glided over her thighs, and then around her bottom, moving with her, then slowly up her back and her ribs, and then his hands smoothed across her breasts, gently caressing her, gliding his palms softly across her hard nipples as she moved, sending jolts of desire coiling through her belly as she braced her hands on his strong shoulders, and rolled her head back, her long hair brushing back against their thighs.

"Caroline, I-" Lucian murmured and stopped as she put her fingers at his lips.

"Don't tell me... show me," she breathed. Her words made his eyes flash and he sat up bringing their chests into contact, he pulled her face to his, cradling it between his hands, and kissed her deeply, hungrily. She wrapped her legs around his torso, and clung on, as he lit fire all over her, within her, and she heard a low moan rise from deep in her chest. The sheets became tangled and discarded, the pillows strewn around the floor, as they ignored the ticking of time and the night turned endless, sliding more slowly toward a pink dawn.

❀

Sometime in the halflight before a new morning, Caroline slipped from the bed and went to check on Ellie and the baby. She sighed a heavy breath of deep contentment as she looked down on each of them in their cots, breathing in the scent of them, stroking their little cheeks gently enough not to wake them.

As she made her way back to her own bed, her white nightgown shimmered in the light, ethereal again. Perhaps she was a ghost and that night she had died and been reborn. Perhaps in the morning she would be someone different. Someone who could leave the past like so many ashes burned by the fire of their lives, and walk away, hand in Lucian's, toward their future without looking back.

She climbed gently into the bed, and sank back, turning to look at the face lying near her, painted in shadows and thinning moonlight. She carefully placed her hand to his forehead and smoothed the lines there, the dreams that troubled him.

Settling her head on his shoulder, she pulled his heavy arm over her, resting it on her hip. It felt right, she realised. They felt like a family, and she felt safe and more loved than she had in years. And so, like that, cradled against his chest, hearing his heart beat under her ear, that heart that she had fought so fiercely to keep alive, she felt more complete than she could remember being in a very long time, more at home, with their family all tucked safely in their beds, than perhaps ever before.

🐚

*T*he next morning, Caroline opened her eyes, and looked around, vaguely disoriented. She looked to the clock, and gasped as she saw the time. It was after lunch. A time completely unheard of to be in bed. As she moved, she felt the exertions of the previous night shot through her, and she blushed. Her brazenness surprised her, and yet, nothing had ever felt more right to her.

She dressed quickly and went downstairs to the drawing-room. The house was extremely quiet. She rang for tea, and asked a maid where Ellie was.

"With her father, ma'am," the maid replied as she poured the tea. Caroline sipped it and tried to sort through her feelings from the previous night. Her reverie was interrupted by the front door, however, and soon Ellie was upon her.

"Mother! Are you feeling better?" Ellie asked, as Caroline set her cup down to avoid it being spilled by her daughter's energetic greetings. Caroline registered that Lucian had entered the room behind her, and her cheeks immediately warmed.

"Yes, I am quite well."

"Father said you were very tired," Ellie continued. Caroline raised her eyes briefly to see Lucian regarding her, with a smirk.

"Yes, well, I am feeling much better. But, it is time for your nap."

"Yes, I know, that is why father brought me home. Otherwise, we might have stayed at the fair all day! He is frightfully jolly today-"

"Sweetheart, why do you not go and pick a story for us to read?" Lucian interrupted quickly. Ellie scrambled off Caroline and nodded happily. She disappeared from the room, leaving a vacuum in her wake. Caroline picked her tea up again and hid her face in it as she sipped. It was quiet, she could feel the nerves springing back up between them. She risked a glance upwards and saw Lucian was perched on the arm of a chair.

"Tea?" she asked, trying to break that building awkwardness with this man whom she had shared everything, held nothing back from, mere hours ago.

"Thank you," he murmured, watching her as she stood and poured the tea and then coming over to him, offered it with a half-smile. He accepted it, and as their hands touched, Caroline finally met his eyes. She stood beside him, arrested by the look in them.

"You... look well," he said softly, tilting his head, scrutinising her.

"As do you... if perhaps a little... worn out," she said, raising an eyebrow, drawing a surprised laugh from him.

"Well, I did not sleep much. I was kept up all night," he said, his eyes warm on her as she retreated to her seat.

"That is a shame, I slept famously," she replied, her eyes still teasing. He opened his mouth to speak, when a maid arrived at the door, knocking.

"Lord Ashford, your daughter is asking for you," the girl said, curtseying as she left. He stood immediately, nodded and started toward the door. On the threshold, he called back to her.

"I am glad of your good rest and conserved energy, Lady Ashford... you will be in need of it."

🐚

*A*s the house settled, and with Lucian busy with Ellie, Caroline decided that only a bath could ease her aching muscles. She had one drawn, and then, dismissing all help, sank deep into the hot water. She must have drifted off again, when a shiver of cold air awoke her suddenly, forgetting where she was. She was still submerged in the bath, and the water was quite cool now. She raised her arms over her head, and suddenly froze as she realised she was not alone. She turned her head and saw Lucian, sitting comfortably in an armchair by a bright, blazing fire. His sleeves were rolled up, his waistcoat removed, and his hands were streaked with charcoal. He glanced up as he realised she was awake, and set his parchment aside.

"Shouldn't you gain permission before you draw someone, especially in a state of undress," she asked archly, feeling exposed.

"Forgive me, I did not think you would object..." he trailed off.

"After last night?" she asked, deciding not to shy away from the subject. He watched her and nodded. "Let me see," she demanded, holding her hand out. He shuffled the papers and dropped them to the floor.

"I cannot, they do you no justice... I am out of practice, I haven't drawn..."

"Since when?"

"Since I last saw you... since Westmere," he confessed. She frowned, knowing how his art was his escape, and how he must have needed that more than ever.

"Why not?"

"Lack of inspiration, I suppose," he said, standing and walking to a large bath sheet. He picked it up and walked toward her.

"The water will be getting cold, and you don't want to take a chill," he said as he held it open in front of him. Caroline panicked at the thought of appearing before him, her body changed since the baby, in the bright afternoon light, naked and standing, having no more secrets.

"Can you not turn away?" she asked, and he rolled his eyes incredulously.

"Never," he said, "I have never been able to," taking her hand and helping her to stand. Her hands instinctively went to her abdomen.

"What is it?" he asked. Caroline avoided his gaze

"Nothing," she said as she climbed out the tub and tried to wrap the towel around herself. His hand stopped her, and she felt tears sting her eyelids, suddenly she felt so vulnerable, she could not stand it.

"Stop," she whispered as he tugged the towel gently away from her. She closed her eyes and clenched her teeth.

Suddenly his hands were on her waist steadying her, and she felt him sink to his knees before her. She opened her eyes to see him staring at the jagged scar that marred her lower abdomen. He traced it with his fingers, his face emptier and more pained than ever.

"Ellie," she whispered softly, in explanation. He closed his eyes at her words, and then, without warning, pressed forward and kissed the ugly mark. She was transported back to the night she told him she was with his child.

Now he knelt before her, having almost lost everything, a life lying in ruins around them, and kissed her with feverish gratitude.

She felt tears begin behind her eyes. Tears that stemmed from all the nights of fear and pain, of loneliness and utter heartbreak. The dark place inside, where she dared not look, the burden of sorrow that she had carried these long years, it threatened to break open, and spill its hard-earned contents.

Her tears began to fall as she put her hands to his head and held it close against her skin, finding she was not alone in her tears, as his wet cheek pressed against her. Gradually, she pulled back from him and sank to her knees next to him. His eyes were lowered, his eyelashes wet, his blue eyes so sad. She put her fingers under his chin and pulled it upward until he met her gaze. Her tears ran freely down her face and dripped from her chin and she leaned forward and embraced him. She buried her head in his shoulder and felt his face burrow into her hair.

It was the union of people who have suffered a particular pain, one that only they could inflict on each other, one that comes from missing someone, someone you truly love, someone who you need to be near in order to live, to feel happiness, to laugh and smile. Someone, without whom, it is questionable whether you are truly alive.

She cried as she hadn't in years. She cried for their time apart, for the years of terrifying loneliness and heartbreak. She cried for the life he had led, apart from his family, she cried for the man that had thought he had lost his child for so long, for the baby that had lost both his parents as she once had. She cried for all they had lost, something she could never truly grieve over without him, as it was something only they could share together.

***

*H*e had no idea how long they sat entwined. The fire burned lower and lower still, and still they held on, anchored for the first time in years. He finally noticed the tremble in Caroline's arms, her exhaustion, and his own. He felt more tired than he could ever remember and leaning away from her, he saw her weariness, her face washed clean by her tears. He carefully stood, unsteady on his feet. Overcome by a tiredness, akin to overindulgence, he steadied himself before reaching down to help Caroline up. She clung to him, as though she had been adrift for weeks in an angry sea, and had only now reached land. He picked her up and carried her to bed, and she curled against his chest.

"Sleep, Caroline," he whispered softly, as he gently traced the shape of her cheek, smoothing back her hair, wiping her tears away. She looked at him, her eyes blue pools, weary and peaceful. He slid into bed next to her and pulled her close, as he breathed in the smell of her, encasing him, sinking through him. She gripped his arms, pulling him closer as she sank into that welcoming sleep, her mind washed bare of thoughts, empty and at rest.

How he envied her that calm emptiness and absence of worries, how he wished he could follow her there. Yet, a particular piece of correspondence he had received that afternoon kept him from sleep, held him back from one of the most important nights of his life to date. Mixed in other mail, hand-delivered, it simply read:

"Do you know where your child is? The time has come to pay your debts, boy. I'll be seeing you soon."

CHAPTER 12

~December 1815~
Charlottesville

*T*he Virginian winter sun, crisp and all so familiar, crept through the leather of Caroline's glove as she leant her arm against the window of her childhood room. She looked down and over the lawn, blanketed in white snow, ringed by trees, which had cast away their leaves, and a large fountain, frozen over, its icicles glittering under the sun.

The sky was cornflower blue, deceptively cold, wisps of cloud drifting lazily, threatening more snow. Childish laughter pulled her attention below, and she saw Ellie run out of the house, hotly pursued by Jeremy Taylor. Caroline saw Rebecca wrapped in wool and furs, calling them over for a hot drink, her British voice cutting through the gentile American murmurs of Caroline's childhood.

The journey West had taken five long and arduous days in a bumpy carriage. The distance might have been travelled in two, but they had decided to take their time, the baby disapproving of long hours in the carriage, and the others enjoying the regular stops, and the sights along the way. The sight of Ellie and her father passing the time chatting, playing with the little one, reading together as he slept, looking out the window, while they shared a blanket and Lucian regaled her with stories of distant shores and adventures, had filled Caroline's heart up enough to forget any hardship or distance endured.

Between Lucian and Caroline, there were few words, long gazes, and secret smiles. She had started to feel complete again, as though a missing limb had been returned suddenly, and she could function again. The long days dissolved into long, dark nights, of tangled sheets, low burning fires and whispered confessions. Each night, each inn, they had passed exploring each other, remembering each other, relearning every slope, each curve, warming away the cold from each other's skin, telling and retelling stories, so many days to recount, so much missed, so much time to reclaim.

As they drew nearer the Fairfax estate, everything reminding her of the winters of her childhood, Caroline had tried to avoid thinking about what lay over the mountains, a small way off in the distance. Though she had not seen it since that night, she was sure that little remained, charred ruins, a family of dust and painful memories. She avoided it at all costs, and yet found her mind returning to it constantly.

Caroline sighed her worries away one more time - at least, down on the lawn, a beautiful distraction to cast her eyes upon.

✿

"I am sure that Katherine will be satisfied with the preparations, considering she is responsible for most of them," Charles was saying.

"Even so, a surprise, a romantic gesture, trust me brother, if there is not something you feel proud of inventing on the day to show her how you care for her, you will feel it keenly in the years to come. Benefit from my experience of the matter," Lucian insisted.

"And I suppose you feel the day of your nuptials lacked something? I am certain Caroline did not feel it."

"It wasn't everything she deserved," Lucian said in a final tone.

She had been happy at their ceremony, he remembered, thinking back at the way she had smiled with him with a sweetness that made his chest ache. Then, of course, the memory that always eroded through the happier ones, the reception, the candlesticks, her face. At the thought of his father, his mind instantly darkened and went to the note, carelessly scrawled, its words, cold and calculating. An icy wind swept through him. He had still not told anyone of it, and he did not plan to. Silus was dead, he had done the deed himself, and he would not let his demons, imaginary or real, seep in to taint this happy time, his second chance at living.

It was that time in the afternoon for the baby to sleep, and soon Ellie too before she tired to the point of crankiness, and Lucian did not wish to dally, as he hoped that he and Caroline might have a little lie down themselves. With the wedding in a few days time, everyone had been far too busy to take notice when the two of them slipped away to warm themselves up.

🍥

*T*he night before the wedding, guests had gathered from far and wide, wearing warm clothes in festive colours. Flaming touches lined the stairs and footmen waited just inside the hall to greet travellers with hot cider and take their cloaks when they came in. He ascended the stair and paused as a butler approached carrying a package. He felt a pang of nervousness in his gut as he looked at the brown paper and attached note. He had not received anything further from his mysterious source, not a surprise seeing as they had been travelling for several days, and had departed almost immediately after the last note.

He nodded his thanks to the butler and took the note and package through to one of the studies. Inside, he closed the door, and set the offending items on the desk, frowning as he searched for some sign of delivery, of which there was none.

He finally grabbed a letter opener and sliced the string tying the brown paper parcel. It was soft, and he easily tore the paper, his hands stilling as he saw the contents.

A doll, hand-sewn and delicate, its pale skin and honey-coloured curls so reminiscent of his daughter, and seen often tucked in the crook of her little arm. It was Ellie's doll, Tabitha, Lucian thought of how his daughter never allowed the toy far from her sight.

But, what froze his blood in his veins, was the side of the jagged cut, a slash, running from one of Tabitha's ears to the next, her stuffing sagging from her gashed throat. He swallowed, feeling a surge of pure anger scorch through his body. He carefully put the doll down, and picked up the note.

The dirty fruit of your bastard loins next, boy.

He felt his hand tremble with repressed rage as he read and reread those lines. Someone was threatening his family, someone, if the tone of the note was to be believed, who should be dead.

"Lucian?"

Caroline lingered in the doorway wearing a simple dressing robe over a bathing gown. He turned toward her, leaving the items on the desk, hidden from view by his back.

"Is something wrong? The dressing gong rang ten minutes ago, and you know Rebecca. Do not give her cause to scold you- you know how she loves it," Caroline said with a light smile, watching his face carefully. She walked toward him, her hand going to his cheek, as she leant into him, and stroked the side of his face, her eyes scanning his.

"Lucian, what is it?"

"Oh, it's nothing at all, my heart-"

"Honesty. Did we not promise?" she said softly, her eyes implored him, and he could no more deny her than he could his need to breathe. He sighed and picked up the note and doll from the table.

"Is that not Tabitha? Ellie has been driving us all crazy looking for her." Caroline's eyes grew wide as she stared at the slashed throat, instinctively raising her own hand to cover the delicate column of her neck.

"Who did this?" she whispered.

"I confess I do not know. I... I can't be sure... it's impossible..." Lucian broke off and strode over to the fire, drawing Caroline to an armchair positioned in front of it. She sank down, watching him closely, her brow drawn.

"Who? Tell me," she demanded as he started to pace in front of the fire. He looked back to her, and then handed her the note. She stared at it silently for a few moments, the blood draining from her face. He sat down beside her.

"Well?"

"It cannot be... he–"

"He is dead, I know," Lucian said, drawing her into his side, and wrapping an arm around her.

"Can you think of anyone else? Someone who might want to hurt you... us?" she asked. Lucian shot her a sardonic look.

"How would one narrow such a list? I have led a disreputable life, and I have earned many enemies. But..."

"How do they know about Silus, about your relationship with him? Only he would speak to you in such a tone," Caroline whispered, and Lucian nodded slowly.

"I am not sure. Perhaps he survived? Perhaps ruining me was worth disappearing for so long? I do not know. It is impossible."

"But, he was dead, I saw... I saw you kill him," she said, and Lucian gave her credit for the fact that her voice did not shake. He gave her a pained look, and she stroked the back of his hand soothingly.

"I barely remember, I only remember you coming to save me, you protecting me," she said, and he shook his head.

"I was too late."

"No, you were just in time," she said and looked back to the fire as a log fell, showering sparks. She heard the sound of heels on the polished marble floor outside.

"Dinner. We must dress," she said firmly, clearly trying to pull them both from the nightmare, and firmly back into the real world. She stood up and pulled Lucian to his feet also.

"I'm sorry to burden you with this," he said.

"My love, the only burden I cannot bear is for you to keep things from me. Whatever this is, whoever it is, we shall face it together," she said with a reassuring smile.

Together they went upstairs, avoiding Rebecca's narrowed eyes as she came down, already dressed, tsking one stair at a time. Lucian slowly climbed the stairs behind his wife, and wished he could feel her certainty, instead of the creeping cold suspicion that everything that they were trying so hard to rebuild was about to be destroyed.

✿

*T*he next few days passed in a state of anxiety for Lucian, who watched the estate, and everyone he and Caroline came into contact with, with a suspicious and wary eye. He did not want to worry the rest of his family, not now and here, one the eve of his brother's wedding, one that had been postponed much too long. Ellie was kept in, which she rebelled against greatly, and he escorted her outside whenever he could, consoling her with riding lessons, never far and always with an Ashford brother or two in tow. Caroline, careful and level headed as always, was often occupied with the other ladies, and looking after the children, and he felt safer knowing she was protected by company, and smiled graciously putting up with Lucian's protective watchfulness.

The night before the wedding approached, the evening where males and females would be divided until the church the next day. Lucian went along with the preparations, and helped his brother to relax, drank some, gambled a little. However, Charles, true to his nature, was not interested in mindless diversions on the eve of his wedding. Lucian looked for him, noting his absence from the card room, on that evening, and saw the balcony door slightly ajar. He poured two glasses of fine bourbon and stepped out onto the moonlit terrace. His brother was standing against the railing, looking out over the snowy Virginian nightscape, as the freshly set sun gilded the white-tipped mountains in the distance.

"Trying to escape your own party. I always knew we had something in common," he joked as he reached Charles's side, and offered him the glass. His elder brother smiled, and accepted it, cradling it in his hand to warm it.

"We have plenty in common, brother... much of the traits I have, and am proud of, I believe we share." Lucian raised his eyebrows, quite surprised.

"Such as?"

"Commitment to family, dedication to the women we love... to our children," he finished, and Lucian managed to keep the shock off his face.

"Meaning..."

"Katherine is with child," Charles confirmed. Lucian nodded, rocking back on his heels, he shot an amused look at his brother.

"Who would have thought it, the good and proper Charles?"

"Well, change comes to us all..." Charles smiled, and Lucian was struck by the warm look in his eye. "She's changed me. Challenged me... showed me a different world," he continued and Lucian found himself nodding. After a period of silence, he looked up to the moon.

"How on earth are we deserving of these women?" Lucian asked, and then turned to Charles. "Of course, you have a much better track record than I, without a shadow of a doubt. Yet, how did reserved-"

"Stuck up, cold and snobbish Charles ever capture the heart of Katherine Fairfax, without a doubt the most challenging, infuriating, inspiring and fascinating woman to grace this earth?"

"One of them, anyway," Lucian smiled, his mind flitting to his own personal enigma. They stared out at the moon and sipped their drinks.

"To us, brother, for..." Charles turned to Lucian raising his glass, and trailing off as he found he didn't know how to capture the words.

"...being so much luckier than cads like us have any right to," Lucian finished, seeing his smile echoed in Charles's face as he nodded.

"Looks like I am missing the real party," Wesley called as he joined them on the terrace.

"What are we toasting to?" he asked, popping open a bottle of Champagne.

"To our inexplicable good fortune," Charles said.

"I will certainly drink to that," Wesley said with a smile and a glance over his shoulder, as the Ashfords toasted again.

"I do not plan to get to sleep late, and I am not drinking anything and feeling horrible tomorrow," Katherine said, thinking how the bubbles had been regrettably making her nauseous of late, as she checked her hair was still pinned perfectly to create perfect curls for her wedding day.

"You have to have some champagne," Rebecca said indignantly and scowled as Katherine firmly shook her head.

"No. I must look like a princess."

"I have never known you to turn down bubbles before..." Caroline teased, missing the look Katherine shot her.

"I have waited long enough for tomorrow, I will not spoil it now."

"Well, if we are not drinking, what are we supposed to do?" Rebecca asked, before turning to Caroline.

"What about a card game? I leant my set to Ellie."

"Yes I know, I had to take them off her. She was using them to dig a maze in the snow for her marbles."

"Do not tell me one word more, or I may have to reverse my opinion on the good and fine breeding of Miss Elspeth Ashford!" Rebecca cried, as Caroline laughed at her outrage.

"I'll go fetch them." As she went to the door, Rebecca suddenly called.

"I am certain she would never have gotten such an idea before Lucian returned, and corrupted her manners and sense of social decorum. You have your job cut out for you with those two, thick as thieves in their bad behaviour, and a third one growing bigger each day!"

"I know! I'm looking forward to it," Caroline called with a laugh, leaving the sitting room, and starting upstairs.

She sighed as she reached the top of the stairs and moved toward the nursery. The house was quiet, the lamplight a soft glow, and the fresh flowers that had arrived for the wedding tomorrow were almost overpowering in the late evening, with all the windows shut, making a greenhouse. Caroline caught a sharp note in one of the displays, and paused. It smelled rotten, for an instant, stale and offensive. Then, the next moment, it was gone.

Shaking her head, she arrived at the nursery doorway, and paused, seeing the candles were already out, and the fire cast only a soft light. She saw Jeremy and Sophie curled up in their beds, and Callen in his cot, and yet, Ellie's bed was empty. She frowned and looked around the room, but there was nowhere for her wayward daughter to hide.

Caroline started back toward her and Lucian's bedroom, located in the family wing, separated from the main house for privacy. There was nothing Ellie loved more lately than to sleep in her parents' bed, now that they actually shared one. The novelty had not yet worn off, and Ellie loved to be the centre of attention, cradled between her mother and father, and neither of them had the will to send her away. Caroline walked the quiet halls, feeling quite calm and peaceful. Everything was prepared for the wedding, the bride and groom were more than ready, and Caroline felt light with the happiness that Katherine and Charles were finally getting their happy ending.

She reached her door, and quietly opened it, finding thick darkness greet her. She leaned out to the hall and picked up the prepared candle waiting beside the door, lighting it and slowly stepping into the room.

"Ellie, sweetheart?"

"Mummy?" Ellie whispered, and Caroline felt the hair along her arms raise slightly at the tone of her voice.

"What are you doing in here, love?" she asked gently, and froze as she smelt it, the smell, the rotting refuse scent - it was strong in here. She recognised it now, not as old rotting flowers, but an unwashed and unclean man. She surged forward into the room, her eyes searching for her daughter, her heart suddenly in her mouth.

"Why... she's with me." His voice was English, and not unfamiliar, yet worn by time and hardship. The candle trembled in her hands as she spun around trying to locate the source. She suddenly saw Ellie, sitting by the window, her knees drawn up and her arms wrapped around them, her tear-stained face pale, and her scared eyes shining at her in the darkness.

"Ellie!" Caroline gasped as she started forward, and then gagged as a cold, dirty hand clamped around her mouth, silencing her, his unclean fingers slipping against her teeth, cutting off her breath, and his face was suddenly by her ear.

"Quiet down, there's a good girl. We are going to be nice and quiet, and prepare a lovely little surprise for Lord Ashford when he returns. Now, can I trust you to be quiet?" Caroline swallowed, beginning to feel faint at the lack of air and the putrid smell of his hand. She nodded.

He cautiously withdrew his hand, and she took a deep breath, before instinctively opening her mouth and letting out a blood-curdling scream. It was cut abruptly short as he hit her hard across the jaw, and she felt her teeth rattle as she fell to the floor, dropping the candle in the process, the room going dark.

"Mummy!" Ellie screamed, and Caroline shook her head trying to clear the pounding, and crawled toward the window, reaching out her hand to calm her daughter.

"Shhh, it's alright, sweetheart," she said and gasped as she felt her hair being yanked, forcing her to her feet. He held her head close to his, his spittle flecking her face as he spoke.

"Listen you worthless bitch, no one can hear you up here. Your family is far away, your husband drinking and gambling. Keep your mouth shut, or the next time I hit someone, it'll be the girl, understand?" he asked aggressively. She nodded, fear coursing through her.

"Good. Now, make her stop whimpering, or I will," he said, thrusting Caroline in the direction of the window seat. She landed hard against it, and let out her breath in a rush, collecting herself, when she felt little hands on hers.

"Mummy?" Ellie sobbed. Caroline sat down and pulled her daughter into her lap, and held her tightly, rocking her.

"Shhh, it's alright, my darling, everything shall be well," she whispered, feeling her lip beginning to swell already, her voice muffled by a lisp. Ellie hiccupped with her sobs and finally started to quiet.

"Well done. At least you have some use," the man snapped, and Caroline saw him bending to fetch the extinguished candle from the floor, her eyes finally adjusting to the moonlight. As he straightened Caroline gasped, his face finally in view.

He sank into a crouch in front of them. He looked over her, and Caroline felt sick as his eyes lingered on her body lasciviously.

"I must say, you look much better than you did the last time we met, Lady Ashford," he murmured, his fingers going to her chin and jerking it up for his inspection. She shot him a venomous look and pulled her face away.

"Do not touch me. My husband will kill you," she promised, tightening her grasp on Ellie as the man came closer, suddenly grabbing her hair and jerking her head roughly toward him, his vile lips touching her cheek and forehead as he ran his nose across her skin.

"You smell so... clean... so...enticing," he breathed and eventually leaned back, and Caroline, unable to help herself, spat at his hovering face. He let go of her face, rising before her.

"You are going to regret that, my Lady. And as for who is going to be doing the killing, and who will be dying... we shall see... now we just need to wait for the bastard, and we can get on with it. How should we pass the time?"

𑁍

*L*ucian grasped the case of cigars and congratulated himself on his prowess in escaping the sedate party, celebrating his brother's final night of bachelorhood.

In truth, he had reached his limit. He disliked being away from Caroline for any length of time, as so much of it had been lost, and there was no time to waste, there never would be again. As he smiled to himself, thinking of surprising her, he turned the corner and spotted his sister coming along the passageway, a reticule hanging from her wrist. She stopped in his path and crossed her arms over her chest as she narrowed her eyes at him playfully.

"Well, smile you might, Luke, always so selfish... but you'll not spoil our fun tonight, more than Caroline can lay claim to a deck of cards," she said with a triumphant smile, swinging the pink satin reticule before his face.

"Why, my dearest sister, why anyone should try to spoil your fun, I confess I do not know... but I can hardly be to blame, when I have only just left the company of the groom-to-be and your husband."

"Aha, so... it is the little imp who bears the blame, I suppose I can hardly be surprised... she is much more irresistible than you."

A laugh broke out from the sitting room to their right, and Lucian stepped past his sister.

"I do not wish to be blamed by Katherine for stealing not one, but two card bearers, so, pray, go about your business," he said with a grin as he started up the nearby grand staircase, leaving his sister attempting to swat him with her bag, before giving up and turning back to her waiting party.

He took the stairs two at a time, as always his step quickening in anticipation of seeing his ladies. He reached the top landing and started along it. Reaching the nursery, he quietly opened the door and poked his head around it. Not there. It was oddly deflating as he looked for a sign of his wife or daughter, yet there was no sign of either. At least Callen's soft, fat cheeks and soft snores were some consolation, as he pressed a gentle kiss onto his fuzzy head.

He turned on his heel and started toward their bedroom. If he knew his daughter, there was no place she'd rather sleep than in her mother's bed. He reached the door and gently turned the knob, hoping not to wake them as he entered the dark room quietly, finding the room surprisingly bright, the light of the moon washing the walls a ghostly pale.

Next, time seemed to flash by in a series of disjointed stills. The empty bed, the sound of his daughter crying, the rough grunt of the stranger's curse and the whimper from Caroline as a pistol pressed into her forehead, the cold click of the metal in the barrel.

It all rushed in on him, overwhelmed him all at once, almost brought him to his knees. To come so close to a life worth living, one which, for one shining moment had almost been within his reach. The most sickening thud in the silence that followed was Lucian's realisation that no matter how he fought, how he tried to be a better man, his past, his crimes, his regrets would always follow him, and hurt the ones he loved the most.

"Close the door. Now. Get your hands up," the voice floated across the whitewashed space. He followed the instructions, disbelief lodged in his throat. He felt the door click quietly shut, sealing them from the rest of the house.

He slowly raised his hands, already thinking of what might be used as a weapon, should the opportunity present itself.

"Now, Ashford," he said the name with a sardonic sneer, "unless you want to accelerate the evening festivities with your pretty little wife here," Lucian felt a fist clench his heart as his eyes, adjusting to the pale, silvery light from the window saw Caroline tighten her mouth as the shadowed man caressed her neck with his fingers.

"Who are you?" he finally brought himself to ask, his blood starting to rage in his ears, anger starting to build, fear, frustration... terror so bone-deep, it almost struck him dumb.

"Who am I?" he laughed. "I shouldn't have expected you to know, I suppose. Tie him up," the man spat, his voice turning dangerously low as he threw a rope at Caroline's feet, stepping back, pistol still trained on her.

Caroline bit her tongue until the copper taste of blood stained her mouth, the torrent of words, the mad urge to dash for her daughter, almost uncontrollable, she ground her teeth and raised her chin defiantly.

"No," she said quietly, and turned her cheek, yet did not shrink back as the man raised a hand against her. He paused there, before slowly bringing his arm down, and running a rough finger down her cheek.

"What fire... I like that, I do. Some men don't, but I quite enjoy it. This shall be fun... yes, indeed," the man said, and Lucian moved forward, rage pulsing through him, until, suddenly lightning quick the man was sitting beside Ellie on the window seat, his arm gathering her in close. She whimpered in fear, and both her parents froze, their mouths stretched in protest.

"Now, where were we? Tie him up. Now. On that chair. Or for each minute you make me wait, I shall break one fat little finger." He tapped each of Ellie's fingers in turn gently with the end of his pistol. "These little things are so soft, that it would hardly take any doing at all."

Caroline, frozen in fear, stood rigid and trembling, unable to tear her eyes from her daughter. "Please. Anything."

The man motioned to the rope, casually resting the pistol on his knee, the end facing Ellie, who was staring at them both, tears running down her ruddy cheeks and into her open mouth.

"Caroline... sweetheart," Lucian called softly, waiting for her attention to shift to him, which it did, at length, her eyes carrying the image that had seared its way across her soul with them. "Caroline, do as he says," he said, coming slowly into the room, and waiting patiently as Caroline looked back to the man for permission. He nodded, smiling now, enjoying having them both under his command.

"And make it good, Lady Ashford," he added. "You do not want to toy with me. If he gets loose, I shall shoot him in the stomach so that he will die slowly and you can watch."

Caroline felt as though her joints had been unhinged as she turned around and stumbled toward her husband. His face was white with tension and shock. She stood before him, unsure of what to do. He slowly sat down on the chair set out, placing his hands on the chair arms, seeing the trembling of Caroline's fingers as she gripped the rope.

"Here you are love, tie it at the wrist," he murmured softly, his heart shattering as her loosened hair, hung askew and the soft tendrils brushed his face, its fragrance taking him to their time in the library at Westmere, so many evenings spent curled on the chaise together, her head tucked under his chin, as she read to him.

He gulped as he felt her fingers scrambling to tie the knots and pull them tight. She was so close and so afraid, and Ellie's little body racked with sobs, and all he could do was watch.

"Get over there, on the bed," the rough voice commanded, and Lucian felt his heart stop in that moment. There was a rustle of silk, as his wife sat gingerly on the edge of the bed, the pulse in her neck beating rapidly, her eyes looking feverishly about the room, and over to Ellie and he watched as the shadow stood from the window ledge.

"Who are you? I demand you tell me why you are doing this... what right have you?" Lucian shouted in anger, as the man stopped in front of him.

"Why, Lord Ashford, it upsets you doesn't it? Something out of your control? Of course, it does - your entire life you have had everything. Everything you wanted... everything I should have had... everything father should have given to me... you weren't even *his* bastard, and yet, you got everything while I got nothing," the man spat and his barely recognisable features suddenly fell into place. Lucian stared hard at him, the mists of his memory shrouding him, the misery of worry of Caroline and the baby, the memory of his father's blood on his hands, surprisingly hot and sticky, his sister's ashen face.

"You. The detective that worked my father's death... Hughes."

"Our father's," the man corrected, smiling then, a manic mask, so clownishly gleeful that Lucian felt his blood run cold. "Nice to formally meet you, brother... I suppose I could call you that, though we don't actually share blood, we share family. I've waited a long time for this day," he said, standing swiftly, whipping around and pointing the pistol at Caroline who had been working her way over to the door.

Reaching her in two long strides, he grabbed her by the chin, and spoke into her face,

"I thought I told you to wait on the bed." He shoved her backwards by her chin, and she fell back, landing heavily on the mattress, and Ellie let out a shrill scream at it, her sobs becoming unbearable.

The next instant, he was atop of her, pinning her arms down.

"Such a pretty wife, so young, so willing, so rich. All I've ever had was dark alley doxies. I've never been good enough for the likes of this, despite being my father's son. I should have been at the balls, I should have had mothers pushing their beautiful young daughters in front of me."

He leaned down, and traced his tongue along Caroline's neck to her ear and plunged it inside before he came up licking his lips. "Now, Ashford, you can be the one outside looking in, for a change, while I show you how it's done," he grunted, leaning his face in, as Lucian looked frantically to Ellie who was staring at the scene on the bed in horror, her little mouth working soundlessly.

"Ellie sweetheart…. ELLIE!" he shouted and was relieved when she finally looked at him.

"My love, we are going to play a game, and mother is going to hide first, so you must close your eyes and count, as far as you can," he said urgently, his eyes pleading with his daughter to accept his words, to play along. "Please, Ellie. Do as I say. You don't want to break the rules, do you?" he cajoled and saw her finally screw her eyes up and start to count loudly.

"Bitch!" he heard Hughes shout, and the sound of a ringing slap reached him as Caroline managed to draw blood, and was punished for it. Lucian began to pull at his restraints, swearing when the harsh knots remained ungiving.

"Stop! Mummy!" Ellie had stood up, her little face red with exertion she was glaring at Hughes, her hands in fists as she ran around to the side of the bed.

"Ellie, don't!" Lucian grunted as he started to attempt to stand up and slam down on the chair, the reverberation humming through him as it refused to break. Ellie was climbing up on the side of the bed now, pulling at Hughes's legs and coat, screaming all the while, her face turning redder by the moment, hiccupping with swallowed tears, her little arms and legs working furiously.

"Piss off, brat," Hughes snarled, kicking a blow that connected foot with her chest in a gruesome hollow sound that tore a scream from both her parents. She landed on the floor, her breath knocked out, as she gasped her panic down.

Lucian crouched, hobbled with the chair bending his back, his blood roaring in his ears as he took in the nightmarish scene. Every cell of his body urged him to act, to protect, but he didn't know how. He staggered over to the wall, turning his back and the chair toward it, and threw himself backwards, hitting it hard, feeling his bones and teeth rattle at the collision.

Caroline did not attempt to avoid the man's reaching fingers, even as they wound into her hair, and wrenched her head this way and that, his face on her neck and mouth. Her eyes were wild, Lucian could see even from where he was, as the moonlight struck the grotesque tableau, yet she was outwardly calm, as always. There was no question in his mind that she would sacrifice her body, if only to keep him and Ellie safe for a little bit longer.

"That's better," Hughes hissed, as she stopped struggling, still, acceptance taking her over. "Don't get any ideas, whore."

"I'm not going to try to hurt you," she whispered, so softly Lucian almost didn't catch it.

"Oh, really?"

"I don't have to," she said, as he leaned back finally and took in her face, her utter calmness, her sudden lack of fear.

"And why is that?" he asked, his husky voice matching her whisper.

"Because. That's my job," the voice came from behind his shoulder, and he groped for the gun, forgotten in the bedclothes and his lust.

Hughes lunged forward, going for her throat, but was too late. Lucian's arm swung around his head, and he tightened, hearing the satisfying choke and strangled cry from Hughes. Lucian yanked him backwards off Caroline, his knees hitting the floor hard, as he went down. Lucian stood behind him, his forearms taught with unused fury and a barely contained rage. Lucian registered Caroline slowly sitting up, her eyes burning brightly as she stared defiantly at Hughes, holding her arms out for her daughter, who had climbed up the bed and fell into them.

Hughes's face turned a deep red and then started to be tinged a faint purple as he spluttered and his legs kicked. Lucian's eyes clouded, he could barely make out his wife on the bed, stroking Ellie's hair, could barely hear anything but the scream of bloodlust in his ears, one he hadn't heard since the battle shots were firing, and the men falling beside him, since he was running into that fire with emptiness in his heart, a man who had nothing to lose.

"Lucian…. Lucian!!! Stop. You're killing him," Caroline's voice called to him through that fog, lingered at the edge of his lucid mind, the part of him that had worked so hard to come back, to be a whole man again, a father, a husband. She pulled at his arm, as Hughes lost all control over his legs, and sagged ever further down, piss staining his hose. But Lucian barely weakened as she tugged at him. It was almost done.

"Lucian, don't do this… please," she was begging, her beautiful eyes too close, and too immediate to ignore.

"He deserves to die. He hurt you, he tried to-" he choked on the words, his grip tightening, his mind counting, his mind that knew all too well the number of seconds needed to end a man, counted down another black mark on his soul.

"Daddy?" Ellie was calling, her face reddening again, tears starting to fall as Hughes started to make the ugliest noises, kicking and lashing in a struggle for breath, the sharp tang of his piss in the air.

"Caroline, remove her, both of you must leave. Now," he said, his voice rough with the force he was exerting.

"No," the word was quiet, solemn, final. He glanced to her then, and saw her, as she went back to the edge of the bed and sat, gathering her daughter into her arms, they looked at him then, asking him to answer for his wretched soul.

"Caroline, don't ask me for this. I cannot leave him unpunished," he said, and saw the resolve only harden in her eyes.

"Lucian Ashford, I am not leaving, I shall not. If you wish to jeopardise your soul, our family, if you need your vengeance, your pride to be slated, above all else, then… I wish Ellie to know who her father is. That he is a man without mercy," her words washed over his red hot anger, and he looked at her disbelievingly.

His hands loosened marginally as he stared, locked into a blue gaze of total honesty. He stared that truth in the eye, he saw himself, through her eyes, his wildness, his hunger, and the murder in his eyes.

He heard Hughes gargle a gasp through his spitty, purple lips and immediately tightened his grip once more, the man letting out a long gurgling sound.

"Mercy? I cannot show mercy to this man!"

"Yes, you can. You can choose to, you can choose to be better than him, better than your father."

He closed his eyes, as her words sank through him, and there they waited, in silence. Caroline finally asking him to prove that he had become a better man, Ellie watching her father, her hero, and waited to see what was right and what was wrong.

Slowly, he let his grip loosen from the rope around Hughes's neck, and the man fell forward, choking in small shallow breaths, through a bruised throat. Lucian stepped back, stumbled almost, and felt Caroline's arm go around him, as Ellie latched onto his leg, her hug as tight as a vice.

"Ellie, run and get your uncles," Caroline was saying as Lucian stared at the man rolling limply on the floor.

He felt an indescribable lightening in his chest, fragile and featherlight. It felt a lot like hope.

CHAPTER 13

"If I may, I would like to make a toast. I promise decorum, Charles. In earnest, I do not think our esteemed guests could take another display of dazzling wit after our dear brother Wesley's heartfelt words." Lucian paused as the assembled party laughed, the chink of glasses and the soft crackle of fireplaces burning. Lit by a thousand candles, the soft glow of the dinner rivalled the golden halcyon of the sunset outside the many windows, painting the freshly fallen snow and the lake which was glistening pink, and had begun to sparkle back at the emerging stars. Katherine, at the head of the table looked like the queen of winter, in beaded golden velvet, white fur, and diamonds. Lucian took a sip of water and waited for quiet to continue.

"Love. The importance of it, the need for it, the sheer power of it cannot be overestimated. We are helpless without it, we are weaker, we are poorer... we are less.

Love is family, wherever we may find it, it is friendship and good-ness. It is the root of kindness. It is hope, for a better future, for a fairer world.

Most importantly... love is the right of every soul, put upon this lonely earth... and yet it is a responsibility in the same turn... it is earned and fought for, it is won and it must be cherished.

Love is a choice. It leaves no measure for selfishness, it has no time for pride. Vengeance and retribution, jealousy and suspicion cannot face it, cannot exist long in true love's presence." He paused then and lifted his glass, the sparkling liquid glowing in the light as he raised it, turning to his brother and his new wife.

"My advice to you, and it has been hard-won in my case, is to choose love, choose each other, tonight, and tomorrow, next week, and next year, and for all the days that come afterward. Choose to love each other, above all else... every day... and do not cease for anything in this world.

"I present this toast, to the bride and groom," he said, listening as his words were echoed, and glasses clinked.

Charles watched his brother and knew that those were the words that he would remember him by, his brother, who had lost too much and suffered too harshly, someone who had learned the truth of the words he gave them that night, a gift to carry him with them, all of them, always. Someone risen from the ashes, someone redeemed, and looking over at a glowing Katherine, Charles understood him completely.

❀

"It's really quite incredible, and yet so tremendously predictable. We all knew that father must have other sons or daughters somewhere, though somehow we never heard of them. But to meet one finally.... under such circumstances," Rebecca said as Isaac gently turned her around, their bodies occasionally straying closer than the proper distance required for the dance.

"Where have they taken him?" Isaac inquired, moving through the dance steps with ease, spying his brother and Eva dancing with Sophie and Jeremy off to the side, Eli proving to be as poor a teacher as he was a participant.

"Just now he is residing in the local jail, however, the sheriff said that a doctor would be arriving to examine him shortly, he thinks he shows symptoms of illness, a brain fever he has seen before, likely contracted in the streets of London, no doubt..." she trailed off.

"Lues?" Isaac enquired and she nodded, twirling under his arm. "It certainly would explain a great deal, his fixation, his final breakdown. Well... the criminal deserves to rot in a cell," Isaac was saying when Rebecca shook her head sharply.

"Don't. He is dangerous and did something horrible, yes, but I cannot help but feel for him. Our father ruined his life, by not acknowledging him, by letting pride and society stand in the way of doing the honourable thing, and providing, at least, for his family. We should leave the blame where it belongs," she said sadly, her brown eyes large.

"Indeed. Of course, my love. Forgive me. Your heart, as ever, is astonishingly big, and capable of more than I might ever hope to understand," Isaac said softly, drawing her close, his eyes full of love for the strong, independent woman he had been most fortunate to win the heart of. He caught her eyes drifting over to the children at the edge of the dancing space, a wistful look in her eyes. "Lady Ashford, I suggest we retire, do you not feel a headache coming on?" he asked as they started toward the edge of the dance floor.

"Yes, quite, I must say I do... all this...erm... fresh air, it is really too invigorating."

"I'll say," he agreed, clasping her slender hand in his.

"*P*lease, do not give Wesley Ashford another deck of cards, or he'll have our shirts!" Mateo laughed.

"You sound like a man speaking from experience, doctor," Virgil Tilman joked.

"You bet, I am!" Mateo laughed again, and his brown eyes sparkled at Wesley over his glass, sending Westley a flutter in his stomach that had nothing to do with the champagne. "You must take my word for it, Mr Tilman, my housemate is the most dangerous card sharp in all of Richmond." They laughed and drank, everyone happily in their cups. Joshua Lee sat across from them, and he had brought with him a young woman from Tennessee, and Wesley was happy to see it. She was funny and had a loud, contagious laugh, and Wesley liked her immensely.

"Play for us, Wesley," Mateo whispered, risking catching his eye while the others were distracted. "Promise you'll play for us later, when everything has died down. Nothing could make this night more beautiful."

"Well," Wesley said, unable to keep the smile off his face, "another couple of drinks, and it won't take much convincing."

"Do I have your word?" Mateo asked, his voice low, making Wesley wonder if they were still talking about music.

"You do," he said just as quietly, thrilling at the intimacy of their private conversation. "But only if you will sing." Mateo smiled and nodded. "In Italian," Wesley specified, and Mateo's smile got a little bit wider.

"You have yourself a deal, Lord Ashford, and I will be quite pleased to hold you to it."

✿

"*W*ill you still love me, when we are old and bored of each other?" Katherine asked the man sitting to her right and felt his hand instantly envelop her own.

"I cannot predict the future; however, I feel a fair amount of certainty that we shall never be bored. For you, Katherine my love, are anything but boring," he said, and she tore her eyes away from the spot where she had been watching her parents dancing, and turned to her new husband.

"They fight all the time, and manipulate each other, and withhold things, but… everything still works, somehow," she said, gesturing to her parents.

"That is because their love for each other, and their love for you and your sisters, binds them," he answered, stroking a strawberry blond curl back. She nodded a little, and turned and smiled at him.

"Katherine, Lady Katherine Ashford, I have loved you, from first I met you, with your outrageous laugh and your scandalous smile, and your optimistic heart, so naïve and so trusting. And I have waited for you, a lifetime, and I'd wait a lifetime more, for you are my home, soon to be home to three," he said, with the barest touch of her stomach. She smiled, a slow, lazy smile that spread across her mouth, her eyes glinting with her affection. "Besides, if that little one is anything like her mother, I fear that, in all the rest of our lives, we shall never be bored again for even a moment!"

❀

"*I* think that Ellie may be a resident in our bed, for a good long while to come," Caroline said to Eva as she watched Ellie following Jeremy around. Jeremey, a sensitive boy, waited for her, holding out his hand, and running to look for the Fairfaxes spaniel.

"It's only natural, and completely understandable Caroline, though Ellie may surprise you. Children are remarkably resistant," Eva said.

"You may be right, and for her sake, I sincerely hope so."

"You know you need not stay - you must be quite exhausted. How have you managed through this day?"

"Katherine and Charles have waited long enough, and anyway, I confess, it is though a great weight has been lifted. Nothing is waiting in the shadows, there is no one intending us harm," Caroline said, trying to describe the lightness inside her, unable to explain the gravity of Lucian's decisions as of late, for openness and honesty, mercy, that he had not believed himself capable of, but that Caroline never doubted.

"I am afraid to interrupt, but if I may, I believe a dance is in order, if you'd consent, my Lady," Lucian's voice pulled her around, and she found him standing before her, looking so very much like she had first glimpsed him in his formal best, standing above her, casually leaning on the balustrade of a grand ballroom - a world away, and a lifetime ago.

She could remember the way his golden hair had caught the candle-light, as he had raised his glass of champagne to her, the girl who had never been chosen first or noticed much, the girl without family or fortune.

She felt his hand slip into the crook of her arm, as it had so many times, as he led her to the dance floor. The band struck up a waltz, and he gave her a formal bow, and offered her his hand, his blue eyes shining as she dropped into a slow curtsy, before stepping closer to him, feeling his hand draw her nearer still, settling on her lower back, his full mouth quirked in his customary smirk.

He turned her, without words under the candlelight, and her mind couldn't help tracing their journey, skipping over all the steps that had brought them here, to be together.

She spied Charles dancing with Katherine, and smiled, thinking of how the years, taking their heavy toll, had changed them all so very much and yet, hardly at all. Yet, one person had changed, that she knew now, and would never doubt.

She felt him pull her closer, as though her thoughts were words to him, and she gently rested her forehead against his chin, propriety be damned. They danced on, surrounded by their family, bound together by more than blood. They had endured together, and suffered together, and now they laughed together and loved all the more for it.

Tomorrow, she could not know, and yet, she knew she would not be alone, and that, for her, was more than enough - it was everything.

EPILOGUE

~March 1816~
Charlottesville

There were only two things that were demanding enough to pull Caroline from the warm embrace of her bed. One was playing outside, and the other, she could see in the distance, walking with his brother. They cut fine figures striding across the green lawn, dressed for riding, smiling and talking together, Lucian and Charles.

Caroline smiled as Lucian suddenly lifted his head and caught her eye. His answering grin lit his face up as he took her in and then lifted his watch from his pocket and tapped the large face. Nodding, Caroline backed away from the window, and shrugged off her silk wrapper, getting dressed without the help of her ladies maid, as she knew poor Mary was busily helping Nanny Lehmann with the baby, who had grown bigger and stronger by the day, and who had just discovered the week prior what his legs were for, and had decided to put them to good use. The baby had been christened Callen William Paterson Campbell Ashford, which Lucian had said was quite the right amount of names for a young earl, and he had stolen their hearts, every one.

There. Not quite the outrageous ensemble she had subjected her husband to at Westmere, yet, not far off, she thought, as she smoothed everything into place a last time and left the room, gathering her crop and hat.

"It's breathtaking, brother, you've never seen anything like those mountains, I promise you," Charles was saying as they walked.

"But, Charles, twenty two thousand acres…. what on earth will you do with it all? How will we ever find you?" Charles laughed and clapped him on the back.

"Say you'll come see it! How about next month? Did I tell you about the bears? Bears, Lucian!" Charles shook his shoulder for emphasis, but Lucian had become distracted by the sight of his wife appearing through the door. He swallowed as he saw her approach. She had had a riding habit made to mimic his clothes as she used to wear them, but these fitted her form perfectly. Thick white linen shirt sleeves had been made into a bodice, tight and structured, supporting her breasts without the need for short stays, buttoning up her torso, she had left a few buttons open at the neckline in a way that made Lucian imagine unbuttoning them all. She wore tan suede breeks, so soft that it fell like fabric, loose at the bottom so as to appear modestly like a lady's skirts, but fitted across her waist, and across the top of her voluptuous bottom. Slung over her shoulder, he noticed a bright red jacket, with gold and black detail, English in every way.

"If you'll excuse me brother, I have some more pressing matters to take care of," he murmured, his eyes never leaving Caroline's as he started forward, presenting her his arm, leaving an amused Charles in his wake.

"Lady Ashford, you are quite ravishing," Lucian murmured as he pulled her close and started them in the direction of the waiting horses.

"Well, if you must know, I had a more traditional riding habit made, but found after its first outing that I could not endure the rigours of such a garment. How women are supposed to ride comfortably, heaven knows."

"I am quite pleased to notice your… adaptations."

"Innovative, are they not?"

"I can only imagine by the cut of your trousers, Lady Ashford, that you mean to ride astride."

"Of course."

"I am so glad to hear it," he rumbled, and she caught his eye, his appreciation not going unnoticed. "I shall be quite pleased at the view, I daresay."

"That is, of course, assuming you can keep up, Lord Ashford," she replied with a smile, before sweeping ahead, already eager to make contact with the horse prepared for her, its chestnut flanks gleaming in the sun.

They rode away from the estate, with Caroline leading the way. She picked up a trail that she used to ride down with her father as a girl. They moved over open fields and entered a red oak wood. The new leaves were chartreuse and emerald, with a touch of pink here and there, and the sun fell through the gaps, moving lazily over them as they finally slowed and rode in companionable silence, side by side. The air was fresh and cool, but the bright sun in the crisp, cloudless sky warmed them, and they stopped at a secluded spot by a river.

Lucian helped Caroline down from her mount. His hands running up the sides of the snug bodice, before lifting her down, standing so close that their bodies slid against each other. Lucian reached up to pull Caroline's hat from her head, and smiled as her raven hair tumbled from it, its pins already giving up their duties. Caroline shook her head back, shaking the last of it loose, and ran her hands up his chest, warming him through with the undisguised affection. They picnicked by the water, the sun through their lashes, their hands in the fresh grass, and the pleasant silence of the place, the gently running river and soft snort of the resting horses, settled on them.

"You look awfully warm in that leather ensemble, my dear. As your husband, I am responsible for your well being. I would be dangerously remiss if I did not remedy the situation immediately," Lucian murmured lazily as he reached over and slowly slid a hand at the open collar of her shirt at the neck, and grazed the warm skin underneath.

"How kind of you, my Lord, to notice. You are generosity itself."

At the sight of her crooked smile, he moved his hand ever so slowly down until he came to a button, and pretending at a patience he did not have, slowly unbuttoned the first, and then the second.

Her hair hung between them, their faces close, and he could see a playfulness there that they were beginning to rediscover.

"My Lord, that is better already. I imagine with the loss of a third button, I might be made to feel even more... comfortable," she breathed, "if you would be so obliging." He went on to unbutton the next, and his fingers slid inward to one of the hard nipples he could see pushing against the tight linen. Her breast was so full and warm, heavier lately, and more sensitive, if he was not mistaken, and as he had spent much of the past few hours appreciating the curve of them, it was an unbearable struggle to hold himself back, as he reached the point, and rolled his fingertips across it, making Caroline close her eyes, and hang her head back slightly, her shining hair falling behind her.

The expanse of her honeyed skin of her smooth neck in the sun made his mouth eager for her, and he took a sip of cool water from the canteen and put his cold mouth to her hot skin. She groaned as he pressed slow, open kisses over her neck, his hand still pressed between the tight linen and her skin, and she ran her hand through his hair, pulling him closer, and down with her as she laid back in the grass.

Lucian kissed his way up her neck, tasting the salt on her skin, and then along the ridge of her chin, to her waiting mouth, which still tasted of the lemon cake which had been wrapped with their lunch. He kissed her slowly and deeply until he felt her writhe under him with impatience.

He leaned back and looked at her for a moment lying there, her raven hair tangled in the grass, the curve of her breasts visible between the unbuttoned gap in her shirt, soft suede and hard leather boots, so American, against the Englishness of the red military jacket, now thrown carelessly to the side. He wished he had paints, as the dappled sun filtered through the leaves and danced across her face, obscuring her eyes for one breath, and then making them glow in another. Her lips were so full and kissed dark pink, that he could wait no longer.

His hands went again to her buttons, and without delay, he unbuttoned the remainder, pulling the hem free from her trousers, and opening the linen wide exposing her perfect form to the navel. Lucian growled, and she laughed, as he set his mouth to the skin of her stomach, and licked a long line up her chest before making his way over to each breast, sucking one while using his hand to caress the other until she was panting his name. At the sound of it, he pulsed with need, and went for the buttons of her trousers, unbuttoning them quickly, and wrenching them down and off without waiting another moment.

He sank to his knees before her. Ran his hands over her, fully naked, his eyes drinking in the details, the artist never resting.

"My love... you must know that you need nothing to entice me... but if you ever wonder, then know this - this is my preferred view of you, stripped bare, for my eyes only. Perfection. Heaven. Paradise." As he spoke, Caroline started to unbutton his coat, tugging it off his broad shoulders and pulling at the ties of his shirt.

She undressed him with a smile on her face and an eager gleam in her eye that made Lucian ache for her. He laid her back down gently on the soft grass, and lowered his weight down slowly on top of her, their skin finally meeting, their chests rising together.

He brought both his hands to cup her face, gliding his thumbs across her jaw, and kissed her, slowly at first, and then more deeply, stroking her tongue with his, inhaling her breath, biting gently at her full bottom lip, when he heard a little pleading moan from deep in her throat, and she suddenly grabbed his backside with both hands, wrapped her legs around his thighs, and pulled him into her.

His breath hitched in his chest and she let out another moan as he entered her, and they both laughed at the heady, needy joy of it. He kissed her harder and slid a little further in. Her smooth, tight warmth tensed around the sensitive tip of him, and it felt so good that he groaned and let her pull him the rest of the way in, sliding slowly against the wetness of her eager body.

"Damnit, Caroline," he said softly, trying to hold himself back, control himself. "It feels so good to be inside of you."

Her large eyes opened and flashed at him, green in the sunlight, and she smiled, and he felt a melding of his head and his heart and his body, so whole and complete, so overjoyed, so very lucky.

"Well, then what are you waiting for?" She said with an impish grin and nipped his lip. "I'm not going to last much longer." He burst out laughing at that, and they laughed again together as he pressed his forehead to hers and began to move inside of her.

They moved together as one, knowing each other as they knew themselves, their cries echoing each others as they rose and fell, and were soon carried off together on the backs of the wind.

"And what of this one?" Caroline asked as she inspected Lucian's palm, holding over their heads as they lay scantily covered on the picnic rug by the sun-glistening river.

"This one, I do believe, was from a knife fight, though I recall little of why and where it was," Lucian murmured, his brow creasing as he gazed at her fingers running over his calloused and scarred hand.

"And these?" she said, indicating further scars running up the side of his hand, and clustering around a crooked finger, which looked like it had been broken before.

"This one, I do recall. It happened in France when I was living on the Dubois farm. A horse was caught in an old cart during a storm nearly killing itself in its fear of the thunder," he mused as he flexed the hand, and Caroline felt the little click of the formerly broken joint. She rested her chin on his shoulder, feeling quite swept up by the decadent afternoon, as she watched him fondly.

"I do believe you are the biggest hearted fool when it comes to animals," she teased.

"Well, perhaps that is true, but I have a similar weakness for Ashford women. Two in particular. Though I suppose they too often bray like mules. Ouch!" he cried as she elbowed him in the ribs.

"The pot and the kettle, Lord Ashford. Tell me more of France. What did you do in your time there?"

"Well, I worked the farm, no small task I assure you, and I... I-"

You?" she prompted when he fell silent.

"I... dreamt of you. Of Westmere. I would sit at the window of the cottage and stare across the sea, fancy I could see you there, and you were happy, safe and loved. I would not imagine what you were doing, or who you were with, as I had given up the right to those thoughts when I left, but my memories of you... well, they were mine to do with as I pleased. Some days, I would picture us together at the farm, I was so dazed with sun and back-breaking work that I would be unsure if I was awake or not," he said with a rueful laugh, and Caroline moved over his chest to gaze down at him. She stroked his stubbled cheek.

"I dreamt of you too," she whispered, and she felt tears prickle her nose as he pulled her face down to kiss him.

"Shush, sweetheart, no more tears... for I would repeat every miserable moment to be here with you, to still be loved by you. To know Ellie. To have found Callen, and watch them grow. I would do it all again," he said, pressing a kiss to her forehead. "So, I have something to show you," he said abruptly, surprising Caroline out of her melancholy. He rolled her gently to the side, and stood swiftly, arms eager to pull her up.

They rode for another few hours, until the sun had passed its zenith and the entire valley was awash with a warm afternoon glow.

Nerves had been building in Caroline as she had started to recognise small indications of their destination, and her hands were starting to feel clammy on the reigns. Lucian was up ahead, and she thought of calling him, asking him to stop, to turn back before it was too late, but there was another urge, a deeper one, pushing her on behind him.

They joined the drive from the left and started up the rutted road, an alley of massive oaks on either side making a shady canopy that stretched upward for a mile or more. Nerves gathered in Caroline's throat, choking her, silencing her when she wanted to cry out to him, plead with him to turn back. She felt paralysed with fear, with memories. Lucian glanced back over his shoulder, coming to a stop when he saw her white face and frozen expression.

"I thought it was time we lay our demons to rest," he said softly, coming to her side, and gripping her hand. Her eyes remained fixed ahead, and he slowly squeezed her fingers. "I understand if you wish to turn back, though I wish you would continue."

Caroline swallowed and nodded, her eyes fixed over the rise of the hill. They started forward slowly, and before long, they had topped the slight rise, and Caroline felt her stomach clench as she looked down into the valley that had held her childhood and her family.

Lucian sat expectantly at her side, and her heart pounded as she took in what was happening. Her throat felt thick as memories assaulted her.

"Well, my darling… what do you think?" he asked, and she heard the nervousness in his voice and realised that he was afraid of her answer, afraid he had overstepped, rushed the intimacy of their rekindled relationship, pushed his position in her life again once more too far.

There were no ruins of the charred end of her idyllic childhood, no sign of how it had come crashing down. There had been, of that she was sure, but the earth had been scrubbed clean of such terrors and had come to life again. There were men moving around, there was work being done, and birds, long since forgotten, sung familiar songs from the trees. The ground had recovered, it was green again, vibrant growth where before there had only been death. The old house was gone, and in its place was a large, newly planted garden, fresh and green with promise, the buds of flowers eagerly beginning to push through, and a fountain and benches at its centre.

Nearby, there were stakes planted, stacks of lumber, the rough outline of a home, a new one.

She saw the men cease working as they noticed Lucian and the foreman called a break. Caroline spurred her mount down the road she had trod a lifetime ago and never thought she would return to. Tears stung her eyes, memories flashed through her mind, but they were not the bleak, smoke-streaked memories that had chased her, they were happy memories of her childhood, some that she had forgotten until that moment when the land gently reminded her.

As she got closer she saw the extent of the painstaking work that had been carried out. The foreman was moving to greet them, and as he drew near, Caroline gasped and smiled in recognition.

"Freddy!" she cried, sliding down from her horse.

"Caroline, or I should say, Lady Ashford," Freddy said sheepishly, glancing over at his boss. Caroline gripped his hand hard.

"To you, I will always be Caroline. How did all of this come about - you, working here?" Freddy looked to Lucian, standing behind Caroline watching them.

"Well, I was contacted by Lord Ashford, asking if I wanted to oversee the restoration of your home."

"Our home, of course," Caroline said quietly, still smiling with joy at her childhood friend, reappearing after so long. Freddy shifted a little, bringing Lucian into the conversation.

"Sir, I hope everything is to your liking," he said respectfully, and Caroline could not take her eyes from the man that she had known as a boy, always hanging around the estate, with his father, the caretaker.

"Indeed it is, though, I must admit the real judge is here now, and I shall rely on her good opinion, and we must consult her on the plans before anything else moves forward."

"Of course. Come, Caroline, let me show you," Freddy started as he strode off toward a cart set up on the far side of the site. Silence fell as

Lucian watched Caroline's reaction, but she could hardly breathe. All she could do was turn around and turn again, looking at every detail, her eyes wide as they struggled to take it all in.

"Caroline," Lucian began, as she turned to face him suddenly, her tears threatening to spill, as she tried to find the words to thank him. What could she say? There were no words fit in the English language to tell him what this meant to her. As she stepped closer, her mouth slightly open, he suddenly dropped to a knee.

"Lucian, what are you doing?" she asked, and gasped as he took her hand.

"Caroline, my love, I want you to marry me again, in front of our family, here, where we will build our new life, and say goodbye to the past once and for all. We are different people now than we once were. I have died, perhaps we both did, and you have brought me back. Marry me again, Caroline, be mine again." Caroline stared, completely dumbfounded.

"But we are already married," she whispered, tears gathering in her eyes, unable to break the connection with his blue gaze.

"Marry me again. Let Ellie carry the flowers, and Callen hold the ring, and let us make our first family memory together, here, the site of our future. It will just be for us, just the family, on your family estate. I have wandered the world and longed for you so long. Please, Caroline, vow your love, and put your trust in me once again... and I swear, I shall spend every remaining moment of my life trying to make you happy, for this chance at redemption is a gift," he implored, his low voice speaking to her heart. She broke his gaze, and looked around. The site was bordered by waving grasses, and she felt the afternoon breeze move her as it did them, gently they swayed, undulating under the sun.

'Shall I ever marry? Or am I truly destined to be an old maid like my sister says?'

'You shall marry. Not once, but twice.'

'Twice? Does my husband die then? That sounds very sad...'

'Oh yes, there shall be much sadness, much pain, many tears, but also happiness like you have never known. And there will be love. It shall be a great love, an epic love. A love for the ages.'

Caroline could almost hear the fortune teller's voice, drifting through the meadow, whispered by the grasses. She felt then the weight of fate, her destiny, which had brought them together, ripped them apart, and reunited them, the stormy seas they had battled, the heartache they had endured, to finally end up washed upon the mountains of her family home, this new beginning, this second chance. The circle completed.

She felt his hand grip hers harder for a moment and brought her attention back to the man on a bent knee before her.

"You're mad. Utterly mad. Yes, of course, I will marry you again, Lucian Ashford," she answered, blinking away the tears that finally broke and tumbled down her cheeks. "And I'd marry you a third time, and a fourth, and a fifth, if that would make you happy!" she laughed, and he stood up, and swept her off of her feet, spinning her around, as he kissed her.

"Lord Ashford, I believe you may need some lessons from your brother on how to act in company... you are worse than ever," she laughed as she leant away, smoothing her hat and her riding habit, unable to wipe the grin from her face. Lucian watched her with a smile, his own eyes possessive, and happy beyond measure.

"My dearest bride-to-be, if I have learned anything in these past years, it is that society can hang for all I care. I will kiss you liberally and often, and I shall stop for no man, nor lightning bolt from on high."

"Pray, let us not tempt fate any further, my Lord Ashford, for we have had a goodly share of it already, and I should rather like a break," she said, drawing a laugh from him as he pulled her closer and pressed another hungry kiss onto her smiling lips.

THE END

Thank you for reading and please leave a review or some stars to share your thoughts!

It makes a huge difference to authors when you do x